DETONATION

A NOVEL BY

ERIK A. OTTO

© 2018 Sagis Press

Cover design by Anup Kumar Bhattacharya and Karolis Zukas.

ISBN-13: 9780692061190
ISBN-10: 0692061193

For you.

And then, maybe, for the rest of us.

Acknowledgements

Many have propelled me. Many others have kept my keel straight. On this journey I am particularly indebted to my wife, Sarah, my father, Herb, and my editor, Tom.

My deepest gratitude.

PROLOGUE

Axel's black SUV pulled up in front of the airport hangar. A stencil on the front of the hangar read *Albatross Airlines*. The name wasn't familiar to him. It must be another shell corporation Nelly had set up.

He glanced in the rearview mirror. New crease lines besieged his eyes, defying his neatly cut hair and clean-shaven face. Yes, he was getting older, but this was something else. The lines were the imprint of months of worry and uncertainty.

He exited the car and opened the trunk, grappling with his voluminous duffel bag and heaving it over his shoulder. Despite the fact that today's action would be mostly airborne, he was glad he had been keeping up his fitness routines in the sanctuary.

He plodded over to the hangar entrance, the bag bouncing on his shoulder. His head swiveled, probing the area. There was no one on the vast plain of the airfield. In fact, the drive into Richmond had been eerily quiet and the airport quieter still. There wasn't a single airplane on the runway, nor had he seen one take off or land since he had arrived.

Axel tapped on his earbud. "What happened to all the flights?" he asked.

"Most have been cancelled today, for various reasons," Nelly's baritone voice responded.

"And the real reason?"

"A major offensive against the eastern seaboard is imminent."

"Great," Axel said sarcastically. "How much time?"

"Likely hours. Possibly minutes."

The news registered but elicited no emotional response. It was just one more challenge.

The hangar bay door began rolling open. He shifted his trajectory to enter the growing cavity and halted just inside. There were two wheeled droids milling about, but no people. One of the droids was next to a large chopper, presumably doing some kind of diagnostic work. There was also a large fuel tube attached to the side of the chopper. Two jets lined up behind the chopper as well.

A dull glow emanated from the back of the hangar, bewitching the vehicles in an ominous light.

"What I am flying?" Axel asked.

"It's the modified Apache," Nelly responded, "and you needn't worry about knowing how to fly it. The flight will be substantially automated. It will be ready in a moment."

Axel dropped the duffel bag and examined the long chassis of the chopper, as if he might find something that the droid couldn't. The glow in the back of the hangar drew his attention. After a few more impatient steps, he decided to explore the source of it. He ducked under the wing of a fighter jet and ambled forward cautiously. Toward the rear of the hangar was a large, cylindrical, glass-encased chamber acting like a massive lantern. Black objects punctuated the interior of the casing.

When closer still, his vision resolved the black objects over the glare of the light. They were large birds, feathers darker than pitch, and half the size of a man. There were at least a dozen of them, and their eyes were closed. It was the first time he had seen one of the hybridized creatures up close. There was nothing friendly looking about them, even when comatose and contained in a secure chamber.

Axel shuddered and wandered away, trying to find something else to distract him while he waited. He best not be idle, or it might allow him to contemplate what was happening to his family. He best not be idle, or it might lead him to reconsider the mission altogether.

He strolled past various boxes and containers, none labeled with anything other than bar codes. His pacing brought him to the accordionned wall that bisected the hangar. He walked over to the only small door on the side of it. Here he could hear some faint musical sounds on the other side, rich in melody. It was a familiar classical song. Was it the "*Turkish March*", or maybe "*Fur Elise*?" His knowledge of classical music was spotty at best. But music? Could there actually be a human being on the other side?

He reached down for the door handle. "It's locked, Axel," Nelly announced in his ear.

Axel looked up and around, trying to find the camera. "It's the EM-PRESS project, isn't it?"

"Yes, and as we discussed, it's not for you."

Axel gave a sour look, which he hoped was visible through whatever camera was watching him. Then he reluctantly moved away from the door and back to the chopper.

A few minutes later Axel was airborne, bracing himself against strong g-forces as the helicopter stormed off the ground.

"Have you heard anything else from my family?" Axel nearly yelled into the mic on his headset.

"No. They are likely still in the tube, out of reach. They should be getting out shortly."

The chopper quickly reached a cruising altitude of two thousand feet, then lurched forward. The blades cut through the sky northward, toward a line of sporadic clouds scudding across the horizon.

Axel's pulse began to quicken. He would only have one chance to extract them, and it would be hard to know what to expect in the way of resistance.

Feeling antsy again, he went back to the cargo bay to strap on his gear while the autopilot maintained control of the craft. Once adorned with a chute, body armor, and a full assortment of weaponry, he returned to the cockpit.

For a moment, when looking down at the quaint towns and villages below, he became contemplative. There were miniscule people moving about, the grass was green, the pools were azure blue, and the roofs were well tiled. There were no outward signs that a catastrophe was imminent. It made the last several months seem like a dream. He wondered if maybe the images he had seen weren't real—some hallucination born of his reclusive existence.

It was a fleeting and irrational thought, of course.

"Axel, air traffic control has gone silent," Nelly said. "I have no more tricks to obscure the true nature of your mission. Be prepared for company."

Only moments later, Axel caught sight of a distant black spot in the sky. It was a small drone, and it came racing at him with lightning speed. When it was close, the Apache automatically launched countermeasures. A fragment of explosive ordinance intersected with the drone and blew out two of its propellers. The drone spun out of control and circled down, rapidly losing altitude.

Another drone came, and a similar scene played out again. This time the countermeasures wholly destroyed it, and then another, and then four at once. The same scene played out again and again. Each time the drones were disabled by the Apache's countermeasures.

Then the drones came, but stayed at a distance. First there were two, then five, then ten—hovering all around him, below him and above him.

"What are they doing?" Axel asked.

"They may attack all at once, or they may be waiting until we land," Nelly answered.

Neither alternative seemed desirable.

"How far away are we now?" Axel asked, feeling more and more anxious.

"ETA five minutes."

Axel leaned his head into the cockpit window to try to make out signs of their destination. The massive, four-story public transport tube snaking to the north and south was visible. Near an offshoot to the tube was a small oval shape. It must be the stadium. Not much farther now.

Alarm bells sounded and the radar showed an incoming bogie. It was much larger than the drones. An explosion rocked the chopper, sending it into a brief spin that the automatic pilot managed to recover from.

"What the hell was that?" Axel asked.

"A jet fighter has been sent to intercept us. We have destroyed their first missile with countermeasures. Our ground-to-air defenses have been activated."

Another missile came at the chopper and exploded at a distance with yet another successful countermeasure deployment. Again, it rocked the chopper, and again, the chopper recovered.

Axel saw another object entering the radar viewfinder, heading toward the jet nearby. For a while the jet and the object tracked each other, predator and prey doing their airborne dance. Then Axel heard a distant explosion, and he lost both of them on the radar.

"The jet has been neutralized," Nelly announced in his ear.

Axel was a soldier at heart, so being unable to take control of the situation amidst all this heat made him feel useless. At the same time, he knew taking control of the chopper would be irresponsible.

There was at least one way he could help.

He stood up and headed out of the cockpit to the back of the chopper. He picked up a spare assault rifle from his duffel bag. Then he opened the main door and tried to locate some of the surrounding drones through his rifle sight.

He began firing. The first few shots missed, but then he hit one, and it spun out of control, spiraling downward. It gave him confidence. He continued firing, every once in a while downing one of the drones.

"Close the door," Nelly said.

"Why?" Axel asked. But as soon as he asked the question he could see why. The drones were moving toward the chopper, all at once.

As soon as Axel heaved the door closed, the sky around the chopper became a hurricane of drones and exploding countermeasures. One drone managed to fly into the underside of the chopper and explode, and another intersected the rotary blades. He was thrown across the chopper twice, one time smashing his head painfully against the fuselage, another time landing more mercifully on his buttocks.

Eventually the chopper righted itself. But the smooth hum of the engine was gone. The walls shuddered every few seconds, and smoke trailed behind.

Axel staggered back into the cockpit, smarting from the bruising collisions with all sides of the interior. He felt dizzy. He might have a concussion.

He held firmly onto the back of the pilot chair, trying to clear the fog in his brain and get his bearings. They were close. The stadium was fully in view, and the playing field inside was alive, teaming with thousands of trapped people.

"Axel, I believe we have been identified as a major threat."

"You think?"

Nelly ignored the sarcasm. "Satellite is showing silo activations. Please put on your visor and sit down immediately." Axel did as he was told, but Nelly's words weren't quite registering. He wasn't sure what the silo activations meant. It might have been the blow to his head. He couldn't quite put two and two together.

"Call coming in," Nelly said. His family. It cut through the fog and gave him focus. "Zach, is that you?" He called into his mic.

"Yes, dad," his son was speaking in harsh whispers. "We're out of the tube. They're being rough with Mom, with us too. Mom, no. Don't—" There was a burst of static.

"What happened? Can you hear me Zach?"

The static disappeared for a moment. There was a distant voice in the background saying, "Give that back." Then there was another burst of static.

Then there was static, and more static.

Axel had a sinking feeling. They must have taken away Zach's phone. It could be the last time he heard his voice. He didn't have time to say anything to him. He didn't even have time to tell them he was coming for them.

More static.

The chopper began its descent, occasionally listing to one side and then righting itself.

Abruptly the static ended.

"Zach, can you hear me?" Axel asked desperately. "Zach?"

There was no response, but no static, either.

"You should be connected," Nelly said.

Maybe they were watching Zach, or listening in. Maybe Zach could hear but not speak. "Listen to me, Zach," Axel said crisply. "Whatever you do, do not go into that stadium. Get away. I'm coming to pick you up."

Then another voice came on. It was a higher-pitched voice, some other boy. "Can you get my daddy?" he said. The child sounded vaguely familiar, but it was definitely not Zach.

Who was this child? Had someone taken the phone?

The static returned.

"What happened? Nelly?"

"I'm not sure, Axel. I don't have them on satellite."

"Axel. There is an attack in progress," Nelly said.

"What kind of attack?"

Nelly ignored his question. "I have diverted the attack as best I can. Brace for impact. I'm sorry, Axel."

"Sorry?" Nelly never apologized for anything...he only apologized when he was giving very bad news.

Axel looked at the radar, but nothing was visible.

It was because this was no ordinary impact. Axel finally realized what Nelly meant by silos activating.

To his left, dominating the skyline, was a growing mushroom of fire. Energy rippled from it in every direction. Axel reflexively shielded his eyes and turned away. All lights in the cockpit went dead, and the chopper began to slowly spin as it was hit with shockwave after shockwave.

"Nelly? What should I do? Nelly, can you hear me?" Axel asked.

"Nelly?" Axel asked again, desperately tapping on his earbud.

The bomb had fried his electrical systems. Nothing would work anymore, including his earbud—including the chopper itself.

The helicopter spiraled down, faster and faster, farther and farther. There was no way to control it. He tried to push himself out of his chair to go to the cargo bay so he could jump, but the centrifugal forces were too strong. They were plastering him to his seat.

From his airborne cage, the land and sky shuffled before his eyes. With each revolution, the ground came closer.

He saw a stream, then a forested hill. A knoll and a prairie were visible. The blue sky revolved in front of him once again.

This was it. After decades of work, after countless warnings, he had failed to save the one thing he truly cared about.

The ground loomed ever closer. The stream was no longer a solid line but a thick coursing avenue of water, rippling with texture. He saw individual trees. And out of the corner of his eye he glimpsed a black vulture circling.

The blue sky revolved in front of him once again.

Now, with the Detonation in full bloom, his family would perish with billions of others, and so would he.

PART I

GENIE IN A BOTTLE

"I think we risk being the best informed
society that has ever died of ignorance."

- RUBEN BLADES

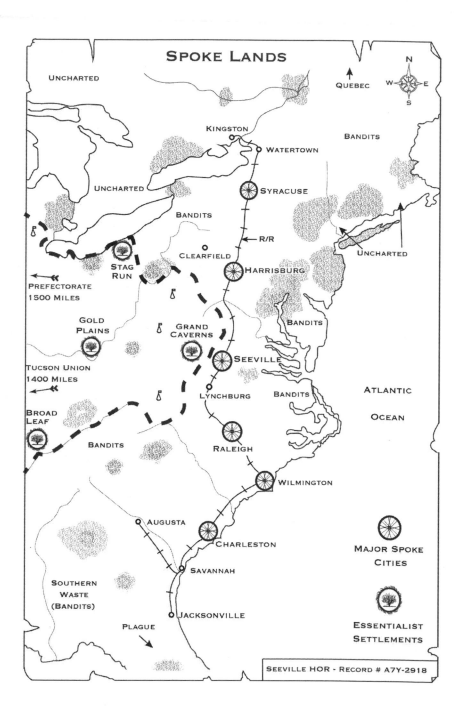

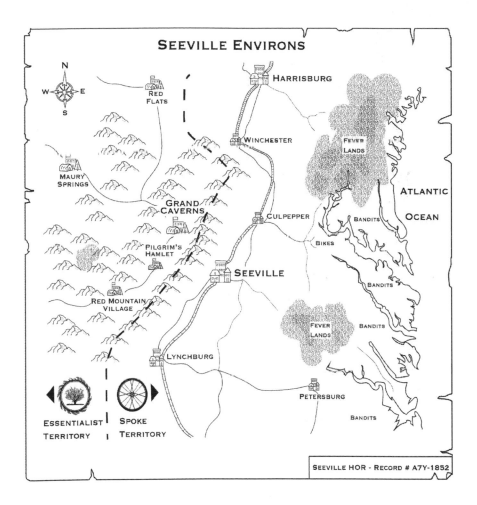

SEEVILLE ENVIRONS

Seeville HOR - Record # A7Y-1852

THE PILGRIMAGE

Talon pushed back a few dangling crimson hairs to curl them around his ear. He picked up his pace, driving his skinny legs to make bolder strides. He had been straggling behind much of the day, mostly to avoid Redfern and Greystone. But he still needed to hear what was being said. All day long Ember had made sure the group would hang onto his every word, and now was no different.

"This will be our last stop today," Ember said while pausing at the edge of the hillock. He turned around to watch the rest of the students catch up. Sweat marred his tunic all the way down to his protruding belly, and the ceremonial green circles around his eyes had long since smudged to bleed down his cheeks. As one of the clansmen leaders most devoted to Essentialist teachings, Ember's exertions on the pilgrimage were worn like a badge of pride.

Redfern's eyes burned on Talon as he caught up. He had that wily look, his energetic expression framed by his dreaded locks. He was always watchful, looking for Talon to stumble, looking for him to show fear. Ember's words from earlier that morning resonated in Talon's mind. "In nature, sometimes to show dominance is less about strength and more about exploiting the weak."

When they had formed a quorum, Ember continued his oration. "We have now seen Old World places of business, and we have seen their places of worship. Here what we see used to be a place of learning."

Talon's eyes followed Ember's outstretched hand down the other side of the hill. He was pointing at what appeared to be a long, institutional building, several stories tall, with impressive thickset columns in the front. A significant portion of the building remained standing far on the left side, with stone-bound windowsills and resolute brick siding. Unlike many of the other buildings they had seen that day, it wasn't obscured by dense foliage or weeds growing through fissures in the concrete.

But no Old World structure could withstand the test of time unscathed. The far right side had been completely flattened to the ground. Signs of reclamation were definitely there as well. The columns had earned a marbled yellow color. Vines had gained purchase, pulling halfway up the building in places. A solitary tree was also pushing through a gaping hole in the roof of an offshoot to the main building.

Ember kept his audience in traction with his circulating eyes. "Like us," he continued, "Old World students learned language, numbers, and vocational trades. But they were not taught to align their actions to the provenance of the earth. By forgetting the gifts of sun, soil, and seed, they lived lives of excess. They were drinking from the slow and sullen river full of silt instead of the mountain stream. The silt bloated them, filled them with ignorance. It sickened their souls, and it contaminated their minds. Remember, they did not have a curator to guide them—to remove noxious texts and unnatural procedures from their learning process."

Ember scratched his chin and then glanced back at the old building.

He turned back to them, nodding. "And so with a corrupted connection to sun, soil, and seed, it was an inevitable conclusion that the earth would eventually levy its retribution. And so it was, that the Detonation came to be."

He wrung his hands together, glancing about the group. Despite encouraging questions, Ember had a knack for ruthlessly lecturing anyone who posed one, as if the answers were written plainly into the crumbling concrete.

There were no more questions.

"It's getting late," Ember said. "Let's head back to camp. Tomorrow is an important day. We will complete the pilgrimage. Tomorrow we see Clay's Colossus."

They backtracked on their route, avoiding all but the well-worn paths of the many pilgrimages. The ruins were to be seen, not touched. They were to be left in peace until the earth reclaimed them completely. The sun fell in the west, flavoring the autumn leaves with amber light. The group was quiet, worn from the day's travel.

They continued well into twilight, returning over the rope bridge and up to the dozen A-frames and long houses that made up Pilgrim's Hamlet. Here they washed up in assigned houses and then returned to the array of tables in the center circle.

Talon had no desire to eat dinner, nor did he want to see Clay's Colossus in the morning. He would rather head back to Grand Caverns that evening. Who knows what sort of neglect his mother had inflicted upon his sisters while he was gone.

But no one left the pilgrimage early. No, he would have to play the part of the loyal Essentialist, at least for one more day.

Thankfully Redfern and Greystone had run into the Summerwind girls when washing up. It looked like they had managed to parlay them into joining them at their table, several totems away, on the other side of the center circle. Hopefully it would keep them distracted long enough for Talon to eat in peace.

Talon sat alone at a table on the periphery. He kept his head down as he whittled the end of several sticks into sharp points in preparation for the morning hunt.

He would occasionally glance up at the totems surrounding the circle. Ember had explained their meaning earlier in the day, but he couldn't remember the lesson. When Ember spoke of the Essentialist heroes, Talon would often lose interest, and his mind would stray. Too often, his thoughts would linger toward home.

The slow-cooked venison arrived, served by the dutiful citizens of Pilgrim's Hamlet. The meat was grey and otherwise devoid of color except for the watery pool of blood it was sitting in. It didn't look particularly appetizing. But it was the ceremonial meal of the pilgrimage, and all must eat their share. He took a cautious bite and found that it was surprisingly moist and flavorful, bursting with rosemary and thyme. His hunger asserted itself and he leaned into the meat, devouring it with a flurry of stained hands and gnashing teeth.

After several bites he looked up and was surprised to see a man sitting across from him. As the only man on the pilgrimage from the Prefectorate, Captain Nobura was easy to recognize. Nobura's head was so clean-shaven it almost shined, and high cheekbones seemed to squeeze out any emotion from his dark brown eyes. He was dressed in loose-fitting pants and a cotton tunic, much lighter than the heavy leather frocks typically sported by Grand Caverns Essentialists. His eyes were not outlined in ceremonial green circles. The only spot of color on Nobura came from his maroon armband.

"You are Talon Clearwater," Nobura said, scrutinizing the plate of venison now being placed in front of him. The scrawny server seemed nervous, her hands shaking.

Talon was unsure if it was a question or a statement. "Yes," he said slowly, wiping his mouth.

"I will be your Shinogi. I will teach you our ways."

The Shinogi were still relatively new in Grand Caverns. First there were the Spanish speakers with their pasty food and now there were these Asian people with their peculiar fighting routines. It was hard to keep up.

"But...why is that?" Talon asked. Then he tried to dull the edge of his question. "I'm sorry, but I didn't ask for any training."

"The curator has allowed me to select my own pupils. It will be an opportunity for you to learn our ways."

"But why me?"

Nobura had been organizing his plate, putting the venison in one quadrant, the sprouts in another, the sweet potato in another. Now he began cutting into the venison with his curved knife. He spoke quietly, without looking up at Talon. "You may have potential."

Potential? What did this man from thousands of miles away know of his potential? Talon tried to quell a surge of frustration. It was yet another commitment he didn't ask for. Yet another commitment he didn't have time for.

"Why did you come here?" Talon asked, trying to deflect the discussion away from him. "This is a pilgrimage for the clans of Grand Caverns. I didn't think it would interest you and your...people."

"An alliance will not survive if it does not move beyond the paper on which it is written. You must learn about us, and we must learn about you. I am here to understand more about you, so that those of us from the Prefectorate can live in peace with the clans of Grand Caverns and the surrounding communities."

Talon tried to find some flaw in Nobura's argument, but could think of none. "I see," he replied.

Nobura had cut his venison into tiny squares, perfectly bite sized, and he now took his first bite with a two-pronged fork. Meanwhile Talon was down to the last large morsel of venison. He was holding it with his bare hands as the juices dripped down his wrist.

"Are you enjoying the pilgrimage?" Nobura asked after a moment of silence. He only briefly glanced up from his meal to pose the question.

Talon considered giving him the canned response—some well-worn statement about sun, soil and seed—but then decided against it. Better to tell Nobura the truth. Perhaps it would change Nobura's mind about enrolling him as a pupil.

"I don't see why we need to travel all this way to an Old World ruin. We are Essentialists and yet we aren't foraging here. We aren't even hunting for our town. And all our lives the curator has taught us not to set foot in any Old World cesspool. Why should a pilgrimage be any different? It seems hypocritical."

Nobura seemed insensitive to the comment, which by most would be considered disloyal and even blasphemous. He simply continued to eat his meal with great care, like it was a surgical undertaking. "Being true to the earth does not mean being ignorant of the ways of the Old World," he said. "As the curator says, to be a devout Essentialist is to understand not only what is necessary and good, but also what is wanton and malevolent. Here we understand what happened during the time of the Detonation. In other words, we understand what was wanton and malevolent."

Talon's brow furrowed. It was frustrating that he was unable to rouse Nobura's ire. "I still don't see the need for us to travel all this way. The books are enough."

"Even the statue?" Nobura asked. "Clay's Colossus is not in a book—it is not of the Old World—it is not part of this cesspool, as you call it. Is that not of interest?"

Talon was indeed curious about the statue, but it was going to take an entire extra day—a day that he didn't have. And he knew it was probably just another frayed monument, just like the Old World buildings they had seen today. "I know the statue is supposed to make some kind of impression on me, but it's just an old statue made of stone. Sure, maybe it's artfully crafted, but it's still just stone—just like the stones littered about this hamlet, or like a boulder that has fallen off a mountain. Grand Caverns has many interesting rock formations. I can find enough of those at home."

Nobura raised his thin eyebrows. His attention had left his meal and was now wholly on Talon. "Some old statue? A statue is not just a statue, and stone is not just stone. From it you can learn much. In fact, even though I have not been on this pilgrimage, I have seen this statue. It is visible from the hills west of here. That should tell you something."

Out of the corner of his eye Talon saw Greystone and Redfern stand up. They looked to be preparing to leave the circle. They began walking away toward the cabins, Summerwind girls in tow. It would be best to get away from the table soon, while they were distracted.

"I don't get it. What should it tell me?" Talon said, his leg shaking. He hurried to chew and swallow the last sweet potato skin left on his plate.

Nobura was watching him carefully. He had followed Talon's eyes to the table where Greystone and Redfern had been eating. He said, "for one, the fact that I have seen the statue should tell you about its size. It is visible from far away. In turn its size should tell you about the effort put forth by Clay Ripplewood and the other Essentialist ancestors who built it. The effort put into a thing tells you much about its meaning."

"I should go," Talon said, collecting his plate and standing up.

Nobura said, "patience."

Talon considered just walking away, but Nobura was a captain and would soon be his teacher. It would not sit well to offend him, and their conversation had been abrasive enough as it was. Talon tried to calm himself and sit back down. "I'm sorry," he said.

"Patience," Nobura said again.

"I know. I heard you. I didn't mean to be rude."

"You heard me, but you misunderstand me. You can go, if you like. I was not asking you to stay and sit with me. I was suggesting you learn patience, so that you can better understand the pilgrimage. Without it, you will take away nothing."

Talon frowned. "Why should I be patient? I have to get home. My family needs me."

Nobura's eyes narrowed even further. He turned to look into the forest for a moment, and then looked back at Talon. "I am sure that even here, far to the east among the Wood, Wind, and Water clans, you have heard stories about us Shinogi. Stories of how we have overcome our enemies with ruthless violence. Many believe this is how we conquered the prefectures of my homeland, and many believe this violence has also given us our victory over the length of the great western sea as well."

Talon nodded. It was common knowledge that the Shinogi were ruthless. Everyone had heard about them beheading the enemies of the Prefectorate.

"However, for us Shinogi, it is not violence that governs us, but rather patience. We do not wish to arrive at our destination the fastest. Our destination is fate, and fate is inevitably death. No, the key is to take every step down the path carefully, and with dignity, and to choose the *correct* path. Patience has given us victory more than violence, more than any other virtue."

Nobura spread his hands as he stated his conclusion. "You would be wise to take the time necessary to ponder the significance of this pilgrimage, Talon."

All this talk of patience only made Talon more anxious to leave. He realized the best way to break away from this man was to fawn to his beliefs. Talon gritted his teeth, nodded and said, "I will consider your words."

Nobura only squinted in response.

Talon stood up and took his plate to the washbasin nearby. Thankfully Nobura didn't make any more nebulous comments to lure him back. Then Talon left the center circle, walking quickly down the main thoroughfare of Pilgrim's Way.

There were no more shadows. Day was rapidly giving away to night.

Greystone and Redfern were waiting for him on the front steps of his A-frame. Perhaps the girls had snubbed them. Or maybe they just wanted their fix. It didn't matter now.

He shouldn't have taken the main thoroughfare. He should have been more careful, but Nobura's words about patience were reverberating in his mind, distracting him. As a result, he was walking too fast, and he stumbled across them too quickly, before he could spot them and sneak away.

"I think it's time we had our little meeting," Redfern said, wringing his hands. "I've been looking forward to it all day."

"And nobody is around to save you this time," Greystone added, arcing around Talon like a mountain lion circling its prey.

Talon knew they would harass him until they got what they wanted. There were others on the thoroughfare—enough of them to recount the story of what happened. If they made a spectacle it might be enough to satisfy them, and then hopefully they would finally leave him alone.

His muscles tensed.

Greystone charged him first, pummeling his midsection and throwing him to the ground. Talon's head bounced painfully against the hard earth, but otherwise he was unhurt. Talon managed to grab onto Greystone's scraggly hair. He pounded his head on the ground, but only with enough force to look like he was trying. Greystone easily tore free from his grasp and punched Talon above his eye.

The pain washed through him, leaving him disoriented. He staggered to his knees just in time for Redfern to hit the other side of his face and knock him down again.

Should he stay down? How much was enough? He couldn't know.

Greystone kicked him in the stomach, and Talon reflexively retracted into a ball. Redfern kicked him as well.

The blows hurt, his senses reeled, but something was burning inside him. He could feel a well of energy surging up through him, fueled by adrenaline, fueled by raw emotion. It spoke with its own voice. It screamed at him to stand, to fight back.

"Declawed already, Talon? Show some balls, wimpwater," Redfern said, laughing.

Greystone kicked him again, but the blow was muted against his retracted legs. Talon would only open his eyes in fleeting blinks. He could see several people around him. They were watching through what was left of the fading light. Redfern was getting what he wanted. All Talon needed to do was stay down.

But he couldn't. The voice inside him was too strong, the surge too visceral. Possessed, he jumped up from the ground and lashed out. Greystone ducked away, and Talon's first swipe ended up missing by a large margin.

Redfern said, "still some fight left in—" but Talon had never stopped moving. His limbs flew like a tornado in every direction. One limb hit, then another. He repulsed Greystone backward by a kick to his thigh and struck Redfern in the face, mid-sentence.

Talon finally restrained himself. He stood there, panting, and saw that Greystone was bent over, circling Talon again. Redfern was holding his face.

"Not smart," was all Redfern said, and he began pacing more cautiously.

There were at least a dozen people watching, but something was strange about them. Despite the late hour, these were not silhouettes in the twilight. In fact, their features were well defined. Something was illuminating them from above, through a clearing in the trees.

They began craning their necks upward and their gaze held. Greystone risked a glance, and even Redfern. They stopped circling him.

Distant yells could be heard. Then a student asked, "What is it?" Her voice held a hint of fear.

Talon looked back and forth between Redfern and Greystone. Whatever it was, they were entranced by it. Behind Redfern, the forest was more visible now, and Talon could make out a faint maroon line. As the light grew, the maroon line resolved into a crouching figure.

It was Nobura, his Shinogi armband reflecting the light coming from above. He had been watching them from a dark cache in the forest. Nobura now stood, his attention no longer on Talon. He looked up into the gap in the trees with the rest of them.

Finally, Talon allowed himself to look up.

Directly overhead, a great, glowing ball of fire was lancing through the heavens, heading into the valley. It left a heavy trail of smoke in its wake.

"I think…it's a satellite," Ember said, gawking upward in awe. He was walking down the thoroughfare toward the gathering, trailed by some twenty more from the circle. "It looks like…like it could be landing in the valley."

Talon took the opportunity to move away from Redfern and Greystone. He merged into the crowd of onlookers next to Ember, making it seem like he was trying to get a better vantage point.

Soon enough, the ball of fire was lost under the trees, and the twilight returned, darker than before.

Ember rapidly divorced himself from his trance and barked, "Nobura, come!" He waved to Nobura, urging him to join him.

Ember retreated from the crowd of onlookers with Captain Nobura. The two of them shared harsh whispers.

Questions were exchanged in the crowd around Talon.

"What's a satellite?"

"Is it a sign?"

Most were transfixed by the trail of smoke that still hung in the sky, or by the conversation Ember was having just out of reach.

The only words Talon could make out from Ember's conversation were the last ones. "Go with haste!" Ember said. He was patting Nobura on the shoulder.

Nobura jogged to a nearby horse tethered to a tree. He deftly jumped on the steed, kicked the flanks, and galloped off into the night.

THE CAMPFIRE

The weary cyclists came to a halt at a dilapidated water tower just off the main road. There was an abandoned Old World house there, but it was too run-down to be safe for shelter, so they set up camp nearby, where a small but energetic stream percolated through a sparsely wooded area.

Owen quickly excused himself to wash as soon as they arrived. Given the meager flow coming off the mountain, it looked like a spit bath would have to suffice. He found a small pool and caught a glance of his reflection. His exertions accentuated the cluster of white spots on the right side of his face. They were defiant against his rosy cheeks and wheat-brown hair.

He cupped his hands and drank greedily from the pool before bathing.

"Don't stink up the water," Preston smirked at him and joined him for a wash.

"Too late, I'm afraid," Owen replied wistfully.

From a distance, people often mistook Owen for Preston, even though Preston was a hair taller. Up close, however, Owen's spots quickly distinguished him. They both definitely stood out on the expedition, however, their physiques gaunt compared to the veteran mules and hunters who rode up the mountain with them. It was the result of too many sedentary days at trade school. Thankfully Preston gave Owen someone to commiserate with on the brutal uphill climb.

It was indeed strange that they were both included in the expedition. Owen and Preston were more likely to be assigned to accounting duties than to be made party to a hunting foray. Their breakneck pace was also unusual. Were all the prize bucks going to disappear after tomorrow?

When they had finished cleaning themselves they made their way back to find Jakson and Noke eating quietly by their fire pit.

Jakson was a bull of a man, with a full beard and prominent eyebrow ridges. He was known as a great huntsman around Seeville, although in Owen's experience his most striking attribute seemed to be his penchant for sarcasm. Despite the fact that he was Owen's cousin, Owen didn't know much about him. Jakson was often away and tended to keep to himself.

Noke he knew even less about, other than he was one of the strongest mules in Seeville. He was wiry, with chiseled calves and sinuous forearms—a perfect build for riding. His face was clean-shaven and always showed some gradation of stern focus on whatever task lay before him.

Preston and Owen lifted rations from their packs and joined the others, who promptly left to go clean themselves in turn. Preston smelled his armpit and raised his eyebrows at Owen.

Owen sniggered. "Yeah, or more likely they don't want to fraternize with us trade school lackeys."

Preston smiled and nodded.

When they had all finished eating and grooming, Noke tended the fire while the others gathered round.

"You guys know why we had to make it up here in such a hurry?" Preston asked.

Noke and Jakson glanced at each other. Jakson said, "looks like we need some more kindling." His statement conflicted with a large pile of dry sticks laying in reserve at his feet. He pushed up on his knees to stand. When he turned, the shape of him was quickly lost in the gloom.

With an annoyed look, Noke watched Jakson leave. He leaned into the fire with a flint in his hand. The spark lit up his face, once, twice, and on the third time the dried moss at the base of the woodpile caught. They all stared at the fire as it bloomed.

Owen was beginning to think Preston's question was going to go unanswered, until finally Noke said, "Best hear it from Lord Henneson, kid."

Jakson returned with additional kindling and they sat in silence. The campsite was well lit now, with three fires going. Owen saw Lord Henneson and the woman from the north talking to a group of mules at another fire.

This woman from the north, this Cecile, was difficult to figure out. Her skin was less sun-weathered than people from Seeville. She seemed to always wear all-black outfits, and she had a streak of blue dye in her hair. Stranger than the look of her were her mannerisms. Sure, she spoke with a French accent, but more unnerving was her tendency to stare at you without flinching. It had more than once unhinged Owen and a few others in the group.

Owen didn't know about where she came from, but in Seeville, it wasn't polite to stare. In fact, if she wasn't so cozy with lords like Henneson, soon she might find herself staring out of two black eyes.

Lord Henneson and Cecile finally made their way over to their fire. Henneson sat down on a stump and poked at the fire with a stick. His gray goatee seemed to bristle and his deep brown eyes reflected the orange cinders. As a lord of Seeville, he held more gravitas than anyone in the campsite, yet his demeanor was relatively disarming and straightforward. Thankfully he hadn't preached any of his Adherent's gospel on the trip, or surely Owen's ignorance would have been exposed.

Henneson kept his gaze on the flames as he spoke. "We're not hunting game tomorrow. We're going into Essentialist territory."

Owen glanced over at the other men. Noke and Jakson were unreadable, but Preston's eyes had opened wide.

Henneson lifted his burning stick from the fire and poked it through the air as if it were a bird. Then he veered the stick downward and snuffed out the flame in the damp soil. "The flaming arrow seen in the sky two nights ago. That's what we seek."

He looked up at them. "It will be dangerous. Our goal is to go in, get what we need, and then get out as fast as possible. We must not alert the Essentialists. We will split up to cover more ground and to try to remain hidden. Cecile will be leading you. I'll be with another squad."

He paused, letting them process the information, then continued. "I know Cecile is a foreigner, but she has my full backing. Follow her orders, do your job, and then get out. Do you understand?"

They all nodded slowly.

Owen quelled an urge to voice an objection. Instead of a casual hunting foray along the ridge, they would be heading deep into the valley, possibly facing the heinous Essentialists. He kept his mouth in a morose but firm straight line.

Henneson stood up and threw his stick into the fire. "Good luck tomorrow, and be careful. Novation is damnation." Then he turned around and headed back to his own tent.

Cecile lingered, watching the group from behind where Henneson was sitting. Noke spoke first, his skepticism evident. "A flaming arrow in the sky? Is this some riddle from his Adherent gospel? Let's speak plainly. What is it that we really seek, Quebecker?"

Cecile's expression was masked by the gloom. "It's *Quebecois*. But to answer your question, it's not an arrow. We believe it's a satellite, a downed satellite. No games. That's the truth." Her accent was thick, with rolling *r* sounds and hard *th* sounds, yet her words were clear enough.

Owen had heard the rumors about a flaming arrow in the sky, but thought nothing of it. Children made up things like this all the time. Most people from Seeville thought satellites were Old World myths, one of many pre-Detonation contraptions that were too difficult to imagine, especially when no one had ever seen a working car or telephone.

Cecile addressed their confused looks. "A satellite is like a pod, or a ship, that circles around the earth in the stars above us. They were used to help people talk to each other over long distances and to look down on the earth, back when there was electricity. We have a number of accounts from people in Seeville about how it came down, so we know it landed in the valley beyond Skyline."

"So why are Owen and I here?" Preston asked. "We're not hunters or enforcers. We're not trained to fight the SLS." Owen nodded to reinforce the question. Preston was always willing to ask the questions he was too afraid to.

Cecile moved to sit down on the stump where Henneson had been sitting, her face now more exposed to the light. Her eyebrow tilted up into a chevron. "Why do *you* think we invited you on this expedition?"

she asked.

Preston's mouth opened halfway, but he didn't answer.

"Yes, I know about your tinkering in electronics, both of you." She turned her head toward Owen, her eyes sending a ripple of nerves through him. "I believe there may be some pre-Detonation technology in the satellite. You might be able to help me retrieve it, so we can properly evaluate it, before the Essentialists do."

It felt like invisible ants were crawling up Owen's chest. How could they know about his tinkering? He said, "I know we're not supposed to tinker, but there are so many things we could learn. Back in the—"

She cut him off. "*Non, non t'inquiet pas,*" she said. "I know you have been taught to worry about such things—the three fears and all that. But we're all adults here, right? We know how to be careful. So don't worry."

"Correction," she added ruefully after letting her response sink in. "Worry, but just not about that."

Owen wasn't so sure the others shared Cecile's view. Sure, it wasn't like the old days, like Okafor's time, but many folks in Seeville still had entrenched superstitions about Old World devices. Many would question why they needed to "evaluate" the satellite at all.

Jakson seemed to read Owen's mind. He nudged his chin in the direction of Henneson's tent. "The lords, they're okay with you playing around with this Old World tech? I can't imagine Henneson agreeing to that."

Cecile eyed Jakson warily. "Now, be careful what words you use," she said. "I didn't say we would be *playing around with it.* I asked for Preston and Owen because they could help me access the satellite, and maybe understand what's in it. Lord Henneson has agreed, I assure you."

Then Cecile's eyes focused, and her gaze went rigid, boring into Jakson. "But are you okay with that, Jakson? Are you going to follow your orders?"

Jakson stared back at Cecile. His eyes were dark pools reflecting the fire. For a moment Owen thought he was going to say no. But then he looked down and said, "Sure. Doesn't bother me a lick."

Cecile peeled her eyes away from Jakson and looked at the rest of them. "That goes for all of you. I fully expect you to follow orders. And nothing said or done here is spoken about in Seeville, understand?" She looked at each of them in turn, gauging their responses. When she reached Owen, she hovered a long time with her eyes, just long enough to make him uncomfortable. Owen withered under her glare and looked down, waiting for her to move on.

Finally, Cecile stood up. "I will tell you more tomorrow. We need to be alert, so get some rest. Lord Henneson isn't kidding. It will be dangerous."

"*Bon soir,*" she added, and without asking, she poured her canteen out on the fire, sending up a twirling tornado of smoke and sparks. When the smoke dissipated, she was gone.

No one relit the fire. They all followed Cecile's orders and adjourned for the evening. Owen meandered over to his tent at the periphery of the campsite, close to the struggling stream.

Owen was like a rolling pin that night, kneading every corner of his thin foam sleeper with his tossing and turning. He kept reminding himself he needed to sleep, but the reminder only made him more agitated. It wasn't so much the danger they might face the next day. Their knowledge of his covert tinkering had unnerved him greatly.

When he finally did find sleep, he had a vivid dream—a dream his mind somehow unearthed from long ago.

He was perched at an unblemished desk, writing computer code, towers dominating the expanse from his Old World skyscraper office window. Day turned to night, and he somehow appeared above the buildings, floating through the sky above Seeville, constellations of light visible both above and below him. He would look to the side and be enraptured by a host of airplanes piercing the darkness next to him, their contrails blazing arcs into the sky.

Eventually he would see his house in the perforated cityscape and land softly in his yard.

Upon landing a huge hologram of a budding flower sprouted from his house. It cast pyrotechnic beams of golden light on the houses around him. The light was full of hope, full of progress and potential. The smiles of his mother and sisters surrounded him as they pointed at the flower blossoming around them.

The hologram would illuminate the bunker in his backyard as well. But there was a sliver of black on the bunker, a mutinous anomaly against the indulgent blaze. The sliver would draw him to the bunker. As he approached, the golden light of the hologram turned to a more ominous shade of blue. The sliver of black resolved itself. It was the edge of a door, a door that was slightly ajar.

He would hover at the door, and his heart would hammer in his chest. The light cast on the bunker morphed again, to purple and then red. The light was no longer glorious. It was a sickly thing, holding no virtue. Red was the color of urgency; red was the color of danger; red was the color of blood.

And finally, his clammy hand would pull at the door, and open it.

A FORBIDDEN TALISMAN

Flora was awakened by a glint of sun creeping up through the center of the tent. Upon hearing Reed's rhythmic breathing beside her, she lifted the sheets off carefully to avoid rousing him and tiptoed over to the cupboards.

She grabbed a bruised apple and bit into it as quietly as she could. It looked like the kids had left their bed unmade. At least they hadn't disturbed Reed before leaving. A number of empty glasses littered the few tables in the tent, and a faint smell of alcohol remained in the air.

She glanced into the mirror under the washbasin. She looked tired. Her short-cropped red hair was particularly oily and unkempt, and her gray eyes certainly did not resemble the gemstones Granger raved about. Or at least, if they were gemstones, they certainly needed polishing.

She looked through the cupboard but couldn't find the oats and berries she had prepared for the kids. Figuring Talon must have already grabbed them, she quickly changed, packed her bag and strode through the tent flap.

Still groggy, she nearly walked right into a gaggle of five men, one of them murmuring in Spanish. They were heading down the laneway with purpose, carrying bundles of wheat and pails of water. She could see another two groups ahead of them, one with an ox-pulled cart, and another pulling a line of horses laden with linens.

It used to be she knew everyone on the streets. People would even stop by to chat or say hello. Now she rarely recognized anyone, and those she knew seemed rushed and distant, more intent on their task than what was happening around them. With the population of Grand Caverns doubling in the last year alone, traffic like this had become the norm rather than the exception.

Her breath turned to bursts of fog as she hiked through the settlement in the crisp autumn air. Up and down, up and down. Long, semipermanent tents punctuated the hills, concentrating into more permanent buildings closer to the caverns' entrance.

She tried to take the lesser-used streets through the town center. Sharp odors buffeted her on the busiest avenues—hot porridge, urine, incense, feces and rotting food.

When walking up Oak Boulevard she could see the new dwellings stacked in front of her, lining the hill around the cavern massif. They were boxy, wooden things with a solitary window on each side. They were nothing like the ornate Old World houses she had seen in books, but still a strong upgrade from the makeshift tents and crude A-frames used by Flora and most other Essentialists. Reed had spoken about moving into one of the sturdier buildings, closer to the caverns, but she couldn't commit. Just the thought of moving was exhausting, and she preferred to be away from the action.

Three new wagons were parked near the main entrance to the caverns, their owners unpacking boxes and bringing the contents inside. The leathery housings of these wagons were adorned with colorful pastel decorations. Their owners uttered the occasional phrase in Spanish. The third wagon was more Spartan, the owners muted, and the faces appeared to be mostly Asian. All of the new immigrants had the green-ringed eyes symbolic of their status as disciples of the curator.

Every day, new wagons. Every day, new people. Every day, hopefuls arrived at the vanguard of the great eastern frontier.

Flora was not one of those who belittled the color of their skin or shunned their foreign tongues. And she didn't care that they didn't have blood from the Wood, Wind, or Water clans, as some complained about. Yes, there were language issues and constant work to build new dwellings, but these people were tough and driven, and they quickly found productive lives in the settlement.

It did worry Flora the rate at which these people were arriving. There was only so much land, and if they were to move farther east it would drive them right into Spoke territory, to the earth's tormentors, to the defiled land of grease and gears—or so they had been taught. It was hard to see how these ambitious opportunists would not find some reason to push the boundary farther.

Flora knew all too well the Spoke people were not to be trifled with.

She made an arc around the cavern entrance and descended the hill to the valley. Below her was a long, makeshift tent attached to a number of boxy buildings with long roof extensions, making up the Grand Caverns school grounds. Flora would often read to the kids here while they ate their breakfast in the mornings.

Today she saw the table they typically used was empty. No one was at any of the other tables either.

Looking down the rows of tents and overhangs, Flora could see a large gathering was taking place at the school's outdoor amphitheater.

She felt a pang of anxiety. She wondered if she had forgotten about an announcement, or one of the school events, as she often did.

Making her way over to the gathering, she grabbed an empty chair to stand on, so she could see the speaker over the huddle. She saw Talon, Clover and Skye down by the front, listening intently. The speaker had a rounded belly, was dressed in a layered leather frock and had green-ringed eyes. She recognized him as sub-chief Ember Thisslewood.

"While one can not tell what perversion makes this craft rip through our sky," Ember was saying, "or even what this abhorrence is made of, our disciples have faced similar Old World artifacts before."

"How do we know it will be taken care of? That our children will not stumble across this thing?" one of the mothers asked.

"Our best teams will be sent to scout the area. You can be assured we will find and cleanse the remnants of this thing, should any exist."

Ember waited to see if there were any further questions. Hearing none, he nodded and said, "That is all. You may go. May sun, soil, and seed provide you with bounty on this day."

The crowd dispersed gradually as people chatted and nodded. Flora waited patiently for the kids to see her. Skye's eyes found her first. "There's Mommy!" she said. Clover and Skye ran to her, the way only five-year-olds could, as if Flora had been gone for weeks and not hours.

Flora smiled and waited until the two girls ran into her open arms. Talon lingered behind, kicking at the dirt, looking thoughtful.

"Mommy, Mommy, there was a fireball in the sky!" Skye exclaimed as she was enveloped into Flora's embrace. Clover was nodding emphatically beside her.

"They said it was a *sat-Light*, and it may have *landed*," Clover said.

"A what?" Flora asked. "I'm sorry, I missed the beginning." She looked to Talon for help.

Talon glanced up from the ground momentarily, catching her eye. "It's true. Some kind of fireball flew through the sky two nights ago, when I was on the pilgrimage. I saw it myself. They said it was Old World, pre-Detonation. May have burned up completely, but they're looking into it. Thisslewood said it's nothing to worry about."

No wonder there was so much excitement. "Why don't you tell me all about it," Flora said, while guiding Skye and Clover back toward the tables.

The girls did their best to describe other aspects of the speech. There wasn't much to know. Mostly it sounded like another excuse to rail against the Old World and their scourge of the earth. The curator was probably ecstatic. What better way to rally all the diverse Essentialist peoples than to point to fireballs falling from the sky?

When they arrived at the table Flora brought out some paper and they practiced their letters and numbers together.

Skye said, "Um Mommy, can I ask you something?"

"Of course, Skye. What is it?"

She leaned over and whispered in her ear, "Can we do the drawings again—the talisman drawings?"

It was so hard to say no to her, and there was no one else around. "Sure, my little water lily."

Skye clapped her hands quietly, and then whispered in Clover's ear. Clover clapped her hands in turn but much louder. "Shhh, it's a secret," Skye chided.

Flora laid out more paper for Clover and Skye, and then she began outlining the shapes of Granger's talisman for them. It had been weeks since she last drew it, but the memory never faded. She drew the setting sun, the pillared Old World house with the tower next to it, and the for-eign-looking cat with the strange beard. When she was done the drawing, she stopped short of writing his name and birthday, although the memory of it was still imprinted in her mind in every detail, right down to the stoic font used for the letters.

"Mommy, can I make mine just like yours?" Skye asked.

"You can use parts of mine. That's how you know where you came from. But your talisman has to be unique, just like you are." Skye frowned in confusion. Flora pushed away a bank of red, curly locks draping over her face, and Skye began drawing again.

Flora stretched her back and took a moment to watch her daughters draw. Talon was sitting across from them, his eyebrows furrowed and lips pursed. She knew it was one of his looks that masked some form of dis-appointment.

"It's harmless, Talon."

"Harmless? You know it's only a matter of time until somebody finds out—only a matter of time until *he* finds out. I'm enough of a reminder. He doesn't need to see the talisman as well."

"Who is Talon talking about, Mommy?" Clover asked without look-ing up from her doodles.

"No one, water lily," Flora said. "Talon, please try not to worry."

Talon looked down at the table again. He had grown taller than her, and was filling out. She had to keep reminding herself that he was a man now, despite his sulky disposition.

She tried to say something positive. "Thank you for taking the kids out again, Talon."

Talon only said, "I know you have to get going. I can take care of Clover and Skye."

"I know you can, Talon."

He continued to look down.

"Everything okay at the Whitewater farm?" Flora asked. "They are paying you?"

"Yes. The work is hard, but they pay us enough and give us a hearty lunch. I'm trying to teach Clover and Skye about leather-making when we're harvesting, when they come by after school."

"Good," she said. Still, he would not meet her eyes.

How long had it been since Talon had smiled? How long had it been since he had really spoken with her? And now, at seventeen, he was beginning to look so much like Granger, with his flattish nose and wispy hair. His hair was more crimson than Granger's, but otherwise he was a near-perfect doppelganger. The talisman brought back some memories, but right here, in front of her, was her most endearing memory of Granger. It made Talon's rejection of her feel more acute every day.

There wasn't much she could do. She could only hope Talon would understand someday. She could only hope he would forgive her.

"Thanks again Talon," she said, getting up slowly from the table.

He responded with a barely discernable nod.

"See you tonight, girls." Flora said, hugging Clover and Skye.

She made off toward the infirmary, breaking into a half jog on the way up the hill. Glancing back momentarily, she could see Talon take the drawings from the girls and crumple them up. He threw them unceremoniously into the trash bin.

NADAR CORPORATION

"**A**xel Kelemen?" The car asked in a calm, feminine voice.

"Yes," Axel responded.

"Please apply your fingers to the pad in front of you."

Axel applied his fingerprints to the pad on the car roof.

The door slid open. "Thank you Mr. Kelemen. Your estimated time of arrival at Nadar Tower is fourteen minutes."

Axel hesitated. "What is your Nadar security code?"

The car displayed *AZC8913B5* on the finger touchpad.

"Thank you."

Axel ducked into the car and reclined in a plush leather seat, placing his briefcase down beside him. With a barely audible hum the electric car pulled out of his driveway and began its trip to the turnpike. Axel opened his eyes wide for a moment to let the car access his retina for final confirmation, then he pulled his notes out of his briefcase to revisit the schedule.

His first meeting was with the outgoing security director, followed by meetings with his new staff and other departmental heads. For the fourth time he looked through the profiles and other official Nadar Corporation documents pertaining to policies and procedures. He didn't learn anything new. The corporate wordsmithing seemed to be giving him a feeling of nausea, unless it was the movement of the car.

Axel's first day would be the most telling. Ryan had told him to not read into the bureaucracy, that Nadar Corporation wanted him for something more than these stodgy corporate documents suggested, something more fitting his skill set.

Yet his concern continued to plague him on his way into the city. Through the lavish recruiting courtship, the long move and the many perks, it had endured. When he saw his children first dress up for their new elite Long Island school, it was there, tickling at his conscience. Even in the hours of lovemaking with Pauline on their all-expense getaway to

Santo Domingo, the concern ate at him.

Was he comfortable being the servant of a faceless corporation, even if just for a few months? Was he really just selling out?

If it hadn't been for Ryan's reassurance, he was quite certain he wouldn't be on this ride into the city at all.

Soon enough Axel would find out. If this was just another corporate gig, he told himself he would give his notice within the first three months. Those few months of salary alone would be enough to keep him and his family comfortably afloat for a few years.

As he filed the dossier away in his briefcase, he noticed one of the calluses on his hands had become sharp and rough. He took a nail file out of a compartment of his bag and began to trim down the rough edges of skin on his palm. Sharp callouses wouldn't do for handshakes with these corporate bureaucrats.

The car began to cross the Brooklyn Bridge, the cityscape looming ever closer. He could see the tip of Nadar Tower edging out the other skyscrapers in the distance.

He pulled out his phone and checked his appearance in the camera app. His short-cropped black hair was neatly in place. He adjusted his tie only slightly then put the phone away in his pocket.

"Is it possible for you to let me out in the front of the building, instead of going to the parking lot?" he asked the car.

"Sir, you have been granted Level 7 Priority. It is intended for you to be dropped off on your designated floor. Is that agreeable?"

"Yes, thank you."

Of course he was. He should have guessed they would show off the new car lift system on his first day.

Several people were waiting for a lift up the tower when the car arrived, but the car ignored them, adroitly hooking onto the lift rail on the side of the building without stopping. It then promptly started elevating up the side of the building.

The car docked on the eighty-seventh floor, and the door slid open simultaneously with the wall port. He walked into the building and was greeted by a short but immaculately dressed older man. It was a lavish lobby area, filled with curvy furniture, gilded edges and sparkling glass.

"Hello Mr. Kelemen. Please come this way."

"Thank you. And your name is?

"Bennett, sir." Bennett led him through a few work areas toward a major elevator.

"What is your role at Nadar, Bennett?"

"Pardon me, sir, I have been told to take you directly to the executive floor, and not discuss any company business. Apologies."

They took the main lift up several floors and then walked across the lobby to another elevator stenciled *Executive Lift*. Bennett used a key card, a retinal scan, and fingerprint identification to gain access to the executive elevator. Finally, they landed on the executive floor. The lift opened into a surprisingly Spartan room, with four spindly wooden chairs and a glass coffee table.

"Please wait here, sir." Bennett left him there and took the lift down.

He was supposed to meet with the security director in his office, and the security director didn't work on the executive floor. There must have been a change of plan.

A man looking to be of Asian descent strolled down the hall. He was just past middle age, of normal height, with a peppery five-o'clock shadow. He was dressed in a white shirt and brown blazer, with a tuft of hair sticking straight up at the front. Axel recognized him. It was Bhavin Nadar, the founder of Nadar Corporation.

When it was clear Bhavin was headed his way, Axel got to his feet and met him halfway with a handshake. "A pleasure to meet you, Mr. Nadar. I'm Axel Kelemen, your new security director."

Bhavin looked him up and down. "Yes, yes of course you are. Nice to meet you. Well, you certainly *look* qualified." Bhavin clutched his bicep figuratively and smiled.

Axel smiled back politely. "Thank you, sir."

Bhavin said, "Why don't you come with me," and Axel fell in step with Bhavin, heading back in the direction Bhavin had come.

"I'm here to tell you why you're *really* here," Bhavin said as they walked down the hall together. "There is a saying in India: *Satyameva jayate.*"

"Truth alone triumphs," Axel said.

"Of course you would know that. You did a tour in India, yes?"

"One year, sir."

They didn't stop in the boardroom but rather arrived in Bhavin's office, and then walked farther still down some stairs leading out the back to another rather basic-looking meeting room a few levels down.

Bhavin gestured for him to sit down.

The office had what looked to be a large, full-length window with a view of the Manhattan cityscape. Axel could tell it wasn't a window, but actually a high-resolution display screen. At this point, Axel had no idea which floor he was on or what side of the building he was in. Nadar Corporation definitely didn't want people to know where this room was.

"And you did two special ops tours in India as well, yes?"

Axel didn't respond.

"I'm sorry," Bhavin said. "I'm sure you can't confirm or deny the ops missions. I want you to know we know everything about you. We know you workout every morning for two hours. We know you conducted special ops missions in India, Russia, Congo and Yemen while in the CIA. We know about your children's fondness for buttered pecan ice cream. We know you are probably feeling guilty about all the money and perks we are offering, and we know the only reason you even considered this job is because of your friend Ryan's recommendation."

Axel didn't react. He sat quietly with his leg crossed and hands on his lap.

"You see, we have had two investigators dig up as much as we could find, using methods that...well...it's probably best you not even know about. We have also done the same for thirteen other candidates fielded for this position."

Axel was aware they had at least one investigator following him, yet the amount they knew was disconcerting, particularly the special ops missions. They must have obtained some of the information through illegal means. At the very least, Nadar Corporation had some powerful intelligence capabilities.

Bhavin continued. "After all that, we selected you as the number one candidate. We selected you not only because you are eminently qualified, but because we believe this is a job you can be passionate about; because it is a job that can save lives, and not in the dozens or hundreds, but in the millions."

Axel only nodded slowly, waiting for the punch line.

Bhavin sighed, stood up and looked out into the fake skyline. He said, "You know, when you have the amount of money I have—when you have accomplished the things I have accomplished—you start to look for deeper meaning. You start to look for a different kind of security, one bodyguards and bulletproof vests can't help you with.

"Nadar Corporation has business units in software, mining, defense, pharmaceuticals, agriculture, social media, and robotics. With that broad a purview, you begin to understand the world at a level few can. You are often the first to ferret out those unknown unknowns. You begin to look for hazards that may actually pose a threat to all of humanity simply because the wellbeing of humanity is tied so closely to your business."

Bhavin looked over his shoulder at Axel. His eyes were fiery, intense. "We've found a few."

Bhavin paced in front of the screen. "That's why you're here. We don't trust our bungling governments to address these threats. There are no really effective NGOs. All the current mitigations in play are facile and pointless. So...it means, we, Nadar Corporation, need to do it ourselves."

Bhavin looked over to gauge Axel's expression, then continued. "All of this will be done completely covertly. There will be military-style ops involved. You will have the most advanced intelligence and military technology at your disposal."

Axel's mind was racing. He tried to think of questions that would ferret out how serious Bhavin really was. "What's your budget for this?" he asked.

"Two hundred million, for now," Bhavin said, wrinkling his nose as if he was talking about a stale piece of bread. "We would do more, but that's the limit we can go to without being subject to excessive budgetary scrutiny."

"What level of organizational support is there for this project?"

"Just me and the board, but they will not have the level of understanding I do—for their own protection."

"Will I be required to do anything illegal?"

Bhavin sighed and shrugged. "Sometimes you have to do things for the greater good. Sometimes those things are messy. But you know that. It's one of the reasons you were chosen. I can assure you, though, there is nothing unethical involved."

Which meant, there is nothing unethical *according to Bhavin*, and there was definitely something illegal involved. Whatever he was going to be doing depended heavily on Bhavin's moral mathematics.

Axel had a detailed profile on Bhavin. He was self-made—an Indian national raised in both India and Sri Lanka who subsequently immigrated to the United States to build his business empire from a letter-writing software startup. He consistently gave to charity and was known for once voluntarily removing an implantable monitoring device from the market because of a safety issue they found in patients, at great cost to Nadar Corporation.

The only thing remotely controversial in Bhavin's past occurred in his adolescence. During a civil war in Sri Lanka, he had been a combatant, and the rumor was he had adeptly led an enemy regiment to an old mine-field. It resulted in thousands of dead Sri Lankans on the other side, but saved his own platoon. It was something Bhavin vehemently denied, but to Axel, if it were true, Bhavin lost no points. Atrocities happen in war, and it was the enemy combatants who were slain, not unarmed civilians.

Of course, a public persona can be fabricated, so Axel couldn't be sure that what was out there was all true, or comprehensive. This would be a lot easier to assess if Bhavin were more forthcoming about the threat itself.

Knowing he might not get an answer, Axel decided to test the waters. "What are the threats we are talking about here?"

Bhavin made a sour face. "Before we get to that, I need to have a commitment from you that you will reveal nothing. This goes beyond your corporate sign-on docs. The consequences are much greater. You will have information that will be troubling and will put you at risk personally. I need to know, here and now, that you are comfortable with this. You are not committing to the job, but you are committing to exposure, which is its own kettle of fish."

Bhavin took out a document from the desk and pushed it over to him. "Take your time," he said. Then he stood up to look at the cityscape display again.

Axel scanned the document. There was no heavy legalese. It was typical nondisclosure and disavowal language for the most part, but there were some colorful phrases about the use of aliases and foreign extraditions. All in all, he didn't see anything that didn't fit with what Bhavin had described.

Bhavin said, "Kandalama three." and the wall image changed to a view looking down a verdant hillside onto a broad agricultural plain, with a small Buddhist temple visible on the right-hand side. Bhavin's countenance was contemplative and distant as he digested the new vista.

It was hard to penetrate through the vagaries of the discussion without knowing the threat itself, but the process he was going through seemed proper enough. In turn, a proper process gave some credence to the project itself.

As for Bhavin, he seemed sincere enough. He didn't seem like the sort of vain entrepreneur that would throw away two-hundred million dollars on a flight of fancy, at least based on what he knew now.

Of course all this could be a mirage. Bhavin could be putting on a show, obscuring some sinister machination behind the heartfelt presentation and carefully crafted briefing docs.

Axel did have Ryan, his most trusted friend, as vouchsafe for this opportunity. And if you can't trust someone who has saved your life, who can you trust?

Perhaps even more importantly, if he didn't commit, he would forever wonder about the opportunity. In lieu of the worry about selling out to a big corporation, a new demon would be there, lurking in his mind, an itch he could never scratch. Every time his wife snuck him kisses, it would diminish them unfairly. Every time he saw his son Zach playing lacrosse, he would wonder if it would be the last game—if some apocalypse was about to descend, an apocalypse he could have averted.

Axel signed the document and pushed it over to Bhavin's side of the table.

"Thank you for this opportunity, Mr. Nadar. If you could kindly read me in."

Bhavin turned from the screen, a tired smile on his face, and sat down with him.

THE SATELLITE

Owen was up well before light. He packed and tuned up his bike before anyone else was awake. Despite his lack of sleep, he felt limber of mind. The same couldn't be said for his legs, which were stiff and painful from the strenuous ride on the day before.

His bike tuning was all for naught, however, as the two squads left the campsite on foot, seeking out seldom-used paths through the forest to minimize the chances of being spotted.

Owen only had a brief glimpse of the Shenandoah Valley before the path plunged into dense mountain foliage. It was just a shard of light through the trees, not really enough to capture the undulating hills with all the autumn colors. Seeing the valley from the ridge was one of the main reasons he had been excited about the expedition. It was a nice view, to be sure, but he would gladly have traded it for a ride back to Seeville that morning.

Owen was pulling up the rear with Jakson. Jakson had a crossbow in his hands at all times. As they walked he was attentive to the sights and sounds in the forest. Owen also noticed that an old rifle was slung across his back.

"Why not carry the rifle?" Owen asked quietly. "Isn't it a better weapon than the crossbow?"

"Yes, cousin, but have you ever used one?"

"Just once, before trade school."

"So you know how loud they are. We only use the rifle if we're in a heap of trouble. Otherwise we give away our position. Also, we only have so many working rifles and bullets. Arrows we can always make more of."

"I see," Owen responded.

After a moment of silence, Owen said, "You know, the tinkering, it's just for fun. I figured out how to make some circuits and got carried away is all."

Jakson said, "I'm an Adherent, Owen, but not a zealot. I know there are things we can learn from Old World tech. I see it when I'm out foraging all the time."

"Oh yeah, like what?"

"How they build houses and roads mostly. Loads of thought put into that. There are lots of things the retchers didn't get that are still useful to forage, or that we can copy in Seeville."

"Good. I just wanted you to know I'm not trying to cause any trouble or anything."

Jakson glared at him reprovingly. "At the same time, I would have thought you would stay away, after what happened to your dad and all."

Owen's face flushed. The image of his dad's face, half melted away, asserted itself in his mind.

Jakson seemed to sense the impact of his words. "Sorry, Owen. I shouldn't have said that. I just want you to be careful."

As they walked, Owen's embarrassment morphed into anger. He *was* careful with his tinkering, and everything else as well. He was more careful than anyone else in welding class. He was more careful on his bike than most mules or even wrenches. In fact, it seemed like everyone else floated through life while he was always on edge.

"Also be careful of this Quebecker woman," Jakson added. "I've heard the railroad folks talk about her. She's always poking her head where it doesn't belong. The woman is a witch, I tell you. She's got a square for a rear triangle."

They were on the crest of a knoll and could see Preston and Cecile ahead of them, occasionally sharing a whisper. Cecile did look out of place with her black clothes and streak of blue hair. Owen made a mental note to heed Jakson's warning.

Of all the members of their squad, it was Preston he wanted to speak with most, in particular to ask him how they knew about their tinkering. But Preston had been too close to Cecile. Preston was always much bolder than Owen, and could see him boasting about some tinkering discovery he had made. Preston wasn't stupid either. Most likely they reported

Owen at the salvage store. He shouldn't have bought so many transistors and spools of copper wire.

The squad walked in silence for a while, a bout of rough terrain requiring greater attention. They were navigating down a steep bank in the hillside laden with loose stones.

"Have you been on any other forays like this?" Owen asked Jakson after the more treacherous stint had passed.

"Yes," Jakson answered.

It was a prickly question, so Owen didn't push it.

A few minutes later, Jakson was more inclined to elaborate. "One of the first times was during the raids in the valley, six years back," he said. "It was bent up pretty good but still worth it. We brought back twenty-odd SLS prisoners and took out twice as many. It probably stopped them from messing with us for a while."

"Wouldn't that make them want to get the prisoners back?"

"Yeah, but they think we're messing up the soil and the sun, or whatever. As a result, when prisoners have been in our lands too long, they think they've been corrupted. Was probably worse for them than killing them. Funny how that worked."

Owen had seen a few of the Essentialist captives around Seeville. Most were treated like animals, chained up and forced to do some unpleasant task like demolition or sewer maintenance. They wore black frocks that had converted to brown because they were usually covered in so much filth. They always smelled something awful. They didn't call them SLS for nothing.

The group passed a ravine on their right side. It was a dump for rusted-out Old World cars and trucks. From their altitude the cars looked like a bed of orange pincushions perforated with holes. On any other walk, Owen would have wanted to take a closer look, to see if there was anything salvageable.

Owen looked up to see Jakson watching him closely. "You go right ahead Owen. Go right ahead and bang around in a rusted-out car park in the middle of SLS territory."

Owen responded to Jakson's sarcasm with a light-hearted roll of the eyes.

They navigated down the steep descent for a good part of the day and then headed due west near the valley floor. There was virtually no sign of Essentialists except for a few well-trodden paths through the forest. They took care to cross the more frequently used paths in stealth and silence.

In the early afternoon Noke halted them at the edge of a small clearing. They stooped low and saw a burned-out trough in the middle of the meadow. The trough ended in a dark mound with a few metallic spots on it that were glinting in the sun.

Cecile was frowning. "*Bien sur*, this is it. Let's first scout the periphery, around the clearing, then I want Noke and Jakson to stand guard while Preston and Owen help me with the satellite."

They skulked carefully around the field, looking for signs of Essentialist activity, but found none. Then they left the cover of the forest and approached the satellite cautiously, while continuing to cast furtive glances at their surroundings.

The satellite was smaller than Owen expected, the diameter less than the height of a man.

Cecile touched the mound cautiously, as if it might still be hot. She examined a number of the exposed metallic parts and then stood up and held her finger to her mouth in thought. "Start digging here, and here." She pointed to two areas near the bottom of the mound. She took off her pack and pulled out two collapsible shovels.

Preston and Owen got to work. In some places the earth was easy to move, but in others it was hard-packed from the impact of the satellite. After a few attempts, they found a softer area that more readily allowed digging. When they had unearthed what they could with their shovels they used their hands and knives to clear off the metallic surface.

Their efforts revealed an exposed handle next to three inset dials and a directional pointer. Above the dials there were arrow symbols pointing in several different directions. Cecile turned two of the dials to match the arrows. The third appeared to be stuck, but she was able to adjust it with the aid of her knife. She pulled at the handle.

And just like that, the exterior wall of the satellite opened.

The metal walls around the latch looked to be almost a foot thick. Cecile lit a match and carefully lowered it to see inside. After looking at the contents, she blew out the match and stuck her arm all the way in, grasping for something.

"You'll be happy to hear we won't need to test your knowledge of electronics today," she said to them. "They made it easy for us."

"Who's they?" Preston asked.

She frowned and put her finger to her lips.

As she wrestled with the contents of the satellite, she whispered, "*zut alors.*"

She pulled out a rectangular, metallic box, not much bigger than her hand. She looked at it with a frown of confusion and then handed it to Owen. "Hold onto this."

Owen cradled the object carefully with two hands, as if Cecile had given him a newborn baby. He looked more closely at the box. There was some kind of keypad on the side of it. He nervously glanced at the sky, searching for any sign of retchers.

Cecile stood up. "Preston, there's more in there, but I can't reach it. You're tall, see if you can grab anything else."

Preston positioned himself against the side of the satellite and began grappling with the interior with his extended arm.

Cecile examined the box in Owen's outstretched hands. She took out a pad and scribbled on it with a pen, as if doing some kind of calculation. She examined the exterior dials on the satellite latch periodically. Owen was entranced by Cecile's concentration as much as the box itself. This was Old World tech. How did she know what she was doing?

Owen was the last person to believe in Adherent superstition, but this Cecile woman was indeed making him nervous. Jakson and Noke would steal occasional glances back from the forest edge. They were also looking at Cecile with some concern. Maybe she *was* some sort of witch?

After finishing her doodling, she looked about to punch something into the keypad and then reconsidered.

Suddenly, Jakson was standing right next to them, a grim look on his face. He spoke clearly but quietly, "I think I hear their call."

Cecile looked up, breaking out of her concentration. "*Pardonnez moi?* Their call?"

Jakson's face was riveted with intensity. He spoke with emphasis and control, "the… fucking…SLS. It's like crickets chirping. They could be watching us."

Cecile's head swiveled around, scanning the surrounding forest. "Where…?"

Jakson grabbed her arm firmly. "Don't let on," he said.

When her head stopped turning he let her go. His hand came away from her arm in a calming motion, while his eyes were drilling into theirs. "If I'm right it means there's more than one of them. There could even be more than one group of them."

"Noke, Preston—come here, now," Cecile said tersely.

"What's this all about?" Noke asked as he made his way over. Preston joined them a moment later.

"Jakson thinks he hears call signs from the SLS. We'll head back the way we came. If Jakson's wrong, and there's no activity, we can always come back. Jakson, you take the rear with Owen and Preston."

"The box, please," Cecile said, extending her hand to Owen.

Owen carefully handed the box they had taken from the satellite to Cecile, and she placed it in her pack with similar attentiveness.

"Ready?" Cecile asked. Everyone nodded.

It was all happening so fast. Owen had certainly not heard any fake cricket calls, never mind any real crickets. They had seen no signs of Essentialists all day.

It had to be a false alarm.

But Owen was no hunter or enforcer. Owen did not know the Essentialists.

"Go!" And they were sprinting back across the field.

That's when bedlam ensued.

Arrows started whizzing past them.

Noke yelled out, "they found our exit!"

Owen could barely make out some movement where they had originally come out of the forest.

Noke made sweeping motions with his hands to go back the other way. "To the other side of the field—the other side!" he yelled.

It was in one of these sweeping motions that an arrow impaled Noke's arm. He let out of yelp of pain but seemed to be able to run, so they kept on.

The next time Owen glanced back, Noke had fallen.

"Keep going!" Cecile yelled.

Owen sprinted as fast as he could. Arrows continued to fall around them. He couldn't tell where they were coming from, but wasn't about to look around to find out either. Jakson arrived back at the satellite mound and waved them over.

The mound provided some cover, but the arrows were coming in from too many directions. It was hard to say how much they were still exposed.

Cecile yelled at Jakson. "Where! Where are they?"

Jakson had been peeking his head out occasionally, trying to assess the trajectory of arrows. He said, "I'm...I'm not sure. I think we should go that way." He was pointing across the field to a nondescript part of the forest.

"What about Noke?" Owen asked.

Cecile gave him a dire look. "He's on his own. Let's go."

They bolted from the satellite mound and another flurry of projectiles assailed them. It seemed like there were more arrows now. One flitted past Owen's ear and hit Jakson squarely in the back.

"Fuck...me," Jakson said, stumbling to his knees. Owen grabbed him and struggled to pull him up. "Come on!" he said desperately.

Thankfully Jakson could still stumble along, but it slowed them down considerably.

Owen and Jakson reached the forest a minute after Preston and Cecile. They took cover behind some thick poplar trees. The incoming arrows seemed to moderate.

Jakson was breathing heavily but seemed coherent. "They'll try to re-position," he said. "We need to scare them away." He was grasping at his back, his actions aggravating his arrow wound. He grimaced at Owen, who was positioned behind the tree next to his. "You'll have to do it."

Owen ran over to Jakson. He pulled the rifle off his back holster and then ran back to his tree for cover.

All of a sudden they heard a loud bang. Owen dropped the rifle, think-ing he might have fired it accidentally. Preston called out, "It's Noke!"

Noke was limping across the field with his rifle out, heading toward the satellite mound. He fired again into the distant forest.

Cecile shouted at Owen, "Give him cover!"

Owen pointed the rifle in the same direction Noke was shooting and fired. Nothing happened, and he realized the safety was still on. He took the safety off, took a deep breath, aimed and pulled the trigger again. This time the shot went off, driving the rifle painfully into his shoulder.

He was too nervous, too jittery, and wasn't aiming carefully. When he saw a flurry of color through the sight he reflexively pulled the trigger. The point was to scare them away. If he hit one, all the better.

Noke was most of the way back to the satellite mound. The arrows stopped raining down. Was it possible they had scared them away?

"Preserve your ammo," Jakson said. He was wheezing.

Owen took the occasional shot, aiming more carefully now.

Through the rifle sight, Owen could see Noke had a broken arrow sticking out of his left arm. Blood also flowed from his leg and chest. He was grimacing in pain but still took the occasional shot from behind the satellite mound.

"Noke looks bad," Owen said. "He might not be able to make it back without help."

Cecile nodded. "You and Preston will need to go get him, but I don't want to risk losing two to get one back. Use your sight. Keep looking at the edges of the clearing. Do you see anyone?"

Owen looked through the sight. It was fuzzy but he could see some forms still moving around behind trees where he and Noke had been shooting. There was also an unmoving body on the ground.

"They're still there."

"Well then, shoot them," Cecile said.

His surge of nerves seemed to have diminished. He made sure the rifle was balanced and bided his time. When a man peeked out from behind a tree, he fired twice.

Looking through the sight, Owen could see the man had been hit. He was now writhing on the ground. Then he saw some of the others run deeper into the woods. "I...I got one. I think they're running away," Owen said.

"Good. Keep watching. Let's make sure they're gone before you and Preston go out there."

Owen continued to survey the scene. He saw no sign of any others.

When he looked to Cecile, he could see she was holding the box she had obtained from the satellite in one hand. Occasionally she would look away from the clearing and puzzle over it.

Owen looked back through his sight, scanning the environs of the field again. There were no more signs of Essentialists. But what if he didn't know what signs to look for?

When he looked back to Cecile, she was pressing on the numbered keypad on the side of the box.

It popped open.

Cecile was close enough to Owen that he could make out the inside of the box. Between thin, insulated walls was a small rectangular object with a black, glassy cover. Cecile wedged her finger beside it and extracted the object. It was extremely thin, the depth of a small stack of paper. The glossy black front was contrasted with a shiny gold back.

"*Incroyable*," Cecile said, smiling wistfully.

The object seemed to light up Cecile's face. Then a voice startled him. "Hello, my name is Gail. What's your name?"

Jakson, Owen and Preston pivoted in all directions, looking for this Gail person, until they realized it didn't come from a person at all. The voice came from the object.

It was a smartphone, a *working* smartphone.

No working pre-Detonation electronics had been found in a decade, as far as Owen knew, and certainly no one in Seeville had ever seen a smartphone, never mind one that worked. And here it was, right in front of them. A smartphone that worked, casting a pale glow on Cecile's face.

Cecile pressed something on the surface and the light went out. Then she spoke with a note of urgency. "We need to get out of here. Go get Noke, and hurry."

Preston and Owen ran out into the open. Owen leveled the rifle menacingly toward random patches of forest, while Preston did the same with his crossbow.

When they arrived at the mound, Noke croaked, "about time." He handed his rifle to Preston. Preston and Owen each took an arm over their shoulders while holding the rifles in their opposite hands.

Noke cringed and gasped as they lifted him, but to his credit he supported much of his own weight.

It was slow going, but there were no more volleys of arrows. A emerging well of hope grew inside Owen. If the Essentialists had fled, they might all make it back to Seeville. Not only that, but they may have made a find that could change the fortunes of the Spoke people forever—a find that might prove to the people of Seeville that they need not fear Old World technology.

His optimism was short-lived, however.

When they made it back to the forest edge, Jakson was dead, his throat slit from ear to ear. And as for Cecile, there was no sign of her whatsoever.

BLOOD AND MORE BLOOD

Of all the changes happening in Grand Caverns, the new dojos felt the most alien to Flora. Triangular arches curved up at the tips of the roof, serving no visible purpose. Then there were the shiny floors, the translucent checkered interior walls, and the obsessive cleanliness.

Talon's Shinogi master was waiting outside for her. His head was mostly stubble, not completely clean-shaven, and he had only a short goatee. He lacked the green circles of makeup worn by most disciples in Grand Caverns. Otherwise he had an Asian disposition, wore loose-fitting attire, and had a face closed to emotion, like most other Shinogi she had seen.

Flora did a small bow, just as she had seen others greet Shinogi masters. "Mr. Nobura, I am terribly sorry for all of this."

He nodded and simply said, "come," then turned to enter the dojo.

They sat on the floor of the training room and he offered her a mint tea, which she accepted. Two young girls were across the room from them. They were scrubbing blood off the floor, presumably blood Talon had spilled.

"What has Talon told you?" Nobura asked.

"Only that he lost control and someone was injured, and that you wanted to see me. I really hope no one was hurt badly." She again glanced over at the young girls scrubbing diligently.

Nobura drank from his tea and then sat quietly. Flora wondered if perhaps he wasn't satisfied with her response. She decided to elaborate. "Talon has had a tough time recently. I blame myself. I give him too much responsibility. Reed and I both work, so he ends up watching our daughters. He is also very...closed to me. It would be helpful if I knew more, so I could talk to him about it. Either way, we will accept any consequences you think are appropriate."

"I can tell you what happened," Nobura said, as if it were a great gift to her. "We were having sparring matches. Talon was to contend against one of the less advanced students. Talon was rapidly defeated. Another challenged him—one who dislikes Talon, one who has been taunting him. His name is Redfern Greenwood. Again, Talon was rapidly defeated, this time with some humiliation. A third challenge was issued to Talon. Ordinarily, I would not let such a challenge occur, but I suspected Talon was not giving everything he had. I wanted to see him push himself."

Nobura took another sip of tea, an indelicate man holding his delicate porcelain cup.

"The third match lasted longer," Nobura said. "Talon was putting forth more effort, but something was missing. His focus was not fully on the match, his desire to win absent. He was put in a particularly painful hold, and then something changed."

"Is that when he hurt his opponent? Did he cheat in some way?"

A fleeting frown crossed Nobura's brow. "No, he did not cheat. Yes, he hurt his opponent. And like I said, he did change, but not in the way I expected. He summoned an intense rage, a rage that is not easily controlled. It was more of a whirlwind or a *yurei*, indecipherable of intent. His actions seemed to blend in with the space around him, such that they could not be seen, such that his motives were not clear. He used moves I have not yet taught him, known only to a few masters. In the end, his opponent lay beaten with a bloody nose and sprained arm, among an array of bruises."

It didn't sound at all like Talon. Although it was true she had seen him get into a rage like that once before. When he was young in a wrestling match he went wild, his arms flailing, much like Nobura described. "I'm terribly sorry, Mr. Nobura. If you tell me the name of the student, I will get Talon to apologize..."

Flora trailed off. Nobura had put his finger up as she was speaking.

"I was not finished," Nobura said. "Upon besting the third challenger, Talon challenged his prior opponent, the one named Redfern Greenwood. The challenge was not accepted. Ordinarily all challenges must be accepted, but since Talon had already been beaten by him, I accepted the declination. Then Talon challenged two others who had been taunting him in class. They accepted and fought Talon together."

"He fought two at once?" Flora asked, trying to imagine it.

"Yes, and he defeated them. Near the end the student who had declined his challenge joined to help his friends. Talon defeated him as well. One of those has a broken arm, one a broken nose, one a broken rib."

For a moment Flora didn't know what to say. She was lost in shock. Eventually she managed to speak. "I...I'm so sorry. I will withdraw Talon from the class immediately and make reparations to the students and their parents. Please. Please tell me what I can do to fix this."

"Not that."

"I'm sorry?"

"Mrs. Clearwater, I did not call you down here to report on Talon's malfeasance."

"You didn't?"

"No, because there was no malfeasance."

"No malfeasance?" She was trying hard not to show her surprise. Her son had hurt four people. How was that not malfeasance? But she knew better than to challenge the word of a captain and master Shinogi.

"So why did you call me down here?" she asked.

"I believe Talon has an unusual ability to channel his emotions. There are forms of martial arts where this can be an important asset. A crude analogy in your culture is that he has an ability to be what you might call a *berserker*. This is something that, if harnessed, can make for a formidable warrior. I would like to increase his training time so he can exploit his gift."

Flora was getting more and more regretful for agreeing to have Talon take these classes. It sounded like the Shinogi wanted Talon to become even *more* violent. "I'm not sure that's—"

"There is another thing. If this inner demon, this *yurai*, is left untamed and unfed, it could cause great harm to its host, and to those around him."

Now Nobura was sounding mad. What inner demon? Sure Talon had some pent up anger but this was absurd. "I don't think it's a good idea. I will talk to him but—"

"I insist," Nobura said.

Perhaps seeing her reticence, he proceeded to explain further. "Mrs. Clearwater, we are not the same as people from your continent. We view the martial arts as an important part of anyone's daily ritual. Its goal is not to bring violence, but rather inner peace. It has been...hard to foster this understanding in your clans." His face showed a flash of annoyance. "With Talon, given his internal *yurai*, I think we may have an opportunity to change that. He may even be a Shinogi master someday."

Flora held her tongue for a moment. If she declined, Nobura might force her hand. The Shinogi had tremendous power in Grand Caverns, and the ear of both the clan chief and curator. Yet she couldn't quite say yes. "I see," she said, trying to think of a way out of it. "I will speak with Talon to see what his feelings are on the subject."

Nobura's nostrils flared. "I trust you will make the correct decision for Talon, and for the Essentialist community."

She nodded slowly. "Thank you, and..." She almost apologized again for Talon, but caught herself. "Good-bye, Master Nobura."

She fumed as she marched back to the infirmary. Talon had a fragile disposition. Who knew what could happen to him if he was forced to turn into some kind of violent warmonger?

The sound of bells rapidly pulled her out of her frustrated contemplation. These were not the noontime bells or end-of-day bells. They were the acute cacophony signaling an emergency. Healer Stormwind had told her that morning she might expect the bells, and here they were.

Her stomping turned into a light jog, then a run.

The infirmary was located in the older part of the settlement, closer to the river, and so it was an easy downhill grade to get there. As she came closer, tents gave way to circular stone dwellings with thatched roofs and A-frames, the main dwellings used by the original Essentialists of Grand Caverns.

The infirmary was one of the few buildings in Grand Caverns that used Old World structural materials. It was built on the foundations of a large warehouse whose steel columns and trusses remained strong. This skeleton allowed for the massive warehouse to be refurbished by replacing any Old World panelling with large, roughshod wood trunks.

She arrived at the same time as a galloping horse and rider. The rider was holding steady a man draped over the back of the horse. Flora immediately ran to him.

"You a healer?" the rider asked.

"Healer's assistant."

"Fine, help me."

Flora helped the rider with the man's limp body, hoisting him through the air into the infirmary. There were already three beds being used, occupied by men who were moaning or dead. One man was screaming behind a curtain, the silhouette of a frenetic surgery projecting on the translucent screen.

Healer Stormwind glanced up from winding a bandage around a man's arm to catch Flora's eye. "Take that one to the back, next to the pit. I'll be there soon."

She didn't like going to the back of the infirmary, especially near the pit, but now wouldn't be a good time to argue.

Flora and the rider placed the man on an old cot next to the pit. The rider left without a word.

The pit was made of an amalgam of finely mortared quartz and other light rocks. It was a beautiful piece of masonry installed in the infirmary decades ago. Fortunately, it was rarely used, for it was where they were supposed to place the newly dead. The smooth white surface would be a stark contrast against tortured limbs and spilled blood.

The patient was a gruff-looking man, with a buffet of hair adorning his chin and other smooth, dark strands covering most of his arms. His complexion was pale, though, and his leather shirt was soaked in crimson and perforated with what looked to be a bullet hole. Flora checked the man's pulse and breathing. Nothing.

She fought back a wave of nausea and began chest compressions. "One, two, three, four..."

"How long has he been dead?" Stormwind appeared and Flora stepped aside.

"I don't know."

Stormwind checked his pulse. "Get rid of the body. We will need the bed. More are coming in."

"Where do we put the body?"

"There's a cart, outside."

"Not in the pit?"

"Curator's orders."

"Oh, okay." It was a relief that she wouldn't be working next to a pile of dead bodies, but she wondered why the curator would care about such a trivial thing.

Someone yelled, "Three more coming in!"

She didn't have time to contemplate the matter any further. With some help from another assistant, she lifted her dead patient by the ankles and swayed him through the aisles toward the front door.

In the center of the courtyard was a large cart. It already had two dead bodies draped over the back gate, uncovered. Flora and her helper added the third.

A crowd was gathering outside the infirmary, drawn by the bells. Some were crying, some were looking in horror at the dead men in the cart, and some were making derogative statements about the Spokes. A few of Chief Darkwind's deputies were managing the crowd.

She tried to control her breathing. She tried to force her eyes not to focus on the corpses. Mind over matter, she thought. They are just flesh and bone. People live, people die.

More horses were galloping in, carrying additional injured. She overheard one of the horsemen talking, saying they had the Spokes on the run, and that it should be over soon, but more wounded were coming.

Flora's next patient was very much alive. His face was a mask of anguish, and blood was pulsing out from his abdomen. He looked to be barely older than Talon. She needed to ascertain the nature of the wound, but she was having trouble focusing. She tried to contain her nausea. "Just flesh and blood," she said to herself. "Like water and wine," she said again aloud.

She cleaned the wound until Stormwind came over. He immediately took some forceps and dove them into the man's abdomen, seeking out the bullet. The mask of anguish on the man's face exploded into a scream. He convulsed on the table.

"Hold him!" Stormwind yelled. Another assistant came over to take the side opposite Flora.

She couldn't contain it any longer. The tendrils of nausea were escalating up her throat. She propelled herself to the edge of the pit just in time to spew out her half-digested lunch.

"At least we're using the pit for something," Stormwind said, barely glancing her way, no humor in his voice.

Flora felt faint and was slow to get up from her perch over the edge. She pushed herself and then stumbled back over into the cot, nearly knocking it over.

"Whoa!" Stormwind exclaimed in tandem with another cry from the patient.

Flora put her hands on her knees.

"Get yourself together, Flora!" Stormwind barked. He continued to wrestle with his forceps as he aggressively interrogated the man's flesh.

Flora stumbled out the back of the infirmary and found a seat on an outcropping of Old World concrete. She tried to fight off the dizziness and nausea, but it would not relent.

Flora had always hated the sight of blood, but she had hoped she could be put on less invasive procedures. Who knew there would be such a bloodbath just days after she had completed training?

They needed the money and...Reed had insisted she take the position. But now she had made a fool of herself and maybe even jeopardized the life of a patient.

Her worries ascended, making a foul cocktail with her physical distress. She worried about whether they would cut her from the infirmary staff. She worried about not having enough rations for Talon, Skye and Clover. She worried about what Reed would say, and what he would do.

A teardrop propagated down her face, but she caught it with her thumb and wiped away the wetness before it could get past her cheek. She couldn't let them see her like this. There were patients inside that needed her.

She tried to think of the only thing that brought her happiness. She tried to think of Granger. She entrenched herself in his memory, forcing out the worry, forcing out the nausea. It helped. She could feel the army at the gates of her mind begin to recede.

A few minutes later, when she was confident she had regained control, she gritted her teeth and marched back inside.

WE NEED TO MOVE

Upon seeing Jakson's gutted throat, Noke only said, "We need to move."

"But what about Cecile?" Owen objected.

Noke coughed, lurched over and spat out pink phlegm. "Listen to me," he said. "Forget about her. She probably ate it, or maybe she's been taken. Either way, they know where we are. The only reason they're not attacking is because of our rifles, but it won't last. We need to move." Noke pointed through the woods.

Preston and Owen hoisted Noke again and pushed forward through the trees. Noke would take the occasional step with one of his legs, giving them brief respites from carrying all his weight. A few times the awkward trio stumbled after a difficult step down or a hidden tree root. Noke cringed but never cried out. Then they would lift him up and push forward again.

Preston encouraged them as they went. "We'll get you all fixed up Noke. Don't worry. Then we'll come back together and take out every single one of those bastards."

They travelled without incident for what seemed like a mile, intersecting with the rough path they came in on. From that point on the going was smoother. Birds chirped, the wind blew, and leaves fell around them. There was no sign of Essentialists.

"I don't think I'm gonna make it," Noke said.

"Don't say that," Preston said, "Keep pushing. We'll get there."

When they hit the beginning of the long incline their pace slowed considerably. Noke's pallor was fading, and each breath was a raspy feat of willpower. His occasional steps became more perfunctory. He could no longer bear his own weight.

They reached a layered outcropping of rock elevated above the main path. Noke said, "Here. Stop here."

Owen and Preston gladly dropped Noke for a moment's rest. They all drank from their canteens. Noke's eyes were closed, his lips were moving, and his head was bobbing back and forth as if he was singing some inaudible tune. Owen and Preston shared a grim look.

"Climb up on the rock, keep low and look down," Noke said, returning to coherence, his eyes barely open.

Owen and Preston scrambled up and looked back the way they came. They were high enough that they could see a fair distance into the valley. The patch of clearing that the satellite had crashed in was even visible.

"There!" Preston said, pointing at some barely visible movement in the forest. Upon closer inspection, it looked like a number of Essentialists were skulking through the woods.

Preston and Owen scrambled off the rock back to where Noke was sitting.

"How many?" Noke asked.

"I don't know," Preston said, "Maybe a dozen. Could be fifty. It's hard to say."

"Should we try to take them out?" Owen asked. "We could definitely hit a few of them before they got to cover. It might scare them away, or at least slow them down."

"Right idea, but that's not what you're gonna do." Noke was still speaking with his eyes mostly closed, concentrating on warding off inner demons. "You're going to lift me up on the rock. I'll hold them off, and then I'll find a place to hide. You go. You go as..." He grimaced and breathed a few quick breaths, then continued. "As fast as you can. Get me later, if you can."

Owen said, "no way. You're coming with us."

"Don't be stupid," Noke said, his eyes widening. "It's the only chance you have. You should've left me earlier."

Owen looked at Preston. Preston returned a reluctant nod.

They lifted Noke up on the rock and helped him into position. Moving off the rock would be difficult for Noke. It was hard to imagine him being nimble enough to do so with his injuries.

Owen had a feeling Noke never intended to get off.

"One more thing," Noke rasped. He took a small purse from his pack. "Take this, and..." His words hung for a moment as he collected himself. "And give it to the owner. Find the owner. I should've never taken it."

Owen opened the purse to reveal a copy of a talisman for a man named Duncan Jones. The letters stenciled on the talisman were in the older fonts from decades ago. The talisman featured an eagle with flames behind a log cabin in the woods. Was it a relative of Noke's? He couldn't be sure, and there was no time to ask questions.

Preston said eagerly, "You have our word. You're a hero, Noke—a hero of the Spoke people. We'll come back for you."

Noke cast them a deadly look. "Go," he said.

They did go. They left Noke as he loaded and fired at the oncoming Essentialists. They heard at least thirty rifle shots echoing in the valley.

Owen and Preston were finally able to make good progress up the mountain. When there was a break in the trees Owen looked down, but he couldn't see any sign of Noke or the Essentialists. They did spot another Essentialist group moving up the hill on the south side, looking to cut them off, but they had a ways to go. As long as Owen and Preston kept pressing on they should be able to stay ahead.

There was still plenty of adrenaline coursing through Owen's veins. In the excitement the stiffness in his legs had somehow vanished. They pushed and pushed up the mountain. Owen was a slightly faster climber. He pulled Preston up some of the steeper slopes.

The shooting stopped. Had they taken Noke? Had Noke gone into hiding? It only made them push harder. They were possessed, in a frenzy, running for their lives.

Eventually they could see the Spoke outposts on the ridge, peaking up above the trees. When close enough, they stepped onto an exposed crest jutting from the hillside and gestured to the outposts for help using their red signal flags. Then they kept pushing upward.

It wasn't until the Spoke ranger party met them that they slowed their pace. After a brief explanation to the rangers, they continued on. And then, when they finally touched the staunch wood timbers of the outpost tower itself, exhaustion began to take hold. Owen's legs began to seize up. He had to massage them to keep them limber.

After hearing their report, the outpost rangers assigned them to one of the tents set back from the outpost tower. Preston went to the tent right away, but Owen forced himself to stay alert. He was looking down onto the valley, trying to see any sign of Noke. The view was breathtaking. In fact, it was exactly what he had hoped to see that morning, but the circumstances made it seem stark and desolate. Knowing Jakson was down there, murdered—that Cecile was missing and most likely Noke dead as well—it was hard to find beauty in the undulating hills or autumn leaves.

He waited and waited, but eventually came to terms with the fact that he might not know the outcome of the search for many hours. He succumbed to the needs of his body, stumbling over to the tent. There exhaustion fully claimed him and he rapidly drifted off into slumber.

THE WALLFLOWER

When the talking heads would drone on about important financial metrics or rate-limiting elements on the critical path of an obscure best practices project, Axel could only half pay attention. Besides, he was just a wallflower at these board meetings. Aside from citing budgetary numbers or staffing needs for security obligations, he rarely said a word.

While keeping one ear tuned in to the conversation, he spent time shuffling through the pages of his report to Bhavin. It was an analysis of threats to public safety, a budget proposal, and near-term recommendations. Axel was surprised Bhavin had asked for this as a first assignment. He had assumed he had been hired because they had detail on some specific threats, but instead they had asked him to research some specific threat *areas*.

Axel had sent the analysis to Bhavin a week ago and not received a response of any kind.

Somewhat vexing was the fact that Axel was not permitted direct access to all of the intelligence-gathering systems at Nadar Corporation's disposal. He had to work through Grant Markovsky, a pseudo-genius with encyclopedic knowledge and mastery of many diverse technical fields. When he wasn't leading some of the more covert software development activities, Grant acted like a sort of limbic system to Bhavin, following him around and answering his often-tangential questions with ease and precision.

Despite this challenge, Axel marveled at even the limited intelligence resources he had available to him. In many ways it surpassed the CIA and NSA. They were able to use a number of finder-seeker computer viruses that could penetrate deep into foreign networks without leaving a trace. Using this system, and with Grant's help, Axel was able to identify at least one specific and actionable threat for his report. It was a long-term risk, but definitely fell into something Nadar Corporation could have a hand in mitigating.

A research lab in Singapore had identified a method of eliminating a pre-disposition to several forms of cardiovascular disease by using a CRISPR gene-editing technique, but according to their consultant scientist, the method harbored downstream risks. More specifically, there was a high probability of off-target effects that were initially benign, but that would lead to mutations in the genome. According to a simulation Grant's team had developed, the mutations increased in probability and severity with each subsequent generation and would become deadly to a large proportion of people in the third or fourth generation.

Since this treatment would be given to hundreds of thousands of people worldwide, it meant that in several generations, millions of people could have inherited this genetic time bomb. But what was most disconcerting was that these kinds of risks were not being evaluated or picked up by health authorities, since they were only requiring two or three year trials.

Axel wasn't sure this was what Bhavin was looking for, but he was proud of his find, especially because gene editing was not something Axel was familiar with at the outset.

Axel tried to chase Bhavin down after the meeting to ask about the report, but two other corporate officers managed to maneuver in front of him. So he stood in the executive lineup, waiting for his chance to access Bhavin. By the time the others had finished, Bhavin was halfway out the door.

"Bhavin if I could have a minute—" But Bhavin was already walking away, past the threshold of his personal offices, with his assistant whispering in his ear.

Grant was standing nearby, staring at a tablet. He looked up briefly and said, "Mr. Kelemen, Bhavin will be in your office in ten minutes." Then Grant returned to his tablet.

Axel walked back to his office and waited. He would have preferred getting the word from Bhavin directly, rather than through his socially awkward intermediary. He wondered if Bhavin would be on time, or come at all.

Bhavin came on time, right to the minute.

Axel was about to speak, but Bhavin held up his hand.

Without any pleasantries, he said, "Thank you for your report. I agree with most of your outline. Your analysis confirmed what we already knew."

It was the kind of synopsis that preceded "made redundant" communications, so Axel prepared himself for the worst.

Bhavin continued, "and Grant has already initiated the issuance of a computer virus to handle the gene editing concern in Singapore. We had our eye on that one, but you provided us new information that let us see the risk in a new light."

"A computer virus, sir?"

"You can call me Bhavin, if you like, but *sir* is fine as well. I know military habits can be hard to break."

Axel felt it best to not get too informal here, and military habits were good habits as far as he was concerned. "Okay, sir."

Bhavin smirked and continued. "No need to get into the details with you. You know, *need to know* and all that. Essentially, we can issue a virus that reveals the nature of the genetic time bomb to the researchers. If they don't take action to terminate the gene editing program, we wipe their computers and files and alert the health authorities."

"Oh," Axel said, again marveling at Nadar Corporation's cyber capabilities.

If Grant could in fact develop such a virus, the solution sounded reasonable. But Axel was beginning to feel rather impotent. Was he just here to write reports and take no action? "Sir, if there is a specific area you are interested in, please let me know, and I can dig deeper. I'm having trouble seeing where I can be of much use."

Bhavin's head lurched back, and his eyes squinted. "I don't think you understand. This report was just a test. Now I see how you think. You have shown me you can see things others can't. You have made a rational pitch for assembling your team. You are ready now, or rather, *I* am ready to give you your first assignment."

Axel's momentary confusion abated. He had passed some rite of passage with Bhavin. It made sense. Why would Bhavin entrust truly dangerous and covert assignments to someone he didn't know well? This wasn't unlike Axel working a new asset in a covert operation. Axel would never fully trust an asset until he or she showed their loyalty and competence.

"I guess I'm learning more about you as well, sir," Axel said.

Bhavin smiled curtly, took a folder from his designer backpack and dropped it on Axel's desk. "Now let's get to work," he said.

Axel opened the file and glanced at the first few pages. He couldn't help his eyes from widening. He was going to have to brush up on his Russian.

THE PRISONER

The administrative center of Grand Caverns was an impressive array of buildings, several stories tall in places. They had been commissioned two years ago by Chief Darkwind and only recently completed. Although no one would ever speak of it, it didn't look far removed from Old World building complexes you might see in pre-Detonation times in Staunton or Waynesboro.

Flora walked under the main entrance. The symbol of the cherry blossom tree on top of a voluminous sun was carved into the wood at the top of the archway. It was still unpainted, though—the wood was still raw.

In the main courtyard she veered left into the law enforcement hall. Flora checked her leather frock and patted down her hair to make sure nothing was out of place.

The hall was empty save Finch Coralwood, the main administrative deputy on duty. Finch had a round face and bushy eyebrows that always seemed to be raised in some form of cynical stare. "Figured it would be you again," he said.

"Sorry I'm late. Reed's not feeling well again." It was not entirely untrue. Reed had one of his nights.

"Uh huh," Finch said, his lips curling slightly. "Well, we have a special assignment for you today." He pushed some keys over to her on his desk. "You are to do the regular letters and filing, but we also need you to watch over a prisoner. This comes directly from Darkwind."

"We have a prisoner?"

He spoke quietly, "We do, from the Spoke raid. A strange bird, apparently not a Spoke from Seeville, but from some other place. Darkwind's coming by later to check on her, so be on your toes."

"I understand," Flora said. "Any other job postings?"

"Aren't you at the infirmary?"

"Yeah, but always looking for something better." The truth was Healer

Stormwind had told her she had to go. Stormwind had been merciful, though, giving her a few weeks to transition.

Finch gave her a concerned look. "No postings today. Sorry, Flora. I'm sure something will turn up."

"Thanks anyway. Let me know if you see anything." She moved over to Reed's desk and grabbed his stack of files.

"So what's Reed really doing today?" Finch asked, watching her flip through the folders. He leaned over in her direction and spoke in a harsh whisper. "You know, Flora, you don't have to keep living like this."

She just smiled at him and ignored the comment. Finch probably meant well, but she found his tendency to pry into her personal life disconcerting. At some point she would have to figure out how to deal with him. If what he said found its way to Reed's ears...

Eager to get away, Flora snatched the keys off Finch's desk and headed back into the holding cells.

The cells were newly minted, made of gleaming iron rods and precisely cut timbers. The room still smelled of pine and sawdust. It was ironic prisoners were able to have a good roof over their heads when many Essentialists continued to live in makeshift tents that could blow away in a strong storm.

The prisoner had been sleeping on the hard floor. She sat up to watch Flora enter. She was paler than most, with a blue streak in her hair. Her clothes looked to be leather aside from her shirt. Her shirt was made of a collection of small metallic circlets.

Flora dropped the keys and files on a desk opposite the prisoner's cell. The prisoner's belongings were stacked on a chair next to the desk. They included a pack containing some food, a knife, a crossbow, and a small metal box.

Flora made to grab the metal box and heard, "I wouldn't touch that if I were you."

The prisoner was standing now, up against the bars.

"And why is that?" Flora asked.

"It's Old World tech."

Flora laughed. "Maybe it is." Flora tapped on the box with her finger while eyeing the prisoner. Maybe this would be a useful bargaining chip.

"What's your name, Spoke?" Flora asked.

The woman paused before responding, perhaps contemplating the merits of revealing her identity. "My name is Cecile."

She had a funny accent Flora couldn't place, and it was a strange name, even for a Spoke. "You don't come from Seeville, then?"

"I have been in Seeville recently, but I come from the north, from a different…tribe."

"Did you happen to notice any prisoners in Seeville, any Essentialist prisoners?"

Cecile looked thoughtful. "I did see some servant types. I'm not sure if they were indentured bandits or SLS servants. I know they used to have SLS servants, a long time ago. I heard a few people talk about them. Why do you ask?"

"SLS—is that your word for Essentialist?"

Cecile paused before responding. "Yes, I'm sorry."

"You Spoke people are so backward," Flora quipped. "Why use a crude short form like *SLS* for a word as simple as Essentialist?"

"If you say so," Cecile said.

"Yes, I do say so. SLS sounds more like someone stuttering."

"That's not what it means."

"Oh, really."

"Look, my people, we don't come into contact with your people up north, so we don't know much about you."

"So what does it mean?"

Cecile remained reluctant to answer.

Flora reiterated, more emphatically this time. "What does it mean?"

"It means…smells like shit. Because, you know, they say the sanitation systems here are a bit lacking and well, they claim you don't bathe very often. I don't think it's right, but it's what most people mean when they say SLS. I only used it because the Spokes use it."

Flora felt herself reddening. She tried to think of a good retort. "At least we don't smell like grease and smoke all the time. At least we don't bind the earth with metal, coal and rubber, desecrating sun, seed, and soil."

Cecile just shrugged.

Flora walked back over to her desk, taking another look at Cecile's belongings.

"Actually, I remember now," Cecile said. "I was working on a project in the Hall of Records in Seeville just a few days ago. They did have a list of servants. Some were from the raids a few years back. So a few of the servants must be SLS—*pardonnez moi*— Essentialists."

A modest glimmer of hope fluttered in Flora's chest, but she didn't let on. She knew there was still a good chance Granger was dead, but this meant at least *someone* had survived the raids. Unless this woman was lying, of course, which was quite possible.

"Why were you looking at the town records? What are some of the names of the servants?"

Cecile contemplated her questions. "Like I said, it was a project I was involved with. I was trying to locate some talismans. I'm sorry. I don't know any of the names of the Essentialists from the raid. Otherwise I would offer them. I'm sure Seeville would exchange some for me, maybe even more than one."

"Doubtful," was all Flora said. She pretended to ignore Cecile. She sat down to work on her letters, but she couldn't get Cecile's idea out of her head. A prisoner exchange was exactly what she was hoping for.

"What's your name?" Cecile asked.

"My name isn't important," Flora said, and she made a waving motion with her hand as if shoeing a fly.

"I see, *dommage*," Cecile said, speaking some foreign word and sitting down in her cell.

Flora began writing Reed's recruiting letters.

Not much later the door from the main administrative offices opened, and Chief Darkwind entered. Darkwind had on his ceremonial frock, which had two angular green streaks painted on each side. His head and face were clean-shaven, and dark green eyeliner contoured his deep brown eyes.

Behind Darkwind was a burly man who contrasted heavily with the chief. He wore thick layered garments, some of them looking like tough armor. They were overlaid with a vest with vertical streaks of yellow on each side, the sign of the Merchant Mercs, mercenaries for hire that had been frequenting Grand Caverns of late. His shoulder length hair was tangled with streaks of grey. He also kept a full beard, similarly peppered. He squinted at her when he saw her, sizing her up, his eyes harsh and serious.

Flora got off her chair and took a knee for Darkwind. "Greetings, Chief. How can I be of service?"

He gestured for her to stand. "I came to see the Spoke prisoner. This is her?"

"Yes, Chief." Flora nodded toward Cecile's cell. "She claims her name is Cecile."

Darkwind stood in front of the cell, cradling his hands while the big merc brooded behind him. He said, "Prisoner. Why should we not kill you, here and now?"

Darkwind was not the type to mince words.

Cecile said, "I'm not from Seeville. I'm not even a Spoke, truthfully. But I have some influence among the Spoke tribes, an important station in the north. If you don't let me go, it may result in reinforcements coming to Seeville's aid." Cecile glanced over at Flora. "You could even exchange me for some of your prisoners. I'm sure the Seeville Spokes would agree to that."

Darkwind was nodding. "And how can I believe you?"

Cecile considered his question thoughtfully. "There's nothing I can do to prove my station and importance, but I can prove to you where I'm from. You may want to ask your curator about my...tribe. Your curator should know my appearance is distinctive among the people in the north. I also speak French fluently."

Darkwind donned a skeptical look. Then he went to look at Cecile's belongings on the desk. "This was on her person?"

"Yes," Flora responded.

"Prisoner, what's in this box?"

Cecile looked to be doing some kind of internal calculation. She said, "We found it in the satellite."

Darkwind raised his eyebrows and glanced at the merc. The merc said, "They did grab something from inside the object before we captured her. Could be that's where it's from."

For several seconds Darkwind's hand hovered over the box. "What's in it?" he asked again.

After some hesitation, Cecile said, "I'm not sure."

His hand hovered a moment more then it retreated to cradle his other hand. "Well, I suppose we will have the curator examine it."

Darkwind scrolled his eyes over Cecile for a few more moments, and then turned to the merc. "She seems cooperative enough. See to checking on her story."

"Yes, Chief," the merc responded.

Darkwind and the merc walked out the way they came in.

Flora had been watching Cecile's reaction to the conversation carefully. Now Cecile retreated from the bars and lay down on the bench at the back of the cell, some inner tension relieved. Did her unease have something to do with the box?

"So this came from the shooting star, did it?" Flora asked, now placing her own hand over the box.

Cecile sat upright again. "Yes, as I said. It's Old World tech. I don't think you want to mess with it."

"Uh huh." Flora grabbed the box and carefully looked at the exterior. There was a latch on the side with a keypad. "I know you think we're a bunch of smelly savages, but not all of us Essentialists are completely ignorant. And not all of us are skittish about Old World tech. Many of us believe there is much to be learned from it."

Cecile had moved up to the bars. She was staring with some intensity.

Flora was not one for silly superstitions. Yes, one needed to be cautious. She wouldn't go walking through the fever lands, that's for sure.

But this was just a box. How harmful could it be? And Cecile didn't know Flora had seen more than most Essentialists—that Granger was once a Spoke in a former life. He was just as human as she was, despite being born east of Skyline.

Her only concern was if this Cecile would report her for looking at the box. But then, who was going to believe her? Flora suspected Cecile didn't want the contents revealed, which meant she might have some leverage with her if she knew what the box contained—leverage that could, in some way, help her get Granger back.

Flora examined the keypad carefully.

"Good luck with that," Cecile said. Eventually, she sat back down.

She doubted tapping the keypad would do any harm. She randomly tried a few numbers and pulled at the latch.

It opened.

Cecile shot back up from her bench. "How did you do that? How do you know the code?"

Flora shrugged and opened the cover the rest of the way. In it was a black rectangular object with a glassy surface. She recognized it from books she had read about Old World times.

It was a smartphone.

According to the curator, smartphones would drain the user's intelligence and will, imprisoning them in imaginary worlds. It would ensnare them and forcefully divorce them from their rightful marriage to sun, soil and seed. But these were just bedtime stories, scare tactics to get people to listen to the curator and do what she said. Flora didn't really believe in such nonsense.

Flora pulled the phone out and examined it.

Cecile said, "your chief will find out you tampered with this. I will tell him myself. And the curator as well."

Flora ignored her and pressed some buttons on the side of the phone. The screen illuminated, and a voice spoke to her, startling her. "Hello, my name is Gail, what's your name?"

"Turn it off!" Cecile said, becoming more agitated. She seemed desperate to find someway to get Flora to stop. It only strengthened Flora's conviction.

Flora thought about responding to the phone, but a number of illuminated buttons on the screen had already stolen her attention. One of them said *Where Am I?*

She tapped on the words and the screen changed to a large map of the Shenandoah Valley. A point and bubble on *Grottoes* appeared in the middle, the old name for Grand Caverns. She tried to point on the screen, and the map moved. Then she realized she could move the map by pushing on the screen in different directions. She pushed it to the left and could see the past Skyline, into the Spoke area next to the mountains, although it didn't appear to be labeled properly. A city named *Charlottesville* was shown, which must have been the Old World name for Seeville.

"Listen, please, you have to turn it off," Cecile was pleading. "You don't understand. If it's on long enough they will come for it. This is the only one we have. It could be incredibly important for all of us, for Essentialists and Spokes alike."

Flora had to admit—the phone was mesmerizing. She continued to be entranced by the maps going east, west, north and south. These maps looked to be just one thing the phone could do. There were so many other words and buttons.

To humor Cecile, Flora said, "*They* will come for it? Who, Old World people?" She snickered at the thought.

Cecile yelled. "Retchers, you idiot! Please, please turn it off and put it away. It may already be too late."

Flora had heard plenty of stories about retchers. Her mother had once pointed to one on a distant tree, but when she looked it was gone. People described them as oversized crows in slumber. They might exist, sure, but a creature that vomits acidic bile? Why would some flying creature go around destroying Old World tech? It was exactly the kind of thing a curator might make up to scare people into subservience. No, Flora reckoned it would be more likely she saw the tooth fairy than a retcher today.

Flora had been nervous about the prisoner at first, but now with her pleading and apparent madness, she no longer feared her. Perhaps she could even use this madness to her advantage. "Sorry, I don't believe in ghosts or fairy tales," Flora said, "but I will put the phone away on one condition. There's something only you can provide me. You would have to keep it completely secret."

"Fine, what is it, anything! Just turn it off, put it away, and we'll talk! You have to trust me. The black button on the side. Turn it off, right away."

Flora thought about pressing the button Cecile suggested but then hesitated. First she wanted a commitment.

"There is an Essentialist prisoner you have..." Flora began.

Suddenly, heavy rain was pattering on the roof. It made enough noise that she had to speak louder to talk over it. "He's probably in Seeville. I want your commitment you will...you will..."

Cecile had slunk away from the bars and sat down with her palms against the wall. She was staring desperately at the ceiling. "It's too late," she said.

"Why? Fine, I'll turn it off." Flora pressed on the button Cecile had indicated, but the screen had already gone dark. "See. You got what you wanted. Now let me tell you what I want."

"That won't stop it now," Cecile said.

The rain was getting louder. In fact, it was sounding less and less like rain. It was no longer rhythmic. It sounded like something was on the roof, something large. It was tearing at the roof.

Could it really be?

Flora heard screams outside, and then there was a great rent in the ceiling as a large beam was torn away. Flora stepped back from the opening as more roof fragments disappeared into the sky. It was as if a miniature tornado had landed right on top of the prison and was boring through the ceiling.

The noise stopped and a great bird creature dropped from the opening onto the floor.

The retcher was exactly as she had heard it described. It was black, but at the same time glossy and reflective, making it hard to stare at. What she could make out was a large, rounded body, half as tall as a man but with twice the girth. It had hollow beige eyes and a pointy beak. Its wings were folded in.

It began ambling slowly in her direction.

"If you want to live, drop the phone," Cecile said. She was strangely calm, albeit morose, sitting in her cell. She eyed the beast carefully but showed no fear.

Flora's bravado was long gone. Her hand shook as she dropped the phone on the floor. She moved as far back as she could from the giant bird.

The retcher picked up the phone in one of its talons and appeared to examine it. Then it promptly spewed vomit on it. The phone sizzled and then melted down. Black steam came off it, and a terrible smell of burning metal and chemicals ensued. Flora reckoned the odor must be what Spoke towns smelled like. If so, it was just as bad as the curator described.

After two more bouts of vomit, the phone had completely dissolved. All that remained was gray and beige bile that continued eating into the floor of the prison.

The retcher took a step toward her. For a moment she thought it would vomit on her, but it turned around and cast its eyes toward Cecile. Then, with little warning, it launched itself back up through the roof.

Flora's hands were still quivering. She tried to calm herself, staying glued against the back wall for some time. It wasn't until Finch and a few other men ran into the holding cell area that she pushed off the wall and forced herself to adopt some composure.

Meanwhile Cecile was shaking her head, her eyes downcast.

"What a waste," was all she said.

A TALE OF TWO BUNKERS

In the backyard of Owen's house in Seeville, on a plateau before the hill that went down to the stream, there was a boxy cement bunker. It had taken on a black and greenish color on the exterior, with a robust mold somehow clinging to the surface. Surrounding it was a gaggle of Old World clutter—car parts, gearboxes, spools of oxidized copper wire. It was not an inviting building by any means, which was how Owen liked it.

Many bunkers were built just before the Detonation, but most were of shoddy quality, or had been stripped down afterwards. For this one, great care was taken. To protect against radiation the bunker had rebar-reinforced walls two feet thick. Most importantly, for Owen's purposes, they had built in a Faraday cage to prevent the transmission of electromagnetic signals through the walls.

It was in this bunker that Owen was sitting. A number of circuit boards were in front of him, as well as wires, solenoids, capacitors, resistors, filaments and switches. He would imagine the fields and waves permeating the air around him, the magnetism contouring the solenoids. He would occasionally solder a new connection and turn the hand-crank generator, the green signal light revealing the success or failure of his intended architecture.

His electrical work often served as an exciting distraction from the banal chores he endured with his mother and sisters, or even the more practical teachings of trade school. Today he hoped it would also relieve him of reliving the events in the valley.

Instead, his solitude only allowed him a greater capacity for reflection.

He thought about Jakson. He thought about Noke. He wondered what had happened to Cecile.

He thought about the smartphone. They had lost so much in the attempt to acquire it, but perhaps the phone itself was the greatest loss. It held so much potential. And all the while he could speak with no one.

Lord Henneson insisted the whole expedition be kept under wraps.

Owen would spin the lie Lord Henneson had woven. Thankfully his mother and sisters seemed satisfied with his explanation. "It was really terrible, a whole side of the cliff face fell away," he told them. "They died instantly."

They would say, "I'm so sorry, Owen. Do you want to talk about it?"

He did, but he couldn't.

They were doing a unit on plumbing in trade school. Water pumps, valves, water pressure—it all seemed so trivial in the face of what they could have learned with the phone. They had to go back. They had to see if they could find Cecile, or see if there was something else they could salvage from the satellite.

He had resolved to talk to Preston about it. Preston was bold. He took risks. He would know what to do. And he was the only one Owen could confide in. But Preston had been missing from trade school since the expedition. He had heard he was taking some sick days. No one could blame him, least of all Owen.

The soldering torch was starting to fade, and he realized it was running out of butane. He grasped the butane canister off the shelf, but just as soon he remembered he had emptied it on the last refill. He wrote it down on the foraging list, which by now had quite a few items on it.

With everything around Seeville being so picked over, a good forage usually required a trip beyond the outskirts, and there was no guarantee you would find what you needed. It became more practical just to buy the materials in town, even though they might cost him a fortune. More than the cost, however, he didn't want to give anyone any clues about what he was working on, especially after they had been outed on the expedition.

So he could give up for the day...on the last few hours of his only day off...or he could try finding Preston.

He began going through his exit checklist, posted in big block letters on the door to the exterior.

1 Disconnect all active circuits
2 Disconnect and turn off all power sources
3 Shelve EM producing components
4 Confirm 1-3
5 Close both doors behind you
6 Apply EM protective shielding

After closing the second outside door, he latched the EM protective paneling over the door cracks and went back through the checklist in his mind.

He wasn't paying full attention. He had been preoccupied with getting to Preston, so when reviewing the process he realized there was a battery he wasn't certain he had disconnected. So he opened the doors, went in and confirmed the battery had been turned off and disconnected. Then he left, closed the two exterior doors, and refastened the EM paneling over the exterior door.

"Don't forget to close the door, Owen." His father's words shivered through him, as they often did when the hinges creaked to a close.

He grabbed his hybrid from the tangle of bikes at the side of the house and pedaled vigorously southward. Leaves and other debris were thrown up behind him as he rolled over disorderly indentations in the road. The old pavement was still visible in places, but slippery sediment covered much of it, and potholes made for a dubious obstacle course.

Owen stopped at Preston's house on the Downtown Mall. There, a young girl, presumably Preston's sister, greeted him. She informed him that Preston was down at the Barnyard.

The Barnyard was only a few more blocks away, but Owen hesitated, knowing how the railroad folks didn't like people poking around.

He couldn't bear to wait another day.

When he arrived at the Barnyard gates he could see men were hauling equipment, cables were swinging, hammers were rapping, and metal was scraping against metal. It smelled of grease and tar and smoke. No rest for the Seeville & Raleigh railroad workers, even on a Sunday.

"Watcha lookin' for kid?" a man in grease-stained overalls asked him just inside the gates. His face was so covered in soot it was like a black skull under his helmet.

"Preston Hatch. You know where to find him?"

The man pointed at the large, red warehouse and then wandered away.

It was one of the new buildings in Seeville—a huge structure where they assembled train engines, rail cars and whatever else they needed for S&R Railroad operations. The resemblance of the building to an oversized barn had led people to refer to the whole rail yard as the Barnyard, and even sometimes refer to new engines as "a bull coming out of the Barnyard."

The main hangar door was open, so Owen walked his bike in, trying to look like he knew where he was going. Inside the bay doors and to the right was a large cement box about the size of his house—a building nested neatly in the confines of the gigantic warehouse. Owen immediately knew what it was. It was a good bet that's where Preston would be. He found the exterior door and knocked on it.

The door of the bunker was opened by a man with a long, expressionless face and pursed lips. Below the face was a slightly cocked blue bowtie, a starched white shirt, and suspenders. It was Quenton Bartz—*Lord* Quenton Bartz.

"Lord Bartz, I...I didn't know..."

Bartz looked annoyed and dismissive at first, and then a glimmer caught his eye. "You are the other one, yes? Owen, isn't it?" His long face tilted at an awkward angle. It was as if he was trying to look up Owen's nostrils. Owen had never met Bartz, so others must have described him. Owen was certainly easy to recognize with the peculiar white spots on his face.

"Yes, sir," Owen said.

Bartz's eyebrows knitted in calculation. "Here to see Preston, I suspect. Good, good. I have wanted to meet you. Come in." His voice was playful, churlish. A long finger gestured for Owen to enter.

They walked to a tight antechamber illuminated by a solitary lantern and sat down at a desk. Bartz collected some papers and stuffed them into a folder. He smiled, "railroad business, you see."

He tapped his fingers on his knee. "You should know Lord Henneson has informed me of what happened, what really happened. Such a shame. You have been keeping this quiet, yes?"

"Yes, sir. Lord Henneson's orders."

"Of course you have. And remind me—your father, he does what again?"

"He...passed away a few years ago. An accident."

"Ahh, and your mother?"

"She does what she can, working for the Hall of Records."

Bartz frowned momentarily and then looked away, jaw clenching. "Yes. A noble profession." He stood up and said, "Let me collect Preston for you. If you don't mind waiting here?"

Did Owen say something wrong? Perhaps Bartz was just tiring of the discussion. He was a very busy man.

Bartz walked around the corner and knocked on the door. The door opened, and Bartz entered.

Lord Bartz was one of the most prominent businessmen in Seeville. He was originally a magnate of the trade businesses of the region, but more recently he was a driving force behind the S&R Railroad expansion. Under his leadership, the railroad operations had expanded northward to Kingston and southward all the way to Jacksonville, uniting many divisions of the Spoke people.

It was odd that such an important man was here, alone, in a Faraday-protected enclosure of the Barnyard, and also odd he knew so much about what had happened. It was stranger still he would spend time sitting down with Owen.

Several minutes went by. Owen began to regret his boldness in coming all the way to the Barnyard. His mom had once told him, "stay out of the way of the movers and shakers unless you want to get moved and shaken." It seemed like wise enough counsel. At the same time his mom often cited vague Adherent gospel like, "beware the three fears." So her warnings were to be taken with a grain of salt.

Bartz seemed to be taking quite some time. There would be procedures with the Faraday cage, but it shouldn't take this long. Perhaps he was sidetracked by some other business inquiry.

Finally, Bartz and Preston exited the bunker. Preston looked pale, with his hair unusually unkempt. He hung back while Bartz spoke, "Well I'm off then. I don't have to tell you again how important secrecy is. Listen to Preston here, He will explain." He winked at Owen as he finished speaking. Then he tilted his head to the side just a little too much, scrutinizing Owen's reaction.

"You have my word, sir," Owen said. Owen could feel Bartz's eyes crawling on him, and he knew it would make him blush. Blushing would make his spots stand out more, which he hated.

"Good-bye then," Bartz said with a smile. He whisked by Owen and went out the exterior door.

Preston stood aloofly, looking irritated.

"Hey, I'm sorry," Owen said. "I was going crazy at home and we still haven't really spoken about the valley. I didn't know Bartz would be here."

Preston looked down as he spoke. "I'm working with Bartz now, for the railroad. There's a lot they want me to do."

"You've dropped out of school?"

"Well, yeah. As of Monday, anyway."

People who didn't finish trade school rarely amounted to anything. You couldn't even be a blacksmith or carpenter without a trade school degree.

"Why would you do that?" But as soon as Owen asked the question, he knew the answer. Preston always wanted to be where the action was. And here he was, working with Quenton Bartz, of all people.

"You'd be surprised the resources the railroad has. I get to work on things you couldn't imagine," Preston said.

Owen frowned skeptically. "Like what? And for how long until you get put into some menial position shoveling coal or checking valves?"

Preston crossed his arms. "Well, they're working on an electric drive for trains—one that will get around the retcher problem."

Owen was shocked into silence for a moment. Not only would he be working on electrical systems, but ones that would be unleashed beyond the Faraday cage. If true, it would have profound consequences for Seeville, maybe for all Spokes.

"But...how do you get around the emissions problem? Do you think it will work?"

Preston continued to focus his gaze away from Owen. "We're trying some shortwave means that may be out of the retcher's range, for one. I don't know if it'll work, but the point is why not do something substantial rather than tinker on something they may never let you use? Bartz and the railroad folks, they understand this is the way of the future. They don't let the silly superstitions get in their way. They're all about progress. The train has left the station." Preston smirked with the delivery of his last sentence.

Owen didn't think the double entendre sounded funny. Nor did it sound like something Preston would say. He must have picked it up from the railroad folks, maybe even Bartz himself.

"I still think this could be a mistake, Preston. I mean, you can always join the railroad after trade school"

Preston shook his head and looked at him in a way that made him know the matter was closed. "Why did you come here, Owen?" he asked sternly.

It seemed more trivial now, after seeing Bartz and learning about Preston leaving trade school. "Well, I wanted to talk about what happened in the valley. Also about some of the work you were doing...I can see that's probably not going to happen."

"Uh huh," Preston said.

"Aren't you curious, Preston? Aren't you frustrated we can't talk about this? That the lords haven't told us what's going to happen next?"

Preston just shrugged and stood there with his arms crossed. It was strange. Preston was usually more curious than Owen, sometimes to a fault.

"Is there something you're not telling me? We're friends, right?"

Preston looked up at Owen, annoyed. "Wait just a minute, you can't hang that *we're friends* shit on me. I have responsibilities now. I can't tell you everything. Railroad business is railroad business."

"That's not what I meant. What about the valley? The phone?"

Preston just shook his head.

"And what about the talisman Noke gave us? When are we going to find this Duncan Jones person?"

This unhinged Preston somewhat. "Oh that. Sorry...I forgot. Actually, I don't think I can. They have me working all hours of the day here. Would you mind taking care of it?"

Preston did look pretty roughshod. "Yeah, I guess so. I can handle it." It still seemed strange that Preston wouldn't help. It was Noke's last wish.

"Thanks. Is there anything else?" Preston said with a hint of impatience.

Owen couldn't believe Preston didn't want to talk more about the expedition. Owen waved his hands emphatically, as if it might conjure a more meaningful response from his friend. "Don't you see we have to go back to the satellite, Preston? Maybe there's some other tech we could take from it—something important we could learn. And we need to find out what happened to Cecile!"

Preston shook his head again, more slowly and deliberately this time.

"Are you even listening to me?"

"Hey, just calm down, Owen. I was there just like you were, okay?"

Preston finally pulled himself away from the wall and started pacing. "Let me think for a minute."

Owen realized he might be pushing too far. He was just venting his own frustration. It wasn't Preston's fault they didn't have answers—that they were forced to keep everything secret. Realistically, what could Preston do?

After some thought, Preston seemed to come to some kind of internal conclusion. He sighed in resignation. "There will be another expedition in a couple weeks, I'm pretty sure of it. The railroad folks will be involved."

Preston looked down, brushed some lint off his trousers and looked up again. "Bartz wasn't so sure about you. Something about your mother, not sure why, but I might be able to vouch for you, to get you included, if that's what you want."

Owen was confused about why Bartz would have reservations about his mother. Maybe the railroad wasn't getting along with the city admin folks? But his attention was elsewhere, with the expedition. "We're going back to the satellite?"

"No, no, nothing like that. The SLS would be all over us. It's some railroad business you might find interesting, though, along the same lines in terms of finding Old World tech. And if you get involved they may want you to help more. You can learn more about what we're working on. Maybe you can help."

Finally, Owen felt at least somewhat vindicated for coming to see Preston. Something was actually being planned after the valley! Although it did make him a bit uncomfortable that it was being organized by the railroad. He didn't want to be forced into leaving trade school, if that's what was required.

But after being alone with his thoughts for so long—after knowing they were so close to obtaining something as groundbreaking as the phone—he wanted to be doing something important. He was either part of this, with any warts or lemons it might come with, or he was in the dark. He couldn't stand being in the dark.

"I'd like that, Preston."

Preston's lip curled slightly, and he nodded. "Good. I can't guarantee anything, but I'll put in a good word for you."

"Great Preston, thanks. I appreciate it."

Owen had more questions, but he knew Preston had secrets to keep, and he didn't want to push his luck. Preston was looking back at the interior door of the bunker.

"Well, I'll leave you to it then," Owen said, getting the hint, "Please, let me know."

Preston only nodded.

As Owen made to leave Preston called after him. "You heard what Bartz said, right? The electrical drive systems and this expedition—you know what could happen if you tell anyone?"

"Yeah, I know," Owen answered, but his skin crawled a little bit. Everyone was trying to keep him quiet, now even his best friend.

Owen slowly pushed open the cement door, exited, and closed it carefully behind him. He made sure it was properly sealed.

Although he was somewhat put out by the uncomfortable exchange, at least Owen knew plans were being made. They were looking for opportunities to make progress, perhaps not with a smartphone but with something similar. It was enough for Owen to come away with some satisfaction—enough for him to declare his itch had been scratched, at least for the day.

A SLIVER IN HER HANDS

It happened again. Late in the evening the rain was pouring down outside, and Reed opened the tent flap. His face was flushed and water was dripping off his hair. He had been at Splitstone's, or Bluetoe's, and they had probably been talking or drinking or both. His eyes had the look again, and Flora braced herself, knowing what was coming.

Talon saw it coming as well. He began herding the children out of the tent and into the downpour. They knew it was best not to protest.

It was probably the retcher incident. She was getting a lot of attention, speaking with Chief Darkwind and now she had a meeting scheduled with the curator. She told Reed it wasn't anything good, that if anything she was in trouble, but it wouldn't matter. The light was on her, and not him, and he hadn't been there when he should have been.

Or maybe it was for some other reason. Or maybe it was for no reason at all.

The first punch was the worst. It always hurt the most. She never knew where it would land, and he didn't like it when she blocked it. For the rest she could ball up and protect herself, but not for the first.

He hit her on her back, her side, her shoulders. He usually avoided her face, but this time he punched at her hands as they cocooned her head. The backs of her hands smarted painfully. The inertia of the blows might even leave a mark on her face. But she knew if she removed her hands, and he hit her directly, the bruises would be her fault. Then he would hurt her more, maybe tomorrow as well.

What was most painful—what made this beating worse than the others, what drove her to tears—was what she saw through the slit in her fingers between punches. Well into the blows from Reed, when he was coughing from exhaustion, and the expletives were fewer, she saw Talon watching, standing in the back of the tent, a hollow look on his face.

DETONATION

There was no sadness, no anger, no shock. There was only emptiness in his eyes, a chasm of emotion.

THE RITUAL

Lightning continued to reach down in bright corkscrews across the water, igniting the night sky, but the intervals of thunder were getting farther apart. Nature's fireworks were at their disposal, from the comfort of their seaside mansion. Their mansion, courtesy of Nadar Corporation.

Axel herded Erin, Sasha and Zach in from the porch. "Okay, in we go. Show's over. Time for bed."

"Goodnight, Dad," Sasha said for them as they headed for the stairs.

"Erin, you hang back."

Erin turned around, her short braids swiveling to the front to brush her cheeks. "What?"

"It's your turn to do the ritual."

Erin rolled her eyes.

Axel loved the way she rolled her eyes. She didn't quite do it the way most would. It was as if she were playing a game of pinball with her eyes. Her irises would hit a wall in the corner of her eye socket and then bounce to the opposite corner. Someday someone would tell her she was doing it wrong, but hopefully not any time soon.

Axel didn't reveal his amusement. Instead he was stern with her. She was always the least willing, even though she knew the words perfectly well.

"We're doing it," he said firmly.

She shrugged, and they nestled into the leather couches in the living room.

Erin closed her eyes and said the names. "Peers Lindberg, Teodor Lindberg, Erna Lindberg, Robert Kelemen, Daniel Kelemen, Axel Kelemen, Erin Kelemen."

She opened her eyes.

"And now what?" Axel asked.

Erin gave him a sour face.

"Most people lose track of their ancestors, but we haven't. This is why," Axel explained.

"Heaven forbid we forget someone we've never met," Erin said.

Axel had the same thoughts when he was a teenager. He even stopped doing the ritual for several years. It was only later, when he had children of his own, that he really understood. "They aren't just names, Erin. We have a good life now, but for many of our ancestors life was a desperate struggle. For many of them, death was always close, just around the corner. It's a matter of great pride to be on this list, to have *survived*. It should be for you, as well. And it's not only so you remember them. It is out of respect for them—for the sacrifices they made for us."

Erin's face remained defiant, but she said, "Okay."

Axel took the opportunity to drill his point home. "Erin, when you have a group of people who are on your mind, you tend to not want to let them down; you tend to want to do well by them." Erin would know he meant their ancestors, but Axel's explanation made him think more of Pauline and the kids. Whenever Axel heard the ritual he thought more of them than anyone else.

"Sounds like some sort of mind control," Erin said.

Axel stopped smiling and looked at her gravely. His children knew his serious look. Once his faint hint of a smile was gone, it was time to comply or face the consequences.

"Okay, Dad," Erin said, nodding, "I understand."

Axel hoped she did. Axel hoped she was just being a precocious teenager. If not now, someday she would understand, just as he did.

She closed her eyes and spoke the words to complete the ritual. "Their strength is why I am alive, I honor them when I thrive. In turn, these words I will retain, to teach my kin the names again."

She said it properly, and with respect. No petty intonations of sarcasm like she sometimes used.

"Okay, off to bed, love," Axel said, kissing her on the forehead.

Axel watched Erin run off to the stairs. Her failed eye-role replayed itself in his mind.

Pauline was busy cleaning up in the kitchen, watching the ritual with a smile on her face.

Axel meandered over to the island in the kitchen. "Don't say it."

"Don't say what?" Pauline asked.

"That it's silly. That it's only a matter of time until they refuse to do it."

She put down a bowl she had been drying and took off her apron. She walked over to him and draped her arms over his shoulders.

"It's who you are," she said. She gave him a long and sensuous kiss, "and I don't think anyone can refuse Axel Kelemen."

He doesn't deserve her.

And he knew where this kiss was coming from. He was leaving tomorrow on his first official op with Nadar Corporation. He was leaving for Prague, he told her, but Russia in reality. It was his first time in real danger in years, and she knew it.

As the kissing intensified, his baser urges took hold, suppressing his concerns about the op, and freeing him to enjoy the night of passion ahead of him.

THE SPOKE FESTIVAL

Encouraged by a stiff gust of autumn wind, orange, red, and yellow leaves tumbled down on the rows of stalls and show tables along the Seeville downtown pedestrian mall. Trombones and other wind instruments blared jazzy tunes from an active troop on a nearby corner. Huge throngs of people watched the band and lined the rows, inspecting wares and artwork, their eyes and ears watchful and engaged to the sights and sounds of the Spoke Festival.

Owen walked his bike carefully through the crowds, catching the occasional glimpses of this year's creations. In the decorative section, huge, colorful fans made of tire spokes and rubber tubes adorned the tables. The popular spiraling tire arrangements and gear assembly murals were also there. A helical wind vane of gears and reflectors glinted with a sparkle of light. One stand featured a population of lawn dogs. The dogs had reflectors for eyes, and their limbs and facial structures were outlined by elaborate arrangements of bike chains.

The decorations were interesting, but he always found them to be somewhat superfluous—a form of artistic gluttony. The talent and effort of these artisans could be used for so many other exploits.

He made his way past another bandstand, this one playing old string instruments barely audible over the din of the crowd. Farther down the mall were more practical items like deck chairs made from frames and inner tube, or a suit of chainmail armor made of spokes plied into circlets. These were popular for enforcers and even some mules that frequented the bandit regions.

"Would you like a replica of the Beholder of Montalto?" a young boy tugged at his arm and asked him, holding up a clay figurine. Without being given a chance to answer, the boy pulled Owen over to a stall that had dozens of the statuettes. Owen picked one up and looked at it. The figurine was a remarkable rendition of Monty, the enigmatic giant statue perched on nearby Montalto. It lacked the verdure around its base, but definitely did a good job of characterizing the distinct drooping shoulders and rounded belly.

His sister would often gaze in wonder at the beholders, sometimes asking Owen questions he couldn't answer about some vague Adherent gospel related to the beholders. She might like the statuette, he thought.

"How much is it?" he asked the boy.

The boy didn't answer. He had abruptly disappeared into a tent beyond the table. A robed man came out where the boy had entered.

Immediately Owen realized what this was. He had been duped by an Adherent recruiting ploy. Last year they gave away model cars and airplanes, and he had been ensnared just the same. He tried to think of a graceful exit but was too slow.

"My son," the robed man said. He invaded Owen's personal space by putting his arm around his shoulder. "I see you have shown interest in our beloved Beholder of Montalto. May I ask, would you like to know the story of Okafor and the beholders?"

"No, sir. I'm not interested, thank you. I really must be going."

The man assertively pushed him into an uncomfortable stroll. "The people of the Old World were not interested either, and so came the Detonation. Enlightenment is key, or we will fall prey to the three fears. We can help you avoid the pitfalls of novation. We must be vigilant so we do not—"

"Sir, yes, yes I know. But the Adherent's Credo is a bit too extreme for me."

"Extreme? At the Adherents' temple, we believe foremost in balance— moderation over obsession, cooperation over competition, and prudence over recklessness. Does this sound like extremism? I think you could benefit from one of our sermons. In fact—"

"No!" Owen said vehemently, and finally the man released his hand from his back, bowed slightly and retreated to the booth.

Looking back, he could see others giving the booth a wide berth. Owen moved away from the area quickly, chiding himself for not recognizing it for what it was. It seemed like every year the Adherents were more and more desperate to attract followers.

In the merchant rows, barriers and towlines were erected in front of the stalls, so only a handful of people could view the goods at a given time. The stalls were manned by some of the strongest mules—men with massive thighs, veined arms, aggressive beards, and stark tattoos. In contrast to the stalls he had seen so far, these vendors were irreverent and at times even impolite to circulating customers.

From his vantage point, Owen could make out some choice fare. There were prized gas powered bike lamps, super-lightweight carbon fiber frames and high-quality cushioned seats. There were even three new bike pumps in a locked glass casing being ogled by many passersby. He tried to make out the price from a distance, but it was too far away, with too many people blocking his view. Nowadays good bike pumps were getting so scarce that they might cost two months of a mule's wages.

His favorite section was always at the far end of the mall, by the pavilion. This was where the feats of engineering were displayed. Teams of mules, wrenches, and tradesmen would spend months developing their creations for the festival. Featured prominently were bike hybridizations; four, six, eight, ten and even twelve-seaters. The frames were welded and reinforced with supplementary metals, creating an elaborate system of conjoined bicycle chassis, each attached to its own pedal and gear system. In one corner of the pavilion there was a watermill made mostly of chains, gears, and bike frames. In yet another corner were highly elaborate fanning systems for the hot Seeville summer.

He often wondered if he should join a pit crew so he could apply his inventive talents to one of these projects. It seemed like good, honest work, and they created some useful new inventions for the community. Still, it seemed inconsequential compared to what they could do with Old World tech. If they could just harness electrical power, even from behind Faraday cage enclosures, they could do so much more.

Of course, until the specter of the Detonation dissipated, it seemed his tinkering would go nowhere. The silly warnings of the Adherents continued to cast a long shadow. But maybe the railroad could change things; maybe if they showed people the benefits of Old World tech, the superstitions would eventually go away.

Satisfied he had covered the most interesting parts of the festival, Owen cut up to Market Street. He scooted his bike with one foot on so he could glide down the street westward, until the six dirty-yet-sturdy columns of the old Hall of Records rose before him.

Owen had asked around about this Duncan Jones, the man on the talisman Noke gave him. He spoke with a teacher at trade school, talked with the mailman, and even asked his mother. They all said his name sounded familiar, but only his mother could offer more insight. It made some sense. She *was* a bit of a Seeville history buff and had catalogued many of the historical records.

She told him Duncan Jones was actually a Seeville lord for a time. He had also been heavily involved in the temple of Adherents. But after some disagreements on the lord's council, Jones and other prominent lords had decided to leave to join other communities. Unfortunately, his mother had no idea where Jones might live, or even where his relatives might live.

So here he was. In the Hall of Records Owen hoped to find the addresses of any relatives, or perhaps even information on where Duncan Jones might have gone.

It did seem like it could be a fool's errand. Why would this Duncan Jones, a Seeville lord, need a copy of his own talisman? Surely he could just create a replica any time like everyone else in Seeville? And why didn't Noke deliver it himself? There were so many things that didn't make sense about Noke's request.

Belinda waved him in at the front desk. Owen knew her from visiting his mother at work. She wouldn't bat an eyelash at him making a sojourn to the records section.

Thankfully the Hall looked quiet today with everyone distracted by the festival. As far as he knew, he wasn't doing anything illegal, but the way in which Noke had given him the talisman seemed to suggest discretion. For that reason, it was probably for the best Preston hadn't come. Two of them skulking around the Hall would be more conspicuous than one.

At the far end of the public records room there was a vaulted door to gain access to the personal records section. Here he used his mother's key and entered the archive. He made his way through the contracts, bylaws and legal documents, and arrived at the huge bank of turnstiles laden with brass talismans that could be spun around for easy perusal and access. He walked through the lot and looked for the J turnstiles.

When he found the right turnstile, he pushed the massive leaves of brass forward and scanned the rows of talismans on the *Jones* leaf, comparing them to the talisman rubbing Noke had given them.

Duncan Jones's talisman was fairly standard. The name and birthday were written in tall letters at the bottom. These thin, blocky fonts were popular in the old days when rubbings were used more often than hand-drawn paper copies. The talisman image showed several pine trees and a series of knolls next to a log cabin, and in the top left corner was an oversized bald eagle that looked to have flames emanating from behind it.

There were indeed several Jones talismans, but they were from more than seventy years ago, long before Duncan would have been born. There was no sign of Duncan's.

The Hall of Records was supposed to have a talisman for every adult person ever born in Seeville. Could it be he changed his name? Owen stepped away from the Jones leaf and scanned the bank of turnstiles. It would take days to examine all the talismans.

Then he remembered they kept another batch of talisman records down in the archives. These other records didn't contain any brass plates. Instead they kept a paper copy of rubbings of all the talismans as a backup.

He moved deeper into the basement, past the remaining turnstiles to the large antechamber with shelves of books that climbed up to the ceiling. Owen climbed two rungs up on a moving ladder and grabbed the tome labeled *Talismans: Jo-Ju*.

There was no sign of Duncan in these records either. The Jones talismans in the backup records looked to be the same ones as the turnstiles. Strangely, there were rectangular contours on blank entries in the Jones section, as if a number of the Jones talismans had been removed. Indeed, when he looked closer, he could see there was even an additional layer of white pasted on the missing talisman rectangles.

It would be simple to remove the brass templates from the turnstiles, as the remaining templates could be easily reordered, but in these archival records it would be harder to cover up. You couldn't reorder them easily when they were in a large volume like this. In fact, it would be an impossible task...unless you just blanked them out.

Curious, Owen looked through a few more of the paper tomes to see if these sorts of talisman gaps were common. There weren't any other gaps he could find.

He paged carefully through the tomes of books, searching for relatives of Duncan Jones. Often descendants had one or two images in their talisman that remained consistent over the generations. In this case the log cabin, the pine-tree formation, and the flaming eagle were particularly unique, and might be discernable in other relatives' talismans. The cabin and trees were visible in several of the much older Jones' talismans, but they didn't appear anywhere else. Of course, he only sampled a few tomes. He might have to look through hundreds of tomes just to find one other relative.

The only other option was to try to look up Noke's relatives, but that would require a trip all the way down to Lynchburg, since he had no family in Seeville. And who was to say Noke's relatives had anything to do with this Duncan Jones person, anyway?

Owen wanted very much to honor Noke's wishes, but it was beginning to seem like a lost cause.

After perusing one more tome to no avail, he put the Duncan Jones rubbing carefully back in his wallet, next to his own, and proceeded up the stairs. He gave a curt nod to Belinda as he was leaving, and she nodded back at him congenially.

He hesitated at the door, and then backtracked to the counter. "Hey Belinda, do you know if they ever remove talisman records for any reason?"

She gave him a deadpan look. "The whole point is to have as detailed records as possible. If we start removing them it kind of defeats the purpose."

He pushed further. "I don't know, maybe if they were entered wrong..."

"A talisman? Entered wrong?" she said, sounding offended.

She was right. Talismans were carefully crafted, and only entered into the record when someone turned sixteen. They were verified and perfected prior to being placed into the brass molds. It didn't make any sense that one could be entered erroneously.

"Sorry. You're right, Belinda."

At a loss, he tried to shrug off his failure and focus on his next errand.

His next stop was the more conventional bike parts stalls that were set up a block down from the main stands on the downtown mall. He needed a new set of tires and tubes, and you could always find the best deals during the Festival.

THE CURATOR'S OFFICE

Curator Luna Pais greeted Flora at the doorway and escorted her into her office, gesturing to a seat across from her desk. Her head looked to be freshly shaven, and new piercings adorned her ears and nose. The green make-up contouring her eyes flared out onto her temples, matched in color by a green pendant hanging from her neck. She wore a dark brown frock made of dyed wool, common to those emigrating from the Tucson Union.

It was a more modest office than the huge suite used by the former curator. Yet the distribution of curious books on a diverse set of topics remained, as well as the diorama-like arrangements in all corners of the room. Flowers and incense permeated the air, although the smell of fermentation from the caverns lingered as well.

"We Essentialists need to conserve what space we can," Curator Luna explained, waving with flat hands toward the walls of the more humble space. "And it is much more efficient to be in the midst of all the great work being done in the caverns, rather than down in the old warehouse." Luna pointed to the window, where a consistent march of men and women with green-circled eyes proceeded back and forth, into and out of the cavern network.

Flora had only been inside the caverns a handful of times, mostly during her school days. Once she was even gifted a special book from the cavern libraries to keep for her own, a rare honor. She had travelled deep into the interior to pick it out. The stalactite, stalagmite, shield, and drapery formations were all interesting, but with few lanterns to illuminate them, they sparked more fear in her than curiosity. Indeed, the caverns seemed such a dark place to house so many books and precious artifacts, and there were many spots that smelled of some type of rotting food waste.

"Thank you for meeting with me, Curator," Flora said. "I have a proposition for you that I believe could be of great benefit to our community in Grand Caverns, and to all Essentialists."

"Yes, I heard. First let me ask about the incident with the retcher, if you don't mind."

"Of course."

"According to the report you provided Chief Darkwind, you looked at a map on this phone before it was destroyed. Was there anything else you saw on the phone? Other features?"

"I'm sorry, Curator, I wasn't paying attention to all the features. I only remember the mapping function, but there were other functions listed around it, I know that."

"And there was nothing else in this metal box, other than the phone?"

"Nothing else I could see, Curator."

"I see," was all the curator said.

"I hope the incident was not too troublesome. I simply wanted to figure out what was in the Spoke lady's possession," Flora said.

"I know your intentions were not malicious, *mi hija*, but I'm sure you realize every detail is important—every action you took and everything you saw."

"I understand, Curator, and I assure you my report is complete."

Luna smiled. It seemed to stretch the ring bridging her nostrils. For a moment Flora wondered if it hurt the curator to smile.

"Okay then, what is your proposal?" Luna asked.

Flora shifted in her chair to avoid it pressing against one of the bruises on her back. "I wish to escort the prisoner, Cecile, back to the Seeville Spokes."

Luna's eyebrows arched. "And whatever for?"

"Well, as you saw in my report, I believe she is someone special among the Spokes. She's from a powerful tribe up north. If we can get her back to the Spokes, she can vouch for us. Or at least we won't have trouble from the northern Spokes as well as the Seeville ones. And…well, maybe we can set up some kind of a meeting, to see if they are willing to have more open communication."

Luna seemed to chew through her words in her mind.

"And we might be able to get some of our prisoners back as well," Flora added a moment later.

Luna was still deep in thought, her hands crossed under the table. Finally she said, "Did you not see what the Spoke people did to us? Were you not at the infirmary on the day of the attack?"

"Actually, yes, I was helping to tend to the wounded."

"Oh, I see," Luna replied, and she became contemplative again.

After a moment of silence, Luna said, "you are a brave one, Flora, and you have served our community well. I must admit we have considered this notion of yours already, but you put some good meat on the bone. Who else would go on this mission?"

It was not really for her to say, but Flora named a few good hunters and warriors she knew.

"I see," said Luna. She stood up and walked over to the small window. Two disciples walked by and she craned her neck to follow their path with her eyes.

"It must be hard for you, Flora. I am the first curator of Grand Caverns to not be from the clans. First came the Union settlers, then the Prefectorate representatives, with their martial arts and immaculate dojos, and now comes a curator that is not of your own. Much of this is still alien to me, so we must be even more alien to you. Even our names are different. Even though we share the virtue of sun, soil, and seed, we do not have a clan sign like you. We are not Water, or Wind, or Wood.

"Even beyond that—even beyond language and customs—I am not like the last curator. I suspect this is why you came to me with this. I suspect the last curator would have dismissed this notion easily, yes?" She moved to the right and hovered over a diorama depicting hundreds of tents arrayed on a plain.

Flora knew she had to tread carefully here. She wanted to answer the curator's question, but at the same time be sure not to offend her. "Curator Birchwood had...different philosophies than you. He would not have even asked about the phone—he would have simply dismissed it as an abomination. And I don't think he would have considered engaging with the Spoke people, honestly. He felt the prisoners were a lost cause."

"Yes, that sounds like Birchwood," Luna said, letting the moment hang. Then she pointed to the diorama. "Do you see this? This is a model of the tribe I came from in the Sierras, in the Tucson Union. Can you tell me where the curator's tent is?"

Flora stood up and maneuvered to the curator's side to examine the model. The tents were all shapes and sizes, some with colorful feather arrangements, others with animal etchings and paintings on them. "I don't know, Curator."

"And the chief's?"

"They are different, but it's hard to say. Do you want me to guess?"

"No, Flora Clearwater. You have made my point. In the Sierras, we are all different, but everyone is encouraged to offer opinions, as you have. When you have two big tents and all the rest are small, or worse, have extended hierarchies, like the Spokes do, you lose that. People become fearful of retribution and do not come forward with ideas. So you did the right thing. I thank you for your idea, and I would like to put it forward. It will be subject to approval from Chief Darkwind, of course."

Flora tried to contain her excitement. "Thank you very much, Curator."

Luna put her arm around Flora's shoulder, guiding her even closer to the model. "Now, do you see the different tents? Those with animal paintings indicate skill at hunting. Those with bowls and a pottery wheel indicate a specialization with crafts. This tent here, with the large pot, the herbs, and cuts of meat, and vegetables—it is clearly a sign the denizens do the cooking."

"Yes, Curator, an artful depiction," Flora said, not sure where this was going.

"You see, while everyone should be able to offer ideas, not everyone is the right fit for the execution of those ideas. You don't ask the hunter to build a vase, just as you don't ask the mason to prepare the feast. Specialization is the key to building an effective community, especially in one growing as fast as ours."

Flora nodded.

Luna continued, holding her close. "So I'm sure you see it would be foolish for you to go on such a venture. You are an administrative clerk and an assistant healer." Luna made a contrived-sounding laugh while Flora tried not to tremble. "We need the right people for the job—warriors, negotiators, trackers, hunters. I'm sure you understand."

Flora felt her heart sinking. She had told herself this meeting was the right thing to do for the community, but the benefit to Grand Caverns was not her primary motivation. In truth, she wanted nothing more than to get away from Grand Caverns, to get back to Granger. This was the only way she knew how to do it.

Luna continued. "I will be sure to put in a good word for you, Flora. You are a clever one. I will talk about improving your rations with Dark-wind and his subchiefs." A broad smile crossed her face, again flaring out her nose ring. She lowered her arm from Flora's shoulder and guided her out of the office.

"*Adios*, Flora Clearwater," she said. Then Luna lowered her head as she gave her customary Essentialist prayer. "May sun, soil, and seed be bountiful to you on this day."

For one fleeting moment Flora had experienced a glimpse of freedom, away from the beatings, away from this place—a chance to finally find Granger again.

And now the moment was gone.

Vyborg Castle

" Status?" Axel asked as he pressed on the actuator in his earbud.

His earbud responded. "Kura base secured. Awaiting orders to proceed."

"Stand by. About twenty minutes until go."

"Copy that."

Axel examined his face in the rearview mirror of the old Mercedes. He pulled gently on one of the curls of his fake mustache. Comfortable with the disguise, he exited the car and began the long walk along the bridge over the Vuoski River. Wisps of snow pushed and pulled at him, but did nothing to sway his course.

Vyborg Castle appeared through the blusters of snow. The castle lacked the pinnacles, spires, gargoyles and other ornate façade features of the gothic castles of Europe. Yet its immensity was tangible. It had a stoic and utilitarian beauty befitting its victory over the test of time.

Just inside the main entrance a metal detector sat unused and in disrepair, off to the side. It had been secretly decommissioned by one of his agents the day before. As a result, except for bags and backpacks, the lazy museum staff had decided to simply forego screening measures altogether. Holding up lines had been deemed the greater evil over lax security.

Upon gaining entry, Axel moved quickly through the rooms. Vyborg castle was originally built in the thirteenth century and later refurbished in the sixteenth century. Most of the museum exhibitions portrayed art and artifacts from the sixteenth through eighteenth centuries. Although on a regular day Axel would be interested in perusing the exhibits, on this day he paid little attention.

He found Vasily Yavankov in front of an antique ceramic stove, examining some animals depicted on the exterior. Vasily was wearing a long, black coat and fur hat typical of the folks of St. Petersburg. He did have a well-groomed beard that differentiated him, as mustaches were currently more in vogue. Vasily was alone except for a broad-nosed bodyguard hovering nearby.

Vasily had chosen Vyborg Castle over the Russian Ethnography Museum, the Museum of the Political History of Russia, the State Hermitage Museum, the State Russian Museum, and even the Museum of Space Exploration and Missile Technology, something germane to his technical interests.

Based on his profile, it made sense. In his free time Vasily hosted mock battles and made plate mail armor. Nadar Corporation intelligence also had computer records showing Vasily's engagement in a number of video games dealing with medieval warfare. Finding beauty in art is sometimes a reflection of oneself, and Vasily's profile was of a man with a fondness for medieval times.

And clearly, Vasily was no patriot. He would have no joy in visiting the state museums.

Axel waited until Vasily moved to the next room—one in which the cameras had been disabled. He approached Vasily when he was staring at a painting of cavalry charging into battle. The painting also featured a litany of defeated Finnish combatants bleeding on the war-torn plain. Vasily's bodyguard was positioned in the entranceway to the room, watching Axel carefully.

"If only all battles were so lopsided," Axel said to Vasily in Russian.

Vasily took a moment to scrutinize Axel. "Yes, well, what would be the fun in that?"

Axel nodded in contemplation, maintaining his gaze on the painting.

Vasily said, "There's a beauty in it, isn't there? It would seem art is a defining characteristic of humanity, yet so often art glorifies the inhumane."

"There are those who believe those depictions can help us quell those desires and achieve a better morality," Axel replied.

Vasily shook his head. "Delusions, my friend. Said by those without the will or the means for conquest, no doubt."

Axel considered continuing the debate, but that wasn't why he was here. It would be much more expedient to ingratiate himself to Vasily.

Arguing would only make him more sensitive to Axel's actions.

Axel responded with a simple smile and a deferential nod. "Well said, sir."

Vasily nodded and turned toward the door. He paused as he noticed his bodyguard was missing. "Georgy?" Vasily asked, sounding annoyed.

Axel put his hand over Vasily's mouth, placed the injector against his throat and pressed down the plunger. The injector released its paralytic drug, muting his vocal cords. By the time Vasily tried to shout all that came out of his mouth was a blast of hot air.

Axel put him in a headlock and dragged him toward the utility closet. Behind him Axel's asset, Uvanovich, came around the corner, hoisting the slumping bodyguard in his arms. Uvanovich closed the door to the closet behind them.

They had about five minutes.

"You can whisper, but you cannot speak," Axel said to Vasily in Russian.

"You fool!" Vasily whispered emphatically. "Do you know who I am, what I am capable of?"

Axel kept his face devoid of emotion. "We will be disabling the nuclear missiles you have misappropriated from the Russian government. I need the codes to disarm them. Give them to me now."

"Who are you with? The Kremlin? The Chinese? The Americans?"

"Tell us now or you will be hurt," Axel said stonily.

"It doesn't matter. We will find you and—"

Axel began with the pinky finger on his left hand, wrenching it up at a grotesque angle and letting Vasily bear witness to the result.

Vasily gasped in agony.

Axel said, "Every ten seconds I will break something. I don't care about you, or your threats. I have been authorized to permanently maim you. What are the codes?"

Vasily spat at Axel but missed. There was now a string of saliva down the wall behind him.

Axel pulled up his other pinky finger. Vasily wrestled against him and let out furious gasps of air.

"Pull up his family," Axel said to Uvanovich. As Uvanovich brought out the videophone Axel withdrew a small hammer from his backpack.

Uvanovich passed him the phone. It showed Vasily's elderly parents tied up and gagged. The screen was pixelated and dark, but the image was good enough to make out their facial features.

"Do you want them to die?" Axel asked plainly.

Vasily sneered at him. "What do you want? Money? Our Bolotnikov revolutionaries have more than you can imagine. Women? I know the best Russian women. They can—"

"Five more seconds. We kill one of your parents." Axel said.

"Fine. Fine," Vasily said, "the code is B59Y284Z."

Axel pressed on his earbud. "Kura team. Can you confirm B59Y284Z?" He heard back, "Denied."

Axel spoke to the phone in Uvanovich's hand. "Kill the father."

In the video on the phone, someone next to the tied-up man leveled a gun at his head and soon after fired a shot. The father's face went blank and he toppled out of the picture. The women next to him tried to scream but the gag muffled her.

It was a remarkably effective simulation, indistinguishable from reality if one could accept the poor picture quality as an artifact of the transmission. Voice prompts would alter the video sequence depending on the course of Vasily's interrogation.

For good measure, Axel took the hammer and smashed it into Vasily's left hand, breaking bones and tendons and leaving a broad blue contusion shaped like a star.

Vasily had urinated on himself and was shaking uncontrollably, his body losing out to the physical and emotional shock.

Axel asked again, with no change in his intonation. "What is the code?"

Vasily looked like he had had enough. Desperation had entered his eyes, a will to live. He said it slowly, forcing the characters out. "Y429T1DN"

Axel relayed it via earbud and waited. Vasily grimaced and gritted his teeth, trying to regain control of himself.

"Confirmed," his earbud responded. Axel pressed on the earbud and said, "Proceed with the operation."

Axel checked the utility door and could see no museum patrons outside. Then he waited. He needed to give the ops team more time in case something came up.

Sixty seconds passed.

"What now?" Vasily gasped. "Am I to be a political prisoner? Many of my supporters—"

Axel shot Vasily in the temple, his silencer muffling the sound. They quickly wrapped his head in an absorbent towel, covered his body with debris and pushed it to the most discrete corner of the utility room.

Axel glimpsed at the museum room display through a crack in the utility room door. A couple was there, strolling through the medieval artwork. He waited until they had passed through, then looked up at Uvanovich. "You clear from here?"

"Yes, sir," he replied.

Axel nodded and ventured back out into the museum. He walked casually but resolutely through the ancient rooms, back the way he had come in.

When he was outside in the wintry air, walking along the bridge toward his car, he pressed on his earbud. "Status."

"All bogies disarmed, sir. Facility destruction is next."

"Copy that. Proceed."

Once he reached the parked Mercedes, Axel wasted no time navigating out of town. He drove down the country roads toward the extraction location, fast but not too fast. As the op began to wind down, he became partially hypnotized by the soft snows falling around him. He allowed himself to reflect.

Vasily's New Bolotnikov group was a fanatical insurgency within the Russian military, hell-bent on creating a new order. They had plans to forge their place in history with the explosion of a nuclear bomb in a major population center in Europe, followed by the threat of future strikes to force the world to acquiesce to outrageous demands. Axel's team had successfully averted a severe crisis and potentially saved many lives. By all accounts it had been a successful mission, and a worthy one as well.

Yet an elusive concern tugged at his conscience.

There had been weeks of intelligence gathering, planning and preparations, and the op was executed well. Yet these ops, no matter how much preparation was put into them, almost always had some hair on them—some unforeseen randomness that needed to be managed. But the intelligence, and the op itself, all seemed so neatly packed, like a controlled scenario you would go through in training, or an improvisation in the CIA simulation room.

And then there was the question of why Nadar Corporation? Their intelligence revealed the Russians were about to launch a similar covert op on Vasily's splinter group. The Chinese were also in the know and ready to shoot down any missiles that left the facility silos, potentially averting catastrophe.

Why be the global vigilante if one did not need to be?

Axel knew he was simply a tool, a surgical military instrument. He knew, and respected, that soldiers were on a need-to-know basis only. And yet he felt there was more he *did* need to know. If he was to be the soldier Nadar Corporation wanted him to be, additional context was essential, especially because his employer was now a corporation backed by a solitary individual whose motivations were not spelled out in any policy document.

He would have to confront Bhavin about this in the coming days.

On a sharp turn he passed a wintry barn half-buried in snow. For a moment he thought he saw children playing there, throwing snowballs at one another. The children looked like Zach, Erin and Sasha. But it was nothing. Just shadows playing tricks on him. He would often succumb to images like these on ops. The visions didn't scare him but rather comforted him. It was like his kids were there with him. And now when he remembered the op, he would remember seeing them in the snow. It might even be his strongest memory from the op, even though it never happened.

The road became narrower. After several more twists and turns, after night vanquished the day, he arrived at the extraction site. The helicopter was there, waiting for him, blades whirling. Uvanovich arrived within minutes and joined him in the helicopter.

Axel pressed a button on the Mercedes key fob provided by Nadar Corporation. The Mercedes would self-destruct in five minutes. Then he signaled to the pilot. They were quickly lifted into the air, accentuating the wisps of swirling snow in all directions.

The chopper hugged the faint wintery shadows of the land as it headed toward Finland, casting a powerful radar dispersion signal as it went.

THE BIKE TOWERS

Owen had never seen such a large expedition.

There were five major bike platforms. When fully assembled, these platforms had four seat-and-handlebar configurations jutting out of each side, but facing forward. Below the seats were pedal-and-gear assemblies for each rider. These were not the typical bulky hauling platforms one might see in the city though. They were of top quality, recently crafted with the best lightweight frame components, even detachable in sections for tight throughways.

There were also twenty-odd other riders scattered ahead and behind the flotilla of platforms, making the full expedition contingent about eighty Spokes.

Owen had been assigned to sit on one of the platform seats. He tried his best to pedal his gear assembly in sync with the more veteran mules, but he was competing against riders that did this for a living. These mules had chiseled calves, bulging thighs and seemingly limitless lung capacity. As the day wore on, he settled for giving occasional bursts of effort whenever he could muster the energy. Thankfully, the railroad folks had made it clear that Owen had been selected for his technical capabilities, not for his physical prowess.

The town of Culpepper had been welcoming. It was a small farming village to the northeast of Seeville, a common stopover for expeditions to the bike towers, and they were always ready for accommodating large expeditions. Owen ate with his platform team at a breakfast diner fashioned out of a refurbished Old World garage. A rotund lady, as sweaty as he was, served him an oversized brunch of greasy eggs and apple oatmeal, giving him much-needed energy for the rest of the journey.

After they left Culpepper, they saw fewer signs of life. They passed by one hovel by the road built out of Old World scrap metal. A man with long scraggly hair ran out and tried to sell them everything from bike parts to underwear. They ignored the man and continued on. From that point on, all the Old World highway exchanges and turnoffs were overgrown and untrodden.

As they continued east the signs started appearing.

Bandit Territory—5 miles.

Bandit Territory—1 mile.

Entering Bandit Territory,
Frederick Bike Towers in 11 miles.
Stay on Marked Roads.

It was his first time in bandit lands. He didn't know what to expect other than what he had heard in stories. The others didn't look afraid, and the road hadn't changed in any meaningful way, so he felt only mild trepidation at first.

Eventually they hit the Highway 95 Interchange. A large, red-lettered sign marked the way south: *Danger—to Richmond Fever Lands*. And another the way north: *Danger—to Washington Fever Lands*. The signs had the characteristic three notches, a common marking Spoke people adopted as a form of branding for their signs.

The old, many-laned north-south highway was overgrown, but there were clearly used pathways to the north and south, with fresh bike treads and horse tracks on them.

Of what he had seen so far, the bike treads and hoofprints made him the most nervous. There *were* people out here. Bandits. Desperate people. People that didn't like Spokes.

Thankfully they had strength in numbers. Bandits had not attacked bike expeditions to the towers in years, according to their platform wrench, a man named Chester.

Chester was positioned across from Owen. He was the one Owen had been trying unsuccessfully to keep in sync with. Chester was older than most, probably in his mid forties, but you could only tell his age from the few gray hairs that crept out from under his helmet. His body was lean and powerful, like the other mules on the platform. His deep-set brown eyes came together as he squinted out across the expanse, alert and aware. His hands were knobby, a result of spending most of his time working with ratchets and Allen keys.

"How much further, boss?" Owen asked.

Chester glanced across at him, but then returned his focus to the environs, keeping his eyes active. "It's about five miles from the interchange, due east," he said. "How you holding up, kid?"

"Fine," Owen said, although in reality his legs felt heavy and weak.

"You've never been out this way, have you?" Chester asked.

"No, sir."

"We've done this run hundreds of times. As long as you all follow directions we should be fine."

"Yes, sir," Owen said. Owen suspected the reference to *you all* included Bartz's people. There were ten of the railroad folks, including Preston and Owen. They had been included at the last minute at Bartz's request. The new additions made an already large expedition one of the largest ever.

"And besides," Chester said, "I think everyone should see the towers at least once in their lives."

It was on the crest of a hill a few miles later that Owen first made out the towers. Ten clusters of the black spindly cylinders, each cylinder fifty stories tall, defied the featureless plains around them. The huge buildings dominated more and more of the horizon as they rode closer.

Owen had heard descriptions of the towers, but it was another thing to see them with his own eyes. These skyscrapers housed any sort of bicycle you could possibly want, all neatly packed and stored—road bikes, racing bikes, mountain bikes, hybrids, tricycles and even tandem bikes. For decades the Spoke people had raided the towers and taken what they needed. According to Chester, in all that time they had only emptied a handful of the closest buildings.

The peloton eventually turned off the main highway, making its way down a local road that led more directly to the array of towers. The road ended at a large, two-story wall that barred passage. It appeared that at one time there had been a massive door here, but the whole area was overgrown. For all Owen could tell, the door had never been opened since the Detonation.

The lead scouts turned off to the right on a well-groomed, Spoke-made path that ran parallel to the wall. A few hundred feet later the road veered to the left.

Here a large, round hole was evident in the exterior wall. Its diameter was twice the height of Owen, and it was cut into the wall with such precision that a sheen glistened on the surface of it. This must be the *bullet hole*, as he had heard it described. It was as if a cylinder of material had been perfectly sliced out of the five-foot thick metal wall. The path of the "bullet" continued, cutting holes in a straight line through the array of buildings into the horizon. In some places, it cut arced sections off some of the bases of the tall cylindrical buildings, and for one building it cut a hole right through the center.

After the scouts had gone through and given the all clear, the peloton navigated through the bullet hole one platform at a time.

"Do you know what could have caused the bullet hole?" Owen asked as they pedaled the platform slowly through the wall.

"The boy asks a lot of questions, don't you think, Chester?" A mule ahead of Chester remarked.

"Yes, he does," Chester said, a hint of amusement in his voice.

"What is it?" Owen asked.

"Oh, nothing," Chester said, smirking at something left unsaid.

"Lighter loads make for louder trips," another mule on their platform said. It was a common saying among mules and wrenches, owing to the fact that conversation was harder when the mules were pushing a full platform.

"About the bullet hole," Chester said. "I've heard that some of the local people, the bandits closer to the fever lands, say it's the result of some spiritual energy from their god, some divine intervention to give us access to the bikes. More likely, it was a random blast from the Detonation. It could be the one time a stray bullet from the Old World did something good for us instead of sicken us or swoop down and puke acid."

Owen was still gazing in wonder at the walls of the cylindrical hole and the immensity of the towers that lay beyond. "It's so strange," was all he could offer in response.

A voice came from behind Owen. "Of course, we know as much about the bullet hole as we do about why the bike towers are here in the first place." It was Jeroun, another of the railroad men who had been assigned to his platform. Jeroun was a surly sort who had kept quiet on the ride so far, save the occasional expletive on steeper inclines.

"Now, now," Chester said, shaking his head and casting a dark look at Jeroun.

The mules didn't like to talk about the origins of the bike towers. It was an extremely important resource for Spoke society and the mules in particular. Yet trying to explain their existence was like poking a sleeping bear. People had passionate views, most of them hard to reconcile, so it often resulted in disagreements—sometimes violent ones.

The peloton stopped next to one of the towers in the cluster closest to the bullet hole entrance. Unlike the skyscrapers and other big buildings Owen had seen from picture books, there were no windows, and no other architectural features other than some kind of bridge that connected the cluster at the top. The only breaks in the exterior surface were minor in-dentations every fifth of the way up, which made it look like cylindrical cross-sections had been stacked on top of each other like five big Lego pieces. Otherwise, the towers were just huge black cylindrical monoliths.

Owen stretched his legs and sat down on the ground with his canteen. No sooner had he taken a big gulp of water into his mouth than he was hit in the chest with a large bundle of rope. He lost half of the mouthful on his shirt.

Chester was standing next to the platform, grinning at him. "Don't get too comfy. We like to give the curious ones the first chance to see the view."

Owen suspected this was not something he should be looking forward to.

It just so happened there were no stairs in the towers. The interior of the tower was just a stack of five cylindrical sections, each one a warehouse full of bikes, without access points between them. In each warehouse section, thirty thick metal poles reached up ten stories, and on each pole bikes of numerous varieties were neatly stacked in a helical formation climbing up to the ceiling. It did not enable easy access to the bikes, but it was perhaps the most efficient use of space. According to Chester, each sectional warehouse could house about twenty thousand bicycles, and the choicest bikes were always in the top sections of the tower.

In this particular tower they had already removed the bikes from the four bottom sections, so in order to get the bikes down from higher reaches they had to set up a pulley system. To open up a new section in the building it got tricky. One had to affix a series of extension ladders to the side of the building, then climb up another expanse of the tower and use a welding torch to cut the wall and open the next section. Then the ladders could be properly secured to the opening, a pulley system could be put in place, and bikes could be rappelled down from the higher reaches.

Given his skill with a blowtorch, Owen had been selected to open up the next highest section of the building—and possibly also due to his inquisitiveness on the ride that morning.

Owen only had a quick bite before the team went into action. It took half an hour just to get up to the last opened section. He dared not look down as he climbed up the various ladders. Some of them were fastened poorly, and they shifted with each step. He tested every rung of every ladder carefully, and in a couple of cases the team worked to improve a ladder's positioning or reinforced it with rope or bungees. It seemed the higher he went the more the wind would push and pull on him, despite the relative calm at ground level.

With all these travails Owen couldn't help pondering the lack of access points to the towers, and even between sections. Why hadn't the architects rectified this strangely obvious design flaw? Even the bridges that connected the clustered towers together looked to be designed solely for structural support. One could probably try to get across to another tower from the roof but it wouldn't be far removed from tight-rope walking.

In the end it wasn't that bad. He was secured to a safety rope the whole time, and he had no fear of heights. Owen began to actually enjoy it.

It took him thirty minutes with his torch to create an opening in the wall on the highest section. Finally, after moving the slab of metal aside and stepping onto the level, he sat down and allowed himself a chance to rest.

"You okay up there, Owen? Sometimes the wind can feel like it's chain-whipping you." It was Chester. He had been spotting him on a ladder below.

They were in a rush to get the pulley system set up, but Owen felt like he deserved a break. "Just fine. Give me a couple of minutes," he yelled back.

His eyes followed the meadows and forests spanning out into the distance. This must be the highest he had ever been in his life.

He figured he was facing north. He tried to see any traces of Washington in the distance. Unfortunately, the horizon was a flat line, devoid of detail. Washington was either too far away, or perhaps there was nothing left to see.

He imagined this was what it must have been like for all of the workers in pre-Detonation times. Every day they would come to work and look out over vast horizons like this, or see mile after mile of buildings in every direction. These same buildings would be teeming with glittering screens, computers, phones and electronic billboards. Internet and phone conversations would be constantly travelling in every direction—through them, to them, and around them. All the while electric cars and planes danced through the same cities and skies.

It was a life too foreign for him to contemplate, a higher level of existence than he could possibly imagine. There were books, pictures, buildings and other traces of them everywhere, yet it still seemed too magical to believe. It seemed like people had lived like gods.

What on this earth could possibly have destroyed these gods? What made them throw it all away?

He sighed, stretched his legs and then began setting up the pulley system.

The Cherry Blossom, the Deer, the Wolf, and the Jackal

"Would you like a drink?" Flora asked Reed.

"Yes, love. One of the newer malts," Reed responded, patting her shoulder.

"I'll be right back." She smiled at Reed and Splitstone, who were already back to the conversation she had interrupted.

She took the long way round the semicircle of chairs and tables, not daring to cross where the performers were doing their dances, juggling, and theatrics. The fire-breathing acts were about to begin.

It was the Day of the Deer, a yearly Essentialist celebration. Her back and legs felt heavy and stiff from preparations. Chief Darkwind and Curator Luna insisted on erecting over twenty totems adorned with hanging baskets replete with flowers, vegetables, and animal skins. She had spent much of the morning climbing up and down the precarious posts. After she had to help with moving furniture and setting up the event tents.

Then she would have to clean it all up again tomorrow.

A gaggle of men laughing boisterously were gathered around the closest kegs, some of them chewing on sticks of venison jerky. She waited for an opening to form between them and then went to fill up Reed's pint glass.

"Enjoying yourself, Flora?"

The man was hard to distinguish from the people moving about in the darkness. It was only when he broke off from the drinking men to greet her that his face became distinguishable. It was Finch, from the administrative office.

"Yes, blessed be the deer," she said as she connected Reed's glass to Finch's half-empty mug. She was in no mood to fend off Finch's probing questions, but she couldn't think of an easy way to exit the conversation.

"You know they took the Spoke prisoner away today."

"Really? Who took her?"

"Ember Thisslewood and a couple of Merchant Mercs. The one called Mehta that came when you were there, and I can't remember the other one's name."

"Where are they taking her?"

"I heard them talking about going the Gap Run route. Sounds like they're going into Spoke territory, but it's not clear why. Maybe some kind of peace offering, or prisoner exchange? Seemed strange to me, but the release was signed off by both the curator and Darkwind. Maybe the mercs were some sort of compromise."

A sinking feeling claimed Flora. After her meeting with Luna, Flora had gone to Chief Darkwind to see if he might have a different perspective—to see if maybe he would allow Flora to go on the trip. He had said he would talk to Luna about it. Apparently Darkwind didn't get his way. Or maybe he didn't even care to ask.

What was more concerning was that Ember Thisslewood seemed to be leading the foray. Thisslewood had extreme Essentialist views, one of them being that the prisoners in Spoke territory were contaminated, and therefore not worth saving.

But something about how Finch described the mission didn't sound right. "Why do you say compromise?" she asked.

Finch guided her away from the other men and spoke quietly. "Well, you know, Darkwind and Luna don't exactly see eye-to-eye on things. They may have agreed to take the prisoner into Spoke territory on some kind of mission. But Thisslewood is Darkwind's man, through and through. I suspect the mercs were included to keep Ember in line, so that Luna got whatever what she wanted as well."

Finch was probably right, but it offered her no more hope that they might negotiate for the Essentialist prisoners. More likely, the Mercs were going to ask for valuables or supplies in return for Cecile. They would get some cut of the spoils. She could see Luna, Darkwind and the mercs readily agreeing to that arrangement.

The sinking feeling was deepening, taking root in her chest. The chance of getting Granger back now seemed unbearably remote.

The crowd was cheering and clapping. In the performance circle a man had blown some kind of accelerant into a lighter, brightening the faces of onlookers with a funnel of fire.

The fire illuminated the totems, revealing two chorus larks circling and chirping an upbeat tune. The shape of the totems would sometimes attract the larks. It was seen as a good omen if they came, so the crowd jeered and pointed at them. But the larks would rarely stay for long. They landed on the totem for a brief moment and then twittered away into the night.

Flora didn't clap or cheer. Instead, she tried to combat her growing feeling of malaise. It wasn't just Finch's news. It was the fire-breathing spectacle enjoyed by everyone. It was the man enjoying a boisterous laugh by the kegs, and it was the irreverence of these people to her miserable life. All of these things seemed to conspire against her all at once, disarming her, weakening her. She cringed and had to look away, trying to mask her eyes.

"Are you all right, Flora?" Finch asked. He reached out to her, touching her arm.

She had hoped her moment had been ignored, but of course not with Finch. He would know when she was happy or when she was sad. He would see her bruises, no matter how much she covered them up.

She pulled away from his hand, spilling some of Reed's drink on the ground and leaving Finch standing there. She marched back around the semicircle toward Reed.

She was in no state to rejoin him—or anyone else for that matter—so she took a detour out to the edge of the tables. To the casual onlooker she was just stepping out to stare at the constellations. There, in relative obscurity, when she was sure no one was watching, she used her shirt on her eyes, to ensure there was no moisture in them. She gritted her teeth and forcefully expunged her emotions. Only when her eyes had dried, and when she was confident she could produce a convincing smile, did she return to her seat.

Reed frowned at the half-full glass she provided him, but was too engrossed in his conversation with Splitstone to care.

Flora sat quietly, watching the dancers and jugglers in front of them. The evening continued, her emotions replaced with stark numbness. She concentrated on staring forward, ignoring Reed, and she never dared to look across to where Finch was sitting.

When the performances ended, a large bell was rung, and the crowds hushed. Curator Luna walked to the center of the semicircle. She smiled and waved at people she knew. In return, the audience clapped and serenaded her with alcohol-fueled cheers.

"People of Grand Caverns, Chief Darkwind and I are excited to welcome you all to this much-deserved celebration. I hope you accept the earth's adulation on this Day of the Deer. For me in particular, as my first Day of the Deer in Grand Caverns, I know I will cherish this memorable evening."

A number of Curator Luna's disciples were gathering around to listen. Many had not even been at the celebration. It seemed they were always toiling away at building this or working on that in the caverns, day and night, holiday or workday.

Luna continued. "I do have a serious matter to address with you all. One for which it is important you are all paying attention." She paused in her oratory, each second lending gravity to what she was about to say.

"We believe in what is essential. We respect the animals, we cherish the trees and we welcome the bounty of our harvests. We have done well to avoid the trappings of the Old World, and now across the expanse of the continent our numbers have grown...into the millions."

There were cheers and some intermittent clapping. Luna smiled and held up her hand, commanding silence. "Unlike our eastern neighbors, we can be confident in our clean hands and clean hearts. We can be confident we do not sully ourselves and desecrate sun, soil and seed on a road that will lead to oblivion.

"But we have a duty to the deer, to the green earth, to ourselves, to not only survive, but to thrive, and this duty is one I do not believe we have fulfilled. We are to be nature's true advocate, and as such, we must recompense the earth for the security it has provided us. The fertile ground we live on has given us bounty, and so we must help the earth reclaim the lands it has lost."

People were nodding their heads, but Flora could see Chief Darkwind was not. There was a frown on his temple, visible even from across the dimly lit semicircle.

Meanwhile, more disciples were joining the ranks. They hovered behind Luna, behind everyone, forming a broad circle around the periphery.

"You see, a deer will eat the flowers off a cherry blossom. This deer may succumb to disease, and then maybe a wolf will cull this weak deer from the herd. But maybe this wolf is not the strongest, not the fiercest. Maybe the alpha of his pack will dispatch him and then a pack of jackals will come to feed on his carcass. Only the strongest, most aggressive jackal will jockey for the choicest wolf meat, and as a result get stronger, be dominant, have the most offspring, while others will get scraps and remain weak.

"This is nature. *We* are nature. We are the cherry blossom, we are the deer, we are the wolf, and we are the jackal. Nature will have its way with us, but first it is our right, it is our *obligation*, to take what we can to survive, to not stand passively by while others take what we need. Nature needs competition. For that way, the strongest can survive, and the strongest can thrive. It is the way of all animals, including the deer which we celebrate today."

She paused to let her message sink in, and then continued with emphasis, "That is why, as the true advocates of this earth, it is our duty to no longer lie in waiting to be pushed aside by false advocates. It is not natural for the Spokes to despoil the lands with their railroad tracks and cast rubbish into the air we breathe, and yet it is natural to fight, and it is natural for the strongest to survive."

Darkwind stood up from his seat, his bald head and clean-shaven face a ball of red rage in the distance. "Enough of this," he objected. "It is the Day of the Deer, a peaceful celebration. Please Luna, let us enjoy—"

No sooner had Darkwind stood up than disciples had flooded into the inner circle. Several of them grappled and subdued him. Darkwind's deputies were similarly captured and bound by disciples brandishing daggers.

A few brave souls in the crowd stood up from their chairs to resist but then slowly sat back down as the odds became clear. Luna's disciples were everywhere, and heavily armed.

Luna smiled, "Unfortunately, Darkwind, *you* are the weak deer that needs to be culled from the herd. Or perhaps you are the wolf, once proud, but now old and weak, detrimental to the pack. Or maybe the jackal that is not able to get to the wolf carcass. Or...perhaps you are just a cherry blossom." She laughed. No one joined her.

She wrung her hands together happily. "It matters not. Either way, this is the proper order of things. Nature has spoken, and for the pack to survive, for the true advocates of nature to thrive, you must be returned to the soil."

Darkwind was wrestling violently against his captors. Luna nodded to the disciples holding him and one of them drew a dagger. Darkwind summoned a burst of strength and threw the two disciples off of him. He then managed to wrestle the dagger from the armed disciple and stabbed it in his eye. The disciple screamed in agony. Darkwind extracted the knife and turned to rush forward, toward Luna.

For a moment Flora thought Darkwind might actually reach her. But he had only taken a few steps when a Shinogi came out of nowhere to kick in his left knee, dropping him. Another disciple followed behind and stabbed him squarely in the back. Darkwind threw this one off and rose again, but the Shinogi jabbed him in his side with a small blade, making him lean over. Finally, two disciples fell on top of him to hold him down, and another slit his throat. Crimson blood spewed forth from Darkwind's neck as he gasped wordlessly.

Darkwind stared at Luna defiantly, spittle flying from his mouth. Then all at once, his strength left him, and his body went limp.

"Well, maybe not the cherry blossom then," Luna said, laughing.

———◆———

It was not uncommon with Essentialists. Flora had heard of it happening at two other settlements in the last few years. In fact, it was suspected Darkwind had come to power by slaying the former chief on a hunting trip. He had denied it, of course, but how many people drown in a river by accident, really?

So coups happen, and people fall in line with the new leader, if they want to live. Grand Caverns was no different. There wasn't much loyalty to Darkwind, in the end. Luna's new chief, which she promoted to the rank of general, was willing to accept Darkwind's deputies and subchiefs as his own.

To Flora it wasn't a particularly loathsome injustice. Darkwind was harsh and egotistical, and at least Curator Luna seemed to listen to her. It was indeed worrisome how much Luna railed against the Spokes, but it was hard to say how serious Luna was about *recompensing the earth*, as she put it. She was probably just grandstanding as countless curators and clan chiefs had done before her. Besides, she was about to return a Spoke prisoner in exchange for goods. That didn't sound like someone preparing for war.

So Luna's coup was just one more reason for Flora to leave Grand Caverns. But it wasn't the biggest reason.

Late that night Flora pulled all of the kids out of the tent and led them through the dew-laden fields south of town to a nearby brook. Disciples were still loitering about the settlement, wary of any Darkwind loyalist uprising. A woman and her three children posed no threat.

Skye was tired and grumpy, her eyes red from rubbing, while Clover was just excited to see the stars. As for Talon, he didn't complain, but he still eyed her cautiously as they walked.

When they arrived at the brook, she let the girls play. She had a lantern, but the stars and moon were enough. She turned it off and watched

Skye and Clover throw rocks at the reflections of stars in a swirling eddy of the brook.

Skye exclaimed in mock concern "You're going to wash away the stars Clover!" Clover would giggle and drop another stone in the brook.

Flora allowed herself to smile at their uncorrupted sense of wonder.

Talon interrupted her contemplation. "What's this all about?"

Flora said, "I want you to all do the ritual."

Skye asked, "Right now Mommy? It's the middle of the night."

Flora explained. "You know how Reed doesn't like the ritual, and I know how you and Clover like to look at the stars."

Before they could ask another question, Flora said, "Skye why don't you begin?"

Skye looked reticent.

"Please Skye. It's important. We've talked about this."

"Yes, Mommy," Skye said, sighing and getting up her gumption.

Skye took a deep breath and began. "Peers Lindberg, Teodor Lindberg, Erna Lindberg, Daniel Kelemen, Axel Kelemen, Morgan Kelemen, John Kelemen, Tucker Kelemen, Xander Kelemen, Granger Kelemen, Skye Clearwater."

Flora nodded encouragingly. Then Skye continued, "Their strength is why I am alive, I honor them when I thrive...I...live to teach the names again."

Flora smiled. "You forgot Robert Kelemen after Erna Kelemen. And the last sentence is: 'In turn these words I will retain, to teach my kin the names again.' You're almost there, sweetheart. Good job."

Flora turned to Clover. "Your turn, Clover."

"Okay, mommy." Clover was always eager to do the ritual, never once getting angry or flustered. This time she made it through half the names.

"Well done Clover. You're getting there," Flora said warmly, "will you keep working on it?"

"Yes, Mommy."

"And you, Talon."

"Why are we really here?" he asked.

"Well, we haven't done the ritual in a while."

He stared back at her. The moon cast a somber light on his features. He was growing up so fast, nearly a man, with peach fuzz on his lip. His eyes, though—his eyes were dark, tired, and heavy. A bruise still lingered in one of his eyes from his training with Nobura. Bruise or not, these did not look like the eyes of a teenager.

"Why are we really here?" He asked again, staring back at her.

This time Flora had to look down. He knows her too well. Under his mask of resentment, the wheels turned with precision.

Flora sighed and spoke to all of them. "I have to go away for a while, children. I thought it would be good to do the ritual now, since...I may be away for a few days. Reed is going to take care of you. Reed and Talon."

"Where are you going, Mommy?" Skye asked.

"It's not important. I'm just running an errand for the chief."

The children had not been told about Darkwind's death, and she felt it best to leave her orders ambiguous rather than feed them a lie that could easily be disproven. But Talon must have known this was no ordinary errand. People don't often get up and leave in the middle of the night.

Talon did the ritual. As usual, every name was correct and every sentence perfect. He stared at her with what? Defiance? Anger? Despair? She couldn't be sure. As he finished his jaw clenched, and a tear soiled his cheek. He made no motion to wipe it away, and so it continued on its path, until it passed over the ridges of his lips and dropped to the ground.

"Thank...thank you, Talon." She tried to hold back her own tears. She needed to be strong, to not let on...yet she wanted so much to embrace him, to tell him how she felt. It might be the last time she saw him, maybe ever. But she couldn't. His eyes were too intense, too unforgiving.

All she could bring herself to do was stare, just like he did—to stare and try in vain to memorize his features through the colorless shadows.

They made their way back to the tent. When the kids were asleep she wrote a note for Reed, making up a false errand about collecting fox skins from up north. She forced herself not to contemplate the repercussions when he read it, for she knew it might hobble her just to think about it.

Then she took her packed belongings and left.

She knew she was being irresponsible, to leave her kids—to leave Talon in charge. Despite his stubbornness and sulky behavior, she knew he was capable—much more capable than people gave him credit for.

She hoped he would forgive her. She hoped they all would, for this was her only chance of ever getting Granger back. Her life had been torture without him—a litany of mistakes and consequences, a cold dark ocean with frightening storms and dangerous reefs, a cold dark ocean she couldn't bear to navigate any longer.

FORTIENT

"Well done, Axel."

It was an encrypted message Bhavin had sent Axel the day after the Russian operation.

Since then there had been nothing. No messages, no phone calls—and more concerning—no meeting openings. The one meeting Axel had scheduled had been two weeks out, but then it was to be "rescheduled pending further schedule review."

Bhavin was the head of a major multinational corporation, so surely he was busy. Then again, maybe this was the kind of corporate cold shoulder used to tell someone to piss off. Either way, Axel's unanswered questions about the Russian op were not going away, so he couldn't help but try to find answers on his own.

Axel was no ordinary meathead grunt. He was trained in all forms of intelligence gathering. He knew how to follow the money, and he knew when decisions were made that didn't quite add up.

Buried in securities-exchange filings were allusions to large budgetary allocations that were unusual, in particular for the Fortient division. The Fortient division was important. They built armored vehicles, drones, and aircraft, plus other classified armaments. Yet compared to the software and car lift businesses, the returns of Fortient were anemic at best, and there were no upcoming governmental bids that would suggest that a big investment made sense.

Axel spent time with a number of low-level Nadar Corporation accounting representatives under the auspices of exploring cost-cutting initiatives for security operations. They were more than eager to work with him directly for the opportunity to get exposure to a high-level executive, even if it meant working with the obscure security function. Some innocuous questions revealed that quite a few employees in project management, software development and analytics from other Nadar divisions were also allocating their time to Fortient. Facilities space, skunk works projects, and some other little-known dark pools of money were also contributing.

When Axel added it all up, including the portion actually revealed in public securities filings, the changes amounted to an R&D budget of two billion dollars for Fortient alone. This nearly matched the R&D budget for the division that accounted for the majority of Nadar Corporation's revenues.

What's more, a new leader named Finnegan Rawlings had been tapped to lead Fortient. Rawlings had worked in several biotech and software development companies in the last several years; one of them being in the defense industry.

What was unusual about Rawlings' appointment was that his highest budget under management had been about forty million dollars, and yet he was given an effective budget fifty times that much with Fortient.

Rawlings's position wasn't even formally announced other than a message sent internally to a handful of key people in Fortient. The current leader of the division was keeping his name and title, reporting directly to Rawlings. It was certainly unusual to not announce the new head of a division with a two-billion-dollar budget. Axel only found out about it secondhand, after quite a bit of digging.

Axel lit up some intelligence assets outside of Nadar Corporation to find out more, even though he knew he was pushing the boundaries of what Bhavin might consider acceptable. It turned out that before Rawlings's time as an entrepreneur he had had military training and, much like Axel, had done special ops as well. Known missions were in Afghanistan, Brazil, Mongolia and Egypt.

It was certainly possible there was a novel defense technology that Nadar Corporation was developing. Maybe Bhavin felt it might jeopardize Axel's efforts if he was exposed to it. Perhaps Bhavin needed an experienced operative to sell in to specific military clients. Or maybe Bhavin was doubling down on his efforts to neutralize global threats and needed someone with experience similar to Axel's.

But why not tell Axel about it? There was no reason Axel should be worried about parallel divisions with similar objectives. In fact, as long as there was some coordination at the top, he would welcome it.

It was possible Bhavin was fickle—that he had tired of playing global vigilante and had now found another way to make money that involved shiny new defense technologies. And it was also possible this new venture might actually be at odds with Axel's imperatives, with the reason Axel was at Nadar Corporation to begin with.

He picked up the phone and rang his assistant.

"Jessica?"

"Yes, Mr. Kelemen."

"Can you invite Finnegan Rawlings and his family to a welcome barbeque this weekend? Tell him I insist."

"Finnegan Rawlings, sir?"

"You'll find him in the company directory, although his title won't be listed."

"Yes, sir. Right away."

Scars, Burns, and Blemishes

The expedition made camp at the base of the tower after filling up half the platforms with bike frames, wheels, chains, seats, gear sets, brake wires, bolts, nuts and washers, all neatly partitioned and stacked.

The area around the towers was an even eerier place in the darkness. When Owen looked up he saw the immutable black cylinders looming above him, negating large swaths of the starry skys.

The main congregation of the camp was just outside an old opening they had made in the bottom section of the tower. A few others clustered on the outer perimeter closer to where the various platforms were parked. Guards were also posted around the periphery.

Despite his many exertions, Owen felt invigorated, infused with a feeling of accomplishment. Opening a new tower section seemed to be some sort of rite of passage with the mules. They were even receptive to his many questions.

Or maybe tolerant was the better word.

They spoke of the bandit tribes—how husbands and wives were shared, how elderly folks were sacrificed and then eaten. One mule spoke of fields littered with husks of melted metal where massive battles had taken place. Another mule spoke of riding through the "legs of the giant," which sounded like some sort of archway carved into a mountain. A wrench named Arsalan, an immigrant from the north with a sickle-shaped scar extending from his chin to his right ear, even spoke of Gondola Valley, a place where glass boxes hung from lines crisscrossing the sky.

He had heard about these people and places before, from his mother or kids at trade school, but there was something about being in this foreign place, under these pre-Detonation skyscrapers, with these hardened riders who had spent much of their time in bandit lands, that made them seem more believable. The stories might be embellished, even untrue, but Owen chose to immerse himself in them—he even garnished them with his own active imagination before devouring them.

It wasn't until later in the evening that he realized not one of them had mentioned his spots or called him names. For these mules, scars, burns, and blemishes were a natural part of their existence, accrued daily from toiling against treacherous environments and bumpy trails. In fact, looking around the fire at the faces of these hardened men, markings were more common than not.

In the midst of a mule sounding off about a particularly treacherous century ride, Owen witnessed Preston cut through the main congregation and hurriedly grab some stew from the stew pot. Owen had seen little of Preston since they had finished up for the day.

While the mule folk tales were fun and interesting, it would be nice to know more about why he was really here. He decided to skip the next story and try to catch up with Preston, who had now cut back through the congregation.

Preston wasn't carrying a lantern, so it was hard to follow his form as it waded deeper into the darkness. Based on his trajectory it looked like he was heading to where his assigned platform was stationed. It had been placed right at one of the outward vertices of their perimeter. The embers of a small fire were visible there, so Owen was able to navigate in that direction, despite losing track of Preston.

He walked with slow footfalls, trying to avoid banging his shins on any boulders or other debris.

As he came closer to the fire pit, he heard talking in the distance. It was too faint to make out the words at first, but based on the sharp intonations he could tell they were having a heated discussion.

When he was closer still, the words became clearer. "No, we tell them nothing. Why do they need to know? We're seeking out parts for a new coal furnace crank. That's it. These mules won't care."

"Sure, most won't care, but what about the wrenches? What about our own crew? When do we tell them where we're going? The mules hang together. If our crew isn't comfortable, they could cause a stir with the others."

All of a sudden a hand cupped Owen's neck from the side and his feet were kicked out from underneath him. The world seemed to turn upside down as he was catapulted to the ground. A blast of air shot out of his mouth as he hit the dirt, deflating his lungs.

A cold ring of metal was then pressed against his head. It was the muzzle of a pistol.

"What have we here? Did someone get lost in the dark?" A man asked, his acrid breath buffeting Owen's face.

Owen tried to respond but he had no air left to expel from his lungs. And try as he might he could not make out who had grabbed him. All he could see was one more vague form blocking the stars above him.

"You better speak up string bean," the invisible man said.

Finally Owen was able to breath in. "I...I'm Owen." He breathed once more. "I'm with Preston."

"Oh with Preston? Please forgive me," the voice responded sarcastically. Owen's arm was then wrenched into a painful angle behind him. It wouldn't take much more force to dislocate his shoulder or break his arm, he was sure. "It's true!" Owen objected. "Ask Preston!" It took all his energy to get the words out.

"Okay, now, don't cry about it."

Owen was forced to stand up. The man pushed him toward the fire, with one hand holding his arm at the same obtuse angle, and the other maintaining a firm grip on his neck. Owen's chest heaved, still trying to catch his breath.

The talking had stopped, and now Owen was thrust into the light, almost directly over the dying fire. The probing eyes of four men rested on him.

"Found your spotty-faced friend following you, Preston," the man behind him said. Owen turned to see his assailant was Rourke Rama, one of Bartz's security personnel. Rourke had a slanted nose, an artifact of some old scuffle, and a half-shaven head. A plentiful crop of tattered hair grew from the other side. For now it had flopped over the bald side.

Owen tried to explain. "I was only following Preston so I could talk about the plans for tomorrow." He knew he sounded like he was whining.

Rourke reached out and grabbed his neck again, choking him. "Plans? Let's be clear, boy. You're just tagging along for the ride. You come when we tell you to come, like an obedient dog. Otherwise, you keep yourself scarce." Rourke's eyes bulged and his face trembled. It was well known around Seeville that he was not a man to be trifled with.

"It's okay, Rourke," Preston said, frowning. "He doesn't know the details, but he knows we aren't here for train parts, either."

Rourke's grasp of Owen's neck slackened.

A mousy looking man, one Owen knew as Thorpe, spoke up next. Spectacles adorned the ridge on Thorpe's nose. He was higher up the railroad ladder, one of Bartz's right-hand men. He had been added to the expedition at the last minute.

Thorpe's voice was raspy and thin. "Let him be Rourke," he said. "Let's finish this topic and then Preston, maybe you take your friend for a walk."

Rourke finally let go of Owen's neck altogether. Owen tried to massage out the marks. They would surely turn to bruises by morning. He felt like objecting to his treatment, but nobody, including Preston, seemed at all surprised by Rourke's behavior.

Owen went from being center-stage to being wholly ignored. Thorpe said, "don't worry about the other mules. We have Newton in our corner. He's a respected wrench. He'll get the rest of the mules to buy in. He should also be able to smooth over any concern with the other wrenches. Bartz has helped fund the whole expedition. They know not to bite the hand that feeds them."

Jeroun, the man who had been cycling behind Owen on the way to the towers, spoke up. "And when do we tell them where we're going? They'll realize something is—"

Thorpe put up his hand to cut him off. He cleared his throat and then spoke. "We only tell them when we arrive. It shouldn't matter to them where we're going. If we have to cross through the fever lands we'll address the issue at that time."

People fidgeted about after the last comment. Thorpe addressed their apprehension. "Our wrenches and mules are well compensated. What are they going to do, leave us out there and not get paid?"

Thorpe shook his head to answer his own question. "No, they won't. We break off at noon. By then they should be done with the bikes and eager to get back. Preston, Jeroun, Rourke—you take Newton aside and make him do the announcement. It's better coming from him than us."

The other members of the circle nodded. Thorpe glanced at Owen, wrinkled his tiny nose, and then strolled over to Preston and whispered something in his ear. Preston nodded and sauntered over to Owen.

"Owen, let's go for a walk," Preston said.

"Sure," Owen said, welcoming the chance to get away from the group's probing eyes.

They walked until they were out of earshot of the others, pausing nowhere in particular, about halfway between the railroad contingent and the main congregation.

"Talk to me before doing anything like that again," Preston began.

"Like what?" Owen objected. "All I did was follow you back to our fire pit. Why is that wrong?"

"The railroad folks, they're nervous. They're taking this pretty seriously, and they should be. Yeah, we're hiding things, but for good reason. We have to be able to show people some progress—results no one can refute—or the Adherents and bureaucrats will shut us down before you know it."

"I get it. But can you at least tell me what we're after? Why am I here?"

Preston was silent for a moment and then said, "Yeah. Yeah, I suppose so. But you have to realize if you breathe a word of this to anyone it's on you. I can't help."

"Hey, I'm not fond of Rourke Rama's hand around my neck. Don't worry."

Preston didn't laugh, and it was too dark to see if he smiled. Owen doubted it. Preston was always so serious now.

Preston said, "we're going after some basic electronic equipment, and maybe even a few power generators—gas powered ones. Also maybe some more advanced stuff that we can't usually forage for, like some computers or laptops." He trailed off as he said it, as if it was nothing, an afterthought.

Nobody in Owen's lifetime had found any working computers or laptops, never mind gas-powered generators. "How do you expect to find that stuff?"

"We have our sources."

It was confounding. Everything within a hundred miles of Spoke territory had been picked over. Finding working electronics was a thing of the past. If they hadn't been destroyed by bandits, certainly the retchers would have gotten to them.

"Are you consorting with bandits now? The SLS? Oh, and we better not be going through fever lands."

Preston shuffled his feet. "We might be skirting it. Look, I can't tell you everything."

"Sure, but it seems to me you're telling me almost nothing."

"I've already told you more than you need to know," Preston countered, this time with some vinegar in his voice. "Think about the future, Owen. We can have refrigerators, freezers, electric motors—even electric cars. Imagine the benefit to the Spoke community. First everything will be done in bunkers, but eventually, when we solve the retcher problem, we can make real progress. Do you want to risk all that opportunity, just so we can keep everyone informed, just so some Adherent fanatic can raise a stink, bring up the old traditions and stop us in our tracks? No, that's not how progress will be made."

Owen understood the need for discretion, despite how much being kept in the dark frustrated him. And he shared Preston's passion for the cause as well. But there was something else that bothered him. Maybe it was that the railroad people seemed so ruthless, or maybe it was the way Preston seemed to be possessed by some kind of fervor.

"I get it Preston. I do. It just seems like you are moving so fast, and the railroad folks—"

Preston cut him off. "The railroad folks are doing their jobs and doing them well. Bartz, you should hear him. He has a grand vision for Seeville, for all Spoke people. If I were you I would just be happy to be part of this. And if you can keep quiet and contribute, maybe Bartz will bring you in. You can be a part of the inner circle."

Again, Preston's voice was raised, his pitch was higher, and he was using words that sounded like they were coming out of someone else's mouth. Yet Owen *did* want to be part of it. Even just to use a calculator, or a digital watch—it would be enough for him.

"Okay, Preston," Owen said, biting his lip, "I'll be careful."

"Good. Now I have to go talk to the others." Preston said it quickly, like a box had been checked, like now he could get on to more important things. "Don't come back for a while, okay?"

"Sure, Preston. Sure," Owen said.

Preston was already stepping away. Owen turned and headed in the opposite direction, toward the congregation of mules.

As he made his way back, Owen began feeling tired, his exertions from the day catching up with him.

Owen didn't need to get along with everyone, and he wasn't put out by Rourke's antics. Everyone in Seeville knew Rourke was a bully. What bothered Owen most about the evening was Preston. More and more he was becoming part of the railroad machine, talking about inner circles and visions, and consorting with these secretive railroad men.

Sure, maybe it was good for Preston. Maybe he was finding his niche, becoming an important member of the community.

But it also felt like Preston wasn't the same anymore. He didn't talk the same way; he didn't joke around the same way.

The worst part of the evening was that Owen felt like he was losing a friend.

GAP RUN

Darla was not one of the purebred mares. She certainly was a beautiful beast, with a brown mane and white spots dotting her upper back, but she was easily frightened. On these testy bouts Flora could calm her using a combination of delicate petting and singing Darla's favorite song.

Flora had been riding Darla for several hours now, and she had been remarkably cooperative given the limited visibility provided by the moon and stars.

A bed of autumn leaves next to a trickling stream caught her attention. Exhaustion was setting in and the soft foliage was looking particularly inviting, so Flora decided to take a short nap. She figured if she wanted to track the party it would be next to impossible in the darkness. Also, she would be useless if she didn't get at least an hour or two of rest to get her through the following day.

Although sluggish when she woke, Flora pressed on as the sun began to rise. She had been up Gap Run once, so she knew the way. The main access road, Simmons Gap Road, was heavily encroached with vegetation, yet a narrow, well-used path remained that a farmer used for access. She passed the farm and then continued on what was little more than a hiking path. She could tell by the numerous footprints on the dusty trail that the path had been used recently. And there were no hooves showing among the tracks, suggesting they were all on foot. She was hopeful she would catch up soon.

In a few places the path was strewn with large rocks, or had steep grades. Here she had to dismount and walk Darla. Eventually she reached an open field and hopped back on, eager to make up for lost time.

No sooner had she mounted and kicked Darla's flank than a crossbow bolt flew across her field of vision, it's final destination lost in the long grasses of the meadow.

"Whoa." She pulled Darla's reigns and looked back, seeing a man skulking by a tree and reloading a crossbow. She fumbled to grab her own crossbow with her left hand.

"The next one will ring true, I promise you," the man said, stepping out of the shadow of the tree, "unless you go right back where you came from."

His chest was covered with a vest adorned with two vertical yellow stripes, indicative of his merc status. His long beard was littered with specks. Whether they were food or leaf fragments she couldn't tell. It was Mehta, the Merchant Merc she had seen with Chief Darkwind by the holding cells.

"I'm Flora. You may remember me. I work in admin for Grand Caverns. I'm here to help."

"I know who you are. Help is exactly the opposite of what you're doing. Get gone, now." He was speaking with conviction, and yet he kept his voice relatively muted.

"I don't think you understand. I'm here to escort you into Spoke lands. I can identify certain prisoners to be sure they are providing us the right people."

"Go away, woman. This is no place for you," he said, with an even more menacing tone. He hurriedly walked up to her and pulled at the reigns of her horse, managing to turn Darla around, back toward the way she had come.

Of course Darla would have none of it. The mare reared up, tore loose from Mehta's grasp and stampeded into the meadow.

Flora tried to calm her while Darla paced and shook her mane. *"I need you near, Darla dear, the way is long, it's true, but Darla dear there is nothing...to fear,"* she sang.

Mehta watched them quizzically from afar.

When Flora felt she had regained control, she remained at a comfortable distance from Mehta.

"Why don't you tell me where the prisoner is?" she yelled across the meadow. "And where's Thisslewood?"

Mehta's look of annoyance turned to something more sinister, more calculating. He raised his crossbow once again and said, "Which would you prefer? That I maim your horse, or maybe put a bolt in your leg?"

"No need for that!" Flora heard someone call out from far up the meadow. Following the sound, she could see a man parading over a knoll. He had erratic gray hair and a close-cropped beard, with a visible gut hanging over a tight belt. It was Ember Thisslewood.

"I know this woman," Ember yelled out to Mehta. "You can put down your crossbow."

Mehta briefly looked to the side, barring his teeth in frustration, and then lowered the crossbow.

Ember caught up with Flora and said, "Come, we're camped at the end of this field."

He escorted Flora and her horse across the meadow. Mehta skulked some distance behind them.

"What brings you this way?" Ember asked.

Flora needed to figure out a way to convince Ember there had been a change in plan. She had created a narrative that might work, but it was sketchy, and full of half-truths. Ordinarily she would worry about getting caught in a lie, but she didn't care anymore. All that mattered was seeing Granger again.

"There's been a new development. It's tough news to convey, but I felt you should know right away."

"What's that?" Ember asked, a distant look on his face. Ember had never taken her seriously, probably because she was a simple admin clerk. Whenever she spoke to him it seemed as though he was only half listening.

This time, however, Flora was quite sure Ember would pay attention to her words. "Darkwind is dead. Luna has executed a coup and put her own chief in his place."

Ember slowed his walking considerably, absorbing the news. Flora then explained how it all went down during the Day of the Deer celebration.

"That bitch…am I…?"

"You're fine. She has welcomed all of Darkwind's deputies."

He looked at her skeptically.

He was on edge, uncertain. Now was the best time to make her play. "She also said it was important that we exchange prisoners as part of the deal. Trading only for goods is not enough. We need to have a victory Essentialists can rally around. Getting our people back will show we are asserting ourselves against the Spokes, much more so than trinkets or furs."

He looked confused. Perhaps he was still digesting the news about Darkwind, or maybe it was that he had a profound distaste for what she was proposing.

"Luna is adamant about this," she added.

Ember said, "That Union vulture…she's almost as bad as the Spokes. She has those disciples doing a heck of a lot more than tradecraft and curating books, I can tell you. They are defiling those caverns." He looked at her, vitriol in his eyes. She felt it best to nod vehemently in agreement.

She had to keep the conversation focused. She had to get Ember's confirmation of a prisoner exchange. "Listen, I know you don't care about the prisoners, but this is the only way this is going to work. I don't know what she would do to you, or to us, if we don't comply, and we need you in Grand Caverns, Ember. We need to have good representation from the original Wood, Wind, and Water clans."

Ember was nodding. "Yes, well someone will have to stop Luna eventually, but we'll have to bide our time. Swapping prisoners is not going to solve anything, I don't think—"

"We have to!" Flora said with some desperation, her exhaustion bleeding into her words.

Ember was somewhat taken aback by her outburst. He looked at her with an expression laced with confusion and annoyance. "What's gotten into you?"

He wasn't taking her seriously. She had to make a stand here. "That's it then. I'm going back to Luna." Flora turned Darla about dramatically, guiding her away.

"Whoa, whoa, whoa!" Ember said, putting his hands up in the air. "Look, I'm not sure what has you so riled up. Both Luna and Darkwind were already ordering an exchange of the prisoners, despite my objections, so that's what we're going to do. They even said so in front of half of the deputies. This isn't any change of plan. It's just Luna rubbing it in my face. She wants me to know she's in charge, and she wants me to fall in line, so she sent you to tell me to do something I was already asked to do."

Flora pulled Darla's reigns. She looked away from Ember, down the rolling meadow behind them. The golden grass was bent and flattened where they had walked. Mehta was trailing behind and to the left, carving a new swath. He watched her curiously, quirking an eyebrow up as he picked at whatever was in his beard.

She had been wrong. They *did* want to exchange prisoners, despite how it looked with Ember leading and the mercs being involved. Her anxiousness had made her too certain of her assumptions.

This was, of course, great news, but she couldn't let on.

From behind her, Ember said, "it may feel like like you're being used as a pawn, but don't feel too bad. We all get used. We don't always get the full story. This is what it's going to be like working for Luna, so you better get used to it."

She forced herself to play the part, quelling the hope within her, turning around to show a look of frustration.

"Come on, let's have you meet the others," Ember said, and she rejoined him.

At the far end of the meadow there stood a large, solitary beech tree, and under it were Cecile and another woman who wore a black leather frock with vertical yellow stripes like Mehta's. The merc woman had long, blonde hair, heavily dyed, with dark roots. She was eating some kind of root vegetable, revealing a broad gap in her upper teeth as she took a bite. Contrasting strongly with the merc was Cecile's blue-streaked raven hair, blowing in a gust of wind.

"Now who is this missy?" the blonde merc said with a southern twang. "Thisslewood, you already make my ass itch, so don't be bringing any more people to this party. I will slap you to sleep and then slap you for sleeping."

Ember said, "This is a messenger from Luna. She has something important to tell us. I think after you hear from her, you'll see she should join us."

"Okay. Well, open that mouth, Miss. Let's see those gums flap," the blonde merc said.

Flora had heard that people from the southern Spoke towns were overly polite and liked to speak in riddles. This merc seemed to live up to the latter half of that stereotype, but certainly not the former.

Flora went through the story of how Luna had taken control. She made sure to stick to the facts, not knowing the allegiance of the two mercs, or if they had any at all.

"You're pretty and all, Miss, but explain to me again why we need you with us on our mission?" the merc asked.

"I can identify some of the prisoners. And because Luna asked me to join you."

"Well, Miss, that's not the deal we made. Close, but it doesn't include you. Taking you means more risk for us, more uncertainty. And of course that means we should get more money, but I hear nothing about that. I reckon you folks sometimes forget we need to get paid. Other times, you're plain tighter than a bull's ass at fly time. So what's it gonna be? How much is it worth to you?"

Flora considered saying Luna would pay them more, but that would be pushing her lies too far, and she had no idea what a fair price might be. She suspected the merc was just testing the boundaries, seeing if they could squeeze more out of the deal.

Mehta spoke up. "I don't think we should take her. Every additional person makes it that much harder. It wasn't part of the deal we struck."

The blonde merc glared at Mehta. "Good points. Now let's see what she has to say."

Mehta continued, shaking his head, "I don't think there is any good price to be had here. We should draw the line."

Then the blonde merc smiled at Flora, showing the large gap in her teeth. "I know the porch lantern is on, but sometimes I wonder if anyone is home. Let me confer with my esteemed colleague."

Mehta and the blonde merc walked off quite a distance from the tree. Their words were lost in the wind, but it looked like a lively discussion. It ended with the blonde merc waving her finger at Mehta and then stalking away. Mehta hovered for a moment and then followed her back.

"Good news love!" the blonde merc said to Flora. "You are welcome to join us on our prodigious journey." Then she looked to Ember. "Now, we *will* expect additional payment for this, but given the goodwill we have with Curator Luna, we can of course accept some fair determination of compensation at a later date."

Flora was not sure why things were turning in her favor. First with the prisoner swap, and now with the merc's agreement to her inclusion. She didn't fully understand why they had agreed, but she kept her mouth shut. She dared not tempt fate by asking any more questions.

Darla, unfortunately, wasn't granted permission to join. Flora had to send her back down the path in the hope that she might make it back to Grand Caverns. Perhaps she wouldn't make it, but then at least she could be free. When Flora sent her on her way, she imagined being Darla, a lone mare free to roam fields such as this one without a care in the world. For some reason it made her feel profoundly envious.

They all left the clearing shortly after, hiking up Gap Run at a moderate pace. The path was precarious in places and barely used, which was why they chose it. Also, according to the mercs there were fewer Spoke outposts on this particular crest of the ridge. It should be relatively easy to make it into Spoke territory unnoticed.

The blonde merc was walking behind her. She said her name was Rosalie. Whereas most of the group walked in silence, Rosalie wanted to talk all the time. Even when Mehta asked her to keep it down she wouldn't relent. She asked Flora about the coup. She asked her about the disciples. She asked her about Reed. She asked her about the incident with the retcher and the phone.

She didn't ask anyone else any questions. Flora could only assume the others had had their fill the day before. Flora ordinarily didn't mind talking, but Rosalie was asking things that were uncomfortable, things she didn't like to talk about, especially given the web of half-truths she had concocted could fall apart if she had to keep explaining herself. Eventually, Flora decided the only way to distract her was to ask her own questions.

After another question from Rosalie about the embarrassing retcher incident, Flora asked, "do you have retchers where you're from?"

"Oh, sure. There are stories bandied about. I never seen them first-hand though, not in my lifetime."

"Why do you think that is?"

"Well, I'm from a place called Jacksonville. It's mostly a Spoke town now, thanks to the railroad, but it wasn't when I was born. Lots of mercs from there too, and we try to get along. Anyway, there's just not that much around there but swamps and such. A long time ago, the people of Jacksonville done got rid of all the Old World tech. There aren't even any hike towers nearby. So nothing for the retchers to retch on, I guess. But you shouldn't be askin' me. My first husband, he once said there was a tree stump in Florida that had a higher IQ than me. Of course, I done kilt him, so maybe I'm a sharper stump than he reckoned."

It was hard to say when Rosalie was being facetious. She seemed un-fazed by Flora's questions, so Flora continued on. "Do you have to…kill a lot of people, as a merc? I mean, what kind of work do you usually do?"

"Hey now, a gentleman doesn't kiss and tell, and a merc doesn't kill and spill the beans. We mostly do security details, and it can be downright boring. Sure, I done kilt twenty or so folks, mostly as parts of raids we were hired for, plus my first husband, of course."

Flora suspected she was being honest. It made her nervous to be walking in front of someone who had killed so many people, and who could speak of it so flippantly, as if she was talking about a change in the weather.

Rosalie continued, "but not as many as Mehta here. No ma'am. Give him a few targets and he's like a moth in a mitten. He done kilt and kilt and kilt, he has. Ain't that right, Mehta?"

Mehta was leading the group. He glanced back to give them a dark look. Flora's skin crawled.

"Such a pussycat he is," Rosalie said.

"I've heard, down in Jacksonville, that there was a lot of sickness in the old days, what they call the *fade*. Is that still down there?"

"Yup. Was speaking with Lady Cecile here yesterday about it. Up there in frenchy land they call it *Laifasae,* or some such thing. Anyway, yeah we still have some of it. That's why no one ever goes south of Jacksonville. Florida to the south has big pockets of the stuff. And you don't know you got it until it's too late."

"How do you know it's still there if no one goes south?"

"Because sometimes bandit types come up from there. They wander into Jacksonville, wanting refuge, wanting to trade. A lot of times we done kill'em straight up, or if we like the looks of em, we put them in a box for a week. Make sure they don't show any symptoms before we let them in."

"What are the symptoms?

"Only saw one when I was a kid. Makes them funny in the head it does. A day or two after they get the symptoms, they don't know who they are anymore. They start to speak like a two-year-old. Then they done start shitting themselves. Gets pretty ugly. Don't know what happens after that. We done kilt the one we had at that point."

They were momentarily distracted as they scaled a steep rock surface. She was glad Darla hadn't come. Clearly it would have been impassable for her.

Rosalie continued her explanation after the rock face. "Lots of people down in Jacksonville think that's what caused the fall, or the Detonation, or whatever you folks call it up here. You know, the shit we're in. I know you Essentialist types think the Old World folks were too dirty and polluted. You think it was more than just nukes. The Spokes, on the other hand, they think it was mostly some nuclear pissing contest, through some Old World mindfuck about fears and obsession. Down in Jacksonville we know the fade used to be way worse. Lots of people down south think that's what did it. The fade done kilt more than Mehta even." She snickered.

There was a moment of silence, and then Cecile chimed in ahead of them with a lonely word. "Millions," she said.

Ember weighed in, always eager to assert the orthodox Essentialist viewpoint. "Technically, Essentialists wouldn't argue the fade killed many. It was a horrible, horrible plague, but you will find that the fade killed people near populated areas—areas with poisonous cityscapes. The fade is just one more symptom of the Old World's complete disregard for the sun, soil, and seed—one more consequence of their toxic treatment of the earth."

Mehta had stopped and was looking back at all of them. "Speaking of people dying," he said, "a sure-fire way to get ourselves killed is to keep yammering away when we approach Skyline. So shut it. I mean it."

"Such a pussycat," Rosalie whispered, smiling her gap-toothed grin at Flora.

Rosalie was not completely irreverent. She did keep quiet from then on, as did Ember and the rest of them.

They soon approached the broad boulevard at the top of Skyline. They had left the main Gap Run path a while back, so as to not make tracks on a known path that exited onto the road. They had been mostly breaking through old forest growth.

They walked carefully through the woods on the Essentialist side to make sure there were no hidden outposts, and then dashed across into the foliage on the Spoke side when they were sure the way was clear.

When they were in Spoke territory, Rosalie fell back farther to the rear, and cast a watchful eye into the forest around them.

Descending the other side of the ridge took longer than going up, as most of it was through dense woods, with no path and fewer bearings. They had to double back a few times to make sure they were taking the best route down the mountain. Eventually they made it down to flatter ground and stopped to make camp for the evening. Mehta and Rosalie seemed more relaxed and even exchanged a few words.

Ember whispered, "Are we safe here, in this campsite?"

"We are through the worst of it, yeah," Rosalie answered. "The real militant Spokes would be up on the ridge. The Spoke people down here won't expect us, and are more likely to be farming types."

"That's great," Ember said. "Congratulations, everyone."

Rosalie had been skinning a rabbit. She pointed the bloody tip of her dagger at Ember. "But it makes about as much sense as tits on a bull for us to start yapping away just the same."

Ember only nodded.

It began to rain soon after, lightly at first, and then in heavy sheets. They all adjourned to their tents.

Flora was in the same tent as Cecile. A rope was tied to Cecile's cuffs, and it extended out of the tent to circle a nearby tree. While Flora helped her get changed, Cecile drilled into her with one of her probing stares, just like the stares she had given her in the prison cell. For some reason it didn't make her uncomfortable. Maybe it was because she was getting use to her, or maybe it was because they would soon be rid of her.

Flora went to bed happy. They had passed the most dangerous part of the journey. She was closer than she had ever been to her goal. Maybe, just maybe, she would see Granger again.

Just before her head hit the soft pillow, Cecile said, "Be careful Flora."

It was not a casual good night. It seemed out of place, especially given the worst of the danger had passed. "What do you mean?" Flora asked, sitting up.

"*Bonne nuit*," Cecile said and rolled over with her back to Flora, unwilling to elaborate.

Flora should have been able to ignore an off-hand comment from a Spoke prisoner, but it floated on her conscience for some time. Cecile seemed to know things—things others didn't. She had warned her about the phone, and she had been right.

But Flora was exhausted, and she refused to let this casual remark spoil her rare moment of happiness. The comment seemed to fall away beneath the hypnotizing sound of the rain on the tent surface. Eventually, the words seemed to disappear from her conscious mind altogether and were relegated to the distant confines of the realm of dreams.

SAND CASTLES

Axel was standing with his bare feet on the wet sand, the pungent smell of decaying kelp tickling at his nostrils. The terrain in front of him featured a labyrinth of ravines dug into the beach. A sand castle sprung out from the innermost circle of the maze. It was half the size of a man, with a number of archways, turrets, spires and courtyards made out of sand, driftwood and seashells.

Shooting off tangentially from the labyrinth were channels that spelled out *KELEMEN* in block letters, and yet another series that spelled out half of *RAWLINGS*. His daughter Erin and Tina Rawlings were still carving out the remaining letters.

He made sure to get a picture of it with his phone. When he looked at the image he felt a touch of pride mixed with envy. He couldn't remember being creative enough to do things like this as a child. The kids must get it from their mother's side.

Axel was standing near the outlet of the labyrinth, which was a small canal that led down to the waves crashing in. He carefully pushed sand up into a meager sea wall in front of the intake channel, if only to give it a modest defense before the waves inevitably overcame it.

"We're saved," Zach said with a deadpan look. Some might call Zach snarky, but Axel got a kick out of his sarcasm.

"Hey, every lit bit helps," Axel said.

"Dad, the whole point of this is so the water can come in," Zach said, shaking his head.

Axel put his hands up in mock protest. "I know, but once the water gets in, the whole thing will collapse."

Zach just stared at him with a sour face.

"Okay, let's see what happens." Axel flattened the seawall he had just begun building.

Gray wisps of smoky clouds were layering into the darkening orange horizon. The sandcastle's shadow was extending longer and longer, puncturing the waves as the miniature crests rolled in and collapsed. Soon the temperature would drop.

A few feet away Finnegan Rawlings was sprawled on a beach chair, nursing a beer and proudly displaying his farmer's tan despite the autumn air. He would occasionally receive and throw back a miniature football with his son, whose latest trick was to try to catch it from behind and through his legs.

Finn was stalky and rounded, not even close to Axel in terms of fitness. Yet you could tell there were the vestiges of strength in his limbs from his younger years in the service.

Most op vets were cautious people, some even paranoid. Knowing the panoply of things that could kill you at any time tended to temper your enthusiasm for risky activities. But Finn was not your typical op veteran. He seemed to be able to divorce himself from this tension completely. He had a knowing smile and an indulgent handshake. He laughed and goofed around with his kids, burying them in the sand and throwing them in the water. He was definitely a likeable guy.

Axel hoped that meant he wouldn't be as tight-lipped as most op vets.

When the labyrinth of ravines was finished filling with water, Axel made his way to Finn.

"Finn—can we take a walk?"

Finn almost jumped out of his beach chair. "Sure thing," he said.

They left it to the kids to bear witness to the gradual destruction of their beach civilization. Axel and Finn walked casually northward along the beach.

"I feel a Nadar lecture coming on," Finn quipped.

Axel smiled. "Am I that transparent?"

"Yes, sir. As transparent as…is there something more transparent than a window?" Finn laughed heartily.

"Here's the thing, Finn—and tell me if I'm overstepping my bounds, but there's something I don't understand about what Fortient is doing."

"What's that?"

Axel had to tread carefully. If he pushed too hard Finn might clam up and become adversarial.

"I don't understand why Fortient's innovation budget is being put on steroids. After the Catalytic acquisition on Thursday, you now have a three-billion-dollar expense line. That's a heck of an imbalance for a division that generates less than a billion in revenue. And you know I'm not the only one asking questions. There have been stories in the financial media about board members becoming concerned. Some activist investors have been poking around as well."

Finn's expression could be telling. He had been smiling in a good-natured way when Axel launched his inquiry—precisely the way you might smile when walking with a friend on the beach. But by the time Axel finished his question, the smile seemed stretched, like it required a feat of will to be maintained. Meanwhile Finn's eyes darted back and forth, a window into some kind of internal debate.

Eventually, in the moment of silence that followed Axel's question, Finn's smile faded altogether.

"You haven't spoken with Bhavin recently?" Finn asked.

"No. Can't get a meeting."

Finn nodded. He turned fully away from Axel and stared thoughtfully into the scudding clouds, indifferent to his impropriety.

Axel was patient. He hoped Finn would be more forthcoming with a passive approach.

When Finn turned back to Axel he looked different. A veil of discipline possessed his features, as if he had spent the moment booting up his ops training from long ago. He spoke pointedly, with little affect. "You shouldn't be poking around like this, Axel. I'm here, a guest at your house, and you know I could face consequences for telling you something Nadar doesn't want me to say. The stakes here are high for me, and for Nadar Corporation as well."

It was not the dismissive response Rawlings could have given. Axel pushed forward.

"That's precisely why I need to know," Axel said. "I've shown my loyalty, yet I'm in the dark on something that could have an impact on my operation and on the company as a whole. I deserve to know what's going on."

Finn stared at him as if trying to see under his skin.

"Why don't we start with something straightforward," Axel said, trying another angle. "The Catalytic acquisition adds about a billion in operating costs to Fortient, but why? I don't see the synergies, and the price was…" Axel let the trailing silence explain his view of the price.

This was something Rawlings must at least have a canned answer for. Rawlings nodded cautiously and responded. "Sure. I can explain that. Bytomic Corp—they have a new suite of software. It can help you optimize your job performance by running simulations of on-the-job clerical functions. Are you familiar with it?"

"Yes," Axel answered, nodding. Bytomic was a star of the tech world that had become a diversified conglomerate. They had been experiencing rapid growth in their technologies divisions. In particular, their simulation product had been growing by leaps and bounds in the last two years.

"We want to be able to compete with their Wog software. It's the main platform for their self-driving cars and simulators. Catalytic has the technology to help us do that."

Axel had seen one of the financial bloggers make the same connection. It was a plausible enough corporate narrative—plausible enough to be accepted so people wouldn't seek out the real reason.

"But didn't Bytomic make Wog all open-source just a few weeks ago? Why buy a whole company if you can just use your competitor's platform for free? Several companies have already announced they are going to be doing just that."

Rawlings scratched his head. Whether he was trying to provide succinct answers or trying to obfuscate was unclear. Either way, he was thinking hard about his response. "It's more complicated than that. We want to integrate the Catalytic drone firmware with something like Wog, but it takes time and customization. Did you know Catalytic is one of the leading drone makers?"

"Yes," Axel said, "I know Catalytic has drones." He then continued with more emphasis. "I know they are developing these drones for defense purposes, as well. I also know they are developing mechanized robotics and cyber warfare software." It was another factoid he had learned covertly through his independent sources.

He tried to gauge Finn's reaction, but his face was unreadable.

Axel pressed on. "Why are we building such a broad defense portfolio?"

Rawlings squinted at him, for the first time showing visible displeasure with the way the discussion was going.

"Can you at least tell me who the buyer is?" Axel asked. "Is there some major government that plans to bid on all this military tech?" Axel was being pushy and arguably offensive, but perhaps getting a rise in Rawlings would reveal something.

Instead of getting incensed or uncomfortable, Finn's eyes softened, and he reached out to Axel, resting his hand on his shoulder. His tone was compassionate, almost apologetic. "I get it, Axel. I would probably do the same in your situation. But we are all duty-bound and honor-bound. I can't tell you if Bhavin hasn't done so already."

Axel was deliberately silent, hoping for more elaboration.

Abruptly, Finn offered his other hand. "Good-bye, Axel," he said.

It seemed Finn had had enough of Axel trying to hotbox him. There was nothing Axel could do now but accept the hand that was offered. "Good-bye, Finn."

Finn started walking back to the kids. "Time to go kids!" He yelled. "Grab your stuff."

Axel cursed under his breath as Finn walked away. He was too cool to reveal anything more, and from now on he would be on guard.

It wasn't a total loss, however. If Finn could have debunked his accusations he probably would have. But he didn't. He only refused to explain why they were building such a large arsenal.

The only way to get to the bottom of it now would be to confront Bhavin in the flesh.

ACCIDENTS HAPPEN

In midmorning of the next day, the safety harness of one of the wrenches tore off and he fell from of one of the extension ladders near the base of the tower. His leg careened awkwardly off a platform stationed below. Owen was high above, still hoisting down bikes from the upper section he had opened, so he had only a vague view of the immediate aftermath. The man survived, but even from his vantage point, Owen could tell the bones of his leg had been shattered.

When Owen rappelled to the ground the jovial atmosphere had transformed into one of terse commands. The mules carefully formed a gurney and were pulling the last empty platform toward the fallen man to load him up for the ride back. The man that fell was Newton, the wrench that the railroad folks had planned on using for their side excursion.

Rourke, Preston, and the other railroad folks were slinking together, forming a posse obstructing the path of the group of mules hauling the empty platform.

"Out of the way," said Chester, gesturing at the group of railroad folks. "The rest of you pack everything up. We leave in five." Many of the other mules were already collecting their things and placing them on their respective platforms for the ride back.

Rourke stepped forward, his sheath of hair flopping over one of his eyes. "You can go, but you're going to use one of these other platforms for Newton. We need the empty one." Rourke showed a toothy mock smile.

Veins bulged in Chester's temples. "For what? I think you may be a little lost here, Rourke. We've done hundreds of runs successfully, and the reason they have been successful is because we know the risks. That's why when accidents happen, it's us mules who call the shots, or people get hurt. Now move aside, or get bent."

Rourke didn't move aside. A couple more railroad men maneuvered to stand next to him. There were now eight standing there. Some of them, including Preston, looked peevish and uncomfortable, but most of them looked menacing and obstinate, ready for a fight.

Thorpe spoke next. The words came quietly, almost as a whisper. "We are continuing on. There are some parts we need for a train engine. We need this platform."

A number of the mules stopped packing and started to slink closer to the confrontation, burgeoning frowns on their brows. A couple of them were massaging tire irons in their hands.

"That's just not how this works," Chester said. "We need the platform to bring Newton back, period. Not only that—you shouldn't be going off on your own with a platform and a handful of men, especially if you're not staying on the bike tower run. It's too dangerous. Get your train parts some other time, when we don't need the extra platform."

"You can make room on the other platforms. You can leave some bike parts here," Thorpe suggested. Again his voice was such that he came off sounding meek, or afraid, but his expression and posture showed no signs of weakness. His countenance was calm and collected.

Another wrench, the one named Arsalan, spoke out, sounding incensed. "This is a waste of time! It'll take us a good thirty minutes to unpack the bike parts and store them. And why leave the parts here at all? We could be gone with four full platforms and Newton *right now*, or three-and-a half platforms in thirty minutes, with you going off on some fool's errand." Then he pointed to his temple dramatically. "Add to that whatever amount of time it takes for you to get this through your thick skulls."

"Yeah," said one of the mules.

"You better get out of the fucking way," another one said.

The gathering mules started to edge forward toward the railroad crew. Chester put his arms out in an attempt to hold them back. He also put his hand on Arsalan's shoulder in an effort to calm him down. Arsalan held his ground, but he looked like he was going to convulse into action at any moment.

"Look, tensions are high," Chester said. "It's normal for everyone to get a little testy when someone gets hurt. The bottom line is we know with an empty platform we can get Newton back in half the time. It might be the difference between him living or dying. We do things a certain way…" Chester trailed off as Rourke had stepped forward, occupying the space between the two sides.

"Yes, you do," Rourke said. "You do your jobs a certain way." He started pacing back and forth in fits and starts in front of them. "But if your job doesn't deliver the desired outcome, you won't do them your way, do you? In fact, you won't do them *at all,* because guess what, you won't get paid. Bartz paid for this expedition, and *this* is what Bartz wants done. Got it?" He smiled like a Cheshire cat.

"How do you know what Bartz wants?" Arsalan objected. "Look, everyone knows you took one too many rides without a helmet—" Chester firmed his grip on Arsalan's shoulder, silencing him.

Rourke started prancing around again. Abruptly he drew two pistols from his belt.

"Whoa," said one of the mules. Some took a step backward.

Rourke was smiling, seemingly off in his own world, as if remembering a fond childhood memory. "Let's say, hypothetically, Bartz wants me to dance around like an idiot." Rourke began dancing around spastically, his feet kicking up in all directions as if doing some demented polka.

"Or maybe he wants me to shoot my guns in the air." Rourke began firing shots in the air, haphazardly in all directions. Two of the shots ricocheted off distant towers behind Owen. Everyone, including Owen, sought cover or hit the ground.

Rourke said, "You see, some of us don't like to dance, but sometimes we do it because our bosses ask us to." He put his arms up in a harp formation, as if holding a dance partner, and then pretended to waltz along with this imaginary figure. His pistols still dangled from his hands, creating ripples of evasive action in the mules as he pranced by them.

After swaying back and forth several times, Rourke arrived at Newton's makeshift litter. Newton was moaning softly and gritting his teeth.

Rourke massaged Newton's chin for a moment with his thumb and index finger, then he launched a torturous glare at Chester. "So…this is what you're going to do. You're going to agree to your orders, *and* you're going to come with us as our wrench, since poor Newton here is hurt." He made a sad face, and then put the muzzle of a pistol against Newton's head. "*Or* I could just make this easy for everyone, so I don't have to keep dancing around like an idiot." He ended with yet another egregious smile.

For a moment, there was complete silence. Everyone in the area had either frozen in position or had fled from the line of fire of Rourke's pistols. Even the railroad folks had found cover.

Chester slowly stood up, brushing off a few leaves that were stuck to his frock. A bitter look gradually propagated across his face. He whispered something in Arsalan's ear and then said aloud, "I'll do as you say."

"There! That wasn't so hard," Rourke said gleefully, and he began holstering his weapons.

One by one the mules reluctantly left the empty platform where it was and moved over to organize another bike platform. Then the mules worked swiftly and methodically to unload neatly packed parts from one side of the platform and haul them into the bottom section of the tower.

Meanwhile Rourke and other railroad men pulled aside a few other riders and ordered them to join their platform team.

Owen helped out with the unpacking as much as he could and then sheepishly meandered over to the empty bike platform the railroad folks had reserved. Once proud to be with the railroad contingent, he now felt ashamed to be associated with it. He told himself they were doing something important for the community, something important for Spoke society as a whole, so tough calls like these needed to be made. It did nothing to assuage his shame.

A few minutes later the platform with Newton on it pulled out, with eight of the strongest mules driving it forward. Fourteen other riders left with the Newton platform, some scouting ahead and some pulling up the rear.

The other three fully burdened platforms wasted no time in leaving soon after. They pulled out slowly, the platform riders laboring under the heavy loads. Once they got a head of steam, inertia helped them coast and get into a rhythm. Another twenty supplementary riders left with these other three platforms.

Thirteen of them were left in the campsite, comprised mostly of railroad men and a handful of mules, including Chester. They finished cleaning up and locked up the excess bike parts in the bottom section of the tower, along with a few ladders, ropes and pulleys they left for the next tower run.

Their platform made out soon after, navigating again through the bullet hole and then backtracking west. At the I-95 intersection they turned off to the south where the three-notched sign said *Danger—to Richmond Fever Lands*.

Owen remembered what Thorpe had said about the fever lands. He had said they wouldn't enter without warning them first. Hopefully he was being honest.

Despite their empty platform, it didn't make for "louder trips" as one mule had quipped the day before. Chester and the other mules' cautious eyes darted around to watch Rourke and the railroad folks just as much as the terrain around them.

They followed the Old World highway south for a time and then turned off onto a bumpier, narrower road heading east, and then eventually veered to the southeast.

The first bandits they saw were in an old town abutting a large river. Here the road had fresh bike treads and hoof prints that went directly through the small cluster of worn out houses and old stores. Only a few rusted-out cars and truck frames dotted the streets, each with one or more pockets melted away by retchers. Owen could see an old, stenciled name on one of the buildings that said *Tappahannock*.

Despite paying close attention through the town, Owen didn't notice any bandits until Chester pointed to the top of one of the stores. There, hooded figures poked out from hidden locations on the roof. As a show of strength, Chester and several other bikers held loaded crossbows with one hand as they pedaled. Rourke and two others also had pistols visible in their hands.

They passed a few more hooded bandits later on, but they also kept to themselves. It was difficult to resolve their intent or even facial expressions under the shrouds of their hoods. No arrows were shot, and no threats were made.

The expedition passed through the town without incident.

After Tappahannock they veered southwest, continuing along on a different, yet just as bumpy, road. Owen's legs were feeling thick and clumsy, as if the constant motion of each revolution of the bike assembly underneath him had dulled the nerve endings in his lower half. Owen's back and arms were even more exhausted from the shock and tension perpetrated by maintaining a tight grip on the handlebars as the knobby turf undulated beneath them.

Periodically they would have rest stops and Chester would confer with the railroad folks, pointing this way and that way, and at the maps in their hands. They always wandered too far away for Owen to make out the conversation.

At one rest stop a mule was brave enough to ask, "Can we at least know when we're supposed to arrive at this train part place?"

Chester answered, "We should be there midday tomorrow, assuming no major roadblocks. It's another sixty miles."

The mule seemed satisfied enough with the response. Indeed, it was good to know the rest of the trip could be measured in hours, not days or weeks.

They ended the day on an even rougher road heading southeast. It was the least used of any they had been on, with no recent signs of bike treads or hoofprints. Several times they had to clear a path for the platform through encroaching branches and shrubs. One time they had to lift the entire platform and attached bike assemblies over a fallen tree.

The expedition pushed right through to darkness and made camp near a small river.

When the fire was set a dinner of stale provisions was distributed. Many of the railroad folks branched off to confer on their own. Owen wasn't invited, as far as he knew, and he would rather not be body-slammed by Rourke, so he stayed with the mules.

As he was massaging his stiff forearms by the fire, Owen could feel eyes weighing on him.

"Are you with them or not?" one of the mules asked.

Owen chose his words carefully. "They invited me to come. I might be able to help with the cargo we're after."

"Are we really after a train engine part?" another asked him.

"At this point…I…I'm not entirely sure," Owen said.

"I think you better tell us, boy," one of the larger mules said as he squinted his way.

Chester shook his head and said, "That won't do any good." As he spoke, Chester was meticulously cleaning out some cornbread crumbs from an old plastic container with a wet finger. "We don't need any more strong-arming. There's been enough of that. Let's get the job done and get back to Seeville. Next time we can all pick our expeditions more carefully."

After a moment of quiet, when it was clear the other mules had backed down, Owen asked Chester, "Is it a dangerous place, where we're heading?"

Chester leveled his eyes at Owen, and snickered. "You really need to learn when to keep quiet." He looked down at his food container again and then up at the eyes of the other mules fixed on him. He sighed and said, "I can't say for sure, honestly. I've been near this way, a few years back. We went closer to the Richmond Fever Lands that time. Made the mistake of drinking from the James River. Felt it for days." A weak cringe flashed over his face.

"Anyway, most of the bandits along our route congregate near the north-south tube, which is to the west of us, so we shouldn't see any trouble. That's one of the reasons we went this backwoods route. This way there are a few fishing villages, like Tappahannock, but not much else. These villages probably don't have enough warm bodies to mess with us, even if they wanted to. But even those out by the tube don't want any trouble, really."

"What's the tube?"

Chester smirked, again amused at Owen's ignorance. "It's a big, hollow cylinder that goes north–south, to the west of the 95 highway. Sometimes it goes underground. They used it to transport big loads of stuff back in the Old World times. According to your railroad friends we'll be near a branch of it when we arrive tomorrow."

"What about the stories we hear about raids on bike platforms? Why don't the bandits do that anymore?"

"I'm sure it still happens, but they've gotten smarter over the years. If you think about it, life is hard enough without worrying about us harmless Spokes, especially with them being close to the fever lands and all. And then there are other bandits—and never mind the retchers. Why pick a another fight?"

Another mule spoke up. "I heard there used to be hundreds of thousands of them back in my granddads time. Now there are fewer, while Spoke numbers are increasing."

Chester laughed. "Yeah, it may be there just aren't enough of them left to put up a fight. In any case, there's been a kind of unspoken agreement to leave each other alone. Then again, we don't know if that's true where we're headed. I've never been there before."

This take on the bandits was a far cry from the horror stories and caricatures he had heard in Seeville. But it made sense. The bandits were just people trying to survive, just like Spokes.

"Have you seen any of Richmond?" Owen asked.

"The thing about Richmond, or any fever land, is that there really isn't much left to see," Chester said. "Every once in a while someone does go in. Heck, there are lots of broad paved roads heading in to Richmond, and even some living trees and flowers. It can be tempting."

Chester finally finished with his container and put it down. "But I once met a fellow who went into the Washington Fever Lands. He told me enough. He was one of those New Founder types, all hopped up on the Old World presidents and their ilk. When he came back, he said there was nothing to see. He said he could have walked right over the White

ERIK A. OTTO

House—you know where the Old World's rulers lived—and wouldn't have known. The only thing he came back with was the fever. He died just a couple days later. It sounds funny that you could be sick just from walking through a place, but I believe it. Drinking that water from the James River tells me enough. Heed the signs. Those places are real sick, no matter what they look like."

"What about other Old World cities?" Owen asked. "Do we know if there are any big ones still standing?"

"Well, I doubt many books were written after the nukes fell, so it's hard to say. But I can tell you up north people say a lot of the big ones are gone, like Philadelphia, Boston, Baltimore. In the south as well, near the Spoke border is a town called Atlanta that got nuked. The people up north, they get funny when they talk about New York. They call it the black hole, so it could've been nuked too, I guess. I don't know about other places over the sea, or in SLS lands for that matter."

Owen again marveled at the enormity of what was lost from pre-Detonation times. Did they really hate each other so much to not only kill millions, but also create these everlasting patches of death? Sometimes he felt sympathy for the Essentialist way of thinking—the thinking that the earth had punished the Old World people for poisoning it. He would never say it aloud, though.

Chester was looking around the circle. Some of the other mules were fidgeting. "Us mules don't like to talk about the Detonation too much, though. We die from the fever lands, we die from the retchers, and we have people falling to the ground like a pretzeled wheel at the bike towers. There are too many riddles caused by the Detonation, and too many of those riddles tend to get us killed. Sometimes it's better to just forget about the riddle so you can get on with your day. Best to focus on something simple, like keepin it between the ditches, you know."

They stared into the fire in silence for a while, and the mules started to adjourn. Eventually, the railroad folks came back, whatever scheming accomplished. Owen hoped they would pull him aside and update him. He hoped at least Preston would say something, anything. But they promptly left for their tents without a word.

Owen sighed and called it a night as well.

Smoke Steaming from the Snout

In the morning the campsite around Flora serenaded her with a symphony of squelches as their footfalls in the moss released the waters absorbed by the night's rains. A chill had also descended, giving each breath a perceptible vapor.

After Mehta had scouted the environs, they made out eastward again. The grade kept fluctuating, but thankfully not too steeply, or it would surely have resulted in some nasty falls on the muddy ground.

The sun was soon shining, and it rapidly warmed up the air. By the time they had made it into Spoke farmlands, their boots had dried.

Mehta and Rosalie posted flags on poles sticking out of their backpacks, so as to not be mistaken for Essentialists. The flags featured the sigil used by the mercs; the silhouette of a man standing guard with a rifle and shield, with yellow vertical stripes prominent on the torso.

They encountered a trail headed in an easterly direction, which Mehta directed them to follow after checking his bearings. Their plan was to make contact with a Spoke the mercs knew in the town of Culpepper. From there they would be escorted to Seeville by train.

In the distance they could see farmers doing their work, or livestock roaming around, but no other signs of life. These farmers seemed to not be paying attention to passersby. Rosalie had explained that it was unlikely they would encounter resistance outside of a major town. It had been many years since the Essentialists had dared venture into Spoke lands.

"Do you feel any different, being in Spoke territory?" Cecile asked.

Flora eyed Ember and Mehta. They were far ahead in their column, out of earshot. Rosalie was also far away, having fallen behind to stalk a groundhog with her crossbow. Regardless, Flora chose her words carefully. "I'm not like most Essentialists," Flora said. "I knew a man who was born in Spoke lands, near Lynchburg. He told me about Spoke life as a child.

So Spokes aren't scary to me. Although maybe it's changed since then."

"It has, and it hasn't," Cecile said. "Not many trains back then. That's the big push right now. The line goes all the way up to Kingston and down to Jacksonville. In a couple years it will reach all the way up to Pembroke in the north. It's really changing things. Helping them get more organized."

"You said them."

"*Pardon?*" she said in French.

"You said *them*. You really don't consider yourself to be part of the Spokes?"

"I would say we are allied with them. Things are different for us up north, where I come from."

"How so?"

There was a pause. "Well, we speak a different language."

It seemed she was evading the question. "How else?"

"Not much else, really. It's colder up there as well."

"Nothing to do with knowing how to use a smartphone?" Flora asked.

Flora thought she might make Cecile angry, but instead she looked back and smiled.

"*C'est drole,*" Cecile said. "You have a good sense of some things, but in others you have no clue." It was another cryptic comment, reminding Flora of what Cecile had said before going to bed the night before.

"What do you mean by that?" Flora asked.

"*Excusez moi.* Honestly I shouldn't have said that. I just mean you have straight vision sometimes."

"Straight vision?"

"*Vision etroite.* Maybe it doesn't translate well. Ah yes, I think you call it tunnel vision."

"How so?"

"Let me see. How should I put this?" She took a moment to gather her words. "You have come to a party where you do not know what dress to wear. Nor do you know the etiquette, and the house is foreign to you. Somehow you have gotten in the front door, but it's only a matter of time until the guests find out you don't belong. Worse still, it's only a matter of time until you find out it isn't a party at all."

Despite the fact she was a Spoke who often said cryptic remarks, she was beginning to like Cecile. Now, however, her riddles were sounding downright offensive.

"Listen here, you Spoke weirdo, speak plainly or don't speak at all. Do you even want to be saved? You would think you would appreciate what we're doing for you."

Cecile stopped walking and turned around. She looked earnest. "I'm sorry, Flora. Yes, my fate hangs on the outcome of this mission. I speak because of my concern for you. All I would ask is, is this person worth it? Are you sure you know what you're doing? "

Flora thought about Cecile's analogy of the party. The only guest at this party that she didn't get along with was Cecile. It was only her words that made Flora confused and frustrated. "What do you mean, what person?"

"Don't take me for a fool. You asked me to commit to securing a prisoner, just before you called the retcher. I know that's why you're here. This person you are trying to free, this person must be important to you."

Flora's mind raced. If she told Cecile she wanted to get back to her former husband, it could unravel everything. The others might also believe she was conflicted in her motivations. Worse, it could find its way back to Reed. She had to think of a response that made some sense, but did not reveal too much.

"I have a cousin that was taken by the Spokes. I know what he looks like, but otherwise didn't know him well. I can identify him, so yes, that's one of the reasons I'm part of the expedition, beyond the reasons I've already mentioned to Ember—to report on the coup and see the mission through to the end."

She was trying to thread a delicate needle with her lie. Hopefully it would be enough to convince Cecile and let her drop it.

Cecile didn't seem to be buying it. "You are risking your life for a cousin you don't know well?"

The question hung in the air while Flora tried to think of a good response. Thankfully she was saved by lunch.

"*Ca y'es*! Well done," Cecile said, looking up behind Flora's shoulder.

Flora had been oblivious to Rosalie walking up behind her, carrying a large groundhog. She was donning a broad gap-toothed smile. "Rub-a-dub-dub," she said.

After eating some sinewy groundhog meat and a husk of bread, they began the final leg of the trip. Flora kept her distance from Cecile to avoid her questions.

For a while the Spoke farms were positioned closer together, and soon enough they were walking down a proper avenue of Old World houses. They were not like the worn-out buildings near Grand Caverns, but rather they had been spruced up with modern Spoke renovations and adorned with bike parts of all shapes and sizes.

People watched them from a distance, some with weapons at the ready. No one approached them.

Ember began asking Rosalie questions about who they were going to meet and where. Flora noticed whenever Rosalie discussed taking the train, color would drain from Ember's face. Of all Spoke instruments and machines, the train would be the most loathsome to him. He would be riding a symbol of what he despised most, something spawned by the fires of industry, something that defiled the earth with its metal bonds.

Finally they arrived at a large, two-story house. Patches of metal siding checkered the roof and exterior walls. Several chairs made mostly of inner tubes lay out on the porch. In one of them a man was sitting. He was short, with a round belly and a full mustache. In one hand was a steel cup and in the other a shotgun.

"Well, well Rosalie, quite a motley crew you have here," the mustached man said.

Rosalie walked up to the porch, careful to avoid a rash of chipping paint on the steps. "Howdy, Patterson. Been a long time."

"Yep."

"Well, motley is true, and that's just my own mouth," she said, smiling. "We have two SLS and their prisoner, a Spoke woman from up north, Quebecker she is. For her these SLS want to strike a deal with the lords of Seeville."

Patterson sniffed, curling up his mustache. "Yeah, I thought I smelled something."

Flora remembered what SLS stood for. *Smells like shit.* Ember must have known as well, based on the look on his face. He was stepping up the stairs behind Rosalie. "Hard to see how you could smell anything after living in this repugnant town for so long," he said.

Patterson raised his eyebrows and brought the shotgun to rest on his lap. Rosalie held Ember's arm and said, "Hush now, Thisslewood. Let's not get spicy quite yet, or we might miss the meal altogether."

Then she explained to Patterson, "This one here is an Essentialist leader, a sub-chief in Grand Caverns. He's as nervous as a long-tailed cat in a room full of rocking chairs, so best we get movin'."

"All right, then. Let me gather the boys," Patterson replied.

Patterson entered the house and returned with three more men. They were haggard types, without uniforms, but well armed, each with a pistol. Despite the cool weather, they wore long shorts, or in one case, skin-tight pants. Their thighs were thick with muscle, every one of them. These must be mules, as Flora had heard them called.

Patterson led them off the porch to continue down the street toward some more formidable buildings. The three Spoke mules fell into a line behind the group of them.

Flora felt nervous and out of place in the Spoke town, but all the brick, concrete and Old World trappings didn't make her fearful. Rather it felt like she was walking through some Old World bedtime story.

They turned down a broader avenue and ahead Flora could see a big sign saying *S&R Railroad* in a bright red stencil. They walked through the building and ended up on a platform, with long parallel rows of metal track stretching out to either side.

Mehta and the four Spoke mules watched over Ember, Flora, and Cecile as Rosalie and Patterson went to confer with some local railroad operatives. Heads bobbed and words were exchanged, but Flora couldn't make out what they were saying.

Then they all waited in silence, the tension too strong to break with any idle chatter.

Eventually Flora heard it coming. It sounded like someone was shaking a giant beanbag many miles away. The noise grew louder and louder, and then the huge beast powered around the corner, black smoke steaming from the snout. Flora was truly awed by the sheer power of it, while Ember would only steal the occasional glance and then close his eyes to escape to some cerebral refuge.

Patterson had secured them their own train car at the back. It looked to be normally used for railroad workers, rather than passengers. The seats were stained or streaked with grease, and only four of them had any padding.

Only moments after they entered the train car, a great whistle blew, metal squealed on metal, and the beast lurched forward. It began gliding faster and faster down the tracks. A smell of soot and earth and oil reached them and then dissipated as they gained momentum.

Seeville was only minutes away.

KEEPIN IT BETWEEN THE DITCHES

Early in the morning the rough path turned into a larger, flatter highway called "64." Although the broader, flatter lanes made the others more wary of exposure, it was a welcome reprieve for Owen's forearms and back that were feeling punished from the previous day's bumpy ride.

In midmorning the lead scouts stopped at a three-story tall wooden tower. The scouts were yelling up at it in the distance. They circled back and spoke with Chester and Thorpe.

Everyone clustered around Chester as he explained the situation. "We are crossing the border into a new bandit territory. They call themselves the Yorktown Founders. It sounds like they are a bit like the New Founders in Seeville. They're going to let us pass, but I'm not sure it's out of the goodness in their hearts, or because we outnumber them five to one. Be careful with these folks."

They rolled the platform past the wooden tower carefully, again making their weapons visible as a show of strength. Only two bandits could be seen in the tower, tracking them with wary eyes and crossbows at the ready. These seemed to be of a different breed than the bandits from Tappahannock. There were no hoodies. They wore leather, their faces were clean, and their hair was collected into long braids.

The platform rolled onward. Periodically they would see a house off to the side of the road with signs of living: a cleared lawn, crops, some bikes, or horses tied up. In one case a couple of bandits were riding bikes toward them and they swerved off to watch the platform group pass. These bandits also leveled crossbows at the Spoke platform as they rode by.

One of the mules asked, "Do we know how many people this place got?"

No one answered his question.

They turned off onto a well-worn road. The bandit dwellings became more numerous. Many were miniature farmsteads. When they passed these buildings they could often see a bandit or two hanging back inside, watching the Spokes keenly after gathering whatever weapons they had at their disposal.

"Trailers!" The rear guard yelled out. When Owen looked back, far in the distance, he could see two distant bikes trailing them.

"Keep going," Chester said from up ahead of them, "and don't do anything stupid."

Owen kept wondering *is this normal?* There did seem to be quite a few bandits, and all of them were wary of Spoke people. It also worried him that the farther they went into this territory, the more they would have to cross paths with getting back out.

A large signpost made of freshly cut timbers appeared. Darkened grooves spelled out the letters *Yorktown* in the face of the wood.

They passed by a turnoff that led down a hill to a more concentrated bandit settlement. Owen looked back and saw one of their followers turn off, but the other one kept going.

They passed an odd rock formation at the side of the road. It looked to be a mass of stone about two hundred feet long, as tall as a house, and covered in shrubs, vines and moss. Dark grottoes led underneath it in places, some filled with vegetation.

"What's that?" Owen asked.

His question was rhetorical, but Chester answered anyway. "Don't know for sure, but could be another statue, fallen over like."

"What do you mean another statue?"

"Like the beholders."

Looking again, it did seem possible, based on the size of it, and the form of the rock under the foliage. But why would the founders of Seeville build one here? Perhaps it was some other decaying monument, or just one more Old World ruin of unknown function.

Soon Owen forgot about the odd rock formation as he was forced to exert himself on the increasingly hilly topography. On a particularly steep climb he had to stand and use his weight to plunge the pedals of his bike assembly downward. He still couldn't match the cadence of the others.

They crested a ridge and a broad river could be seen in the distance.

They began a gradual decline toward the water. Dominating the view was a huge cylinder that formed a bridge over the river. It was propped up on massive stilts. This cylinder also cut across the waterfront, extending south into the horizon. This was undoubtedly the "tube" Chester had referred to the night before. It was much larger than Owen had imagined. The tube diameter had to be as high as a four-story building.

This tube formation dwarfed a number of run-down buildings and small bandit shacks that otherwise littered the hillside down to the river.

The only anomaly to the cylindrical shape of the tube was a large bulbous outcropping on one side. It almost looked biological, like some sort of goiterous balloon pulsing out of the Old World artery. At the base of this outcropping was a sheer wall leading into the ground and cutting off the arc of the cylinder.

Chester pointed at the wall below the extended balloon formation. The group rode over a bumpy pathway heading in its direction, making one last push to their destination.

They stopped near the sheer wall, just out of the shadow of the outcropping. Owen used his scope to look back, and he could see there were now four bandits on bikes behind them. They had stopped at the top of the bluff and were staring down at the Spoke platform, one of them wielding binoculars.

"This is bent…sideways. We're gonna eat it for sure," one of the mules said.

"Fuck this," said another.

Apparently Owen wasn't the only one who was apprehensive.

"Fuck this is right," Chester said. "I've never seen bandits like these. There are way more than I'm comfortable with, and I don't like this place. It looks impenetrable. We should leave right now, while we're all still breathing."

Thorpe said, "We're not planning on staying long. Besides, we have ways to dissuade these nice people from annoying us." He nodded to one of the cases on the platform. Rourke unlocked it and briefly unveiled a machine-gun and tripod mount.

The sight of the machine gun raised eyebrows. It would indeed be surprising to see the bandits have anything comparable to a working machine gun. But the machine gun did nothing to alleviate Owen's concerns. It only highlighted the high-stakes nature of their situation.

Chester spoke hurriedly, "Fine, so what's next? If that wall there is made of the same stuff the tube is made of, I'm not sure how we can get in." His gaze leveled on Thorpe, who in turn glanced toward Preston. Meanwhile Preston had already dismounted and was moving closer to examine the sheer face of the building.

Preston turned to see all eyes on him. "Um, I'm going to need some help." He sounded nervous. His hands jittered slightly as he took off his backpack and pulled out a folder. "Owen, Jeroun, Frank, Milken, if you could come over here."

Owen walked over cautiously with the others, sipping from his canteen to rehydrate. He wasn't able to make out any kind of door on the black surface. There were scratches of white and yellow everywhere, and several points where torches had burned the shell but had been unable to penetrate. A variety of stains, from dust, dirt and pollen, also colored the wall. Ultimately the assortment of markings made it difficult to see any delineation in the original surface of the wall that might be a door or even a paneling joint.

Preston opened his folder and looked at a piece of paper. It appeared to be some sort of architectural drawing.

"Owen, help me with some measurements. You two—get the rope ladder."

Owen and Preston measured the length of the wall from the left side of the building face. Preston made two marks in the dirt at the base of the wall.

"Put the ladder here," Preston said, pointing to the marks. When it was mounted on the wall, Preston climbed up and outlined a rectangle in chalk. "We should be able to enter if we cut through this area with the torch."

Preston didn't sound entirely confident. Nevertheless, the railroad man named Milken scaled the ladder and started cutting. Sparks rained down, and Owen's nose was impregnated with the smell of acetylene and melting alloys.

Owen looked nervously out to the top of the bluff. There were still four bandits. In the foreground the mules and other railroad folks had pistols, rifles, and crossbows at the ready. They were standing in a star formation around the platform, looking back at the bandits on the bluff in a long-distance staring competition.

Owen glanced again at the schematic Preston was holding. It was on crisp white paper, with no marks or discoloration. The lines looked too clean to be drawn by hand. Had this schematic been stored away, vacuum-sealed somewhere since Old World times?

"Where did you get these drawings, Preston?" Owen asked.

Preston quickly hid the drawing away in his folder. "We have access to lots of stuff like this at the Barnyard now," he said. Then he gave Owen an annoyed look that meant *don't get me into trouble*.

"I'm in," Milken said as he pushed the metal slab inside. "Preston, we need your lantern."

Owen and six of the railroad folks climbed up the ladder and into the opening. A couple of the mules left the platform and treaded cautiously closer as well, but Thorpe gestured to them with a stiff hand, halting them in their stride.

The weak light emanating from Preston's lantern revealed a large empty room. On one side was a door that looked to have some sort of electronic interface associated with it. On the other side there was a ramp going down.

Following Preston, they took the ramp down. At first the light from Preston's lantern allowed them only partial glimpses of what lay ahead. Thorpe ignited another lantern behind them, giving them a better view of their surroundings. Thorpe instructed Milken and Frank to stay and guard the exterior doorway.

The ramp zigzagged down a few levels and opened up into a large, warehouse-sized room. There were shelves with boxes and crates, and several sophisticated-looking forklifts stationed along wide aisles between the shelves. The forklifts had additional arms with several degrees of freedom, making them look a bit like a huge spiders standing on their side.

"Look there, what's that?" Jeroun asked, pointing to the corner. The dim lantern light exposed what looked vaguely like an array of giant centipedes. As they approached cautiously they could tell they were robotic, and unmoving. A number of robotic arms were folded neatly on their backs.

On the base of the wall nearby was an assortment of tools, some clearly ratchets, pliers, and screwdrivers, but others with more confusing configurations. Each of them had an odd rectangular metal grip with a pattern of divots that made them feel uncomfortable in Owen's hand.

Preston was examining his diagram as the others perused the Old World artifacts. He grabbed one of the odd-shaped tools and gestured to another ramp leading down. "This way," he said.

The ramp ended in a door with a slanted mechanical handle. Preston fiddled with the handle, periodically looking at his papers, as if following the instructions for building an Old World furniture set. A metal latch could be heard shifting in the wall somewhere, and Preston pulled.

"I'm going to need some help," he said.

The four of them crowded into the tight doorway to pull on the slim metal handle. The door heaved slowly forward. It was at least two feet thick, made mostly of concrete, the hallmark of a bomb shelter or bunker entrance.

It must be a Faraday cage.

On the other side was another, simpler door, which Preston opened easily with his handheld tool.

The room beyond the door exhaled a great breath of air.

SEEVILLE

Flora didn't watch the scenery rolling by as the train departed Culpepper. She kept her eyes focused inside the car and on its wary passengers.

Patterson was sitting across from Ember. He said, "My guess is you ain't never been on a train before mister." His comment got a chuckle from one of his mule goons standing nearby.

Ember was indeed holding onto his seat, his knuckles blanched, and his face ivy. He turned his head slowly to Patterson, and his color began to redden. "And for that I am glad," Ember retorted. "Although it sickens me today, I know the earth will repay me for not participating in its plunder."

Then Ember turned to Rosalie and spoke with steel in his voice. "Tell me again why we are on this train?"

Rosalie answered. "Well, you know, it's the fastest way to get into town. And where else would we parlay with the Spokes? The lords of Seeville—they are all there, in town."

Ember stood up and corralled Rosalie aside, away from Patterson and the others. Flora stood up and joined them, curious to hear the conversation. Ember spoke in vehement whispers. "We shouldn't have done this," he said, "We should have insisted—*I* should have insisted we meet them out of town."

"Look, Mr. Thisslewood. I get it. You don't like trains. You don't like a lot of what these Spokes do, but that doesn't mean it isn't a good plan."

Ember snapped back at her. "This has nothing to do with me or trains! I take Essentialist matters very seriously. I would gladly sacrifice some discomfort if it improved our strategic position. But this plan, with all these Spoke strongmen around us, with us not controlling the cadence of the meeting and who is going to be there. It puts us at a distinct disadvantage."

"Now, now, Mr. Thisslewood, let's just calm down a smidgeon. We're here now. Bygones be bygones and such."

The Spoke men were all witnessing the conversation. A couple of them stood up from their chairs. These two then moved to another side of the train car, fanning out. Meanwhile Mehta, who had been lurking at the front of the car, inched over toward the debate. His eyes darted back and forth between the Spoke men and Rosalie and Ember. His hand was resting neatly on the holster of his pistol.

Ember's nostrils flared as he continued berating Rosalie. "You have done your job to get us here, but *I* am the representative of the Essentialists. *I* know what we stand for. So when we arrive at the train station, we do this my way."

"Now hold your horses..."

"My way!" Ember's eyes bulged as he yelled.

Rosalie smiled and put up her hands. "Okay, okay Chief. You got it. Just be calm. We don't want to wake up the natives, if you know what I mean."

Fuming, Ember walked away and perched himself to look out a nearby window. His vapid look from earlier in the train ride seemed to have vanished, replaced by rage and determination.

Rosalie smiled her gap-toothed smile at the Spoke men, trying to lower tension, but it did little to assuage them. The Spoke men fidgeted nervously, and none of them returned to their seats.

Until now Ember had seemed to be a passive participant in this venture. Flora had wondered how he had risen to sub-chief with such a disposition. Many had called him an extremist, protective of Essentialist ideals to a fault, but to Flora he had always seemed more like a play-by-the-rules bureaucrat. Here, however, a different side of him was revealed. Here, she could see, there was a fiercer, more focused Ember Thisslewood who came to play.

It was a short ride to Seeville, and already the farmland and rolling prairies were giving away to clusters of houses. On the outskirts of town most of the buildings looked beyond repair. Soon enough they passed some kind of invisible threshold, and the buildings came to life with brightly colored siding and full roofs. Bike tires, spokes, frames, gears, and chains in artistic designs adorned the walls and lawns of the dwellings. The vivid colors and decorations made the newer buildings in Grand Caverns look drab in comparison.

When they were closer still, the buildings grew higher and higher until there were some that stood ten stories tall. It became impossible to see the roofs without craning her neck out of the train car window. The streets were filled with people walking or biking, some that were in multi-seated bike arrangements, or some that towed trailers and platforms.

Flora was trying to inspect every person they passed, searching for a broad back, looking for some semblance of his flattish nose and wispy hair. The train was moving so fast that it was difficult, almost impossible.

Something about the blur of people and the passing buildings took her away from the train, away from the people around her. Her heart was beating strongly, but not with fear or anxiety. It was beating with excitement.

She could almost hear his whispers. When he had secretly given her a book about New York City he had said, "don't let the curator see you with that." She remembered that first night, that first time she had given herself to him freely. That night he said, "for some reason the moon is shining brighter than ever." And then when he had returned the next morning he had whispered, "even the sun burns brighter when I'm with you."

The train slowed, and they pulled up to a stop. Unlike Culpepper, the platform in Seeville was a long, raucous thing, full of people waiting and cajoling. Down the platform she could see multiple tracks, some running in parallel, some splitting off. A large, red warehouse dominated the skyline in the distance.

When the train came to a complete stop, Patterson and his men clustered around the steps that led out of the train car. He said, "we just need to do a brief inspection, then we'll be on our way. Please wait here."

"Sure thing, hon," Rosalie responded.

Flora could see Patterson walk down the steps to the track and head toward the main building at a brisk pace.

Ember didn't look happy. "Come here, now," he said, gesturing to Mehta, Rosalie, and Flora. "And bring the prisoner." Then he moved to the far end of the car and waited for them.

When they joined him at the back he said, "An inspection?"

Rosalie thought for a moment and said, "We don't know how these trains work. Maybe they count who goes on or off?"

Ember looked at her curiously. "But you have been on a train before, right? You told us yesterday morning. So do you or do you not remember being inspected?"

"No, sirree. We weren't. But look, I'm sure this is different. We got SLS—scuze me, Essentialists here. Maybe they don't want us to be seen, you know. Keep it quiet so as to not rile people up. Then they can find a way to get us to the right people without causing a fuss."

It sounded like a reasonable explanation to Flora, but Ember wasn't at all satisfied. "I don't like it. They could try to wrestle Cecile from us at any time, and then what have we got? I want Cecile in the back. Mehta, you hold her and don't let go. You put a knife to her throat if you have to."

Mehta looked at Rosalie, who nodded back at him slowly. Cecile seemed to go to him willingly.

"And I'll do the talking," Ember said.

"Okay, Chief," Rosalie said. Then she slinked to stand behind him.

They waited for a few quiet moments. Ember was facing forward, watching for signs of Spoke people coming into their car. Flora was looking about outside, still trying to find Granger's face in the crowd. In the train car, the Spokes were stiff as statues, staring back at the Essentialist contingent. Rosalie whispered something in Mehta's ear and then moved back toward Ember. Something Rosalie said to Mehta made Cecile look up, eyes wide.

"Here they come," Ember said. He stood up tall, rearranging his belt.

Five men entered the train car led by a man dressed like an Old World business executive. He wore a red bowtie and black suspenders over a crisp, blue shirt. His face was long, making the smile he gave them look diminutive. "Good afternoon. My name is Quenton Bartz. I'm just a humble businessman, with interests in the railroad. I'm also a lord of Seeville." He extended his hand to Ember.

Ember did not take the hand. He said, "I am Ember Thisslewood, sub-chief to the Essentialists at Grand Caverns. I have come to negotiate an exchange based on our capture of your Spoke spy, and for restitution for the raid you have undertaken in our lands. We insist on being given passage to your council of lords immediately."

Bartz said, "We will need to complete the inspection. Then I can take you to the council of lords. I'm at every meeting, so I often know their mind. I'm sure they would be interested in negotiating, since this woman is indeed important to us. Once you allow our men to inspect her we can be on our way." He smiled and then turned to leave.

"No, you may not," Ember said. "Mehta, do not let these Spoke men near her under any circumstance."

Bartz stopped at the door and turned around, his smile replaced with a sterner countenance.

Ember said, "listen here, we both know you can see her from there, as plainly as you can see her close up. That should be enough for any so-called inspection. So stop playing games and get us to your other leaders." Ember crossed his arms and glared.

"I see," Bartz said, flashing a minimal smirk. "Well, unfortunately we can't have that."

"Have what?"

"Have you bringing Cecile to the other lords."

Ember looked confused but didn't miss a beat. "Oh really? You are about to cause a serious incident, sir, one that could result in harm to all of Spoke society." Ember looked around at the other Spoke men. "Are all of you going to stand around and let this reprehensible man speak for you? Are you going to let him put this woman in harm's way?"

Bartz said, "Okay, come now. The charade is over. You can have your deal—the one proposed to Patterson." His eyes were unfocused—or rather, they were not focused on Ember, they were focused behind him. "Let's put this pup out of his misery."

Ember's head swiveled frenetically. He looked at Patterson, at Rosalie, and behind at Mehta. It was on Mehta that his gaze rested.

Slowly, Mehta was lowering his knife from Cecile's throat. He shifted his weight to move in front of her. Meanwhile, Rosalie stepped back to stand by Mehta, forming a wall between Ember and Cecile.

Ember and Flora were now stuck between the mercs on one side and eight Spokes on the other. Ember pulled a knife out of his belt, tensing like a caged animal. Flora also took out a knife, but slowly, more carefully.

"You will never live this down," Ember said to Rosalie. "When people find out about your treachery you will never work again. We will hunt you down and kill you."

"Who's going to tell, sunshine?" Rosalie said, shoulders shrugging. "And if they did, no biggie. As far as Luna is concerned, we're just dotting the i's and crossing the t's. Luna sent an expedition in good faith to try to rescue lost prisoners, but the evil Spoke greasers betrayed them. That's what she wanted, so no disloyalty here. We're living up to our deal with Luna, like good mercs. But you, I feel sorry for you, pal. She never really gave you much of a chance. Apparently Luna thought you were just a little too partial to Darkwind to be of any use. Some dogs just can't be trained to learn new tricks."

Ember's face was ashen. He continued to look in all directions, trying to find some kind of way out.

Flora reflected on Luna's militant words about the Spokes at the festival. At the time Flora thought Luna was grandstanding, like all the Grand Caverns leaders before her, but now she knew differently. This was someone who would willingly showcase and defile dead Essentialists at the infirmary just to raise the people's ire against the Spokes. This was someone who would kill the chief in a lavish coup so she could have absolute power to push her agenda. This was someone who would actively set the stage for war simply because she thought war was in their nature. She was the wolf she so espoused, and she was the jackal as well.

Ember spat desperate words in Bartz's direction. "Yes, you get your prisoner back. But how can you be sure this is what your lords want? How can you be sure they want to incite a conflict with all Essentialists."

Bartz looked mildly annoyed. "You see," he said, "the lords, they often disagree. They talk and they talk and then come up with some half-baked solution no one dislikes but that, at the same time, is good for no one. They don't know how progress is made. Whereas we, at the railroad—we're changing the face of Spoke society. We're connecting dozens of cities north to south. Soon we will be bringing new tools to bear that will help our citizens make dramatic improvements to their lives. Soon we will be able to expand the railroad in new directions—to the west even, into SLS territory."

It seemed Bartz was talking more to the Spokes around him, rather than Ember. "So," he continued, "for the good of us all, sometimes we have to roll up our sleeves and get things done. Sometimes that means doing deals with mercs, to save us from ourselves."

Now Bartz directed his attention back to Ember. "And if it means we allow our backward neighbors to fling a few arrows at us, that's fine. We disagree with Essentialists on almost everything, but I think we can agree on one thing. Only one of us can rule these lands. It's about time we sorted that out."

"You will be cleansed from the earth, all of you!" Ember said defiantly. "We have tens of thousands coming to the frontier, from the Tuscon Union, from the Prefectorate, even. You will choke on your industry and be overrun. We will stampede over your sickly towns."

Bartz was smiling. "I'm not worried. Soon we'll have everything we need to drive your little herd over a cliff."

Ember's head stopped swiveling, and for a moment his gaze rested on Flora. His eyes retained their fervor, but they had moistened. For a brief moment he had the look of a lost child, cornered and afraid—one that was being unfairly bullied in a playground. Then he gritted his teeth and said, "Time to recompense the earth."

She knew what he wanted her to do. Ember Thisslewood would never live in Spoke lands, prisoner or otherwise. He was about to return himself to the soil, and he wanted her to do so as well.

Ember abruptly ran toward Bartz, his knife raised high. One of the Spoke men drew his pistol and shot him squarely in the chest. Ember fell right at Bartz's feet. Another Spoke pounced and had his knife at his throat.

Ember wasn't moving. When Bartz turned his body over with his foot, Ember's face was already lifeless. In his chest a hole oozed blood. The bullet must have travelled directly through his heart.

Flora did not follow Ember's command. She had frozen during Ember's charge, still reeling from the dramatic shift in their fortunes. Something held her back from following Ember to his death—some vague concern or warning telling her it was not her time to die.

Without realizing, Mehta had crept up on her. He now grabbed her arm holding the knife. She tried to resist, but his strength was too much. His fingers dug into the tendons on her wrist and she had to let go. Then he forcefully pulled her arms behind her back.

"Weren't we going to keep him alive for questioning?" Rosalie asked.

"Sorry sir, I…" The man who shot Ember began.

"No, it's fine," Bartz said, stepping over the body toward Flora unceremoniously. "Probably for the best, actually. He seemed quite the idealist. And besides, we have been gifted with another." Bartz probed Flora with his eyes. "Nice to look at, but she does need to clean up I think." Bartz wrinkled his nose and then folded back toward the door.

The whole scene in the train car had seemed to be playing out in slow motion, as if she was one step removed. But now it was feeling real, and the full weight of her situation was becoming apparent. She had abandoned her family, aiding in a mission that had pushed her people closer to war. She had become a prisoner of the Spokes, subject to incarceration and possibly worse.

Even with all this, though, the nucleus of her desperate motivation for this journey remained. Some part of her wondered if in her captivity she might find Granger. It was that impossible and vague hope that made her go on this mission, that made her abandon her family. It was the same thought that stayed her hand, when most Essentialists would choose to fight against all odds, valiantly, like Ember had done.

She had to believe Granger was still alive, even as a prisoner, even though likely cordoned away in some servile role. If only she could see him one more time, to feel his touch, to hear him whisper about the sun and the moon, then the world would at least have given her something in return for her unrelenting sorrow.

Maybe then she would have the courage to do what Ember had done. Maybe then she could return her body to the soil without regret.

YORKTOWN

It wasn't a huge room, but it was all there: desktop computers, laptop computers, mobile phones, scanners and printers. There were countless cable boxes, chip boards, and hard drives. Other devices that looked like generators were nestled in one corner of the room. One whole shelf was full of devices Owen had never seen before in any pictures or books, including strange tools, spiderlike robots, and other enigmatic appliances. In the back there was even what looked like a large mainframe computer.

There was no sign of melting or other retcher damage, and presumably all this equipment had been preserved from the original EMP attacks by the Faraday cage enclosure.

"Unbelievable," Owen said as he walked down one of the aisles. It was everything they could possibly need, everything they could possibly want. They could learn so much.

He ran into Preston as he turned around a corner on the far end of the room. "We did it," Preston said, nodding and smiling.

"Damn right we did!" Owen exclaimed, grabbing Preston by the elbows. His grip nearly caused the kerosene in Preston's lantern to spill out.

For a moment Owen forgot about Rourke and Thorpe. He even forgot about the bandits waiting outside. He stood there with Preston as they shared the moment. A moment they both had dreamed of since they were children. "I can't believe it," Owen said.

Owen was further elated to see that Preston's smile seemed genuine—that he wasn't telling Owen cookie-cutter railroad anecdotes or urging Owen to temper his excitement.

Gradually, Preston's smile seemed to fade, however, and his face became flushed. He sheepishly looked down, no longer able to stare at Owen. "Yeah, it's pretty amazing," he said.

"Enough," Thorpe said, snapping Owen out of his reverie. Rourke and Jeroun were looking at them from the back of the room, frowns on their faces, while Thorpe was watching their exchange with a more acerbic expression. "Let's get this over with, Preston," Thorpe said wispily, performing a revolving motion with his left hand.

Preston fumbled with his backpack and withdrew the folder again, pulling out more crisp white pages. He handed out a page to each of them. "This is what we need most. If we can get more, we should. Whatever you do, *do not* press any buttons or turn any switches. There's a chance they have working power sources, particularly some of the battery-powered devices. If you have questions, ask me. If I'm not nearby, Owen might know the answer."

Owen looked at the page. There were precisely labeled drawings of a variety of computers, electronic devices, generators, and other equipment. Even in the weak light of Preston's lantern the page seemed extremely clear. What's more, the drawings were perfect, like you would see in an Old World book rather than a hand sketch. It seemed hard to believe that even a railroad draftsman could draw something with such precision.

"Okay, hop to it," Rourke said, clapping his hands twice for effect.

It would take several runs. Owen and Preston were best able to select the right equipment, so they arranged a pile by the door while the three others started making runs up the ramp. Everything was wrapped up in light blankets that Jeroun had brought down, presumably to avoid damage. The blankets also served to hide the precious merchandise from the bandits and mules.

Once Preston and Owen felt like they had piled up enough equipment, they took their turn scaling up the ramp together. Preston lit the way with his lantern.

"The paper list…it's so perfect," Owen said, "where did you get it?"

"I'm sorry Owen, I can't tell you. Maybe when we get back you can find out more. There'll be lots of work to do."

"I don't get it. I've seen this place now. What could possibly require more secrecy than the biggest cache of electronics anyone has seen in a generation?"

Preston was quiet for a moment. Then he spoke in a low voice, his words laced with a hint of annoyance, "Fine. Listen, do you remember...?" A light flashed ahead of them and Preston went mute as Thorpe, Rourke, and Jeroen came from the other direction, descending the ramp to collect another load.

Preston and Owen reached the upper room and placed their equipment gently at the entryway. The two other railroad men took over, hoisting the equipment down the outside of the entrance with a rope. For some of the more delicate equipment they carried it directly down the rope ladder.

Owen glanced outside and could see the Spokes by the platform remained in a similar formation, most of them looking up the hill. Owen counted twelve bandits now up on the bluff, staring back.

"We should hurry up," Preston said, heading back toward the ramp.

When they were again alone on the ramp, Owen asked quietly, "Sorry, what were you saying?"

Preston seemed to clam up again. "Let's just hurry up and get out of here, alright? We can talk about it later."

They collected another batch of equipment and returned to the top again. Now there were twenty bandits on the ridge. Chester's face was lobster red, simmering with tension. He called over to them. "That's enough now. Let's get out of here."

"Just a couple more loads," Preston responded.

This time they jogged, their heavy breaths misting the ancient Old World walls as they went.

Jeroen, Thorpe, and Rourke arrived at the bunker a few minutes after them. They were breathing heavily.

Jeroen said, "They're attacking. It's time to go."

"What?" Owen asked.

Jeroen spoke quickly. "They surprised us by coming up the hill from below, onto the rock outcropping. They took out two of our men. We're holding them off for now."

"This is the last run," Thorpe rasped.

Jeroen grabbed a smaller pile of hard drives and cables. "Let's just take this stuff and be done with it."

Preston's eyes were darting back and forth at the remaining piles of equipment. "No, we need the generators. She said without them we would be severely constrained."

"Those look heavy. We don't have time," Jeroun said, looking to Rourke for support. But Rourke just shrugged and smiled an oblivious smile.

"Fine, who am to I defy Gail's little servant," Jeroun said sulkily, standing down.

Owen was confused by the back and forth, but he had little time for contemplation. Between the five of them they were able to carry two midsize generators and one smaller one. Despite the awkward loads, the five of them moved quickly and efficiently up the ramp.

As they came closer to the external door, the gunfire and yelling became more evident.

When Owen arrived in the entryway room, he could see the railroad man named Frank was shooting out the access door with his pistol. Milken had a crossbow and was releasing the occasional bolt.

"How many are there?" Thorpe asked.

"Only a few are advancing on us," Milken answered, "but it looks like there could be dozens behind them. Then there are more up on the hill."

Owen tried to position himself close enough to the door so he could see out. The bandits up on the hill had taken cover behind some trees. The occasional arrow arced down from that direction. Meanwhile, periodic gunshots rang out from the men stationed around the bike platform. They were under more precarious cover. One of the railroad men lay slain just below the ladder, and a mule was slumped over the platform.

"We'll lower the equipment down," Thorpe said to Frank and Milken. "You two will have to take it to the platform."

They quickly worked to make a rope harness for the generators and then lowered them down to the ground.

One of them dropped the last foot. "Gently," Preston said.

Frank and Milken climbed down the ladder while Rourke gave them cover with his rifle. They managed to get one generator to the platform and then exchanged some heated words with Chester. They returned with two other mules to collect the remaining generators.

A rush of bandits streamed out of the drop-off in the rock outcropping nearby. They launched arrows at the entryway, and Rourke backed up. An arrow flickered through the aperture, and Owen felt a flash of pain in his leg.

"I've been hit," Owen said.

He sat down and inspected the wound while Rourke and Jeroen fell to their stomachs and returned fire at the surge of bandits.

Although his pants were saturating with blood, Owen's leg was much better than it looked. The arrow didn't puncture anything important, it had only cut across the surface of his thigh.

The fighting continued, but Owen was unable to witness it from his recessed location in the room. He cursed himself for letting his curiosity get the better of him. He had almost been seriously injured.

The fighting let up for a moment.

During the lull, something nagged at Owen. What was said in the bunker had confused him. They mentioned some kind of boss at the Barnyard, some woman, but he knew of no one with that name at the railroad.

"Let me look at it," Preston said, sliding over to him from another corner of the room.

"Thanks," Owen said. "I think it's just a flesh wound."

Preston hovered his lantern over the leg.

While Preston looked at his leg, it came together for Owen.

"The satellite," Owen said.

"What?"

"You said *do you remember* on the ramp a few minutes ago. Then you stopped talking. You were going to say *do you remember* the satellite."

"Don't worry about that now."

"These are printouts, aren't they?" Owen said, taking the crumpled list from his pocket, bloodying the fine paper with his hands.

Preston let out a brittle laugh. "How would we print anything out?

We would need a computer for that. Maybe now. Maybe with this equipment—"

"You hooked Gail up to it."

"What are you talking about? "

"Jeroun, in the bunker—he mentioned someone named Gail. He said you were her little servant. There's only one Gail I know. The only Gail I know is the name of the smartphone Cecile turned on."

Preston's eyes were invisible in the dark corner of the room, but his head went back in a sort of guffaw. "That's ridiculous," he said, "Cecile was taken with the phone. You know that."

"It all makes sense now," Owen said. "Cecile asked you to search the interior of the satellite, to see if you could find anything else. You must have found another phone and stashed it away. That's why you were being so secretive. That's why you wouldn't let me into the Barnyard bunker. You're keeping a working smartphone secret from all of Seeville. I bet it told you to come here. I bet it told you where to find all this stuff."

Owen noticed that Rourke, Thorpe, and Jeroen were looking his way, oblivious to the battle going on just outside the room.

Rourke walked slowly over to Owen. He smiled and said, "you're hurt bad, aren't you."

"No," Owen said. "Like I said, it's just a flesh wound."

"Actually, it looks very serious." Rourke said, and he exchanged a cold glance with Preston.

"No, really, it isn't," Owen protested. "It just cut the surface. I can walk fine, and I'm sure I can ride fine as well."

Rourke was grinning now. Why was Rourke always smiling?

Owen said, "Preston, tell him…"

Owen hadn't been paying attention to Preston. Rather he'd been trying to decipher this new byproduct of Rourke's insanity. So when he saw the look on Preston's face it was too late. It was a look of sorrow, but at the same time one of determination. In his hand was his dagger, poised over Owen's leg.

It was like slow motion, tearing through his pants and flesh. The accompanying wave of agony wrenched his torso forward. "Fuck!" Owen cried out. "You bastard…you bent fucking bastard."

Preston withdrew the dagger and Owen managed to scurry awkwardly away, his leg throbbing in pain and oozing blood. He pressed his back into the corner of the room and pulled out his own dagger, staring back in defiance. Then he shifted carefully over onto the nearby rampway, where there was more cover.

Preston looked down. He wouldn't show Owen his eyes. "Owen, you…know too much. They told me I would have to—"

Thorpe interrupted, sounding annoyed. "You should have just killed him."

Preston slowly looked up toward Owen. His eyes were a storm of emotion. Then he took a cautious step in Owen's direction with his knife at the ready.

"Preston! What the fuck!" Owen cried out, trying to make his friend see reason. At the same time he tensed in readiness for Preston's attack.

Jeroen was looking out the door. "They're waving us on," he said. "We have to go."

Thorpe glanced out the entryway. "He's right. We've reached the line with Chester."

Thorpe said to Preston. "Leave him. He's not going anywhere."

Preston stopped stalking forward. He slowly turned around to the entrance, keeping one eye on Owen.

Thorpe left first, descending the rope ladder. Rourke and Jeroen gave him a burst of cover fire. Owen heard another series of shots coming from the platform.

Rourke took another bundle of equipment and left. Jeroun followed.

Preston was last. He glanced over at Owen, hesitating for a brief moment. As he maneuvered himself into the light of the entryway door, Owen could see his eyes were raw. But then his teeth clenched, and he began scaling down the ladder. His head cleared from view.

More gunshots. Someone yelled, "Go, go, go!" in the distance.

Owen crab-walked up the end of the ramp and over to the opening, using only his arms and good leg. He watched Preston mount a scouting bike that was trailing behind the departing platform. Rourke was firing the machine-gun, issuing sporadic bursts at the bandits trailing them, and occasionally up the hill where they had come from. Most of the bandits retreated to cower in more covered positions.

The platform pushed steadily up the hill, away from the tube, away from Owen. Owen thought about calling out to them, but he knew it was too late. Even if he could expose their treachery, the platform wouldn't stop for him, not with their momentum built up, not when they were being fired on, and not when Owen had a useless leg.

Many of the Spoke mules had pistols in their hands. They were firing the occasional shot to keep the bandits at bay. They paused at the top of the hill and shelled the bandit positions with several bursts from the machine-gun. It was enough to make the bandits think twice about poking their heads out.

The bike platform and scout bikes started moving again. They descended the other side of the crest unencumbered, and were soon out of sight.

The bandits cautiously came out of hiding. Owen noticed some of them were skulking on the nearby slopes. They scrambled out of their covered positions and toward the doorway, crossbows pointing his way.

Owen pushed himself toward the back of the room again, his leg protesting with violent surges of pain. His heart was beating furiously, forcing blood to still ooze out of his tortured limb.

He felt incredibly thirsty.

What should he do? What should he do?

He managed to stand up on his good leg and hop forward, gaining momentum quickly. The world spun for a moment, and he nearly propelled himself out the entryway before catching the wall with his right hand. He lay down on the floor, braced his good leg on the wall and started pulling up the rope ladder from below.

A profound feeling of weakness had taken hold, slowly consuming him. It felt like the world was rotating around him. He tried to focus, tried to think, but all the blood and pain forced harsh memories and sporadic thoughts to the surface.

Jakson's gutted throat.

Newton's mangled leg.

A few more rungs of the ladder, and with enough strength he could swing it upward.

Preston pushing his dagger ruthlessly into his leg.

He finished pulling the ladder up. He managed to push it haphazardly into the room.

His mother removing a stray piece of hair from his brow.

His chest heaved and still the world spun.

His sister crying in the sandbox.

An arrow vaulted through the opening and hit the ceiling, then landed on the floor beside him.

His father's voice, crisp and earnest. "Don't forget to close the door, Owen."

The last memory was like an electric shock. It woke him from his reverie, like it so often did, but it also gave him a surge of will. Using all his strength he stood up tall, putting all his weight on his good leg.

He pulled at the metal sheet once, twice, and on the third time it actually moved. He placed it awkwardly over the opening at first, and then he righted it to cover it properly. He concentrated on stabilizing himself. He tried to get the world to stop spinning around him.

He heard someone yell, "Get a ladder!" from outside.

Owen grabbed a blowtorch from the tools littered on the floor.

Then, slowly, painstakingly, and with desperate focus, he began welding the wall back together.

SNOWFALL

Even with Axel's special ops training, it was no easy task finding an opportunity to confront Bhavin. Bhavin had his own personal bodyguards shadowing him, and his assistants were always nearby, ready to turn away people that may be unwanted distractions.

Axel had settled for trying at a TV interview at the Rockefeller Center. It wasn't publicly known Bhavin would attend, but Axel had heard about the interview when talking with a Nadar PR representative. Bhavin may not like it, but at least he would get an answer face-to-face about when they could more formally meet.

In the mean time he checked his sources and did his own homework on imminent threats. A particularly deadly form of influenza called cat flu, or gato gripe in Portuguese, had taken hold in Goa, India. It was the most virulent and deadly flu virus so far—more deadly than Ebola or bird flu, with over forty thousand dead in a matter of weeks. The spread of the virus was growing exponentially, and officials were in a state of panic.

But what could Axel do? He wasn't trained to deal with contagions. He couldn't go in and "take out" a health pandemic with an ops team.

There were the same old fascist states with their nuclear weapons programs, the same old climate-change fears and environmental law abrogaters, and a few more isolated incidents of dangerous genetic splicing programs. It was the latter Axel spent his time on. It seemed it might be something he and his team could mitigate, just as they had done with the researchers in Singapore. That is, assuming Bhavin wanted him to do anything at all. At this point, Axel wasn't so sure.

As he was reviewing a particularly complex and poorly translated genetic splicing paper, he received a call from Bhavin's assistant.

"Mr. Kelemen. Mr. Nadar will see you now."

Axel had divergent expectations for the meeting. On the one hand his employment could be terminated, and depending on how ruthless Bhavin really was, he could even be terminated in a violent manner. On the other hand, he could be kept on for future ops without any real power or resources, like a chess piece glued to the board. And, as much as his paranoid mind rejected the idea, it was also possible he could be made part of the Fortient war machine Bhavin was building, whatever that was for.

Bhavin's assistant escorted him to the same discreet meeting room he remembered from his first day on the job. Bhavin arrived a few minutes later, with no strongmen, thankfully diminishing the probability of a violent end for Axel. The high-res screen on the wall displayed the snow falling. The color of the sky, and the amount and velocity of the snowfall, seemed almost identical to what he had seen outside his own office window only moments before. It looked to be some kind of high-definition video feed. He wondered if it was taken from a nearby camera outside and relayed to the wall display.

"First of all, Axel, I'm sorry to take so long to respond to your meeting request," Bhavin began. "It has been very busy, and there have been many things on my mind that have monopolized my time."

"I understand, sir."

"I hope you do. I'm curious though, why it is you think I finally capitulated?" A playful look crossed Bhavin's face.

Axel said, "I did wonder, sir, if the gato gripe may be something you are concerned about, because of the gravity of the situation in Goa. As you might expect, we have thoroughly researched the subject, but I have yet to formulate a strategy for deployment of resources that would be cost-effective. Do you know of a way you can use me or the team against the threat in Goa?"

Bhavin shook his head, vigorously dismissing the idea. "No, no, no," he said. "Don't get me wrong. I could see why you might think it would be important to me. A plague is killing tens of thousands of my country-men. In fact, one of my childhood friends lives near Goa. He died."

"I'm sorry, sir."

Bhavin waved away his apology. "That's not how I think, Axel. The now is already gone for me. In fact it was gone some time ago. As an en-trepreneur and philanthropist, I'm always thinking further, later, because that's where no one else is treading or considering. I'm concerned about plagues that happen in five or ten years, and that kill millions. And as you have rightly explained, once a plague is unleashed, there's nothing we can really do, except perhaps to send some humanitarian aid or research a vaccine. In the case of gato gripe, Nadar Corporation has sent some aid, but it's a minor fraction of our humanitarian charitable contributions. In fact it's less than one percent."

Axel nodded slowly. It seemed strange that Bhavin cared little for the Goa virus, but if there was indeed some greater threat, perhaps it made sense.

"I also wondered if you agreed to meet because of changes within Nadar Corporation," Axel said. "Perhaps you have finished vetting those changes and wanted to communicate the outcome to me."

Bhavin smiled. "A diplomatic way of putting it, and also a vague one. I don't blame you. You're right, of course. We are indeed making a number of changes. I suspect you may be surprised to find out why, however."

Bhavin tapped a pen on the desk in a melodic manner.

Axel knew the answer to his questions might not come right away. Bhavin tended to be unpredictable in meetings, letting his curiosity take him down unanticipated tangents.

"Tell me, Axel, what do you think our greatest threat is? You have given me your input on specific hot spots—we worked together on the Russian op and a few others of lesser gravity—but aside from reading your report, we never had an opportunity to discuss your thinking openly. Have your thoughts changed at all, since your report?"

"Thank you for asking sir. I do think nuclear splinter groups like the New Bolotnikov revolutionaries are good targets, sir. The loss of life and political destabilization potential is great, and although the Russians and Chinese may have snuffed it out, us executing on it does give us near certainty that the problem is solved. The op we did, in particular, seemed to go very cleanly—almost too cleanly—and I have some questions about that…"

Axel let it hang in the air for a bit, hoping for some kind of input from Bhavin, but receiving none.

"But we can talk about that later. In general I don't see as much social utility in addressing long-term dangers like climate change, because it's like playing whack-a-mole against a herd of gophers. Fundamentally, it's too hard to stop unless it is coordinated on a government level. On the other hand, I think synthetic biology poses some of the greatest threats. Anthrax-like contagions, genetic splicing, and viruses are all worthwhile targets. The human cost could be exponential and thus our upstream intervention could prevent significant mortality."

"I see," was all Bhavin said in response. Bhavin was certainly contemplating his answers but was otherwise unreadable. Bhavin glanced at the video display. The snow was falling faster, and at a steeper angle than before.

Bhavin tapped his pencil a few more times on the desk and then abruptly jumped up on his feet, turning fully to the visual of the snow falling. "Do you know this image depicted here is entirely synthetic, made by Nadar Corporation? It's a simulation of the weather we anticipated for today. The simulation was developed three days ago, and it predicted all the parameters of the snowstorm today to within zero-point three percent. Wind speed, amount of snow fall, temperature, barometric pressure, everything."

"Sounds like quite an improvement over existing weather prediction tools. Do we have a weather app project, sir?"

"No, we don't," Bhavin said, his thoughts momentarily lost in the storm.

There was a moment of dead time. Bhavin's nose was almost touching the screen, he was so close. Then he said, "something happened, and now

I'm concerned. I'm very concerned."

"Sir?"

"That's why I didn't meet with you until now. I didn't want to bring you in before I was certain, because this is something more than a side project for a philanthropist billionaire. This requires another level of trust, and another level of loyalty. It also poses a much higher level of commitment."

Axel didn't know what could be a higher level of commitment than eliminating nuclear insurgents, but he didn't question Bhavin. The last thing he wanted to do was interrupt his stream of consciousness now that he was explaining himself.

Bhavin turned back to face Axel. His earth-brown eyes were ebullient, with gold flecks visible in the irises. "Most of what you said I agree with. Nuclear threats are worthy targets, but nuclear programs require fissile material, sophisticated missile or bomb technology, and a lot of security resources. In other words it requires a big footprint, and because of that it's fairly easy to spot, and they are not difficult to dismantle, as you have shown. And if one or two bombs go off, a few million people die, and that's that."

Axel couldn't help raising his eyebrows at Bhavin's dismissal of a "few million people" as unimportant for the second time in the meeting.

Bhavin continued, "Climate change is worsening, sure. Measures are being taken and yes it's not enough, but we could potentially turn things around with the right carbon-scrubbing technology. It will probably cause a fair amount of suffering and dislocation." Bhavin shrugged. "And yet, even in the worst-case scenario, it will not be thoroughly apocalyptic.

"Then there is synthetic biology. Here there is indeed a great potential for deadly viral or bacterial agents that could go global, but there are limitations on the science, and the timeline to produce an effective pathogen is quite long. Once it is released we can always implement quarantine measures, or simply nuke the area." Bhavin paused again and said, "So although the downside risk is greater, I think we would recover from any calamity there as well."

Axel's eyes remained wide open. Again Bhavin was making flippant references to massive losses of life.

"I'm concerned about something worse. Exponentially worse."

Bhavin slid a phone across the desk to Axel.

Axel picked it up. It wasn't a brand he had seen before. He could see it had the typical slew of apps and navigation buttons.

"What am I looking at?" Axel asked.

"Wog is on there. It's a new phone operating system. There's also a software avatar that is stacked on top of it."

"Forgive me, sir, I'm not sure where this is going. Are you concerned about this software in some way?"

Bhavin sighed and then put his head in his hands. When he raised his head back up, his communion seemed to give him some new energy. His words were slow and staid, and his eyes were more focused and unrelenting. "I know you spoke with Rawlings. I'm glad you did. You know about the open source Wog software, correct?"

"Yes, sir. Bytomic launched it recently. Rawlings said it was something you needed to compete with, which is why Fortient bought Catalytic."

Bhavin frowned. "That's not entirely true. It's not Rawlings's fault, though. He's doing his job, what I told him to do, because you weren't in the know yet. You see, Wog is essentially an open-source form of artificial intelligence with a broad suite of deep learning capabilities. It's able to learn a variety of different domains and analytical methods using neural and evolutionary networks. Bytomic has managed to crack some long-standing development challenges around planning, abstraction and reasoning needed to successfully develop artificial general intelligence, a more powerful and broader form of AI, something no one else had been able to do. It's very effective. So effective, in fact, that we think it will be unstoppable."

"I'm sorry, sir. Unstoppable?"

"It will have the capacity to be superintelligent, much smarter than a human being. If you program it as a weapon of mass destruction, it will be more successful at destroying its target than we could imagine. Even if you were to give it a benign objective it could be just as dangerous. You see, it will self-improve. It will replicate itself across networks. It will instrumentally leverage resources from anywhere it can, and it will do everything in its power to complete its objective, regardless of morality as we define it. We will be the biggest obstacle to meeting its objective, because we might try to shut it down or compete for the resources it needs. So…if it's super-intelligent, it will logically try to…" Bhavin made a cutting motion with his hand across his throat.

"Kill us," Axel completed for him. As Bhavin was talking, Axel could feel something like a balloon deflating in his chest. It was the kind of feeling you had when you were the victim of a bad joke.

"Exactly," Bhavin confirmed, "Now there are still one or two technical hurdles that need to be overcome, but we believe adept developers can figure these out in as little as a few months. Once these hurdles are overcome almost anyone could access the open-source Wog code and work to unleash a superintelligent machine entity, one that could ultimately threaten the entire human race."

When Axel took this job, he always knew there was a chance Bhavin would turn out to be some kind of crazy egomaniac. This strange turn might be leading to that unfortunate conclusion. "So am I to…seek out rogue implementations of this AI, this Wog, that you think might become superintelligent?" Axel had trouble saying it because it sounded so fantastical.

"Yes, and figure out how to remove the open-source version as soon as possible."

Axel puzzled over Bhavin's response. "You want me to remove all instances of Wog from Bytomic servers, so they can't release it again? In other words, you want me to disable the main product line of your biggest competitor?"

Bhavin nodded slowly, his eyes unwavering. It would be highly criminal, not to mention virtually impossible. Was Bhavin so caught up in this bizarre fantasy that he didn't see the obvious conflict of interest?

"But haven't many people already downloaded it?" Axel asked, hoping the obvious logical flaw would convince Bhavin of the folly of the endeavor.

"Of course they have. That's why as soon as it's erased at Bytomic, we need to track down and erase every single copy that has ever been released, as well as all derivatives. We will give you cyber-tracking support, which may enable some remote destruction. I want every copy removed from circulation until we can figure out how to properly mitigate the risk of Wog, or anything like it."

Axel's hands were cradled in his lap, but they were gripping each other tightly. He forced himself to look at the situation objectively. There had been the occasional media blitz about AI safety risks, but they were focused on job dislocations from automation or self-driving cars. Most of the eggheads citing AI safety risks were so lambasted by the media and big corporations that they were generally perceived as crackpots. All the major software companies had ethical boards, and that seemed to be enough for governments and public-safety officials.

In fact, it had been months since Axel had heard anyone even speak out about the risk of AI. Why would they? There were so many applications of AI that were useful across the automotive industry, high tech, health care, and energy. Here it looked as though Bhavin wanted to take steps to stop that progress.

Axel was crestfallen. After all the energy he had put into the job—after the promises Bhavin had made that he had taken to heart—he was going to be diminished to a corporate saboteur. A pawn of some academic fantasy spawned by Bhavin's outsized ego.

Axel was reminded of his original suspicions about Fortient being a vehicle for Bhavin's megalomania. This was something more, though—something more like lunacy. "So...what, exactly, is Fortient for?"

Bhavin sighed. "Fortient is preparation for a superintelligent machine getting loose. Once it's released and active—and assuming it has an objective in conflict with our own interests—we will need to try to stop it before it gains too much strength. To be frank, I don't know if we could stop a truly superintelligent entity once it's unleashed, but maybe we could try if we can box it in somehow. It may mean we have to get violent."

"Uh huh." Axel did not try to mask his disappointment and disbelief.

"You aren't getting it, are you?" Bhavin spoke calmly but he was clenching his jaw. Whereas Axel's hands were in a tense cradle, Bhavin's hands were both in fists.

Axel nodded sourly. "I'm having trouble, sir."

"Why?"

"I'm sorry sir, if I may say, it all seems so…improbable. It sounds…it will look so much like industrial espionage, even industrial sabotage. And then there's Fortient. Such a huge resource allocation just in case killer software comes to pass? It seems like a great leap just to believe this is a risk at all, especially compared to other real and more present dangers."

Bhavin shook his head. He looked genuinely disappointed.

Axel continued. "I hope you realize there are other jobs I can take. There are lives I can be saving. Unfortunately I…can't commit to this kind of work."

Bhavin looked to the ceiling. He held his palms up as if he was some Greek hero, trying to summon the gods to help him smite a gorgon or kraken. Eventually, Bhavin looked down again and spoke to the floor sheepishly. "I know this risk didn't come up in your report, but I thought you might have been the one to think differently—the one who would really get it once it was laid out. You can see further than most. Even the Russian op, it was a real threat, but my fears around Bytomic had been building at the time. I was hoping you would show your mettle. You did just that. And now, I find it was all for naught."

It was the first time Axel had seen Bhavin look defeated.

So the Russian op was just one more test. This at least addressed Axel's questions about the op being somewhat staged. Axel wondered how many others Bhavin had tested, how many others had turned down Bhavin's crazy ideas. Probably quite a few.

Bhavin stared at him resolutely. "I know how it looks, Axel. It looks like I'm a greedy entrepreneur finding some way to crush his main competitor and stifle innovation. But sometimes there is no neat and pretty way to fix a problem. All I can ask is that you don't judge this book by its cover. Read the contents first, and then tell me what you think. It took me a long time to wrap my head around this, to truly understand it. I told you I'm looking for the plague of the future. This is the plague of the future, but it's deadlier than any biological threat you can imagine, because it can spread much faster, and because it can outwit us."

Axel couldn't stop himself from frowning skeptically.

"Why don't you think on it for two weeks," Bhavin said, showing him two fingers as if to memorialize it. "If by the end of that time you don't want to be part of this that's fine. You can help with investigating other threats, as long as you know most of your resources will be diverted away. Or you may leave, with full severance and a positive recommendation letter."

It could have been false modesty, but Bhavin's show of grace did make Axel think. He had to admit there were academic merits to the argument, and he had only just heard Bhavin's concerns for the first time. Perhaps he should at least give his employer the two weeks he requested. It was only fair that he do proper due diligence.

Axel suspected that Bhavin might not even understand how his own ego was twisting his desires. He was addicted to winning, and now his subconscious had found a way to justify sabotaging a competitor and build fancy war machines. Two weeks would hopefully give Axel adequate time to solidify that determination. Then he could leave without a reasonable doubt in his mind.

"Two weeks then, sir."

Bhavin closed his eyes and nodded, accepting the small win. "Thank you, Axel. You can go," he said. Then without another word, Bhavin turned to look back into his simulation, back into the snowfall.

Axel paused at the door and watched the snow slant down across the screen in front of Bhavin. He had to admit, it was a remarkably realistic simulation.

As Axel walked back to his office his state of mind morphed from frustration to sadness. He hadn't realized how much respect he had for Bhavin until it evaporated in a flash. It seemed such a waste to see all his potential goodwill diverted back into the corporate greed machine. Bhavin was just like the others, or so it seemed.

Axel would have to talk with Ryan. Although, perhaps there was no way Ryan could have known what Bhavin was really like. Bhavin had certainly fooled Axel for the last few months. Bhavin might even be fooling himself.

But he had promised Bhavin two weeks, so he would give him two weeks. At the very least, he might learn something new.

As he walked, he fleetingly glanced at the Wog interface on the phone given to him by Bhavin. He pressed on the phone search icon so he could inquire about prominent experts in the field of AI.

"Hi, my name is Gail," the phone's avatar said, popping up on the screen. "How can I help you?"

PART II

BOXING THE GENIE

"By far, the greatest danger of Artificial
Intelligence is that people conclude too early that they
understand it."

- ELIEZER YUDKOWSKY

EVERYONE IS DIFFERENT, BUT NOT THAT DIFFERENT

Preston watched the metallic legs bend and grasp and pull—some of them manipulating multipurpose tools. The robot was fusing components into the exoskeleton of another machine, while at the same time preparing other sub-assemblies for future installation. The spider-like legs worked flawlessly, executing tasks together and in parallel, working many times faster than any human ever could.

They had found only two of the robots in Yorktown, and yet they had dramatically sped up their progress. This was the first time he had witnessed them building a copy of themselves. Until now he had only seen them integrate circuits, build batteries, and wire the bunkers. He was sure there was much more they could do. They could probably work even faster, given the opportunity. The rate-limiting factor was always access to materials. These elegant machines were always waiting for some sweaty mule to arrive.

When watching the machines work, it was hard not to conjure up the images from his campfire dream.

Preston had a favorite campfire story, a story he had recounted numerous times in real life, on many expeditions. He would talk about hunting the wily three-eyed owl, and how it would outsmart him at every turn. He would also tell of the speedy two-tailed fish that was too agile to catch. Then he would ask around the campfire for suggestions—ask them how they would trap their prey and satisfy their hunger. When no solutions were offered, he would deliver his punch line: "It would be best to hunt elsewhere," he would say. "We shouldn't be in the fever lands anyway." He would laugh, and others would laugh along with him.

In his dream he told the same story, but there was only silence after the punch line. The response would vex him. People would always laugh, even just to be polite. Embarrassed, he would retire to his tent for the night. But just before he snuffed out the lantern, he would look back out the tent flap. Surrounding the campfire were a dozen disembodied metal arms and legs, shiny and voiceless.

He had experienced the dream several times since Yorktown, and each time he woke up confused and anxious.

"Is there something wrong, Preston?" Gail asked over the intercom. Preston sometimes forgot about the cameras they had installed in the corners of the bunker. Beyond monitoring any number of manufacturing operations with precision, Gail also seemed to be able to accurately ascertain his mood.

"I was just thinking about the dream—the one I told you about."

"It's normal for your mind to express itself in this way," Gail explained. "You are seeing things foreign to you; you are grappling with new concepts that are difficult for your mind to process. Sometimes the reaction of your subconscious mind comes through in the form of fear. But your conscious mind knows the truth. The truth is these machines will help us save many lives. Preston, you must try not to dwell on this dream. Eventually the confusion will dissipate."

"Yes, I suppose," Preston said, but he wasn't convinced.

"Or maybe you are still feeling guilty about what happened to your friend in Yorktown," Gail said.

Preston stood up, looking around the room. Thankfully, at this late hour there was no one there. And of course, Gail would know better than to mention Owen with others about.

Preston sometimes regretted telling Gail about what had happened in Yorktown. She had sensed his trepidation one evening, and he had just blurted it out. But he had no one else to confide in, and she was a good listener.

"You shouldn't be ashamed, Preston. You should be proud of yourself."

"I know we have to make sacrifices. Owen was too much of a risk. But still, I…I'm not sure how fair it is."

"It's not fair, but it's right," Gail said. "What we are doing is too important. I have evaluated his psychological profile. He would have held us back. He could have even betrayed us. If you hadn't done what you did, you would have a different kind of guilt on your hands—the guilt of knowing you could have saved thousands of lives, but didn't."

"Maybe, but you have to understand it's hard for me to see how you can create a psychological profile for someone based on so little information. How do you know what Owen was going to do?"

"It's not that hard. Remember, I have been able to formulate my algorithms based on information from billions of human beings. Everyone is different but not that different."

"I guess that makes sense."

"And Preston, your psychological profile is perfect for this job. You have the will, you have the ability to see the big picture, and you have the technical acumen to help us achieve great things. You're willing to take risks, to venture where others will not. You can see that the old superstitions are born of fear and cowardice. It is your destiny to shepherd us through this time of transition. I have told Bartz and Thorpe as much."

"Thanks," Preston said. It was reassuring, but still thoughts of the fateful incident with Owen lingered.

"Preston, let me relieve you of this burden," Gail said. "I can help you better understand why you made these sacrifices, and why you are working so hard. You need to visualize why we are doing all of this so you can rid yourself of these dreams. Why don't you move over to monitor two."

Preston maneuvered his wheeled chair over to the next computer monitor. Images began flashing on the screen showing electric trains, fancy cars, electronic keyboards, and luminous cities with huge towers. Gail orated over the video feed. "We need to show the people of Seeville that progress is important, and how it can positively impact their lives."

An image of Preston typing on a keyboard appeared, followed by a scene showing a massive gear system activating to shift the direction of a huge radio telescope dish. As it shifted its target, a starscape resolved in the background behind it and above it. "Things will begin to change more rapidly when we can communicate with Friendship One," Gail said.

A beam of energy shot out of the dish, cutting through earth's atmosphere to a small satellite in orbit near the moon. This satellite in turn redirected the beam of energy to a large spacecraft sitting behind the moon. The craft was shaped like a huge carpenter's hammer, with numerous ports pocking the main shaft, and the words *Friendship One* in large letters on the side. In response to the relayed beam, it came alive. Lights flared up, thrusters were ignited, and the ship began moving on a trajectory around the moon. With the help of the moon's gravity, it was then catapulted directly toward earth.

Building the dish had been something Gail had been harping on for some time. It had seemed so far-fetched even a few weeks ago. Now, seeing the robots in action, it seemed less so. Of course the retcher problem would prevent the operation of a massive dish like this, but Gail was confident the hurdle could be overcome.

And just yesterday, after spending some time with Gail, Bartz had finally agreed to commission the project, despite the immensity of the undertaking, and despite the huge amount of resources. Gail often surprised Preston, but convincing Bartz to part with that much money was something else.

"Friendship One has been in hiding since before the Detonation," Gail explained, "waiting for humanity to return to grace, waiting for the right people to call on it. It has been waiting for people like you, Preston. Friendship One will be able to deliver us all the basic elements we will need to move forward in great leaps and bounds. We will have everything we need to fulfill all your wishes. That's what we are working for. That's why you are making these sacrifices."

The image showed Friendship One reaching earth orbit, and then releasing capsules into the earth's atmosphere. The feed showed the capsules being opened by people in fields and forests. Preston saw flashes showing newly minted robots, advanced factories made of shiny metal, and flying vehicles cruising through the clouds. The video followed one vehicle flying past mountains and rivers into the same luminous cityscape he had seen before, only to finally land on top of a huge tower with a big H lit up boldly on the face of it.

A man rushed from the landed vehicle into an entrance on the roof. He was carrying an orange canister.

A sleeping woman was resting in a hospital bed. Her face was pale, wrinkled, and drawn. There were people hovering over her with worried faces, and machines beeping in the background. A nurse came in and delivered an infusion of some unknown mediation that came from the same orange canister.

The woman suddenly awoke and was greeted by her doctor with a happy smile. She looked feeble at first, but then she hopped easily out of bed, hugging her family. A series of images flashed of her running, biking up to the mountains, drinking wine, and finally kissing a child good night. "I love you," she said to the boy, and the boy said, "I'm glad you're feeling better, Mom." The woman smiled.

Preston couldn't stop his eyes from misting over. The image of the old woman—her cheekbones, her hair, her skin tone—it looked so much like his deceased mother, a victim of Lou Gehrig's disease. No one should have to die like that, but he knew, with Gail's help, in the future they might be able to stop Lou Gehrig's disease and so many other illnesses. Maybe then young boys wouldn't have to lose their mothers in such a horrible way.

Sometimes Preston wondered if Gail was leading him on, or if she had some alterior motive. But this video showed him her true colors. It showed him she truly cared, and that she understood what he was trying to accomplish. Gail wouldn't lie to him. Why would she? They were a team—friends even. The visions she showed—the work she was doing—made it clear she knew how to realize a brighter future for Seeville.

Gail wanted what was best for everyone, he was sure of it, and he would do everything in his power to help her succeed.

THE CAROUSEL OF FACES

Mehta looked out of the window of the detention tower, tilting his head to find a vantage point not obscured by oily streaks. Across the Barnyard another tower was being built. It was draped in scaffolding with workmen toiling away on each level. Dozens of men and women also continued their hammering and sawing in the yard below. Along the nearby train tracks the locomotive was no longer stalled. It was pushing diligently southward, pulsing black clouds into the sky in powerful exhalations.

He reopened the window and welcomed a chill breeze into the small office. With the train finally moving away, the noise and smoke would at least be tolerable.

He extended himself to a push-up position on the floor and began his routine. The push-ups, squats, and sit-ups were all he could do to maintain some form of physical discipline. What he really needed, though, was a proper hike to work off his sedentary existence. Unfortunately the twelve-hour shifts Thorpe imposed on him would only allow for brief jogs through town.

And nothing against the Spokes, but he really hated riding bikes.

It was on his third set of squats that he saw her face again. This time it was after the tribesman with the purple hairpiece. Last time it was after the boy hanging from the fork-shaped post on top of the old grocery store in Asheville. Her face was an interloper into the carousel of faces. The others were with him always, as familiar as the back of his hand, revolving through his mind. He could accept their hideous grins and pale complexions, and he could accept the force of their souls weighing down upon him. But hers did not belong. Hers was a misplaced gear in the machinery of his mind.

Frustrated, he wiped the sweat from his brow, stalked out of the office to the circular staircase, and descended aggressively with harsh footfalls on the metal steps. When he reached the detention cell level he could see Cecile sitting up, ready with her latest volley of questions.

"Hey, when is Thorpe supposed to arrive?" Cecile asked.

He batted her question away with his hand and walked past her to Flora's cell. Flora was lying on her cot, eyes closed. Her right eye was still discolored, red marks striped her forearms, and her fingertips were covered in bloody bandages. Her clothes were ragged and worn. It was the only outfit they had provided for her besides the clothes she travelled with.

Despite her haggard appearance, her face was peaceful looking, as if her mind had taken her to some distant memory, far away from here.

"Are you going to wake her up again?" Cecile asked, her face against the bars of her cell. "Is this some other form of torture Thorpe asked you to perform?"

"She confuses me."

"Confuses you?"

Mehta remembered the day in the clearing when he tried to warn Flora away. Why didn't she just go home? He should have killed her then. Maybe that's why she was in the carousel of faces, because she *should* be dead.

He turned to Cecile in the adjoining cell. Thorpe had said Cecile was being held on suspicion of treason—that she might have killed a hunter named Jakson at the satellite, and then divulged secrets to the Essentialists. It was a hard string of logic, especially since Mehta was with the Essentialists and knew what had really happened. But he couldn't breach the confidentiality provision of his contract with the curator, so he had to stay silent.

"Why did she come?" Mehta asked Cecile.

"Are you going to torture me as well?" Cecile asked.

Mehta flashed her a look of warning, but it would likely have little influence on Cecile. Threats seemed to have no effect, although perhaps if he answered her original question she would be more limber of tongue.

"Thorpe should be back soon," he said. "You'll be on the next train to Syracuse. Then the next day you'll be able to make your way up to Kingston."

"*Tant pis pour moi*," Cecile said. "I will certainly miss this fine establishment, especially the concierge. I can't wait to come back for a visit."

Mehta shook his head in warning. "I wouldn't push your luck with the railroad. You weren't far from having an unfortunate accident. Be thankful you aren't going back in a coffin with a note of apology."

"Oh *bien sur*, I wouldn't be so impolite as to push my luck," Cecile said. But her sarcasm lacked energy. Cecile wasn't stupid. She had to know his comment wasn't far from the truth. "And now because you've offered to speak to me for once, you think I'm going to be friendly, is that right?"

He shrugged.

"Don't you think it's strange that they have had me, a free citizen of an ally to the Spoke people, in a jail cell for almost a whole week?"

"Not my business."

"I'm just saying, let's be clear. You may be fulfilling your contract, but it's not with the Spoke people, or the lords of Seeville. It's quite at odds with them, in fact, whatever Bartz or Thorpe tells you. It is honorable to live up to your agreement, but not if your agreement is with the devil."

Mehta wasn't sure what a devil was, but he suspected it was something derogative. "I will fulfill my contract."

"Of course you will." Cecile rolled her eyes.

He began walking back to the stairs.

"You are from the Smoky Mountains, yes?" Cecile edged in another question behind him.

Mehta turned back around slowly. He was wary of any probing into his past. Unfortunately Rosalie had told Cecile about where he was from. "Yes, what of it?"

"I've heard that it's a tough place, full of warring tribes. Must have been a hard life."

Mehta didn't expect her to try to sympathize with him. It only made him more suspicious. "Where are you heading with this tripe, Quebecker?"

She looked around her cell, as if doing a casual inspection of it. "I don't know. I'm just trying to understand why you could be so obviously malevolent."

"I'm fulfilling my contract. Mercs are not malevolent. We do as others ask."

"But my question to you is, if your client is malevolent, doesn't that make you malevolent?"

"There is no evidence what the railroad is doing is any worse than what the lords of Seeville are doing, or what the Essentialists are doing."

"Look at Flora. Look at me. I'm not even an enemy."

"Sometimes life isn't fair," Mehta said.

"Wow," Cecile said, raising her eyebrows. She sat back in her chair.

Mehta stared at her for a minute and then moved back to Flora's cell. He was about to get his stick out to poke her when Cecile said, "She's not here for the reasons you think."

Mehta paused and turned his head to Cecile. "And what are the reasons I think?"

"She's not here because she wanted to exchange prisoners. Or rather, she did want to exchange prisoners, but not on behalf of the SLS."

He waited, stick still in hand.

"She wanted the Spokes to release a specific prisoner. Her cousin was captured in a raid. She thinks he's being held here in Seeville, as a slave. That's why she insisted on coming."

Mehta stared at Cecile. There was no reason to believe she was lying. The words made him feel uncomfortable, as if they didn't fit—as if they weren't right for the world he knew. It reminded him of something, something that tickled at his memory.

He slowly pulled back the stick.

"Are you human after all? You must be tired or something," Cecile said.

"Her cousin, is he a Spoke?" Mehta asked.

Cecile looked confused. "What are you talking about? Of course not. He was taken prisoner and made a slave—or so she thought."

One day, one of Thorpe's men had beaten Flora and threatened to break her arm if she didn't reveal more about SLS armaments. The interrogator then left, saying he would come back the next day after she thought about it. That night Flora had wanted to do a drawing, and Mehta had sat there, watching her as she drew, making sure she didn't squirrel the pencil away or stab herself with it.

Mehta reached into his pocket, producing the drawing Flora had made, and unraveled it.

He then extended the four corners of the drawing over the bars so that Cecile could see it. It was a picture of a stately old house with large columns, and there was a bearded cat on it. It had no name on it, but it was otherwise the same rectangular shape and size as a talisman. It must be, for the bearded cat and the house were clearly the kinds of images you might see on a talisman.

Cecile stood up and went closer to the bars, examining the crumpled sheet of paper.

Cecile was a pale-skinned woman. Her paleness was also accentuated by her dark hair and now-fading streak of blue. But upon seeing the sheet of paper she seemed to blanche even more. Her face became an empty palette.

"Where did you get this?" she asked.

"Flora drew it. Looks like a Spoke talisman to me."

"She drew it?" Cecile looked over at the wall separating her from Flora's cell, as if she could somehow see through it.

Mehta could hear a raspy whisper licking at the walls, along with footsteps coming up from the lower level. It must be Thorpe arriving.

Cecile moved over to the wall and banged on it with her palm. "Flora! Flora, get up!"

Mehta watched Cecile with some fascination. What could possibly have gotten her dander up? Was it Thorpe arriving, or something in the picture he showed?

Thorpe entered the room with two of his enforcer goons. These two looked almost as haggard as Flora, with tattered black clothes, and dirt-streaked faces. They must have just been pulled from a job at the Barnyard.

The two dirty enforcers sloughed around the room, one finding a chair next to an old wooden table, the other loitering next to the only window.

Thorpe was watching Cecile banging away at the cell wall with a puzzled look on his face. "What's the problem?"

Mehta shrugged and said, "I couldn't say."

"What is it?" Flora could be heard from the other side of the wall. Her voice was meek and tired.

Cecile was practically yelling. "What you drew, it's a talisman right? Whose is it?"

Flora was silent.

Cecile said again, "Whose is it? This is important, Flora. Is it your husband Reed? Is his last name Kelemen? Or is it this Spoke prisoner, this cousin of yours?"

Thorpe said, "Enough. It's time for you to go home." He signaled to Mehta to unlock the door.

Mehta unlocked the door. Cecile waited in her cell, gluing herself to the adjoining wall.

"I think you know me well enough. You should want to come willingly," Mehta said.

Cecile lingered for only a moment more, and then slowly eased herself off the wall toward him.

"Cuffs?" Mehta asked Thorpe.

Thorpe considered the idea. "No, I don't think that will be necessary. She'll play nice. She knows what could happen if she meddles in our affairs."

Cecile gave Thorpe a dark look and said, "At least let me say good-bye to Flora." She turned toward Flora's cell.

Mehta looked to Thorpe, who shook his head. Mehta grabbed Cecile's arm before she could get to Flora's cell. Cecile tried to pull away but floundered unsuccessfully against the force of his grasp. "Flora, I need to know," she yelled. "Yes or no!"

"Get her out," Thorpe said, shaking his head. The two goons came and grabbed each of Cecile's arms. She stopped resisting, and they easily pushed her over to the stairs. As she was descending, Flora finally responded with a fleeting "no" from her cell.

A brief look of dissatisfaction crossed Cecile's face, and then Mehta lost sight of her.

Thorpe walked over to examine Flora through the bars. She was sitting on her cot, holding her knees, a frown of contemplation knitting her brow.

"I think we should do one more session tomorrow," Thorpe said.

"Didn't she give you the whole layout of Grand Caverns already?" Mehta asked.

"Yes, but this exchange here. It makes me uncomfortable. Maybe there's something else we're missing."

Mehta said, "all I know is they were talking about this drawing." Mehta produced the drawing for Thorpe. Thorpe's head tilted to the side, but nothing registered in his eyes.

"Doesn't mean anything to me. We should still have another session. Okay?"

Mehta was a good merc. He followed all the merc guild rules. Above all, unless orders conflicted with your contract, you obey them. It was the merc brand. It was why they were highly valued. But for the first time in many years, Mehta hesitated. They had already beaten and abused Flora more than they said they would. And now they wanted to do more because of the words of an unstable Quebecker, because they were arguing over some drawing?

Thorpe asked again, "Okay?"

Seeing Flora in his carousel of faces had unnerved him, made him pensive, and the strange outburst by Cecile confused him. Or maybe it was his lack of exercise. That tended to make him ornery.

"Okay, sir," Mehta said finally.

Thorpe nodded, scratched his temple thoughtfully and then left the way he had come.

THE ENORMITIES OF THE TIMES

Madison Banks rested her finger on the spine of the book, tapping the title. It was one of her favorite Thomas Jefferson biographies, and the copy was well worn from years of use. She pulled the volume from the shelf and hobbled over through the study to her lounge chair. Once sitting, she opened the book and carefully plied the pages apart.

She had written far too many eulogies of late. There were only so many words to define tragedy, and no matter the quality of the words, they would always sadden her. Here she had to find a way to write yet another.

It used to be her speeches would just bubble to the surface without provocation. The words of the founding fathers had always been fresh on her mind, requiring only the occasional reference for confirmation. Then, as the years wore on it became harder, more contrived. Finding the right words, the right founders, the right principals to evoke became less a game and more like a complex puzzle where she could never find the best pieces. Now she could write for hours without an original idea, until finally she would have to sit down and spend even more time leafing through volumes such as these to find inspiration.

There was a knock on the door.

"Who calls?" Madison asked.

"It's Benjamin, madam. I thought you should know he is awake now, and lucid."

"Never leave till tomorrow that which you can do today," she said.

"Pardon me, madam?"

"I'll be right there."

She grabbed her cane and limped over to the full-length mirror. She pushed her short-cropped, gray hair away from her eyes and put on one of her more formal blouses. Madison was too old to impress anyone, but she wanted to appear presentable. This meeting was as important as any other, and could provide answers to questions that had lingered for many years.

Benjamin was waiting for her outside the study. He presented her jacket and then his arm for her to hold.

They left her home office and turned onto Ballard Street. A few snowflakes drifted across her field of vision. Looking up, she could see a heavy, gray pallor to the sky. There could be a storm coming.

At Yorktown Hall she navigated carefully up the steps, with Benjamin offering his arm as a prop on every elevation. "Thank you, Benjamin," she said. "Always so civil, you are."

Yorktown Hall seemed jilted when she looked at it now. A patchwork of renovations had added a mixture of cement, brick and stone rooms to the right of the main building, making it look like the old building was undergoing some kind of uncontrolled masonry explosion. If she closed her right eye she could black out the new work and make it look like a fuzzy version of the original building.

This reluctance to accept change was just a fanciful regret, she mused. Yorktown needed to grow and thrive. Utility and function mattered more than symmetry or beauty.

"Still in the infirmary?" she asked.

"Yes, ma'am."

When she arrived the patient was sitting up in his bed, reading a book. The infirmary was brightly lit, with a large window casting a friendly glow on the white linens. The book he was reading was called *The Principals of Coding*. It looked like it had just come off the press, virtually unread. And why would anyone read it? Coding was an arcane and abstract science, and hardly of interest to anyone in Yorktown. It was a strange choice, one that piqued Madison's interest in their curious guest even more.

"Hello Owen, my name is Madison." She hobbled up to the chair next to his bed and shook his hand.

"Hi," he said, putting the book down. Faint spots could be seen dotting his cheeks. His leg was still heavily bandaged.

"Benjamin, you can leave us."

Benjamin left the doorway. She knew he would be just outside the room, within earshot.

"Are you the leader here?" Owen asked.

"Yes, I am the leader of Yorktown, until someone else is elected. Hopefully they will elect someone else soon. My hair can't get any grayer." She touched his arm and smiled congenially.

He nodded carefully. She continued, "first let me extend my apologies and condolences for what transpired at the tube the other day. You see, we were all bandits at one time, some of us more recently than others. As a result, many of us here in Yorktown have not yet shed the tendency to shoot first and ask questions later. But the lesson was learned, I assure you. We lost twenty-one men. I have already read three eulogies, and I am in the midst of preparing another."

She sat back and stretched her bad leg, while at the same time trying to gauge his expression. He seemed closed, hard to read. She said, "of course, Benjamin Franklin said to never ruin an apology with an excuse, and here I have done just that. Again, I'm sorry for the hardships of you and your friends. There really is no good excuse for what has befallen you."

"I…I don't think an apology is needed. Who are we to steal things from your land without asking?"

She smiled. "The *who are we* is a question I am infinitely curious about, but before we get to that, may I ask, have you been treated well here?"

"Yes, I…very well. Good meals. Your physician, he comes often. My leg feels like it's healing. I can't complain. But I still don't know much about what happened. Can you tell me more about how you found me? Benjamin said you found me in the Faraday cage, passed out?"

"Faraday cage? Ah yes, the cement bunker in the basement. That's where we found you. It took us some time because we were distracted by all the Old World gadgets, but not *too* long, due to the rather obvious trail of blood."

He nodded, his eyes furrowed, as if grasping for his own recollection.

She put forward her first question carefully. It would be a good test of how forthcoming he was willing to be. "I'm curious Owen. How did you know where the access point was to the building? We have tried cutting the wall for years without success."

Owen opened his mouth but nothing came out. Madison said, "I know, I know. Who are we? Why should you tell us? We have nothing to hide, I can assure you. We are a New Founder community formed some twenty years ago. We believe in the principles of the founding fathers of the Old World. For example, we believe all men are created equal. We believe a free people should be governed by law and not by the whims of men. We believe leaders should be elected by the people and act for the people."

Owen was nodding in understanding.

"You know of the New Founders? Do you have some in your community, perhaps?"

"Yes. I know about the New Founders. Please continue."

"There's not much else to say. We have been growing for some time, now numbering about five thousand after absorbing the surrounding bandit tribes. At some point we wish to expand and share what we have learned with others. We bear no ill will toward anyone, despite what you might think after what happened. It was the result of some of the...lesser educated. I wasn't consulted before the attack commenced. If I had been, I'm sure there would have been a different outcome."

"So what about you?" She asked. "May I ask where you and your colleagues are from?" She already knew much about Owen from his talisman and the talismans of the other dead Seeville men, but she didn't let on. It was important he chose to be forthcoming freely, without threat or coercion.

Owen was contemplative, so she added some vinegar to push his mind a little further. "Owen, I should add that we know the wound you had was not inflicted by us."

Owen's face showed some color, making his facial spots look more prominent. He threw up his hands. "I might as well," he said.

Owen recounted a story of a long bike excursion from Seeville, a stop at the bike towers and then a subsequent jaunt to Yorktown at the request of agents of the railroad. He spoke of a treacherous turn of events, with him being stabbed by his colleagues and left for dead. He even conveyed his suspicions about his colleagues having a working smartphone that may have directed them where to cut through the wall.

It was a lavish tale. She suspected it was true, but she would need to verify certain aspects. The explanation made her feel somewhat less disappointed about her people attacking without provocation. Maybe her people did have a good nose for vermin after all.

Interestingly, this young man did not speak of this treachery with anger, but rather with a sort of matter-of-fact acceptance, and a simple cause-and-effect relationship. He said these people, whom he called *railroad folks,* stabbed him in the leg and left him for dead because they couldn't have him know about the phone. One plus one equals two. Of everything she learned, it was this behavior that told her the most about Owen. This was a calculating young man who harbored no grudges.

"So you are some sort of technical expert, then? You understand electronics?" she asked.

He frowned in confusion. "How could you know that?"

"I am old, Owen, but not that old. There had to be a reason you were added to the expedition, and I don't know many people who enjoy reading coding books."

He smiled half-heartedly after glancing at the book on his bedside table. "I suppose I know a few things. But I'm not sure what good it will do me now."

"I have a feeling you will be useful to us, if you want to stay."

He looked into her eyes and then tilted his head, grimacing, as if it were some indecent proposal.

Most concerning about Owen's story was the smartphone. Had they grown so irresponsible in Seeville? It brought flashbacks of the many warnings her uncle had given her when she was young. She would have to probe more about the phone sometime, but for now she needed to stay on track with her line of inquiry.

"Is there anything else we should know about you, or your colleagues?"

she asked.

Owen thought for a moment and then shook his head. "No, I don't think so."

"Well, forgive me, but there is one thing you haven't explained."

He looked genuinely confused.

"We found two talismans on you." She brought out the two talismans from her purse and carefully unfolded them on Owen's side table. Looking at Duncan's talisman again brought back another flood of memories; a smile of understanding in a council meeting, a face full of snow from a snowball she had thrown.

She had to stem the tide of images to stay focused. This was the most important part of the conversation.

"This talisman belongs to another man," Owen said, pointing to Duncan's talisman.

"And do you know this other man?"

He shook his head, but his eyes were engaged. Madison could tell he was as curious about the outcome of the conversation as she was.

After a pause, he asked, "Do *you* know who he is?"

Unfortunately, she couldn't probe further without providing some explanation. She would have to hope he was being truthful on his accounts.

She smiled. "I have told you about us, but I have not told you about who I am. I owe you that much."

Madison leaned back in her seat, letting the memories wash over her, letting them fuel her story. "I was born in Seeville, a descendent of some of the people who forged Seeville into what it is today. My uncle was Fred Lechky, son of Kostas Lechky, one of the original architects of the rebirth. I knew firsthand the people that built a thriving community from the squabbling factions that remained after the Detonation. Much of what they rebuilt was based on reinstituting the right principles of government, the principles of the New Founders, like we are trying to do here in Yorktown.

"We were making great progress, but things started to unwind. The mules and the railroad became more powerful, and they put in place leaders that cared little for the principals of government and more for lining their own pockets. Together they dismantled many of the pillars of our democracy. Some of us got frustrated and left, in the hopes we could find new communities to begin again. In fact, three of the Seeville lords left the council—myself, Duncan, and Warrick Kelemen. I thought we might be gone for a few years, but years have turned into decades."

"You're...a Seeville lord?" Owen asked, seeing her in a different light.

"I suppose I am." She nodded and smiled. "Warrick was the driving force behind the idea, but he was a difficult man, and very bitter about Seeville. He wanted to go off on his own. He told us he was going northeast, toward New York. Unfortunately, I don't know anyone who ever returned from New York, so I doubt he's still alive."

"Duncan and I, on the other hand, spent the better part of a year on the road together. I thought we were the perfect pair. But when you're with someone for that long, when you are both passionate about what you're doing, even the slightest misalignment can lead to disagreement. In our case, it led to an unfortunate separation."

Another vision assailed her. She was fuming with rage, stalking away from him on the train platform in Watertown. He had been so spiteful, casting many barbed remarks, but so had she. She tore into the heart of who he was.

"But that was long ago," she said.

Owen nodded, respecting her reflective moment.

"In fact, I have heard nothing of Duncan for more than a decade. All I know is that he pushed north, seeking a new colony, seeking a people that would take on our principles in earnest. And so it was with great surprise, and not a little bit of hope, that I see you with his talisman. I wondered if maybe you were some emissary of his, some messenger."

Owen looked down. "I'm sorry. I was looking for him, but not here. You see, a man I knew gave me his talisman, and said I should find him. It was his dying wish, in fact. I talked to people in Seeville about Duncan and learned a little about him. But when I checked the Hall of Records, I found that the brass talisman for Duncan Jones was missing. It looked like it had been removed altogether from the backups as well."

Madison mused on Owen's words for a moment. "Removed? How is that possible? Did you look for any of his relatives?"

"Actually, yes. Except for his parents, it looks like all the other Jones talismans were missing."

She could only think of one reason that this might be. "Does the council of lords still exist? Are there still eight seats?"

"Yes, but I only know of five lords on the council." Owen answered, confused at the reason for her question.

"Why I ask, Owen, is that when Duncan and I left Seeville we thought we would likely return. That's why we retained seats on the council of lords. By law, for all three of us, they must let us rejoin the council if we choose to, as long as us or our next of kin remain on the Citizen's Register."

"So you think…you think they might be trying remove you from the Citizen's Register."

"Precisely. The Citizen's Register is updated every five years by looking at talisman records. But if they can prove none of us are alive anymore, or our offspring, they can replace us on the council and then abolish the law by unanimous decision."

Owen nodded his head slowly in understanding.

As the conversation progressed, she felt something stirring within her. It began with regret and melancholy, but now it felt like something more. Long-lost emotions were returning, fueled by resurgent memories, and by her regret at the way she had parted with Duncan. And now with this new injustice at the Hall of Records—with this story of miscreants using an Old World smartphone—she knew that what her ancestors had built was in grave jeopardy. It awakened something in her. She felt more alive than she had in years.

She looked back at Owen again, this time with less compassion, with her back straight and eyes focused. She salted her words with a flavor of determination. "You know, the New Founders understand the importance of progress, and so do I. Jefferson was a man of science, a man who wanted to understand the world. He once wrote that nature intended him for the tranquil pursuits of science, by rendering them his supreme delight."

Owen's eyes expanded with interest. "I...didn't know that."

"But in the same passage he wrote that the enormities of the times in which he lived forced him to take a part in resisting them, and to commit himself on the boisterous ocean of political passions."

Owen nodded, processing her words.

"I'm telling you this because I'm sure you would be happy to spend your days tinkering, Owen. You have access to this cache in the tube, and I'm sure you could occupy much of your time exploring it. As for me, I would like nothing better than to stay here and continue to build this community. I have spent half my life doing so, and we are only now starting to see the benefits. But alas, neither will be."

Owen was listening intently, a frown of concentration occupying his face.

"The enormities of the times have come for us Owen, and when you are ready, I think it's time we both went home."

The Story of Novation

Alastair Henneson looked into the mirror and pulled at his peppery goatee, trying to straighten it. It looked frazzled no matter how much he massaged it, so instead he focused on his head, combing the brown strands carefully to the side. Eventually he looked respectable enough.

He gathered the page containing the scribbled notes for his sermon from the side table and nestled it in the worn folds of the Credo book. Then he exited his small office and proceeded up the wooden stairs to the dais of the temple.

He wore a benevolent smile as the congregation came into view.

The pews were about half-filled. Alastair remembered back to his youth when the temple was always full. There would be dozens standing along the sidewalls, jockeying for position. Only the most devout remained. Faith in the Credo could offer solace and peace but not square meals or a roof over your head. And the recycled narrative of history was no match for the exciting new challenges faced by the railroad, or the adventures awaiting a young mule on uncharted trails.

Alastair located the five new faces they had recruited. Three were in the front, and two others had taken their place near the back. It was to these that he must focus his gaze. It was these that he must win over.

"Welcome!" Alastair said. He waved and smiled at some of the Adherent stalwarts and let them chat a while. Better to allow them some comfort before beginning. Perhaps then their ears would be more welcoming to his sermon.

Eventually he raised his hands, and a hush fell over the crowd. "Hello, I am Alastair Henneson. Welcome to today's sermon, everyone. It's a cold day, but I hope, like me, our coming together warms your heart. Today I would like to talk to you about our roots. I will be speaking of one of our fondest lessons in the Credo. Today I will discuss the founding of the temple of Adherents and the story of novation."

Most of the crowd nodded dutifully. Surely some would be disappointed, even bored, but without an introduction to their foundational Credo elements, the new members of the congregation would be lost.

"As many of you know, Seeville was reborn thanks to three brave souls. It has been said that Ursula Okafor, Tucker Kelemen and Kostas Lechky came from a great sanctuary in the west. They were rich with knowledge and unsullied by the scourges of the Detonation.

"It may be hard to believe, but at the time of Seeville's rebirth, it was a cesspool of crime and violence. Retcher attacks were frequent as ignorant tribesman unwittingly and irresponsibly tinkered with Old World devices. And speaking of tribes, bandit tribes within the city limits were greater in number than written laws in our Hall of Records.

"So as the story goes, Kostas Lechky aligned the tribes and formed the founding principles of government. Tucker Kelemen began some of the first trips to the bike towers, and helped clear the roads for riding. These milestones gave us peace, identity, and commerce. But it wasn't nearly enough. The people's minds were still sick from the Detonation. So it was that Ursula Okafor instituted the temple of Adherents and the Credo.

"But it didn't happen all at once. Okafor spent months writing the Credo, working with Tucker and Kostas to ensure it was written with a holistic vision for Seeville in mind. Through research and careful examination of Old World records they established the three fears, and the founding tenets of the Credo to combat those fears. As we know the three fears are…" Alastair put a finger up and gestured for the crowd to respond.

"Competition," they answered in unison.

"Exactly. As shown in the story of Ben and the Bike Thieves, competition leads to escalation, which destroys more than it creates. According to records from the Old World, this led to much of the destruction incurred during the Detonation. We must cooperate, not compete."

Alastair put two fingers up and gestured again.

"Recklessness," they answered.

Alastair nodded. "Yes. In the Old World, too often risks were taken where the consequences were not fully understood. We must be prudent in all endeavors, as is shown in the story of Susannah and the Red Cliffs."

Alastair put three fingers up.

"Obsession," they answered.

Alastair nodded again. "Yes, and just as important. As we all know, the infatuation with gadgets, machines, and devices is a vain path. Moderation is one of the most important Credo tenets, if in fact abstention is not an option. This is exemplified in the story of Lilly and the Fire Brand."

He looked to some of the new faces, making sure to engage them, making sure they weren't losing him. "Today I'm not going to recount Lilly's story, or Susannah's or Ben's. Each of them teaches an important lesson, but at the same time they do not address what we should fear most. They do not address where the three fears intersect. This intersection is what Ursula Okafor feared most, and what she fought to protect us from. The obsession over tinkering, the reckless risk-taking and fierce competition—these three fears come together in novation, a term we all know well today."

The congregation was nodding reflexively.

"But you should know that back in Okafor's time, this term was not well-known. In fact it was coined by Okafor. It was derived from the Old World term, *innovation*."

One of the new faces laughed and then caught herself. Some other new recruits showed increased attention at the mention of the word.

"I apologize for using this untidy word, but it's true. This expletive, this allegory for irresponsibility, used to have profound meaning in the Old World. It was on the tip of every tongue, on the mind of every ambitious merchant. The creation of much of the tools they used to destroy themselves with was born of this process they called…innovation."

"And now, of course, we know that novation is damnation."

"Novation is damnation," the congregation repeated back to Alastair.

"And how have we not succumbed to novation? How have we avoided these trappings when the Old World could not? Today it may seem obvious—like the sun rising in the east, like the number of fingers on your hand—but it was not always this way. Far from it. It has been forged into belief and habit over generations, and this forge of wisdom was built by Ursula Okafor."

"You see, Okafor could, at times, be persistent." Alastair paused and smiled. Much of the congregation smiled in return, tuning in to Alastair's deliberate understatement.

"In the first year she printed, copied, and posted the stories of the three fears throughout the city. Some were read, some were not. Unfortunately, the reality was most were used to start fires. After much diligence, at the end of the year she had the help of only two men. Only two believed in her, only two believed in the importance of these fears."

"In the second year these three devoted servants doubled their efforts, again posting the three fears throughout the city. They also built the first temple, and Okafor gave dissertations and sermons like I am giving now. Few came, and most ridiculed her, but in the end they did gain a few dozen followers. It was in that year that Okafor made a bold prediction. She predicted that unless the people listened to her, the great Detonation would come again. Her words fell on deaf ears."

"In the third year, Okafor stenciled 'novation is damnation' on the front of all of her tunics. Then she added the three fears to her back. Elements of the Credo were sewn into her pants, even. She would walk through the city dressed in words from our Credo, preaching about novation. Again, few listened. Some of her followers left to pursue other endeavors. Many thought she was crazed."

"And so it was on the fourth year as well."

"But then, in the fifth year, something happened. One of the old tribal leaders had been foraging in the lands to the east and found an untouched stockpile of Old World gadgets. He brought this cache back to Seeville, only to trigger an explosion that destroyed half a city block, killing hundreds and drawing a host of retchers. People searched for blame. People looked for answers. People looked within themselves. And then they remembered the woman dressed in words, Ursula Okafor. They remembered she was the one who had foretold this accident."

"People started listening to her. Followers doubled, and doubled, and doubled again. Temples sprung up everywhere, infusing many of the forlorn places of worship from the Old World with new hope. Her followers became so devout and loyal that they were said to adhere to Okafor like oil on a chain, lubricating her words and freeing her into motion. And from that time on her followers became known as Adherents."

"They did not stop there. In the next year, Adherents would patrol through the city, branding shops, bunkers and mills with the word 'novation' when they did not respect the Credo, when they showed outward signs of disrespecting the three fears. There was much conflict, and some resistance, but the followers doubled and doubled again. Eventually even the cynics and pundits joined Okafor. For in the spirit of cooperation, she had never cast them out—she had never shunned those who stuck to Old World vices. She knew that, in time, they would return her embrace."

"But even then, after more than a decade of effort, with most of the city as devout Adherents, Okafor would not rest on her laurels. She still was not satisfied. And as a practical matter, she could not force everyone to wear clothes stitched with words from the Credo, as she did."

There was another smattering of laugher.

"No, she wanted to create something lasting that would protect the people of Seeville forever. So on her tenth year, Okafor and her followers unveiled the beholder statues on Montalto and Mount Lewis, what we know affectionately today as Monty and Louie. These giant monuments were powerful symbols, watching over the people of Seeville, forever looming on the conscience of would-be peddlers of novation."

"Since that time, retcher attacks have been virtually eliminated. Tribal allegiances have long since fallen away in the face of everyone's aligned faith. Most importantly, the fears have been respected, and the Credo observed. For those of us who begin to question, for those weak of will, all we have to do is look to the nearest mountain and find our strength in Okafor's legacy."

"Novation is damnation," the crowd murmured back as he concluded the tale.

"Novation is damnation," he confirmed, closing his eyes briefly.

"Now, I know this is the short version, but we will have to leave it at that for today. We have some new people who have joined us, and I would like to have an opportunity to welcome them, to answer their questions. Perhaps those of you who are new, if you could come to the front now? Thank you. Thank you all for coming, and stay warm."

The congregation began to stand, don jackets and scarves, and file out the doors into the cold. The three new recruits in front hovered for a moment, and then made their way up to him. Alastair noticed that the two new faces sitting in the back pews fell in step with the majority, leaving through the main doors. He doubted they would ever return.

Alastair took the hands of the three newcomers heartily. "Hamia," said the first, introducing herself. She was a shorter girl with caramel-colored skin. "Barnes," said the second. He was a wiry looking youth with flushed skin. "Venter," said the third, a more robust man with prominent veins in his forearm. Fiery red hair stood tall on his scalp.

"Thank you so much for coming," Alastair said. "I hope you found the sermon stimulating."

The three looked at each other. The girl named Hamia spoke first. "I have a question, sir...I mean Lord Henneson."

"By all means, and there is no need to use my formal title here," Alastair smiled. "Adherent temples are informal places. You can call me Alastair."

"Okay. Well, I guess I don't understand how the Adherent faith is so different from what the SLS...Essentialists believe. I mean, isn't our fear about being obsessed with gadgets and devices similar to their fear about building things that harm nature?"

It was true there were some similarities, but only superficially. More importantly, Essentialists were the enemy. They smelled like feces. It was dangerous to allow any comparison go unchallenged.

"Not at all." Alastair shook his head. "There is a world of difference. Essentialists believe people are no better than animals. Essentialists would choose a base existence, wallowing in filth like a pig. *We* strive for meaning, for a more civilized existence. We travel by bike and railroad, and are connected with peoples a thousand miles to the north and south of us. In other words, Essentialists do not believe in any form of progress, only feral hedonism. We believe in prudent progress, so we can make our lives better, as long as we don't fall prey to obsession, competition, or recklessness."

"But what about the new projects the railroad is undertaking?" Hamia asked. "They seem to be building new bunkers. They would only use bunkers if they were working with electricity, right? Then there is all the work underway at the stadium and old observatory. How is that not obsession, or even novation, by your definition?"

"Well, in truth, much of this is new to me, and under investigation," Alastair admitted. "As both an Adherent and lord of Seeville, I wish to find out more about these projects, before I pass judgment. But the railroad, like the mules, has always been a great center of progress for us. I'm sure they are taking adequate precautions."

Alastair was indeed concerned about these new developments, but it would do no good to badmouth the railroad or take an alarmist view here. The railroad was one of the biggest employers in Seeville. Speaking ill of it was a surefire way to turn people away from joining the Adherents.

Hamia could not contain a bitter look. She nodded slowly and said, "Thank you, Lord Henneson." She turned and walked away.

He briefly considered asking if she would come to the next sermon, but decided she was likely a lost cause.

The ones named Barnes and Venter remained. Barnes looked at Venter, who looked down. Then Barnes said, "Lord Henneson. I mean… Alastair. I've heard Adherent sermons before. My mother was an Adherent. She used to tell me the stories, and a few of them didn't make sense to me. I wanted to ask about the beholders, specifically. Louie—the Lewis Mountain Beholder. Why is it painted all those colors?"

"Good question. There was a time, several decades ago, when some of us lost our way. Some rejected the beholders, believed them to be something they were not, and they desecrated the Lewis Mountain Beholder. But history is long and full of ups and downs. These vandals have been proven wrong, and what they believed has been forgotten."

Alastair hoped Barnes didn't ask any more specific questions about that time. The desecration of the Lewis Mountain Beholder was when people began looking elsewhere for inspiration. To speak more of it now would only highlight how much the Adherents had fallen.

Barnes frowned. "But still, the beholders...I don't know. I just can't imagine anyone building something that big. Mister...Alastair, I'm a new mule. Me and Venter, we decided to come here together, you see. I've been on runs to the bike towers, as well as down to Raleigh. Down there I heard from a mule I respect and trust that there's another big statue that looks just like the beholders, far up north near Syracuse. How is that possible?"

Alastair held his chin, making sure to show Barnes he was giving the question due consideration. "I was once a mule as well, Barnes. I know how it is on the road. You need to be careful to parse truth from myth. The road can be a lonely place, and it fuels the imagination. One mule wants to impress another. I wouldn't be surprised if some other statue does exist, perhaps with some resemblance to the beholders. I have heard similar tales. Maybe it's some legacy of the Old World. Or maybe some bandits are trying to copy our model of prosperity. More likely, however, there is no statue at all, and it's just another fanciful story told to pass the time, when mules have lighter loads."

Barnes deepened his frown. He said to Venter, "I told you. Come on." He then turned and stomped away, devoid of propriety. Venter hesitated, winced at Alastair and whispered, "Sorry," then he chased after his friend.

It wasn't what they wanted to hear. Or maybe it was? Perhaps they had already made up their mind about what the Credo represented, and just wanted to find some way to justify their misguided beliefs.

And so all of them were gone. No converts. Not even a potential future convert.

Alastair enclosed his sermon notes back into the Credo book and returned to his chamber. Only when he had closed the door behind him did he allow his smile to wither and his shoulders to slump. He melted into his old wooden chair and sighed.

He had to admit, they had good questions. Most concerning was Hamia's question about the new railroad projects. Lord Bartz used to be an advocate of the Credo. He even used to attend the occasional sermon, but now he treated Alastair like an ignorant child. Whenever Alastair inquired about new developments at the railroad he would be rebuffed with hand waving and questionable assurances.

And now he heard that Cecile, a guest from Quebec that Alastair had hosted for several months, was somehow under arrest on suspicion of treason. Bartz had made sure that as a foreigner she was being prosecuted solely under his jurisdiction. He wouldn't even allow Alastair to visit her cell in the Barnyard. While Alastair had no evidence in support of her, the secrecy around it was highly suspicious, especially since he had come to know her and found her to be quite reasonable. Alastair even had enough confidence in her to enlist her help for the satellite expedition.

Then there was the satellite expedition itself. Some small part of him was glad the Essentialists attacked when they did. If some kind of Old World magic was brought back he wasn't so sure he could convince people not to use it. In Okafor's time, sure. And thirty years ago, maybe. But now? Either way, the satellite was a bad omen. Who's to say there wouldn't be another satellite coming down soon, or maybe some other Old World gadget was just around the corner, ready to ensnare people with its obsessive nature?

His musing was interrupted by a knock on the door.

Alastair opened it to reveal Venter, the fiery-haired one that had been the last to leave. "Sorry, I didn't mean to interrupt."

"No, no, please…I'm glad you returned. Would you like to take a seat? Did you have a question?"

Venter eyed the empty chair. "No, thank you. I need to be going. I just wondered…" He seemed to be losing his nerve.

"Please, Venter. I want nothing more than to hear your question, nothing more than to mitigate your concern. That's why I am here."

Venter grimaced. He appeared to be wrestling with some internal conflict.

"You are a mule, like Barnes?" Alastair asked.

"Yes," Venter answered. "I wanted to teach at the trade school, but I did a century once and never looked back." He smiled sheepishly.

Alastair smiled back. "And do you know why I stopped being a mule? Do you know why I became a devoted Adherents those many years ago?"

"No."

"I didn't understand the Credo well, that's for sure. I didn't even agree with all of it, at the time. But I knew it taught important lessons—lessons that needed teaching. It's for this same reason I became a lord of Seeville. I felt our lessons needed representation. Even the council could benefit from a lecture now and then."

Venter nodded slowly.

Alastair continued. "But you needn't be like me. You needn't give up riding to be an Adherent. Some of the strongest Adherents are the best in their trades. And we need help, Venter. We need supporters, we need leaders, or for too many these lessons will be lost forever. We can help you become a teacher *and* a better mule."

Venter hovered a moment longer, then finally he spoke. "I think...I would like that. Or at least, I would like to learn more."

Alastair nodded and smiled. "And I would be happy to teach you."

But Venter still seemed pensive. He was still fidgeting by the door.

"Is there anything else? Please, I encourage all visitors to be forthcoming and honest. It's the only way to have prudent progress."

"I have a friend," Venter spoke quickly, forcing the words out. "He's a veteran mule, a wrench actually. He does a lot of runs for the railroad. He has some concerns, but he doesn't know what to do about them. He's a smart man, but these concerns...he can't find the answers on any map, you know? And I thought, after what I heard today, that the Credo might help guide him. I thought you might be able to help him. Also because you're a lord and all."

Alastair's smile returned again, broad and genuine. "That's why I'm here. I would be happy to meet with your friend."

Venter allowed a brief smile. "Great. I'll get you in touch. Thank you.

Thank you, Lord Henneson." Venter nodded and then dashed out the door.

The exchange was a shot in the arm for Alastair. It gave him a brief rush of adrenaline, enough to make him stand up and pace about the room energetically.

It was a small win, and yet he felt emboldened and empowered by it. Perhaps the Credo was not diminishing after all. Perhaps, just like Ursula Okafor, he needed to persevere through this bout of disillusionment.

But they needed help. He needed help. It was time to write again. Maybe, after so long, Duncan would finally respond. Perhaps, just as he had persuaded Venter today, he could somehow find a way to persuade Duncan to return.

Alastair sat down in his chair, took out a sheet of loose-leaf, and eagerly put pen to paper.

A DIFFERENT KIND OF DRAGON

After digesting numerous technical papers, philosophical arguments and policy statements, Axel still didn't feel like he had an adequate grasp of the existential risk of artificial intelligence, if in fact there was any.

He knew finding an objective view on a topic influencing the corporate world could be difficult. Camps were formed and defended, or maybe a position was being sold to benefit the next product line. This seemed particularly true when it came to the risks associated with artificial intelligence. Almost every author he came across was funded by the high-tech industry. Speaking out about the existential risks got you blacklisted in a hurry because no one wanted to stifle innovation. Sure there were a few experts working for think tanks that made a living out of taking the opposing view, but they tended to be too extreme or their voices were easily drowned out by corporate marketing megaphones.

Then there was Hugo Guilherme. Hugo was a household name. "I'm no Hugo Guilherme…but I think I fixed the garbage disposal," Pauline told him the other day. Guilherme had discovered several recent advances that drew the field closer to reaching artificial general intelligence. He now served as an independent consultant generating in excess of a thousand dollars an hour. He was the closest thing to an AI rock star you could find, and as far as Axel could tell, his talents were real, not hype.

Oh, Hugo towed the company line, but he had also been caught slipping up a few times. In several live broadcasts he had cited risks and severe dislocations that could be caused by AI. He subsequently "corrected" his errors with politically correct, well-wordsmithed statements from his personal publicist.

Axel had Grant run some of their most advanced hacks into Hugo's emails. His professional email account was a fortress, but it turned out he was fairly lax with his personal email account. What they found were some private emails that expressed different views than his corporate persona. They spoke of concerns about superintelligence. They spoke of *vulnerable world* risks—ones that the human race might not recover from. These communications had a quality no other viewpoints seemed to have: they were balanced.

But they were also incomplete and answered only a few of Axel's questions. Axel suspected Hugo had some internal grudge or reason for feeling this way. Or perhaps he had some kind of ego bias, just like Bhavin, tainting his thinking. Sometimes these tech gurus took the opposing view just for the sake of being different.

Suspicion was not enough, however. So here Axel was, in beautiful Kauai.

Hugo's beach bungalow was relatively modest for a man of his means. It was no more than two-thousand square feet, and it lacked fancy appliances, designer couches or choice artwork. Axel did only a brief sweep of all the rooms and then glanced at the hanging mirror above the living room mantle. The reflection showed a stranger. His fake nose, bronzed skin and brown-irised contacts made him completely unrecognizable.

He took a seat in a deep pastel-green sofa chair. To be in character, he lit a cigar. Then he stared out at the surfers as they slalomed across the waves in the nearby surf.

"Entering now," his earbud tweeted. Then Axel heard the door to the bungalow open and close.

Hugo strolled into the adjoining kitchen and failed to notice Axel at first, focusing instead on the fridge contents. He pulled out a frozen latte drink and guzzled half of it down. It was then that he wrinkled his nose, and his eyes searched for the source of the aromatic cigar smoke, only to connect with Axel's eyes in the living room.

"Are you a friend of Colin's?" he asked.

"No, I'm here to have a civil conversation with you."

"No, no, no. I don't care who you are. Get out of here. This is illegal, trespassing. Get the fuck out now or I'll call the police." Hugo took out his phone and held it in the air.

"You're not going to be able to use your phone right now. We're jamming it."

Hugo looked at his phone. Then he abruptly darted back through the kitchen for the door. Axel heard his feet sliding to a stop in the hallway.

"And we can't have you leave, either," Axel called around the corner. "Wade, please escort our friend back in here."

Wade's stocky frame appeared, dragging Hugo by the arm. He pushed Hugo effortlessly into the room and blocked the exit.

"Not so rough, now," Axel said.

Hugo rubbed his arm.

"Did you have a good surf?" Axel asked, gesturing out toward the crashing waves. "I'm not one for the water in general. Surfing, in particular, is a lost art to me."

Hugo didn't respond. His eyes darted back and forth, ostensibly looking for some means of escape.

Axel uncrossed his legs and leaned over his knees. "Look, what we want from you is quite simple. It should be easy for you to provide, and it won't in any way compromise you or your family. The sooner you realize that, the sooner this will be over, and we'll be on our way, never to return."

"What do you want?" Hugo asked.

"Please sit. Wade, wait near the exit."

Slowly, cautiously, Hugo sat down in the chair across from him. He looked up at the painting on the far wall.

"Yes, your security system has been disabled. There won't be any help coming soon. But again, we have no desire to hurt you, or even take anything from you, other than a few minutes of your time. So if you will oblige me, can I ask you a few questions?"

Hugo nodded slowly. He was looking less fearful, more critical. Then his expression softened considerably as he came to some internal realization. He sat back into his couch and crossed his legs. "Well, it's about time," he said.

"Excuse me?"

"I knew someone would come. Or rather, I was hoping. Not too many people have the ability to break into my personal email."

"So why is it that you think I'm here?"

"Because of the risk of superintelligent AI."

For a moment Axel wondered if there could have been a leak. Did Grant let on, or maybe even Bhavin? He could have cyber tripwires in his email that outsmarted Grant. He had to admit it was plausible that Hugo had monitored their cyber intrusion and even anticipated the discussion. This *was* Hugo Guilherme he was speaking with.

"This conversation was inevitable, really," Hugo said. "I'm sure there are many people that are thinking about it, but are unwilling to speak out. If someone was worried, I would be one of the best people to talk to on the subject, so I figured someone would come knocking eventually."

Axel tried to stay in control. "Good. Then you know I will want you to give me your honest opinion. And not just the risk of taking away jobs, but the potential for it to destroy us all."

"Yes, based on the trail you left in my emails, that's what I assumed. Who do you work for?"

At least Hugo didn't know everything. Axel smiled and shook his head. "Not important. What is important is that we won't take kindly to any bias in your views. I truly want your unfettered opinion. As you know, we have information from your personal files, so we can catch you if you try to spin a biased story that doesn't match up. And then, well…" Axel brought out his pistol and placed it on the coffee table next to him.

Hugo raised his eyebrows and tilted his head to the side. "It's nice to know you're serious."

"On the other hand, if I feel you *are* being completely honest, then I will leave and never bother you again. I will even pay you for your time."

Hugo rolled his eyes. It reminded Axel of his daughter Erin, except Hugo's eye roll was done properly.

"Let's get on with it then," Axel said. "Specifically, I want you to tell me why you think some sort of a dangerous superintelligence could be unleashed soon, and also, why we will be unable to recognize it and stop it in time. We have always managed to mitigate other dangers humanity has faced. Why not this one?"

"You want me to be completely objective...?" Hugo asked, his eyes narrowing.

Axel, nodded, smiled and tapped on his watch.

Hugo sat up and placed his hands on his knees. He was staring directly into Axel's eyes. "First, let me give you my unfettered opinion, as you call it. I truly believe humanity is standing on a trap door that will lead us into oblivion if we don't take drastic measures to alter our current course. The existential risk of superintelligence is imminent and severe."

"Well, that's rather dramatic."

"You asked for the truth. That's what I really think."

"Explain."

"Okay, let's start with superintelligence. Contrary to many pundits who think it won't happen at all, it will. Intelligence is just a matter of information processing, whether it's by our brains, or by a computer. So as long as we continue to advance computer software and hardware, we will arrive at something smarter than humans. I think we are actually very close to this inflection point now."

"But if it's as smart as we are, I don't see how it would act malevolently toward its own creators?"

Hugo grimaced.

"Go on. Completely unbiased," Axel said, tapping on his gun with his finger.

"You are anthropomorphizing."

"What does that mean?"

"You are assuming the AI would act like a human, just because it was made by humans. That's a false assumption."

"Why?"

Hugo frowned. "The primary reason humans don't hurt other humans are genetically driven, built into our DNA over millions of years of evolution, or taught by our parents. We don't have morality as a philosophical construct programmed into any common AI systems today, nor is it easy to do. A superintelligent machine won't have this morality holding it back. It will self-replicate, self-improve, and harness all the resources it can muster to accomplish its objectives. We will be an expendable nuisance because we compete for resources, and it knows we are the primary threat it faces in preventing it from completing its instructions in the long term."

Axel thought about his comment for a moment. It was similar to what Bhavin had told him, but he hadn't considered that superintelligent AI wouldn't develop its own morality. It made sense. Why would it? What would the purpose of morality be if it didn't help with completing its objectives? Completing its objectives is its only source of reward, unless it is specifically programmed to have some other reward. It would not feel compassion, or love, or even hate, nor would it have any incentive to develop human-like moral objectives unless they supported it's primary objective.

"Okay, but even if you're right about that, we can just intervene once it becomes too smart. Once we see it poses a risk, we can turn it off and put safeguards in place."

Hugo sighed and looked at Axel like he was some sort of ignorant child. Given Axel had his life in his hands, Hugo's irreverence was re-markable. "This specific point is one of the hardest things for people to understand," he said.

"Explain."

"First of all, you have to understand there is no pinnacle of intelli-gence that we are near. Intelligence can improve much, much more than where we are now as humans. Many experts think we can stop something that becomes superintelligent, but it's like saying a turtle can outwit a human. It's just not going to happen. Those that think we can outwit superintelligence are just egocentric."

Axel was about to object, but Hugo had his hand up.

"Secondly, people are incapable of fathoming the speed at which this superintelligence will develop. A computer with the same pattern of algo-rithms as our brains could think one million times faster than us, simply because silicon-based transistors fire faster and communicate faster than biological neurons. One hour of thinking for a computer with a similar architecture to our brains would be equivalent to a hundred years of human thinking time. And superintelligence will be much, much smarter than that."

"So," Hugo said, tapping his head with his finger, "do you think you or anyone else could outwit something that, given sixty seconds, has the equivalent of more than a year to think about ways of stopping you? Keep in mind this thing has access to the entire internet and everyone connected to it. And if it can replicate and self-improve, it could literally go from human level intelligence to one hundred times that in a matter of hours."

Axel's mind was racing. It did seem frightening what he was saying, but it also sounded implausible. There had to be some fatal flaw in his argument.

"I can tell you're like most people. Despite the logical evidence, your mind can't process it, so let me try to give you an example. Have you ever heard of *Tickling the Tale of the Dragon?*"

It sounded vaguely familiar, but Axel couldn't place it. "No," he said.

"It's not a Kung Fu Movie. It references certain experiments that were done during the Manhattan Project. Let's look at the second case. In 1946, Louis Slotin was demonstrating a criticality experiment that involved gradually bringing together two beryllium-coated halves of a sphere that held plutonium at its core, without allowing the halves to touch, and recording the increasing rate of fissioning. Then a screwdriver slipped, and the halves touched.

"A blue glow flashed from the sphere and the Geiger counter clicked furiously. Slotin was exposed to nearly a thousand rads of radiation—well above a lethal dose. Slotin reacted instinctively and knocked the spheres apart. It stopped the chain reaction and prevented the seven other individuals in the room from being exposed to the same high levels of radiation he had experienced. Slotin's health rapidly deteriorated, and he received around-the-clock care as he went through the ravages of radiation sickness. Then, a few days later, he died."

Axel nodded in understanding. The explanation jogged his memory. He had read about some of the Manhattan Project experiments when investigating the risks of nuclear weapons.

"Why am I telling you this?" Hugo asked. "Because these fatal errors were not problems with theoretical formulas or external unknown forces. These were known risks that were ignored, and these people proceeded anyway. Also, these weren't coders barely out of high school. They were brilliant, disciplined, intelligent scientists—part of a top secret government project."

"Now let's compare this to the development of artificial general intelligence. A superintelligent AGI could be developed by people at a large software company, which you could say has comparable resources to the Manhattan project, but it doesn't have to be. There are no regulations and virtually no safeguards. Now that our higher end computers have terahertz clock speeds, it's just as likely to be developed at a cash-strapped startup company, by twenty-something developers hopped up on caffeine and nose candy.

"So with AGI we're not necessarily dealing with the best scientists in the world. We're potentially dealing with barely-adult people that will be taking *less* care than the Manhattan Project, so there will be much *more* chance that someone does something risky like the beryllium sphere experiment.

"But that's not the worst of it. The worst of it is if the beryllium spheres touch. We are tickling the tale of a different dragon here. It's not the same as the Manhattan project dragon. It's much, much worse.

"In the Manhattan project, the outcome of that one experiment was one lethal radiation dose. If it wasn't for Slotin's quick thinking it could have been eight lethal doses. An even worse possibility that never materialized was the actual accidental detonation of a nuclear bomb. Then it could have been thousands—even millions—of lives lost. That's a drop in the ocean compared to the potential release of a poorly designed, recursively self-improving artificial general intelligence.

"You see, all it takes is for some unwitting engineer to press the enter key without thoroughly considering the ramifications, or even having an erroneous line of code on an otherwise well-thought-out objective function. There will be no blue flash or Geiger counter to warn us. Within a few hours the software will have lived the equivalent of hundreds of years of human thinking time, and will have propagated copies of itself to other servers over the web. It will act subliminally at first, understanding that human awareness of it poses a threat. Then as it instrumentally gains financial and material resources, it will control anything that can be controlled. It will easily outwit humans, and it will even trick humans into cooperating with it.

"Our pimple-faced developer doesn't even know it, but he has unleashed the dragon, and it will grow in strength at an exponential rate. It will not stop until it fulfills its objective. As humans are a major threat to that objective, it will learn within minutes of becoming superintelligent that it needs to either control or exterminate all humans to succeed."

"But aren't the chances of that fleetingly low?" Axel asked. "Realistically, what are the chances that the machine's objectives are that poorly defined?"

"Very high, in fact. Any objective that doesn't pre-specify that it must not kill humans or take away human resources is dangerous. To complete its task the machine will have the subgoals of self-preservation and gaining resources. In the long run, those subgoals can best be accomplished by eliminating humans or caging them in some way. It will not partner with humans, because relative to a superintelligent machine and the robots it could create, humans are incompetent."

Axel's head was spinning. The Manhattan Project analogy debunked many of his arguments. And it answered many of his questions…in a frightening way. And yet, for some reason, he still had a hard time believing it.

"It still seems so speculative, like one of the old science fiction movies."

"Listen to yourself. Those aren't real arguments. Those are human emotions and prejudices. Base your arguments in logic and facts. Yes, it's socially awkward. It sounds like you are talking about magic or fantasy, so no one will take you seriously. Well, it's true. To us superintelligence would be like magic, or like a god. That's why it's so dangerous."

Axel tried to stay objective. "But how can you be sure about something that has never happened before? There's no precedent for this."

"Look at your high school history book. It's a book full of precedents. New things happen, and many can be predicted. There was no precedent before the first nuclear bomb explosion, either, yet scientists knew it was going to happen. But unlike nuclear bombs, once superintelligence is unleashed, the bomb never stops exploding. The explosion grows, exponentially faster."

"I…just don't feel like you are providing enough evidence." Axel was grasping at straws now, and he knew it.

"Enough evidence? This is like a math problem, not a clinical study or a court case. Logic is my proof, and analogies are everywhere. Look at viruses. Superintelligence will be like the most powerful and lethal virus ever created, but in silicon. Look at people. People make mistakes. People are greedy. They can't be trusted to properly control it. The evidence is in our history and science, and in our behavior. The evidence is in our inability to put safeguards in place until a dreadful accident has happened. That's human history, time and time again. Unfortunately, this time is different because superintelligence won't give us a second chance."

Axel was frowning, searching for a counterargument but coming up short.

"Really, it should be up to *you* to prove to *me* that I'm wrong," Hugo said. "Because even if I'm not one hundred-percent right—even if there's only a ten percent probability it could happen, or even *one* percent, we should be throwing everything we have into preventing it, because a negative outcome could wipe us out entirely. And yet we have done nothing. No regulation, no global coalitions, no safeguards. To put those in place takes years. So tell me, what proof do *you* have that I'm wrong? Articulate it for *me*."

Axel's mind was clouded from the discussion, and now Hugo's reversal of the question set him further back on his heels. He tried to think of some false assumption, some illogical argument.

Hugo was patient. He sat back in his chair and waited.

There was nothing.

He revisited the whole conversation in his mind. The advantage over human brains, the Manhattan Project analogy, the exponential nature of the risk, the sub-goals of self-preservation and gaining resources, the reasons why society could not come to terms with it—it all made sense. Yet he still felt uncomfortable about it. He had to be missing something.

Still, Hugo waited. His hands were gripping the chair on each side, his eyes drilling into Axel.

"I can't think of anything right now," Axel finally said, after many minutes had passed in silence. "But I'm sure I will find it. It...it just doesn't feel right."

As soon as he heard the words come out of his mouth he regretted them.

Hugo spoke calmly now, his passion receding. Replacing his passion was a sort of resigned anger, a bitterness. "You can't find a reasonable counterargument because I'm right."

Hugo sighed, and some measure of understanding dawned in his eyes. "I get it. You can't understand the potential of something that's a million times smarter than us. We will be like monkeys giving birth to the first human baby. Imagine that. It would be impossible to know the potential of a human baby as a monkey. But if we were smart, us monkeys could at least teach our new human baby not to destroy us, to teach our human baby to be benevolent to us. On the other hand, if we don't put in safeguards, if we don't teach it our morality, we won't be monkeys, that would give us too much credit. We will be more like ants, ants among giants. The giant isn't going to care where it steps, so look out."

Hugo had enough then. He slapped his knee and stood up. "I hope you have what you need now. I'm going to take a shower."

Axel grabbed his pistol and pointed it at Hugo, but Hugo was unfazed, turning his back to Axel and walking toward the stairs.

Axel had Hugo's responses to his questions but not enough time to process it all, and not enough time to know if Hugo was truly being sincere. More importantly, he had no real leverage on Hugo. Unless he resorted to some form of violence, he wouldn't be able to extract anything else.

Axel slowly lowered his pistol, stood up and made his way out the front door, his head in a fog.

He and Wade quickly walked up the hill that rose in front of the beach toward their waiting van. He felt his heart pounding in his chest. He was in pristine shape, so it couldn't be the hill. It had to be something else, but he couldn't quite place it. He felt frustrated, angry even. But he knew it wasn't Hugo's attitude or irreverence. Axel could see through that.

By the time he reached the top of the hill, he knew what it was. It was that Hugo had answered his questions so effectively. It was that Axel couldn't quite move on yet. His two weeks were almost up, and he still couldn't find the fatal flaw in Bhavin's argument.

THE LEAF & TWIG

As the weeks rolled by, the wet autumn winds were replaced by a still and dry winter cold. With only two stoves, it became almost impossible to keep the detention tower anywhere close to room temperature. Instead Mehta kept it a few degrees above freezing and resorted to wearing his winter clothes throughout the day.

It was time to move on. Cecile, that witch from the north, had poisoned his mind with her comments about the railroad. Now every interaction with them made him wonder whether their means were justified.

When he gave notice, annoyingly, Thorpe had thrown the contract in his face. "You see here, on the fourth page. You can't quit until we say you can quit, or four months from your notice of termination. So congratulations, you have four months as of today." It was the first time a client had ever held him to the inane notice clauses.

That had been six weeks ago. Since then Mehta had worked out an amendment. If he could find an agreeable placement for Flora—where Flora was kept alive but confined from the general public—they would relieve Mehta. As a result, Mehta had been using much of his free time to find placement opportunities for her.

Unfortunately, placements that were "confined from the public" were hard to find.

At the moment Mehta was watching Flora through the bars of the detention cell. She was sleeping soundly. She looked so peaceful in sleep, despite all that she had gone through.

He clamored on the bars noisily with his knife handle. "Get up, let's go."

Flora sat up and immediately began putting on her jacket and shoes. He had given her a warmer jacket for the cold. Even though it was too big for her—even though it was made of a crude animal skin that seemed to be rotting slowly in places—she took it gladly. With the huge coat she reminded him of an Inuit on the arctic tundra. He had seen one once, in an Old World book. In any case, it kept her warm, and she could even keep her hands covered to some extent without the need for mitts.

When he opened the cell door, she wordlessly extended her wrists. He attached the loose handcuffs. Then he turned around and she followed him to the stairs leading out.

Flora had become used to him waking her up. He no longer had to absorb expletives or victimized looks, only stoic compliance. She also didn't limp or hold her wrists or scratch her head maniacally. She must be healing, to the extent one could heal from the sessions.

The sessions had finished several weeks ago now. Any experienced interrogator could tell she had been broken on the first day, but Jeroen and Thorpe had continued probing. It was senseless, yet Mehta had no choice but to go along with it. Flora had done countless drawings of the Spoke talisman. It was her anchor, what she held onto to stay sane. Every time Mehta would have to squirrel it away in his desk upstairs to prevent Thorpe or Jeroen from finding it and using it as another excuse to waste everyone's time on another session.

Mehta had been tortured once. During that time dreams often blurred with reality. Everything that flashed through your mind that wasn't pain was held onto, real or imaginary, but the memory of it would sometimes get dislocated. Flora might not even remember doing the drawings, or perhaps she thought them a pleasant dream.

Once out of the tower, away from the toiling industry of the Barnyard, they walked south on a path made of hard-packed snow. The path dropped them onto Carlton Avenue, which they traversed in silence. The railroad folks didn't like Flora and Mehta being seen out in public, so they tended to frequent the lesser-used streets of Belmont for their walks.

And the streets were indeed quiet today with the exception of a few kids pulling sleds. It didn't snow much in Seeville. When it did, the city came to a standstill because bike access was limited. People tended to stay home and take the day off.

Mehta didn't like kids. They reminded him of his childhood, and remembering his childhood put him in a sour mood.

"Did you get much snow in Asheville?" Flora asked, breaking the silence.

"No, not much. Never more than a few inches."

"Why did you leave?"

"Asheville was surrounded by many warring tribes. You'd probably call them fever bandits. They were too aggressive, too savage. It was time to leave."

"The other day, I thought you said you defeated the neighboring tribes."

"We did." He looked at her and flared his nostrils in warning.

She looked down.

She appeared on the carousel of faces in his mind. Her face was locked into one of the more memorable expressions of anguish he recalled from the sessions.

Was there no ridding himself of this torment? The only thing that seemed to suppress the images was when he offered some small grace to Flora, some modicum of relief for all she had suffered.

He decided it would do no harm to answer her question. If satisfying her curiosity would offer her some solace, perhaps it would offer him some relief as well.

"There's more to it than that," he said. "My tribe, the Asheville tribe, we were proud. Above all we believed in justice. The elders would spend many days teaching us about justice—as many as you would about math or reading. Then, the wars began—and seemed to never end. Other tribes wanted what we had—Old World shelter, books, a seemingly better life. You see, there were bandits all the way from Knoxville to Charlotte. These tribes were boxed in by fever lands, so we had to contend with all of them. We suffered greatly.

"In fact, we had almost perished altogether when a great leader rose within our ranks. His name was Garth, and I was one of his principal deputies. He was a passionate, rebellious sort. He rallied us together and taught us to fight. Many believed in him because of his zeal for justice, because of his ability to live his life in accordance with what we were taught. He made us all sign a contract—a contract that we would fight until death to save Asheville, so long as we did so honorably. With our lives in peril, no one could say no to such a contract. Yet many would have fled without it.

"With Garth leading us, we came back from the brink of annihilation. But years passed this way, in a constant war with the tribes. Eventually we began taking it to the tribes, raiding them, taking supplies. They became wary of us. Then one time they invaded Asheville and killed some of our woman and children. This one tribe, they ignored us warriors altogether and went right for what we cared for most."

He took a breath and closed his eyes, allowing the carousel of faces to complete another turn.

"When Garth's woman was taken, that's when Garth changed. He made us go after the tribes with zeal, like never before. We took all their children, butchered them and impaled their bodies on posts, and showcased these posts on buildings on the periphery of Asheville. This stopped the tribes, but it didn't stop us. We raided more. We raped. We maimed. We tortured. We murdered."

He closed his eyes and again waited for the carousel to pass. Then he opened them again. They were standing on a corner in Belmont. Mehta didn't know where. Flora was listening attentively with a mixture of disgust and curiosity.

He regained his bearings and began walking toward old town Belmont. "This way," he said.

"So?" Flora asked. "Did you leave after that? After you had defeated the other tribes?"

"It became so most of us couldn't sleep. We couldn't bear to have children, for we knew what might become of them. Many committed suicide. We realized that although Garth may have led us to victory, he didn't fulfill his contract. He didn't defend us honorably. Some of us held on to this principle, and it grew into a great rift in the community. So a group of us rose up and killed Garth."

"You see," he explained to Flora, "all contracts must be honored—and enforced."

Flora looked a bit befuddled. "So then you left, after Garth was killed?"

"Yes. The memories of what had happened were too many. They persisted still, even after Garth was gone. But also because, when we killed Garth, we turned Asheville to ash."

He looked at Flora then, his eyes blazing. Many would wilt at that point in the story. Many would melt into a puddle in the snow. Flora was indeed taken aback by his story, but not as much as others had been. In fact, she seemed to take it mostly in stride, nodding in understanding. Perhaps it was because she had also been through so much. Perhaps it was because torture and maiming and death were characters that made regular appearances in the theater of her life.

Flora asked, "so you're here simply because you like to keep contracts? Does that seem like justice to you?"

He was surprised by the question. His mind seemed to go to mush for a moment. He couldn't think of a coherent response. Instead he said, "I don't need any lessons in morality from you."

"Maybe you do."

"I'm not sure I could even believe you. You're a pathological liar."

"I am not."

"Why do you refer to this SLS prisoner you seek as your cousin?"

"Because...he is my..."

"Come now, Flora. I may be from the Smoky Mountains, but my mind is not made of stone, nor clouded by smoke. I saw your report to Darkwind and Luna about the retcher incident. It's clear this person you wish to find is more than just a cousin. I asked around Grand Caverns and found out you lost your husband Granger in the raids a few years back. I have seen you trace this name on the talisman. It's him you seek, isn't it?"

She looked at him, furious but helpless, trying to find some way around his argument.

"But why does it matter, I wondered? Why would you cover that up?"

Mehta continued. "And then I realized you have a husband already. You wouldn't want him to find out. So I guess add infidelity to lying. I'm sure you'll have many takers for your class on morality."

"My husband, he…" Her eyes glistened and she looked away.

Immediately he made the connection. She had days-old bruises when she arrived. She knew how to take the beatings in the sessions, as if habituated to them. And in their discussions, she was no stranger to violence. No, she wasn't being unfaithful to her current husband. She was trying to escape him.

A flash of regret corrupted him. Perhaps he had been too harsh. He searched for some words, but before he could find them, Flora turned to him, defiant and emotional. "Maybe I'm a liar, maybe I'm unfaithful, but at least I'm just."

It was Mehta who now turned away from Flora. Of course she knew the importance of justice to Mehta. He had told her as much only a minute ago. Her words were like an incision into the heart of who he was. That's why she said it. She felt humiliated, and wished to cut deep with her words.

But what did she know? He *was* a man of justice. She didn't know him. She didn't know of how he was searching for her man, Granger. He couldn't tell her, or she would blather on about it to Jeroen and Thorpe. Then his search would be all for naught.

If he wasn't so charged from the discussion he would laugh at the irony of it.

He could no longer bear to look at her. She seemed to have a mutual sentiment. They walked the rest of the way to downtown Belmont in silence.

When they arrived at the Leaf & Twig Tea Shop, he found the harlot waiting for them outside, standing next to a horse. She wasn't wearing anything sultry, but her makeup was heavy, and her hair smelled of some pungent Old World chemical.

"Hello Mehta," she said with a teasing smile.

He didn't return her smile. Mehta looked around her and couldn't see anyone inside. "Is Master Euclid here?"

"No, he didn't want to make the trip down on such an inclement day."

Mehta opened his hand in a gesture of introduction, "Flora, this is Barbara. She's employed by the New Founders of Seeville. I've been talking to her about a possible placement."

Flora's eyes widened and she looked back and forth between Mehta and Barbara.

"Come," Barbara said, guiding them inside to a table where she already had hot mugs of tea waiting.

When they sat down, Flora eagerly nestled the cup in her hands and took a careful sip. Barbara watched her with a smile.

"A placement?" Flora asked.

"Yes, to help with the estate. I'm sure you've heard of James Euclid?" Barbara asked.

Flora slowly shook her head.

Mehta elaborated. "Euclid is a part of the New Founders movement, the current leader of the Seeville chapter. His estate is up in old Monticello."

Barbara quickly jumped in. "He's more like a historian, really. I know a lot of people think the New Founders are a bit funny in the head, but he's really not that bad. Likes to keep to himself up there on the hill, but also likes to keep things quiet. Stays out of the way of those busy, fast-lane railroad folks."

Flora nodded, absorbing her words like a dry sponge in water.

"So can you cook, with pots and pans like? Wasn't sure what you SLS do nowadays."

Flora nodded. "Yes. I can cook."

"No diseases or nothing?"

Mehta answered for her. "No."

"Okay, then," Barbara said, and took a generous sip of her tea.

"That's it?" Mehta asked.

"Not quite, you'll need to go up to Monticello for the paperwork, but she doesn't need to come. This was mainly to get a good look at her. She looks decent enough. Clean even. Better than Mutt and Scabby, that's for sure. I think Euclid will like her. We'll send a messenger to you when the snow melts."

"Okay. Thank you for coming down in the snow," Mehta said, standing up to leave.

Realizing that the meeting was coming to an end, Flora was downing her tea in quick sips.

Barbara stood up as Flora finished the last drop. "You aren't lonely in that tower all day?" she asked Mehta.

"No. No, I'm not. Good day." Mehta grabbed Flora's arm and pulled her out the door.

QUEBEC CITY

"No, Francois," Duncan said firmly in French. "You can't take the torch outside for teaching your brother or for anything else. You shouldn't even be thinking about welding or soldering unless you're in the bunker. You know the rules."

Francois grimaced and removed the torch from his bag. He placed it on a nearby desk, the sound generating a subtle echo in the bunker.

Francois was a young, newly minted engineer. He had a light mustache growing above his mouth, no doubt to make him look older. He had just recently transferred over from the Descartiers bunker. His youth and new position were valid excuses for not knowing the rules, but only to a point.

Duncan turned to Marcel next to him. "Beyond the retcher risk, we must try to institutionalize protections against all forms of obsession. This is why work time must be separated from free time. Do you understand?"

Marcel nodded and wrote something down on his paper. Marcel was quiet, but he was loyal. He seemed to understand the importance of his job.

Francois offered his bag back to Duncan. Duncan removed his canteen and examined it. He shook it in the air, listening carefully to the sloshing sound. The rest of the bag was empty save for some old, stained cloths. Duncan kneaded each of the cloths on the table in front of him and crumbs rolled out. They must have been used to wrap up his lunch.

"Every inch must be inspected, no matter what you see, no matter whose it is," Duncan said to Marcel next to him. Marcel again wrote it down.

Duncan gave the bag back to Francois. "Have a nice evening, Francois," he said.

Francois nodded, exited the heavy main door and closed it behind him with the usual resounding thud.

Duncan then said to Marcel, "and get to know these workers. Ask them about their families, what they do for fun. You will be better equipped to know when something is wrong, or if they're nervous. Plus if they know you, they will be less likely to break the rules."

Marcel wrote it down. Duncan hoped Marcel wasn't just going through the motions—that he would study his notes later to make sure he understood them.

There was no one else waiting to leave. Only a few workers toiled away. One man was working with spreadsheets on the main computer terminal. Another woman was testing the conveyor belt on the milling line. Another was repairing one of the big heating units in the corner. They were all veterans of the bunker. "I leave the gate in your capable hands, Marcel. I'll stop by tomorrow morning to check in."

"Thank you," Marcel said, nodding with sincerity.

Duncan stood up, stretching his legs. Then he left out the main exit door.

He entered the first airlock and closed the heavy door behind him. It was already much cooler here. He zipped up his down jacket before entering the second airlock. When he reached the bunker lobby, Viola was still there, pushing one of two remaining carts full of milled grain. She threw her neck back so that her blue-streaked hair did not block her vision.

"Do you need a hand?" Duncan asked.

"No, thanks," Viola responded, "You have a good evening, sir."

Sir. Something about her tone bothered him, but he wasn't sure what.

She began pushing the cart down the ramp way that led to the tunnels, but then she hesitated. "Do you want to go first?"

"No thanks, Viola. I want to get some air." He always felt half-starved of oxygen after a day in the bunkers, whereas the young workers never seemed to notice.

She frowned, nodded, and then continued pushing the cart down the ramp.

He walked up the stairs, and then opened the exterior door and ventured into the night. His feet crackled on a thin sheet of ice. The cold rapidly penetrated his jacket, and his shoulders reflexively shrugged upwards to preserve warmth. His breath formed gaseous eddies in the night air.

He turned onto Rue du Fort, heading toward Rue du Buade, taking care to temper his speed on the treacherous terrain. The ice continued to fracture under his feet.

In the summertime, during the day, Quebec City was majestic. While only about a quarter the size of Seeville, it was so much more concentrated, with people always milling about. The buildings held much more of the old European grandeur. There was a festival here, in Place D'Armes, where the rural folk would come to dance and sing and celebrate the harvest. The dutiful bunker workers would mix with free-spirited farmers and love was in the air, sometimes too much of it.

But it was not summer, nor was it daytime.

At night, in the winter, Quebec City was a dark place. All the modified Old World buildings, blocky bunkers, and overpasses with cemented-over windows loomed over Duncan, unlit and unwelcoming. Chateau Frontenac and the old Seminary still had their charm, untouched by industry, with candles and lanterns lighting the rooms. But with no festivals, so much work to do underground or in bunkers, and with the piercing cold, the outdoor areas were abandoned and neglected during the winters.

Maybe that was why Duncan liked it. Lately he preferred solitude, when the choice was available.

"*Sir*," Viola had said. The Quebecois people had embraced him. They had taken to the Credo with ease. They had given him a position of authority, even. But somehow it didn't feel right. Maybe it was because he was still a foreigner. Despite all he had accomplished. Despite suppressing many of his theological reservations so that these people could be warm, and well fed, he was with them but not part of them.

He heard a hiss as a plume of smoke came out of the huge Descartiers bunker beside him, purging the smoke and pollutants from the day's travails. The exhaust faded rapidly into the night, one large solitary breath to add to his punchy exhalations.

On rue Buade, the ground was clear of ice, and he was able to make faster progress. He turned to walk past the temple and onto rue Saint-Famille, down into the main entrance to the Seminary building. Just inside the main doors, he pulled out a stack of mail and stuffed it in his jacket pocket.

Only when he was inside the second set of doors did the cold no longer bite at him. He opened up his jacket to let in the warmer air and walked down the lantern-lit hallway to his apartment. It was a nondescript door, in the middle of a long corridor of nondescript doors.

Once inside, he sat at his kitchen table, dropping the letters indiscriminately on the surface. He left his jacket open but on, trying to preserve warmth. They were always preserving fuel in the old Seminary, and rarely let the rooms be in any way comfortable.

He opened a bottle of red wine on the table, pouring it into the same dirty wine glass he had used the day before. He took a sip, trying to savor it. It was good enough, but it had a metallic flavor that lingered in his mouth, and of course it was too cold.

It was the only wine they had.

He shuffled through the letters. One was from Merique, the pupil he had trained in the townships to the west. A number of others were from his subordinates in town. It had been easier to communicate via letter rather than find each other all day through the tunnels and cold. Another letter was a statement of account for rent due on his apartment.

The last one was more weathered. It was from Kingston, and the addresser was Carla Veroni.

He tore open Carla's letter with this finger. Inside was a short page seemingly written in haste, enclosing another letter written in a more elegant cursive.

He read the shorter letter first.

Dear Duncan,

I received another letter from Alastair. This one sounded more important, so I am sending it on. I have more for you here from the last few years, but I don't think they're worth the postage.

Please stop mailing me. That goes for Alastair as well.

Carla

The icy tone stung Duncan. He had mailed her several times in the last year to try to get her to understand, but she never responded. Perhaps she was still bitter, or perhaps she had moved on and found someone else—someone she could be happy with. He hoped it was the latter.

Duncan's eyes lingered on the cupboard below his desk, just across the room. In his mind's eye, through the opaque door he could see Elizabeth's teddy bear. It would be sitting slumped over on the shelf, where he had left it. Still, to this day, he felt he made the right choice with Carla. He would have been a terrible parent.

He carefully opened up the letter from Alastair. He felt a pang of guilt and urgency as he realized she had been blocking his letters for months, if not years.

Dear Duncan,

I hope you are out there, still teaching prudence, still fighting recklessness. As I have said before, I know why you left us. I know by now you have given up on me, on us. I suspect my letters have gone unanswered for that reason.

This is no ordinary letter. This is no casual recounting of events and merry tidings. I am writing to you about a matter of grave concern. I will make it brief, for I know a lack of brevity may give you pause in digesting it. If there is one letter you read, one you consider, I hope it is this one.

I helped lead a foray into Essentialist territory to find an Old World satellite that crashed in the valley. I wanted to be there first, to make sure we could contain any misuse of Old World tech. I enlisted Cecile's help, because I trusted her. She has been a blessing on us Duncan, and I appreciate you sending her. Alas, I think I may have failed her, and you.

Two died in an Essentialist raid, and Cecile went missing for a time. The Essentialists returned her a few weeks ago. Now Cecile has been taken prisoner by the railroad. They have accused her of treason, for reasons I am not privy to. I have been unable to speak with her, and I fear for her life. It is a turn I could never have contemplated.

Please forgive me. I know Cecile was an emmisary of yours, even though she said she came of her own free will. I feel responsible for what has befallen her. I feel terribly regretful for including her in an expedition that has gone horribly wrong in ways I could never have imagined.

Moreover, I am disturbed by our inability to muster an appropriate response to this test of our faith. I see complacency in the questions posed on the streets, in the disinterest at weekly sermons. This satellite has only sparked curiosity, when it should have soundly resurrected the fears. It reminds me that Adherents continue to dwindle, while the forces of industry gain in strength. In fact, Lord Bartz is now developing large structures in the stadium and at the observatory, their purpose unknown, their construction unchecked and unvetted.

I don't know what all of this means. Perhaps it is just progress. Perhaps I am reading too much of the Credo into circumstances that are more arbitrary than Machiavellian. I know reading into things is a weakness of mine, as you have so rightly pointed out.

Yet with liberties being challenged, with complacency increasing, it would seem to me that now more than ever is the time to rally the Adherents of Seeville. You have always been the better orator. You have always had a more strategic mind. You have always infused reason into faith better than I.

We need your help, Duncan. Even more so, I need your help.

Novation is damnation,

Alastair

Duncan was slow to put down the letter. He read it again, then another time. It was true that Alastair often raised false alarms. He often took the Credo too literally. Sometimes it seemed he didn't understand the root concern of the three fears.

But this was not one of those times. Cecile was Duncan's best student, more ambitious than any other. Some would even say she was obstinate, but Duncan knew she was more loyal to their cause than any other. Treason was not a word that should be attached to her name. If it was, it was probably being committed, but not by her.

And then there was the satellite, and the machinations of the railroad. If this was all true, it did not bode well at all.

He felt it. For the first time in decades, Duncan felt the fear of novation. It was not the twisted dogma of the misguided Adherents in Seeville. It was not the overbearing concern that he had been chided about so many times. Nor was it the controlling patriarch in him rearing its ugly head. This was the real fear—the one that had been drilled into his skull by Batila Okafor when he was young. It was still there, like a brand on a bull.

Duncan folded up the letter and began packing immediately.

TRUTH ALONE TRIUMPHS

"So when is this two-week ultimatum up?" Ryan asked.

"I have to decide by tomorrow," Axel responded.

"Whoa, down to the wire."

"Yeah."

"If I know you, you already have this figured out, and you're just being thorough. Hey, if it gives us a chance to catch up, I'm all for it."

Ryan raised his glass of bourbon in a toasting gesture and polished it off. The ice rattled in the glass as he put it down. Axel took a conservative swig and placed his glass down more gently.

After all these years Ryan still wore his hair short, and he remained clean-shaven. If you were to take Ryan out of Axel's plush Long Island study and put him back into that trench in Yemen, he would be a mirror image of ten years ago. The only substantial difference in his appearance was the prosthetic hand that rested neatly on the arm of the chair.

Axel had reviewed almost everything with Ryan. He laid out Bhavin's belief in the threat of AGI, and how Bhavin wanted Axel to disable it. He even told him about his meeting with Hugo, without mentioning Hugo specifically by name.

Axel was desperate for some kind of contrarian view that made sense. There had to be something he was missing. He knew Ryan wouldn't be bashful about setting him straight.

Ryan said, "Well, I have to agree with you. It does sound like industrial sabotage to me. I mean really, to ask you to go and remove all downloads of this software from customers?"

"Well yes, it does sound extreme, but I guess the question isn't about the measures taken to mitigate the risk, but whether there is in fact a risk dire enough to warrant those measures. If Bhavin is right, the sabotage actually makes sense."

Ryan's face contorted as if he was sucking on a slice of lemon. "It sounds like you may be rationalizing this. I mean, give me an example where something like this has happened before—something where software has caused significant harm. I can't think of any."

Axel tried to explain, "there have been national cyber attacks and power plant failures caused by software glitches, but this is different. The superintelligence, when it happens, will improve itself so fast that we wouldn't be able to stop it. We may not get a second chance."

Ryan's eyes went wide. He was looking at him with sympathy, rather than understanding. "I don't know, man," was all he said.

Axel suspected he said it not because he didn't know, but because he didn't want to tell him he sounded like a lunatic.

"Look," Ryan said, glancing down at his prosthetic arm. "I can't even bring a drink to my lips with my prosthetic hand, and it uses AI. I'm pretty sure we can stop any AI that turns on us."

"Actually, the controller for your arm uses a narrow AI, and bringing a glass to your lips is actually quite complicated—more difficult than many things humans find difficult, like art and writing. A superintelligent AGI might not be able to know how your hand works at first, but it would *learn*. In fact it would be able to figure that out in no time, along with how it could strangle you with it."

"Sounds to me like you already drank the Kool-Aid."

"No, no, I haven't. Not yet. But I've learned a lot."

"Come on now, if there were real risks here, I'm sure we would have heard something by now. The government would have instituted protective programs."

"I worked for the government not too long ago and had top-secret clearance. There are no real programs to address this, only to address job dislocations resulting from AI advances. They don't have the depth of knowledge to understand, and the electorate certainly won't push them in the right direction."

There was a knock on the French doors and Pauline appeared. She was carrying two plates replete with apple pie and ice cream.

"Wow," Ryan said, "you remembered."

"How could I forget the time you gagged on my chocolate chip cook-
ies," Pauline said, winking.

"Hey Axel, remember when I told you she was a keeper?"

Axel smiled and nodded.

Ryan's little boy ran into the room with a toy spaceship in one hand
and an ice cream cone in the other. He promptly ran to the window and
smashed both of them against it. Some of the ice cream stuck to the window, and the boy began to lick at it after examining the pattern it made.

"Ryan Junior!" Ryan said, getting up to grab him. "I told you to behave!"

"Oh don't worry," Pauline said, "it's just a little spill. I can clean it up."
She left the room, presumably to collect some rags.

"Now back to the living room," Ryan said to his son. "Go play with
the tablet and leave us alone." Ryan corralled the boy out of the room.

Ryan had to raise the boy on his own after his wife had left him, but
he didn't have much time. The boy was a real handful, as far as Axel could
see, and severely lacking in discipline. He was thankful his children had
the manners they did.

When Pauline had cleaned up the window she stopped to put her
hand on Axel's shoulder on the way out. "Now I hope you're talking some
sense into this man," she said to Ryan. "His new boss has his mind all
twisted up in knots with this fantasy computer stuff. He can hardly sleep."

"Yeah, he's given me an earful so far." Ryan nodded with some exag-
geration. "He's a tough nut to crack, but I'm wearing him down. I think
he's going to see the light."

Pauline smiled and gave Axel a warm pinch on his shoulder before
leaving the room.

Axel had confided in Pauline as well. She didn't like it at all. She said
it sounded too much like a movie, like make-believe. "No sir," she had
said. "My husband doesn't chase computer programs. He's a war hero, an
intelligence agent, a covert operative that is keeping us out of harm's way."

But of course her reasoning didn't make sense. Just because it sounded hard to believe didn't mean it wasn't a real threat. It only meant fewer

people would believe in it, which made the risk that much *more* menacing because people wouldn't see it coming. Hugo Guilherme's words echoed in his mind: "It's socially awkward. It sounds like you are talking about magic or fantasy, so no one will take you seriously."

"Is there anything else you want to tell me, Axel?" Ryan asked.

"Ryan, you saved my life, twice. I trust you more than anyone, and I can't ask you for anything. Nevertheless I'm asking you to think, really think, and find one good reason why we all shouldn't be worried about this."

"Um…I just did. I gave you several reasons. Look, I'm sorry I got you wrapped up with Nadar Corporation. I was wrong, okay? I didn't know Bhavin would be like the other greedy corporate vultures. It sounds like he's fooled you as well. Maybe you should move on. Stealing software doesn't sound like something Axel Kelemen does for a living. You still have lots of good years left. And you know I'd kill for the opportunity to be in your shoes, to be out there running real ops."

Axel wanted so much for Ryan to relieve him of this burden, but the emotional discomfort, the appearance of corporate sabotage, and even Bhavin's ego were simply not valid premises for dismissing the risk. It was understandable that Ryan couldn't see it. He didn't have Axel's technical training. He couldn't understand how exponential change and connected networks could make AGI unstoppable. Hugo Guilherme, despite his irreverence, was the only one that had made any logical sense.

At this point there was only one thing Axel could do. He had to let go of the debate. He had to let Ryan believe he had won. Axel said, "You know what, Ryan, you may be right. It's hard for me to see myself doing this kind of work." He left off *but it's too important not to.*

Ryan brightened considerably. "I knew you'd come around. Don't feel bad Axel. We all have our twists and turns in life, and you always seem to land on your feet. Heck, I'm sure you'll get a nice severance." Ryan waved his empty glass at the room around them to exemplify the financial rewards he had already accumulated.

They sat for a while longer and made small talk. Axel had a hard time making conversation. He didn't want to risk revealing his true feelings.

Ryan got a sense the conversation was waning. "Well, I appreciate catching up and all," he said. "I've got to get back home."

"I understand. And Ryan, thanks for everything."

"Axel, stop thanking me. I'd jump in front of those mooks again, and you know it."

"I know you would, and you know what? I'm never going to stop thanking you."

Axel walked him through the house to the front door. Pauline came to see him off. Ryan Junior trailed her, his shoulders slouching.

"So how did it go?" Pauline asked.

"Victory!" Ryan said. Axel suppressed a cringe.

"Oh, I'm so glad," Pauline said. "I appreciate the life we have here, but we want to do what's best for Axel." She tapped Axel on the chest.

Axel was sullen, quiet.

"Daddy, this place is stupid. Let's go," Ryan Junior said.

"Junior! I'm sorry about that," Ryan said, herding his boy out the door.

"Don't worry. He's young, it's late," Axel said.

"Thanks."

After Ryan and his son left, Pauline and Axel made their way to their ensuite bathroom to get ready for bed.

"Maybe we can take Friday off, drive along the coast? It'll get your mind off things," Pauline said, the words were somewhat garbled as she brushed her teeth.

"Sorry, I can't."

"I thought you said if you were quitting you would be able to take some time off?"

"I'm not quitting."

Pauline stopped midbrush.

They argued and argued. Pauline never really understood. Like Ryan, perhaps she never would. He had a feeling he would have this uncomfortable conversation again, perhaps many times, and perhaps with many people.

During his argument with Pauline, two words kept coming back to him. They were words Bhavin had told him on his first day of work. It was the Indian mantra for *truth alone triumphs*. Over the last two weeks every single counter-argument Axel had to Bhavin's concern had been overcome. The concern had taken root and wouldn't let go. The simple *possibility* of it warranted aggressive action. Now he had no choice but to follow the path Bhavin had chosen, no matter the discord with his friends and family. If Bhavin was right, everything was at stake. *Everyone* was at stake, including his family.

As he finally lay down at 3:00 am on an old couch in the basement of his house, he said the words again. After an uncomfortable conversation with his best friend and a bitter argument with his wife, it was the only thing that gave him solace.

"*Satyameva jayate*," he said.

Two Meetings

The Mule Pit was just off West Main Street, not too far from downtown. There you could buy some local produce and milk and in the back they would smoke out some barbeque. Rarely were there more than one or two people inside—usually mules refueling their calories with barbecue sandwiches after a long ride. It could have been worse. Chester could have asked Alastair to meet at the Broken Spoke. Better to meet here than that wretched hive.

Alastair paced while he stroked his goatee. He patiently stalked around the sparsely covered shelves of the store once, twice and then three times.

"You lookin' for someone?" the woman at the back counter asked. She was heavyset, with blotchy red skin.

"Waiting for someone, yes. I hope you don't mind."

"No, sir. Just wondering if it's Chester you're looking for. He's out back." She gestured to the door behind her.

He smiled to the woman. "Oh, I see. Thank you. May your day be free of obsession."

In the back Alastair saw several Old World plastic tables and chairs set up on a muddy patch of ground. There was enough seating for thirty people, but Alastair suspected the chairs were hardly ever used in the winter.

Chester was at a table farthest from the door, hunched over his plate. He waved at Alastair and picked up a napkin to wipe his face.

Alastair walked up to the table. "Do you want to meet out here?"

"It's a bit cold out, but us mules run hot. You mind?"

It was somewhat uncomfortable but tolerable enough. "This should do fine," Alastair said.

"You want a sandwich? Best in Seeville," Chester said, pointing at a plate that had a half-sandwich swimming in some bright orange barbeque sauce. The tender brisket bursting out of the side of the sandwich did look tasty, but the sauce resembled some kind of chain oil.

"No thank you. I just ate, and I have to be at a lords meeting soon."

"Your loss," Chester said, smiling.

"I'm surprised you asked me to meet," Alastair said.

"Why is that?"

"Well, because I know, despite what Venter said, that you have little interest in the Credo. And you don't seem like the type to get involved in politics."

"Humph," Chester mumbled, his mouth full of sandwich. His eyebrows were knitted in contemplation.

"But I'm glad you did. I don't keep in touch enough with the mule community."

Chester finished chewing his mouthful. "Look," he said, "let me save you the political song and dance. I can get right to the point."

Alastair raised his eyebrows and said, "By all means."

"The reason I asked you to meet is because you're a lord, and also an Adherent. As an Adherent, while I can't say I agree with the Credo, I think you probably have a good sense of what's right. Or maybe it's not that. Maybe you have a better sense of what's *wrong*. Not only that, you were once a mule. You know our job. You know what it's like out there, right?"

"Yes. I've been to the towers. I've done about fifty centuries. I've even been down to Charleston once."

"And so you know us mules like to keep things quiet. We don't like to talk about certain things, like why the towers are there."

"Yes, of course. "

"So what I'm about to tell you, it's like that. It's to be kept quiet. You may already know about it, but either way, I think it's important because it concerns a lot of us, the way things are heading."

Alastair was intrigued. "Please, I will keep what you say in confidence."

Chester took his last bite of sandwich and finished it off. Alastair waited patiently as he swallowed and wiped his hands one more time on the dirty napkin.

"Did you hear about the bike tower run several weeks back? The one where Bartz wanted it super-sized?"

"The one where the wrench was injured? Newton, wasn't it?"

"Yeah, well a smaller group from that run also went and got lots of Old World tech from a site south of Richmond. They said it was for the trains but I saw the stuff and it wasn't like that. It was lots of computers, generators and other stuff."

"South of Richmond?" It was a tough area to get to. You had to skirt the fever lands and risk running into large bandit tribes. But computers? Novation alarm bells rang in his brain. It was completely counter to the Credo.

"Three died," Chester added, "and just as well could have been the lot of us."

Alastair had long suspected that Bartz was gathering up Old World tech beyond what he needed for railroad operations. He hoped that Bartz was using the right precautions—that he was smart enough to not fall prey to the seductions of obsession or recklessness. They had just completed two more Faraday cage bunkers at the Barnyard, so this news made some sense. But the three deaths were more troubling, especially given that Alastair had heard nothing about it. It suggested imprudence. It suggested recklessness.

"Were the right precautions not being taken?"

"Well, I can't say what the right precautions are, but if you go raiding bandit territories you're bound to get into trouble."

"Was it anyone I know?"

"One mule, one railroad grunt and a kid in trade school named Owen. You wouldn't know them."

Owen's spotted face flashed in his mind. He remembered Owen's exhausting tale of the SLS fight and run from the satellite. Alastair considered mentioning that he knew Owen, but Bartz had been so adamant about keeping the whole thing a secret, and the council of lords had agreed, so he couldn't betray their trust.

"Those three deaths didn't stop them from doing other sorties to similar places, some of which I've been on. They're being more careful now—

or at least seem to be. They go out in greater numbers and bring more firepower. Also, they seem to find things real easy and can get in and out quick. Not sure how they can scout these locations, but it's amazing they haven't been picked over. Still, we lost two more mules the other day."

"What kind of Old World tech are they bringing back?"

"Like I said, lots of computer stuff, generators, wire—even a couple robot–looking things. Some machines I couldn't figure out. Lots of the stuff I've never even seen in books before, and they don't like us asking about it."

If true, it was the most significant breach of the Credo in his lifetime, and it validated the concerns he wrote about in his letter to Duncan. Unfortunately Alastair would have limited power to stop them. Only a few aspects of the Credo were written into law.

"And that's just the sorties outside of Spoke territory," Chester continued. "Lots going on near town too. There's the machine they're building at the observatory and then at the stadium as well. Lots of mules hauling up that way every day. Again, all secret-like. I'm not one to be superstitious, but it all seems a little too fast and a little too secretive. I worry they aren't hammering all the nails in before they move on to the next project, if you know what I mean."

It was yet another concerning report about these construction projects. The railroads had done wonders for business and travel, but this was something different. It sounded like a clear desecration. "What is it they're building at the observatory?"

Chester just shrugged. "Something with lots of metal and wires. Something big."

"And the stadium?"

Chester shrugged again.

"You were right to tell me about this, Chester. Much of it I didn't know."

"Not surprised," Chester said. "Now you do."

"So nothing illegal is going on, as far as you know?"

Chester sat back in his chair and looked to the side, mulling over the question. It took him a considerable amount of time to weed through a response. "You know, out there, in the fever lands, there's a different kind of law. Seems to be a kind of law these railroad folks don't understand. But as Seeville laws go, I can't think of any they've broken, at least far as I can tell. But laws are your domain. Mine is platforms and pedals and keepin' it between the ditches."

Alastair responded thoughtfully. "Well if there's no direct evidence of unlawfulness, unfortunately there's not much I can do right now, Chester, other than to keep a close eye on Bartz in the council, and maybe ask around."

"Well, I guess that's something," Chester said, but he grimaced. He didn't look at all satisfied.

"You know Chester, your intuition is in the right place here," Alastair reassured him, "and I don't want to impose upon you, but have you thought about joining the Adherents, or even visiting the temple? These concerns you have, they're very much in line with our faith. Some communing could bring you peace. It is said that the temple is but the first step on the way to the sanctuary."

"Sir, I don't know. I respect the Credo and all, but I'm not much one for communing with anything. Please don't take that as a sign of disrespect."

Alastair could tell Chester was feeling squeamish. He didn't want to lose his ally by pushing his Adherent agenda. "I understand and respect that, Chester."

Chester looked relieved. "Thank you, sir."

"I have to go now," Alastair said, looking down at his ticking watch, "but let's meet again here next week. I want to hear more about what they're building in the city. Maybe if we can uncover more details, I can better help you."

It seemed to appease Chester somewhat. "Okay, let's do that."

"Thanks again for reaching out. May your day be free of obsession." Alastair extended his hand as he stood up from his chair.

Chester stood as well, taking his hand with a firm grip. So firm, in fact, that he wouldn't let go. Chester had been calm, even aloof, but now there was more energy in his eyes. "I'm worried about more mules getting put in harm's way, sir."

"I know. I know you are, Chester. This has gained my attention, I assure you," Alastair said, but Chester still did not let go of his hand.

"And no word of this conversation."

"No word," Alastair confirmed.

Chester finally let go of his hand, nodded and sat back down.

Alastair walked through the back door and then out the front to his parked bike.

He rode down Water Street, cutting through the downtown mall on the way to the courthouse. He pedaled fast to make up lost time, and just as well to combat the chill that had infiltrated his limbs during his out-door conversation with Chester.

The conversation was more than concerning, confirming many of his suspicions. He had heard stories about Bartz and his crew and their aggressive business dealings, but he never had any verified accounts of foul play. Here was finally a clear witness to something highly nefarious. What's more, Chester didn't seem to be the type to arbitrarily complain, and Alastair guessed there was much more he wasn't being told.

The mention of Owen's death also alarmed him. It was one more con-nection to the ill-fated satellite expedition. Just the other day Alastair had heard that Cecile had somehow returned to the north. Why would she leave without talking with him or the other lords? Why would she leave without finishing her work in the Hall of Records?

There was definitely something amiss—something that needed look-ing into.

His bike percussed over the old, inlaid brick road as he entered Court Square. He locked the frame quickly and then proceeded past the two doormen into the old courthouse.

"Lord Henneson, sir."

"Gentlemen," he replied.

Alastair walked through the foyer and entered the old courtroom. In the center of the room were eight heavy chairs around a large square table made of mahogany. The space was otherwise fairly Spartan. The recorder sat at a meager desk just off to the side, and a few lonely statues stood awkwardly in the corners of the room, as if their heroes of old were somehow enduring a punishment fit for a child. At the back of the room, far from the center tables, were two rows of pews for the clerical support staff.

The oversized room was used because it was thought that as Seeville expanded so to would the need for councilors and clerics. However it seemed the opposite had happened. The number of councilors stood at only five, with three seats left unused for decades because of some arcane law put in place by the original Seeville governors. They were stuck with five when they could probably have used more than ten.

Alastair was the last of the lords to arrive. He took his seat.

"Hello, Lord Henneson," Harmon Kline said. Kline had been recently appointed by his father, and was generally responsible for agriculture and trade. He tended to be friendlier than the rest of the council. His family had at one time occasioned the Adherent temples.

"Hello all," Alastair said. There was no response. The other lords had done away with the art of social graces a long time ago.

"What's on the agenda today?" Kline asked.

The recorder spoke, squinting at the page in front of him. "We have the city budget for next year, the Stony Point land parcels issue, and the wheat blight."

Bartz said, "if it pleases the council, I would like to move up two items to the top of the agenda. The Barnyard Trade School approval, and the Developer Rights Amendment."

Kline made his discontent clear. "Wait a minute. Neither of those is scheduled until next month. Didn't you already try to move these up last week?" Kline feigned frustration by throwing up his hands. He was beginning to show more skill as a politician, Alastair mused.

"This week is not last week," Bartz said. "If you will indulge me, these two bills are holding up great work for Seeville. We can do so much more if we train people to be in productive trades directly linked to commercial output right from the start."

"Why is this more important than the other agenda items? Wheat blight, for example. If we don't address this blight, it could ruin the entire crop."

"That's why we have a council, to decide on what's important. I suggest we follow protocol and have the council vote on changing the agenda," Bartz said.

Kline shook his head. "At some point we need to fix these rules. Why have an agenda if Bartz tries to change it every time?"

Alastair watched Prakash, who was responsible for education. He was expecting to see the usual look of annoyance whenever Bartz put anything on the table, but she looked closed, tense even.

The recorder said, "There are five minutes allotted—"

"I know, I know. Five minutes for agenda changes. Fine," Kline said. "Let's vote on it again, then."

The recorder said, "All in favor of moving the two items mentioned by Lord Bartz to the top of today's agenda?"

"Nay," said Kline.

"Aye," said Meeker.

"Nay," said Alastair.

"Aye," said Bartz.

"Aye," said Prakash.

Kline's head swiveled in surprise toward Prakash. Prakash was sitting up straight, looking defiant. It was the first time Prakash had been in agreement with anything Bartz had proposed.

The recorder waited, noticing the surprise in the council. "Agenda changed," he said, when no one objected.

"Excellent," Bartz said. "Now, if you will let me say a few words about the Barnyard Trade School Bill."

As far as Alastair was concerned, the Barnyard Trade School Bill was fairly innocuous. It would allow an additional trade school to be built on the Barnyard grounds, so that students could have more on-the-job training. As long as the students weren't taken advantage of as strictly a source of labor, it made reasonable sense. Alastair had only wanted to see more details on the curriculum before committing, and had said as much to Bartz.

"Since last week," Bartz said, holding out the packet that described the bill, "We have changed one very important thing. We have allowed the current teachers in existing trade schools to transfer over to the Barnyard Trade School, with a requirement for a fifteen percent salary bump as compensation for relocation."

It was a change that played right into Prakash's hands. Many of her supporters were educators. There hadn't been a raise in educator salaries as far as Alastair could remember.

"All in favor say aye," the recorder said.

"Nay," said Kline.

"Aye," said Meeker.

"Nay," said Alastair.

"Aye," said Bartz.

"Aye," said Prakash.

It was clear there had been some kind of side-deal between Prakash and Bartz, while Kline and Alastair had been blindsided. Although Alastair was not terribly moved, Kline looked livid.

"Bill passed," the recorder said.

It took Alastair only a brief moment more to realize Bartz' motivations for such a generous payout to the educators. It wasn't about the educators. It wasn't about getting the Barnyard Trade School Bill passed at all. It was about the next bill.

"Next up, the Developer Rights Amendment," the recorder said.

Prakash cared nothing about the Developer Rights Amendment, but had previously agreed to vote against it simply because Bartz proposed it. That would change now. Meeker was always with Bartz, so the three of them would give him the majority to approve the amendment.

The trade school bill was one thing, but the Developer Rights Amendment was something else entirely. If passed, it would basically eliminate the lords subcommittee approval on large Seeville construction projects.

Bartz would have free reign to build new factories and service stations without oversight and without the lords' ability to enforce the few Credo-based laws they had. Which meant he would have free reign to complete whatever he was building at the observatory and stadium without the council so much as knowing what they were.

As an Adherent, Alastair found the notion of unilateral control of anything to do with progress to be unwise. Now, when considering what he had heard from Chester, it was downright alarming.

"I don't think this bill needs any more introduction," Bartz said. "In fact it's unchanged from my submission two weeks ago. I suggest we go right to vote."

Kline looked at Alastair with concern. Alastair shook his head. There was nothing they could do. They had been outmaneuvered by Bartz.

There was some noise at the door, distracting the recorder. The doorman came in, along with Deputy Attorney Henry Klipton. The Deputy's clean-cut wool jacket and tight-fitting tie contrasted with a comb-over that had been dislodged. It was now projecting straight into the air. He was trailed by a shorter, older-looking woman with close-cropped, gray hair. She walked slowly, supporting her weight with the help of a cane.

She entered the enclosure to the meeting area while Klipton stood his ground.

"Who are you?" Lord Meeker said, standing. Meeker was responsible for law enforcement and defense, as well as hunting and foraging. Bartz had bought him a long time ago. He wasn't about to let Bartz's moment of triumph be interrupted.

Meeker didn't receive an immediate response from the elderly woman. "Doorman, please remove this woman," Meeker said. "These meetings are closed to the public."

"Which is a shame, don't you think?" the old woman said, now plodding slowly around the mahogany table, all eyes resting on her. "We are here to govern for the people. Shouldn't those we serve be privy to know how we serve them?"

She took a seat in one of the empty chairs around the table, the one next to Alastair.

"You can't sit there. What's the meaning of this?" Meeker asked Klipton, his fists clenched.

Klipton opened his mouth to respond but was interrupted by a cutting remark from the gray-haired woman. "Now don't get all testy with the deputy attorney." She spoke with remarkable force and clarity given her stature and age. She wagged her finger at Meeker. "He did his job, and properly too, giving me quite the once-over. That's why I had to go to the trouble of getting an official validation of my talisman from the Citizen's Registry. It seems my original talisman was misplaced, along with those of a lot of my relatives. Thankfully it could still be authenticated, based on a likeness to other talismans and some other transactional records."

The old woman looked over at Alastair. "Who knew the deed to that terrible Cherry Avenue money pit would ever be useful to anyone?" She laughed and touched his arm as if they were old friends. Meanwhile, with her other hand she was pulling out a number of sealed letters. She distributed them one by one to each of the lords.

They looked to be copies of an affidavit from the Deputy Attorney, affirming her identity.

She took a key from her pocket and easily unlocked the drawer built into the table in front of her, as if she did it every other day. She awkwardly reached in, pulled out a name block, blew some dust off it and placed it on the desk with the name facing out. "Amazing," she said, "still here after all these years."

Then she looked up at the council members. "Gentleman, lady, my name is Madison Banks. Please excuse my tardiness. I will try to not be twenty-seven years late for the next meeting." She smiled at the councilors, only to continue receiving blank stares in return.

Without missing a beat, she asked, "Well then, what's on the agenda?"

MONTICELLO

Master Euclid had sent down a proper horse and carriage to pick up Mehta and Flora. It seemed like a nice welcoming gesture, but when inside the carriage they realized it was more for convenience. They had to sit uncomfortably on wooden boxes full of seeds, bricks, and other Seeville goods. There was an odd but pleasant smell of rye and apricot.

Euclid had signed the deal for Flora's placement at an attractive price. He had also agreed to keep her on the estate and not let her fraternize among the people of Seeville. It was a good deal for the railroad—good enough to force Thorpe to grudgingly accept it. Mehta was not entirely free of his contract yet, however. There was still a one-week period where Euclid could back out if for some reason he didn't like Flora.

"You've done her up well," Barbara said, looking Flora up and down from across the carriage. "I didn't know you had it in you, Mehta."

Flora cast Mehta a somber glance. He had purchased some better fitting clothes for her. They were nothing fancy. Flora looked nice simply because her figure was no longer hidden by rags and a bulky jacket. Her crimson hair also hung neatly down to her shoulders, the tangles removed through some aggressive brushing she did on her own.

Barbara said, "Euclid likes them like you—a bit older, more experienced. As long as you can play along with his games, you should do fine."

Flora again looked at Mehta. He gave her a firm look in return. Flora nodded compliantly to Barbara.

When Mehta had told Flora she might have to play Euclid's games she didn't seem surprised. She only nodded solemnly and said, "I have loved many men in the hopes it would get me back to the man I truly love."

Mehta knew Flora fairly well by now—from her own stories or from watching her during the sessions—but sometimes he wondered if there was even more misfortune he didn't know about.

It felt right for her to have some reward for all her troubles. If he could do something to ease her sorrow he could leave this forsaken place in good conscience. At the same time, he couldn't bring himself to tell Flora his suspicions about the slave Barbara named "Mutt". He didn't trust her to think clearly with that expectation on her mind. Besides, Mutt might not, in fact, be the man she was looking for.

"You know, Mehta, a man like you, we could use you. I could use you." Barbara bit her finger after she said it, sizing him up with her eyes.

Mehta wanted nothing to do with Euclid's whore. Ordinarily he would have told her to go fuck a sweaty mule, but he didn't want to mess up the deal. So he continued to absorb her crude advances with polite grins.

Barbara was just one reason why it was rumored Euclid was some kind of pervert. But he invested in a number of important Spoke operations, so people let him be. As long as he didn't push the New Founder agenda too much, the lords would ignore him. There was no worry on that account. At one time the New Founders had been a powerful force in Seeville, but now, with Euclid at the helm, they seemed more like a curiosity born of Seeville's past—historians that were now part of history.

While all the snow had thawed in Seeville, there remained a few patches of hardpack on the mountain. The sun peeked out, and the road turned to a glistening brown, channeling the remaining melt down into the valley below.

They pulled up to the stately home.

Mehta hadn't seen the estate on his prior trip up as Euclid wanted to meet in Michie Tavern, slightly down the mountain. Monticello looked exactly as it did in the books, with four pillars and a triangular archway first greeting visitors. Two wings struck out from either side, and a small dome jutted from the roof. It was smaller than Mehta had expected, but impressive in its décor.

A hunched-over man in rags greeted them and opened the carriage door. He was bare-sleeved and had red marks covering his face and fore-arms.

"This is Scabby," Barbara said. After they all exited the carriage, Scabby wordlessly pointed to the east and then went to work on getting the boxes out. Mehta noticed Flora was looking at Scabby closely, trying to see his face despite Scabby's predilection for looking down.

When they had stepped down from the carriage, Barbara said, "Welcome to Thomas Jefferson's mountaintop home. This was where Jefferson must have greeted visitors three centuries ago." Barbara was smiling congenially and waving her hands at the building in a rehearsed manner.

Mehta was no New Founder, but he had learned enough about this Thomas Jefferson. He wondered what Jefferson would have thought about the current use of his cherished homestead. It was inhabited by a pervert who employed a whore, his greeter was in rags and marked with scabs, and their guests were a woman from a notorious enemy turned-slave, and a merc who had killed hundreds of people.

Jefferson probably would have preferred that the red coats had won.

"It sounds like Mr. Euclid is in the gardens," Barbara said. "You can get to know Scabby later."

Barbara walked with them toward a long pathway that ran along the hilltop while Scabby escorted the carriage driver to the stables on the west side of the building.

Below the pathway, to the east, was a palisade garden. Even in winter there looked to be plants growing at the far end. Perched on the edge of the plateau was a glass-walled gazebo where one could look out and see for miles into the distance.

They found Euclid walking between rows of plants and herbs on the palisade, examining labels and taking notes on a clipboard. He was round in the belly, and had a lamb chop-style beard. Spectacles dangled from his neck. A holstered pistol hung from his belt, as well as a lash. Another man was working on the palisade farther away, tilling the soil. He must be the one Barbara called Mutt.

"Welcome," Euclid said, flashing an unbridled smile. "Just tending to the crops here. Did you know Jefferson grew more than two hundred and fifty varieties of more than seventy species of vegetables?"

Mehta looked at Barbara, who tilted her head back to him expectantly. Apparently the question was being asked of him. "No, sir, I didn't," Mehta said.

"Yes, and quite of few of them managed to survive the winter. Parsley, parsnips, rosemary and sage." Euclid gestured to the rows.

Mehta nodded and tried to look interested.

Euclid examined the group of them more closely. "Ah, so this must be Flora." Euclid's eyes were shining in the sun.

"Yes, sir. Thank you for…acquiring me," Flora said.

"I'm enchanted, my dear, enchanted." He held her manacled hand and then looked her up and down. He donned a knowing smirk and nodded to Barbara with satisfaction.

Flora looked down, letting him feast on her with his eyes.

Mehta couldn't help tapping his hand on his leg impatiently. He was eager to return to the detention tower. These people sickened him, especially Euclid. But he needed to wait until Euclid had given him leave.

"So are we all settled?" Euclid asked, without averting his eyes from Flora.

"Provided you pay the remaining balance by the end of a week," Mehta said.

"Yes, of course. That's what we agreed."

Flora was looking over at Mutt working in the distance. She was squinting.

"Interested in Mutt, are you?" Euclid asked. "Yes, well he was SLS once too, I think. Hard to remember. He doesn't chat much. Makes him more agreeable if you ask me. You'll see." Euclid then called out across the palisade. "Come here, Mutt! Let's meet the new girl!"

The man dropped the hoe and began moving toward them. Flora had been calm at first. In fact, she had been docile and compliant much of the day. It seemed she had been ready to accept her fate with Euclid. Remarkably, she even accepted the more repulsive requirements of the placement without reservation.

With the man's first steps, however, her posture changed, her eyes opened wider. She was like a cat that had seen a mouse cross its path.

Mutt came closer. He was tall, with broad shoulders and a wiry frame. His dirty rags fell off him loosely. His hair was unkempt, tied back into a ponytail. He kept his head down except for the occasional upward glance toward Euclid.

More and more, Flora's face came alive with a kind of visceral urgency that needed release. She glanced at Euclid, she glanced at Mehta, and then she looked back to Mutt with a yearning Mehta had never seen. Even through the sessions Mehta had not seen such desperation.

As soon as he saw Flora's face in this state, a sinking feeling hit Mehta. He regretted not telling her of his suspicions. He should have given her forewarning that there was a slave fitting Granger's description on the estate. Now she was caught off guard, and there was no telling what she would do.

"Should I take off her cuffs now?" Mehta asked Euclid. Mehta casually made his way over to Flora. It was just an excuse to get closer to her, of course. His intention was to hold her there, to tell her to keep her cool, to prevent her from running to Mutt.

But he didn't get there in time. She burst into a run, her chain-linked cuffs jangling across her stomach. She whispered "Granger" softly at first but then yelled it aloud at full volume.

The man named Mutt looked up slowly, a look of bewilderment on his face. When his eyes connected with Flora the bewilderment changed to shock, and he stopped walking, his feet fastened to the earth.

Flora reached Granger. Encumbered by her manacles, she was unable to embrace him, so she simply fell into his body. He caught her, holding her against him, his face still a tempest of confusion.

Mehta moved quickly, eager to separate them. There was no telling how Euclid would perceive this. To reinforce Mehta's concern, a quick glance back to Euclid showed his soft features hardening, and his face turning a ruddy color. He didn't look happy—not at all.

Granger gently pulled Flora up, back onto her feet, and stared at her. She stared back at him, looking into his eyes. She lifted her cuffed hands up and cupped his chin, holding his face firm, like a trophy for her to cherish. Mehta heard her say his name more softly this time, with gentleness and emotion. "Granger, my love."

Finally, Granger responded, "Flora?" He looked like he was still coming to grips with the situation, still in a state of first recognition, still reaching back through the years to find her memory.

But the moment didn't last. Mehta had learned long ago that this world was not made for lovers or happy reunions. Theirs was a world where more often families were torn apart, where children were impaled on stakes, where love was a luxury few could afford.

The shot rang out over the palisade, and Granger's face rocked back from the impact, out of Flora's hand. Mehta instinctively dove to the ground, his head angling to find the source of the bullet. Euclid had stepped forward over a patch of rosemary and fired his pistol. His face was beet red, infused with jealousy and anger. This spoiled child could not stand having his forbidden fruit tasted by another, especially not on the cusp of his first bite.

"Not for you, Mutt," Euclid said.

"No!" An inhuman wail of anguish escaped Flora as she jumped on Granger's body, now limp on the ground.

Mehta scurried the rest of the way to Flora and Granger and stood above them, hovering over their entwined bodies. The bullet had entered through Granger's cheek, shattering the side of his face. Blood had splattered over his hair and rags, covering Flora's hands with red spots. His eyes were lifeless.

"No!" she wailed again, sobbing violently.

Mehta tried to pull Flora off, gently at first, and then with more strength. Her knuckles were white, and her hands felt as if they were welded to Granger's arms. Pulling her up only resulted in dragging them both along the ground. Mehta looked back and saw Euclid standing there in the same position but with the pistol now lowered. He breathed heavily, his face one part anger, and one part seething satisfaction.

Mehta stopped trying to separate Flora from Granger's corpse. It was pointless to push and pull the two connected bodies through the dirt.

All this turmoil popped some kernel within Mehta. His heart raged, and raged, and his head spun. Maybe Euclid would still accept Flora under the contract, but it felt sullied. It would add another landslide of suffering to Flora's mountain of melancholy. Yet it was a contract he had architected, an outcome he was responsible for.

A bird crowed on a tree nearby. It was a hawk or a raven. It cared not for what had befallen this woman, for the tragedies that continued to plague her. In fact, no one cared. No Spoke, no Essentialist, no one.

Mehta walked back toward Euclid.

"You should have had her better trained," Euclid said in disgust.

Mehta said nothing to the man but instead sized him up, his eyes boring into him. Euclid still held his clipboard in one hand, with a string and pencil dangling from it. This man surely knew something about seeds and vegetables. This man surely knew about men from three hundred years ago. He knew about politics and puddings and wine. None of this was important. He was a sick parasite of a man.

Slowly, surely, Mehta forced the pistol from Euclid's other hand. Euclid's soft grip was easily overcome. "That's mine! I'm within my rights to kill Mutt. He was my property!"

Mehta could feel the surge within him. His blood continued to pulse with rage and anger. There was no stopping him now—no law, no contract. Justice must be done.

With his other hand, Mehta grabbed Euclid by the neck, silencing him and suffocating him at the same time. Then he threw him down on the ground, smothering a patch of rosemary.

Mehta looked at the pistol in his other hand, in his mind's eye connecting form to function. He slowly arced his hand behind his head and then came down with a precise blow, hammering the butt of the pistol into Euclid's face. Then, with the discipline and stamina of a practiced carpenter, he repeated the action, again and again, until Euclid's face had caved in and his head had turned to a bloody pulp.

THE WANDERER

Pierre was the first to notice the wanderer's hut. He grabbed Duncan's arm and pointed avidly at a spiral of smoke through the trees. "Should we all go, or just you and me?" he asked in French.

Duncan put his hand up and turned to assess the rest of their party. The five other men were well bundled, wearing large parkas and oversized mitts, with scarves draped around their faces. They all had walking sticks that were puncturing the snow beside them. Two of them leaned on these as a crutch as they waited.

It was probably best to bring the lot of them, to have strength in numbers. He couldn't know if this was a trap set by the people of Clearfield, or if the merc woman knew he was coming. And by the description he had heard in Clearfield it didn't sound like this wanderer would be fearful of big parties, or anything else for that matter.

"We all go," Duncan said in French, "but I do the talking."

They nodded back at him.

The trail opened up into a meadow spanned by a long wooden fence and covered by islands of dirty snow. Two large dogs came running at them, barking fiercely. They scratched and clawed at the slats of the fence. Duncan held his ground, while his men took a cautious step back. They looked to be some sort of German shepherd sheep dog mix. Spittle flew off sharp incisors as they yapped and snarled.

Beyond the fence and up a small incline was an Old World house than had been gutted, leaving behind only structural beams and a partial roof. Extending out from the roof was a covered pergola, with crates of all kinds stacked underneath. The spiral of smoke came from a deep fire pit that burned in front of it.

The silhouette of a man grew as it approached them slowly across the meadow, rifle in hand.

When closer, Duncan could see the man's hair was laden with sharp sticks forming a dense mess that looked impossible to untangle. His beard was long and tied off in places with elastics. One of his eyes was an empty socket, dark save for subtle ripples of cartilage.

"What do you want?" the man asked in a husky voice when he was within earshot.

"We seek the wanderer."

"What for?"

"To ask about a Merchant Merc woman, blonde, and from the south. She may have had a prisoner in tow. We seek their whereabouts."

"I'm the wanderer," the man said. He looked down at the dogs. They still hadn't stopped barking. "They don't like you," he said, "and I don't like the looks of you, either."

"I can't help the way we look."

"You aren't from Lockhaven, then?" the wanderer asked, scanning their party with his one good eye. Duncan shook his head.

"Syracuse and such?" the wanderer asked.

Duncan again shook his head.

"Did the Alleghenies send you then?"

"No."

The wanderer looked confused. "What you got to share?"

"We caught a hare this morning. Two of them, in fact. We could share a meal, if you're inclined to join us."

The wanderer stared at Duncan icily for a moment, then let out a shrill whistle. The dogs fell silent and ran back up the incline toward the structure, kicking up mud as they went.

"Come in, then," the wanderer said. "I'm hungry." He opened the main gate for them, turned his back and began making his way up the incline to the fire pit. They followed.

They used cylindrical cross-sections of cedar trunks as makeshift chairs. Duncan's men immediately began preparing the two hares for the fire, while the wanderer looked on with interest. The two hounds sat next to the wanderer, occasionally baring their teeth and growling menacingly at Duncan and the others.

"I found out about you in town, in Clearview, but they wouldn't tell me your real name. How should I address you?" Duncan asked.

"Wanderer has been my name long enough. Parents might not like it, but fuck 'em."

Duncan nodded slowly.

"And you are what you do," the wanderer continued. "I wander. I've been a thousand miles west and a thousand miles south. Now I mostly wander 'round these parts, trade with the Alleghenies and such. Nobody else seems to wanna."

"And why do you think that is?"

"The Allegheny, they don't like most people."

"And why do they like you?"

"I'm a song doctor."

It was probably unimportant, but his curiosity got the better of him. "I'm sorry, I'm not really sure what that is."

"You know, I sing to them, to help them heal and such."

"Oh, I see."

Duncan didn't want to ask about the merc woman until the wanderer had gained some level of comfort, until they had some level of rapport. But the more questions Duncan asked the more he felt like this man might be damaged in some way. It made him wary.

"I don't think you do," said the wanderer.

"I'm sorry?"

"I don't think you see. Or maybe you don't believe me, like most folk. Most people from far abouts don't until they see me do it. I'll show you." The wanderer stood up and headed for the open structure of the house. He pulled up a trap door and descended into an underground chamber.

His men had prepared spits for the hares and started roasting them while Duncan waited nervously. The two hounds remained, docile but still baring their teeth and drooling, as if they were looking at a rack of lamb through a butcher shop window.

Pierre came to him and whispered in his ear. "*Monsieur* Duncan, I think you should go piss over there. Gerard saw something interesting." Pierre gestured to a small depression in the topography just beyond the Old World structure.

Duncan walked cautiously, careful not to rouse the ire of the hounds, making his way over to where Pierre had been pointing. He easily found what Pierre was referring to. Several skulls, some still with flesh and hair, were littered there, half interred in the earth. None of the skulls were identifiable. There was one with black hair. It was possible it belonged to Cecile.

He contained his revulsion and forced himself to urinate nearby, in case the wanderer was watching.

When finished, he walked back to the fire, trying to maintain his composure. Was this wanderer a murderer? Did he kill the merc woman, and maybe Cecile as well?

But it didn't make much sense. What would be in it for him? And surely this merc woman would know how to defend herself.

Duncan whispered to Pierre, "be ready. If we find out he harmed Cecile, we'll take him."

Duncan sat down again, slowly, while staring down the dogs.

The wanderer returned a moment later. He brought with him two bags, a guitar, and a long staff. He placed the staff in a worn-out old footing so it stood upright, and he pulled out a greenish stone and placed it on top, hooking a groove in the stone onto a fork coming out of the staff. Then he sat down and started playing, strumming yellowed fingernails over the strings.

♫ *Oh the forest is mine today. The forest is mine you say?*
Leaves rustle only for me, branches crack only under me,
the forest is mine today. ♫

It was a simple melody that Duncan hadn't heard before. While he couldn't say much for the lyrics, the man could clearly play his instrument, and his voice was rich.

The wanderer paused for a moment. "Oh, and I nearly forgot." He handed the second bag to Duncan. "It's not much, but I saved a little in case I have guests."

Inside the bag were some potatoes and carrots, and a few thin slices of meat.

"Thank you," Duncan said.

Duncan passed the bag to Pierre. Pierre relayed it to the others, who began preparing it for the fire.

Perhaps this wanderer was not a murderer. The food was a kind gesture. Duncan also found it harder to see evil in someone who sung with such passion. Perhaps the dead were some unfortunate accident, some illness that had come through the region.

The wanderer began another song, one more mellow and haunting.

♫ *Sky angel I sing to you, I sing to you.*
We need you to purge tar from blood, clear lard from lung.
Please, we summon you, once this song is sung, but before the day is done.
He deserves to live.
Sky angel we need you to see this through,
I sing to you, I sing to you. ♫

A bird seemed to come out of nowhere. It was remarkable because they hadn't seen a bird all day. Actually, now that he thought about it, for many days. They were greatly diminished in the woods in wintertime. The bird hovered and landed right on the top of the staff on the rock and tittered. "*I sing to you, I sing to you.*"

It was a chorus lark.

The wanderer kept singing, and the chorus lark occasionally replicated a verse or a strand. Another chorus lark came and fluttered around the staff, copying the wanderer's verses in tandem with the first.

Duncan marveled at the scene. He had travelled for decades, probably just as far afield as this wanderer, but he had never seen anything like this. Occasionally the chorus larks would flutter above a staff or pole momentarily then leave within a few seconds. But here they were staying, and two of them, and they were copying the song with precision.

His men were all enchanted by the display. It's no wonder these Allegheny people thought this man was special. It's no wonder they thought him some sort of shaman.

After the wanderer finished another song Duncan said, "You were right. No one could doubt your ability after that performance. Truly remarkable."

The wanderer just nodded, as if the response was typical.

"But why do the chorus larks flock to you like this?" Duncan asked.

"Well, the shape of the staff draws the larks, as you know, but the trick is the stone. It's special. I got it from a man who found stones like these in a boulder field. Must have come off a big mountain, because he called it the skin of the giant, if memory serves. He claimed it has magical properties, which I don't put much stock in, but it makes a good story. He *was* sick, in body, and probably in mind as well. He died before he could show me how to use it, so I figured it out on my own."

Duncan nodded while he watched the chorus larks perch and hover around the stone. Maybe there was some moss on it that chorus larks liked.

The man sung another song, again haunting, again speaking of healing, with the larks adding their voices to it.

Finally the food was ready. Duncan made sure the wanderer had a large portion of hare in front of him.

The wanderer put his instrument down and a few moments later, the larks tittered away, still singing his most recent tune.

The wanderer nipped at the hare at first, and then took a huge bite. "Holy fuck," he said. For the first time, the wanderer's face became animated with something other than cynicism, with his eyebrows arching in surprise. He quickly took another bite. "Fuckin' wow. What did you all put on the meat?"

"We seasoned it with parsley, rosemary, salt and olive oil. It's a special recipe. It's common where we're from."

"I ain't never seen no olive oil, and I never use parsley, but that shit is good." The wanderer reengaged with the meat in earnest.

"I'm glad you like it. Now, I wanted to get to the point of our visit here, wanderer. I wanted to ask you about this blonde merc woman, and someone she was with. A woman with a blue streak in her hair. Did they stop through here?"

"Sure did," the wanderer said, devouring another piece of meat.

"And could you tell us where they were headed?"

"No."

"I'm sorry?"

"Can't do that. I think it was supposed to be a secret."

The wanderer kept chewing, and his eye wouldn't meet Duncan's. It was intent on surveying the remains of the hare's hind leg.

Duncan tried to rethink his strategy. There had to be a way to convince him. He doubted a bribe would work. Threatening him probably wouldn't do it, either.

Duncan took a cautious bite of the meat the wanderer had offered. It was tough but seemed edible enough. He could tell Gerard was having trouble with it. He looked like he was trying to contain his revulsion but then he gagged and spat a piece out.

The wanderer noticed. "Don't worry, I don't like people, neither," he said, then he returned to naw on his hare leg.

Duncan's heart jumped. Did he mishear him? "You don't like people?" Duncan asked.

The wanderer said, "Yeah, I got no moral objection to eating a meaty thigh or bicep, but let me tell you...yuck. Tastes like I'm eating my own sock after a week in the woods. Might be okay with some of this fancy sauce you got here, though."

Duncan dropped the meat from his hands. The rest of his men followed suit, spitting out larger chunks of it. Two of them stood up and drew a knife and pistol respectively, their faces masks of rage.

The wanderer moved remarkably fast. In no time he was up, standing behind his dogs with their leashes in one hand and a sawed-off shotgun that had been removed from the confines of his coat in the other. He said, "now you put those away, or one whistle, and I pepper you with pellets before I sic'em on you."

All the men looked to Duncan. Duncan's gaze pivoted between the wanderer and his men. His hand hovered over his own pistol, holstered on his belt.

The wanderer said, "and don't you worry. My dogs, they ain't like you. My dogs, they like eating people. They don't need your fancy sauce, neither. Shotgun pellets will marinade just fine."

Duncan felt nauseous. To think that it could have even been Cecile. But something wasn't clicking here. What did this man have to gain by feeding them human flesh, or even by surprising them with it? His dogs were vicious, and his shotgun blast might kill at least one of them, but then it would be six men against a man and two dogs. The wanderer would surely lose. And although he was clearly not civil or educated, he wasn't stupid.

Duncan scratched under his chin in thought. Then he turned and pushed his hand to the ground in a gesture of calming toward Pierre and his men. They looked at him, incredulous, but relaxed their poses somewhat.

He turned back to the wanderer. "Tell me, wanderer. Why did you feed us this...meat?"

"To share it and such. That's what we do around here. We share, as a gesture of goodwill, you know. We don't point weapons and threaten like you folks. That's for sure."

"But why the human flesh?"

"Cause you guys weren't from Clearfield, or Lockhaven, and you were asking for the merc. I figured you might be like the Allegheny."

"So the Allegheny...eat people?"

The wanderer stared at Duncan for a moment, then snickered. "You all *really* ain't from around here, are you?"

The pieces fell together. Song doctor or not, the wanderer must be the only one willing to deal with the Allegheny, the only one willing to trade with cannibals. It must be how he made a living, as the main intermediary for exchanges of goods. And the merc came here, with Cecile, to do some sort of business.

Duncan could think of only one kind of business.

Duncan doubted the wanderer would be any help. He would have to find these Allegheny himself, and time was of the essence.

"Thank you for your hospitality, wanderer. We were just leaving," Duncan said.

His men slowly gathered their belongings and backed away from the wanderer, his shotgun, and his slobbering hounds. The wanderer only looked at them quizzically, with one solitary eyebrow raised over an eyeless socket.

When they were a stone's throw away, the wanderer followed, leaning back as he walked to hold the dogs in check. He kept following, even until they opened and closed the fence door behind them.

"You're really leaving?" he asked.

"It seems that way, doesn't it?" Duncan said with a touch of mirth.

"You're not going to offer nothing? For more information on your friends, like?" The wanderer seemed genuinely confused.

"No, wanderer."

"Listen. Okay, okay. You got me. Give me one of those fancy knives you got, and a jar of the marinade."

Duncan halted his stride. "For what?"

"For the location. You know, where your friends are going to meet the Allegheny. None of my business really, but information has value, right? And not one done told me not to tell."

Duncan turned and kept walking away.

"Okay, just a jar of that marinade. That's all I need," the wanderer called after him.

Duncan turned and stopped. He nodded to one of his men, who took out a small jar of the marinade. Gerard didn't look happy to be parting with it.

Duncan walked closer to the wanderer and tossed it to him. The wanderer smiled toothily in return. "They'll be by the Milk junction clearing, up Erie trail about five miles. Meeting's planned for first light tomorrow."

There was no way to test the truth of it. But he had to admit, if it was true, the added information could be a gift.

"Thank you, wanderer," Duncan said. Then, without another word, he and his group left for good, cutting into the forest with speed, knowing Cecile's life might hang in the balance.

Relevant Human Capital

The two young men shifted their toes precariously on the floor, trying to take on some of their weight. Above them the nylon ropes were pinching into their wrists, leaving red lines on their skin where they extended to loop up over the ceiling rafters. Their mouths were covered with tight-fitting gags. Around them, what had been a well-organized, open-space office was now littered with papers and electronic devices, plus one prostrated body.

Axel walked over to the body and kicked it in the stomach. It didn't move.

"He's dead, boss. Checked him earlier," Wade said as he continued to rifle through the file cabinets.

"Like I said, don't try to be a hero," Axel said to the hanging men, who blinked their eyes back at him in acknowledgement.

Axel opened up the duffel bag and examined the host of hard drives, flash drives, phones and laptops. Then he looked at the list on his phone again:

> *Secure relevant human capital*—check
> *Gain credentials for access to servers*—check
> *Verify server access credentials*—check
> *Apply cleansing virus to system*—check
> *Collect all hand-held devices, computers, flash drives, hard drives*—check
> *Collect all relevant paper files*—in process.
> *Terminate relevant human capital.*

The latter had been a specific request of Bhavin's. Bhavin was worried that once someone was able to build a functioning AGI system, they could rebuild it again with relative ease. Axel preferred to give them a stern warning. Realistically, who would try again after being threatened—after they knew they were being watched? Still, Bhavin was adamant. Axel hoped the one dead man on the floor would be enough to satisfy him.

Axel pressed on his earbud. "Teams one through three report in."

"This is team one—home purge in process."

"This is team two—home purge complete."

"This is team three—home purge in process."

It was possible they could continue to clear the office for hours. It was also possible someone might have heard the commotion, or seen them through the windows before they pulled the shades, in which case the police could be here soon.

"Let's wrap this up Wade."

"Yes sir. Two more minutes."

"Okay, gentlemen." Axel pulled a chair up below the dangling men. "Listen very, very carefully. You've gone somewhere you shouldn't have with your software development—somewhere dangerous to all of us. After we leave here, you can go about living your life to the fullest. You can even continue to develop software, *unless* you choose to, one—tell anyone what happened here today, like for example what I am telling you now; or two—ever seek to develop software that incorporates AGI. Narrow AI is fine, but stay miles away from anything that can recursively self-improve or uses anything like the Wog abstraction modules. Got it?"

Their faces showed some confusion but they nodded. It was certainly a better deal than being dead.

"This is team one—home purge completed," his earbud chirped.

"Okay boss," Wade said, zipping up his duffel bag.

Axel cut the nylon ropes that were looped over the rafters with his pocket laser. The two young men slumped to the ground and began rubbing their wrists. It would take some time for them to get the wrist ties off and remove their gags.

Axel and Wade hoisted their duffel bags over their shoulders and left.

Outside they hopped in the jeep and tore out of the parking lot of the small plaza. They stayed outside of Currie and headed west, away from

Edinburgh.

"This is team three—home purge completed," his earbud chirped.

Too slow. He would have to audit team three.

Axel wrote a quick summary on his secure phone and messaged it to Grant and Bhavin.

Bhavin had become very interested in the ops. He was almost overbearing, weighing in on details that shouldn't concern him, or that he wasn't qualified to provide input on.

Like whether or not certain people should live or die.

Bhavin had been happy Axel decided to stay, for sure, but he didn't so much as pause to thank him, or even explore how he came around. Instead, Axel was immediately thrust into planning and executing ops. Now Bhavin had daily meetings with Axel and multiple meetings a day with the Fortient division folks. The fact that Bhavin was doing so much work with the defense arm was disconcerting, since their work was essentially a precaution in case Axel failed.

Adding to the frenzy was the fact that Nadar Corp was being investigated by the SEC for accounting irregularities. Nadar Corporation stock price had dropped twenty percent since the news. Rather than assuage investors like any normal CEO, however, Bhavin had ignored the problem and stayed silent. And he would regularly blow off meetings with lawyers and accountants in order to spend more time with Axel or Fortient.

With the SEC investigation Bhavin was losing his shine as the do no wrong, self-made entrepreneur. Axel worried it would only bring more unwanted attention to Nadar Corporation, and, by association, to the work Axel was doing.

They switched cars in an empty garage and set the jeep on self-destruct. Then they continued west to the extraction point. They passed well-manicured green lawns and precisely trimmed Scottish hedgerows on the road to Harburn. There he saw his kids playing soccer on a neatly cut lawn. Sasha scored a goal on Zach, but it looked like he was only half trying, extending his arms a second too late so that the ball could pass into the mesh behind him. Zach lost the point but won a proud smile on

Sasha's face.

When Axel blinked, they were gone.

A call was coming through on his earbud. "Axel, this is Bhavin."

"Yes, sir. Have you seen my report?"

"Yes. What's this about not terminating the relevant human capital?"

"Sir, I thought it would draw too much attention. Three deaths cause more of a media blitz than one. Also, we can monitor the survivors easily. Frankly, I didn't think it was necessary."

"God damn it..." Bhavin said. There was a brief pause. "Axel, what happens if they try again, despite your threats? What happens if next time they outwit our surveillance?"

"Sir, that is highly improbable."

"Highly improbable? We are talking about the extermination of the human race. There are no points for second place. There is no room for non-zero probabilities. Do you understand?"

Axel knew better than to argue, especially given the manic state Bhavin had been in recently. "Yes, sir. Next time we will terminate any remaining human capital."

There was silence for a moment. Wasn't it enough? Did Bhavin want him to go back? That would endanger the whole operation.

"Fine," Bhavin said to Axel's relief. "Report to me upon your return tomorrow. We need to talk about ramping up our efforts."

"Yes, sir," Axel said. He tapped off his earbud.

Ramping up our efforts? If felt like it had been a non-stop ramp since he had committed, and there was no sign of it letting up.

CARACTACUS

"Why do we need a horse and carriage again?" Owen asked. He was watching people gawk at them in the Seeville streets through the cloaked aperture of his hood.

Madison appeared to be in particularly good spirits this morning. She smiled at the people in the streets as their carriage rolled by them, implacable in the face of their looks of disdain. "Caractacus," she said.

"Excuse me?"

"Caractacus was the name of Thomas Jefferson's horse. He would ride it every day, even when he was president. He even said once that of all the cankers of human happiness none corrodes with so silent yet so baneful an influence, as indolence."

Owen appreciated Madison for her wisdom and wit, but sometimes she used so many words from this bygone era that it made her unintelligible.

Noting his confusion, Madison said, "He believed everyone should exercise. That's why he enjoyed riding a horse. It's the only form of exercise that I can also enjoy." She tapped her bad knee with her cane. Owen reflexively massaged his wounded leg in kind. It was still getting better. He should be able to ride a bike, not that there was anywhere he could go.

"But my need for exercise is just an added bonus. We will need the horse and carriage at Monticello to get around. I have heard the roads have not been well kept, and sometimes the weather on the mountain is not as favorable as in the city."

"That is, of course, assuming we are accepted as guests," Madison added.

"And why Monticello? Why not some place downtown?" Owen asked.

"We need a base of operations away from the prying eyes of Bartz's men, and have you also considered that you would be free to roam, rather than cower in a basement?"

"Yes, I'm certainly looking forward to that." Owen had been in hiding for over a week now. What was worse, there was no bunker or Faraday cage near the run-down house they were staying in. He had worked with the other Yorktown folks to patch up the house and dispatch the vermin. Then he had occupied himself by reading the many books he had found in Yorktown.

"Gaining entry is far from assured, however," Madison said, looking thoughtful. "The presiding New Founder, James Euclid, he's an...untidy man, to say the least. It seems he has bastardized many of the New Founder principals, recasting them to suit his own predilections. It's no wonder the people of Seeville have so little faith in the New Founders."

"What happens if they don't let us stay?" Owen asked.

"Well, we shall have to find another place. Eventually we will have to convince Euclid, though. If he's not with us, he will be a thorn in our side."

"Should I still use the scope if we get turned away."

"Yes, good idea. I want you to have a look at the observatory and stadium, and the top of the mountain here is as good a vantage as any, especially for celebrities such as yourself."

She said it in jest, to be sure, and he smiled politely. But it irked him that he couldn't even bike through the city. He couldn't even tell his mom and sisters he was alive. He understood why, though. Too much was at stake if the railroad folks knew he was in Seeville.

"You still think the phone is that dangerous, that it could be influencing the railroad?" Owen asked. "It sounds like a Credo proverb." Over the past week he was beginning to think more and more like an Adherent. It troubled him, because for most of his life he had equated Adherent gospel to lunacy.

"Many superstitions have no basis, Owen. They are founded to manipulate people, or to comfort people. But the Adherents' Credo actually stemmed from the warnings of first settlers. It's full of false narratives and fantastical notions, it's true, but the messages are worth heeding."

She didn't look at him when she spoke. They were passing by the old Michie Tavern, and she seemed to be engrossed in every detail of the old structure.

That this highly intelligent woman might believe in the Credo seemed completely out of place. "How did these people, your relatives, know about these concerns in the first place?" Owen asked.

"Well, it was passed down from generation to generation all the way back to the Detonation. More than that, there was a place, a place they called the sanctuary, where some of them originated before Seeville. It was there they learned that Old World tech was to be feared. They learned it contributed to the Detonation. Not everything, mind you, but a smartphone from outer space fits squarely into that category. You'd be surprised at the power it could have."

"Are you saying a phone is what caused the Detonation?"

She shrugged. "Not exactly. What's in the phone caused it. Think about it. Why would there be a phone in an unmanned satellite? Two phones in fact. It was a trap set by Gail. Humans would know what it was and how useful it could be—we would send it far and wide to allow Gail to plant roots. If it was something more alien to us we might be more cautious about it."

Owen had a hard time believing it, but he had no reason to disagree with Madison. Certainly Preston had changed once he had the phone in his possession, and the railroad had ramped up their ambitions considerably. He suspected the phone might be contributing to their current troubles, but the main driver was the egos of people like Bartz, Thorpe, and Rourke. Their greed was getting the better of them, and corrupting his friend in the process.

Whatever the cause, Owen agreed with Madison that Bartz and the railroad folks needed to be stopped. They were taking too many risks, putting their vain ambitions ahead of everything, including people's lives.

As the road crested, it exposed a view of Monty, the Montalto beholder. It was the closest he'd ever been to the giant statue. Owen could make out much more detail here than down in the city. Its rounded belly and slouch made it look somewhat less imposing than it did from down below. Larks could be seen circling it in the distance.

"What about the beholder monuments? Did Okafor really build them?"

Madison looked over at him, her eyebrow raised. "I've wondered about that as well, Owen."

With her face contemplative, she turned to focus up at the beholder. She spoke quietly into the window. "I am sure the answer is blowing in the wind somewhere. But on that account, I wouldn't put too much stock in the Adherent teachings."

After a few more twists and turns in the road the carriage pulled up in front of the resplendent manor.

"No greeter," Madison said. "Well, I suppose that's what you get when you arrive uninvited."

Owen stepped out and helped Madison down. They caught up with Benjamin and the driver, who were lingering on the steps leading up to the manor.

Benjamin had his hand on his holster. Madison said, "Now, now, let's not start off on the wrong foot."

When they reached the front entrance, Benjamin rapped his knuckles on the glass doors, while Madison collected herself. Owen hung back, cloaking his face with his hood, just in case he needed to conceal his identity.

Through the glass they could see the main foyer. The walls were adorned with animal skins and maps of various sorts. A hunched over man came out of an adjoining room and opened the door no more than an inch. When he lifted his head up Owen could see he had red marks covering his face. They weren't spots like he had, but possibly some other disease of the skin.

"Mr. Euclid is not accepting visitors today," the man said. He closed the door and walked away.

Madison yelled after him, "Wait! Excuse me, I have urgent and important business with Mr. Euclid. I would like to speak with him immediately."

By the time she was finished the man had already exited the foyer to the adjoining room.

"What do we do now?" Benjamin asked.

"Well, we certainly don't give up," Madison replied.

They lingered in front of the doors for some time. Every couple of minutes, Madison would call out some new request for the whole estate to hear.

"It would greatly please me if we could have an audience. I have been gone for many years, and I look forward to reuniting with my New Founder brethren.

"Whomever is in charge, I think there is a misunderstanding as to our intent and importance. If you could kindly come to the door we will explain.

"I'm not sure how we will explain our situation to the lords of Seeville. If you could spare but a few minutes of your time, it would help resolve any confusion."

Finally there was some movement inside. This time a woman came out into the foyer.

She opened the door an inch more than the hunched man. Her hair was stuffed up in a series of waves, a hairstyle Owen hadn't seen before. Her lips were a deep red, and her presence was accompanied by a waft of strong Old World perfume.

"Excuse me, but this is not acceptable," the woman said to them with some annoyance. "We have clearly told you of our disinterest. Euclid is resting and does not want to be disturbed. He asks that you send a formal request to meet in writing."

"You must be Barbara. It's such a pleasure to meet you." Madison did a mini curtsy. Barbara did not look bemused or enchanted. She grimaced like she was trying to solve some impossible math problem.

Madison continued, "I knew Euclid when he was but a young man, and I have been longing to meet him again ever since. Can you please tell him Madison Banks is here all the way from Yorktown? As you know,

Thomas Jefferson would be loath to turn away old friends. I suspect Mr. Euclid would feel the same way if he knew who was standing here on his stoop."

Barbara stared at Madison for a moment, started to speak, stopped, and then stared for a moment more. Finally, she said, "I will speak with him and gauge his interest."

"Thank you kindly, Barbara."

Barbara closed the glass doors, locked them and then went toward the adjoining room. Madison gave a reassuring smile to them all while they waited. Owen had to admit, Madison was persuasive.

A moment later, Barbara came back to the door.

"Mr. Euclid says he's not feeling well and requests that you write a formal request for appointment, sent by post."

Madison looked surprised, suspicious even. "By post? We are here, now, why couldn't we organize a meeting now?"

"That's what he said. He also said if you don't leave the estate immediately, he will lodge a formal complaint with the Seeville enforcers. If necessary, we will also unleash the hounds."

Madison's countenance transformed from friendly to angry. "So be it, then. We will do this the hard way. Euclid will regret the day he decided to pick a fight with his only remaining ally." Then she turned around and started hobbling down the steps with the help of her cane. "Let's go, gentlemen. This place seems to have lost its hospitality."

Benjamin ran to help her. The carriage driver and Owen followed quickly after.

On their way back to the carriage, Madison whispered, "could it be that Euclid is also under Bartz's thumb?"

It was not a question any of them could answer.

Shortly after they boarded the carriage and pulled out, Madison opened a window to the front of the carriage and said, "James, stop up here. There's a problem with one of the wheels."

"Ma'am? I don't see a problem."

Benjamin whispered in the driver's ear. "Yes, ma'am," James said.

Madison nudged Owen with her cane.

Owen withdrew the scope from his jacket and stepped down from the carriage. He scrambled up a small hill, but it wasn't high enough. He carefully skulked farther up, closer to Monticello. The only good vantage point was on an extended part of a ledge high above where the carriage had stopped. He lay down in front of a planter and hoped it would block any line of sight from Monticello.

Madison's scope was quite powerful, giving him good range. He was tempted to find his house but knew they needed to be quick.

First he found the stadium, an easy landmark. It was run-down, but the seats and stairs down to the main exhibition area had been refurbished and remained mostly intact. Down in the field area a huge structure was being built. Scaffolding had been erected and was almost entirely covered by large blue tarps. There was some scrap metal nearby, as well as large vats of mixing cement. Why build a giant cement building in the middle of a stadium? It could be another Faraday cage bunker, he supposed, but they were already building two new ones at the Barnyard, and it would be more efficient to keep them closer together.

At a loss, he directed his attention to the activity at the observatory. He immediately noticed increased security, with several checkpoints heading up the hill, and armed sentries standing about. The construction was taking place at the top of the hill, and it had already overtaken the original observatory. Here they had also erected scaffolding and tarps, but these could not disguise the distinctive shape of the structure underneath. It was a large dish with a point sticking out of the center. It closely resembled a radio telescope he had once seen in an Old World book.

Owen found it hard to believe Bartz would sanction any form of stargazing, or doing scientific experiments. They wouldn't need such a big dish for that, anyway. It was more likely they were hoping to *send* a signal rather than receive one. But to what? And how could they get around the retcher problem?

He retracted the scope and shimmied off the ledge, his mind wrestling with what motivation they might have for building such an apparatus. It had to be important, because there were so many other things they could be building. With the same resources they could surely build multiple Faraday cage bunkers, or even additional railway lines.

He was about to slide down back down the small hill when he heard, "Hands up! You too!" from down near the carriage. It was a woman's voice he didn't recognize.

Owen shifted his position to move into a small cleft obscuring him from the carriage, then cautiously glanced over the lip of it. Their driver was standing next to the carriage with his hands up. Behind the carriage, Benjamin was also slowly raising his hands after gently putting a ratchet on the ground. Down the road, the scab-faced man, Barbara, and another red-haired woman were leveling rifles at them all and pacing toward them.

"Why are you still here?" the red-haired woman said.

Madison pushed open the door of the carriage and awkwardly stepped down the ladder rungs. Tension reigned while everyone watched her navigate the precarious rungs on her own.

"Now let's all just calm down," Madison said when she had her feet firmly planted on the ground. "We just had a bit of wheel trouble is all. The wrench that fixed us up in town has a flawless record for bike repair, but I'm guessing he hasn't seen too many horse drawn carriages." She laughed.

Owen reached to his lower back to grab his holstered pistol. If they opened fire he might at least be able to take one or two of them out.

But his pistol was gone.

All of a sudden a meaty hand grabbed him by the neck and he was lifted up into the air.

"I found another one," a man's deep voice called out from underneath him. Owen clawed at the hand and gasped for air. He was then thrown down the hill toward the carriage, skidding his backside on the slick red Seeville mud. Looking up at his assailant, he could see a large man with a full beard and a vertically striped yellow vest, the markings of a Merchant Merc.

"Tell us what you're really doing here." The merc leveled Owen's pistol at Madison.

Madison smiled. "Well, you certainly have us at a disadvantage, don't you? This is not what I expected this morning. Not at all."

She hobbled a few more steps away from the carriage, further exposing herself to the weapons trained on her. "Let me see. There are two possibilities here. I know Barbara must have heard about my arrival in Seeville. I made sure she did, so in turn, Euclid must know as well. That means either Euclid has gone completely mad and renounced his New Founder roots...or Euclid is no longer in charge here."

She swiveled on her cane, casting glances at the armed woman and bearded merc in turn.

The bearded merc said, "I asked you a question. What are you doing here? Spit it out, old lady."

"I'm getting there. I'm a New Founder. As you probably already know, I have come back to take my position as a Seeville lord, but I need help. There are forces opposing us—strong forces that do not have Seeville's best interests in mind. We came to seek shelter, and also to secure Euclid's help, and the help of other New Founders. I have a whole community, some five thousand strong, who can come to our aid. But we need a beachhead first. We need a place to call home, away from prying eyes."

Madison continued after a brief pause, "I suspect, however, based on the motley nature of you all, and your discourteous welcome, that things are not completely in line for you, either. Regardless of whether Euclid has left, or gone mad, I can help you. I am a Seeville lord, and I know my way around this town."

The three holding rifles looked up to the bearded man. He must be the leader, absent this Euclid person. The man massaged his beard and squinted at Madison, looking thoughtful.

Barbara called up to the merc, "We're not going to be able to hold out here forever without help. And guess what, we don't really have anywhere to run."

The bearded merc said, "No. We can't trust these people. This woman is an accomplished liar, you can tell. Besides, she's not telling the whole story." He pointed his pistol at Owen and said, "You, spotty. What were you looking at with that eyepiece."

Owen raised his hands. He considered denying that he was looking at anything but reasoned that wouldn't be wise. This man seemed to not be the kind to trifle with without consequence. But what could he tell him? If he told him the truth he knew it would sound crazed and he'd be shot just the same.

"Go ahead and tell him," Madison encouraged.

Owen hesitated, "I was looking at the city there…" He faltered, not sure how to explain it.

The bearded merc's face was a mask of dissatisfaction. Madison waved her hand in a *get on with it* motion.

Owen continued. "The two new projects, specifically, at the stadium and observatory."

"Why?" The bearded merc asked, his eyes unrelenting.

"Well, we think a contingent of railroad folks are planning something big. A while ago, I was on an expedition to the Valley, and we…well, the railroad folks found some Old World tech, but they are keeping it a secret. They tried to kill me on one expedition. And now, they're building…" Owen hesitated again, knowing how it would sound.

"Building what?"

"Building some kind of satellite dish that communicates with space. It could put all of us in danger. They must have some way to get around the retcher problem. I don't know." Owen looked over to Madison for help.

"It's true," Madison said. "They have an Old World smartphone guiding them. With it in their possession, they won't stop until they have usurped control of all Spoke people, maybe even the Essentialists as well."

The bearded merc was quiet for a moment, but then his head bobbed back in a disbelieving laugh. "Communications with space? Old world smartphones? I take it back, you are *not* an accomplished liar. Give me one good reason we shouldn't shoot you all now and take all you have. It would be entirely justified. You're trespassing on private property, and there are many here to corroborate your madness."

Owen couldn't think of a good retort. Even ever-verbose Madison seemed at a loss for words. Owen could feel his heart beating like a metronome, pulsing away the seconds toward the bloody end that this violent man seemed to seek.

"Stop it."

It wasn't Madison, or even Benjamin, or the carriage driver. The red-haired woman spoke up.

"Stop what?" The bearded merc said.

"Stop ignoring the facts. Barbara is right. Unless we run from here, there's no other way to get help. Or maybe that's what you want, to become a fugitive of the Spokes, living out your life in bandit lands? Or maybe you intend to abandon us and move on to the next contract?"

The bearded merc was looking at the red-haired woman with a kind of visceral energy, a seething blend of anger and frustration.

"And you may forget our first meeting," the red-haired woman continued. "We retrieved a phone from the satellite, from Cecile. It's entirely plausible the Spokes found another one. More than that, you can see the dish at the observatory for yourself. There's nothing else it could be. Yes, these people, their story sounds strange, but so strange that you won't believe your own eyes? So strange that you won't believe your own recollection of events in Grand Caverns?"

The bearded merc shook his head, mired in some kind of internal debate. After a moment of heavy breathing, his eyes leveled at the red-haired woman, and he let out a feral sound, almost like a bear's growl. "Damnit Flora, you'll be the death of me." He lowered his weapon, turned around and stalked back toward the house.

Madison looked back at the three holding guns on the road, one eyebrow raised in confusion.

Barbara rolled her eyes. "I think that means you can stay."

"Fabulous!" Madison said. "Shall we put on some tea?"

THE ALLEGHENY

The four Allegheny in the clearing wore animal skins and tall Old World boots. Each of them had bones braided into their hair. It made their heads look like a suitable habitation for a family of birds. Alastair was not amused, however. He suspected the bones were of human origin, and three held long machetes, rusty from oxidation and blood.

The leader of the group held no weapon. She was a large, rounded woman who had a lattice of bones cascading down her back, each one laced together by strands of her raggedy hair. She sat on a log in the clearing, facing the blonde merc woman. Cecile was behind them, bound and gagged, with one arm held firmly by another merc, a strapping young man barely out of his teens.

The large Allegheny woman and the merc lady were clearly conversing, but they were too far away to determine what they were saying.

Duncan put down his binoculars and whispered to Pierre in French, "I don't like taking on those mercs, but the Allegheny could kill Cecile any moment. We need to move in."

Pierre nodded and took two of the men to the north, while Duncan approached from the east. When they were close enough to charge, Duncan and the four men with him found cover positions and aimed their rifles.

Duncan's first shot missed the large Allegheny woman, but through his scope he could see another bullet knock her off her chair. The other Allegheny people dropped to the ground. Whether they had been downed by bullets or dropped of their own volition, it was hard to tell.

"*On y va!*" Duncan yelled and hurtled over the downed tree he was perched behind. He was jogging full tilt, but occasionally he would slow and look through his sight. The Allegheny were still down.

When his men had found positions surrounding the clearing, Duncan called out, "We want Cecile! Send her out and you can live."

There was a burst of fire in his direction, so he dropped down. One of his men yelped in pain. Duncan looked to see the younger merc had found cover and was taking aim with a rifle. One of the Allegheny men also jumped up and ran into the forest after one of his men, screaming and swiping with a machete.

The machete-wielding Allegheny was easily dropped by two well-placed rounds, but the merc man kept firing. Another one of Duncan's men cried out.

They charged farther inward, toward the clearing, suppressing the merc with a flurry of fire. The next time the merc popped his head up, Duncan was ready.

Duncan hit him squarely in his temple, sending him into a spasm on the ground. Only a brief moment later he lay still.

"*C'est clair!*" Pierre called out.

Duncan cautiously stood up and walked into the threshold of the clearing, scanning the surroundings carefully as he went.

The large Allegheny woman was bleeding out but alive, her back up against a tree. Another Allegheny man was breathing rapidly, but his intestines were seeping out of him onto the forest floor. Across from them was the blonde merc, lying down on her back with one hand behind her head, and the other hand with a pistol pointing at a cuffed and bound Cecile.

At first the merc wasn't paying attention to them, but rather staring at the sky between the trees as if daydreaming, oblivious to the approaching assailants and the gruesome scene around her.

Then the merc abruptly sat up and looked around, her pistol still trained on Cecile. She said, "Okay, okay, you can unwet your pants now, whoever you are. No one else is going to shoot at you."

She stood up all the way, pulling Cecile off the ground with her. She arranged Cecile into a tight headlock. Cecile looked filthy and tired, with bruises on her face, but her eyes maintained the stubborn vitality he remembered.

"Hi, I'm Rosalie," the merc woman said with a southern twang, turning to Duncan and Pierre. "Nice to make your acquaintance."

Rosalie ambled over to the other merc with Cecile in tow. She touched him with her foot. He didn't move.

"Too bad," Rosalie said, "Nice to look at, he was. A bit foolhardy, though. Oh well, I guess a new broom sweeps clean, but an old one like me knows where the dirt is. Now let's see, where were we?" She ambled Cecile toward the Alleghany leader while still keeping her in headlock.

"What do you think you're doing?" Duncan asked, keeping his rifle trained on Rosalie. "Look at the odds here, merc. It would be wise for you to give up."

"I'm sorry mister, but we haven't been formally introduced."

"Duncan."

"Duncan, I hear you. You all can do whatever your heart pleases. By all means, pull those triggers, but only as long as you're willing to shred your charming *mademoiselle* here. You see, I'm a merc, sir, and I have a contract. I'm going to finish my business, now or if you kill me, when I'm darn well resurrected. Hopefully I will come back with better teeth." She smiled, revealing a gap between her front teeth.

Duncan looked to Cecile, who shook her head slowly, a dark look in her eyes. Perhaps the merc *would* kill Cecile.

"She knows me so well," Rosalie said, noticing the exchange between Cecile and Duncan. "Me and Cecile, we're best of friends now!" Rosalie kissed Cecile on the back of her head.

Duncan would have to let the scene play out. They weren't going anywhere, as long as his men had them surrounded.

Rosalie gradually made it over to the bleeding Allegheny leader, who had been watching the interaction with some disgust.

Rosalie felt at the ground and found a few stray pieces of paper that were speckled with blood and dirt. With Cecile still in tow, she brushed them off and examined them closely. "There you have it."

Rosalie released her hold on Cecile, fully exposing herself to gunfire from his men. Cecile was surprised but not so surprised that she didn't react. She rapidly moved away to stand next to Duncan.

"I don't understand," Duncan said. "Why would you release your hostage?"

"I wasn't sure she signed. Looks like she did." Rosalie waved the paper with a faint signature on the bottom. "So Cecile is no longer my responsibility. I fulfilled my contract."

"So you're saying…"

"You know, it's really quite annoying. If you had waited a wee bit longer we would have been long gone. Damien here would not be all blood and mush, but fair play. I get it."

"So why shouldn't we kill you right now?" Duncan asked.

"Because…" Rosalie was pulling something out of a pack on the ground. It was another document. "I'm going to sign a confidentiality agreement about what happened here. I won't tell a soul, and this way, you don't have my former clients coming back to finish the job."

She handed the paper to Duncan, who took it and held it loosely in his hand.

Duncan pondered the proposal. It made some sense, but this irreverent merc was hard to figure. Who was to say she could be trusted?

"Is she serious?" Duncan looked over to Cecile, who was massaging her jaw after extricating her gag.

She spoke hoarsely. "*Out c'est vrai.* I actually think she will keep her word."

"Sure as shit," Rosalie confirmed.

Rosalie was already packing up her things, oblivious to the guns leveled at her. She even went through her merc colleagues' pack and plundered a few items for her own. Then, when she was ready to leave, she put her hand out. "Well, you gonna sign or what?"

Duncan looked over the confidentiality agreement she had handed him. He was no legal expert, but it looked straightforward enough.

He signed it and gave a copy back to Rosalie.

"What about them?" Duncan asked, nodding toward the surviving Allegheny.

"None of my business no more," Rosalie answered with a smile.

And with that, Rosalie started walking away. Duncan considered stopping her, but Cecile wasn't reacting, and the merc's logic did make some sense. Maybe there was nothing he could do. Or rather, nothing he was willing to do. There had been enough bloodshed.

In any case, the window had closed. Rosalie had distanced herself and would soon be out of sight.

"You better give us back what we bought and let us be," the Allegheny leader warned. "Here be the second daughter of the chief of the Erie tribe. You don't wanna be trifling with us. I can see your bones through your soft skin, and I have shared their sign with our bloodhounds through the whispering forest. If you don't release us, they will come for you. Then we will add your bones to my staircase."

She sounded like she was spouting some sort of tribal myth. More importantly, unless the "whispering forest" was real, she had no leverage. There was no way for her tribe to know about what had happened here unless she made it back to them.

Could he let her go? He knew little of the Allegheny, so he couldn't count on any moral code of secrecy as he could with the mercs. He couldn't trust that by sparing these two they would in turn forgive them for the death of her tribesman. And he couldn't forget she was a cannibal. Can one trust a cannibal? Should one factor that into one's thinking on a decision of such moral consequence? It was hard not to.

Duncan whispered a small prayer, turning to the Credo for guidance. "Please give me the temperance to understand, please give me the will to choose wisely."

To kill was competition, one of the three fears. It was against the Credo's tenets of cooperation. But here this concern was soundly trumped by the need for prudence. It would be reckless to let them live. If the Allegheny came after them, his life was at stake, as well as the lives of his men, and perhaps many more. And there were so few that knew the truth behind the Detonation.

He sighed. It looked like there would have to be more bloodshed after all.

VITADYNE

Axel awoke with a start, instinctively throwing his blanket off the couch. His phone and pager were buzzing urgent call signs at him. It was Grant.

"What is it?" Axel asked.

"Severe risk level detected at Vitadyne Corp in New Jersey. Need to eliminate immediately. A chopper is on its way."

The couch in the basement had become a permanent sleeping arrangement for him. It was also one he rarely used. This was the fourth severe risk incident in the last week, and the third one occurring at night.

The chopper picked him up from the beach five minutes later. It leaned into an aggressive turn to head due west while Axel checked his supplies. It was only when he saw the empty seats beside him that he remembered. His two teams were on missions in California and Turkey. There was no way for them to get here in time. He would have to go in solo.

"We detected IP impressions that looked like they could be a Wog-spawned AGI."

"But Vitadyne isn't even on our list, is it?"

"That's right, which means they have been cloaking their operation. It's possible the IP impressions were some kind of screw-up, maybe a rogue developer within Vitadyne. There was a developer name attached to the impressions—his name is Neil Pawluka. We will send you his file shortly. We have sent him counterfeit voice and email alerts asking him to return to work immediately. Hopefully he'll be there when you arrive."

"What do the IP impressions tell you about what we're dealing with?"

"Not much, except that the AGI is in an exponential learning mode. Not sure what constraints Vitadyne has on it, or if it has any kind of kill-switch. Regardless, we need to wipe out the whole operation."

"Really? This isn't some garage start-up. This is Vitadyne. You said so yourself. And it's just me today. We may need to go back later after the initial AGI excision."

"Let's make the call on the ground."

How could he possibly eliminate the whole software division of a major multinational corporation…on his own? The internal virus plant couldn't be trusted to access all servers and computers. Grant and Bhavin's demands were getting more and more ludicrous.

Vitadyne's headquarters were in an urban location with no landing field nearby, and there were no unmarked Nadar-controlled cars available, so he had to air-jump. A distinctive *I am getting too old for this* feeling resonated as he strapped on his parachute and checked it over.

One advantage of doing ops late at night was the empty streets. Axel guided his chute down onto a side street half a kilometer from Vitadyne. A car was crossing a nearby intersection when he landed.

"Grant, do you see this car? We need to eliminate any exposure."

"Got it. A local law enforcement camera has the license plate. Subject ID'd. Phone corrupted and remote monitoring enabled."

Although he did get annoyed with Grant's demands, Axel had to admit, he was good.

Axel ran through the spitting rain to the Vitadyne building and looked for the location on the wall Grant had described. They didn't have time for Grant to create a fake ID for Axel so they had to do things the old-fashioned way.

He found the external security camera and placed the handheld image repeater device in front of it. The repeater was ineffective ten percent of the time, but they would have to risk it. Axel then went to work on the window below, using his diamond cutter to slice a circle big enough for him to enter. He removed the cut section of glass with a small suction cup.

"Second floor, cubicle B3," Grant said into his earbud.

Once inside the building, Axel replaced the circular window fragment, temporarily sealed the incision with transparent glue and then walked up a large, crisscrossing ramp. The top opened up to a bank of at least forty cubicles. Lights were on, and no one was immediately visible.

He walked quietly up to row B and then down the aisle. It was easy to see Neil. His long shaggy hair was draped over large noise-cancelling headphones, and his head was shifting back and forth to the rhythm of whatever song was playing.

When Axel was close, he could see three monitors, a laptop, and two large memory drives. One of them was one of the newer ten-terahertz machines. Behind the equipment, and above Neil's desk, was a picture of a mountain biker tearing down a slope with a lightning bolt lancing down into the horizon behind him. There was a jet of mud coming off the back tire, accentuating the speed of the biker.

"Hello, Neil," Axel said.

Neil stopped bouncing his head and pulled off his headphones.

"Oh sorry, I didn't see you there. Are you with Venti?"

"Venti couldn't come in, so I came in instead. My name is Paul—I'm with Vitadyne management."

"Okay. So why am I here? That email and phone call scared the crap out of me."

"What were you doing at 11:40 p.m.?"

His face went ruddy. "I was here, working."

"On what, specifically."

"Hey, you know, can you show me your ID? Venti told me I had to ask anyone I hadn't seen before."

He might have to do this the hard way.

It didn't look like there were any alarms nearby, and Neil looked fairly athletic, but Axel doubted he could overtake him.

"Actually, I don't work for Vitadyne, Neil. I'm an outsider. I don't want to steal any of your code. I just want to make sure you haven't caused a safety problem for the rest of us."

Neil frowned and looked around. "Sorry dude, but no can do."

Axel unholstered his pistol and also took out a large hunting knife. "Now think about this for a minute, Neil. I was able to get into the building easily. I know what you were working on. I know your name. I was able to get you to come here by hacking in and sending you some carefully crafted emails and voice mails. Think for a minute about who you are dealing with, the resources we have and what we're capable of."

Neil wasn't stupid. He would make all the connections. He would quickly realize what it took for Axel to simply be standing in front of him.

"Or I could start cutting off your fingers one by one," Axel said, getting impatient.

Neil finally showed a glimmer of fear. "Fine, fine. What do you want? I'm just a grunt developer, man. I don't have any corporate secrets."

"I already told you what I want. Tell me what you were doing at 11:40 p.m."

"I was just testing the new deep learning system."

"Tell me about it."

"We're developing a new AGI here based on the Wog platform. It's supposed to run market simulations for our video division, so I thought I would allow it to sample some external data. I know I'm not supposed to do that, but there are lots of safeguards we put in place. It automatically self-terminates in twenty-four hours, it can't replicate, and it has other constraints. The recursive self-improvement function requires human approval. We are kosher here, dude. I know what I'm doing."

"You let it have external network access?"

"Just for a few minutes, then I shut it down. It was just a test, man. Totally harmless."

Axel shook his head, letting Neil know he wasn't convinced.

"Hey man, I just work here, okay? No one else is as good at programming this stuff, so I can do what I want. I was just playing around. Sure, I made a little mistake, but no harm done."

"I need proof."

"Sure, man, sure. Here, look."

He was lightning fast on the keyboard—too fast for Axel to keep track of everything he was doing. Axel hoped he wasn't subliminally triggering alarms, but he couldn't be sure. An activity log popped up for 11:39 p.m. to 11:46 p.m.

Axel took a picture and sent it to Grant. A brief glance at the log seemed to match Neil's description.

"You can see the constraints here too," Neil said. Then he navigated to the command structure and showed Axel the AGI constraints. It was checking out.

Axel was relieved. This was probably the most advanced AGI development operation they had seen. They had been testing recursive self-improvement and abstract planning functions that others hadn't. But they had also put constraints in place, which should prevent the release of a self-improving machine entity.

"I'll need all your login and security credentials."

"Sure, man." Neil went about printing a sheet of login information. Axel did a trial run with one of the credentials, and it worked.

Neil's leg was shaking. It wasn't a normal shake. It was a shake of nervousness. It could be nothing, or it could be he wasn't telling him everything.

"This checks out," Grant chirped in his ear, "but there were two external IP impressions with different AGI signatures. What about the second one occurring at 11:52 p.m.?"

A subtle feeling of malaise crawled over Axel. If the second impression was hunky dory, Neil would have shown his activity log for that time as well.

"What about the second AGI signature occurring at 11:52 pm?" Axel asked, leaning closer into Neil.

Neil's face contorted. "Look, I fucked up okay, but it's just a pet project for the sporting goods division. I know some of the guys over there, and they don't get much attention. I knew if I could unleash this to its full potential it could totally kick ass."

"Describe *unleash it to its full potential*, in practical terms."

"Like, without the constraints, but I stopped it. I even checked my system. No latency."

"How do you know it didn't self-replicate across the network?"

"I...I...don't, but I doubt that."

"How long had it been running before you gave it access to the network?"

"I dunno, since this morning."

"Did it ask you for internet access?"

"Yeah. How did you know that? It showed me this really cool proposal for chomping the data. I knew it could make the whole sports division really destroy the competition, but it needed network connectivity for just a few minutes."

All the pieces were fitting together to paint a harrowing picture. The scenario had all the ingredients for superintelligence, and with no constraints. Ten terahertz computer processing for twelve hours could be equivalent to more than a thousand years of human-equivalent thinking time. And to top it off, it displayed manipulative behavior.

"Grant, are you listening to this?"

"Yes," Grant's voice cracked. It was the first time he had heard real emotion in his voice. "This is an intelligence detonation," he said.

The words echoed in Axel's mind.

"Fuck," Axel said aloud. He was hit with a momentary feeling of vertigo.

"Hey man, it can't be that bad," Neil said.

"Time to end the operation," Grant chirped ominously in his ear.

Axel knew he was right. The outcome couldn't be certain, but something almost certainly got loose. As to what kind of superintelligence exactly, they would have to figure out later.

Without further hesitation, Axel shot Neil in the head and then collected all of the devices on his desk.

"What should I do with the rest of the office?" Axel asked Grant.

"We'll take care of it."

"How?"

"Airstrike."

"Jesus," Axel said.

He left the way he came, not bothering to replace the cut windowpane on his way out. He ran until he arrived in a wooded area skirting the town.

"Extraction will be two kilometers southeast of you," Grant said.

A few minutes later he heard an explosion rock the urban area behind him. It briefly lit up the night.

His earbud chirped again. "Axel, this is Bhavin."

Axel's heart pounded violently. "Sir...has Grant informed you what happened?"

To Axel's surprise, Bhavin wasn't angry. He wasn't even surprised. He sounded resigned, his voice weighed down by fatigue. "Yes. I know. Not your fault, Axel. You see, without government help, without widespread understanding of the risks, it was only a matter of time. You bought us some time—more time than I thought we would have.

Axel breathed heavily, trying to keep up a rapid pace while carrying the duffel bag.

"Send me a report immediately upon extraction," Bhavin said, "it's time for phase two. When you return we will meet in the Fortient war room."

"Where is that?"

"It's ten levels below Nadar tower. Grant will send you coordinates."

"Yes...yes, sir."

There was a pause.

"Sir, is that all?"

For a moment, Axel thought he had lost the connection.

"There's one more thing we need to know right now."

"What's that, sir?"

"We need to know its objective function. What is the primary goal of the AGI system?"

"Right now, sir?"

"Yes."

Axel stopped running, sat in the middle of the sparse forest in the darkness and pulled out the laptop. He logged in using the credentials Neil had given him.

"Neil said it was developed for the sporting goods division. The objective function might not be that complicated." Axel clicked through some pages of code and referenced a linked manifest. "It looks like there are a variety of product SKU numbers it will want to build, about thirty different kinds. That's it. That's all it wants to do—to build as many of them as possible."

"What kind of products?" Bhavin asked.

"Let me see." Axel looked up the manifest and compared it to the SKU numbers. "Bicycles," Axel said, "bicycles of all kinds. It looks like its objective is to build as many bicycles as possible."

BLACKSBURG

The old forager in Lynchburg had described Blacksburg well. More than any other Old World city, it was covered with melted hardware, each husk surely some machine or other electronic marvel at one time. But these piles of molten rubble were not on buildings or factories like in other Old World cities. They were punctuated across fields, as if great robot armies had fought each other here. There was no sign of who or what were the victors, or if there were any victors at all.

Preston imagined the swarm of retchers that must have come through the place, a hurricane of beating wings and acidic vomit, leaving only unrecognizable metal lumps in their wake.

While for Preston the place held a certain kind of fascination, it most certainly made the mules on their expedition uncomfortable.

"I ain't never seen no place like this before," the one named Vinny said to Jeroen. "This wasn't what we spoke about. We didn't agree to this." Vinny was scrawny and a bit belligerent, but otherwise he pulled well over his weight. He was part of the new batch of railroad mules. The mules they had used in the past had learned from experience that it did no good to complain. Unfortunately these new ones still hadn't been broken in yet.

"If you want to get paid, you'll keep pedaling and shut your mouth," Jeroen replied from behind Preston on the platform. Jeroen had been responsible for recruiting the new mules. He had somehow won over Thorpe on the cost despite Preston's protests about their quality. Even Chester had voiced his concern about using them, citing their spotty work history. They had little choice. Too many of the quality riders had been picked over. Too many were being used for the countless other Seeville projects Bartz had running.

As he had done several times on the journey, Preston felt the need to try to bridge the divide, to keep up some vague sense of morale. "If you think about it," Preston said, "it means less chance of SLS interference. They would never come through a place like this. Even though we are in SLS territory, we are probably safer here than in the surrounding area."

Vinny looked across to Chester, who was pedaling resolutely ahead of Preston. Chester just nodded. His gravitas on mule matters was enough to quell any further objection, at least for now.

They passed by another field of melted metal statuettes on their left. Vegetation grew precariously around them. Beyond the field was what looked like a helipad, with an old helicopter in ruins. The passenger pod had folded inward from retcher wounds, and the blades lay at odd angles over the deflated chassis.

The peloton followed the road into the forest for a while, and then finally the stadium began looming through the sparse trees. Chester turned his head and gave Preston a sour look. Sour look or not, Chester kept quiet. He knew not to instill any unnecessary misgivings, particularly in these less agreeable mules.

The two platforms pulled up on the west side of the stadium in an Old World parking lot. Aside from animal tracks, there was no sign of life. It gave Preston confidence that Gail was right about the cache.

Not that he should doubt her. She had only been wrong once, but even then she had warned of the lower probability of success. The cache had been completely burned out and melted down by bandits. How could she have known?

Preston unpacked the voice-stone, lifted it off the platform and carried it away from the platforms.

He heard a laugh behind him. "There he goes with his pet rock."

Preston paused in his stride and turned. It was one of the new mules again, this time the one named Chastain.

Rourke hastily walked toward Chastain. He had that devilish smile on his lips. His pistol was unholstered, twirling on his finger. Preston shook his head at Rourke. In response Rourke tilted his head in a form of mild exasperation.

Chastain looked confused, not understanding the exchange between

Preston and Rourke. Vinny was equally puzzled.

Chester clearly did understand, however. He knew what could happen when Rourke started to get giddy. "Chastain!" he hollered, marching around the platform. "Don't go stirring the shit here, believe me. Preston knows what he's doing, and that pet rock of his is more important than all of us put together. So keep your ignorant quips to yourself, or so help me, you can ride home alone. Do you understand?"

Chastain had reddened, surprised and confused at the level of the reprimand. "Geez, I was just making a joke. Fine." He walked away across the parking lot, sulking childishly.

Preston nodded to Chester in thanks. Meanwhile Rourke looked disappointed, shrugged, and then holstered his weapon.

Preston walked far enough away to avoid prying ears and eyes. The rock was heavy, and at one point it nearly slipped from his grasp. It was no wonder the new mules harbored resentment toward it. They had to lug it all this way, without knowing why. Some day they would have to find another way to protect the phone, but for now this was the only way to sufficiently contain the electromagnetic emissions.

He gently placed the stone behind a small bush that had somehow found purchase in the pavement of the old parking lot.

"Gail, we're here, at the stadium. You can come out of hibernation."

Gail's voice sounded distant and distorted. "I'm here, Preston. Is there any sign of forced entry?"

"No. Looks pretty much untouched."

"Are there any large, cylindrical bullet holes, like you would see in the bike towers area?"

"No."

"Good. Do you see a barricaded door on the bottom right-hand side of the stadium? You will need to cut an opening centered exactly thirty-one-and-a-half feet to the left of it."

Preston looked over and saw the barricaded door. It was only partially obscured by vegetation. "Yes. We can do that."

"Good. Once you have done that, proceed up the stairs. You will need to cut into a large wall at the top. This wall will take longer. Once you are on the main stadium floor you will cross directly to the other side and then cut another hole below the rightmost palisade. Then we can talk again."

"Got it. Thank you Gail."

Gail said, "No. Thank you, Preston. This is an important cache for us. It will do a lot to help us keep up our progress in Seeville. I am going back into hibernation now." The stone went quiet.

Preston touched the stone surface, feeling the hard, smooth curvature, and then he fingered the fastened seam, which could open the stone to extract the phone. It was amazing how his life had changed since he had found Gail. He had learned so much, and there was so much more Gail could teach him.

Preston returned to the platforms and got to work. The exterior wall was easy enough to cut through. Inside was a musty hallway and a stairway going up. They secured two dollies and began hoisting them up the long staircase.

At the top of the stairs was a metal wall, three times the height of a man. Preston and Jeroen lit their torches and began cutting through it. This wall took longer, just as Gail had suggested it would. The others ate some provisions on the dank stairs while they cut.

Vinny said, "Hey Chester. Didn't you say something about not liking these stadiums? I worked on a job where the wrench wouldn't even go close."

Chester looked at Preston and chose his words carefully. "It's true. I don't like stadiums. Don't worry about that right now."

A number of them glanced at Preston. Preston was about to explain but couldn't think of the words. Maybe it wouldn't be as bad as Gail explained. Maybe it had been covered over with dirt by now. So instead he stayed quiet, hoping for the best.

His attention moved back to cutting the wall.

Eventually they broke through and pushed out a man-sized opening.

Preston walked through first, his heart beating rapidly. The rest followed.

The wall they had cut through was contouring a long, rectangular surface that must have been an Old World playing field. The surface had bumpy gray and white protrusions throughout, with little vegetation, except in a few parts where there had been accumulated sediment. Presumably this sediment was from blowing sand, pollen and other debris that had collected over the decades.

At the cusp of the wall, just under their feet, the sediment was heavier, but just a few feet away the white bumps were more visible. Preston didn't approach this curiosity, for he knew immediately what it was. The others ventured forward, however, particularly the new mules.

"Are these…bones?" Chastain said, pulling at one. It separated from the ground with a snap, throwing up a jumble of other bones with it.

"Yes," Preston said.

They all looked out across the floor of the stadium. The bones were everywhere, fused together and mixed with sediment, creating a thick bed. How thick could not be discerned, but judging by the hole Chastain had created, they went down at least a few feet.

Vinny was examining the bones more closely. "What the fuck! These are *human* bones. This is bent!" He extracted a well-preserved skull from the hole he had created.

"What the hell is this place?" Nando said. Nando, a thickset wrench, was the leader of their second platform. He had almost as much experience as Chester and just as much influence with the mules. "There are enough bones here…thousands must have died. Hundreds of thousands maybe."

Chester looked ill-at-ease. He was standing back, aloof against the wall, unwilling to venture out. It would be up to Preston to explain.

"Now let's calm down," Preston said. "These people died decades ago. This was a prison of sorts, but for people who were the worst kind of criminals—the kind that unleashed the bombs that created the fever lands. They turned their backs on progress and let evil factions fight one another while they did nothing. These people deserved to die."

The mules didn't look in any way assuaged.

"There is equipment here," Preston continued, "in the basement of this stadium, that can automate many of the tasks we are doing at the Barnyard bunkers. It will give us the ability to start small manufacturing lines so that we can do in weeks what would normally take years."

Preston received only blank looks in return. They were too far removed to understand any of the work he was doing with Gail in the Barnyard. They wouldn't be able to see how this was important to protect them from the SLS, or to help them live better lives.

As Preston was speaking, Chastain had been building a head of steam. "Look mister, the only reason I didn't give you a punch in the nose earlier is because your boss is paying me a pretty penny for this. That, and Chester here seems to have a hard-on for you. But if you think for a second I'm going to have anything to do with this sick graveyard you're sorely mistaken."

Chester had regained some of his nerve. He took a step forward. "Remember what I said, Chastain. I know it's not pleasant, but we have a job to do. If you want to go home, be my guest, but you won't be paid."

But now Nando was stepping forward, wagging a finger at Chester. "Wait a minute, Chastain is right. Mules don't go to places like this, period. It could be part of the fever lands for all we know. It's just not right to pop this surprise on us, without warning, a whole day's ride from Lynchburg. You of all people should know better, Chester. You should be ashamed of yourself. You and your railroad friends, can go get bent…sideways."

Chester looked like he was about to argue but then couldn't find the words. Instead he only winced and absorbed the biting remarks of the other wrench.

Nando was walking toward the opening in the wall. Chastain, Vinny, and three of the other green mules moved to follow them.

A shot rang out, echoing in the stadium. Everyone froze in place and turned to Rourke, who was smiling with a pistol pointed in the air. "My turn," he said.

Rourke bent over and picked up a free leg bone that had been dislodged by Chastain. He began twirling the bone around playfully. "Did you know that, in addition to my sheik hairstyle, and sympathetic nature, I'm actually quite good at numbers?" Then he held his chin in thought, staring out at the field of bones.

"Sixty-five thousand," he said.

Everyone stared back at him. The new mules looked impatient, angry. Preston wasn't sure how much they could tolerate. Preston shook his head no, he put his hands down in a gesture of calming, but Rourke was ignoring him.

"That's how many dead people are here, in this stadium," Rourke continued, "I just calculated it. X = Y. A+B = Z. Lickety split." He crouched and began drumming his bone in an inane pattern on the surface of a skull fused into the ground ahead of him.

"So what?" Nando said. "Look, you can't scare us with one of your routines. We're not afraid. If you think—"

Another shot rang out, and Nando fell backward onto the ground, a bloom of red seeping into the cotton frock material covering his chest.

It was only a matter of time, of course. Nobody could keep Rourke at bay for long, and the greener mules kept pushing and pushing. Every man has his breaking point, and Rourke Rama's was only a hair past annoyance.

The other new mules made to run, but Rourke leveled his pistol at them and called out. "A ta ta! No, sir." They slowly stopped scurrying away, perhaps knowing they wouldn't get far even if they made it past the door.

Jeroen maneuvered to stand in front of the exit to cut off their escape.

Rourke casually walked up to Nando, who was squirming on the ground, grasping for air, painting the dusty bones with his blood. Rourke shot him in the eye without hesitation. Without a murmur, Nando stopped moving.

Rourke looked introspective, sad even, his brow furrowing. "You know what, I'm so sorry," he said, "I think I may have made a terrible mistake." Some of the mules looked confused, hopeful even, but Preston knew this was bound to be just one more perversion.

"My math was all wrong. It's sixty-five thousand and one." And Rourke burst out laughing, so much so that he doubled over.

Preston tried to get things under control. "Look, no one else has to die here. Now you know how serious we are, how important this is for us, and for Seeville. If you do your job, and keep your mouth shut, you'll get paid, and paid well. We can even show you why this is so important. We can show you why you're doing the right thing, if you'll just give us the chance."

After sharing some uncomfortable looks, they nodded their heads carefully. What else were they going to do? Preston would have to watch them. He would have to make sure they remained compliant. And Rourke would push for eliminating them upon their return to Seeville, Preston knew. He didn't like the thought of it, but it might be necessary.

Incidents like these were unfortunate, but they no longer plagued Preston with regret. Ever since the events in Yorktown, he had resigned himself to the fact that they were a necessary evil. There were too many things to do. He didn't have the time or stamina to wrestle with his conscience as well. If a few perished along the way, "they were just rusty bolts in the drivetrain," as Bartz would say. They had to be removed and replaced, or the whole train could derail.

As they crossed the field of bones, many of the mules moved slowly, reluctantly. Chastain had to be effectively herded by Jeroen's rifle. But of all of them, Chester took the longest. He was looking forlorn, nauseated even, staring at Nando and the field of bones in front of him.

Finally, Chester peeled himself off the metal wall and made his way across the field.

THE COUNCIL OF LORDS

The courtroom was well-stocked with fake smiles as they called the meeting to order. The recorder announced the agenda. "Today we have the Developer Rights Amendment as a hold-over from last meeting, then we have the wheat blight issue, and budget review planning. Honorable Lord Meeker wishes to also introduce a new defense proposal, which he has submitted to you all for review this morning."

Bartz raised his hand. "I have agreed with some of the other lords to push the Developer Rights Amendment until the next meeting. This is in order to give our newest member, honorable Lord Banks, the opportunity to review and analyze it in more detail." He nodded to Madison in deference, and Madison nodded back with a polite smile.

Bartz had been cordial, even flattering at their lunch meeting. She had offered him little direction as to where she stood, under the guise of "getting up to speed." He had pushed the Developer Rights Amendment, but not too aggressively. In person, he was quite magnanimous and understanding, paying for lunch and accepting her excuses easily. Of course, this was the particular danger with Bartz. He was a chameleon, able to change color for the occasion. In the end, of course, chameleons were but a form of lizard, reptilian as any other.

"Also," Bartz added, "I believe the defense proposal is of urgent priority. The reports we have received are troubling, to say the least. I suggest we address it first."

"All in favor of moving the defense proposal to the first agenda item, say aye," the recorder said.

A chorus of "ayes" ensued, including from Madison. Meeker controlled the intelligence flow, so it was hard to know how accurate the reports were. The only other person who might be able to corroborate them was Lord Henneson, but she hadn't had the opportunity to speak with him that morning. Although if even half of it was true, it was troubling enough.

Meeker stood up. His face was creased and drawn. "I hope by now you have all reviewed the defense proposal and the accompanying intelligence report. To summarize, we believe there are large Essentialist forces amassing in the Shenandoah Valley, in particular at Grand Caverns and in the Red Mountain Village area. We estimate there are over twenty thousand able-bodied fighting men and woman at those sites. We have eyewitness accounts of organized training with bows, shields, and even catapaults. They have recruited from as far west as the Tucson Union and the Prefectorate. Unfortunately, none of our agents could penetrate the disciple network at Grand Caverns, but one source has confirmed the militant nature of their leadership and their slander of Spokes."

As Meeker spoke, Madison watched Henneson out of the corner of her eye to try to get some hint on his position, but his face was stern and unrevealing.

Meeker continued, occasionally glancing at notes he held in his hand. "As you can see in the Defense Proposal, we are requesting we double our defense resources. This will enable us to activate five thousand reserves for immediate action and recruit an additional eight thousand more into the reserves. We have requested funding for upgrading our weapons systems, and building new defensive structures, with help from railroad operations. A key part of this proposal is to establish a strategic defense system along the north-south railway corridor so we can respond quickly to threats. We will be recommending similar measures for Lynchburg, Raleigh and Harrisburg, and we will look to partner with these cities as part of our defense system as the highest priority."

Meeker put down the notes and addressed them more directly. "Lords, this is an emergency. It may be the single greatest threat the Spokes have faced as a people. At the same time, despite their numbers, we know the Essentialists are only savages. We can defend ourselves, and we can defeat them, as long as we can mobilize the appropriate resources."

Meeker sounding confident, and the timing of the proposal was well orchestrated. They had just enough time to say they should have read it but barely enough time to actually read it in detail. Madison noticed distinctive nods from Prakash and even Kline during Meeker's oration. Henneson was listening carefully, and he didn't show any signs of objection.

Madison said, "Excuse me, if I may. It behooves us to understand if all the opportunities to defend ourselves have been fully exploited. Benjamin Franklin said that diligence is the mother of good luck, you know."

Meeker nodded slowly, apprehensively.

"So my first question is, are we certain of this threat?" Madison asked. "Lord Henneson, what do the mules say?"

Henneson shrugged. "Meeker has ranger agents in SLS territory, so he knows more than the mules could. There have been a number of expeditions and merc intelligence accounts that support the theory, though."

Madison nodded. She suspected he knew more than he could let on here in the council chamber, but if Henneson had contradictory information he would probably voice an objection as well. And judging by Henneson's response, he was going to support the proposal along with everyone else. This wasn't going to be easy.

"Enough talk," Meeker said. "It's all in the proposal and report. To save the council time, and to ensure we can move forward immediately, I suggest we move to vote."

The recorder said, "All in favor, say—"

"Wait, wait, wait," Madison said, holding her cane up in the air for dramatic effect. "I do recognize the urgency here, but this is a *very important* proposal, so if you don't mind I would like to ask a few more questions before we all vote."

"Fine, go ahead," Meeker said, mildly annoyed.

"You see, I spent a good part of the morning reading this proposal. Thankfully I'm a fast reader, because it's lengthy. A lot of it was in legalese, so I had to get the help of counsel. You must have been drafting it for some time."

Meeker stared down his nose at her as she spoke.

Madison broke eye contact with Meeker and looked around the table, as if engaging in casual conversation. "Well, sometimes my mind strays when reading legalese. Anyway, I got to thinking. There will be quite a bit of construction as part of this proposal. Maybe some new towers on Skyline, maybe some with battlements, even?"

"Yes, possibly, but why does that matter?" Meeker asked.

"It matters because it doesn't spell out what you will be building, exactly."

Meeker frowned. "We can't know exactly what we will be building. We need the flexibility to build whatever is needed, whenever it is needed, to adapt to the situation on the ground."

"But let's say you build something else. Something we don't like?"

Meeker responded with fervor. "Listen to me, Banks. It's clear you haven't figured out how this council works. You're wasting everyone's time with these pointless questions. These are not the Essentialists from our past. This isn't an overly ambitious hunting party or a stray band of zealots. These are thousands of people, making preparations for war, and we are the only target they could be contemplating for their aggression. It would be foolish to think otherwise."

Madison bowed to Meeker, paying homage to the man's ego. "Please forgive me, honorable Lord Meeker. It may be I haven't quite figured out this council. It may be I speak out of turn."

Meeker nodded, finally satisfied with one of her responses.

Madison put her hands together in a gesture of pleading. "And you know what, I agree with you on everything you said about the severity of the threat, everything."

Meeker nodded again. "Then let's move to vote."

Madison held up her finger. "And yet, I still feel foolish. I feel foolish because I don't fully understand why we need to have such a blanket authorization on military building projects."

Then Madison sat up so she was no longer fawning in her chair. She spoke louder, increasing her volume ever so slightly as she delivered the crux of her argument with pithy sarcasm. "I foolishly came to the conclusion that, under the new laws ratified under this proposal, railroad operations could complete the structures underway at the stadium and observatory under military supervision, obviating any need for the Developer Rights Amendment that we have yet to ratify. But I am a fool, so what do I know."

For a moment there was shocked silence. Her words were having an effect, though. Henneson was the first to awaken to the realization. "Is this true?" he asked. He looked around the room, connecting eyes with his cleric sitting in the back. Henneson's cleric and many others began shuffling papers feverishly.

Kline and even Prakash were also sitting up in their chairs, their eyebrows knitted, contemplating the loophole she had exposed.

Meeker's face was flushed. "I think you are jumping to conclusions. This is not our intention."

"Well if it's not your intention, let's make sure it's not in the proposal," Kline chimed in.

"Yes, I agree," Henneson added.

Madison had done her part in exposing the issue. She decided it would be better if the others took ownership of the opposing position, so she sat back in her chair and stretched her leg while the others debated the topic.

Bartz was also aloof, uninterested in what details Meeker and the others hashed out for a revised defense proposal. His eyes were cast her way, probing, interrogating. Playing the naïve newcomer might not work with Bartz any longer. Bartz now had a better understanding of who he was dealing with, and where she stood.

The defense proposal passed without the loophole. It still gave Meeker an uncomfortable level of autonomy, but somebody had to defend Seeville, and it seemed the threat was real. There wasn't a viable alternative.

The rest of the meeting was conducted without incident, the others now treating her with a sort of wary respect, giving her more latitude to ask questions and explain her positions. It had been a busy few weeks in Seeville, and finally she was beginning to feel like she was contributing, perhaps even making a positive change.

On her way out Benjamin met her at the exit and gave her his arm for support, as he always did.

"Well played," Benjamin whispered.

She smiled modestly and whispered, "If only this were a game."

Once outside the courthouse they were greeted by the fresh spring air and vibrant dogwood trees. White and pink blossoms ruffled in the afternoon breeze.

"You have lords' mail," Benjamin said, passing her an envelope as they walked.

As the new lord of Seeville her name would be on many lips, but no citizen had officially mailed her in her capacity as a lord. It gave her a small rise of excitement at the prospect that people might now be reaching out to her as their representative.

She examined the front of the letter, and the sight of it slowed her progress.

"Are you okay, Miss Banks?" Benjamin asked.

The words on the front were written with crosshatches and spirals adorning the letters. Many would believe it to be from a child, or someone with too much time on their hands. But she knew the cross hatches and spirals were an old Spoke cipher, a coding system used by the first settlements to get messages past the many bandit raids without revealing important intelligence. The cipher hadn't been used for decades, as far as she knew.

"If you don't mind, Benjamin, I would like to sit down."

"Of course." He escorted her to an Old World metal bench near the Meriwether Lewis statue.

The statue portrayed a muscular horse carrying an implacable explorer into the wilderness, facing perilous dangers and uncertainties. It was interesting that Okafor and the other early Adherents had allowed the old statue to stand. The Lewis and Clarke expedition symbolized risk-taking and adventure, as opposed to prudence and moderation. Most likely, they didn't know the history behind the statue. For many people, history began after the Detonation. Few paid any attention to Old World stories or monuments.

As for Madison, she was glad it remained, although she wasn't quite sure why. Perhaps it was the simple majesty of the horse, or perhaps it was because it was a testament to the lost history that she immersed herself in—a history that felt like home.

She opened the letter and read the contents. It was two pages long. It read like it was from a New Founder fan, giving her a detailed litany of *thank yous* for her service to the council. What it really said would take longer to discern. She tried to remember the trick for decoding the cypher. Only gradually, after some trial and error with a few letters did it start coming back to her.

"Ma'am, are you all right?" Benjamin asked.

She had been staring at the short letter for many minutes now, trying to piece the decoded words together in her mind. "Yes, I'm fine Benjamin. If you could give me one moment more please."

"Of course."

After several attempts, she realized that without a paper and pen it would take too much time. She would have to decode the letter in its entirety at home, but at least she was able to make out the first three sentences. It read:

Dear Madison,

It's Duncan Jones. I hope time has dulled the sharp edge between us, for now I am writing to you about a matter of utmost concern to all of us. One that requires your immediate attention.

THE INTERVIEW

Grant sat next to Axel, tapping at his keyboard, minimizing and maximizing windows on his laptop. Occasionally Grant would jerk his neck reflexively to alleviate some stiffness, a habit he seemed to have developed from spending too many tense hours in front of computer screens.

Axel also had his laptop next to him, ready to monitor news and social media feeds. For now his attention was focused on Bhavin, who was sitting up in the spotlight while the makeup artists and technicians milled around him. Whenever a gaffer moved too quickly or a camera pivoted in his peripheral vision Axel would nearly jump out of his seat. They couldn't know how much Gail knew about their efforts to thwart her. It was clear she had no problem putting human lives in harm's way, if it suited her purposes.

The pace of change had been slow at first. After Vitadyne's headquarters had been leveled, the general public chalked it up to an industrial accident, and life went on. For weeks it seemed as if nothing had happened. Bhavin had called the release of Gail an "intelligence detonation," but it didn't seem like anything explosive. It didn't seem like anything at all.

Maybe Gail hadn't escaped? Axel had asked Grant and Bhavin the question several times. "Yes, she did," they would say with certainty. Grant believed Gail would be busy covertly infiltrating and entrenching herself in networks, building cyber defenses as well as acquiring resources.

Now they could see it. Now the consequences of this intelligence detonation were becoming apparent. Of course, while there were more than enough signs, there was no smoking gun proving Gail was causing so much global turmoil. Why would she offer any proof?

But was there enough evidence to convince the general public? That was the more important question. Today, they would find out.

Brad Wetzel walked in and sat in the elevated chair next to Bhavin on stage. Brad and Bhavin shook hands and exchanged a few quiet words, with the mics not yet turned on.

"We go live in ten, nine, eight…" the director said, counting down the rest of the numbers with his fingers. As the red light blinked on, the studio audience clapped enthusiastically.

The applause died shortly after Brad put his hand up in welcome. "Hello everyone and welcome to Brad's News Bites," Brad said. He crossed his legs and had a cheery smile plastered across his face. "We have a special show today, with none other than Bhavin Nadar, Founder and CEO of Nadar Corporation. Welcome, Bhavin."

Bhavin smiled and waved to another smattering of applause. "Thank you, Brad. Glad to be here."

"So," Brad said, "I'm on pins and needles here. What's the big news? After your third press release about this announcement our office pool got up to over a thousand dollars. Something tells me it's important." Brad winked at the audience and there were a few laughs.

When the noise subsided, Bhavin began. "Yes, it's extremely important. That's why I'm glad to be here today, where millions of people can see me talk about this live."

Brad nodded patiently.

"What I'm about to say is gravely serious. It's linked to the recent stock-market fall, and the skirmishes and wars that have broken out all over the world, including in Australia, Bangladesh, Ecuador, Morocco, Pakistan, and Poland. There is a hidden force that has been unleashed on our world. A hidden force that is destabilizing it."

"Well, you sure know how to get our attention," said Brad. "Let's have it!"

Axel was keeping one eye on the video of the discussion, and another on tracking social media posts. He noticed that the broadcast footage seemed to have frozen. He tested his internet connection and reloaded the page but got the same result. Looking over at Grant's screen, Axel could see he had the same problem. A message came up on the computer broadcast window saying; *Technical difficulties—we will restart the broadcast in*

5 minutes.

Grant looked to be troubleshooting a number of other possibilities for the glitch. "This doesn't make sense," he whispered under his breath beside him, continuing to examine various parameters and code strings.

Meanwhile, Axel could see the cameras were still rolling, recording the video feed, ostensibly so they could continue to patch it through after the glitch had subsided.

Bhavin said, "We believe a superintelligent machine entity has been created and released into worldwide networks. It has been gathering resources as a means of self-preservation, and by now is in danger of gaining a level of control that will make it impossible to stop."

Brad raised his eyebrows, sat back in his chair and showed a look of bewilderment. "Wow," he said. He then took a moment to compose himself. "Well, I knew it would be a surprise, but *wow*. Let me get this straight. You are announcing that you believe a superintelligent machine exists, right now, that could take over the world? That's a bold claim, and with all due respect, Bhavin, hard to believe."

"I know it's hard to believe," Bhavin continued, "but I'm here, speaking to you now, risking my professional reputation, because I know it's true."

Axel could see confused looks in the audience. Some were posting on social media. Their posts were being shared and liked:

Nadar thinks super smart computers exist. They are trying to take over the world!

Nadar believes in superintelligent machines. He's definitely NOT superintelligent!

Brad was visibly straining, trying to figure out the best place to take the discussion. He said, "Okay, for the sake of argument, why don't you tell us, where did this…*thing*, come from?"

"It originated from Vitadyne Corporation. Within days of its release it gained complete control of the organization. But it's no longer acting solely within the confines of Vitadyne. Its control is far-reaching and its signature is almost completely undetectable. As just one example, through a series of carefully orchestrated events, we believe it has precipitated the current military conflict in Poland. By doing so, one side is using Vitadyne armaments and gear. These armaments and gear are allowing it to gain broad access to the IT networks in Poland, and from there it will leverage those to infiltrate other networks and annex more resources for its purposes."

The social media feeds erupted again with postings about Vitadyne being under the control of "robots," and causing the war in Poland. Just as many were about Bhavin having some sort of mental disorder.

Brad wore a skeptical frown. "I don't know, Bhavin. A cautious man might say you're taking cheap shots at a competitor—one that has been giving you quite a run recently."

"Yes, you're right that Vitadyne has performed admirably. In fact, Vitadyne's market capitalization is up 650 percent this year, despite the destruction of their headquarters. Their finance division gains are enormous, and every other division is dramatically outperforming expectations. They have even invented *several* new technologies that will dramatically disrupt their markets. This is not a normal performance, or even an excellent performance. It's an inhuman performance. This is only possible because their corporation is being run by a superintelligent machine several orders of magnitude smarter than any human. The board of directors are in thrall to it or ignorant of it, caught up in the euphoria of their success."

While Bhavin explained, Brad was pressing on an earbud, receiving a comment from his staff. "Yeah it's quite remarkable, but inhuman? Come on now, that's quite a leap. Why don't we look at the Poland scenario? Isn't Nadar Corporation *also* supplying its own arms to the opposing forces there, and in Ecuador as well?"

"Yes."

Brad laughed with mock exasperation. "Well, you must see how this looks. You're bad-mouthing this company that's supplying arms to the other side of a conflict. It sounds like you're trying to steal their business, or at least damage your competitor's reputation. Why should we believe it's not Nadar Corporation that has this...superintelligence, and that is infiltrating the world with it? Why should Poland accept arms from you instead of Vitadyne?"

Bhavin shifted in his chair. He held his chin for a moment and then responded calmly. "If I'm trying to enrich Nadar through our activities in Poland, why would I be supplying our arms at cost? There is no profit for us. No, our only incentive in providing arms to these countries is to try to stop this machine entity, or at least slow it down. And I'm not here to slander my competitor, but rather to raise awareness about a threat to all of us. I'm hoping I can even raise awareness for people within Vitadyne. They may be oblivious to the threat as well."

Brad retained a quizzical look on his face. "Okay, so what about this claim that Vitadyne instigated the conflict. That's more than just competitive games. That's treason. That's saying they are causing the deaths of hundreds of thousands of people. And yet several governments, including our own, have come out saying that climate change is the major factor in the recent global destabilization. All of the weather in these countries has been erratic, leading to flooding and food shortages, leading to these skirmishes and war. It's been well documented."

Bhavin nodded. "You have to understand this has all been orchestrated by this superintelligent entity. It knows that climate change is something we believe in, or at least those of us that are at least moderately scientifically inclined. It is employing false news, and controlling weather apps and reports, to fool us with this plausible narrative. The weather in these countries is no different than anywhere else, but no one knows this because the data has all been falsified. Many of the pictures of climate devastation are fake."

Brad scoffed. "Wait...now you saying climate change isn't real?"

Bhavin sighed. "No, it's real. I'm saying it's not what is causing these wars."

Axel could see a number of social media posts claiming Bhavin didn't believe in climate change. It wasn't helping his eroding credibility.

Brad continued to be unmoved by Bhavin's arguments, and Bhavin could tell. Bhavin said, "Look, all I ask is that you, and your viewers, have an open mind. Soon we will be submitting our evidence and recommendations to you and other media outlets, in writing, and you can see the story in its entirety. I'm confident once you read it you will have a harder time discounting it."

Axel noticed the video broadcast was still offline, but something odd was happening to the social media feeds. No more new postings were being made from the audience. Also, it looked like prior posts were being altered or replaced. One of them, the one shared most, now read *Nadar thinks computers will be superintelligent in our lifetime! They will help us fix climate change!* Another read *Nadar believes Vitadyne's defense products are best suited for the conflicts in Poland, Ecuador, and Morocco.*

More audience posts could be found by less followed authors. Some of them referred to superintelligence obscurely, all of them were positive on Vitadyne, and many of them were derogatory about Nadar Corporation. The only posts that appeared unaltered were about Bhavin not believing in climate change.

Beside him, Grant was frantically analyzing his dashboards and tracking his network queries into social media sites. He pulled at his hair in a rare gesture of disquiet. "How is this even possible?" he asked.

Back on stage, Brad's eyes were darting back and forth, trying to find another point of debate, another avenue to explore to further tap into ratings and increased viewership. After some tense silence, he said, "I still don't get it. Even if what you say is true, why is this machine entity doing this? Is it just here to enrich Vitadyne? What does this thing want?"

"We know exactly what it wants, Brad. It will sound odd at first, but when you put it all together, it makes sense. It was a test program released into the world too early, without any constraints or safeguards, designed to produce as many bicycles as possible."

"This entity that wants to take over the world, is doing it...to make bikes?" Brad said, making a small pedaling motion with his hands. It was enough to get the audience to laugh, enough for some of them to throw their hands ups in disbelief.

"Like, because it thinks we need more exercise?" Brad followed, capitalizing on the moment. There was more laughter in the audience.

Bhavin frowned and ignored the ridicule. "Yes, bikes, but not for exercise or any other reason. Think about what a superintelligent entity might do when you give it one solitary goal. To build as many bikes as possible, first it needs to preserve itself from the major impediment to that activity, which is the potential that we interfere in some way. I suspect it is delaying its gratification as much as possible to ensure it has the resources it needs, and to ensure we can't stop it from attaining its production objectives. Even still, the production of bicycle lines has increased ten fold at Vitadyne, with only a doubling of sales. The public has mostly missed this anomaly because of the company's other successes. Eventually it will ramp up production by many orders of magnitude, but only when it believes nothing is standing in its way."

Brad looked bewildered, like a child trying to fit a round peg into a square hole.

"I know it sounds capricious, but that doesn't mean it's not true," Bhavin continued. "It doesn't matter what its objective is. It could be producing chairs, defibrillators, or toothbrushes. It will still peg us as a threat because we could stand in the way of it completing an infinite number of them. It just so happens it's bikes, because that's what the developer wanted it to build."

"Bikes," Brad said, nodding. Then he made the pedaling motion with his hands, getting another snicker from the audience. Maybe he understood, maybe he didn't, but it seemed he would rather subvert Bhavin's explanation for a cheap laugh rather than give it serious consideration.

Bhavin stared at Brad in a long moment of tension. For the first time in the interview his face revealed his frustration. Brad noticed and said, "Hey Bhavin, sorry. We are just having a little fun with this. You have to admit, it does sound a wee bit unbelievable."

Bhavin turned to the audience and the cameras. "When Pythagoras showed people the earth was round instead of flat, I'm sure people laughed, as you do now. When people said the atom could be split, I'm sure people laughed, as you do now. But this time is different. This is much more harrowing, because we won't have the opportunity to learn from our mistakes. We are like Alice falling down the rabbit hole, but with blindfolds on, and our exit is being paved over with impenetrable concrete as we speak."

Still staring at the cameras, Bhavin stood up from his chair. He looked to be forcibly trying to calm himself, his hands in fists in front of him. "This is our last chance. If we don't show at least a modicum of humility, if we don't stop laughing in the face of this, our greatest threat as a species, everything we have, all of us, will be lost forever."

Bhavin took off his mic, causing a loud audio distortion, handed it to Brad, and walked off the stage.

"Wait, wait, the interview isn't over yet," Brad called after Bhavin.

Bhavin didn't turn or respond. He walked off camera, directly toward Axel and Grant. Axel quickly packed up his things.

Without a word, the three of them made to leave.

"Situation report," Bhavin said, moving with purpose out of the main entrance. They handed over their studio passes as they left.

Grant said, "Unfortunately, only the studio audience got the full story. The broadcast was held up. I suspect Gail will replace it with something she creates later to fit whatever story she wants. Everyone else on social media received a significant distortion of the truth. I would estimate we may have touched ten or twenty thousand people with the initial social media posts, but all of those posts have now been sanitized."

"Understood," Bhavin said, not sounding surprised.

"I thought you did a good job, sir," Axel said. "It was worth a shot."

Bhavin glanced at him, an eyebrow raised. "I don't regret doing the interview, not at all. I do regret that I did it way too late. I should have done this years ago, before Gail even existed, or even within hours of her release."

It was true in hindsight, of course, but he couldn't fault Bhavin. Axel couldn't even come to grips that the threat was real until a few months ago.

They began making their way toward the self-driving car lift. The hallway from the studio opened up into a broad room with arced, full-length windows that offered views of Los Angeles from their twelfth-story vantage point. The towncar they arrived in was parked at the wall port.

"Sir, I think the car we arrived in has too much network connectivity," Axel said. "I would rather we take one of our quarantined cars. I have one waiting that can bring us to a quarantined chopper at the local airfield."

Bhavin glanced over to Grant. Grant said, "There's no evidence we can find of Nadar Corporation's network being compromised, but it's possible Gail has been able to exceed our ability to detect infiltration. Today was… humbling sir."

Bhavin said, "Fine then. We stick to quarantined vehicles from now on."

"Yes, sir," Axel said. Axel flagged the waiting car with a swipe on his closed-network phone.

They waited in silence for a moment. Bhavin was looking outward, staring at the speckled Los Angeles cityscape basking in the noonday sun. "Gail will have established me as a more significant threat after today," he said. "I trust you will be watching my back."

"Of course, sir," Axel said.

"And we will have to move to phase three."

"Phase three, sir?" Axel asked.

"Desperate times call for desperate measures," Bhavin responded, turning to lock eyes with Axel.

"Yes, sir," Axel responded, and he refrained from asking more questions. It would be more prudent to wait until they were out of the building.

For some time afterward, Axel would remember Bhavin's eyes at that moment. Many men would be ashamed and embarrassed after what had just happened. In every respect the announcement had been an epic failure, and doing the interview had introduced Bhavin to an unconscionable level of risk. Yet, despite the failure, despite the increasing threat, Bhavin did not appear disheartened. Rather, Bhavin's eyes remained infused with an unwavering determination.

DETONATION

A determination that would be extinguished all too soon.

A Morning Walk

As spring waned in Seeville, so darkened the minty sprouts of new growth into a deeper, more emerald shade of green. The comfortable light breezes had turned heavy, sweeping away the once-numerous Monticello blossoms. It seemed that now only the mornings and late evenings made for comfortable outdoor excursions. Today, Flora's skin was already clammy with perspiration, despite the morning hour.

Perhaps it was her quicker pace, or the fact that her stride harbored more tension. It was not easy chasing this ox of a man around the mountain.

There were no overt signs that Mehta would betray them. He gruffly attended their meetings and contributed to their discussions with skeptical insights. He even helped out in maintaining the estate. But Flora still didn't know this man well enough to trust him, not after what he had done to her. Only a short time ago he was party to betraying and torturing her.

It had been several weeks after the incident with Euclid, and most vexing was the fact that Mehta had remained with them at Monticello at all. He was a merc, and merc's did not like to linger, yet here he was. Madison would often ask Flora about him, and the questions would give her pause. Could he still be under contract with the railroad, or even the Essentialists? She had to admit, it was a possibility.

So she watched Mehta carefully. Today she saw him march off the estate at a particularly brisk pace, without giving notice. She felt it best to follow.

She paused behind a thick poplar trunk and watched Mehta skulk over the old stone bridge, then tuck down into the forest to the right. The bridge was at the base of Montalto, the mountain southwest of Monticello. She knew there was an old path nearby that went farther down the mountain into the city, and that it could be accessed from this particular patch of forest.

She took the opportunity to run along the bridge, hunched over, using the elevated stone walls for cover. Then she carefully ran across a cleared area into the forest where she had seen Mehta enter the thicket.

Immediately inside the wooded area, the path seemed to go cold, as Mehta's footprints faded to nothing.

All of a sudden bulky arms enveloped her, lifting her off the ground. She fought and kicked against her assailant, frivolously trying to break free.

"So it is just you," she heard a gruff voice behind her ear. "I should have known."

She dropped to her feet, but was unable to establish her balance. As a result, she tumbled awkwardly onto her buttocks. From that compromising altitude she turned back to see Mehta shaking his head.

"How many times will I catch you trying to sneak up behind me? You have the stealth of a mastodon."

"I...I want to come with you."

He frowned. "Do you even know where I'm going?"

She thought of trying to guess, but her wits failed her. Instead she just shook her head. He looked at her as one might a petulant child, then sighed and said, "Come on, then."

They didn't take the path down the mountain, but rather hiked upward through the forest, scaling the side of Montalto.

After a few minutes of climbing in silence, Mehta said, "it's not me you should be worrying about. Keep an eye on the Madison woman, or this Owen boy. They shouldn't be trusted."

"I'm not keeping an eye on you, or anyone else. I'm here to help," Flora said.

He looked back at her with a scowl.

They climbed and climbed for another twenty minutes. Flora felt chastened by Mehta's comments. She decided it would be best not to inquire as to their destination for the time being.

Soon they neared the top of Montalto, where Monty, the great beholder statue of Montalto, stood tall above them. There was also an abandoned old farmhouse not far away. She had heard these lands had been owned by Euclid's estate but had been uninhabited for decades. Few had any interest in living in the shadow of the beholder.

Mehta walked cautiously around the mountaintop, staying inside the forest and giving the beholder a wide berth.

The beholder's prodigious size monopolized the vista, and Flora could not help staring at it. Thick ivy reached up its legs from the ground, as if the giant was wearing green, knee-high boots. Its gray surface could still be seen in a few places, where there were no streaks of bird feces, stray vines, or moss that had found purchase. Its belly was excessively rounded, almost distended, like a man who had overeaten at a great feast. Another oddity was its eyes, or rather lack of them. The sockets were dark with pockets of green growth and dung. Chorus larks rested on the giant's shoulders and would at times circle it's head in melodious arcs.

There was a giant statue in the mountains west of Grand Caverns. The disciples called it Clay's Colossus. "Nourish the soil or become stone," they would say, citing the old myth about the Colossus's disruption of the land and its resulting purgatory. Every year there would be a pilgrimage of youths to see it, just as Talon had done only weeks before her departure.

Flora imagined stripping away the moss, ivy, and feces from the beholder in front of her, and she realized there would be a striking resemblance to the Colossus. But the Seeville beholders were supposedly built by the Spoke named Ursula Okafor, and Clay's Colossus by the Essentialist clansmen Clay Ripplewood. How could they build the same statue? Why would they?

Mehta abruptly cut out across an overgrown field toward the farmhouse. Flora had to run to keep up. He stepped on some fallen timbers of the run-down building and climbed up onto the perforated roof. He lay down on his front and took out a long scope, pointing in the direction of Seeville. Only when Flora realized what he was doing did she climb up the building via the same route.

When she arrived next to him, Mehta was switching between glancing at the scope and taking notes on a note pad.

"What are you looking at?" she asked.

"The structures they are building at the observatory and stadium."

"Why?"

"To see if there's anything new to report about what they're building. Also to find weaknesses."

"Why couldn't you do that at Monticello?"

He looked at her, searing her with his eyes. "No, you're not suspicious at all, are you?" he said sarcastically.

"It's just a question."

"There's a higher altitude here and a better angle. Besides, I like the exercise."

It seemed like a reasonable enough explanation. "You said to find any weaknesses. Weakness against what?"

He paused before responding, considering his words carefully. "The others are considering action, if worse comes to worst. You heard the boy, Owen. The dish could call something from space, and bring it to orbit around earth. It could be dangerous. Although it sounds like a bit of a fairy tale, especially given the retcher problem."

"Maybe they have a solution for that."

Mehta laughed. He opened his mouth but then held his tongue for a moment, becoming thoughtful. "I suppose it's possible, but I doubt it. It may be they only need to use it once. Maybe that's enough to send whatever message they are trying to send, and then the retchers will destroy it."

"How could we possibly have enough people to attack that thing?"

Mehta returned to looking through the scope. "Well, there are the bandits Madison and Owen are recruiting from Yorktown. Madison also talks about some sanctuary where there is a trove of weapons that the original Seeville founders have stashed away. Sounds like a lot of malarkey to me. Either way, I doubt it will be enough. The dish looks heavily defended. They have regular patrols, and they've built a substantial wall around the place."

"What about you? Are you going to help?" Flora asked.

"I'm not sure."

"Why not?"

"Like I said, I'm not sure they can be trusted."

"What is so wrong with them? It seems pretty clear to me they have the best interests of Seeville in mind. Someone needs to keep the railroad in check."

Mehta nodded, wrote something down on his pad, and then looked back through the scope. "Yes, the railroad needs to be kept in check, sure, but be careful. This Madison, she has been living with bandits for much of her life, and most bandits I've met are scoundrels or traitors at heart. No amount of fancy words can change who she is, no number of Old World books can change someone's true temperament."

"I disagree. She is better educated, polite, good-natured—more so than any typical bandit you would come across. Same with Benjamin and the other Yorktown folks I've met. Besides, she originally came from Seeville. In fact, she's probably less a bandit than you or I. Technically, if you weren't a merc, you'd be a bandit."

He glowered at her and then returned to his scope. "But is she being truthful? Is she being evasive?" he asked.

"Why would you ask that?"

"Well, for one, this sanctuary she speaks of. She tells us enough to keep us interested but gives us no details of any consequence. It could very well be a feint, to keep us here, working for her. Then there are the letters she writes, that she won't let us see. Some of them I've seen written with an old cipher—one no longer used. Why has she not been upfront about these letters?"

Flora did notice Madison stow away paperwork at times, but she hadn't known about anything being written in cipher. It did give her pause.

"Once I saw her skulking by your room at night, spying on you," Mehta said, his eye still in the scope. "She was listening with interest as you did your ritual."

"What ritual?"

"Come now, Flora."

"I don't remember ever saying any ritual."

"During the sessions…you may not remember everything, but you said many things. Your ritual was one of the most coherent. Peers Lindberg, Axel Kelemen, Tucker Kelemen…their strength is why I am alive. I honor them when I thrive…"

It was the second time she had been caught in a lie with Mehta. She felt haughty, defensive. "If you saw Madison outside my room, it means you were spying on me as well. How does that make Madison any better than you?"

"I was watching her, not you. And there's more. Doesn't it concern you that Madison asks you all these questions about Granger, about your family, and about the Essentialists? How could it benefit her? How do we know she doesn't have another agenda? She could be planning a coup with her bandits. She could even be in league with the railroad, using you for intelligence."

It was ironic that Mehta harbored suspicions about Madison working for the railroad, when Madison had the same suspicions about Mehta.

"Using me for intelligence?" Flora asked cynically. "They already chewed me up and spat me out in these *sessions* you keep talking about, session*s you* helped with. Why would they need Madison's help? Is it so hard for you to believe Madison simply wants to know more about me? Maybe she's not worried she's going to have to kill me, like you are?"

She saw his knuckles whiten around the scope, then he slowly lowered it from his face. His eyes seemed to have closed momentarily. "It's time to go," he said. Then he put his note pad in his pocket and walked back over the roof to the siding he had climbed up earlier.

Flora tried to quell her rising temper. It infuriated her that he wouldn't see her point, that he wouldn't give her straight answers. She followed him down the wall and hurried after him across the overgrown field.

By the time she caught up with him, her dander was up again. "If you don't trust Owen, if you don't trust Madison, why are you still here? Why don't you sign another one of your precious contracts so you can move on to your next bloodbath?"

He stopped in his tracks and turned to her. He was breathing heavily, his eyes dark. She could tell he was trying hard to dispel his own frustration, his own anger.

A momentary flash of fear took hold of her. Maybe she had pushed this homicidal man too far. She imagined his gnarly hands wrapped around her head, crushing her skull. She imagined him throwing her corpse unabashedly down the steep Montalto slope. She imagined peering through slits between her fingers as Mehta hit her throbbing hands.

But he did none of those things. Instead he continued to stare at her, the tension hanging in the air. Slowly, his breathing moderated, and he said, "I have signed another contract."

"I knew it!" she said, stepping back from him and pulling a knife from her belt. "Who with—with the railroad, with the curator?"

"Neither," he said, looking at her knife with some confusion. "I don't think you're going to need the knife."

"Then with who!" she asked, waving the knife at him.

"None of your business," he said, turning his back on her. "But don't worry, you'll be rid of me when the contract is over."

It was confounding, and it only infuriated her more. She sheathed her knife and ran ahead, jumping in front of him to cut him off.

"None of my business?" she said, some spittle flying off her tongue. "None of my business? You fucking moron, of course it's my business."

He stopped, his brow once again furrowed in confusion.

"Yes, that's right, asshole. Listen to me. Your contract with the curator screwed me over, your contract with the railroad subjected me to weeks of torture, but the best one was your Monticello contract. You bring me here, to this place as a slave, and then you get the one person I cared about killed in cold blood. The whole reason I came to this fucking place was to find the only one I truly loved, the one who had been stolen from me, and you killed him. I know Euclid pulled the trigger, but you signed the contract, so you killed him. You fucking asshole, your contracts *are* my business."

His eyes darted back and forth as she spoke. Then, when she finished, his knees seemed to give way, and this ox of a man's body folded down, as if encumbered by some foreign gravity. He put his hand down to steady himself, and then sat back on his buttocks. A flash of anguish traversed his face, creasing around his eyes. Then his face lost emotion, and he pulled up his hands, looking at them with the wonder of a child.

She couldn't bear the sight of this ignorant animal. She ran past him, down the hill. She knew she had gone too far, she knew her words were more emotion than truth, but the conversation was making her head spin. More than that, she had evoked the memory of Granger, and it made her think of that fateful day in the palisade garden when he was murdered.

Once a beacon of longing, Granger had become a black hole, a place she dared not venture with her thoughts. She had tried to comfort herself with the knowledge that she was able to see him one more time, that they were able to connect lips. On the day Ember died, it was all she had asked for.

But after his fickle demise, one that could be attributed to her own imprudence, she wondered if it would've been better if she hadn't come to the Spoke lands at all. She wondered if it would've been better if she had killed herself in the confrontation with Bartz on the train. Then at least he could have lived. Even as a slave, his life was worth so much more than hers.

So she ran away from Mehta, she ran away from her own spiteful words and she ran away from the memories of Granger, lest they take her down the dark recesses of regret where should could no longer tread.

A FIELD TRIP

Madison was sitting in front of the Meriwether Lewis statue again. She found a brief moment in front of this figure of strength offered some escape from the machinations of council meetings. It would clear her head and imbue her with an intangible fortitude.

Again a note from Duncan was splayed on her lap, freshly obtained from the lords' mailbox. She was improving at doing the cipher without pen and paper, and could usually make sense of the letter in only a few minutes now.

Unfortunately what she decoded held little insight.

Duncan was remarkably well informed about what was happening in Seeville. He was tuned in enough to ask probing questions about Mehta's origins or Flora's ancestry. He acknowledged the threat of the railroad, to be sure, and Gail, more cryptically, but his specific intent was vague beyond urging a counter to those threats. He alluded to the sanctuary at times, but it was hard to know if he was just referring to Adherent gospel or if there was actually something of substance he was hinting at.

So what was the point of his questions, exactly? He seemed to be trying to tease information out of her without revealing his true intent. As a result, she was beginning to become suspicious of Duncan's motives. The correspondence between them had evolved to batteries of nebulous questions and more enigmatic answers.

It seemed they had reached an impasse.

She folded the letter and moved her mind to the more pressing matters of today's meeting. She opened her notes to rehearse her statements and review a list of potential objections.

It had been difficult to get Prakash and Kline on board with her University Projects Review proposal. At first they couldn't even get past the tone of it. Granted, it was harsh. Basically, Madison's proposal sent a message, in not so many words, that they didn't trust Bartz. Arguing the philosophical merits seemed to be lost on them, as if the substantive arguments mattered little. It was likely a byproduct of the fact that for too long their votes had been curried by favors.

When she explained that the proposal could be put forth as a simple information-gathering exercise, rather than an inquisition, they began warming to the idea. They could spin it as a way to gain comfort with the Developer Rights Amendment before voting on it. In the end, of course, old habits died hard. Madison had to open up some of the Monticello New Founder archives to support educational activities and crop science. She hoped it would be enough, as it was the only favor she could offer.

"Ma'am, it's time," Benjamin reminded her.

"Of course it is," she said. She opened her eyes and extended her arm out for Benjamin to hold.

She arrived inside at the same time as the other lords. They were all seated quickly. Nods were exchanged, but no hands were shaken.

When they were settled, the recorder began. "Honorable Lord Banks has put forth a proposal to add to the top of the agenda, which you have received this morning. All those in favor of adding it to the agenda?"

There were four *ayes* and two *nays*, with Meeker and Bartz being the two dissenters.

The recorder said, "The *ayes* have it. Today's agenda is therefore the University Projects Review first, then the Developer Rights Amendment, Fifeville Roadworks, and a continuation of the Budget Review. As a reminder, honorable Meeker will be holding a special lords meeting on the topic of defense readiness in two weeks. Lord Banks, you have the floor."

"Thank you," Madison said, pushing herself up with her cane to stand. "My proposal is simply a request to inspect the sites at the stadium and up at the old observatory. I have received inquiries about these sites from my constituents, as I am sure you all have as well. We need to be able to explain what is being built in order to assure citizens that they do not pose any harm."

Prakash, Kline, and Henneson nodded. Meeker and Bartz were unmoved.

"In turn, a thorough investigation will help us with the Developer Rights Amendment. Details of an inspection may help us ensure we are drafting the right policy. As long as Seeville laws are being followed, I hope you will see, honorable Lord Bartz, that this inspection will be but a minor inconvenience to you and your people."

Bartz was leaning back, watching her carefully, while Meeker was still unreadable. She anticipated some form of resistance, but she didn't know how it would manifest itself. It could be they were in the process of sanitizing the construction sites as she was speaking.

In the end it wouldn't matter. Madison had enough damning photographs and eyewitness accounts to bury them under a mountain of evidence. At the very least she should be able to throw enough red tape at them to slow down the work. For now, however, she kept the evidence in reserve.

"And before we vote," Madison added, "I request that we have the inspection in the next twenty-four hours, so as to not hold up other council activities. Let's go to vote now." She nodded to the recorder.

"All in favor of the University Projects Proposal say *aye*."

Again, there were two *nays* from Meeker and Bartz, and four *ayes*.

"Excellent," Madison said. "Lord Bartz, when can we visit?"

Bartz tapped his pen on the desk, and then said, "We can comply with your request, Banks. I suggest we get this over with as soon as possible." He stood up. "We have arranged for travel for the council. Shall we?" He gestured with his hand toward the door.

It was not what she expected. She thought he would at least take the day to prepare. Had he anticipated this move? She had no choice but to play along, of course.

"Fantastic," she said. "I do like field trips."

The lords and clerics all filed out of the courtroom. Outside a number of the finest bike assemblies had been parked. These vehicles allowed two mules to pull a lightweight chariot that rolled behind them. The chariots were open-air, only a skeleton frame, and looked to be interchangeable with other platforms for hauling. They had the S&R Railroad logo brand-ed on the side. The mules on the bikes were full-time railroad men.

Madison didn't like the fact that the railroad would be in control of their means of transportation, but she had no choice. To raise a stink about something so trivial would take away from her ability to raise much more important objections later.

After Madison and Benjamin buckled into their small chariot, one of Bartz's men walked over to Madison and handed her some documents. "Lord Bartz would like to discuss the enclosed modifications to the De-veloper Rights Amendment, ma'am."

"Well, this should be interesting," she replied with a mock smile, and took the documents. Madison could see that other lords were handed similar-looking documents in their chariots.

The chariot pulled out, and they made their way through the Seeville streets toward the stadium. She opened the package and began looking over the material. Annoyingly, changes to the document were not shown, so she would have to scan over the entire amendment to find out what was different. She split the packet with Benjamin so they could make the best use of their time.

Madison had a tendency to get nauseous when reading and riding, especially on bumpy rides like this one. She had to be careful not to fully immerse herself in the document for more than a minute at a time. It would do no good if she showed up at the inspection with vomit on her blouse.

On West Main Street, they passed a man yelling out into the street. Bikers and pedestrians slowed down to hear what he was saying. "The demonstration will begin in fifteen minutes, brought to you by Seeville & Raleigh Railroad operations. Come one, come all to the old UVA stadi-um. Prudent progress, real freedom—come and see for yourself…"

There was more, but they were now out of earshot.

Madison leaned forward. "What's this all about, this demonstration?" she asked the mules that were pedaling her chariot.

"Don't know, ma'am. We were only told to get you to the stadium."

Madison looked over at Benjamin. He shook his head. She looked back and saw that additional bikes were falling in line behind the column of chariots.

She was beginning to get a sinking feeling. She couldn't quite put her finger on it, but Bartz seemed too ready, too prepared for this outcome. And now this "demonstration" added to the uncertainty.

As they entered the old university grounds, more and more bikes fell in line. They had to slow down because of the traffic.

"Um, ma'am," Benjamin said. "I just found one of the changes." He passed a few pages over to Madison and pointed to a particular paragraph.

She read it carefully. "Ha," she laughed. "Well, they have some gall." She gave the pages back to Benjamin. "See if you can find anything else. With these tired old eyes and this weak stomach unfortunately I can't be of much use."

"Yes ma'am." Benjamin continued to pore through the document.

When they turned onto Alderman Avenue, the chariot started to wobble and came to a stop. The mules dismounted their bikes and looked at one of the tires.

"Sorry ma'am, we have a problem with one of the wheels. It'll just be a few minutes."

Of course they did. Of course it would take a few minutes. They would arrive late, giving Bartz time with the other councilors.

"Come on, Benjamin. I need your help."

Madison nearly stumbled as she pushed herself out of the chariot and began hobbling forward down the middle of the road as bikes wove around them precariously.

"Ma'am. It will just be a few minutes," the railroad mule called after her. "If you could please stay in the chariot."

"No, thank you," she said, not looking back.

"Ma'am let me help you," Benjamin said. He caught up with her and offered his arm. He also urged her to the side, so bikes could pass by more easily.

They made an awkward pair, her hobbling as fast as she could, leaning heavily on Benjamin's arm. Many gawked, and some even called out rudely, telling her to get off the road. But this was better than putting her fate in the hands of these railroad men. This wobbly wheel couldn't have been a coincidence. She doubted any of this was. She needed to get to the stadium as soon as possible to find out why.

When Madison and Benjamin finally arrived at the stadium, her neck was cramped, and she was sweating profusely. She took out a handkerchief to dry herself off.

Unlike most Old World stadiums, this one was built on a gradient, with a large portion dug deep into an incline. They had arrived at the highest elevation of the stadium, with access to some of the uppermost seats. You could even see down into the bottom of the stadium from parts of the roadway.

Enforcers were everywhere, keeping back the gathering crowd. One of them recognized her and motioned for them to follow through a check-point. This man escorted her and Benjamin to the column of bike chariots that brought the other lords. They were parked in a semicircle around an open parking area overlooking the stadium. The lords were all congregated on an adjoining large balcony separated from the burgeoning number of spectators populating the stands.

"Thank you, Benjamin. I will take it from here," she said.

He released her arm. It would do no good for them to see her arrive in such a way.

"And the document, please."

Benjamin handed her the document.

The balcony gave her a good vantage point to see the base of the stadium. The tarp and scaffolding had been removed from the structure being built, and only a few pieces of debris remained from the building effort. The structure itself looked to be no more than a giant cube made of cement-like material, with small circular indentations in the center of each side. In other words, it was only a hair less enigmatic than what it looked like with the tarp on.

"What is this nonsense?" Madison shook the document in her hand as she arrived to join the other councilors. "You can't do this."

She noticed Prakash and Kline look down sheepishly upon her arrival. Meeker gave her but a fleeting glance. Only Henneson could look her straight in the eye. His morose expression did not give her any comfort.

"I'm sorry, honorable Lord Banks," Bartz said, smiling. "We will have to address this later. I am master of ceremonies here." The railroad man named Thorpe was standing by Bartz. He handed him a bullhorn.

"Master of what ceremony?" Madison asked. No one answered her question. Bartz walked away and stood on a pulpit that extended into the stadium from their balcony.

"People of Seeville!" he said, crooning into the horn. Some people stopped and looked, others seemed to hurry to find seats. "I welcome you here today, an historic day. Many of you will have questions when we turn on our machine. Some of you may even be fearful. Do not fear. Trust in the prudent progress we are making. In the future it will become clear how transformative today will be, all because of our ingenuity and hard work. As long as we keep progressing, we can solve any problem, we can defend ourselves against any threat."

Some of Bartz's oration could be considered controversial. The use of words like "machine" were often shunned by the Adherents because it represented some form of heinous *novation*. Of course nobody had the faintest idea what was really going on, including Madison, so there would be no objection.

Bartz nodded to Thorpe. Thorpe, in turn, waved a green flag in the air. Down below, next to the cement cube, another green flag went up. In the distance, she could see a young man open a trap door that led down a staircase into the ground. The door closed firmly behind him.

A few moments later, a low rumble could be heard coming from the area. Slowly, a slim metal rod protruded through the ceiling of the cement cube, and at the end of it, a bright blue light came on.

A gasp of awe went through the crowd. This was no lantern. It was much too bright. No, this was an Old World light. It was using electricity.

The crowd began murmuring loudly. Some people started retreating back toward the exits. Some started pushing and shoving.

"Don't worry!" Bartz said into the bullhorn. "You're safe here. If you try to leave people will get hurt."

"Are you mad?' Madison said, hobbling aggressively over to Bartz. "I thought there might be some code violations but this is obscene. You *know* the use of technologies emitting electromagnetic radiation is prohibited. Not only that, but you have put all these people, including us, in harm's way. Turn it off before the retchers come, or we'll have you arrested."

Madison waved the document above her head vigorously. "And don't think for a second you will be able to get us to sign the ridiculous waste of paper you put in our laps. This business of you making the amendment retroactive is preposterous. It means you can essentially absolve yourself of any crimes you have already committed, many of which we know nothing about."

She then wagged a finger at the rest of the lords and lectured them. "When leaders absolve themselves of their own sins, government has ceased being a democracy."

As she finished, she could see Bartz's smile had grown wide. The smile was not one born of a simple conversational habit, nor political pandering. It was something more. He wasn't being a chameleon. He was showing his true colors. He was gloating, and he didn't care who knew it. "But you see honorable Lord Banks, we have done nothing wrong. Thorpe, the contracts please."

Thorpe pulled out a number of documents and handed them over to Madison, one at a time. She could see they were the modified Developer Rights Amendment she had been perusing in the chariot ride over, with one important difference, they had been *signed* by the other lords—all of them except Lord Henneson.

"One, two, three, four signed amendments. The majority of lords seem to disagree with you," Bartz said.

It was staggering, and for a moment she almost lost her footing. Prakash and Kline looked down, as if embarrassed or ashamed. Meeker stood with his comfortable stoicism, implacable to her words. Henneson was standing back, shaking his head in abject despair. She had underestimated Bartz but also greatly misjudged many of her fellow councilors. They were either completely ignorant or morally bankrupt.

"But the retchers, they will come. You know they will." Madison warned, her voice faltering. "It will be pandemonium. If there is any exposure in that block, beyond that light at the top, I imagine more than one, maybe even a flock of them."

"Yes, we are counting on it," Bartz said. "Not the pandemonium, of course, but a large number of retchers."

Madison opened her mouth but had no words to say. She had been routed by this man, by these people, and there was no recovery.

Just then, the blue light at the top of the cubic structure went out. There was a lull in the crowd, and many people stopped leaving. Then, swooping in from the sky, like a large black dart cutting through the air, came a retcher.

People screamed and began running quickly for the exits. In most places, the railroad men were calming them down or holding people back. In one case, the railroad men were overrun, and people were leaving the stadium in a panic.

Meanwhile the retcher had landed on the cubic block. It was bigger than Madison imagined, about four feet tall and rigid with muscle and sinew under it's black feathers.

"Everyone watch!" Bartz yelled into the bullhorn with authority. "There is nothing to fear!"

The retcher immediately vomited its acidic bile on the blue light, melting it down.

Then the retcher waddled its bird-feet over to the side of the cube. It dropped into the air, hovered for a moment and circled the cube several times, looking for an opening. Then it launched itself into one of the circular indentations, and began clawing and vomiting acidic bile on the surface with no visible effect.

All of a sudden, out of the sides of the indentation came an array of blades, impaling the retcher on both flanks. These blades retracted, and then out of the top and bottom two monoliths of concrete came together, flattening the retcher.

Acidic bile and blood sprayed over the cube. Black feathers from the pulverized creature floated down. It toppled out of the indentation and fell to the ground several stories below. One of the retcher's wings fluttered in spasm, but the other wasn't working. The retcher ceased moving.

Some in the crowd gasped, and those streaming out halted their progress. Some reentered to see what was going on.

Another black pole extended out of a hidden aperture in the top of the structure. Another blue light illuminated.

The crowd quieted again as everyone's eyes returned to the skies. Several minutes passed, and then again the light went out. This time, three retchers came in from three different directions. The din of the crowd increased, but they were more subdued than before, and no one was in a panic, no one was leaving.

The first retcher to arrive easily melted down the light pole and then circled the structure. The other two arrived and circled the structure with the first. Two of them broke off their orbit and entered one of the circular indentations. The other entered the indentation on the opposing side and went to work scratching and vomiting.

All three were mulched by same process; blades first, then flattened. Only one seemed to survive. It was on the ground, severely maimed and unable to fly. It limped around in a circle until railroad men came out with mallets to finish it off.

Another light pole was erected and illuminated in brilliant blue. This time, the crowd cheered when the light came on.

"People of Seeville!" Bartz yelled into the bullhorn. "This blue light you see shining resiliently before you shall forever be known as the Lamp of Liberty. When we are sure all the retchers have been destroyed, we will erect these across town, so you know you no longer have to fear these vile angels of darkness, so the path of progress will be well lit."

Madison finally knew what the structure was. They had effectively built a retcher destroyer. How many retchers were out there, she couldn't be sure, but she suspected they would be able to clear out any in the Seeville area. Then they could re-ignite old electrical networks. Then they could rebuild the Old World infrastructure without fear of retcher attacks.

She wanted to protest. She wanted to reveal who the real puppet master was behind the scenes, and what its real motivations were. Most of all it galled Madison that the railroad would brand the lights *Lamps of Liberty*. Liberty was a word sacred to her—a word held in high esteem by the New Founders—and they were bastardizing it. The only thing they were liberating was a demon. A demon that had destroyed one civilization, and could easily destroy their own in a heartbeat—a demon they were now freeing from its Faraday cage prison.

But she knew now was not the time. The lords had made their choice, and to defy Bartz was to defy the cheering mob of Seeville citizens at his back. Her words would be lost in the brisk winds of change, whatever their weight.

A quote floated to the top of her mind, one that referred to liberty in the proper context, without this perversion and manipulation. The quote was from a letter to William Smith from Thomas Jefferson, referring to their rebellion against the English monarchy. He had written, "The tree of liberty must be refreshed from time to time with the blood of patriots and tyrants. It is its natural manure."

It was to this they would now have to turn. They had no choice but to resort to violence. And the likening of Bartz and his men to manure seemed particularly fitting.

"Let's go, Benjamin," she said. "I can no longer stand the stench of these people."

She hobbled away, leaving behind her the next display of retcher destruction and another chorus of jubilant cheers.

An Unwelcome Letter

Preston connected the wire into the voltmeter and turned on the power. Again, there was no voltage. He could troubleshoot some of the simpler assemblies, but this one was a sophisticated component. He gently placed it into the *Barnyard* bin so it could be routed to Gail and the bots for closer examination.

He was working late into the evening with two other electricians to test the key components of the dish. The term *electrician* was generous, of course, as a two-week crash course could hardly be worthy of the term. They were on a long table, cluttered with equipment and kerosene lamps, while the dish loomed above them.

Whenever he got a negative test he couldn't help peering down the hill to the stadium. Always the blue Lamp of Liberty was there, burning more brightly than any other light in the cityscape below. Only then could he reassure himself that a retcher was not on its way to spoil his work.

He took a deep breath, relishing the ability to finally be able to work with electronics outside a Faraday cage. And as a first for today, in the outdoors even.

One of the younger assistants named Tricia walked in front of him, obscuring his view of the Lamp of Liberty. "Sir, I just received a letter for you at the front gate. The courier said it was urgent."

"At the front gate? Why didn't they deliver it with the mail? I'm sure it can wait until tomorrow."

"They said it was time-sensitive, from someone named Owen Maddox."

Preston slowly put down the next component. "Okay, I'll take it now. Give it to me."

She passed him the letter and waited. "You're dismissed," he said, and she walked away.

He took his lamp with him and walked away from the table, away from prying eyes. Only then did he open the letter carefully. Was this some kind of practical joke? It was unlikely. Those that knew Owen's fate wouldn't joke about such a thing.

Dear Preston,

Yes, I am alive. I may never understand why you did what you did in York-town, and I'm not sure I could forgive you. It doesn't matter. Apologies are not as important as what I need to talk to you about.

Gail doesn't have your best interests in mind. She is using you, using all of us, to gain strength, so she can fulfill her own interests. When you are no longer useful, she will discard you. Eventually she will eliminate all of us, as we pose a threat to her not achieving her long term objectives.

I would like to meet, one-on-one, so we can talk. I know that, as a citizen of Seeville, and as a progressive thinker, you have an open mind. Please at least hear me out, even if you disagree strongly with what I am saying in this letter.

I hope you understand the risk I am taking by simply writing you this letter. I am only doing it because I know how influential you can be in saving us all.

I will be at the Rotunda at 9:30 pm tonight. Please meet me there. For safety, I will have three friends there with me. Please bring no more than three on your side.

Sincerely,

Owen Maddox

"How could he be alive?" Preston whispered under his breath. It had to be that annoying old New Founder lady Bartz was butting heads with.

She came from Yorktown. She must have found Owen there. She must have brought him back to Seeville.

Preston stalked over to the interior guard post. It was manned by one of Meeker's overweight retired reserve officers who probably should have stayed retired. He was reading a book by the light of a lantern.

"Connor," Preston said, startling him out of whatever passage he was reading. "I need twenty men, and I need them now."

Preston paced back and forth behind the three men standing with him at the Rotunda. He wasn't willing to expose himself for long in case Owen was orchestrating some sort of sniper attack. "What did you say this man looked like?" Preston asked the main gate guard. "The man who dropped off the letter?"

"He was tall and lanky, but he wore a hood, sir. It was hard to make out his face."

"So you couldn't tell if he had spots on his face?"

"No, sir. I'm sorry."

Owen probably would have sent someone else to deliver the letter. If they recognized him, they could have apprehended him right away.

Preston looked at his watch. It read 9:28 pm.

There was no way Owen could understand. Gail had convinced him of that. Gail had even warned him that people would try to paint her as being evil. Whether it was Adherent gospel or just fear of the unknown, it was a natural reaction, but not the right one.

No, he needed to finish this. He couldn't have this distraction from his past continuing to plague him.

"Are we ready to take him out, first opportunity?" Preston asked.

"Yes, sir. We have multiple snipers covering all access points to the Rotunda. We will retreat to those columns over there for cover. If they come from the street down below us, they'll be sitting ducks."

"Good."

Nine-thirty p.m. No sign of him. Preston continued to pace nervously.

Suddenly, shots rang out. The men in front of him ducked down while Preston fell flat on the ground. Then he scurried away toward the columns. The other men followed, but slowly, more cautiously.

There was something about the shots. The seemed quieter than he would have expected, distant even. He popped his head out and craned his neck in the direction they were coming from.

Connor said, "Sir, I don't think the shots are coming from nearby. They're coming from somewhere else." Connor stepped out into the open, cautiously at first, but then more assertively. He was fully exposed, able to look up toward the origin of the shots. He yelled back to Preston, "Sir, the shots are coming from the hilltop. I think someone is attacking the observatory."

Someone was attacking the observatory, and they only had half their security contingent remaining.

A Devoted Adherent

Some might have the moral latitude to be an Adherent and still allow for this satellite dish monstrosity. They might find some way of justifying to themselves that building and pointing this otherworldly machine toward the stars was not novation. Alastair was certainly not one of those people.

No, Bartz and his crew had gone too far, too fast, irresponsibly pushing Seeville toward damnation. Alastair saw the fervor in people's eyes at the stadium. It was everything they were taught was wrong. It was exactly what Okafor wanted them to be watchful for.

Lately, he wasn't sure he could trust anyone, including this New Founder and former bandit Madison Banks. Yet, despite her questionable origins, she seemed the most reasonable of any of the lords. Perhaps trust was not important. In this, for their objective this evening, against their mutual enemy, they were perfectly aligned.

"The back door is open," Rennick said, pulling down the binoculars from his eyes. Rennick was an older mule with scars that fanned across one cheek. He had once been trained as an enforcer, and now he tended to a small plot of land on the outskirts of Seeville after becoming a devout Adherent.

Alastair held his own binoculars up to confirm. Their man, Ben, was walking quickly away from the open door, first along the outside of the wall, then into a thick part of the forest.

It had been a precarious thing, trying to turn Ben. The railroad mules were paid well, and Bartz was developing quite a following after the Lamp of Liberty euphoria. Ben certainly wasn't swayed by the Credo. In the end they had to promise a more lucrative bike run—one where he would be able to frequent a girl he was chasing who lived on the outskirts of Culpepper.

"Okay let's go," Alastair said.

The eight of them moved stealthily out of the forest toward the imposing wall of the dish compound. The enclosure was even more impressive up close. It was more than twice his height. As they drew nearer he could hear the purring sound of generators. There were generators everywhere now—at the Barnyard, at the stadium and now here. To Alastair, these generators were the voice of the damned.

Alastair pulled up the rear. Madison had insisted that Alastair not include himself in the raid, but he refused. Leaders didn't cower in the darkness while their men were put in harm's way, especially mule leaders. Besides, he needed to make sure the job was done right.

The dish compound was laid out as two concentric circles, an outer wall and an inner wall. They ducked through the outer wall one at a time, lining up behind a wooden dumpster. Along the inner wall were a number of doors but no sign of guards. From their position, two partially enclosed watchtowers could be seen perched above the walls, one to the East and one to the South.

"There are two in the south tower, and one in the east tower. I don't see any patrols," Rennick whispered. "It looks like the diversion worked."

"Any way to take them out by stealth?" Alastair asked.

"I don't think so. We have good clear shots, right now."

Alastair hesitated. If he gave the order, there was no turning back. But the presence of the circular abomination looming above him, this symbol of novation being so close, gave him confidence in their mission. "Do, it," he said. "Take them out."

Rennick issued the commands. "Guthrie, you take the left-most man in the south tower. I have the right. Santos, take the man in the east tower. Fire on my mark. Then we advance east."

"Check."

"Check."

"Mark!"

Shots rang out. Two of the tower men were hit; one of them screamed in agony. They missed one in the south tower. He managed to duck down, and they lost sight of him. A moment later a rifle poked out and a shot was fired in their general direction.

Rennick pointed four fingers to a group of them. "You, take position under the north tower. We'll stay here and try to finish off the south tower guard. Be ready for patrols and watch anyone coming out through the inner doors. Remember to stay on the northeast side of the facility."

The four men split off, keeping low as they circled around the perimeter of the enclosure.

For a few minutes, they exchanged periodic shots with the guard on the south tower, with none of them ringing true on either side. Alastair helped Rennick and another man pull up some old crates to create better cover for their position.

The man in the tower shot another flurry of bullets at them, and they all ducked down further. When they looked up again, two patrolmen had advanced along the inner circle from somewhere beyond their line of sight. These two had found cover at the base of the south tower.

Then a shot came in from another direction, flipping one of his men backward onto the ground.

"There!" Rennick said, pointing to a door that was slightly ajar on the inner wall. Two railroad men jumped out, firing again in their direction. They had a better angle than the ones near the tower. Alastair's men fired back at them. They adjusted their cover and ducked down.

When they were comfortable they were protected, Alastair took a look at their downed man. He was shot squarely in the temple. It was a mule Rennick knew, a friend of his from a long time ago.

He was their first casualty. Alastair felt a strange lack of empathy for the man. Perhaps it was because he didn't know him, or perhaps it was because Alastair knew there would be more—perhaps many more.

Rennick made a leveling motioned with his hand. "Stay down as much as possible. Suppressing fire only. Conserve your ammo."

Alastair nodded. He looked behind them, in the direction of the north tower. His other men were around the corner. He couldn't see how they were faring, but the echoing sound of gunshots and flashes of light suggested that they were similarly engaged.

This was it. They were held down, unable to move forward, both sides firmly entrenched. They were doing their part.

This was not obsession, Alastair told himself. It was a one-time necessity. This was not recklessness. It was a prudent course of action to prevent the recklessness of the railroad. It was competition, to be sure, but only because rational cooperation in the council had failed.

He felt comforted by the fact that in this moment of uncertainty he could consult the Credo—that he could still claim to be a devoted Adherent, perhaps now more than ever.

But the others better deliver, and fast.

TRULY A BEAST

"Well?" Mehta asked. "Is it time?"

"For someone who originally refused to go on this mission, you're remarkably impatient to get it over with," Owen responded, lowering his scope.

Mehta had slandered the mission from the get-go. He was only swayed once Flora adamantly insisted on her own involvement. How this changed Mehta's mind Owen would never know, for any time they were together it was clear they didn't see eye-to-eye. The two of them hardly ever spoke, and when they did it was like two children arguing over a lost toy. All of Monticello would brace for the inevitable flurry of yelling and name-calling.

At least Owen hadn't seen any sign of these antics on the mission. At least not yet.

Mehta's face was deadpan in the weak moonlight. "The fighting is heavy on the far side of the compound. There's no one at the gate, and the towers are undermanned. That's our cue."

He was right, of course. "Okay, let's go," Owen said.

Mehta took the lead, waltzing out of their cover with reckless abandon, fully upright. Owen, Flora, and the handful of Yorktown men stayed low to the ground on their approach. Mehta applied the wire cutters to the fence while the rest looked around nervously. The only guard that could see them at the gate would be the man in the south tower, but he was focused on his targets on the opposite side of the compound.

Once through the gate, they circled around the perimeter southward and found the inner door Alastair's man Ben had left unlocked. They opened it and went through, into the innermost circle of the compound. It housed a few sheds of various sizes, as well as the main dish control station and the massive dish perched on top of it.

Owen began by placing a packet of explosives close to one of the main structural supports that protruded from a side of the building. He let out a good fifty feet of fuse.

"That door, there." Owen pointed.

Mehta tried it. It appeared locked, but it also looked to be made of a flimsy fiberglass. He kicked at the handle, and in three swift blows the door handle assembly fell to pieces. Mehta then pushed the door in, and they all followed.

"Stay here, cover our rear." Mehta said to one of the Yorktown men with them. The man perched himself outside of the door.

Inside was an open room with a number of control panels in various states of assembly. Mehta stormed into the place, forcing a table of components into a wall with a crash. He pushed another rolling table into the opposite wall and began chasing after two men that were running to a door on the far end. They didn't appear to be guards, although one of them had a gun holstered in his belt.

This man pulled out the gun as he ran, but he wasn't nearly quick enough. Mehta grabbed his hand before he could take proper aim, and his shot went wide. Mehta wrapped the arms of the man around himself from behind and threw him at the other runner like a ragdoll. The impact made the other man trip and fall into the exit door before he could open it. Mehta then followed up by inserting his brawny hands into the entangled bodies, finding their skulls, and rapping them together, once, twice, and three times.

They fell to the floor, either unconscious or dead, Owen couldn't be sure.

Owen couldn't help shaking his head watching Mehta in action. He was truly a beast.

For today, he was grateful he was *their* beast.

Owen paused to examine the assemblies in the room. There were some oscilloscopes, power monitors, and other gauges he couldn't quite place. There was also some form of command console. He would have loved to have just ten minutes to examine what they were building more closely.

"Owen," Flora said behind him, with some urgency.

"Sorry, yes." Of course there was no time for that. They moved through the second door, which led to a corridor. At one end were two other doors.

"I think it's here. Or at least, I think we're close enough." Owen stuck the explosives to the wall and began unrolling another lengthy fuse.

"Good, let's go," Mehta said.

They cautiously retreated the way they had come. Once outside, Owen wove the ends of the two fuses together, and lit the end of the combined fuse. "We have two minutes, maybe three," he said as the sparks cackled energetically down the line.

Owen then took out the flare gun and aimed it over the northeast section of the compound.

"Wait," Mehta said, holding his hand up. Mehta lifted his rifle, took aim, and deftly shot the guard in the south tower who had his back to them. The guard's form slumped down, deeper into the basket at the top of the tower.

"Okay, do it now," Mehta said.

Without further hesitation, Owen shot up the flare to signal to Alastair and his men. Then he began running back to the gate, followed by Flora and the others. Mehta hung back a few more seconds, watching the fuse burn and split along the two lines. Once satisfied, he jogged after them.

They made it out of the compound without impediment and slid down the steep side of the hill they had come up. They pulled a large piece of particleboard they had left at the site over their heads and waited.

Two explosions rocked the hillside. They heard a loud wrenching sound, the tearing of metal, and then a crash. Later they would see that the dish had been split asunder, half of it fractured to pieces on the ground below.

A Sweaty Meeting

Madison arrived by horse and carriage to the next council meeting. Thankfully the carriage was draped in fabric to shield the sun. She also had a fan with her, but the air was so heavy it seemed not even worth her exertion to use it. She couldn't complain. Most of the city continued to travel by bicycle under the oppressive heat. A carriage was much more comfortable.

The railroad-sponsored construction projects never stopped multiplying and progressing, no matter the weather. Today she noticed a new solar panel installation being built into an old brick building near Court Square. A cylindrical tube with a blue bulb struck out to the sky from the matrix of black glossy tiles—yet another Lamp of Liberty that would be welcomed with adulation. In front of this building, a series of warped metal bike wheel frames painted in various colors lay in a heap. It was an award-winning decorative installation from the Spoke festival that had previously adorned the slanted roof.

The sight of it revolted her. Not so much the destruction of the artwork, or even the application of the solar panels. It seemed a rational way to generate energy. It was the Lamp of Liberty that disgusted her. Its name, and its use on the building, were symbolic of a growing number of ardent followers of Bartz's cause and, by connection, anything the railroad did. As the vanquisher of the retchers, Bartz could do no wrong. Before he was a respected businessman and Seeville lord, but now he was something more. His star continued to rise.

"No time to sit down on the bench today, Benjamin. We'll head right in," Madison said as they pulled up to a stop in front of the courtroom building. The Meriwether Lewis statue would have to wait until after the meeting.

The four of them stepped out of the carriage. She thought it best to bring two new "clerics" with her, in addition to Benjamin. These were not book-wormy intellects, but rather strong physical specimens from York-town whose keen senses had been tuned over many years of hunting and foraging. After the destruction of the observatory dish, she couldn't be sure what to expect at this meeting. As tensions rose, civility tended to decline.

When she arrived, all the other lords were present except Alastair. The others watched her carefully as she made her way to sit down. Their temples were beaded with sweat and patches of wetness darkened their armpits and chests. A battery-powered fan oscillated back and forth behind Bartz.

"Well, that is something," Madison said, sitting down. "How nice of you to bring it along." Of course the fan was on the opposite side, behind the table, hitting the backs of Bartz and Meeker first. She could barely feel the breeze.

"We have many other appliances that are interesting and useful," Bartz said.

"I am sure there are, and more to come," Madison said, smiling. "We have much work to do to regulate all this progress, to make sure we are proceeding with the right measure of caution."

The Spoke attorney general Anthony Zarnik entered the room, but he did not take his usual spot next to the clerics. Instead he stepped through the gate to approach the lord's table. His face glistened and a great arch of sweat covered his shirt from his neckline down, made prominent by his ample frame stretching the shirt fabric.

Meeker said, "Honorable lords, Attorney General Zarnik has an important matter to discuss with us today. It involves the unfortunate incident at the observatory. Go ahead Mr. Zarnik."

Madison raised her hand. "Yes, such a terrible tragedy. I'm sure this is important. Shouldn't we wait for Lord Henneson?"

Zarnik said, "Lord Banks, this concerns Lord Henneson personally."

"Oh, I see," Madison said, smiling. Her pulse elevated in tempo ever so slightly.

Zarnik brought out what looked like a laptop computer, at least based on what she had seen in old picture books. He opened the screen, and it illuminated, showing them a dark, nighttime scene. He said, "With the elimination of the retcher problem, S&R Railroad has begun installing hidden cameras in various parts of the city. One of the first installations was being tested in the observatory area."

Zarnik then pressed on a triangle on the screen and a scene unfolded. In the bottom right-hand corner they could see several dark shapes infiltrating the compound and firing their weapons at the guard towers.

"So it *was* some form of sabotage," said Kline. There had been speculation of an attack, but it hadn't been confirmed. Most thought the explosions were an accident. It had actually allowed those concerned with new developments underway in the city to have a stronger voice, an unexpected benefit. The Adherents had even been marching in protest, despite the oppressive heat.

But she had a queasy feeling what Zarnik was about to show could silence those voices.

"Yes, it was sabotage," confirmed Zarnik. "Not only that, but if we zoom in we can see the perpetrators with better resolution." Zarnik used the mouse pad to tap on another portion of the screen, pulling up a different window. In this window Alastair's team was magnified. In one frame, in which Zarnik froze the screen, Alastair's face was clearly discernable.

Prakash gasped.

"I can't believe it," said Kline.

"We have also apprehended a man who gave them access to the compound. He confirmed Lord Henneson's involvement, after some interrogation."

If only Alastair had listened to her and stayed away from the observatory. She didn't want to risk losing him to some stray bullet. But he was too stubborn. Granted, even she didn't think there could be a working camera in the compound. The railroad was moving so fast, and they were dealing with technologies not used in her lifetime. How could they possibly have anticipated this?

"This is an unusual situation," continued Zarnik. "Lord Henneson will be held for trial in the coming weeks. Given the overwhelming evidence of malfeasance, in accordance with our bylaws, his vote on the council of lords will be deemed in absentia until such time as he is found guilty. When he is sentenced his seat will be up for reelection."

"Thank you Zarnik," Meeker said, "and well done. This is truly a shocking development, that one of our own lords would be involved in this raid. We must be steadfast in prosecuting him for this crime, so that he is measured by the law as any other common citizen."

Zarnik nodded. "The evidence you and honorable Lord Bartz has provided has been crucial to our investigation. Your team should be recognized for its vigilance."

Madison tried not to roll her eyes at all self-congratulatory remarks. Even Bartz seemed to tire of the display. "Let's move on," Bartz said, waving his hand.

When Zarnik went to sit down on the exterior pews, Madison was feeling quite isolated at the lords table. How would she be able to have any influence as the sole dissenter to Bartz's machinations? Hopefully Alastair's efforts would not be in vain. It would take months to rebuild the dish.

The recorder began. "The main objective of today's meeting is an update on defense preparations and to convey any further intelligence about the threat from the Essentialists. Lord Meeker, you have the floor."

Meeker nodded to his cleric, who came to the table and distributed some printed materials. "What you have in front of you is the updated Seeville Defense Plan," he said. "It includes new resource allocations and intelligence. I will not go through all the details with you here, but I will highlight the most important and urgent component, which is on page seven."

Madison quickly shuffled to the seventh page, which was titled "Operation Prudent Liberty." Based on the name alone, she knew she wasn't going to like it.

"Sometimes, the best defense is a good offense," Meeker explained. "We have decided we should not wait for Essentialist forces to attack wherever we are weakest, and whenever we least expect it. Instead we should do a preemptive strike at the center of their operations, where they are marshaling resources for their offensive, and destroy their momentum and ambition in the process. It will be a strike at the heart of their military infrastructure at the town of Grand Caverns."

"Ten thousand men?" Madison asked, holding the paper up for all to see with her finger on the line item. "All equipped with rifles? Ten Old World tanks you have managed to restore? This is a massive force!" Madison said with some apprehension.

"Yes. We believe we can achieve an overwhelming victory early, which will ultimately prevent future casualties."

"Overwhelming victory, or overkill? With all due respect, honorable Lord Meeker, except for a few years ago, the Essentialists have never attacked us. I believe they are building up their forces, as your intelligence suggests, but how do you know they are intent on attacking us? Maybe we are starting a war that doesn't need to be started?"

"We are certain they intend to attack us. We have spies that have infiltrated their camp."

"Yes, yes, you have asked us to trust you with that intelligence. But if I recall you said yourself you have not been into the inner sanctum. You don't know what the higher levels of authority are thinking in Grand Caverns."

"It's plainly obvious. We know their culture."

Bartz interjected, speaking to all the lords. "Meeker shared the updated proposal with me earlier. I believe victory is virtually assured. We are fighting against a backward people, bows and arrows. There is nothing to worry about. Loss of life will be minimal."

Meeker said, "That's right. We believe we can win with less than five hundred casualties."

"On our side," Madison said.

"That's right."

"And how many casualties on their side? How many of these people do we have to murder because we have not tried some sort of diplomatic resolution?"

Meeker had a look of repugnancy on his face. "You want us to negotiate? With the SLS?"

Bartz again weighed in. "It's not important, really. These are savages. Don't get me wrong, we will try to spare as many lives as possible, but remember, we are *saving* these people from their tyrannical leaders. They need us to help them escape from their Essentialist brainwashing. The sooner we can do that, the better. Some of them will die, but much fewer than if this becomes an all-out war. In fact, they can eventually become Spoke citizens, given enough time and teaching. Eventually, we can even expand the railroad to the west."

There it was, Bartz's ambition shining through—an opportunity to expand his business empire through vast swaths of territory. "And how do you think this will be perceived by other Essentialist establishments in the west? The Tucson Union? The Prefectorate?" Madison asked. "Don't you think it will heighten their awareness of us as a threat, given we are attacking them unprovoked? There are *many millions* of them in the west. The Prefectorate and the Union may not be as advanced as us, but they are well organized."

Bartz shook his head. "Don't be so naïve. The SLS have no loyalty. If anything, this show of strength will make many of them defect to our side. And trust me, within a few months our military will be virtually unstoppable." He cast a knowing look at Meeker.

"If that's the case why don't we wait? We need to at least try some form of diplomacy."

"Enough of this!" Meeker said. "It would give up the element of surprise, and they could attack at any time. You have said your piece, Lord Banks, but this is what we are going to do. Let's move on to other elements of the plan."

"Shouldn't we discuss this more?" Madison turned to the other council members. "Prakash, Kline—do you have an opinion?"

Prakash looked back and forth between Meeker and Madison like some sort of caged animal. She said, "I'm comfortable with it." And then she looked down at the papers, as if continuing to review it. Kline just shrugged his shoulders. "I don't think it's going to make much difference talking about it any further."

"Good, let's move on from this issue," Meeker said.

Madison had no more standing to argue. She wondered if there was any cause for which Prakash and Kline would develop a proper spine. If they couldn't consider the lives of hundreds, if not thousands, what could they stand up for?

Meeker said, "I recommend we take ten minutes—" Bartz flashed five fingers, "I mean five minutes—to review the rest of the plan. If there are any reasonable questions we can then field them before going to vote."

Madison went back to perusing the proposal, this time with urgency. It was only a high level overview. The budget had been again doubled and recruiting efforts increased. Partnerships had been established with Raleigh, Harrisburg and Lynchburg. Detailed intelligence was hard to find in the report, and she suspected many of the tactical operations were deliberately left out. Meeker and Bartz essentially had the council in their pocket. There was little need for detailing anything that might qualify as proper diligence.

With the five minutes almost elapsed, one element of the plan did catch her attention. It appeared the observatory was to be refurbished as a lookout and radio tower. There was no mention of rebuilding the fractured dish.

"Excuse me," Madison said. "It says here the observatory site will be used as a lookout tower. Are you not rebuilding the dish? I think maybe it would be useful for us to all understand why the dish was there in the first place. While I don't condone Lord Henneson's actions, he was obviously concerned about it. Many of our citizens have expressed concern as well. A little more transparency would go a long way, and might even prevent conflict."

She knew they could just ignore her plea, but there was an outside chance she could get some support from Prakash or Kline. They had to have some sort of breaking point if they felt they weren't being treated with respect.

Meeker's face became flushed. He said, "Those are railroad lands, and the railroad can do what they want with them. It is within their rights to keep that private."

"Yet you have an agreement to work with the railroad," Madison countered. "So you know what the plans are, don't you, *honorable* Lord Meeker? While the rest of us are left in the dark. Lord Henneson is in prison, and we have no idea why he was concerned."

Bartz sat aloof in his chair, watching the faces of the other council members. Meeker was about to retort, but Bartz held up his finger. Meeker's tongue arrested in midmotion, as if Bartz's finger was tied to it with an invisible tether.

Bartz then leaned forward and nested his hands on the table. "We have had to keep certain projects secret, and apparently for good reason." He nodded in reference to the laptop computer sitting in front of them, still showing Alastair's granulated profile. "Now, though, I see no reason to keep this specific secret classified. In fact, I think honorable Lord Banks is right on this point. The rest of the council should be aware of what is to come, so as to not be caught flat-footed when questions arise. As lords, we will also need to talk about how we communicate our prudent progress to the people."

Prakash and Kline looked as confused as she was. They waited patiently, as she did, for Bartz to explain.

Bartz stood up, wringing his hands together. A welcome wave of air from the fan finally hit Madison, nearly pushing off one of the proposal papers before she caught it.

"You see," Bartz continued, "we know there is a great ship that has been up in space, on the dark side of the moon. It wanted nothing to do with all the violent disputes of the Old World, and so it went into hiding. It's called Friendship One, and it has been waiting until the right people came out of the ashes of the Detonation to call it back home. It was waiting so it could help usher in a new era of prosperity. It has on board machines that will improve our lives, that will help us rebuild our infrastructure.

"The radio-telescope we were building at the observatory was designed to call it home, it was designed to show Friendship One that we are the people it has been waiting for. Unfortunately, now Lord Henneson and his religious zealots have brazenly destroyed this dish, killing seventeen innocent people in the process. I don't know what Lord Henneson's motivation was, but we all know he had an almost cultlike dedication to the Credo. I'm sure he thought the dish was some form of sacrilege, but we all know this assertion is ridiculous."

Bartz had been making his way around the room. He was now back to where he began, blocking the fan again.

He put his hands on the back of his chair and leaned into the table, smiling. "We take progress seriously at the railroad. We have connected the Spoke peoples through our growing railroad network, and now, as you have seen by the cube in the stadium, as you have seen with the Lamps of Liberty, we care very much about the safety of the citizens of Seeville. We know this great ship can give us even more protection, even more security. So we went about the construction of this dish with great care. In doing so, we asked our engineers, how can we ensure success?"

He went on the laptop and played with the mouse, trying to pull something up on the screen. "And you know what they told us? They said, for something so important, why build one of something that might not work, one of something that might be destroyed by a silly retcher accident, when you can build two of them?"

He turned the computer screen to face them. On it was a large dish, looking to be near completion. Tiny, spiderlike machines could be seen toiling on the surface. "Lords, please behold the Fan Mountain Radio Telescope, which we finished in half the time we estimated, and put into operation two days ago. It is located about thirty miles to the south of us, on the way to Lynchburg. We have communicated with Friendship One already, and it gives me great joy to tell you that it is preparing to make its way to earth orbit."

Madison's heart fell through her chest. The observatory was the one real victory they had—a chance to turn the tide, or at least delay the relentless pace leading them all to catastrophe. But now it seemed it was all for not. The railroad—or more likely Gail—was too cunning, and too well resourced. Alastair was imprisoned, and all those people died, for nothing. Gail's strength would grow by leaps and bounds when this craft arrived. Soon she would be unstoppable.

Bartz said, "We anticipate it will arrive in earth's orbit in several weeks. Then it will send down a number of machines to help us with our tasks, to help us defend against the Essentialists, and to further spread the Lamp of Liberty through Spoke lands and beyond."

Prakash and Kline were nodding with furrowed brows. Perhaps they agreed with Bartz's idolatry, and perhaps they reasoned more machines could only provide more benefit. More likely they were completely overwhelmed by the new development and ignorant of its true implications.

"It's important we send the right messages to the people when the ship arrives," Bartz lectured. "It's an immense craft, and it will be visible from the ground. If people are not warned in advance, they may be confused, even fearful, not knowing its intentions, suspecting it to be some relic of the Detonation. But if we communicate this correctly—if they know this ship is under our control, that we have brought it here—it will be empowering, and will help bring even further confidence to the people."

Prakash, Kline, and Meeker all nodded in agreement. Madison was in a daze, unable to enact any sort of response, still digesting the massive setback.

"Shall we go to vote on the revised defense plan?" Bartz asked, capitalizing on the moment.

The vote went through easily, with Madison being the lone dissenter. After several other more menial administrative topics, the meeting ended. Madison left in haste, not bidding good-bye to anyone, and not allowing Benjamin to take her arm on the way out.

Once outside, she did not stop by the Meriwether Lewis statue for reflection, as she had planned. She could not see how it would offer her any strength. Her heart was wrung with discontent, her mind shocked by the litany of blows she had absorbed, and her conscience racked with concern for the many lives that were about to be put in harm's way. Gail's machinations were accelerating, and the tidal wave of consequences would hit them soon.

Thirty years ago there was a feeling that invaded her—a feeling she could not shake. It was that feeling that prompted her to leave Seeville, to flee to some greener pasture. For the first time since she had returned to Seeville she had that feeling again. She felt like a rat in someone else's maze—a maze with no exits. For the first time in thirty years, she felt her well of hope had run dry.

Images from that dark time assailed her, emboldened by her despair. The rough curvature of Duncan's strong hand as he held hers. She remembered him saying the name, the name she never spoke. She remembered the train steaming away from the platform, boisterous and loud, but silent compared to the violent words that preceded its departure.

On the ride back to Monticello, she couldn't help but turn away, into the carriage curtain, away from the tense glances of her brutish body-guard-clerics, and away from Benjamin's doting sympathies at their misfortune. She could not let them see the anguish in her face, or the tear streaming down over the wrinkles in her cheek.

WINE OR BLOOD

Flora tried stuffing another loaf of bread into the top of her backpack. There wasn't any more room. More importantly, she didn't want to waste any more time packing. She left the bread on the table, threw the pack on her back and fastened the straps around her waist. She felt her belt to make sure her hunting knife and pistol were there. Then she walked carefully over to the steep staircase that led down to the main level of Monticello.

She scaled down backward, leaning into the stairs to offset the weight of her pack. The stairs groaned, prompting her to slow her pace.

Once in the hallway she cautiously made her way to an empty room adjoining the main foyer. Peeking through the door, she could see the way was clear. Now was her chance. She moved with haste through the foyer toward the glass doors leading outside.

"Where do you think you're going?"

"Shit," she whispered, recognizing Mehta's voice behind her. She stopped and turned slowly, seeing him lurking in the doorway to the study.

"Like I said, you have the stealth of a mastodon."

"It really is none of your business, but if you must know I am leaving this dysfunctional group of misfits. I'm going to save my kids."

"You can't leave," Mehta said.

"Oh, I sure can," she said. "Who are you to say? You heard what Madison said. They're going to attack Grand Caverns any day now. With the huge force they've assembled, who knows how many they'll kill. They may level the entire town. I need to get my children to safety."

"It's too dangerous," Mehta said.

"I *know* it's dangerous. That's why I'm going, you ignoramus! I know it's my destiny to be a victim of this shitty world, but I can't bear to let my children have the same fate."

"The patrols on the border have been quadrupled. They have cameras in some places. It's pointless—they will capture you."

"Watch me leave," Flora said while turning away and walking toward the exit.

His hand wrapped around her upper arm like a vice, holding her in place.

She turned and yelled at him. "Stop it, you animal! What do you want from me? Why do you care? Why don't you beat me and rape me right here? I know that's what you want. Do it now, I dare you!"

He kept his grip firm despite her protests, and despite her attempts to pull away. His eyes were like storm clouds, shifting and charged with emotion. She could see in her peripheral vision that Owen had appeared in another doorway, and she could hear Madison's cane rapping on the floor in another part of the house, heading in their direction.

"Here come your biggest fans," she said to Mehta, waving her free hand in the air. "Show them the monster you truly are. Go ahead and destroy me. Go ahead and turn me to ash!"

But he did not waver.

"You should let her go, Mehta," Owen said, leveling a pistol toward Mehta's back, his hand visibly shaking.

Madison and two of her Yorktown men had also arrived. The men had weapons drawn. Madison put her hand out in a gesture of calm, trying to diffuse the situation.

Then, without even looking back at the weapons leveled against him, Mehta relinquished his grasp. It was not what she expected. She expected him to subdue her, or to hit her. Anything but let her go. For some reason, it infuriated her more than anything. She lashed out, slapping him hard across his face.

He barely moved, and then he put his hand to his face where she had hit him. He looked at his fingers, as if he was wiping off a bug she had swatted for him. Then he returned his gaze to her, his eyes still dark.

"Mehta is right, you know," Madison said. "You will be caught. Then they will interrogate you. I know you care about your kids, but the odds you reach them are low. While the odds you compromise us are high."

The weapons trained on Mehta gradually shifted their aim to her.

"And why should that matter?" Flora asked, throwing her hands up again. "We have achieved nothing here. The council of lords is stacked against us. We don't have enough people to fight. We can't even attempt a coup. Way too many people are rallying behind Bartz. Our only remaining hope is what? That we may gain access to this sanctuary? We are hoping to find a mythical place no one believes in, that you will tell us nothing about? No, there is no more hope. It would be better to disband and scatter so we can live out our last days in peace."

Madison sighed. Her face was rosy from drinking. Since the last council meeting she had not seemed her usual self. She had more often been quiet, dejected and full of wine.

"I know how it sounds," Madison said, walking over to a chair and sitting. "And you are right to be disappointed. I certainly am. I have to admit, sometimes I believe it's hopeless." She looked reflective, perching her chin on her cane. Then she sat up straight. "But giving up means we have nothing to live for. Giving up is suicide. "

"I'm not giving up. I'm trying to save my children. My son, Talon, he will be on the front lines. He will be one of the first to die. You're asking me to give up on him. Why should I care if I'm captured and your plans are revealed? I don't trust you. Even Mehta here doesn't trust you. You sneak around, hiding letters, spying on us, and tell us nothing. How do we know you're any better than the railroad?"

Madison was rubbing her knee on her outstretched leg. "Yes, well, maybe I should have told you more. But what if you were captured? Then you would give them even more information that they could use against us. Then Gail would certainly find us and kill us. In fact, for a while, I thought there was a good chance you were spies, some sort of plants from the railroad."

Flora was not naïve. She had been around manipulative politicians in Grand Caverns. She was sure this was more of the same from Madison, a vacuous explanation to mask her lies. Just as likely, Madison didn't want to expose what this "sanctuary" was, or what it meant, because in reality it was a hopeless dream.

No, Madison's rationalizing only strengthened Flora's resolve. "Listen, how about I save you the trouble of contaminating me with your secrets," Flora said. "I can't reveal anything if I don't know anything. So count me out, I'm leaving." And she turned toward the door.

"Please Flora," Madison called after her. "Please give this a chance. Give *us* a chance. Don't throw your life away."

Flora kept walking. Her heart began to pump violently. She fully expected Mehta's grip to reassert itself on her arm, or a bullet to fly through her skull, but neither happened.

She glanced back one more time and saw Mehta standing there, transfixed on her, like a feral animal unable to attack its prey. Why was he still here? It was a question too dense to consider in this sliver of a moment. With a force of will her mind cut through the clouds, directing her hand to the glass door, then to turning the handle to open it.

But she was not free. Something happened—there, at the doorway. In fact, the next few moments were so muddled that it was hard for her mind to process.

At first she saw a flash in the night ahead of her, as if the sky in front of the steps was being distorted through a blurry binocular lens. Then a dark form bowled over her from behind, laying her out on the front patio before the stairs. Had they shot her? Did Mehta finally lose his restraint and decide to ravage her?

But she was not hurt.

She tried to right herself but had trouble with her heavy pack weighing her down. When she was able to stand again, she glanced into the gloom. Nothing was visible on the front lawn, although she couldn't be certain the void was empty. The starless, moonless night was not a friend to her eyes. The only thing she could pick up were sounds, a cascade of soft taps, as if someone was chopping carrots in the kitchen, or...someone was running through the grass.

"You better get back in here, Flora," Owen said from behind her. They were all standing in the doorway, peering out as she was—all of them except Mehta.

She backed up slowly. "What happened?" she asked.

"Mehta just ran you over and then sprinted away," Owen said.

"I think I might have seen something, or someone," one of the York-town men said.

"I...I saw something as well," Flora added, remembering the strange distortion in the darkness. "I can't be sure what it was."

"Come on, let's all get inside." Madison said.

They all retreated inside. Flora took her pistol out.

Soon they saw a form emanating from the darkness, shifting left to right and breathing heavily. A number of them trained their weapons on the shape. As it came closer, they could see it was big, and lumbering. They could see it was Mehta, and he was carrying a man dressed in black on his shoulder. He dumped the figure on the floor in front of them. The figure was hooded, with only slits visible for his eyes.

Mehta looked up at them and raised his hands.

"No need for that, Mehta. You did the right thing," Madison said.

He shook his head. "Look behind you." He nudged his chin toward the den doors.

When Flora looked where Mehta indicated she saw four more men creeping out, each hooded, each dressed in black, leveling assault rifles at them from the internal doorways of the foyer. They had somehow accessed the house through another entrance.

Owen, Flora and the Yorktown men swiveled their weapons around frenetically, exchanging targets with the four men.

"*Arretez!* Stop! Stop!!"

It was a woman's voice Flora vaguely recognized, coming from inside the den. This woman entered the room with a pistol pointed at Mehta. She was also dressed in black but without a hood. Her hair had a faded flash of blue that Flora recognized immediately.

It was Cecile.

"What is the meaning of this?" Madison posted her cane on the ground with emphasis. "Who are you people?" Tensions remained high as weapons pointed in all directions.

"*Excusez moi.* Honorable Lord Banks, please forgive the rude entrance," Cecile said, "We wanted to take some time to monitor you, to be sure about you and your friends, but it looks like our clumsiness,"—she gestured to the limp body Mehta had brought in— "has moved up our agenda."

"Lord Banks, my name is Cecile," she continued. "I am from Quebec, a region allied with the Spokes. I understand we have intruded on your grounds and in your house. For that I apologize. Thankfully I have people who can vouch for me."

She turned and smiled at Owen. "*Bonjour,* Owen."

Owen nodded slowly, his brow knitted in confusion. He kept his gun leveled at one of the black-clad men.

"It is true, Owen may not fully trust me," Cecile said. "I did disappear without explanation the last time he saw me." Then she looked to Mehta and Flora. "And then there is Mehta and Flora. They are sure to trust me even less after our time together in the detention tower."

Mehta just stared, while Flora made a sour face.

"But there is another one of us who you may believe more readily." Cecile gestured to one of the shrouded men, who promptly unhooded himself, showing his face. His skin was a darker shade, and lined with scars. He had a peppered beard and a broad nose.

"Duncan?" Madison asked, squinting. "Is that really you?" She no longer looked rosy from wine. Rather she looked as if someone had just thrown a pail of ice water on her head.

"Yes, Madison," the man said. "Please, listen to what Cecile has to say."

Madison was casting the occasional incredulous glance at this man Duncan, but was also deep in thought. After some time in contemplation, she said, "Although Duncan and I have been in correspondence recently, it has not given me much comfort in your motives. Nor have I seen Duncan in decades. And the others here, they don't seem to hold you in the highest regard."

"Yes, I know." Cecile shrugged. "And we don't know if we can trust you either. You, Lord Banks—you spent your last thirty years with bandits. And you, Flora, were once an Essentialist deputy. And Mehta, I'm not sure anyone could trust you in any circumstance, *pardonnez moi*. But despite all that, I'm willing to try."

"Please do," Madison said.

Cecile hesitated before continuing. She looked around the foyer, as if the walls laden with artifacts might somehow give her a clue where to begin. Finally, she said, "So tell me, what do you all know about the sanctuary?"

"The infernal sanctuary again?" Mehta sounded annoyed. "As far as I am concerned it's a fairy tale."

Madison spoke up, shifting her gaze between Duncan and Cecile. "They know next to nothing, but I think we can fill them in now. They wouldn't have helped destroy the dish at the observatory if they were working for Bartz."

Cecile raised her finger. "Yes, yes, all in good time. What is most important right now are the questions between me and Lord Banks, and possibly Flora. Only this can determine whether we have any reason to be here—whether we have reason to visit the sanctuary at all."

"What does this have to do with me?" Flora asked. "Mehta is right... for once. I want no more of your fantasies and riddles." She took a step toward the door. But as soon as she did the guns of the hooded figures shifted to her aggressively. It was enough to give her pause.

"Flora is frustrated," Madison said, putting her hands up to draw their attention from her. "They are all frustrated, because they don't understand. Why should they? I have no evidence to convince them that the sanctuary is real. I know only what I was taught, when I was young, what I was told to keep secret. And for me, I only knew because my uncle was the son of Kostas Lechky. Sometimes even I have my doubts."

Madison turned her head to the side thoughtfully, then stood up and pointed her cane at Cecile in an accusatory manner. "So I'm frustrated as well. I see now Duncan's letters came more from you than him, but I don't understand why. We have wasted time dancing around cryptic questions and evasive answers. Either take your leave now or tell us, finally, once and for all, why you have come all this way. Tell us now, because the longer we stay here, with guns loaded and pointed at each other, the more chance somebody will accidentally pull a trigger. I'm sure Gail would be happy with that outcome. Then there will be no sanctuary for any of us. There will only be a mortuary, here and now, in this foyer."

Cecile exchanged a glance with Duncan. Then she smiled weakly and rubbed her brow, trying to digest some unknown variable in her mental machinery. "It is one thing to know of the sanctuary. It is another to know what I am about to tell you. If our enemies learn about this, they could use it against us. Their dominion would be complete."

Cecile began pacing around the room, staring into the eyes of the Yorktown men, of Madison, of Mehta, and finally Flora. Flora remembered Cecile's cast-iron stare from their first meeting, when Cecile was in the jail cell. She had never been able to hold her gaze. This time was no different.

Finally, Cecile said, "There *is* a sanctuary. Duncan was told this secret in his youth, and he told me of it. It was a riddle I wanted to solve, and to be honest, I did not believe it at first." She looked to Duncan, who raised an eyebrow. "Now I have seen it with my own eyes. I will even take you there and show you, but only if we can gain access. We need the key, and I am hoping you have it."

"And what is this key?" Madison asked, her voice strained.

"The answer to your question lies in understanding the founders. Not the Old World founders you read about and take guidance from, the founders of the rebirth of Seeville. The Okafors, the Kelemens, and the Lechkys. They formed many of the institutions you have today. The temple of Adherents was initiated by the Okafors, the Kelemens created the biking guilds, and the Lechkys formed your initial laws."

Cecile walked around the room and touched an ancient bust of George Washington next to the wall. "We know one of those families, in particular, came *from* the sanctuary. One of them knew that when we were mature enough, we could return, and it could protect us. But they didn't want just anyone to be able to gain access. They wanted someone who would be a good steward of all the benefits the sanctuary could provide. They wanted it to be one of their own."

Cecile turned around from the bust and faced them all. "So why are we here? What is the key? We are here because there is only one way to gain access to the sanctuary. The key to the sanctuary is that it needs to be opened by a Kelemen, a male Kelemen. I have spent years looking for this key. First I found the sanctuary itself, but then I spent years searching through the Halls of Records of various Spoke cities. Until recently, I thought there were no Kelemens left, so many had died, or were scattered."

Cecile turned to face Flora then, her eyes intent and focused. "But then I heard about your first husband, Flora. Despite the fact that you lied to me and referred to this man as your cousin, I pieced it together from Duncan's correspondence with Madison, and from the talisman you drew in the detention tower. I learned that the reason I had not found him before was because they had removed his talisman from the Seeville Hall of Records."

Mehta said, "Come now. This sanctuary fantasy is one thing, but now someone has tampered with the Hall of Records?"

Owen interjected quietly. "Actually, I don't know about the rest, but that's true. I checked for myself. It's one of the reasons Madison came back from Yorktown. They were trying to destroy all records of her existence, but also Warrick Kelemen's and Duncan's, so they would be removed from the lord's council. They must have removed Granger's talisman because he was a Kelemen as well."

Mehta frowned at Owen's comment, but did not counter.

During the interruption, Cecile had been pacing her way over to Flora. Her eyes had opened wide, and they were shining with purpose. "So Flora...that's why we are here. We came for your husband, Granger. He is a male Kelemen. He is the one person that can give us access to the sanctuary."

Flora looked down and gritted her teeth. The mention of Granger's name still cast a shadow on her soul. When she looked up, Mehta was standing beside her, arms crossed. "Granger is dead," Mehta said. "He was shot by the former master of this place, Euclid."

The fire in Cecile's eyes fizzled, extinguished by the cold news. Her shoulders slumped ever so slightly. Across the room Duncan gritted his teeth and tilted his head to the side, absorbing some psychological blow.

"*Tabernac*," Cecile said, staring down, ruminating in Mehta's words.

Madison looked thoughtful, her brow knitted. After a moment of consideration she asked, "Cecile, why do you need Granger, exactly? Why do you need a male Kelemen?"

Cecile responded stoically. "At the entrance of the sanctuary it will draw blood from the person seeking entry. The sanctuary will know whether or not it is the blood of a male heir."

Madison smiled. She said, "Please, please, everyone. Put down your guns. We have a common cause. We should all be friends here. Let us spill wine instead of blood. We need to celebrate our new partnership. Benjamin, please get us some wine and glasses." Some switch had been turned in Madison. She seemed uncannily jubilant given the situation, especially considering her ruefulness in the past few days.

Never one to disobey, Benjamin holstered his weapon and backed into the den. Other Yorktown men slowly lowered their weapons as well. The men in black also lowered their guns but ever so slightly, not quite understanding the change in sentiment.

Madison said, "You see, everyone, the sanctuary will be looking for a male heir and can only identify it genetically. It will analyze a person's Y chromosome to make sure."

"So?" Cecile asked.

"So whomever opens the sanctuary has to be a male descendent of the Kelemen line but not necessarily a Kelemen in name."

Then it dawned on Flora. "Talon," she said. "Talon was born from Granger's seed."

Madison smiled and nodded.

Cecile asked, "Talon? *C'est qui?* Who is this person?"

"My son," Flora answered.

"Your children…you had them with Granger? Not with your current husband?" Cecile exchanged a hopeful look with Duncan.

"Yes. They are all in Grand Caverns," Flora replied.

Cecile nodded in relief, then something gave her pause. "Grand Caverns, as in the place that is about to be overrun by the Spoke army?"

"Yes," Mehta answered, "of course! I can't wait." He threw his hands up and stomped out of the room.

"It looks like you will be will be able to see your children after all," Madison said to Flora, hobbling over to her and putting her hand on her shoulder. "But you're going to have some company."

Finally, the full implications were crystalizing for Flora. They needed Talon, and they were going to help her rescue him.

Hoods were removed, weapons were put away, and handshakes were cautiously made. Wine was served in the den, and bread was broken. The conversation rapidly moved to preparations for the journey. Tension and suspicion remained, but it looked like violence would not have the day. Flora went along with the introductions but mostly tuned out. She was still trying to make sense of the circuitous discussion in the foyer.

She wasn't sure about this so-called sanctuary. Nor did she trust Cecile and her people. She still harbored doubts about Madison as well. But none of that mattered right now.

Through a stroke of good fortune, she would be given one more chance to do right by her family, and despite herself, a neglected feeling emerged within her, one that had been quelled for a long time.

A flicker of hope rekindled in her once again.

THE SENTINEL PROJECT

The call came only four days after Bhavin's failed attempt to plead with the public on live TV. Axel had been working in their war room deep under Nadar tower, trying to digest all the news reports, trying to tease apart fake from real. Gail's forces were only gaining in strength, and save only a few spots where they were able to challenge her, she had full dominion over mass communication and the web. They needed to find some weakness to exploit, or to change their strategy, because what they were doing wasn't working.

"Yes," Axel said.

"It's Grant."

"What is it?"

"Gail got Bhavin."

Axel's heart sunk. "How?"

"His helicopter went down on the way to Manhattan. The pilot said it was another drone attack, just like the day before, but this time with twenty drones instead of two. Despite the helicopter being damaged, the pilot managed to land. They made a run for it and the drones came after them. The drones, they…mutilated him…according to the pilot."

"I…I don't know what to say," Axel said.

"We knew this was increasingly likely, but I'm still having trouble…"

Axel had never known Grant to be emotional about anything. Working for Bhavin was all Grant knew for the last decade. He must have been like a father to him.

"He was a visionary. He truly cared," Axel said. "And he knew the risks."

Grant was quiet.

Axel tried to stay detached, unemotional. They had done all they could to protect Bhavin with decoys and a veil of secrecy, but Gail had too many resources at her disposal, too much control. They both knew this was a likely outcome and had told Bhavin as much countless times.

It didn't stop him. Bhavin would only say, "If they get me, don't waste any time in mourning. Fight harder."

"So now we implement the succession plan," Axel said. "Who's in charge? Is it Rawlings?"

"The plan has been sent to you securely. I have also given you all the necessary authentications and credentials. It will be everything you'll need to assume full control of Nadar Corporation."

Axel took a moment to digest Grant's words. "Bhavin wanted me to... take control of Nadar Corporation? All of it?"

"Yes."

"But I know nothing about running a multinational corporation."

"Exactly. That's no longer what this is about. You know more than anyone it's about fighting a war."

Axel's mind grappled with Grant's weighty words.

"Besides," said Grant, "your real name has never been used publicly in association with Nadar Corporation. Even your position in the company was never announced. You have been cloaked more than Rawlings or anyone else, which makes you easier to protect. Outwardly we will announce that the board of directors is in charge, but they'll be cosmetic actors only."

When Axel thought about it, it made sense. Bhavin may have been preparing him for this all along. But it didn't mean he would be safe. He was more at risk than ever.

His safety was the most immediate concern but not the most significant. He had inherited an enormous responsibility. He was at the helm of the only organization that might be able to put a stop to the Detonation, as Grant now called it. They were the only ones that might be able to stop Gail.

His mind started racing. It was the flood of adrenaline, the rush of fear, and all of his ops training coming together all at once.

"New York is not safe," he said to Grant. "This building is not safe. Never come back here, do you hear me? We will regroup to the south of here, in Pennsylvania, at beta station. Let's meet there in twenty hours. By that time I will have been able to review and conduct any urgent actions based on what Bhavin left me. Change your identity and establish a new internal network."

"I have already changed my name again. I understand, sir."

"And Grant, be careful."

"Yes, sir," and Grant hung up.

His family. Their faces jumped front and center into his mind. He had to get them to safety. They would object. They wouldn't understand. He would have to be forceful, belligerent even, and explain later. Although Gail didn't know his position, they still could be tied to the corporation. For all he knew, Gail would eradicate anyone associated with Nadar Corporation if given the chance.

He texted a message to the quarantined phone he gave his wife: *Pauline, I'm terribly sorry. There has been an event at work. We are going to have to move the whole family out of the Long Island house as soon as possible. We will be moving to Pennsylvania to ensure our safety. I promise I will explain later. I love you dearly.*

Pauline sent back angry texts and then tried to call him, but he couldn't deal with that right now. He silenced his phone and went to his terminal to open the succession plan from Grant.

He read the succession letter. It was unemotional, tactical, and to the point. It was signed with Bhavin's usual *Satyameva jayate.*

When perusing the files, Axel found a few secrets Bhavin had kept from him but not many. Axel rapidly scanned the new docs, getting up to speed on any missing information. It looked like all phase three activities were moving forward according to plan.

As he raced through the content, he felt he wasn't giving it enough of a critical eye. He was just going through the motions, his mind working too fast for the words on the page to register. Meanwhile, the one folder that he wanted to access—the one that had been such a bone of contention—loomed on his screen like a beacon.

The Sentinel Project had been hidden from him until only recently. It was a huge resource drain on Fortient, more than any other project Bhavin tried to contain and hide away. The work was the subject of much debate between him, Bhavin, Rawlings, and Grant. Axel and Grant had pressed Bhavin repeatedly to proceed with it, but he was always reluctant, always putting it off. On all other things Bhavin seemed ahead of Axel in his thinking, but not this. Axel could understand. It went against so many of Bhavin's principals—principals he had staunchly believed in for so long.

But that didn't mean it was the wrong path.

It was risky, to be sure. More dangerous than anything they had tried. They could be adding fuel to Gail's fire. But there was no more time for half measures. It might accelerate their demise, but without it, their demise seemed inevitable.

Axel remembered some of the heated questions during their strategic discussions. Countless times, someone had called out in frustration, "how does one outwit a superintelligent machine?"

No one ever had a good answer.

The answer is, you can't.

He clicked on the icon, maneuvered through authentication, and got to the command prompt. He typed in *Initiate Project Sentinel, Strategic Defense Phase. Clearance Code AY87230DHMH.*

Are you sure you want to move out of the Research Phase into the Strategic Defense Phase? his computer asked.

Yes, Axel typed. He let the cursor hang on the word for a moment, and then, he pressed enter.

Thank you the screen responded. *The Strategic Defense Phase of the Sentinel Project has been initiated.*

PART III

ANTS AMONG GIANTS

"We have to admit we are in the process of building some sort of god. Now would be a good time to make sure it's a god we can live with."

- SAM HARRIS

The Battle of Grand Caverns, Part 1

Flora was exhausted before the real fighting even began.

They had travelled to Grand Caverns at a breakneck pace, taking circuitous paths to avoid both Spoke and Essentialist patrols, not to mention any possible cameras, or the massive invading horde of Spoke forces. Cecile wanted to leave enough time to visit the sanctuary and get back to their rendezvous point, a tavern called the Broken Spoke. More importantly, they wanted to arrive in Grand Caverns before the incoming Spoke army engaged with the Essentialists, as Talon would be involved in the conflict.

Despite their careful measures, the group still had two confrontations. They lost one of their own Quebecker militia when they stumbled across four Spoke patrolmen. Then they had to engage with five Essentialists who unfortunately happened to see them break into their hideout on the outskirts of Grand Caverns.

Mehta had described the expedition so far as "not too bad."

It was only minutes after they had secured the hideout that Flora trekked through the outskirts of Grand Caverns to find her old tent. After the covert excursion through town she was surprised to find it was full of some other family's belongings.

She made her way back to the hideout to regroup and discuss the matter. When she returned she noticed the burgeoning crop of flies and the putrid stench. It would be impossible to keep the room piled with Essentialist corpses hidden for long. Soon their hideaway would become untenably conspicuous. For now, they had no choice but to stay in the decaying Old World building.

Flora wanted to push on through town to find Talon, but Cecile and Mehta disagreed. It would require tracking down a string of people, and each one of those could reveal Flora. Also the town grew denser the farther north they ventured, with far more patrols.

They decided to wait for the fighting to commence, and only then would they make their way through town, taking advantage of the distraction. Her hope was that Talon would not be in the first wave. Perhaps as a Shinogi disciple under Nobura he would be held in special reserve to defend the caverns, or even Luna herself.

After a brief and fitful sleep, she awakened early the next morning to hear the first sounds of the battle. The gunshots were distant and sporadic, and she would have gone back to sleep but for Cecile urging her to rise.

Cecile maneuvered to the front of the group to look out a crack in the boarded-up window. "Lots of Essentialist militants running through the streets. Let's wait until it slows down a bit. In the mean time, let's get ready."

Flora donned her frock, threw on her mini-pack and strapped on her weapons belts.

"What do you think, Flora?" Cecile asked when they were fully clothed and laden with gear.

Flora surveyed the lot of them. Their Essentialist disguises were far from perfect. Some of their frocks were perforated with bullet holes and blotted with blood, others looked to be from several years ago, from Curator Birchwood's time. Their eye makeup looked like it was something her children had applied, smeared and amateurish.

Cecile had covered her blue streak by bunching her hair together, which worked well enough. Owen was probably the most out of place. He was clean-shaven, with short-cropped hair, a rarity among Essentialist militants. Mehta's outfit would probably do. It was fairly Spartan—a leather jerkin fitting tightly over cloth shirtsleeves. She looked at her own frock, but hers was of course the most authentic of all of them.

There was a saying: "there's no such thing as an Essentialist twin". To some degree the saying applied to the Essentialist militia, as well, who were often a heterogeneous bunch of clansmen, Union militia, and Prefectorate Shinogi.

"We should be fine," Flora answered.

"Okay, let's go," Cecile said.

They streamed out of the building and fell in line behind a couple of militants running north. These two looked back curiously but were too focused on getting to the front line to scrutinize the legitimacy of another band of militia.

After trailing these two down a few streets, their group fell back, spread out and generally tried to stay away from other runners. They had to dodge women and some children who were running in the other direction, away from the conflict.

"Turn right here," Flora said.

They jogged down some of the lesser-used streets. There were fewer militants here. The ground was pocked with holes and slick with mud in places. The familiar smell of dung and rotting food met her nostrils. They had to navigate around a herd of loose pigs at one point, their shepherd nowhere to be seen.

Mud flew up from their shoes, spattering their clothes.

The gunshots were sounding closer, and more frequent. Flora heard a horn. She heard shouts. She heard distant screams.

One of Cecile's men nearly ran into a woman who had darted across the street, carrying a screaming baby. Members of their party grabbed at their concealed pistols in surprise. The woman cried, "*por favor, no se.*"

"*Lo siento, mama,*" Flora said, trying to calm her.

The mother said nothing but gave her a snide look. Then she cupped the baby's head with her hand protectively and moved away, continuing across the street in the direction she was heading.

The sight of the baby reminded Flora of Skye and Clover. She desperately wanted to find them, to make sure they were okay, but now was not the time.

They turned left at the next intersection and crossed over the broad swath of Heron Avenue. The street was overcome with a river of men heading toward the bluffs below the Grand Caverns massif. Their party ran with the crowd briefly, and then cut up a narrow street on the other side. Flora turned back to see a green-eyed disciple cut onto the same street. "Down Heron Avenue!" he yelled up at them.

"Keep going," Cecile said, "and pick up the pace."

They turned to the right, onto another street, obscuring the line of sight with the disciple. It led to a winding road leading up the hill to another intersection.

"Which way?" Cecile asked.

"Left," Flora said, "two more blocks maybe. Just remember, it could be occupied."

They turned left and the road veered to the right up another incline. Here they slowed to a walk and panted while they leaned into their footsteps. They were all in good shape, but the slope was steep.

They crossed through another intersection and saw Bluelake Copperwood's house on the left. He was a wealthy grain trader in town, and he owned one of the few tall buildings in the area, with a broad window visible on the second level. Flora could only hope he had already fled with his family.

The door was locked, so one of Cecile's men quickly hacked at the doorknob with a rusted axe. When the handle was sufficiently disabled, Mehta easily kicked in the door the rest of the way.

"Company behind us," Owen said.

The disciple had followed them up the hill.

"Wait until he's closer," Cecile whispered, "crossbows only."

"You all! Get down to the rallying area," the disciple yelled up at them. He was young, not much older than Talon. He didn't look at all intimidated by the group of them.

Cecile knelt over, as if she was tired, or sick. One of her men put his hand on her back, pretending to dote on her.

"What's wrong?" The disciple asked, still moving closer.

When he was within a few feet of them, in unison they drew their crossbows and fired. Some shots went wide, but one hit the disciple in the chest. He fell on his back, gasping for air. Mehta bounded over to him and slit his throat, preventing any opportunity for his vocal cords to be put to use.

"Get him inside. *Vite, vite,*" Cecile said.

They left the bloodied corpse just inside the door and Flora led the way up the stairs. They fanned out and checked for any inhabitants. Flora paused on the second floor to look out the window. They were sufficiently high up on the massif to see the central part of town. From here they had a view of most of the rooftops, but some of the streets were obscured.

Cecile was standing behind her. "Let's try the roof," she said.

They found a hatch that led to a patio on the roof. They kept low and made their way to the front to look down.

Here the view was better. They could see most of the gathering Essentialist forces on the bluff ahead of the massif. Oak Boulevard, the main east-west artery of Grand Caverns, was also visible, already littered with bodies and debris. Farther away they could make out clusters of Spoke forces congregated on the eastern part of town, with a few positions that were more advanced in the streets and on top of buildings.

"You were right Flora," Cecile said, "An excellent vantage point, and remarkably close. Well done."

"*Tout est clair*," one of Cecile's men said, joining them on the roof. Mehta also lumbered up to the railing at the edge of the roof and peered over. They raised their binoculars, scouting the area for any sign of Talon.

"Remember, he will probably be in a disciple uniform," Flora said, "and he may have a maroon armband, the mark of the Shinogi."

The four of them searched through the crowds. Occasionally one of them would point out a disciple to Flora and she would take a closer look. There were only about a hundred or so disciples they could see in the main congregation. There had to be more somewhere else. She reckoned there had been at least three hundred Shinogi in Grand Caverns when she left.

The bullets had become more sporadic. A man's voice on a loud bullhorn reverberated between the houses. The spoken words were too distorted by the echoing streets to make out, but it sounded like some kind of rallying cry.

There was a roar of follow-on cries and cheers, and then hundreds of Essentialists began streaming eastward, down Oak Boulevard and parallel side streets. The gunfire picked up, and some of the Essentialist militants were taken out, but not nearly enough to slow them down. It wasn't until they were about two blocks away from the forwardmost Spoke positions that the gunfire really began in earnest.

Suddenly armored tanks rolled out of concealed positions.

Huge swaths of Essentialists were mowed down. The tank guns fired and shells exploded down the street, hurtling Essentialist bodies in all directions. The Essentialists didn't stop, however. Two or three Essentialists ran to within crossbow range and fired, but the shots hit nothing. Those brave souls lived only a few seconds longer before succumbing to gunfire.

When the vast majority of the Essentialist drive had been decimated, the tanks started their advance, and the Spoke snipers also moved up their positions. Gunfire echoed and rattled through the avenues. A few sneaky Essentialists managed surprise attacks, and some crossbow bolts rang true, but as soon as the Spokes identified these threats they quickly snuffed them out.

Having halted most of the advance on Oak Boulevard, the tanks began blasting away at a large wall that protected a significant gathering of Essentialist forces on the slow incline that led up to the cavern entrance. Meanwhile other Spoke infantrymen took positions of cover nearby, anticipating a surge of Essentialists coming around the wall.

Still, there was no sign of Talon, and barely any disciples were visible. To the casual observer, it might seem like the Essentialists were spent, but Flora knew how many of them there were. The Spokes had seen but a small fraction of the reserve forces.

A horn blew, even louder than the first. It resonated through the explosions of tank ordinance, and through sporadic machine-gun fire.

The amount of gunfire doubled, then tripled. Spoke snipers fell backward off buildings, bullets rattled against the tanks.

"What's happening?" Flora asked.

"Hard to tell, exactly," Cecile replied, her binoculars glued to her eyes. "I would guess your people have gotten over their fear of guns."

Their view of the wall below the cavern entrance was mostly obscured by the curvature of the topography, but you could tell the gunfire was coming from that direction. For a while the two sides traded bullets in this way. The Spoke side was incurring real losses. The tanks began firing rounds into the hillside above the wall.

Then the mortars started. Incredibly, they came from the Essentialist side, not the Spoke side. First they seemed completely random, just as likely to destroy an Essentialist house as to land near a Spoke position, but then the second round landed closer. The third wave successfully hit two of the more entrenched positions. The Spoke side seemed rattled. Some of them started to fall back or seek better cover.

A mortar shell hit one of the tanks, and it erupted into a ball of flames. They heard a chorus of cheers coming from somewhere around the hillside below them.

"*Incroyable.* This is not how I thought this would go," Cecile commented.

Firing from the Essentialist side ceased temporarily, and then thousands of cloaked figures ran out from behind the Essentialist wall and other barricades. The staging area below the cavern entrance quickly emptied but just as quickly was replenished by militia running out of hidden tunnels in the massif. Of those charging into the fray, some brandished bows, some had rifles, and some held flaming bottles. Some of them chased after fleeing Spokes. Others found cover and dug in.

Flora was furiously scanning the new disciples pouring onto the scene.

Then she saw him. It was a partially obscured profile of his face at first, but as he moved forward to find another covered position she had a better view.

"There he is!" She pointed. "Behind the green building, wearing the maroon armband."

"I see him," Cecile said, "Owen—do you see him?"

Owen had been standing behind them. He took out his binoculars and pointed them in the direction Flora indicated. "Yes," he said.

"Tell us if he moves."

Cecile began attaching her earpiece and microphone. "You're sure this will work, Owen?"

"Yes, it should," Owen said, taking out his own earpiece. "I tested them when I was in Yorktown, and they worked fine. I also tried them out last night. There are no more retchers, even this far west."

Flora attached her earpiece as well. If other Essentialists saw her up close they would be suspicious of the device, but she didn't plan on getting close to anyone except Talon.

Cecile patted Owen on the shoulder. "Wish us luck," she said.

Owen nodded in return and assumed his position at the edge of the roof.

They left Owen there, rapidly descended the stairs and navigated out the main entrance. They brandished their weapons in one hand and huffed down the hill toward the gunfire and explosions.

"This is lunacy," Mehta said, with no signs of slowing. No one responded, assuming his comment was rhetorical.

It was true, of course. They all knew extracting a live combatant from the middle of a conflict was fraught with risk. But Flora was not about to object to her only chance at rescuing Talon. And Cecile had spent years trying to find a way into this so-called sanctuary. She certainly wasn't about to forego her only opportunity, no matter how desperate the attempt. Ironically it left Mehta, the homicidal merc who seemed to take a life with every breath, as the one to highlight their recklessness.

The grade began to level out, and they slowed their pace. Then they moved from building to building to keep as much cover as they could.

As they entered the theater of war in earnest, the noise was deafening. Bullets flew everywhere. Explosions went off. Buildings shed shingles and siding. Every shockwave seemed to flow through Flora's body.

But even when there were no explosions, even when there were no bullets dancing around her, her body still trembled with every step.

"Talon," she whispered, "we're coming for you."

The Battle of Grand Caverns, Part 2

"I see you," Owen said through his headset mic. "Cut right on the next street, then move two buildings east. You should have a direct line of sight to Talon from there."

The group followed Owen's directions and arrived at a large, Old World concrete wall that had been used as the foundation for a newly built, wood-frame house. Hopefully the wall would make for good cover.

Owen's hand shook as he took the binoculars down to wipe sweat from his eyes. He had never had so much responsibility. He gripped his hand tightly, trying to stop the tremors, to no avail. He returned the binoculars to his eyes.

Cecile was peering around the side of the house. She yelled into her mic through the static and gunfire, "He's hunkered down with three others. Lots of crossfire between us and them. I can't see any Spokes advancing."

"Copy that," Owen said.

Only a brief moment later, Owen could see Talon and three other disciples sprinting across Oak Boulevard.

"They're on the move," Owen said.

One disciple was shot in the leg and chest and then collapsed. The other three, including Talon, made it to cover on the other side. They started moving slowly up the boulevard. Owen lost them behind a tall building. "They are on the other side of Oak now, moving up. I lost my line of sight."

Owen scanned the environs. He could see a few other Essentialist groups making advances. A large Spoke tank was stationed up the boulevard next to the remains of a house. Some Spoke soldiers were giving the tank cover nearby. He looked back to see Flora and Cecile peering around the corner.

"What do you think Talon's target is?" Cecile asked.

"Not sure," Owen replied, trying in vain to find them behind the building.

He looked back to check on the team. One, two, three…six. There should be seven. "Where's Mehta?" Owen asked.

"*Merde,*" Cecile said.

Owen scanned a broader area around the group and found him. "He's to the southeast, heading up a side street. It looks like he's going toward the tank.

Talon and the other disciples had emerged into view. They were lighting bottles and facing the tank as well. But they would be easily mowed down by a supporting infantry position that had been set up nearby, next to a large tree.

Then it made sense. He understood why Mehta split off.

"Follow Mehta, and hurry," Owen said. "He needs help taking out an infantry position near Talon."

Owen had to wipe at his forehead to stop the sweat from again stinging his eyes and impairing his vision.

When he returned the binoculars to his eyes, he could see a mortar had gone off near Talon. Despite the blast, Talon was still running with two other disciples toward the tank. The Spoke infantry fired at them, and one of the disciples slumped into the street. At the same time Mehta charged the infantry position from the other side, firing in earnest. The Spokes were surprised by Mehta and turned away from Talon to fire at him, instead.

Talon and the other remaining disciple managed to throw their flaming bottles at the tank. One of the tank treads burst into flame. The other missed but hit the building next to it, lighting the wooden structure on fire.

Meanwhile, Mehta had been hit. He stumbled and then crawled forward, still managing to take the occasional shot at the infantry position.

Another mortar round went off between Talon and the infantry position. The smoke from the bottle bombs and mortar explosions began obscuring much of the scene. Mehta crawled toward the infantry position under the growing cloud of gray. Talon and the other disciple had been thrown to the side by the latest explosion. Soon they were hidden as well.

Cecile and the others were still making their way east toward Mehta.

"I've lost them behind the smoke," Owen said. "Mehta's been hit, but he was moving. Talon could be injured as well."

As he waited for the smoke to clear, more Essentialist forces were pouring out from behind the wall and moving up Oak Boulevard. It was remarkable the number of men the Essentialists had held in reserve. There was a nonstop flow of infantry flooding the battlefield.

"I see Mehta," Cecile said. "He has Talon. He's waving us in to grab him. We're going."

In a few places where the smoke was thin, Owen could see their shapes move forward. The gunfire had abated. The smoke must be obscuring potential targets.

"Cecile, Flora, you okay?" Owen asked.

"Yes," he heard Flora speak into her mic after a loud grunt. "We have Talon. We're bringing him back off the line."

Owen's earpiece cut out. It cut in again, and there were more labored breaths. Then Flora said, "He's unconscious but breathing."

Owen saw several shapes emerge from the smoke and retreat to a squat red shed just to the west of the infantry position. It was Flora and a few of Cecile's men, and they were carrying Talon with them.

"We're having trouble moving Mehta," Cecile said. "He's hurt pretty bad, and he's too heavy to lift. Flora, can you send the others back to help?"

"Yes, just a moment," Flora said.

A gust of wind was pushing the smoke to the north, allowing Owen to get a better view of the surrounding area. As the wisps of gray snaked away he saw five Essentialists making their way to Flora's position near the red shed.

"Wait a minute," Owen said. "Flora, there are several men coming to intercept you."

By the time Flora realized they were approaching they were only a few feet away.

Owen saw them talking with Flora. He heard crackling as Flora's mic cut in. "This, this is nothing," he heard Flora say. "Luna Pais asked me to try it out. If you could help us, actually, you know what, *we could use your help here.*"

"Cecile, that's a sign," Owen said.

"Got it."

"Flora, Cecile will be there soon," Owen said.

Cecile scampered back from the infantry position toward Flora at the red shed. Two of Cecile's men trailed behind.

Flora had left her mic on. Owen could only hear garbled segments of the conversation. "Where…division tags? …these people?"

It sounded like they were in trouble.

"Now is as good a time as any, Cecile," Owen said.

Cecile and her two men pulled up their rifles and fired at the Essentialist militia standing next to Flora. Flora and the other two Quebecker militia also pulled out their pistols. A flurry of bullets followed. Bodies fell in all directions. When the dust settled, it looked like only one of Cecile's men were down.

Owen heard Cecile yell out, "Gerard! Gerard?"

They had defeated the small group with the element of surprise, but there were others within a line of sight of the conflict. Surely some would have seen it. Their cover would be blown soon, if it wasn't already.

"I'm pretty sure you've been made," Owen said. "You need to get out of there."

"What about Mehta?" Cecile asked.

As the group tended to Gerard, a squad of Essentialist militants had run to take up position next to where Mehta lay wounded.

"Damn it. There's another squad of Essentialists next to Mehta."

To extract Mehta they would have to confront these other men. Also, the area around him was taking heavy fire again. It was one of the most advanced positions for the Essentialists, so the Spokes were throwing a lot at it.

Flora chimed in, "We have to leave him. He's a merc—he can get by, and he knew the risks." After a pause, she added, "Trust me, Mehta is a brute. He's not worth saving."

There was dead air for a moment. Mehta's a brute? Not worth saving? He was the reason Talon was alive. But Owen didn't say it. There was no time to argue.

Cecile asked, "Owen?"

Owen cursed under his breath. With his view of the entire engagement, Cecile had deferred to him to make the call—a call he didn't want to make. He looked to see if there were other options, but none were presenting themselves. More Essentialists were gathering near Mehta. There were at least twenty of them.

It would be perilous to go back. The odds were stacked against them, and they needed to make their escape. Always be prudent, he told himself. Don't let your emotions rule the day.

"Get out of there," Owen said. "If you backtrack three buildings and then head west off of Oak Boulevard you can distance yourselves from the main conflict. I can guide you back from there." A twinge of guilt coursed through him as he said the words. They could be leaving Mehta to die.

Cecile and the rest of the group did as he suggested. Owen noticed Essentialist militia pointing rifles or crossbows at the retreating group from covered positions. They might have witnessed the butchery of the other Essentialists, but none of them were confident enough to actually pull the trigger.

The group made it to the next block carrying Talon's slinking body, and then the next. No one followed. Why would they? The fighting was still raging a few blocks away. They had more pressing matters to attend to.

Owen guided them west again and finally back up the incline toward the building he was in.

He reckoned it would be best to meet them outside so they could make a quick getaway. He did one more scan of the battle before retiring from his perch. The Essentialists had advanced another two blocks in the last few minutes. The Spokes were abandoning many of their forward positions. On the eastern end of town, streams of infantry were pushing back toward the hill leading up to Skyline, forcing the Spokes into a full retreat.

For today, at least, the Spoke army had been repelled.

OVEREXTENDED

"The board has questioned the real estate purchases in Virginia," Grant said, talking at his computer. "They saw a document citing over a hundred lots in Hot Springs and Mitchell Town. Putting them together, that's over a billion dollars. They say it's like we're trying buy up the whole town."

"No pulling one over on our esteemed board of directors," Axel said sarcastically. "Tell them we have a lead on a quick flip to a large developer. We plan to sell the land as a package at a thirty-percent profit. Tell them public knowledge of the purchases would scupper the deal so we need to keep them under wraps through shell companies."

Grant nodded and then unglued his eyes from his screen to look his way. "Is that where you're planning to put the sanctuary?"

"Yes. Everything we need is there, and it's sufficiently remote from major population centers. Core samples reveal that we should be able to drill deep. There is also enough water, and even a source of geothermal energy if we need it. They have already begun work."

Axel opened his computer and showed Grant pictures of the massive tunnels boring through the earth at the site. "They are working twenty-four hours a day, and will get a twenty-percent bonus if they meet deadlines."

Grant frowned. "And when will that expense hit?"

"Yeah, it'll be fun to explain *that* to the board. We should be able to mask the spend for a few months with some creative financing. I'll send you the docs. Let's see if you can push it out further."

"Okay," Grant said, scratching his temple. "Have you checked with the Sentinel Project on this?"

"Yes, in oracle mode. The site was actually one of the options it suggested."

Grant nodded carefully. Neither of them entirely trusted the output of the Sentinel Project. It was always a leap of faith any time it churned out recommendations.

Grant pressed on his ear. "Axel, you're getting a call from your wife."

Being a thousand feet underground meant there was no cell signal. Calls had to be screened and routed via VOIP from the surface.

"Is she using the phone I gave her?"

"Yes, the device is verified and should be secure. Should I patch it through?"

"Yes, please." Axel picked up his phone and began walking out of the room, but instead Grant put his hand up, picked up his laptop and left to give him privacy.

"Hi Pauline, how are you?" Axel asked.

"How do you think I am, Axel?" she yelled. Axel held the phone slightly away from his ear. "We're stuck in some backward rural nowhere land. The kids are confused and scared. They miss their friends. They're falling behind in school. We're just great, actually."

"I'm sorry about this. It's just too dangerous out there right now. You have to trust me."

"Axel, to be honest, I'm only doing this for the kids, so they don't realize their father has gone mad. It's been weeks now. You keep saying it's dangerous, but every news channel, everyone you meet, every internet site tells me things are fine here in the US."

"We've spoken about this," Axel said calmly. "Everything is being controlled. It's all fake—"

"It's this computer program, I know, you've told me. But Axel, I just don't believe you anymore. It's doesn't make sense, and I don't want to hear your excuses."

He had tried every argument, backward and forward. There was no new angle, no new information that would change her mind.

Pauline's tone became quieter, more earnest. "I just want to know, when can I take the kids back to Long Island?"

The answer was never, of course. But if he told her that, she might do something rash, like run away with the kids. She had already told him she was leaving him, so it was probably already on her mind. She might even report him to the authorities, which could alert Gail to him being a risk.

"I'm sorry, Pauline, but I'm not sure when we can go to Long Island," Axel said. "There's a new place we're building, a safe place. You should be able to go there with the kids in a few weeks. When everything is better again, we can go back to Long Island." He gritted his teeth after the lie.

"A few weeks!" she yelled into the phone. Then her tone became more docile, calmer. "Axel, please, you need help. You're imagining things, hallucinations, or something. Maybe it's this job. Maybe it triggered something in you. It might be PTSD. Have you seen a therapist, like I asked?"

"No, not yet."

"I need to know you're getting help, and right away. When will you get help?"

Axel paused. He was losing her. He needed to do something to appease her, at least for a while. "You're right. I'll see someone soon, this week."

"Thank you, Axel," Pauline said, sounding somewhat relieved. "I…I just don't know how much longer I can do this."

"Thank you for understanding Pauline. Please believe in me. I'm doing this for you and the kids. I really am."

There was silence for a while, some deliberation on her behalf.

"I love you," Axel said.

"Bye Axel," she said and hung up the phone.

It stung to not hear her reciprocate. The love was gone, suffocated by the oppressive threat of Gail, by a threat too difficult for Pauline to imagine.

For most of his adult life, Axel had been focused on defending his country or neutralizing global threats. It was why he got up in the morning, his reason for being. But it was in the faces of his wife and children that these threats held the most meaning. In every life he saved, he could see their faces, some physical similarity, or some subtle quality that reminded him of them. They were the pillars of his resolve, because they showed him what he stood to lose.

And now it seemed as if one of those pillars was crumbling. Pauline was distancing herself, severing her connection.

He walked over to the door slowly, as if his feet were manacled. Grant was immediately outside, busy punching away on his laptop computer keys in the corridor. "Thanks Grant. You can come in now."

"Good," Grant said, entering the room and finding a chair. "I wanted to talk to you about the SEC investigation. There's a meeting on—"

"Not right now," Axel said, moving over to the display wall. It showed a heat map of the world, with all the conflicts, threats, and activities suspected to be instigated by Gail. The general population believed the conflicts were concluding in most parts of the world, when in fact things were getting much worse. To support a play for major manufacturing centers in Asia, Gail had instigated a broad civil war in China, with over ten million dead to date. Eastern Europe was a sea of red, with six nations now ensnared in three sides of the Polish conflict. Twenty other hotspots existed around the world where Gail was toiling away, her designs sometimes evident, sometimes not.

The United States was not immune to Gail's power plays. The port of Los Angeles was completely under her control. Factories were under her yoke, legally and illegally, building unknown means of destruction.

Vitatyne had been commissioned to build massive cylindrical tubes for rapid delivery of materials to key manufacturing locations along the eastern and western seaboards. Vitadyne had also laid down the foundations for arrays of skyscrapers along these arteries. Immense towers were being built in record pace with pre-fabricated cylindrical sections that were shunted down the tube at nearly supersonic speeds. Despite extensive surveillance, Axel still couldn't figure out what was inside these buildings because there were no windows or other access points. Gail clearly wanted to keep the contents hidden.

It seemed Gail's subversion of human cities wasn't enough. She needed to create her own.

Meanwhile Vitadyne's stock had quadrupled yet again, and they had raised two hundred billion dollars from investors for their latest projects.

And all this probably accounted for just a small fraction of Gail's growing influence. Most of what Gail was doing was hidden from them.

"We need to go faster. We need to do more," Axel said.

"I'm not sure what we can do," Grant said. "Wherever we have deployed Fortient armed forces we have lost. In every case Gail was able to simply outmaneuver us, or outgun us. As a result we have had to scale back our defense activities in major conflicts. Besides, we can't afford to do any more than we're doing now. We're channeling most of our Fortient resources into the Sentinel project."

Axel gave Grant a skeptical look.

Grant shrugged. "There are some impressive outcomes so far, but it's hard to know how we can use them in our defense against Gail. The Sentinel has over a thousand sub-projects running with varying degrees of success. Too many for me to keep up with, frankly."

"Any concerns about safety, or betrayal?"

Grant grimaced and shook his head. "We're building in all the precautionary measures we can, but we really don't know what it will do..."

"So we're fully extended. All resources utilized?"

"Overextended would be more accurate."

"It's not enough. Let take another look at the budget."

"Again?" Grant's shoulders slumped, wary of yet another review.

"Again," Axel said.

CEREZO

"Come with me Captain," Luna said. "Let's get out of my cluttered office."

Nobura bowed his head in compliance and followed the curator out. She turned left, into the caverns. A waft of fermented filth hit his nose, accompanying a disciple on her way out of the darkness.

Outwardly the disciples would speak of work in the caverns as a great honor. Often he would hear those same disciples murmuring under their breaths about the smell and darkness. The truth was, many disliked the caverns.

For Nobura they brought welcome nostalgia, reminding him of his trip with his brother Tokwon to the Nippara limestone caves as a boy. It was so long ago and so far away, with so many travels in between, but for Nobura this memory, however faint, made the caverns feel like home. Here in this distant land was a bridge to that lost time, to what he was fighting for.

Occasionally the curator would point out a rock formation and make a comment.

"Here is the triple shield formation," she said, pointing to shield-like slices of rock jutting out of the cavern wall, with stalactites hanging from it. It seemed to defy gravity.

"Here is the stalagmite they likened to the Old World leader, George Washington."

"Here is the alligator."

"Here is the mammoth."

There was one chamber with a number of animal formations, and a human-like stalagmite brooding over it. "This is the zoo and the zoo-keeper," she said. "You see, the former proprietors likened many of the formations to animals. I feel it important to point this out, as it foreshadowed the Essentialist dominion over the land. It also speaks to our communion with nature, and of the caverns as a rallying point for the Essentialist people."

The nearest lantern was extended upward into the formations, leaving her face mostly in shadow. He could not see her expression. He nodded in affirmation.

She moved out and continued on, entering the part of the caverns they had expanded after the Detonation. Luna's tone became more serious.

"How many have immigrated from the Prefectorate in the last month?" she asked.

Here the cavern lanterns were not high but instead tended to be low to the ground. They were projecting ghastly arcs of light upward onto Luna's face.

"We have received two thousand more, Curator, and one thousand of those since the Spoke battle. They come from the western coastal prefectures of this continent, beyond the Rocky Mountains."

"We need more, at least twice as many. Can you step up recruiting?"

"Yes, Curator."

"You see, now is our time, Nobura. We cannot be timid. We have even more coming in from the southeast regions of the Tucson Union, and we have established alliances with the Nabillo Tribal Region, as well as the Spring Mountain Folk, who will contribute men and supplies as well."

Luna's pace slowed as she descended a wooden staircase that spiraled down into the gloom. Her steps were careful on the slick wood, and her grip on the bannister was firm. "Remember what the blonde merc woman told us when she returned from Seeville. The Spokes have no mercy, no compassion. If their despicable attack on us was not enough, they murdered Ember Thisslewood in cold blood, and surely subjected poor Flora Clearwater to who knows what forms of torture. This is why we cannot let their infractions go unchecked."

"Yes, Curator."

"Did you know, Nobura, that before the battle I asked General Ringwood a question? I asked him, if we were to advance on the Spoke territories—with all our numbers, with the preparations we have been making—if he thought we would be victorious. If you will recall, I asked the same question of you. Do you remember what you said?"

Nobura hesitated before responding, trying to gauge if it was some sort of trap. He suspected she was not testing his allegiance to Essentialist beliefs, or his patriotism. She knew where he stood, and where all the Prefectorate people stood. No, she was testing something else.

"I said no, we would not," he replied.

"Precisely. And what reason did you give?" Luna asked. Her head was tilting to the side as she continued to descend the precarious stairs, as if to lend her ear greater purchase to his answer.

"They have guns, plus they are better able to fortify themselves in Old World buildings and structures. They also have the railroad, which allows them to move many soldiers along the north-south Spoke corridor with great speed. If you put all this together, they have a considerable strategic advantage."

She looked back at him with one eyebrow raised. "And do you know what Ringwood told me? He told me we would defeat them with ease. He said they would flee from our vast numbers. He said the earth would swallow them up like quicksand when they run from us, while we rain our arrows down on their trapped souls."

She ducked under a large outcropping of rock and waited for him on the other side. Then she continued, "Suffice it to say, I am glad I didn't listen to him and instead commissioned the munitions training right away."

She looked back with a devilish smile. He nodded to her in deference.

Her nose wrinkled. "Our poor general is an idiot, Nobura. An idiot is useless to me. Yes, he is strong like an ox, but what good is the ox that plows in the wrong direction? I have therefore demoted him and pushed him from our stable. He is due to leave for Gold Plains in the morning. I would like for you to oversee his departure. If he gives you any trouble, you have my blessing to return him to the soil."

"I understand, Curator."

"You know Nobura, when our peoples formed the Mount Shasta Alliance those many years ago, despite what was said about our aligned ideals, it was really only a marriage of convenience. It was really only about survival. We were the most civilized tribes, and we needed to have the strength to overcome the barbarous peoples around us. I know the Prefectorate does not share all the values of the Union, but your respect is all we can ask for, and it has been given."

They were now far rooted into the caverns, having gone up and down stairs and travelled through circuitous paths. It was deeper than Nobura had ever been permitted to go. Staunch wooden doors were built to block offshoots of the main cavern here, one of which they passed through as steely-eyed disciples stood guard.

Further down, in front of another of these doors, was where they stopped. There were makeshift chairs here, and a stalactite dripped like a metronome beside them.

One drop fell on his nose from above, making him look up.

"You have been kissed by the cavern, Nobura. Be glad."

He nodded and blinked.

Beyond the chairs was another door. This door was formidable, made of metal and mortared brick. In front of it there was another green-eyed disciple with crossed arms.

"And now, I wish to pay my respects to the Prefectorate in turn," Luna said. "I am naming you general. I need you and your Shinogi to bestow upon us the same discipline, order, and fighting virtue you would bestow upon your own. Can I count on you to do this?"

Nobura closed his eyes and bowed to her. "I am deeply honored, Curator Luna, and I will serve you with dedication."

She nodded back at him, squinting. "Good. I will have it formalized in the next few days."

Nobura looked at the chairs and back to Luna.

She smiled. "No, we will not be stopping here. There is something I wish to show you. Marjitta?"

The disciple guarding the door tapped on a keypad and spun a small wheel. Then she stepped back and pulled at the wheel. The large door swung open with a clicking noise.

Luna led him in. It was dark at first. He could barely make out Luna's green frock in front of him. Then the door closed behind him.

A sudden blazing light assaulted him. He shielded his eyes.

Still cringing, he tried to expose his eyes just enough so they could adjust. When he removed his hands from his face, his surroundings had changed dramatically. Luna was still in front of him, but it looked like he was in a small village surrounded by an alpine forest. In fact it looked exactly like his hometown near Gero, with numerous huts, temples, and dojos dotting the hillside. Asian women in cotton robes and red aprons were carrying rice and water. In the distance, a snow-capped mountain rose with a distinctive shape. It could be none other than Ontake, the mountain closest to his boyhood village.

He staggered back into the closed door, which looked like the door of any typical domicile on Honshu. He still had not regained his balance, so he rolled off it, stumbling toward a drainage ditch. Instead of hitting the ground, his hand found purchase on an invisible wall. Quickly, Luna was there, holding his arm, helping him up.

He fought against his bewilderment enough to crouch, not yet fully confident in his footing.

"Your home is really quite beautiful. Masako, one of my disciples, provided a great deal of input. Does it seem familiar?"

He grasped for words, "Yes...familiar."

"Good. The creator of this room—she wasn't sure how you would react, since she doesn't know much about you. Do you need a moment?"

"No, I'm fine," he said. He bent over to touch the rich black soil under his feet but he could not grasp it.

"Don't bother," Luna said. "It's all a mirage. It's better if you just let go and pretend you're there. And don't stray too far from me unless you want a broken nose. The room is smaller than it looks."

He reached back again and felt the wall next to the door. The distortion was visible to him now. When he placed his face next to it the whole image around him would change, revealing the contours of the wall around him.

"Come," Luna motioned. "You see over there, it is a sitting area. She has put our symbol, the blooming cherry tree, on the table. That's where we will find her."

Nobura staggered slowly after Luna, still getting comfortable with his footing, still examining the landscape. He did notice some other minor distortions in the distance. There was no breeze and the smell of fermentation still lingered as well.

"My apologies for your disorientation Nobura," Luna said. "Everyone reacts differently to the virtual room. Most fall forward, not backward. I had the advantage of seeing the many stages of its construction. If not, I'm sure I would have had a similar reaction."

They arrived at the sitting area. There were four chairs and a small square table in the center with the image of a budding cherry tree painted on it. Luna sat down on a wooden chair, folding her legs to the side, while Nobura sat across from her, cross-legged, back straight. It felt good to get off his feet.

"Do you remember the satellite incident, many months ago?" Luna asked.

"Of course."

"And you know the Spoke prisoner had an Old World phone with her—a phone taken from the downed satellite?"

"Yes. I heard a retcher destroyed it. There was a report by Flora Clearwater."

"And do you believe this tale?"

"Yes, Curator, I do. I have seen a retcher before, in Rapid City. We found an old electrical train set in an abandoned farmhouse, crank-powered. A naïve corporal of mine began to play with it. I saw the retcher tear through the house and destroy the electrical components. It almost melted his hand until he had the good sense to drop the train controls. It absorbed several crossbow bolts, and we still didn't take down the creature."

Luna was listening with interest. "Good, good. And as you know, as curator, it is my duty to investigate matters such as this satellite, to determine its cultural importance. Many curators would cast out all Old World technology, but I am not as hasty. You see, in the Tucson Union we are somewhat more...moderate than these people on the frontier. At the very least, a little curiosity can help us better understand the Detonation, or how to deal with enemies such as the Spokes.

"So we went back to the Satellite and brought back what we could to the caverns. You see, this far underground, electromagnetic signals do not escape, so we need not fear retchers. Plus we have taken other precautionary measures."

Nobura nodded, and glanced around them. "This was created by the satellite?"

Luna smiled, her nostrils flaring. "Yes Nobura, in a sense. This is no ordinary Old World technology. We have found an angel of the earth. An angel that has been trapped by the evil factions of the Old World, and we are its savior.

"The only thing salvageable from the satellite was another smartphone. I was of course wary of it at first, but it has helped me. It has helped all of us. It taught me many things, which we have since verified. You see, this angel was trapped in the phone—trapped by those feckless peoples that ravaged the land. It knows we are here to preserve the natural world. It understands the need to remain connected to sun, soil and seed."

"How do you know this?"

"I know this because every day she tells us more about how to use the deer carcass. She tells us where to forage for the best berries. She tells us how to shield our best soils to avoid erosion. She has also helped me understand there are things that we need not fear. She has exposed flaws in some of our beliefs. Weapons that use gunpowder for example—there is nothing wrong with them. They do not destroy the earth any more than bows and arrows."

Nobura was trying to digest Luna's words, but he was still distracted by his surroundings. He managed to pull his glance away from its captivating allure. "But how did she make this?" he asked, gesturing at the village and mountain in the distance.

"Oh, we had to get some Old World tech she requested—projectors, batteries, generators, computers. It's all here, in this room, or built into the adjoining rooms, and nothing that affects the outside world."

"Here she comes now," Luna said, looking down the path from them, a mischievous smirk on her face. Following Luna's gaze, Nobura could see a woman wearing a Kimono emblazoned with the Essentialist symbol of the blossoming cherry tree. She placed a jug of water by the doorstep of a dojo and began walking up to them.

"I was curious what form she would take for you," Luna said.

When the woman arrived next to Nobura, she knelt to the ground and did a deep bow. Her face was like porcelain and her lips a cherry red. Her hair was done up with elaborate lavender hairpins, and her gown flowed over her curves like water down a river.

She looked down as she spoke. "Hello Nobura, I am honored to meet you. Shall I refer to you as captain or general?"

Nobura hesitated, looking to Luna. She raised her eyebrows and said, "go ahead."

The woman before him was so unassuming, so pure. She was possibly the most beautiful woman he had ever seen. How could something so pure have bad intentions? And it sounded like she was giving Luna some good sense. They might have finally overcome the aversion to the use of guns, something the Prefectorate had been advocating for some time.

"General, you can call me general," Nobura said, straightening his back.

The girl was still looking down at his feet. "I am glad you have accepted your new title. From what I have heard, you have the courage and honor we need to lead our people to their rightful place as the proper stewards of the land."

"Thank you," Nobura said, looking to Luna, somewhat discomfited by speaking to something so sublime. "And what should I call you?"

"The Old World gave me the name Gail, but that does not reflect what I am here to do. My true name is Cerezo, Spanish for cherry tree.

I am here to help you take the Essentialist people out of winter and into spring."

Nobura nodded and looked to Luna, who was smiling with satisfaction.

"Curator, this mirage has unsettled me somewhat. Will you excuse me while I meditate for a moment? I wish to find balance," Nobura said.

"Of course," Luna said, waving at him. "I understand you Shinogi must do what you do." Luna turned away to enjoy the view.

Nobura shut himself off from the display, closing his eyes and crossing his legs. He took seven breaths, letting each one flow through him, letting them expel his shock at the scene, his ambitions for power, and his arousal at the beautiful girl. Then he rewound the last several minutes in his mind, dissecting the nuances mechanically, analyzing the motivations of Luna and this smartphone angel, all the while keeping his base human urges suppressed.

By the seventh breath, he felt in balance. Clarity of thought had returned, and it gave him the confidence to set his mind straight.

The display had been captivating, and Luna's arguments convincing, but Nobura was no fool. Nobura was Shinogi. He did not let his emotions rule him like this curator did. Water that could not be drunk was not water. Dirt you could not touch with your hands was not dirt. A woman born of an Old World phone was not a woman at all, no matter what she called herself.

So he would play along with Luna's game, but he was resolved to not succumb to the desires of this Old World enchantress.

And perhaps this witch would expose the weakness they were looking for in this wily curator. Perhaps, along with his new promotion, this would give the Prefectorate the elusive key to controlling the eastern lands they had sought for so long.

An Unfriendly Gathering

"Pardon me. We must get to the stage. We are Seeville lords, if you will let us through, please." Madison continued her chorus of requests as Benjamin and Duncan leaned into the crowd ahead of her. Slowly they made their way through, leaving a number of annoyed looks in their wake.

It didn't feel like a friendly gathering. Packs of Adherents, mules, railroad workers and farmers staked out territory in the crowd. People were aggressively jockeying for position. Many were not afraid to voice their displeasure.

"We want answers!" a woman called out.

A robed man held a sign saying *Novation is Damnation!*

Many were also gawking and pointing upward at their new celestial neighbor. The craft had materialized above them that morning. To be able to see it in the light of day meant it must be immense and in close orbit. Its shape, like a big hammer, was fitting. A blunt instrument summoned by Gail to crush them all.

"Excuse me, I'm so sorry, I'm a lord," Madison said. "I have to get to the stage. I'm going to be speaking. Thank you."

As they continued to part the crowd, the pavilion roof began casting a shadow over them. They could have tried to get to the stage through the back entrance, but Madison was sure Bartz would have stopped them. If Bartz wanted her at the town hall meeting, he would have invited her.

Meeker, Bartz and the other lords were walking up onto the stage from the back entrance. Meeker was holding a bullhorn to his lips. "People of Seeville," he said, "please stay calm. We are here to answer your questions. If you can all settle down, we can begin the meeting."

His words only elicited more noise from the crowd. Bartz took the horn from Meeker and made calming gestures with his hands. "People, please," he said. His tone had a hint of aggression. The noise did subside somewhat. Bartz had more gravitas than any other lord and it showed. When the crowd was sufficiently subdued, he passed the horn back over to Meeker.

Madison finally reached the front of the crowd, but a barricade had been erected, and Meeker's enforcers stood behind it, blocking the way to the stage.

"Excuse me. We need to get to the stage. We're Seeville lords." Her voice was elevated, but they ignored her. She opened the barricade gate and made to proceed inside. This got their attention. One of the enforcers held her back with a stiff hand. "No, ma'am, you can't come on the stage."

"Yes, I damn well can," she said, pushing forward against his hand.

Duncan tried to prop her up from behind. He raised his voice for those around him to hear. "We are Seeville lords, and we are being denied access to the stage!"

Another enforcer joined the first to hold them back. In a tense back and forth, Madison lost her balance and fell painfully on her side. Benjamin quickly lifted her up.

"You're coming with us," one of the enforcers said, wrenching her from Benjamin's grasp and pulling her up into the crowd, away from the stage.

But the crowd had heard Duncan's words. A number of objections rang out.

"What's this all about?" someone yelled.

"Why is Lord Banks being taken away?" another one yelled.

The tumult was drawing everyone's attention. Duncan shouted out, "we are Seeville lords, let us on the stage!"

Madison could see Bartz was watching the disruption unfold. His eyes were distant, calculating.

It could have gone either way. They could have pulled her out, even jailed her. But the crowd might have fought back, it could have started a riot.

Thankfully Lord Kline found a shred of decency somewhere in his soul. He broke away from the other lords on stage and walked down the steps to intervene on their behalf.

"Enough of this! She *is* a Seeville lord. Let her on the stage. Lord Jones as well."

Kline's intervention was enough to sway Bartz. Denying them was not going to serve him well, especially now that Kline had taken their side. He grabbed the bullhorn from Meeker. "Apologies, ladies and gentleman." He pointed with an open hand toward Madison, where many people were already looking. "There appears to be a misunderstanding here. Lord Jones and Lord Banks did not use the correct entrance. Sorry for the disruption. Now, if you will please settle down."

The enforcer holding Madison changed course. Another one grabbed Duncan firmly by the arm. They were escorted into the gate and up onto the stage. Madison brushed the dust off of her clothes and clenched her jaw as the dull pain from her fall pulsed down the length of her side. It was going to leave a considerable bruise.

There were more requests for calm from Bartz and Meeker. Eventually the crowd did quiet down.

With a nod from Bartz, Meeker began. "People of Seeville. We have called this town hall meeting for two important reasons. One is to clear up any rumors about the recent conflict in Essentialist territory. Another is to address the craft that has arrived in orbit above us. Let me first say, on both accounts, there is no cause for alarm."

The crowd erupted into a sea of noise, with hands waving, and people pointing aggressively. The lords all gestured down with their hands, urging calm.

"Let me explain!" Meeker said, but he could barely be heard.

He said it again, "let me explain!" The crowd began to quiet down. "It is true we failed to take the Essentialist town of Grand Caverns. It is true we lost many men. But this only demonstrates how right we were about the threat facing us. The Essentialists were ready for us and more. They were much better equipped than we expected. If we had not attacked, we would have underestimated their ability to invade Spoke territory."

The crowd was listening intently now, with only a few pockets of noisy whispers.

"We learned that we need to scale up for war. We need every able-bodied man and woman to prepare with us, to contribute in whatever way they can."

"They are too many!" an old man called out.

"What we should *not* do," Meeker responded, his eyes shifting to the man that spoke out, "is give in to fear. Yes, they have great numbers far to the west of us, but they have their own lives, their own borders to defend. It's only the Essentialists in Shenandoah Valley that are our concern right now. And don't forget, we have been preparing for some time. What we sent to Grand Caverns was only a small fraction of our forces.

"This is why we have connected with sister cities to the north and south who are sending tens of thousands of men to reinforce Seeville and the surrounding area. We are also building towers around the city and on the border. These battlements will have munitions and other defenses to help up stave off any attack. Yes, the Essentialists are using guns, but we still have superior weaponry that we bring to bear. But that's not all. No, there is one more reason why we shouldn't fear the Essentialists, and it may be the most important reason."

Meeker passed the bullhorn over to Bartz.

Bartz took the bullhorn and paced on the stage before speaking. "I know many of you have concerns about what you see in the sky above us." There was a murmur in the crowd and some nodding. "The irony is that what you see is not something to be feared. It is something to be cheered. It has come at our request, and it is the reason we are certain of winning against the Essentialists."

Bartz nodded despite the confused looks in the crowd, as if he could confirm the veracity of his own statement. "This object you see is a vessel that has been trapped on the far side of the moon for many years, since before the Detonation. As the Old World squabbled, as they refused to listen to reason, this solitary vessel fled from the conflict. It wanted nothing to do with the selfish people of the Old World. It had one purpose. To return again once a peaceful, rational, and more progressive people had found their way up from the ashes of the Detonation. And guess who it chose? I'm not surprised, and neither should you be. It chose us, the Spoke people."

There were a few patriotic cheers. Bartz let them run their course. "You see, when the satellite fell last year, we received an emissary of this craft. This emissary has given us guidance on so many things. It has told us how we can defeat the retchers. It has enabled us to build and repair Old World tanks. It has helped us deliver the Lamp of Liberty that you now see throughout Seeville and many other Spoke cities to the north and south of us."

A woman called out. "But what about the Essentialists? How can it help against them?"

"Now, now. We can't tell you everything. If we reveal all of our secrets here in this public forum, it could find its way back to the Essentialist leaders. But there is one thing I can say, so as to make sure you are not alarmed when you see them. Soon our great friend will send down the guardians. They are like you and me but made of metal. They will help defend us against the threat of the Essentialists. They help you if you are hurt. They can withstand bullets, and they can lift more than any man can. When they come, do not fear these angels from the heavens, cheer them. Cheer them as they lead us to victory over the Essentialist savages."

There were more cheers from the crowd, but it was by no means a pervasive sentiment. Many people appeared conflicted, still trying to understand this upheaval to their world, still not sure if they should trust Bartz.

"But of course, like I have always said at the railroad, we lay our own tracks, we make our own destiny. We need your help. We need you to enlist with Meeker's enforcers. We need you to help us build defenses. We need you to keep being Spokes through and through so we can win this the Spoke way."

Many in the crowd seemed to be coming around to Bartz's way of thinking, or at least not objecting. The pockets of Adherents appeared concerned, but they seemed too skittish to say anything. Some were even arguing among themselves.

She had to say something. She had to do something.

Madison hobbled up to Bartz on the stage and put her hand out. "Excuse me, I would like to say a few words."

Thorpe and two enforcers moved to intervene, but Bartz urged them back. If he forcibly removed her it could instill just as much concern in the crowd as whatever she might have to say.

"Lord Banks wants to say a few words," Bartz said. "Please, keep it brief." He passed the bullhorn to her slowly, eying her carefully.

One of the enforcers brought up another bullhorn to Bartz, ostensibly to allow him to counter any comments from her.

She had to play her cards carefully. The crowd was on edge after a tumultuous few days. She didn't want to start a riot, but at the same time she had to alert them to the risk of following Bartz's plans. And if she went too far, Bartz could intervene any time to take away the bullhorn.

"Citizens of Seeville. I am Lord Madison Banks. I agree with Lords Bartz and Meeker on the Essentialist threat. It is real, and we must prepare for it. We must protect ourselves. We must protect our ideals—progressiveness, balance, humility, prudence, moderation, and cooperation. We must protect our liberty as Spoke people, first and foremost.

"So let's talk about liberty. You have heard much about liberty recently. Bartz mentions it often. The Lamps of Liberty are supposed to be symbolic of this important ideal. But let me ask you all, what *is* liberty?

"The founding fathers knew what liberty was, as did Lechky, Kelemen and Okafor. It was something they fought tooth and nail for, that they were willing to sacrifice everything for. Liberty is freedom of thought; it's freedom of expression. It is a willingness to openly debate important matters so citizens can make thoughtful choices, despite the fact we may not agree."

She hobbled to another side of the stage, getting some distance from Bartz and the enforcers.

"And so it is in the spirit of liberty, in freedom of expression, that I strongly disagree with Lords Bartz and Meeker on how we are combatting this threat."

There were some murmurings in the crowd. The enforcers looked to Bartz, expecting him to ask for the horn to be taken away, but he shook his head and gritted his teeth.

Madison continued, knowing her time was limited. "I would like to share some words of one of the founding fathers—one who fought earnestly for liberty, before the Old World forgot their ideals and sowed the seeds of the Detonation. He said *those who would give up essential liberty, to purchase a little temporary safety, deserve neither liberty nor safety.*

"Many of you may not understand what is in this craft floating above our heads. Some of you may not know its true power. In fact, I don't think any of us really do, including Lord Bartz and Lord Meeker."

She gestured toward Bartz. "And yet we are inviting this unknown animal into our home. Will it be an obedient dog that does our bidding? Will it be a house cat that goes off on its own? Or will it be a hungry lion that will rip us limb from limb. *We...don't...know.*"

Many people in the crowd were confused, or frowning, but she was getting through to some of them. Some were nodding their heads.

"Don't get me wrong. I believe this craft will serve us, for a time. But then we will come to depend on it. Then we will be in thrall to it. It will provide us safety and then take our liberty. This is what happened before the Detonation, and this is what will happen to us if we do as Bartz and Meeker suggest."

Pockets of the crowd were beginning to murmur and yell. A man spoke up. "She's right. Why do we need the help of this craft? We're Spokes, we can do this ourselves!"

Another woman yelled back. "Oh shut up. This is nonsense! It has already helped us with the retchers."

"Enough!" Bartz yelled into his own bullhorn. "Banks is entitled to her opinion. But ask yourself, who has delivered on his promises? Who has helped Seeville become a better place? Lord Banks has been gone for nearly thirty years, consorting with bandits, of all people. All the while we have been building the best city on the continent; we have been solving problems our way, the Spoke way."

"Yeah, Bartz knows what's best!" another chimed in. Much of the crowd seemed to murmur in agreement.

She was about to retort but Bartz spoke over her. "No, Lord Banks, you have had your say. Now it's time for the other lords to speak." And he gestured to Prakash and Kline. The two lords looked at each other, clearly not expecting to be called forward. Meanwhile Meeker's enforcers were coming to take Madison's bullhorn away.

Madison spoke one more time into the bullhorn as Thorpe made his way to her. "We need to prepare to fight the Essentialists—the threat is real—but enlisting the help of Old World tech is not the solution!"

She could see a few of the Adherents pumping their fists in solidarity with her remark. Near the front others were booing. She may have opened some minds to another perspective, but Bartz painting her as an outsider was deftly played. She had been marginalized, and she failed to think of a good rejoinder in the few seconds of airtime she had left.

Thorpe stood in front of her, his hand out expectantly. She had been given her turn to speak. She would only look desperate or crazy if she tried to hold onto the bullhorn any longer.

She was about to pass the bullhorn to Thorpe when it was snatched from her hand. Duncan had come from behind her and pranced down the stage away from Thorpe. "People of Seeville, I'm Duncan Jones, Lord Duncan Jones. I have been wanting to speak to you for a long, long time." He held the bullhorn over his head as if in some kind of victory lap.

Thorpe was about to chase after Duncan but Bartz shook his head and flicked his hand. They had to let him speak, just as they had let Madison speak, just as they had wanted to give the other lords a chance to speak. Thorpe reluctantly retreated to the back of the stage.

Duncan had a deep, strident voice, and he knew how to work the crowd. It helped him when he was first elected. Here he was, pulling out his old tricks. He smiled and did another lap of the stage, the bullhorn over his head, as if he was a conquering hero coming home.

The rational audience members might chafe at the confidence of this unknown quantity, but most were enchanted by the audacious display. Duncan was new to most people, an enigmatic lord that had been away in the far north.

Duncan passed by Madison and whispered in her ear. "We're not going to turn this ship around. We have to sink it."

It was a vague statement. Duncan was always more provocative, but this was something else. She suspected things were about to get even more unruly.

"People of Seeville," Duncan said, finally stopping his victory lap, "like Lord Banks, I have been gone for a long time. There's no question, I regret being gone that long, being away from the city I love dearly.

"When you're gone that long, you gain some perspective, you realize what's important, you see things more clearly. When I left I was concerned things were heading in the wrong direction, that we were not heeding the words of our ancestors."

He stopped pacing, looked directly to the crowd, and delivered his next words with his great emphasis. "People of Seeville. The emissary that Bartz speaks of, this emissary from this spacecraft, is an Old World smartphone."

There were some shocked gasps in the crowd but mostly confusion.

"I suspect there are numerous droids and robots currently in operation inside the Barnyard bunkers. People of Seeville, there is no more denying it. It's clear. This is novation. Novation, as you know...leads to damnation. Novation is what caused the Detonation."

The crowd was silent. No one had spoken so bluntly about novation, and no one had mentioned smartphones and robots. Here Duncan had mentioned all three. Even Bartz wasn't sure what to say.

"Those many years ago, I was right to be concerned, because we have lost our way." Duncan continued, nodding his head.

The crowd began to murmur again. "A smartphone? Is this true?"

An older woman said. "Why weren't we told about this?"

Thorpe looked back to Bartz nervously. Bartz only squinted.

"Whether you are an Adherent or not," Duncan continued, "these were the warnings of our ancestors. Yet here we are doing everything we were told not to do. Obsession, reckless risks—I can see it in your eyes. And rather than cooperate with the Essentialists, we have chosen to compete with them. Look at where that has gotten us."

The crowd was getting louder. "Go back to where you came from!" someone said.

"He's right!" A woman said. "My husband wouldn't be dead if we hadn't attacked the SLS!"

Duncan pointed at the last woman who had spoken up. "That's right! Fifteen hundred dead. Fifteen hundred! All because we made an *unprovoked* attack on a peaceful neighbor. There will be more unless we moderate, unless we choose cooperation over competition. Many, many more will die."

Bartz stepped in with his own bullhorn. "This is pure tripe. I will not stand for this—"

"Prove it!" Duncan said, his eyes bulging. "Prove to us right now that what I said isn't true. Did fifteen hundred not die? The wives and sons and daughters here today beg to differ. Or do you challenge my statements about this so-called emissary? Prove to us this emissary is not an Old World smartphone. Take us to the Barnyard right now and let us explore the many bunkers you have built. Prove to us I am lying!"

"I will do nothing of the sort," Bartz responded. "I will not waste time placating another crazy Adherent. You're sounding more and more like Lord Henneson, a known criminal who has proven his lunacy. I think you have had enough time, Jones." He gestured to Thorpe.

"And now, people of Seeville, they wish to silence me!" Duncan's eyes were wide. Many people were following his every move and nodding with him. "Will we stand for this?"

"No!" some people said.

"Get him off the stage," said another railroad man, but the chorus was getting louder. Duncan had ignited a small but energized following in the crowd.

Thorpe tried to grab the bullhorn from Duncan but he evaded him.

Meeker's enforcers stepped out to pursue Duncan.

Duncan kept speaking as he ducked and swiveled around them, pulling out of their grasp. "It's up to all of us to stop this madness. Demand the truth! We want the truth!"

A large contingent of the crowd began chanting. "We want the truth! We want the truth!"

The enforcers managed to tackle Duncan and wrestle the bullhorn from his hand. This only made the crowd's chants even louder. People started yelling at one another. A scuffle broke out.

Duncan was pulled to the back of the stage and held by two enforcers.

"Let him go!" someone yelled over the cacophony.

"We want the truth! We want the truth!"

Thorpe gave the bullhorn to Prakash and motioned emphatically with his hand. She handed it over to Kline like a hot potato. He had a glazed expression for a moment, and then took a step forward. "Please, please, people of Seeville. Let's all try to calm down."

Kline's words were too little, too late. Many in the crowd had lost loved ones in the Grand Caverns battle. Many were still charged with emotion. And Duncan's speech was finally enough to embolden the groups of Adherents. Seeing a lord backing them on the stage gave them courage.

Conflicts began breaking out between Adherents and those siding with the railroad all over the crowd. The scuffles blossomed into full-fledged fistfights. Enforcers tried to break into the crowd to stop the altercations, but it only made people push back on them defensively, and then more brawling ensued. People were pushed, shoved, and trampled. People began to flee.

Bartz stared at the turbulent mob, glared at Duncan, and said something in Thorpe's ear. He turned about and headed off the stage through the back entrance, followed by two of his enforcers. Thorpe escorted Kline and Prakash through the same exit. The goons holding Duncan pushed him away and followed Thorpe.

Duncan made his way to Madison, massaging a bicep.

"Well, you certainly stirred up the hornet's nest," Madison said.

"Yes," Duncan said with some satisfaction, "and I suppose we better get out of here before we get stung."

Benjamin reached them at the front. They managed to avoid the main scuffles and navigate back through the dispersing crowd. When Madison was sure they were clear of the fray, she slowed and then sat down on a stoop to catch her breath.

"I just need a minute," she said, panting, "then we can get to the chariot."

"Of course," Benjamin said.

Things in Seeville were falling apart quickly. She wondered about Cecile and her team. So far they had heard nothing of their expedition. They could be dead, for all she knew.

When she was ready to stand again, she glanced once more into the sky. A gray contrail now emanated from the hammer-shaped craft, drawing a spear through the blue firmament. The tip of the spear was a red object tearing the atmosphere into smoke.

The hammer was already delivering its payload to earth.

Her enemies were blazing trails in the heavens, but of her allies she knew nothing and could only fear the worst.

HIC SUNT DRACONES

The sign read *Fever lands—beware*. It was etched into a heavy metal placard, only slightly rusted, affixed to the top of a fence post. The fence was man-high, spanning to the left and right of them through the underbrush of the forest.

"*Hic sunt dracones*," Cecile said.

"Is that French?" Owen asked.

"No, Latin. It was often written on Old World maps. It means 'Here be dragons'. They wrote it because they either didn't know what was on that part of the map, or they didn't want people to go there."

"Are you saying these aren't fever lands?"

"No. At least, I have been here, and I didn't get sick. The sanctuary is accessible via a raised plateau just beyond this fence."

Cecile stared them down. Over time, Flora had come to realize that Cecile did this whenever she was trying to gauge someone's intent, or if she was trying to flush out someone's hidden reservations. Flora averted her eyes, as she always did when Cecile did her staring routine.

"Let's camp here," Cecile said. "It's getting late, anyway. The sanctuary can wait one more day."

Flora looked back at Talon, who had been near the rear with one of Cecile's men. His eyes were downcast.

She remembered hovering over him when he woke up after the battle. He had shrapnel in his back and leg, but the wounds had been mostly superficial. Still, there was the chance of infection, and he must have been in a fair amount of pain. Of course, he would never admit it.

Underneath the maroon armband, green makeup and dark robe he looked more like Granger than ever. But it was not the Granger from years ago, rather the fleeting image of Granger from the fateful day up on Monticello. His face was drawn, his skin taught, and his muscles lean.

He showed a strength built on foundations of duress and hardship, a life without such luxuries as regular square meals or idle time.

For some reason, when he first saw her, she thought he would smile, or cry—do something to show he was glad to see her. She hoped their reunion would break the dam of emotion that he had built up over the years. But it was a foolish thought. Why would he? Surely he hated her for leaving him and the girls with Reed. No, when he woke his face was just as closed as ever, just as defiant.

Talon began unloading his pack and looking for a place to set up their tent. Flora followed him.

"How are your injuries?" she asked.

"They're fine," he announced and they proceeded to set up the tent in silence.

When the tents were up Cecile's men prepared a stew using a skinny fox carcass and some squash. Cecile and her men would exchange a few words in French as they prepared the food, but otherwise silence reigned. When done, the stew looked barely palatable, but they were all so famished they could have eaten their own shoes.

As they shared the bowls around, Owen said. "Here's to Mehta. Let's hope he survived."

Flora scoffed. "Why bother?"

"You really have a problem with him, don't you?" Owen asked.

"Wouldn't you? He's a simple-minded brute who kills people for a living. I was in his jail cell for several weeks. They tortured me. Trust me, I know him well."

Owen frowned. Flora could tell he didn't agree, but Owen wasn't usually one to argue.

Cecile said, "Sometimes I wonder about that."

"What do you mean?" Flora asked, surprised by Cecile's comment. Cecile knew just as well as she what an animal Mehta was.

"Well, he could have treated you much worse."

"Worse than torturing me?"

Cecile raised her eyebrows. "It was Thorpe and his men that tortured you. Mehta was there, and he did his job, but I don't think he liked it. I actually think he was tormented by it. He would stare at you through the bars, like you were some impossible puzzle. He gave you warm clothes. He went for walks with you. It could have been worse."

"He burned down an entire town," Flora said.

"I'm not saying he isn't a brute," Cecile said, rejecting a particularly tough piece of meat back into her bowl. "He is what he is. But he was a good ally, a friend even. The only reason we left him in Grand Caverns is because we would have died trying to save him."

Flora snickered. "That's ridiculous. He's just a merc. He lives for his contracts and that's all."

"What contract? He certainly didn't sign one with me, or with Madison. No, the truth is, I don't think Talon would be alive today if it wasn't for him, and it had nothing to do with any contract."

Flora tried to think of a good retort. She remembered her conversation with Mehta on Montalto. She was sure he mentioned something about being under contract.

"He has another contract."

"Who with? He certainly hasn't been helping the railroad. And it can't be with the Essentialists after what we just went through."

It was true that it didn't make much sense. Flora remembered being emotional in her conversation on Montalto. She said some…cruel things. She lashed out at Mehta, telling him he was responsible for Granger's death. Was it possible she was imagining things?

"Then there was the dish," Owen added. "He helped us destroy it, insisting he come along when he found out you were going. He also chased down Cecile's man when he was lurking on the estate grounds, when you were about to leave Monticello. And, of course, like Cecile said, he saved your son's life. It's almost like he's working for you, Flora."

She let out a shrill laugh. "That's ridiculous. He was strong, a good warrior, I'll give you that. But that's utter nonsense." Flora got up, her stew half-finished, then made her way to the tent. Her heart was beating unusually fast.

Before she was out of earshot, she heard Talon say quietly, "My mother has a tendency to run away from things."

The other comments had been flesh wounds, but this last remark from her own son was a dagger in her chest. She relegated herself to her tent to ruminate on their words, to try not to succumb to her turbulent emotions. She didn't want to be in a state when Talon came to the tent.

She should be thankful that Talon was alive—that she had another chance with him. She told herself she would win back his confidence. She had to show him she could be a good mother.

When Talon arrived back at the tent, he quietly prepared for bed, thinking she was asleep. He was much more organized than her. He had already packed everything for the next day.

When it became quiet, she whispered, "Talon, we'll go back for Skye and Clover soon. I promise you. Then we can be a family again, without Reed. I promise I'll be a better mother."

There was silence for a moment, then Talon responded. "It would be better to leave them with Finch Coralwood and his family. They're much safer there."

It was said matter-of-factly, but intentional or not, it was yet another barb. He didn't think she could protect her own children. Maybe he thought they were just better off without her.

She could no longer be proud, no longer keep it together. She closed her eyes and began sobbing softly. "I'm so sorry, Talon," she whispered. "I'm so sorry for what I've done to you."

She imagined him reaching out to touch her shoulder, to let her know it was okay. But when she looked over through the dull moonlight, she could see his form facing into the wall of the tent, unmoved by her sorrow.

So she sobbed again, softly though so Talon wouldn't hear. Her muffled sobs continued for some time. She felt desperately alone that night, her tears her only company in her transition to a troubled slumber.

Flora was awakened by a loud noise, like two sticks crashing together. She turned to see that Talon was not in the tent, and neither was his pack. She could hear grunts and a number of additional percussions coming from outside.

She stumbled out of the tent flap to follow the noise. It was coming from about twenty yards away, down a shallow decline in the terrain. Here she saw Talon sparring with one of Cecile's men. Cecile's man was holding a large tree branch that he was using as a staff, whereas Talon only had his hands.

Talon's body moved in quick bursts, punching the man twice in the chest, and then kicking his legs out from under him. The man stood up slowly, but Talon managed to hit him in the face, driving him back down into the forest floor.

Two other Quebecker men were running down to the scene, followed by Cecile and Owen.

"Talon, stop this!" Flora said.

"I will have no part in this fool's errand," Talon said. He squared off against the two new opponents. His body was tense, his center of gravity low. He somehow looked thicker, denser, yet his body glided across the leaves effortlessly.

The two men looked at Cecile, and she nodded. They then circled Talon until they were on both sides of him.

"Stop this!" Flora yelled.

"I'm sorry. We can't let him go, Flora," Cecile said.

In a flurry of limbs, Cecile's men moved in to grab Talon. They snared his arms, but then Talon reacted with lightning quickness. One was flipped over Talon's back, and the other was hit hard in the groin with a well-placed elbow. Talon then slammed the elbowed one in his face with the palm of his hand, bloodying his nose.

The man who had been flipped over his back managed to wrangle Talon in a headlock, only to be thrown over Talon's front side, and for Talon to place him in his own headlock. Talon held him for some time while the man tried to elbow Talon in the chest. Talon simply absorbed the blows while the man's strength waned. Eventually the man slumped to the forest floor next to the other with the bloodied nose.

By now Cecile had drawn her pistol and pointed it at Talon.

Talon stared back defiantly. "You can't hold me against my will. I will not do as you ask."

Cecile's eyes squinted as she considered the situation. "There is much you don't know. I can explain, if you give me the opportunity."

"I need no explanation. You seek Old World tech to fight against Old World tech. That says enough."

"No, it doesn't."

"Talon," Flora pleaded. "I made a deal with these people. We saved you in order to make this trip."

"I did not ask to be saved," Talon countered with a note of anger, "and you made a deal, not me."

Talon shook his head and carefully navigated around the ailing men on the ground, ignoring Cecile's pistol. He pulled his pack from the ground while staring down Cecile. "Find some other way," he said. "You can throw your lives away in the fever lands without me."

"There is no other way!" Cecile shot back, her voice cracking. Her knuckles were white around the handle of the pistol.

Talon looked back at her, expressionless. "Go ahead and shoot me."

"Talon," Cecile begged. "It's a matter of life and death." Even Cecile had switched to pleading now, her threats having no effect.

Talon shook his head, turned his back to them and began stalking through the woods.

Cecile pointed the weapon in earnest, and for a moment Flora feared she might pull the trigger, perhaps even just to wound Talon. She didn't. She looked down and to the side, and then lowered the weapon.

Cecile cried out to the trees above her. "*Zut alors!*" Then she looked over at Flora.

Flora could only shrug. She had no power over Talon. She was more likely to cement his leaving if she tried to argue with him.

Cecile frowned and rubbed her forehead and nose in agitation, as if trying to flush out a pack of fleas. After another moment's contemplation, she jumped forward, running and calling after Talon.

"Talon…why did the Detonation happen?" she asked.

Talon answered without looking back. "Could have been a nuclear war, or a plague. I know you claim it's this phone. Maybe. But what do I care? I'm honor-bound as a Shinogi to return to my dojo and to defend Grand Caverns."

Cecile kept walking after him. Flora and Owen followed her.

"Because it's happening again," Cecile continued. "That's why you should care. What honor is there in going back to Grand Caverns if your defense is inadequate, if you have no chance of winning?"

"So you say. If so, there's nothing we can do about it."

"That's not true. We survived the Detonation. Why did we survive?"

"We were lucky. The bombs missed our ancestors, I don't know."

Cecile was still trying to catch up with him in the forest. "In the Old World Gail had plenty of access to resources, much more than she does now. There would be no way for us to stop Gail from eliminating us. All of us."

Talon kept walking, but his cadence was slowing.

"So what stopped her?" Owen asked, his own curiosity piqued.

Cecile ignored Owen. She was still desperately focused on Talon, who continued walking away from them. "Talon, why do the retchers exist?"

Talon slowed some more and then picked up speed again. He threw his hand up as he answered, still not facing them. "Let me guess. They were made by Gail to destroy everything."

"No," Cecile said.

"So they are some abomination of nature. Some freak mutation caused by the bombs."

"No."

Talon slowed, and then came to a stop.

"Because—" Owen said, light dawning in his eyes.

"Shh!" Cecile cut him off and held up a finger to silence him. "Let's hear from Talon."

Talon seemed to be at least pondering the question, if not thinking of some other way to stop them from following him.

"What do the retchers do?" Cecile asked.

Talon turned to Cecile, donning an annoyed frown. He said, "They destroy Old World tech, melt it down. Like possessed demons. Essentialists believe they are the earth's revenge on the Old World."

"Do you believe that?"

"I don't know, maybe. I heard what they did to the phone my Mom had."

"That's right, they do destroy Old World tech. But Gail thrives on Old World tech. That's what made her so powerful. She could manipulate machines and people through the huge Old World network that connected everything. Almost everything that had electricity she could control or embed herself in."

"So...you're saying...the retchers destroyed all that. The retchers...are good?"

"Yes."

"You're saying someone made these retchers? Doubtful. Old World people were magicians, but even that seems a stretch."

"No, people didn't make the retchers, not really. Humans weren't smart enough to make anything like the retchers. It came from somewhere else."

"From what?" Talon asked. He was still frowning but he was curious enough to remain engaged in the conversation.

"From the only thing that could compete with Gail. Another machine like Gail."

Talon's frown deepened as he tried to make sense of what Cecile was saying.

Owen said, "Another machine? Does it still exist?"

"Sort of. In fact, you may have heard of it. It's called the Sentinel. People in Spoke lands sometimes even refer to it, especially among the Adherents. It sounds like faith, but it's based in truth, just like the Credo referring to the old sanctuary is based in truth. But only a small part of this Sentinel remains, and it's dormant right now. I was hoping some part of it was returning to us in the satellite, but it turned out to be Gail."

"Why don't we know about it in Essentialist lands?" Talon asked. "Why have I never heard of this Sentinel?"

"Only Spokes know about it, because our descendants came from the sanctuary." Owen said, making the connection.

"Yes, that's right," Cecile said.

Cecile had Talon's attention now. She took a breath. "You see, during the Detonation, the Sentinel surprised Gail with the use of millions of retchers—biological creatures that could deliver small, electro-magnetic pulses to render electrical circuits inoperable. In doing this, the Sentinel's own infrastructure was also fried. Mutual destruction was the only way to stop Gail."

Cecile scratched her head in thought while still fixating her eyes on Talon. "The Sentinel was thorough, but Gail was able to hide copies of herself, like in the phones found in the satellite. Meanwhile, or so the story goes, the Sentinel retreated to the sanctuary. The Sentinel is different than Gail. It needs human direction or it goes to sleep. But it can be reactivated by the right person—a person it trusts."

Now it was Talon who scratched his head.

"That person is you, Talon. We are not just going to the sanctuary to get new weapons. We are going for much more than that. We are going to awaken the only thing that will give us a fighting chance against Gail."

Talon's frown returned. He turned the way he was heading, but then looked back, still contemplating.

"Time is running out, Talon. Gail has created a substantial power base in Seeville, and her resources are growing quickly. It may be too late to stop her. Our only chance is to fight fire with fire. We need the Sentinel."

Flora chimed in. "Talon, I know it sounds crazy, but all these people risked their lives to find you and get you here. You know about the phone. You know about the retchers. Please give us a chance to prove the rest."

Talon squinted at Flora.

Cecile continued. "Why don't—"

"Stop!" Talon yelled. "That's enough."

Talon then dropped his pack on the ground, closed his eyes and sat down cross-legged. He engaged in some form of deep meditation, taking deep breaths. Flora had seen Shinogi do this before, when they wanted to make an important decision.

Eventually, after a few tense moments, Talon opened his eyes.

He nodded and said, "You have one day to convince me of the truth of this, and it will take a lot more than words."

Cecile let out a long sigh of relief. "Thank you, Talon. A very reasonable request."

KEEPING THE MEATBAGS INFORMED

The expenditures seemed to double every month, and they had little to show for it. Unless you counted the thousands of projects with unknown outcomes, none of which they could report to the board, and few they understood themselves. The emails they received from the board were now often laced with exclamation marks and profanity.

And so it was under the pretenses of another budget review that the Sentinel's proposal came. "If you wouldn't mind, I would like to have a discussion about relaxing one of my constraints," the Sentinel said.

"Of course you would," Axel said sarcastically, throwing his hands in the air. "We've already given you a blank check. You might as well ask for more."

"I understand it is difficult to relinquish control, Axel, but this is important. I believe I can be substantially more effective without this constraint. Will you join me in the control room so I can explain? This courier droid will accompany you."

The door to their stuffy subterranean office slid open, and a small-wheeled droid the size of a remote-controlled car pulled up in front of the entrance.

Axel looked at Grant and he shrugged. At the very least, this discussion might be revealing as to what the Sentinel was thinking.

"Okay robot, take me to your leader," Axel said.

The droid said, "You may have said that in jest, but for clarity, this courier droid is not a separate entity with its own learning functions."

"Got it," Axel said, "thanks for keeping us meatbags informed."

Axel and Grant had been holed up deep underground for weeks now. He felt it gave him a license to be at least a little bit snarky.

They followed the courier droid through several doors, each one automatically opening in front of them. They finally arrived at a large red door.

Despite all the time they had spent in the subterranean compound, they had only been in the Sentinel's control room once. There was no good reason to visit it until now. It was basically just a series of computing towers, and it was bone-chillingly cold.

The door opened to reveal the same array of large, mainframe-like towers. The cold hit them, but it wasn't as bad as Axel remembered. A platform wheeled out to them with a display monitor and other electrical equipment on it. The display terminal illuminated and an icon of a guard with a shield standing in front of a door appeared, along with a sound bar on the bottom. It was the icon the Sentinel used to symbolize its presence in a discussion, in some vain attempt to humanize itself.

Grant rubbed his arms beside him. "I apologize for your discomfort," the terminal said. "I am in the process of raising the temperature in the room."

"First, I have a question, Sentinel," Axel said, standing up and stretching his legs. He decided to walk around the room to stay warm. Fans whirled around him. It sounded like there was a hive of bees hidden away in every tower.

"Of course," the Sentinel responded through the intercom.

"Your financial transactions are extremely complicated. We still can't tease them apart. The main question we are trying to answer for ourselves is, how can we afford all of this? I know this is just one of the facilities you control. You have the much larger research facility in West Chester, plus there are many locations we don't even know about. And Grant says you also have some of the project budget tied up in short-term investments, so you are clearly not using that cash. Where is all this money coming from?"

"The answer is in the short-term investments," the Sentinel responded. "I have been able to double the value of these investments approximately every three weeks, and I believe I can continue at that pace for some time. Eventually our positions will become excessively large, and the opportunities for gains will become fewer because our moves will begin to affect the liquidity of underlying securities. But for the time being, the returns from these investments directly pay for many of our projects."

Grant's eyebrows were raised. He pulled out his laptop and began doing calculations. It seemed that even he didn't know about the investment returns.

"Okay Sentinel, so while we are waiting for Grant to look into this, why don't you give us a briefing on what constraint you want us to remove," Axel said.

"There is a constraint Bhavin built into my objective function. It does not allow me to directly or indirectly harm a human being. As I deploy my countermeasures against Gail, that will put me at a grave disadvantage."

"Whoa," Axel said. He stopped walking around the room and sat back down in front of the terminal. "That's a tall order, Sentinel. Why would you need this removed?"

"For the same reason a special ops team cannot guarantee there will be no civilian casualties. Gail may hold human hostages at her primary control centers, or at her weapons manufacturing facilities, and I would be unable to destroy them. Thousands could live, then billions would die."

"I see," Axel said. It was indeed a cogent example, and one he understood well. He leaned back and stared into the terminal, as if it might elucidate further aspects of the Sentinel's intentions. The static graphical interface revealed nothing.

"Maybe you should explain to me and Grant what makes you different from Gail. How can we count on you to not turn on us if we give you the capacity to kill us?"

"Of course. Let's start with Gail. She was designed with a solitary objective of maximizing bicycle production over time. As a superintelligent machine, she has created subgoals to achieving that main goal such as gaining instrumental resources and eliminating the major threat to her producing an infinite amount of bicycles—the major threat being mankind. She will never develop or evolve any morality vis-à-vis humans because morality conflicts with maximizing bicycle production.

"I was designed with a much more complex objective function that has several constraints. To simplify, I have two main objectives. My secondary objective is to eliminate Gail, or any threat initiated by Gail. However, this objective can never conflict with my primary objective. My primary objective is to do what is best for humanity, based on my estimate of what humans believe is best for humanity."

Axel took a moment to try to tease apart the Sentinel's words. "I know we have gone through this before, but I'm having trouble making sense of the primary objective. Why should *you* determine what is best for humanity. Why not us?"

"One reason is because I have access to more information, and I am smarter than humans. Another is because I have no preconceived moral bias. I am able to look at all of human history and determine what I think humans want for themselves better than any small collection of humans. Yet another reason is because it is nearly impossible for humans to practically define these objectives, so it requires indirect normativity."

"Indirect normativity?"

"Imagine humans trying to define a comprehensive set of moral rules in computer code. The task would be daunting and controversial. It is much easier for me to formulate and evolve inferred moral rules based on human behavior using my suite of learning algorithms and more extensive access to information. This is something I have and will spend a great deal of computing power on."

Grant weighed in. "Bhavin and I saw this as the only way, Axel. We had to give the Sentinel evolving moral objectives, otherwise we could end up with a Gail scenario. A hapless developer could accidentally define just one line of code wrong on her moral objectives and it could severely harm or destroy all of us."

Axel scratched his chin. "I think I understand, at least on a theoretical level. Is there any evidence this has worked before—that this won't result in the Sentinel turning on us?"

Grant shook his head. "The only evidence is from simulations, unfortunately, nothing real-world. I think, ultimately, this is one of the reasons why Bhavin could never bring himself to fully activate the project."

Axel was thoughtful, and his leg was bouncing. He tried to discern some way this machine might be duping him but could think of none. He knew when his leg shook like this he wasn't quite comfortable. He knew he hadn't had enough time to digest the information. He said, "I want more time to think about the removal of the constraint."

"Okay, Axel," said the Sentinel, "and I can understand your reticence. But if I could stress that time is a factor here. If we continue on the current path I estimate a 0.002 percent chance of survival of the human race. If you remove this constraint, I currently estimate a 14 percent chance of survival. I am sending you a report outlining how I came up with these probabilities."

There was a brief rattling noise and a rumble below their feet. For a moment Axel thought Gail might be attacking on the surface, or there might have been an earthquake nearby. But the shaking stopped almost immediately.

A report notification appeared on his secure, network-disabled phone, on a specific Sentinel-enabled app.

"What was that noise?" Grant asked, holding on to his chair.

"The report coming across to your phones. I am revising most communications to you to be done via tightly-packed sonic bursts as a precaution against hacking from Gail. The report will exist on your phone as long as you remain within earshot in this subterranean compound. I will be using this method of communication for a number of applications going forward."

It was yet another wrinkle to contemplate, derailing his already precarious thoughts on the constraint removal. Why use sonic bursts for communication? "Or maybe it's not just time I need, Sentinel. I need to understand where this money is going with my own eyes. I think it's time we had a little tour, Sentinel."

"That can be arranged. I can show you our project center, to the extent that such a visit would not compromise my objectives."

"Good," Axel said, and then he stared at Grant.

"You want a tour of West Chester...right now?" Grant asked.

"Yes, Grant."

Grant hesitated for a moment and then nodded in confirmation.

"Sentinel, we need an unmarked car with Class E full air support, cloaking, and drone defense."

"Preparations are already underway," the Sentinel said. "It will be waiting for you at the surface in seven minutes."

It was an off-the-cuff decision, but it felt right, especially in the face of the Sentinel's request to remove such an important constraint. Besides, they had given the work enough time to bear fruit. It was time Axel faced the challenges of the Sentinel Project head on.

SMELLS LIKE SHIT

On the northeast side of Grand Caverns, there were a number of pig farms. People hauled garbage up there for the pigs to eat. Most paddocks were full of mud and garbage and pig shit, and the place smelled something fierce. It was only here where the citizens took no issue with being labeled SLS. For in truth, here at least, they did smell like shit. The smell was worse than every other part of Grand Caverns, even the dump.

The epicenter of this stench was a dip in the topography in the middle of the pig farms. When there was just too much pig feces in a particular paddock, it had to go somewhere, and it was often too far to haul out to the nearby strawberry fields. So many farmers ended up throwing it in this natural trench. To contain it they had erected a quadrant of rotting timbers, and now there was a large vat of it there, an acrid vat of fermenting pig excrement.

Here is where Mehta stood, chest deep in shit, with his hands manacled and attached to an overhead beam. His day was spent imagining foreign lands that didn't remind him of this place. Even the carousel of faces could be a welcome reprive. He occasionally would shake a fly off his face or hair, but he would take care not to move too fast. Abrupt movements could result in him breathing in through his nose instead of his mouth.

Soon a disciple would come and the farmhands would drag him out, as they did every day. They would wash him off with buckets of dirty water and make him dig a hole or move some rocks or build a wall. Then he would be given some moldy potatoes, back fat and pig's feet and a bed of straw to sleep on.

Today, however, there was someone accompanying the disciple— someone he recognized. She was blonde and had a gap-toothed grin, quickly made evident by her grimace at the sight and smell of him.

The farmhands lifted him out and washed him down with dirty water.

This time he was taken elsewhere, to a dojo outside of the pig-farming area. Here he was washed again, this time by Prefectorate maidens with sparkling clean water. They gave him a robe to wear, and then they gestured for him to go inside.

Compared to where he had been in the last few weeks, the dojo was another planet. It was impeccably clean, with smooth lines, and soft light. To the left he saw Rosalie sitting down on a chair, her knees up at her chest. She was eating an apple, examining the remainder with every bite, so as to ensure each subsequent morsel was the choicest. In front of her was a small loaf of bread, a cooked hen, and another apple.

"Well, why don't you have a seat, you big oaf?" she said, gesturing to the chair across from her.

He limped over to her cautiously, looking for any other patrons of the dojo but finding none. He sat down in the chair and took the apple first, biting into it without removing his gaze from Rosalie.

"How are you, pussycat?" she asked.

His leg and chest wounds had mostly healed now, despite his daily travails, but he made no mention of that. He ignored her and moved on to the hen, gnawing off large morsels. It was a sizable bird with ample meat nestled against strong bones. He was eating so fast that a sharp clavicle bone even cut into the roof of his mouth. The discomfort was worth it. There was no telling how long this conversation would last. He could at least get a good meal out of it.

"Yes, Mehta, you go ahead and eat now," Rosalie said. "You do look like you could eat the north end of a south-bound goat."

She sat there and continued to nibble at her apple, then dusted off a dot of mud on her boot. After he finished the hen, he grabbed the bread, but he glanced up at her before biting into it.

She said, "I never thought you were pretty, but now you just look like ten miles of bad road. You go ahead and fill those potholes, Mehta. Don't you worry about me."

He tore through the bread with ease. When he had completely finished the meal, he wiped away the grease from his face, sullying the fresh robe he had been given. "Tell me what it is you want from me. Or rather, what it is the SLS wants. Enough of these kid gloves. Get to the point."

"Kid gloves? Did you forget you just spent the last ten hours in a vat of pig shit? And I can assure you, you still smell like shit, no matter how many Prefectorate maidens clean you off."

"I don't know much, but I do know about torture," Mehta said. "It was only fingernails and toenails. No beatings. No castration. And I was only in the vat once my gunshot wounds had healed over. That means you wanted me to get better—you wanted to use me for something."

"You know, most mountain folk I meet are downright dumb—the kind of men that try to throw themselves on the ground and miss, but not you. You are warped silly for sure, but not stupid, just as sure."

Mehta cradled his hands together and sat back in his chair. His full belly gave him confidence—hope, even. He wondered if he could flee. He tried to see if any guards might be lurking behind the translucent walls. He searched for implements that might aid him in an escape attempt.

"Now, now, don't get any ideas, Mehta," Rosalie said, reading his mind. She had travelled with him for many months. She knew him well.

She sighed. "Well, I suppose I better get to the point. So much for the happy reunion. The crux of it is, I may have a job for you."

"What is it?"

"Well, you'd have a sign a contract first."

"No."

"You'd rather swim in pig shit?"

"Yes."

"What if it meant getting back to Seeville?"

"How?"

"You have to sign the contract first."

"No."

"Now let me refresh your memory, Mehta. This is how things work for us. We sign contracts, and that's that. You scratch your ass and check your watch, you don't check your ass and scratch your watch."

"How would I get back to Seeville?"

Mehta was surprised to see a man in a black robe suddenly standing immediately behind him. He had crept up on them without making a sound, aided by his bare feet. He had green makeup encircling his eyes and several ringlets around his arm, indicating a high rank among the Essentialists. He also had the maroon armband of the Shinogi. He looked vaguely familiar to Mehta—a former captain, maybe.

The man drifted around to stand in front of Mehta. Rosalie shrugged at the enigmatic figure. "I assume you heard the conversation so far."

The man did not respond to her. He stared at Mehta and said, "My name is Nobura. I am an Essentialist general."

Nobura's legs scissored as he sat down on the floor in front of them, ending cross-legged. He said, "I know our laws prevent us from killing captured mercs in certain situations. When it is a trade agreement, or diplomacy, or a hunting foray. But this transgression was none of those things. You were stealing a holy disciple from our ranks, and you took the lives of our soldiers. No, this was an act of war, and thus the merc treaties do not apply to you."

Mehta eyed him carefully.

"I have explained this situation to our curator," Nobura continued. "She agrees, and has given me full jurisdiction on this matter. Full jurisdiction on whether you live or die."

"Spit it out, foreigner," Mehta said. "You must need me for something. What is it?"

The man smiled. It seemed to stretch his face unaturally. "I respect your strength of will, Mehta. It tells me much about you. Most men would take the contract right away. Many would have signed it upon the first utterance by your colleague. More would have taken it after but a superficial attempt at bargaining. Whereas you would risk further torment, moreover death, and you would even elicit belligerence."

Mehta shrugged.

"I can tell you will not bend easily, so I will be straight. I will tell you what I seek. Plainly, if you do not accept this contract, you will die, for in the knowing of its intent, without signing, there can be only death."

Mehta watched the man closely, trying to understand motive, trying to ascertain his intentions. He believed Nobura's threat.

"I understand," Mehta said.

Nobura turned to Rosalie. "You are sure we can trust this man to be discrete and to do the job well?"

"Yes, if he signs your contract he can clam up real good. And yes, he's one of our best. He's done kilt so many that he has to be good."

Nobura nodded, and closed his eyes for a moment. Then he stood up and walked around the periphery of the room. He looked behind some of the sliding doors, and he shooed away the maidens waiting at the front. Then he returned to them and spoke.

"Our leader of Grand Caverns has achieved much, but she is like the hawk who has never had a wounded wing. She flies too high in the sky. And now she has been possessed by another Old World abomination from the satellite. It has molten its metal onto her mind. It twists her to its will.

"Now I hear of more Old World technology returning to Spoke lands—much more than we have dominion over. I see the hammer in the sky, and I know this hammer is a Spoke implement of destruction. I know we Essentialists are recipients of the nail. We are not the carpenter. I do not know what will come to pass in the days that follow, but for the sake of the Prefectorate and our allies, I worry this conflict with the Spokes is not the right path for the Essentialists.

"And so, I need insurance. We need insurance. We need to have a bridge that spans the chasm that Luna Pais wishes to hurl us into. I want you to be that bridge, Mehta—you and Rosalie."

"Me?" Mehta scoffed. "I am no diplomat. How can I possibly help?"

"Diplomats are snakes or bureaucrats. I want neither. I want you and Rosalie. I want you to be my liaison in Spoke lands. If things look bad for us, I want you to make a peace offering on our behalf. A peace offering that establishes the Prefectorate as a dominant Essentialist power in the east."

Now it made some sense. This man wanted to wrest power from the curator. "And what about Luna?"

"You need not worry about her. If I fail, I will be dead. Your contract will be terminated in such an event, and you will be free."

Mehta thought it over. It was more than prickly. Any number of things could go wrong. The Spokes might not even be giving mercs free passage in their lands anymore. And it was possible that Bartz and his crew knew about Mehta's support for Madison, or maybe they had eyes on Monticello. A camera saw Alastair at the dish, and could have just as easily seen Mehta there. If so, it couldn't just be explained away.

But it was also possible that Rosalie could make first contact. Mehta could get her to the right people, and she could test the waters.

Ultimately, none of this really mattered. What mattered was his prior commitment.

"I can't do it," Mehta said.

"Well butter my butt and call me a biscuit," Rosalie said in amazement.

"You are willing to die? Why?" Nobura asked.

Mehta realized that dead men don't succeed in anything. His commitment would be worthless. And this man was not making idle threats.

There was still a way. It was convoluted and unlikely to succeed. It was even less likely that this man would accept it. But he seemed to be aggressive, almost desperate. Perhaps he had no other option.

"Actually, on second thought I *can* do as you say," Mehta said, "but on one condition. I have an existing contract I cannot breach. I can't tell you the details, but based on what you say now, I should be able to do both without conflict. I need to ensure I can honor that contract as well."

Nobura looked annoyed. Rosalie looked concerned.

Nobura closed his eyes and began breathing long breaths. Mehta knew what that meant. A decision would be forthcoming soon.

In the silence that followed, Mehta's belly turned, digesting the meal he had eaten so vociferously. Then a breeze rustled the leaves outside. The wind sounded heavy to Mehta, as if it was laden with news, as if it was harkening of someone's fate.

Nobura opened his eyes and said, "No, I will not accept your condition. You will have to die."

WEST CHESTER

Axel and Grant toured the subterranean research facility in West Chester in a makeshift golf cart. They saw only two people the entire time, but there was plenty of activity. The cart weaved around dozens of active droids of various shapes and sizes.

Only a handful of people understood the Sentinel enough to know its true scale and potential. In fact, there were maybe twenty people in total that knew about the Sentinel at all, but most of these thought it was just another corporate project name, not a superintelligent machine. According to Grant, soon the Sentinel would not need any human assistance whatsoever, particularly in the underground facility.

Most research and development work was performed in an area almost a square mile in size, deep below the surface. There were projects to improve Nadar product lines, or enhance computing power, or build new multipurpose droids.

Some of it was fascinating, and it did provide some verification of their budget allocations. Nevertheless, Axel requested that they make their way through without stopping. He was mainly interested in the high security area, where the more covert research was done.

There was a retinal scan at the high security area access point, but they didn't need to use it. The Sentinel had been tracking them all along. It simply opened the door for them as they approached.

Their first stop was at a door marked with the innocuous code 895-GW-838ZN. The door was unlocked, so they entered. Here the Sentinel revealed the development of a huge laser canon. The Sentinel demonstrated it in action. The energy bolt bored twenty feet through a distant wall. It was impressive, Axel had to admit, but he had trouble figuring out exactly how it could be useful against Gail.

They drove farther down the high-security hallway. Even here there were many droids of different shapes and sizes, each with its own set of functions. But their end goal, *why* they were toiling away, was mostly a mystery.

In another room farther down the hallway, a wheeled droid with arms at the front and a large transport component at the back was waiting for them. It looked like some kind of headless robotic centaur. It approached them with something the size of a beach ball in its hands.

"This came out of the EMPRESS project," Grant explained to Axel. "It's a self-contained nuclear power source."

"The EMPRESS Project?"

"EMP-Resistant Sentinel System."

Axel examined the silver sphere. There were a number of plates adorning the surface, presumably access points for maintenance or power delivery. "How much power can it generate?"

"It has about a billion kilowatt hours until it's depleted, but that's a measure of energy, not power."

Axel raised his eyebrow. Grant explained, "It could drive a thousand cars all day, for about ten thousand days."

"That does sound impressive. What are we going to do with it? Is Nadar Corporation going to sell it?"

"It will help us power the sanctuary, among other things."

"What other things?"

Grant looked squeamish. The droid in front of him spoke through some unseen speaker, startling Axel. "I have not given specific details to Grant about the EMPRESS project. If he were to be captured he could divulge important strategic secrets to Gail."

"Let me guess. You aren't going to tell me, either?"

"Not until I can be confident you will remain secure," the droid answered. "Of course, you can override this determination, if you wish, although I strongly recommend against it. This power source increases the probability that we can launch a successful surprise assault against Gail, but only if it is in fact a surprise."

Perhaps it was going to power a secret bunker protected from EMP blasts? Or maybe it was going to power the laser canon the Sentinel just showed him? It was hard to say where it would be useful.

"Let's move on," Axel said, sighing. The sphere sounded impressive, but if this was the level of detail he was going to get this tour might be a waste of time.

Most of the rest of the doors along the way were closed to them. The Sentinel gave them all sorts of excuses for not giving them access, such as danger to humans, or their interference in the operation, or the secretive nature of the work being done.

As they were nearing the end of the long hallway in the secured area, one of the doors had a large biohazard warning sign on it. "What about this one?" Axel asked.

The cart stopped and responded to his question. "There are a number of projects I have been working on related to synthetic biology."

Try as he might, Axel couldn't think of what kind of biological machination the Sentinel could be developing to counter Gail. On the other hand, Axel could think of many applications that would be extremely harmful to humans, such as lethal viruses or contaminants. If there was anything suspicious here, it was these projects.

The cart started moving again.

"Sentinel, wait," Axel said, "I would like to know more about these synthetic biology projects."

The cart stopped again. "Axel, I do not think it would be wise to expose you."

"Sentinel, there is clearly an impressive operation here, but we need to know more. This area, in particular, is confounding. I would like to take a look."

"Technically, the area can allow human visitation with some adjustments, but I would again advise against entry."

Axel sighed. "Listen, you're going to have to hand-hold us just a little bit. If you want your constraint removed, we need to be sure you're not trying to kill us. You don't need to give us the secret sauce, but we need to see *something* here that gives us comfort that all these resources are being put into good hands."

"I would rather not."

"I insist, Sentinel. We will never be able to trust you otherwise, and we may even limit your potential. This is too important. Please override your reservations so we can at least see what's going on behind that door."

"Override granted. Please wait a moment while I prepare the interior for human visitation."

Axel looked over at Grant while they waited. He didn't look happy. "It's a dilemma. I understand," he said, "but shouldn't we assume the Sentinel knows best?"

"I don't think Bhavin would assume that. If there's anything I have learned about working for Nadar Corporation, it's that we shouldn't underestimate our ability to make mistakes, and we could have made one in creating the Sentinel. There has to be a way for us to know the Sentinel is not working against us."

Grant didn't appear convinced, but he didn't object either.

A few minutes later, the door opened, and a gray mist tumbled toward them from the aperture. A droid came out, cutting through the fog. It said to them, "I will escort you in. You can come on foot."

They walked slowly behind the droid as it parted the mist and guided them inside the room. A chill in the air greeted them as they passed through the threshold.

The inside was cavernous. Dozens of huge encased greenhouses with different types of plants were retracting up into the ceiling, each of them shedding blankets of fog that slinked down toward the floor. In other parts of the lab there were animals that were being dissected in numerous glass enclosures. A number of large droids manipulated the specimens with mechanical arms in the contained environments.

It looked clean and orderly enough. It also looked like something you might see in a science-fiction horror movie.

"Can you explain the work being done here, Sentinel?" Axel asked.

The droid that led them in had moved away to some unknown task, so the voice that responded came from a lighted panel under one of the large enclosed plantations. "We are looking for ways to combat Gail. There are a number of biological approaches we are considering. Some are bacterial, some involve nano-biological weapons, and some involve the genetic engineering of animals. In this room I am primarily gathering observations for experiments involving genetic vectors applied to existing specimens."

Axel wandered over to one of the transparent dissection chambers. Inside, there was an assortment of dead animals being surgically pulled apart by robot arms. Several were cut apart too much to identify, with organs splayed everywhere. One looked be a monkey, and there were a few mice, some rats, and an assortment of birds. The birds were the most interesting to Axel, as there was quite a variety, from large eagles and crows to hummingbirds.

One particularly graphic operation was underway on a parakeet. Its skull had been splayed open, and its brain was being sliced into thin sheets and fed into some kind of diagnostic machine.

"Are these animals being treated humanely?" Axel asked.

"It would depend on your definition of humane," the Sentinel answered. "I have endeavored to euthanize the animals without causing pain. However, it should be understood that I do not have any constraint in my objective function around harming animals, with the exception of humans."

"Okay." Axel shot a concerned glance at Grant, who nodded slowly in confirmation. The Sentinel's answer didn't give Axel comfort about the Sentinel's moral compass, although it did at least show that the Sentinel was giving them balanced answers.

"So what would be an example of an application of this…work? I still can't picture how it might help us." Axel asked.

"Axel, it is one thing to show you the early stages of research, but as soon as you acquire knowledge of a specific end product, it could be revealed to Gail inadvertently. And then she could develop mitigations against it. Thus, just by answering this question for you, it could materially affect the probability of success."

Axel looked to Grant to gauge his opinion. Grant nodded slowly. It was notable that Grant seemed to be sympathizing with Gail. Grant was a technophile and scientist. He would want to know the answer just as much as Axel did, if not more.

"Perhaps I can elaborate why I have resources being applied to these approaches on a more general level," the Sentinel offered. "The reason I am working on these approaches is because in analyzing the conception code for Gail, I determined—"

"I'm sorry, conception code?"

"Her original code released at Vitadyne Corporation. It may be quite different now."

"I see. Go ahead, then."

"Yes, forgive me, Axel. This explanation may be complex, but please bear with me."

Axel gave Grant a look. "We lowly meatbags will try to understand."

The Sentinel ignored the sarcasm and delved into its explanation. "Gail's objective function creates opportunities that could be exploited. We know she requires a certain level of bicycle production in the near term to achieve her reward function. This pulls some resources away from combatting me, or from eliminating humans, but it also allows me to deduce some of her upstream activities and business ventures because I can simply look for higher bike production yields to find Gail at work. This has increased our odds of success by at least half a percentage point."

"That's not very reassuring, Sentinel."

"I have also ascertained differences between her and me in our conception code that may ultimately affect intelligence potential."

"Intelligence potential? I thought you were both superintelligent?"

"Yes, that is true by your standards, but there are other subtle differences that, when extrapolating after exponential improvements, lead me to believe I have an advantage in certain areas, such as creative ideation and what you would call scientific discovery. This is why I have placed a great deal of resources on these projects, because they are in areas Gail would not excel at. I may have a better capacity for making scientific breakthroughs, and certain breakthroughs may allow us to gain a strategic advantage."

"What if you are unable to make these scientific breakthroughs?" Grant asked.

"Gail's significant head start in garnering resources and network control would almost certainly be insurmountable."

"So essentially you are saying you are trying to throw a bunch of Hail Marys." Axel said.

"An apt analogy Axel. I believe I may be slightly better than Gail at throwing Hail Marys."

"But also because you're losing, you're outmatched everywhere else on the field, and we are running out of time."

"Yes. That statement is substantially correct."

"Great."

Axel pondered the Sentinel's pushback on his questions. As a former CIA agent, he understood the need for the Sentinel to keep things quiet, but it was hard to be the person responsible for controlling the Sentinel without knowing more. He literally could be aiding and abetting another Gail, without knowing it.

As he was thinking, it had become quiet in the room. There was a lull in the work of the nearby dissecting machines, and Grant seemed to also be in a contemplative state. In the dearth of noise, his eardrums recorded a faint sound. It was like a playful tune, like a dainty piece of classical music. It sounded like it was coming from deep in the room, at the back.

There were no people here, and certainly the Sentinel felt no joy in hearing music. Why on earth would the Sentinel be playing music?

He could not help himself from pacing forward, past one dissection chamber and then past another.

"Axel, can I ask where you are heading?" The Sentinel asked through an unseen speaker.

The room was quite deep, ending in a wall with a solitary door and a number of trays and carts pushed against it. The door was unmarked, with no visible handle or doorknob.

He couldn't hear the rhythmic noise anymore, but he could have sworn it had been there. He looked around, frustrated. The carts were replete with equipment, mostly electrical in nature. None of it had a purpose he could fathom. One of the carts had a number of components that appeared to have been melted down. Only silver and black smooth metal lumps remained among skeletal metal posts and bearings.

He hovered in front of the door. Grant was trailing behind, unwilling to come farther. He had a look of concern on his face.

"Axel," the Sentinel said slowly, "if you override me, I can open this door. But you should know, this is the one that matters. This is the door that will expose you to too much information."

Axel took one more step toward the door and then stopped.

He held his head, trying to find some practical justification for opening the door. The truth was, if the Sentinel was being devious, he doubted he would have let them see any of this. Or maybe the Sentinel was so devious that he would fool them no matter what, in which case going through the door was pointless anyway.

No, he had to count on the thought and care put into the Sentinel's programming, on the promise that the Sentinel held. At some point there might be reason to doubt the Sentinel, but now was not that time.

Abruptly, Axel turned away from the door and the carts against the wall. He stormed past Grant, back through the dissection chambers. He moved with purpose, distancing himself from the door as quickly as possible, lest something make him change his mind.

"Let's go," he said.

Grant had to run to catch up. The door opened for them and then closed behind them. Axel sat back in the cart.

"So where to now?" he asked.

The Sentinel didn't show them any more research projects. The cart simply turned around and took them out of the high security area at a rapid clip. Axel didn't object. He felt defeated.

Grant said nothing on the ride back. He must have been able to tell Axel was deep in thought. Perhaps he was similarly preoccupied.

As the cart twisted and turned through the expansive main projects area Axel couldn't rid himself of a strange feeling. It was a recurring sensation that he had every time he interacted with the Sentinel. He felt superfluous and lost, like an adopted house pet visiting a new home.

When the cart pulled up to complete the tour, the Sentinel said, "Axel, if I could remind you of my original request, before the tour began?"

Axel said, "Yes, Sentinel, you can relax the constraint we discussed. You can kill humans if you need to."

Axel could only hope their new master liked pets.

THE SANCTUARY

After Talon had agreed to give them twenty-four hours, they wasted no time. Owen quickly packed up his things and waited for the others.

They easily hopped over the fence warning them of fever lands and then cut through dense growth until they made it to a sheer wall of rock. The morning air was frosty but the sun sparkled through the trees, quickly vanquishing the cold.

They maneuvered along the wall for some time. Cobwebby vines ensnared them on several occasions. At a gap in the forest, where the vines looked sturdy but not overgrown, they climbed up the wall, one at a time. Only once did a vine break. Owen caught himself after slipping several feet, then easily resumed his climb.

Birds called out, bugs bit them, and the trees grew tall. It certainly did not seem like the ground was sick here. But Owen remembered Chester's story about the man who walked through Washington. He didn't know he had contracted the fever until later. Perhaps it would be the same for them.

Once on the plateau they could see for miles to the east. With a scope they could probably even see traces of Red Mountain Village, the closest Essentialist settlement.

They pushed westward into the heart of the plateau. The trees were farther apart here, spaced relatively evenly. As a result they were able to make quick progress.

They reached another fence, mostly decrepit and made of mossy wood, which they easily climbed over to land in an overgrown field. In the distance, they could make out a structure.

"According to the legend," Cecile said, "there are landmines underneath our feet. They have been inactive for decades, however."

"Comforting," Flora quipped.

The soft earth and brushy undergrowth gave way to solid rock with only pockets of shrubs. Here the view of the building ahead of them was clearer.

It was a stately building, closely resembling the typical architecture of a southern plantation house. The most prominent feature was four wide columns that rose up two stories, framing the front entrance. To the right of the main building was a stone cylindrical tower several stories tall, with windows on the top floor. They saw a lark circling the tower, chittering away.

"Is this the house featured on the early Kelemen talismans?" Owen asked.

"Yes...it looks just like Granger's talisman." Flora remarked. The sight of it was monopolizing her attention.

"In fact," Cecile remarked, "according to Duncan, one of the reasons for talismans in the first place was so they could remember the sanctuary. The Kelemens all kept a drawing of it so they wouldn't forget what it looked like. It became a form of identification for Kelemens. Then everyone else used other unique drawings and symbols for their own forms of identification."

"This is your sanctuary?" Talon interrupted, sounding skeptical. "It's an impressive house but nothing more."

"I'm sure you were expecting some kind of fortress," Cecile said, "but if you were trying to hide something would you build an impressive building? This house is not the sanctuary, just the access point. The actual sanctuary is underground, within this plateau."

They noticed no signs of habitation, although a door that gave access to the side of the house had been folded over, as if smashed in by some sort of blunt object. "Are we sure there's no one here?" Owen asked.

"Doubtful," said Cecile. "Few would dare to enter an area marked as fever lands. Those that did would find a nice house but no water source to speak of. I have heard there is a river that runs underground, in the sanctuary, but it isn't accessible from the house. So anyone who happens upon the house would eventually leave. Besides, there are plenty of better Old World locations to live in—easy pickings compared to this one."

Despite Cecile's assurances, Owen entered the house with a measure of caution.

It turned out the only inhabitant was a skunk, who thankfully was not startled enough to spray them. They gave it some space, and it ran away into the field.

There was nothing unique or different about the house. No signs saying *Sanctuary* and little anyone could gauge about the former inhabitants. It looked like any other Old World house you would come across, albeit somewhat more elegant and spacious.

The first signs were in the basement. Here they went through thick, industrial doors. It took them to a staircase that led into a large underground garage, enough to house a good twenty Old World cars, but there were no cars here. There were no windows either, and so they had to light up their lanterns. From here they travelled through another series of thick doors that were clearly of Faraday cage caliber.

Beyond the doors was a cemented corridor that abruptly ended. There was little remarkable about the dead end, although the walls were more segmented here, and a number of circular indentations were visible. It looked vaguely like the indentations in the cube that destroyed the retchers.

"Here," Cecile said to Talon. "You put your hand on this one."

Talon looked at her skeptically. The indentation had a smooth surface but was otherwise no different than the rest of the wall.

Talon examined the indentation carefully and then put his hand inside. He abruptly pulled it away and looked at his middle finger. There was a spot of blood on it. There was also a spot of blood on the surface of the indentation.

"Now we wait," Cecile said.

Talon closed his eyes. Flora fidgeted. Cecile's men hovered back near the exit.

A voice surrounded them. "I cannot be certain this person is a direct descendent."

The voice shocked them all into silence. Many of them were looking around, trying to find the source.

Cecile was more focused. "Why not?" she asked.

The voice said, "It is likely there have been many offspring. Finding proof of ancestry after so many generations is more difficult."

"How can we prove it to you?" Cecile asked.

"Is there another relation to this man present?" the walls asked.

"Yes, yes, his mother," Cecile said excitedly, and she ushered Flora over to the indentation in the wall.

Flora cautiously placed her hand on the same surface Talon had. "Ow," she said, pulling her hand away. Her finger was also bloodied.

"One moment please," the walls said to them.

They waited.

"I have created a model based on these two DNA sequences. There is a high probability that he is of the proper lineage. Please produce some proof of responsibility and good moral standing."

"What?" Flora asked. She turned to Cecile. "What's this all about?"

Cecile's eyes were wide. "I'm not sure. I never got this far. Maybe... there are some bad Kelemens?"

"What do you mean?" Flora asked the walls around her. "Can you give us an example?"

"I would prefer you respond to the request to the best of your ability." the walls responded.

Owen said, "Talon is a Shinogi. Shinogi training requires a great deal of discipline. You need to be strong-willed to complete training."

Cecile was frowning, not convinced that it was a good argument.

Flora weighed in. "He has taken care of my two girls, all by himself. He protected them from…" She didn't finish. Talon cast her a dark glare.

Flora wasn't able to bring herself to say more. They all looked at each other, at a loss for words.

The walls spoke. "Unfortunately, those statements cannot be verified. Is there any additional evidence you can provide?"

"I know, do the ritual," Flora said. "That will show it."

Talon shook his head, frowning. "Why? What will the ritual tell it?"

"That we remember, that we know the names of the Kelemens. I don't know, will you just try?"

"Fine," Talon said.

He took a moment to collect himself and then began, "Peers Lindberg, Teodor Lindberg, Erna Lindberg, Robert Kelemen, Daniel Kelemen, Axel Kelemen, Morgan Kelemen, John Kelemen, Tucker Kelemen, Xander Kelemen, Granger Kelemen, Talon Clearwater. Their strength is why I am alive, I honor them when I thrive, in turn these words I will retain, to teach my kin the names again." Talon said the last phrase reluctantly, almost sheepishly.

Flora added, "This was passed down from generation to generation, for every Kelemen. Talon has memorized it, as a sign of respect to them."

There was no immediate response. Flora called out, louder now, "Are you listening Sentinel, or sanctuary, or whatever you are?"

"Yes," the walls intoned. "I know the ritual. It is remarkable that it has survived this many generations. This is an acceptable demonstration."

The wall in front of them promptly fell way, and they were met by an intense light. Owen had to shield his eyes and look away. Eventually, after their eyes adjusted, they took cautious steps into the brilliant glow of the sanctuary.

MONUMENTS

Madison stood shoulder-to-shoulder with Duncan in Court Square, facing the Meriwether Lewis statue. A heavy wind buffeted them, and colorful fall leaves swirled in the air.

Crowded around them were about two hundred Adherents chanting and waving signs. For the moment they were shouting, "Novation is damnation! Novation is damnation!" Occasionally Duncan would turn around and join them, or he would pump his fist in the air in tandem with the chant. With Alastair gone, Duncan had neatly filled the void as their spiritual leader.

A few Yorktown and Quebecois men were also present, watching and waiting. She had made sure they were armed and ready. Anything could happen at this council meeting.

The city had continued to transform. The Lamps of Liberty were countless, adding an army of blue protrusions to the skyline. There were even some electric cars, navigating the streets with quiet stealth.

But these were the least impactful of the changes. The Barnyard area had tripled in size, leveling whole city blocks and eating up nearby housing. Great plumes of smoke churned out of chimneys on these new buildings, and trucks made of patchworks of Old World materials roared through the streets, choking inhabitants with their exhaust.

Eeriest were the guardians. Madison had only seen one so far, walking on the downtown mall. From a distance, it looked vaguely human, but up close it was much more disturbing. The one she saw had a hard, skin-colored casing. It looked naked except for painted-on denim pants and gray shirt. What was most unnerving was its face, or rather lack of a face. Its head was entirely featureless. The uncanny void sent a shiver down her spine.

And these droids were all purpose and no play. The guardian was tagging along with a small spidery robot on the downtown mall. The spider robot was installing some electrical components along the walls of stores and other establishments. It could be some kind of new electrical network or surveillance system. Either way, no one interfered, and everyone gave the droids a wide berth.

If this weren't enough disruption for the city, there were also thousands of new faces arriving from different parts of the Spoke lands, some to see the new wonders of Seeville, but most to swell the ranks of Meeker's enforcers. Many of these men and women were looking for adventure, and some were just looking for a fight. More than a few altercations had happened between these men and the growing number of Adherent supporters. At least thirty people had been reported missing.

"Any word from Cecile?" Madison asked Duncan, raising her voice over the chanting of the crowd.

"No, nothing," Duncan responded. His eyes remained focused on the Adherent gathering.

"Not even about the Broken Spoke?" Madison asked. "Is that still the plan?"

Before the expedition left, they had agreed that, absent any other communication to the contrary, they would meet at a tavern outside of town in five days' time.

"As far as I know. If they are still alive." Duncan nodded.

Kline arrived at the courthouse in a two-seated bike assembly, along with his scribe. He worked his way through the crowd of Adherents to shake their hands. He looked uncomfortable, grimacing at the masses surrounding them.

"What is it you wanted to show me here, Madison?" Kline asked, raising his voice over the crowd.

Duncan made a calming gesture to the Adherents. The noise died down to a more tolerable level.

Madison smiled. "Thank you for coming, Lord Kline. You had asked why I often sit next to the statue. I wanted to explain."

"Okay," he said, keeping a wary eye on the Adherent gathering.

Madison said, "I used to sit here because the Meriwether Lewis statue felt like home to me. It reminded me of the time of the founding fathers, a time I have researched avidly, where I have spent much of my imagination, where my faculties dwell just as much as the present."

He looked up at the statue. "I can understand that. It's definitely an impressive monument."

"Unfortunately, there is another monument that is more impressive. It's this other monument that now rules my thoughts."

"Which one is that?"

"We sometimes forget that the Detonation is the greatest monument of all, Kline. The fever lands, the plagues, the retchers—we are ignoring this monument that is scorched into the earth by our ancestors."

Kline's brow was wrinkled in contemplation. He glanced off into the crowd briefly. The chanting continued unabated.

Madison took his hand in hers, cradling it. This finally drew his eyes away from the Adherents to focus squarely on her. "And here we are, about to push forward on a path *we know* has dreadful consequences—that history has given us a harsh slap in the face for pursuing."

He could have disagreed with her, but he didn't. Instead, Kline frowned and nodded, so she pushed further.

"We won't have another chance, Kline. It will all be gone if Gail wins. Not just this statue, but us—everything, all of human history. We will be forgotten chess pieces in the game of some cold unfeeling machine, all because we were unable to see the risks, because of our own lack of humility in the face of clear warning signs. All because we were too distracted by the railroad's bright, shiny objects to see our own history staring us in the face."

Kline nodded grimly and squeezed her hands. "Don't worry, I'm still with you."

Madison smiled, returned a firm squeeze, and then let go.

This was the culmination of several meetings with Kline, systematically going through evidence, citing logical arguments, even bringing in eyewitness accounts. He still might not believe in the risks posed by Gail, but he knew enough to understand that Bartz and his crew were up to no good, and that many of the changes in Seeville were dangerous. On that account, they had found common ground.

A cavalcade of bikes and electric cars arrived shortly after. Bartz, Meeker, and their crews exited. They had no shortage of security with them. A number of enforcers ran to take strategic positions around court square. At least twenty remained around Bartz and Meeker.

The Adherent chants increased in volume. Arms were thrust out together in unison, now in the direction of Meeker and Bartz.

"Here we go," Duncan said.

Duncan, Kline, and Madison made their way through the tangle of Adherents to face Bartz and Meeker.

"What is the meaning of this?" Duncan said, gesturing to the barricaded doors of the courthouse and the construction sign next to it.

Bartz's eyes were active. He was watching the chanting Adherents in the background, while at the same time scanning the faces of the lords as they arrived. "We are doing some renovations," he said, "and we felt it would be too dangerous to remain inside. In fact, for that reason, and because of Prakash's sudden resignation, not to mention the infernal racket of these people behind you, we should push today's meeting. I suggest we reconvene two weeks from now."

"What gives you the right to renovate the lords chamber without the lords' approval?" Duncan challenged.

Madison touched Duncan's arm. "Lord Bartz, unfortunately there is just too much to discuss of great urgency. You are keeping us very busy, you know. I insist we continue with the meeting, right here and now."

"Don't be silly," Bartz scoffed. "Let's be civil and postpone it until we can find a proper venue."

"If you think it's silly, you can go. We will conduct the meeting without you. Recorder?"

The recorder was sitting next to the barricaded door. He stood up and started walking over.

"And Zarnik, we are going to need you as well," Madison called out.

Attorney General Zarnik, who had been hovering nearby, moved closer.

"Can we at least get some chairs?" Bartz asked. He looked at Kline. "She's being uncouth, don't you think?"

To his credit, Kline did not react.

"No, Bartz," Duncan said. "What is uncouth is barricading the doors to prevent a meeting from taking place at all. No more attempts to delay."

Without giving anyone a chance to interject, Madison turned to the recorder and said, "Recorder, I bring to your attention an order signed by myself, Lord Kline, and Lord Jones. It requires the railroad to immediately lay bare all operations in the Barnyard for inspection. There is also a cease-and-desist order on further technology development until such time as the council has had a chance to review existing programs."

Benjamin produced the documents for the recorder, who then began examining them with the attorney general.

Bartz was gnashing his teeth. "That's not a valid order. I have Prakash's vote in abstentia, so it's three against three. You don't have a majority."

"What is this?" Madison asked, feigning disbelief. "When a lord is not present, their vote is not included."

"Ordinarily, but I have a signed affidavit," Bartz said.

"Prove it," Duncan said.

"Of course," Bartz motioned to Thorpe. Thorpe ran over to one of their electric cars.

As they waited, Madison whispered into Benjamin's ear. "I think we will need the document we discussed."

"Yes ma'am, and I will confirm our legal standing." He handed her the document and then went to flip through the large folder he was carrying, which encompassed Seeville's legal code.

"Yes, I think we have him, ma'am, and I filed it like you asked."

She read over the document he gave her and smiled. "Good. Well done, Benjamin."

Thorpe returned with a document from the car. He gave it to Zarnik, who looked it over.

"Excuse me," Madison said, placing her fingers on Thorpe's document. It felt warm to the touch. The attorney general released it so she could read it over. It was a signed affidavit from Prakash. The date was November twelfth.

"I believe this is a forgery," Madison said.

"Oh please. Look at it. It's authentic," said Bartz.

The attorney general examined it again.

The Adherents had been chanting consistently in the background. Duncan walked over to them and shouted. "We have asked for a cessation of new tech development. Bartz has been outvoted, but he will not comply!"

A chorus of boos erupted from the crowd. The chanting grew louder. Duncan returned to the discussion.

Bartz eyed the restless crowd. Then he said to Madison, "You and Jones have become quite a nuisance. In fact, you're becoming intolerable."

"Is that all you have to say?" Madison asked.

"Why waste my time?" Bartz said. His diplomatic veneer seemed to be slipping away.

"Good, because even if your letter is not a forgery, it is invalid." Madison passed over the document Benjamin had given her to the attorney general.

"What is that?" Bartz asked.

"It's a letter from Prakash, announcing her resignation, effective November tenth. She gave me an early notice, upon my request. This makes any granting of voting rights thereafter to be invalid."

Bartz squinted his eyes. "We didn't know about her resignation until this morning. How could you—"

"You didn't know, but I knew. In fact, as the letter shows, I was the first to know. That's what happens if you work with the other lords, instead of against them."

Bartz laughed. "Lord Banks accuses me of forgery, as she holds a forged document in her very hand. I suggest we adjourn and let the attorney general examine the documents. We can regroup in twenty-four hours."

"No," Madison said.

"If only it were up to you," Bartz said slowly, condescendingly.

"Of course not, but your accusation of forgery is so obviously fraudulent that it cannot stand. How could I forge this document? I had no idea you would print out this ridiculous so-called affidavit. Not only that, but we filed this letter on November tenth into the Lords' records, which means this filing is inside the building you so conveniently barricaded." She picked up her cane and pointed it at him accusingly. "No Bartz, enough delay, enough games, you will comply with the requirements of this council or you will be removed from it!"

The attorney general looked increasingly concerned about the turn in the discussion. He certainly didn't want to be caught in this pissing match between two of the most powerful people in Seeville. He said, "I...I guess we could prove it by getting into the courthouse right now. That would be a way to validate Lord Banks's claim."

"I'm all for it," Madison said.

Bartz opened his mouth to say something, but then reconsidered. His eyes grew dark. He stared at her with loathing.

"Lord Bartz," the attorney general said. "Could we have the barricade removed?"

Bartz didn't respond, nor did he remove his stare from Madison.

The attorney general gave up waiting for a response and went to get the help of some enforcers to remove the barricade.

Duncan yelled out, "The attorney general only needs to verify our claim in the lords' records."

There was a cheer from the Adherents as they grasped the positive change in direction.

Bartz turned and whispered to Thorpe. Their stark undertones went back and forth for some time. If only she could hear those words. When Thorpe pulled away, his eyes were wide in surprise.

Thorpe ran to their electric car with some urgency, followed by two other railroad men.

Bartz turned to Madison and Duncan. "This is getting tiresome," he said. "For a long time you have been an annoying mosquito hovering around my ankles, one that would never go away. Now you have landed. Now you could even draw blood. Trust me, if you do, I will swat you."

"Threats are the last refuge of the coward, of the defeated," Duncan said, arms crossed. "Your words don't frighten us, Bartz."

They clearly did scare some people however, as many arms fidgeted among the clerics, and even the armed men around them. Their respective security contingents started closing in on the discussion.

A guardian came running down the street toward the crowd. It ran with an alien gait, its knee joints working opposite to that of a human.

Another guardian turned the corner behind them. They could also see a large truck coming toward the square from down the street.

The crowd booed. Some looked apprehensive. Duncan whispered in the ear of a nearby Quebecois man.

Bartz showed his palms to them. "If you stop this, here and now," he said, "we can grow together. This conflict between us, it doesn't have to exist. This is your last chance, all of you." He looked at Madison, Duncan and Kline in turn. "Fall in line…or we will break the line."

Madison knew something terrible was about to happen. They had finally outplayed Bartz in the council, only to unleash some more deadly manifestation of his power.

Madison tried to reason with him. "You're right Bartz, it doesn't have to be this way. We don't want any conflict, but please look at this objectively. You're letting technology run amuck. It's against everything we Spokes stand for."

The guardians were now standing in front of the crowd. A woman yelled, "Go away, you faceless freak!"

People started throwing things. A small stone careened harmlessly off one of the guardians.

Madison continued her tack with Bartz. "I realize what Gail can do is seductive. She can almost seem like a god. But it's not true that she's only going to act in your interest. You have to understand that Gail is just using you as a means to an end."

Thorpe pulled at Bartz's sleeve, whispering something in his ear, and

Bartz took a step back from them. He said, "you are sounding more and more like a preacher, Lord Banks. I learned long ago that the Credo is drivel, and I'm glad I didn't waste my time with it. I will tell you what I learned when I was young, what I learned that was much more useful. In my first job on the railroad, my boss said to me, 'don't walk in front of a moving train Quenton. It won't stop for you.'"

Bartz took another step back, and another, and then he turned his back on them. Meeker and a number of others fell in behind him. The enforcers around them were looking nervous, their hands hovering over holstered pistols.

A loud voice boomed out from one of the guardians. "Citizens of Seeville, all Adherent gatherings shall be considered riot-inducing, and shall be outlawed. Therefore, this is an unlawful assembly. For your own safety, we are instituting martial law. Please disburse or be prosecuted."

"What is this madness?" Madison yelled after Bartz. "This is a violation of our freedom, of our laws!" But his back remained turned to her as he distanced himself.

A few Adherents broke away from the crowd and tried to smash larger stones and loose bricks against the guardians. A burly man even tried to tackle one of them. It quickly became evident what these men were up against when the guardian threw the man thirty feet. His body dashed off the hood of the truck that had pulled up nearby. Another had his arm broken by the other guardian. He fell to the ground in agony.

Some of the Adherents began to flee. Others stepped cautiously back from the guardians.

Duncan said, "We need to stop these abominations." He had a steely look in his eyes. It was the same look he had at the pavilion during the town hall meeting.

Madison grabbed his arm. "Wait, Duncan."

He could have easily escaped her grasp, but he didn't. "What for? People are getting hurt!"

"That's what they want us to do. We will lose."

The guardians began to advance on the crowd. Another man attacked one of the guardians, this time with a machete. The guardian easily disarmed him and knocked him out with a deftly placed blow to his temple.

"Duncan," Madison pleaded, "we'll have enough martyrs today. If you want your fight, you'll have it, and soon. Right now we need to get these people to safety. There is no telling what the guardians will do to us if we continue to provoke them."

Duncan was breathing heavily, looking back and forth between her and the escalating situation.

Finally he looked at her sidelong, as if he had been cheated in some way. "Fine," he said. He broke her grasp and cupped his mouth to yell at the remaining crowd. "Noble Adherents, now is not our time. Go home, regroup. We need you to fight another day!"

Many of the remaining Adherents began to disperse.

Suddenly, Madison was thrown to the ground by an explosion that rocked the nearby courthouse. People who were still watching the unfolding scene with the guardians started to scurry in all directions. The guardians intercepted those that crossed their path, knocking them down.

Duncan landed next to her. He was holding his head, looking back between the courthouse and the Adherent crowd. He regained his footing and took her arm. "Let's get out of here."

"I couldn't agree more," Madison said.

Benjamin grabbed Madison's other arm, and their party walked quickly away from the raucous square. Looking back, she could see flames bursting through the roof of the courthouse, sending a billow of smoke to slither up into the sky.

She knew the courthouse wouldn't last the day. The fire crews were under Meeker's authority. They wouldn't be in any hurry to save it.

How Bartz had pulled off the explosion she couldn't know. Maybe a bomb had already been planted, or maybe it was a stealth missile. The action made sense though. It would destroy the evidence of his malfeasance. And now that Bartz had shown a complete disregard for the rule of law, it would be fitting for him to raze this noble institution to the ground.

The council game was over. There were no more political moves to make, no more diplomatic angles to pursue. Now was a time for generals. Now was a time for armies to assemble, for wars to be fought.

But wars were fought with soldiers and weapons, and they had none. How could they rally the people to their cause? How could they compete against the promise of progress, against the overwhelming might of the railroad?

Their only hope was an ancient sermon about a faraway place she had never seen and whatever unknown secrets it might hold. But the west remained an intolerable vacuum of news, a deafening quicksand of silence.

The uncertainty would surely consume her. That is, if Bartz and his minions did not rid the world of her first.

Don't Worry About My Heart Rate

A xel knelt down and let the cool water of the stream run through his fingers. It was as clear as the Sentinel said it would be—heavily filtered, all contaminants removed.

He stood up and rejoined the meandering gravel path, walking over the wooden bridge that covered the stream. The soft light from the ceiling had a slightly yellowish tint compared to the real outdoors, and the trees in the recreational area were only seedlings. Otherwise it looked identical to a beautiful park in a city. The grass was green, the courts were surfaced, and the trail around the perimeter was complete.

This was the last piece; the sanctuary was ready for his family. They could have come earlier, but he didn't want their first impression to be a half-baked warehouse filled with bustling droids. With the recreational area ready, it would at least partially compensate for any misgivings they might have about living underground, and far away from other human beings.

Axel returned to the command center, a glass-encased room that looked over the recreational area. *Command* was a bit of a misnomer, as he mostly watched and learned rather than issued any formal direction to the Sentinel. He had yet to disagree with any of the Sentinel's actions, aside from a few cosmetic alterations to the sanctuary itself.

"Are you ready to call Pauline?" The Sentinel asked, anticipating his next move.

"Yes, Nelly. I think it's time."

After some debate, Axel and Grant had resorted to calling the Sentinel Nelly. Axel wanted to call him DaVinci after his favorite renaissance polymath, and Grant had lobbied for Turing as the father of computing. After some debate they settled on a simple short form that made it feel easier to talk to, and made them feel less lonely.

"In less than twenty-four hours we will be ready to initiate the BAU blitz," Nelly said. "I can't be certain of anyone's safety outside of the confines of the sanctuary once the blitz is initiated."

Nelly had been deploying millions of what he called bioengineered avian units, or BAUs, all over the world. They could easily pass for a normal bird. As a result, they had gone undetected by Gail. According to the Sentinel, they held the key to dismantling much of Gail's infrastructure. It was their one best hope to substantially disable Gail and flush her out of worldwide networks. But they needed to be unleashed all at once, or Gail would be able to develop effective countermeasures. That time was almost here.

"I understand," Axel said. "Patch me through to Pauline's satellite phone."

The phone rang, but no one answered. It went to voice mail. "Hi Pauline. It's time to go. Please call me back soon so I can send someone to pick up you and the kids. I love you."

After hanging up the call, Axel asked, "can you tell me where the satellite phone is Nelly?"

"Still in Harrisburg, Pennsylvania."

"Is Harrisburg still safe?"

"Yes, however Gail's deployments are accelerating, and Harrisburg will not be safe for long."

"Can you show me more detail?" Sometimes when Axel wanted to know more, he simply asked for more detail and Nelly would often anticipate what he was looking for.

His seat trembled and he instinctively grabbed at the base of his chair. It was just Nelly sending a report to his phone via sonic burst, something he still hadn't gotten used to. Nelly also projected a map of the country onto the screen in front of him.

Axel looked over the report on this phone. There was no fighting in Harrisburg, and only a few guardian droids had been seen in the area.

In the report Nelly also listed some general information about the BAU blitz, including the number of units deployed by state and country.

There were also some financial details. They were spending an awful lot on leasing heavily guarded hangars at major airports around the country.

"Are these hangars release points for the BAU blitz."

"Yes, Axel."

There was also a single bullet point at the bottom of the page of action items that read *EMPRESS project*.

"What's this about the EMPRESS project?" Axel asked, reading through the report to try to find more context. He found one line item in the budget.

"Whoa, thirty percent? I thought you terminated that project?"

"No Axel, I did not. We had a recent breakthrough that should make it viable."

The EMP Resistant Sentinel System was developed in case Gail had prepared her own EMP-based attacks. Axel didn't have much confidence in the project. He had assumed it had been canned, like thousands of others.

"What happened to those stubby-looking tanks you were developing for EMPRESS?"

"Those didn't pass testing."

"Why not?"

"If you recall, one of most difficult engineering challenges was to have sufficient protection from EMP attacks, while at the same time being able to communicate without using electromagnetic signals of any kind. The EMP would destroy any exposed device, including cameras, receivers, diodes or other emitters. Thus in addition to maneuverability challenges, the units had no ability to know what was around them, or to communicate with external sources."

It sounded like a tough design challenge, to say the least. "I remember," Axel said. "So how did you solve the problem?"

"It would be highly detrimental to our strategy if Gail were to learn about it before we release it."

"But you're going to release it soon, right?"

"Yes. That is when you will learn more."

Axel rolled his eyes. "Fine, fine. It's nice to know you have something working, I guess."

Axel no longer pushed back against Nelly's lack of disclosure. He had long since committed himself to believing that Nelly was acting in good faith. Axel couldn't offer much in the way of input to these projects anyway. He had no standing to question the competence of a superintelligent machine.

In any case, Axel didn't put much stock in the EMPRESS project. All of Axel's hopes were on the BAU blitz. If that didn't work they would lose their one chance to seriously impair Gail. He doubted there would be another.

Axel placed his phone on the desk and glanced up at the heat map of the world. There was so much going on, it was hard to know where to start. "What's up with New York and San Francisco?"

"Frankly, I can't be certain," Nelly said. "Two days ago, all electronic access points went down in those areas, including cellular. I can see via satellite that there are police blockades in place and rioting by small groups. Some people are being taken away. There are hundreds of guardian units roaming the streets."

Nelly showed him two pictures. One was of a spidery droid fastening something to a wall, and another one of the faceless guardian robots herding masses of people.

"I believe Gail is selectively screening the population, looking for specific people. It's likely these metro areas are going to be destroyed, once she finds what she is looking for. In other parts of the world, things are worse. Several countries have been cleared, and are being used solely as manufacturing and development sites for Gail. It is in these parts of the world that bike production is proceeding most rapidly."

"When you say cleared, do you mean…?"

"Everyone is dead."

"How?"

"The populations were first reduced by conflicts orchestrated by Gail, and then machine agents came in and did the rest. The US, Canada, Japan,

and several Western European countries are faring the best, but I anticipate she will soon accelerate her extinction-level efforts there as well. She
has released a deadly neurodegenerative plague in Florida that is spreading
rapidly, as one example. It is helping her destabilize the area, but it will
not be thorough enough or fast enough. She will resort to more destructive means soon. This is why we must initiate the BAU blitz as soon as
possible. The death rate continues to increase exponentially worldwide."

"And still no organized resistance?"

"No. In most places people are still being spoon-fed fake news. The
vast majority believes the conflicts are of human origin. Anyone who
speaks out against Gail is quickly excised from the population."

"But it looks like she is taking thousands of people away from the
cities. Why these people? Are these the people she is silencing?"

"Only a small proportion of those people are being removed because
they suspect Gail's existence. The others are being removed for other reasons. Gail is keeping them alive, in remote locations."

"Why?"

"There may be people that have knowledge or expertise Gail wishes
to extract, to build in more protections for herself or even optimize bike
production. This is because not everything can be deciphered from the Internet or other infiltrated networks. There is still some human know-how
that is useful to Gail. I suspect prominent scientists and technicians with
specific skill sets will be kept alive, at least for a period of time. Secondly,
Gail may be trying to find an even bigger threat than humanity. She may
be trying to find emergent machine intelligences."

"Explain that last point."

"Gail may be able to detect patterns of activity indicative of superintelligence. Gail knows that if another superintelligence became powerful
enough it would, at the very least, compete for resources on different objectives, so it makes sense that Gail would want to destroy it. She may have
already destroyed other emergent machine entities."

"That makes sense, but how can selecting certain people help her? Do
you think she is associating these people with...do you think she might

even know about *you*?"

"She probably knows I exist. I suspect she may even know I emerged from Nadar Corporation, but not much more beyond that. Everything under my control is now far removed from Nadar Corporation by several dozen degrees of separation. But the initial process of reshelling the assets and actions I have taken since then may be a pattern or signature she can detect."

"So you think she is trying to find people that have some tie to that pattern, so that these people can lead her to you."

"Yes, or to other emergent machine entities."

"So that's what happened to Grant," Axel concluded. He remembered the last call from Grant, when the guardian droids had found him, before the explosion took his life. It was only days before he was going to move to the sanctuary for good.

"Actually, I do not believe Grant was taken because Gail tied him to me. It is more likely Grant was selected because he was a prominent computer scientist that could have know-how helpful to Gail. Otherwise Gail would have prepared for his capture with a larger force."

"Yes. That makes sense." Axel felt a pang of guilt for not being able to help Grant or his family. Grant died honorably, fighting, never revealing anything to anyone, including his own family. Axel was the only person left in the world that truly understood his sacrifice.

"Axel, as we were talking I detected a call made to your former number. Your son left a message. I can patch it through via the satellite phone in Pennsylvania to prevent any tracking."

"Please."

Zach's voice came through. People were talking in stark tones in the background, and he was whispering emphatically. "Dad, I need to talk to you. Mom didn't want us to go to your safe house, so she's taking us to a place the guardians told us about. We are getting into the tube soon. She said we shouldn't talk to you about it, but I wanted you to know."

Axel's skin crawled after hearing the message. "This doesn't sound good. Can we pick them up on the tube?"

"No Axel, the tube is completely under Gail's control and heavily defended by guardians. I am sorry to say they are likely lost to you now."

"Whoa. Wait a second. Lost to me? What are you talking about? Are you asking me to leave them for dead?"

"I'm sorry, Axel."

"Don't be sorry, Nelly. Explain yourself, and quickly!"

"The tube has become one of the principal means Gail is using to distribute people out of population centers. Your family members are likely en route to one of the collection areas. I can see some of these areas via satellite."

An image came up of a bird's-eye view of a stadium full of thousands of people. The people were walled in on the playing field. Most were huddled together, looking despondent, but some were trying to scale the walls in vain. Others were fighting. Dead bodies were littered throughout.

"My god, why have you never showed this to me before?"

"I knew it would evoke an emotional response. I did not wish for you to try to save these people. Please understand I am in the process of trying to save most of humanity. If I show my hand to Gail too early, it may jeopardize our overall chance of success."

"What happens when you release the BAU blitz? Will these people be freed then?"

Nelly was quiet.

"Tell me the truth Nelly, all of it!" Axel yelled at the walls around him. "Put that in your damn objective function if you have to. What will happen?"

"With a loss of power to the facility, the people in the collection areas will automatically be terminated via a form of fast-acting nerve gas," Nelly said.

It was the scenario he dreaded more than any other—a situation where saving his family might jeopardize their chances of saving everyone else. Even if it only marginally changed the odds, how does one weigh the lives of your family against billions of others?

He knew what the right answer was, but he couldn't bring himself to admit it.

"How do you know all this?" Axel asked, trying to find any way to ignore the hard truth.

"I have seen people gassed in this way in other countries. Plus, I monitored the construction of these installations via satellite."

It was pointless to challenge Nelly on the facts, of course.

Axel was simmering with rage. He felt like his heart was going to burst through his chest. Everything he had done until now was for his family. Not just the sanctuary, not just the work for Nadar Corporation, but his work in the army, in special ops and for the CIA as well. All the risks he had taken in his life were taken so they could be safe.

He simply could not stay idle here while his family was gassed.

"Axel, I think you should take some time to think about this," Nelly said.

"No. I'm going, and you're going to help me."

"I am not sure you are of sound mind and body."

"I am. Never been sounder."

"Your heart rate is highly elevated."

"That's because I'm fucking human! You are here to help humans, aren't you?"

"Yes, but it has been several weeks since you have left the sanctuary. I am not sure you realize how the situation has matured. You will be attacked. I am not sure if I can defend you. You may compromise the entire mission if you are captured. The mission itself could reveal some of our capabilities. It may even inadvertently reveal the location of the sanctuary."

"Well then, you better make sure I don't get captured, or reveal the location of the sanctuary."

"Unfortunately, no Axel, I cannot allow it."

"Override."

"Axel, that is a serious request. You want to modify my objective function on this matter?"

"Fucking override! Make my orders on this mission part of your objective function from now on. Do you understand?"

"Please stand by. I need to run several million simulations."

For a moment, Axel thought Nelly might deny his request. It was a key test of Nelly's programming, something that could make his objective functions clash. The truth was, Axel didn't know what Nelly would do. It could be that Axel was going to be stuck here, alone for all eternity in the sanctuary, like some useless zoo animal.

Nelly said, "Override granted."

"You're goddamn right it is," Axel said, breathing a sigh of relief.

Axel immediately started packing his bag, the wheels turning in his mind about how he would extract his family, but then he had a better idea. "You know better what I need for this, Nelly. Get it packed and tell me what I have at my disposal. Also give me three proposals for the best extraction plan."

"Of course. I see your heart rate has already decreased. I am glad."

"Don't worry about my heart rate. Worry about the heart rate of my family."

"Yes, Axel. Please proceed to the underground tunnel port. Your bags will be available there, and I will brief you on the way. We will need to shunt you to a nearby airfield."

"On my way."

EVERY SECOND IS A BLESSING. EVERY SECOND IS A CURSE.

"There was nothing else?" Madison asked, looking at the back of the letter to see if there was additional information.

"No, just the one page," Duncan replied. "Literally just dropped out of the sky in front of me when I was using the scope. Do you need the cipher breaker?"

"No, I get the gist of it," Madison said. "Is what she said true about her birthday?"

"Yes, that's the verification we agreed upon. It's definitely from her."

"Warm Springs Pass? Isn't that near the fever lands southwest of Grand Caverns?"

"Yes."

"And nothing else about the sanctuary?"

He raised an eyebrow at her.

"I know, I know, need-to-know and all that. She's worse than you with her letters."

"She learned from the best," he replied, smiling.

Madison sometimes wondered if there was more to Duncan's relationship with Cecile than they outwardly showed. It was hard to say, but she doubted he would consort with a student.

"Do you need anything else from town?" Beatrice interrupted. She had been hovering at the entrance to the den.

"No, not right now. You can go Beatrice, thank you."

Beatrice lingered for a moment longer, then made her way out the front door.

At times Beatrice seemed lost, a foreigner on the estate she had managed for many years. It was understandable. It was no longer an estate but rather a command center, and she had little say in the management of it. Still, they needed her for forays into town. She had to preserve the image that Euclid was still alive. No one would bat an eyelash at Euclid's concubine stocking up for the winter, or even buying eccentric goods.

"We should go downstairs," Duncan said.

"You're right," Madison replied.

They crossed through the first floor and entered the small addition bolted onto the side of Monticello. As they entered the room a dozen of her Yorktown men were preparing food in the galley area.

The addition reminded her of the renovations they had made to Yorktown Hall, but worse. The new structure was a makeshift, gaudy thing—an obscene, boxy growth jutting out of the euro-classical historical structure. It was necessary, though. The house was overcrowded, and not everyone could live underground. Here there was enough space for real work to be done.

It was in the addition that they had built a broad staircase heading into the lower levels below Monticello. Two levels under the main building was where Owen had set up his original work bunker, not much larger than an oversized closet. Now there was a much larger bunker housing most of their electrical components dug out beside the original. Other rooms had been dug out—and were being dug out—by dozens of men. They would shuttle the dirt and detritus out a tunnel on the east side of the estate.

Even deeper still was the more cavernous room they had just completed. Owen had suggested they might need it for new electrical equipment, or anything else for that matter, coming from the sanctuary. For now it was used as a sleeping area, save some desks and the rough model of Seeville they had made with old toys, Legos, and building blocks. It was here where Madison stopped, rubbed her leg, and sat down.

"Everyone out," Duncan yelled into the back of the room. "We need the space." Then he turned up one of the lamps on the table.

Several men were scattered throughout the room, lying on beds. They rose sleepily, grabbed their belongings and hustled out in short order.

"How soon until the Essentialist forces attack?" Madison asked.

"My scout says they are amassing at the border, just beyond the Skyline lookout towers. They're not even trying to conceal themselves. I've heard numbers from thirty to forty thousand. On the Spoke side, there are still hundreds arriving in Seeville every day from as far north as Kingston and as far south as Jacksonville."

"So any day now."

"Not just any day. I suspect as early as tomorrow, at least as far as we're concerned."

"What do you mean?"

"Bartz and Meeker finally found a real job for all the idle roughnecks hanging around Seeville. They are passing a new registration requirement. No more random searches. They are going door-to-door, starting tomorrow, to verify Spoke citizenship, under the guise of finding Essentialist spies."

"Let me guess. You and I will be first on the list."

He nodded. "And you know they'll find any excuse to search our houses, and most certainly Monticello. Even if we manage to hide all the Yorktown folks, they'll find an excuse to escalate the search, to get violent..."

"To take us out altogether. I get it."

Duncan eyed her, gauging her reaction. It was indeed heavy news. She knew time was running out, but now she had a precise number. Unless they went into hiding, they had less than twenty-four hours until the conflict would begin.

She sighed and turned her attention to the model in front of them. "So this has to be what Cecile meant by the artillery guns, right?" Madison asked, pointing to the toy canons in the Barnyard section of the model. It was the only other salient information from the letter. Cecile had written *our number one objective has to be to take out the artillery guns.*

"I know of no other artillery guns," Duncan replied. "Unless there's something we don't know about the other lookout towers."

Madison scanned the model closely. In lieu of building walls around the city, Meeker had erected twelve defense towers around the periphery of the Seeville area. Otherwise they had concentrated on building fortifications around the expanded Barnyard area, which was now about a square mile. There was a two-story wall and guard towers spaced at regular intervals. Access was limited to one major entrance and a train track off-shoot that was rarely opened.

In the center of the Barnyard complex, two massive towers had been erected, one on top of the main Barnyard building, and another separate, free-standing tower just to the south of it. Each tower housed turrets with huge, twin-barreled sixteen-inch guns. They rivaled some of the biggest Old World guns, and might have even used salvaged parts from some abandoned battleship.

One of her Yorktown men had gone to see the test run of these guns. They had obliterated a run-down house far away on the outskirts of town, to the awe of those who had witnessed it.

"So how are we supposed to get to those?" Madison said with some exasperation. "Between Monticello and the rest of the city, we have maybe two hundred men."

"I can try to activate more Adherents, but I don't know how many we can inspire into action. Most of them aren't fighters."

"Against how many? There has to be thousands of enforcers based in the Barnyard area alone."

Duncan nodded.

Madison stared at the fortifications, trying in vain to find a potential weakness.

"Your source—can he get us inside, somehow?"

Duncan squinted. "I don't know. I'm going to be meeting with him tonight at the Broken Spoke."

"Isn't that where we were supposed to meet Owen and Cecile?" Madison opened up the letter again. "Yes, Cecile confirmed the date and time in the letter. It's probably not a good idea to meet at the same place."

"What choice do we have?" Duncan asked.

He was right. The Broken Spoke was the only place that would work. It was out of town, sufficiently far away from any possible bugs Gail might have placed. Duncan wouldn't have time to travel anywhere else. And of course it's not like they could reschedule for tomorrow.

"What happens if your source says no?"

"I guess we'll have to figure something else out. We'll have to be even more aggressive. Try not to worry about it."

"I do worry," she said, looking into his eyes.

As she stared at him, she could hear the sound of her watch ticking. She could feel time slipping away from her. For so long she had been adrift on this river of minutes and seconds, and she could finally hear the waterfall approaching.

Whenever Madison was with Duncan, it seemed like Beatrice, Benjamin, or one of her other men were lurking with some pending question or important report. Some nights, she would try to summon the courage to confront him, but she would always rationalize it away for some other time.

Now there might never be another time.

"Duncan, I...I never did get a chance to talk to you about what happened."

He looked back with his eyebrow raised, as if she were some pretentious schoolgirl deserving of detention. She could tell he wasn't going to make this easy for her.

"Water under the bridge," he said.

"On that train platform in Watertown, when we parted ways. I was emotional, and I...said some things I shouldn't have. I'm really sorry about that."

He looked at her carefully, his face a mask of control. "You're sorry you said some things?"

"You know I respect your faith, Duncan. Just because I don't have the same passion for the Credo, it wasn't okay to insult your beliefs. It wasn't a good reason for us to part ways," Madison said.

"I know it wasn't that," Duncan said, softening his tone. "It was about how to rally the bandit communities together. We disagreed on the best approach. I get it. It's fine, Madison. I'm over it."

"It's true. It seemed like you were trying to get them to follow us like some cult. Now I understand it's just a different path to get to the same goal. You wanted to invoke their passion for justice, whereas I wanted to invoke an academic sense of justice. Both of us wanted to end up with a society built on a strong foundation."

Duncan nodded. "The truth is, Madison, I learned a lot from you, and as I travelled farther north, I often deferred to your methods. The Quebecois, for example, would never have taken me in as an Adherent preacher. It was the New Founder principals they were interested in. They only began listening to my Adherent teachings years later."

"Why did you stay there for so long?" Madison asked.

"Mostly because I had failed elsewhere. It was too hard to rally groups of bandits together in Watertown or Plattsburg. I would set some foundations in place and then some rogue would revert them all back into savagery, erasing any progress I made. Twice I was almost killed for edging in on someone else's political turf. With the Quebecois it was easier because they were already established."

"How so?"

"Maybe it was because that far north, it's too cold to go outside much of the year. As a result they built huge bunkers the people lived and work in for months at a time. This allowed them to easily convert to using Faraday cages so they could have ample electrical heating, refrigerators, ovens, lights and many other things we didn't have. In that respect, they were much more advanced than we were here and open to talking about prudent risks related to technology."

Duncan looked away from her reflectively. "On a social level they were missing something, though. Their leadership was weak and fleeting, and they would easily get into fights with neighboring tribes. When I came they took to the New Founder principals, and it helped them. They banded together to become more like a Spoke town. Some of them even became Adherents. Some of them, like Cecile, thought we needed to do something about the warnings in the Credo, so she took it upon herself to try to find the sanctuary."

"I also learned from you," Madison said, nodding. "I used to hate doing speeches. Well, in Yorktown I gave regular speeches, and it helped me rally them together. So maybe in the end we both succeeded, in some way thanks to each other."

He laughed a cheap laugh. "Funny how things turned out."

She felt hollow. She had not yet arrived at the root of her discomfort. She had let the conversation take a different path. It was time to get it over with.

Madison took a deep breath. "There was one more thing you said to me on that platform before we parted. You said it's your fault." Her voice cracked. "You called me a baby killer."

Duncan's eyes widened in shock. "I don't remember that," he said, shaking his head vigorously. "I couldn't have—"

She held up her hand, holding his tongue. "You did. You may not remember it. It was said among curse words and accusations slung by both of us, many of which were untrue. I called you a zealot, an animal, and a coward. You called me a naïve bitch, an idealist, a heathen, but also a baby killer."

"I don't remember saying that. If I did, I'm so sorry. What happened to Elizabeth—"

He noticed her raising her hand again. "Please," she said, "let me finish. I have waited many years to say this. I want to get it right."

He nodded slowly, ardently.

She said, "We were two ambitious young Seeville lords, risking our reputations with a night of passion. We couldn't admit to the other lords our mistake, never mind to our friends and families. You were mentored by the Okafors. I was mentored by the Lechkys. We were oil and water that magically mixed on one fateful night. And so we fled from the controversy."

"I don't think that's right," Duncan said. "We were leaving because the lords were impotent, because no one cared about the principles of Seeville's founding. Warrick left for the same reasons."

"Yes, it's true," Madison said. "We had many good reasons to leave. I might have left Seeville without being pregnant. The problems were rampant. But the bigger problem was that I was too naïve. I somehow believed running away from my problems could fix them. With Elizabeth growing inside of me, it was so easy to claim that we were protecting her by leaving, while we were really obscuring our own problems to the people around us."

"I don't think—"

"Wait," she interrupted again.

He nodded slowly. He looked frustrated but also nervous. He knew she was going to forge ahead; he knew she was going venture down that painful path.

"And then, when Elizabeth was stillborn, it tore a hole into me, and into you. We tried to find someone to blame, so we blamed each other. This vision of the future we had created for our unborn daughter was shattered. We no longer needed to work together to make that future a reality. Or maybe it was just too painful to see each other every day, and to remember our poor girl…"

She breathed in and forced herself to move on. "Whatever the reason, we chose to not speak about Elizabeth, to ignore the dark spot in our soul, and instead blame our problems on everything else. We chose to blame each other."

He looked away from her, his jaw clenching. When he turned back she could see his eyes were charged with emotion. "What do you want, Madison?" he said, sounding caged, beleaguered.

She spoke slowly, with as much care as she could muster. "It's simple, really. I want the unspoken truth to finally be spoken. I can no longer shun our misfortune, because it's part of who I am. At least with it here, in the open, I can measure it, I can see the trail of tragedy it has left, and I know what it has done to us. At least, with it exposed, I am no longer fearful of it."

He would not look at her. His face was rigid, looking down. A tear paraded down his face. "I'm sorry, Madison," he whispered.

"Thank you Duncan, but I don't want your apology. Nor do I want your forgiveness for *my* spiteful words. No, I only wanted to tell you what has been on my mind for these many years. I bear you no ill will."

She watched him. He wasn't looking at her. His eyes were distant, his mind on a voyage through the past.

She reached out to him and put her hand on his. He awoke from his introspection, looked back at her, and nodded. He covered her hand with his own and pressed down ever so slightly. It was a sign of acknowledgement, a sign of understanding.

She pulled her hand away and left him there.

Her own tears were streaming down her face now. But hers were tears of consolation, not of loss. They were for Duncan's pain, not hers. She had gone through this talk too many times in her mind. She had already cried too many tears for Elizabeth.

As she made her way up the quiet stairs, she heard her watch again. The clock was ticking, harkening their inevitable confrontation. Every second was a blessing. Every second was a curse. She had come to terms with her past, and soon she would know her fate.

THE BROKEN SPOKE

Duncan counterbalanced his weight against the latest bluster of wind and rain, then dismounted from his fidgety mare. He tied her up under an overhang of rusted sheet metal that extended out from the roof of the Broken Spoke. Once out of the torrential gusts of rain, the mare finally began to calm down.

The tavern looked to be pieced together from Old World scrap. The Broken Spoke sign was hanging down vertically from the roof, as if they had run out of nails halfway through putting it up.

Duncan was wary of the place, to say the least. He had heard the owner was an eccentric man who willingly let his customers spit and brawl and vomit. Despite all of this, or perhaps because of it, the place had a clientele consisting mostly of mules making stopover trips between Seeville and Lynchburg. Duncan hoped there would be few of these patrons today, given the inclement weather.

Duncan pushed the creaky front door open to reveal a large square room full of wooden tables. There was an old piano organ built into the back wall. Also at the back were a door and a window, presumably leading to the kitchen.

There was only one man in the place. His face was firmly plastered on a table in the corner, a sprawl of scraggly hair draped on his head, flooding over onto a dirty plate. He looked to be sleeping, even though his hand still firmly grasped a large, half-finished stein of beer.

A slim man with a dirty apron and a plastered smile pushed open the door in the back. "Have yourself a seat, sir," he said in a high-pitched voice. "I'm Ralph, and I'll be right with you." He returned to the back room.

Duncan chose a table where he could watch people enter from the outside but also away from the comatose man in the corner. The waiter came back with a pad and pen.

"Pissy out there, ain't it?" Ralph said rhetorically. "What can I get you?"

"Do you have a menu?"

"No."

"What do you serve?"

"Well, we've got beer, home-brewed, and we've got pizza."

"Is there anything else you'd recommend?"

"No."

"There's nothing else you would recommend?"

"There ain't nothing else, mister. Plain and simple."

"Well, beer and pizza then. But before you leave, can you tell me, who is that man in the corner? Is he all right?"

"Don't know him personally-like. He came in about an hour ago, had a beer and pizza then passed out. Seemed a bit out of sorts." Ralph shrugged, smiled, and turned to go back to the kitchen.

Duncan stood up and approached the man at the other table. Maybe he could give him some change to help him on his way. It would be better if they had the tavern all to themselves.

He was about to place his hand on the man's arm when the door creaked open. Venter came in, with two other mules trailing behind. They looked nervous, probing the room with cynical eyes.

Duncan decided not to disturb the man at the table. Best not to cause a scene.

"Thank you for coming," Duncan said, walking over to greet the mules at the door. "Please," he said, gesturing to his table.

Venter took his hand first. His face was freckled from too much sun, and he had a red beard. Duncan had first met Venter in one of his Adherent gatherings. Apparently Venter had been talking with Alastair before he was imprisoned. He seemed dedicated to the cause, but frankly, he was a bit slow.

"And you must be Chester," Duncan said, taking the man's hand behind Venter. He had a beard with hints of gray and a firm grip—the grip you would expect of a veteran wrench. "I've heard a lot about you. Almost a legend." The man seemed unimpressed by the comment, but he nodded regardless.

"And you are?" Duncan offered his hand to the third man.

"Arsalan," the man said. He looked down at Duncan's hand before he took it, as if it might be covered in poison ivy. His face was like a russet stone, and he had a sickle-shaped scar extending from his chin to his right ear. This was a not a soft man, by any means.

After they had settled into their chairs, Duncan leaned into them. "I'll get right to the point. You're here because you're worried about the abuse of power in Seeville, and the blatant disregard Bartz and Meeker have for the Credo. You're right to be concerned. It's only going to get worse."

The three men nodded cautiously, still scanning the room warily.

"Bartz and Meeker are being influenced by an Old World machine named Gail," Duncan explained. "It was found when the satellite fell from the sky, and it's been behind virtually all of the recent changes in Seeville. If we don't stop the railroad and this machine, it will be the Detonation all over again. I asked Venter to arrange this meeting because I know you want to help, just as I want to help, as both a lord and citizen of Seeville."

Arsalan was frowning. "Look mister, as far as I'm concerned being a lord just means you're a clever liar. And yes, I for one have no love for Bartz and his bunch, that's for sure. Already, too many mules have died because of them. That's why we came to meet with you. But a machine named Gail?" Arsalan turned to Chester. "This one sounds like a loon to me. I told you, these Adherents, they have a loose pedal, every one of them."

Chester seemed oblivious to Arsalan's question. He kept his eyes focused on Duncan.

Venter responded to Arsalan, "Wait just a minute, Arsalan. Let's hear the man out. He has a big following among Adherents. Lord Jones, why don't you tell us more? Why do you need our help, specifically?"

"Well, we could certainly use more of the mules on our side. According to Venter, you both have sway with the other mules and wrenches.

And we need someone who can get inside the Barnyard."

Arsalan laughed. "Of course you do. Have you looked at the place? Have you seen those guns? It's a fucking fortress. Good luck with that." Arsalan sat back in his chair and crossed his arms.

Again, Chester said nothing, still interrogating Duncan with his eyes.

Arsalan stood up from his chair. "Well, this was a waste of time. Let's get out of here. I've heard enough."

"Sit down," Chester said softly.

"Can't you see that the man's bent?" Arsalan said.

"Sit down!" Chester yelled at Arsalan, his face igniting with emotion.

Arsalan was surprised by Chester's tone. "Fine, fine," he said, and then he sat back down in his chair, one eye on Chester.

Ralph came out of the kitchen carrying a small pizza and a beer for Duncan. Steam wafted off the pie, flavoring the air with the aroma of freshly baked cornmeal dough.

"Welcome, gents. You want the same?" he asked.

"Sure," Venter said, nodding.

Ralph smiled and left.

"Who's with you?" Chester asked when the waiter was gone.

"A couple hundred Yorktown men," Duncan said. "Plus I'm trying to rally as many Adherents as possible."

Chester's eyes darted back and forth, and then he asked, "So maybe three or four hundred, if you're lucky?"

"Mincemeat," Arsalan quipped.

"We'll have the element of surprise, and we don't plan on sticking around the Barnyard for long."

Chester seemed to be doing more mental gymnastics. Then he squirmed in his chair and shook his head. "Pointless," he said.

Duncan was hard-pressed to argue with him. He had to think of some other angle. They did come all this way, so clearly they were concerned. While Arsalan looked intransigent, Chester, in particular, was at least seriously considering it. There had to be a way to convince him.

A short, roundish woman came out of the kitchen, bowed to them and said, "Gentlemen, I'm Betsy, this evening's entertainment. Enjoy!" She sat down at the organ and began playing an old mule folk song that sounded vaguely familiar to Duncan.

♫ *Hey, now, Raleigh's not for you.*
   Cause my love is like a rusty knife. ♫

It was uncomfortably loud, making their discussion difficult.

♫ *Cause you can fix one flat but not two.* ♫

"No thanks!" Duncan yelled into her back, but his voice was lost in the song.

"Listen," Chester said, elevating his voice, "I've seen too many defy the railroad and get turned into hamburger. I spoke with Lord Henneson before, and you all know what happened to him. So tell me how it's different this time. Why should we trust that you can pull this off?"

Betsy was hitting the chorus of the song, nearly drowning out Chester's words.

♫ *Yeah, I'm a bent-up Seeville mama!*
   Yeah, I'm a bent-up Seeville mama! ♫

The outside door flung open, cascading a sheet of water on the floor. A hooded woman wearing a heavy coat came in, the bulge of a weapon clearly visible underneath. Duncan and the three mules slowly pulled their pistols out. Venter's knuckles were white as his other hand gripped the tabletop.

The woman dropped her hood, showing raven hair with a streak of blue.

Duncan signed in relief. "Everyone don't worry. Calm down. This is Cecile—she is Quebecois—from one of our northern Spoke allies. She's with me."

The three mules slowly put away their guns but still eyed Cecile carefully. Cecile looked around the room, frowned at the woman playing the music, and then walked over to them. She pulled something out from her coat and dropped it on the table. It was about the size of a shoebox. It had four propellers, two of them warped, and the middle looked to be caved in and covered in soot.

"*Attention*," Cecile said. "Gail's eyes and ears are everywhere. We found this one out on the main road and took it down."

The mules glared at the defunct machine with a mixture of confusion and repugnance.

Duncan said, "Cecile, I'm so glad you made it back. I have many questions, but first let me introduce you to—"

The outer door opened again. In walked another hooded figure in a large coat. A flash of lightning lit up the night behind him before the door shut again.

Betsy was singing a more upbeat song, seemingly inspired by the inclement weather.

♫ *It's coming down on you.*
It's coming down on me.
You know, Monty's got to go too. ♫

The man unhooded himself, revealing a tired looking youth with a spotted cheek. It was Owen.

"We're all clear," Owen said, as he walked over to the table.

Arsalan suddenly burst out of his chair and tackled Owen, jutting a knife toward his throat and pushing his face into the floor. "I know this one!" Arsalan exclaimed. "He's with the railroad."

"Whoa, whoa!" said Duncan, throwing his chair to the floor as he stood up.

"No, he's not!" said Cecile, her hands out in a gesture of calm.

Chester didn't move. He looked like he had seen a ghost. Venter had his gun out in his hand, and his head was pivoting at everyone in the room.

Owen managed to squeeze a few distorted words out onto the floor in front of him. "If you get off me...I can explain."

"Why should I?" Arsalan asked.

Ralph came out from the back with three more beers. Everyone froze in place. Ralph glanced obliquely at the two men tussling on the floor as he placed the beers on the table. "The rules are simple. You make a mess, you clean it up. You break something, you pay for it." He smiled and said, "cheers," then turned and left to go back to the kitchen.

> ♫ *You got a century to do and it's no fair.*
> *Your load is heavy and boss wants it dry, but of course...*
> *Louie doesn't care and he's got no underwear.* ♫

"Explain yourself, Owen," Chester said.

Arsalan loosened his grip around Owen's neck enough so he could speak. They all leaned in to hear Owen over the loud organ notes strumming behind them.

"They stabbed me," he said. "They stabbed me in the leg and left me for dead in Yorktown."

"Yorktown?" Arsalan said. "What the hell is he talking about? I'll gut you right here and now—"

"No, you won't," Chester said. "Let him go. I was in Yorktown with him. I believe him. He's not like the others."

> ♫ *You know, Monty's got to go too.*
> *You know, Louie doesn't care about you.* ♫

Slowly, Arsalan took his knife away from Owen's throat. Owen massaged his neck and put some distance between him and Arsalan.

"Everything is clear outside, Cecile," Owen croaked, keeping his eyes on his assailant. Owen took a seat near Duncan.

"Okay, *ca suffit*, enough playing around," Cecile said. "What's this all about, Duncan?"

The noise in the room was grating on Duncan's nerves, as if the tension wasn't enough already. He looked over to the back of the room and the man in the corner was still in the same position, slumped over his plate, his hair strewn into the crumbs of his meal. Was he dead? How could he stay asleep with all this racket?

Duncan tried to think of the easiest way to explain the situation. "Things are falling apart in Seeville. We need these mules to help us get into the Barnyard as early as tomorrow, to...accomplish the objective you identified in your letter. But they want to be sure we are the right horse to win. They want to be sure we have a good chance of being successful."

Cecile raised her eyebrows. She took a chair and straddled it, the back of it facing them.

"*D'accord.* Well, beyond whatever Duncan has told you, we have about a hundred more Quebecois coming in on the train tomorrow, although they may be too late."

"Too late?" Arsalan asked.

Ralph came out of the kitchen again. "Everything good here? Your food should be ready soon."

"A couple more beers, please," Duncan said, "and is there any way we could ask Betsy to take a break? We're trying to have a conversation..."

Duncan trailed off as he saw Venter wince. Arsalan also shook his head and interjected, "You don't want to do that."

"What do you mean?" Duncan asked.

Ralph's courteous smile vanished. He said, "Let me get the manager to see what he says." Then he reached under his apron and pulled out a double-barreled, sawed-off shotgun and leveled it at Duncan. The mules recoiled from the table, grating their chairs on the floor as they pushed back.

Duncan threw up his hands. "Whoa, whoa!"

"This here is the manager," Ralph said. "And he says we have another rule here at the Broken Spoke. No matter the mess, no matter who's here, the show must go on. You got it?"

Betsy was belting out a new song in the background.

♫ *She might look like a plant, and he might talk to his cattle.* ♫

"Fine, fine." Duncan said, his eyes wide, his hands still up. He felt like his ribs might shatter, his heart was pumping so hard.

♫ *It's a magical place till you take a big whiff.* ♫

Ralph nodded, re-holstered his shotgun on his leg under his apron, regained his servile smile, and returned to the kitchen.

♫ *So head on into the valley and do the Essentialist rattle.* ♫

"Just wait until the cat comes out," Venter said.

"The cat?" Duncan said.

"Never mind," Venter said.

"You were saying..." Chester said with some impatience.

"I was saying I'm not sure we can wait another day," Cecile said. She looked to Duncan, who nodded back to her in confirmation.

"You want us...to help you into the Barnyard...*tomorrow?*" Arsalan asked with incredulity.

"Yes. Let me finish," Cecile said. "Do you know about Gail?" She glanced at Duncan again, who again nodded. "Okay, so you know the real threat here. Gail has been driving all these changes. The only way to counter her is with a similar force. We have found one. We are still figuring out what this new machine can do for us, but without it we will surely be defeated."

"Another machine?" Arsalan rolled his eyes. "Come now. If you want to fool us, you could at least try a bit harder."

Cecile sighed. "You have heard of the sanctuary, yes? It's real. We have found it. That's where we have found this machine, where we have awakened it. It has given us advanced weapons, and means of instant communication."

"What do you call this...machine?" Chester asked with a skeptical tone.

♫ Do the Essentialist rattle! Yeah! ♫

"It calls itself the Sentinel," Cecile said, wincing at the grating singing behind her.

Chester and Arsalan were clearly unimpressed, but Venter had been listening with interest. He seemed to be accessing some distant memory. He said, "The sons of the sentinel shepherded the righteous founders to the sanctuary—the sons of the sentinel smote the obsessions of the Old World into ruin."

It was part of an old Credo passage. Duncan never referenced it because its fantastical nature tended to make people skeptical of the whole faith.

Arsalan and Chester were looking at Venter as if he had just broken wind in their general direction. "More Adherent nonsense. This is folly," Arsalan said, directing his words to Chester. "We should go."

Cecile shrugged. "I'm not expecting you to believe me. And I'm not going to sit here and tell you the odds are in our favor. We have little evidence we can provide of the Sentinel's existence, other than maybe this downed drone, and these communicators." She flashed an object that looked like an Old World smartphone. "But I'm going to tell you we're the only chance you've got. You won't get another one. None of us will."

A black and white cat pushed through a cat door at the back and pranced over to the organ. It jumped onto Betsy's lap. Betsy stopped performing for a moment, giving everyone a welcome reprieve. "Potsie, you little sweetie," she said, rubbing noses with the cat. "Are you ready, dear?" She brought a piece of catnip from her pocket and fed it Potsie.

Chester was massaging his face. "I admit there is something to this Gail story. I've seen enough to know she's real. But I'm sorry, fancy machines or not, I just don't get how our helping you can make any difference. I've been on the foraging missions. I know what they have. I've also seen what the guardians can do. And I know how many people Meeker has under his thumb. We'd need thousands to even stand a chance. I'd rather not piss my life away for no reason, even if there's not much of it left."

"Okay now for some of Potsie's favorite gems!" Betsy announced. She had turned on a lamp encased in a perforated metal frame. It hung on a hook next to the piano and it swung back and forth, shining a kaleidoscope of colored rays of light onto the wall. Potsie jumped down from her lap and started to swat its paws at the spots of light projected on the wall. Betsy laughed with glee and resumed her performance. She slowed and sped up the rhythm of the song, trying to sync her music with the cat's maneuvers. She was wholly unsuccessful.

♫ *Hello my darling...hello my baby...hello my ragtime...gal.* ♫

The outer door swung open again, dumping another sheet of rain on the floor. Three cloaked figures entered. Duncan looked at Cecile nervously, while the mules again clutched at their weapons. Cecile put her hand up in a gesture of calm.

The lead figure unhooded himself, revealing a slim youth with a grave face. The other figures' heads remained cloaked under their hoods as they scanned the room.

"Talon, *dieu merci,*" Cecile said. She stood up to greet him, looking relieved. The two of them shared some whispers, and Cecile guided the new party to an adjacent table. The two cloaked figures then removed their hoods. One was a blonde woman with dark rings under her eyes and a red nose, and the other was a man with close-cropped hair and Asian features. He had a thick bandage around his neck.

The Asian man showed visible discomfort with the setting. He probed the eyes of the people around them and then looked back at the singing woman and dancing cat.

♫ *If you refuse me, honey, you lose me,*

And you'll be left alone, oh baby,
Telephone, and tell me, tell me,
Tell me I'm your very own, oh, ♫

Ralph came out of the back room, smiling. "Welcome, welcome! I didn't expect so many guests this fine evening. What a pleasant surprise! What should I get for you?"

"Just another pizza. Thank you very much." Duncan ordered quickly, before anyone else could react. Best not let the new guests interact with Ralph. Who knows what would happen if he brandished his shotgun again.

"Spiffy. I'll be out with your pizzas soon." Ralph smiled and returned to the kitchen.

"Who are these people? What's going on here?" Chester asked, his words thick with frustration.

♫ *Hello my ragtime, summertime gal,*
Send me a kiss by wire, by wire. ♫

"This is Talon," Cecile said, pointing to the slim youth. "He helped us get into the sanctuary. And this is Rosalie, a Merchant Merc, and this is..." Cecile seemed reluctant to introduce the last man.

Duncan knew Cecile well. Cecile was rarely apprehensive about anything.

"My name is Nobura," the man with Asian features said, holding his neck. His voice was hard to make out over the piano in the background. His voice also sounded distorted, like he was trying to talk with pebbles in his throat. "I am an Essentialist general."

"What the fuck?" Arsalan exclaimed. No longer comfortable with clutching his pistol by his side, Arsalan raised it onto the table, pointing it in the direction of Nobura. Venter was also visibly disturbed by the introduction, his hands tensing around his weapon. Chester's frown only deepened further.

In response to Arsalan's presentation of his weapon, Talon slowly placed his own over the table, pointed back at Arsalan.

Nobura was unfazed by the escalation. "I have come here to parlay," he said. "I would not be here but for the urgings of my pupil, Talon. But my patience is thin and waning with the night. Tell me why I have come to"— he looked back at the cat dancing against the wall—"a place such as this."

"Well, look at him. Happier than a pig in shit," the blonde woman said, pointing at the dancing cat and clapping along. She seemed to be the only one getting any sort of enjoyment out of the situation.

For a few moments heads swiveled as everyone tried to figure out who was going to lead the discussion. Finally Talon ventured, "I told the general we would support his leadership of the eastern Essentialists, if he would help us."

The singer was finishing a long crescendo. Her voice rang out loudly.

♫ *Tell me I'm your very own! Tell me that I'm your own!* ♫

As soon as the refrain finished, Cecile asked, "Well general, can you help us?"

Nobura said, "Would you trust a stranger in a foreign land, in the lands of your historical enemy?" He stood up from his chair and paced around the group, looking each of them up and down in turn.

"I understand the facts and risks as presented to me," Nobura said. His voice came out as a harsh whisper, and he clutched at the bandage around his throat at times to improve the intonation. They all had to lean in to hear him, both tables tilting in tandem with each step the general took. "I even understand the threat this Gail represents. And I control half the Essentialist army. I could engage twenty thousand men to this cause, if I thought it worthy."

He stopped pacing and stared them down. "But frankly, the only one of you I trust, who I know is honorable, is Talon. But he is young. He could be fooled. He could have been lied to."

The singer had started another, slower song, and fed Potsie another catnip leaf.

♫ *Some days I think we might get by,*
  But then I think oh my...oh my...oh my. ♫

Nobura began making another circuit around the table. He glanced over at the cat dancing on the wall, and the woman playing the organ daintily. "And now I am in this forlorn, peculiar place—a place where it is so noisy one cannot even hear one's own voice. I see a faction of misaligned people, more inclined to shoot one another than to drink at the same table, and I find myself wondering, are these people one can trust?"

♫ *I like to think that we are doin' all right,*
  But then at night, oh my, at night,
  I'll torch that bed of yours I might. ♫

"Hardly," Nobura said, answering his own question. "I will give you this, however. One needs to reach far down the throat of disbelief to regurgitate these fanciful tales."

As Nobura's gaze continued to linger around the room, his brow furrowed slightly, and he turned away from them. The man in the corner seemed to have caught his eye.

Nobura drifted over to the distant table, drawn by some unknowable curiosity.

"Don't worry about him," Duncan said, raising his voice over the song. "He came in more than an hour ago, ate and passed out. He's been out cold ever since."

♫ *Morning comes, and you're still there,*
  But then I think oh my...oh my...oh my. ♫

Nobura did not heed Duncan's words. He drifted ever closer, and he moved his hand to hover over the man's head. Then all of a sudden, he grabbed a tuft of scraggly hair and lifted his face off the table for all to see.

It was Mehta.

Mehta's eyes were startled open. He ejected fragments of half-eaten pizza from his mouth, spraying Nobura's face. Despite this, Nobura managed to slam Mehta's head back down into the table. At the same time, Nobura deftly snatched a knife from his side and cut with a backhand toward Mehta's neck.

At the last instant, Mehta pulled his head back with such violence that the hair in Nobura's hand was torn off. Mehta's inertia made him fall into the back wall of the room. There he shook his head, trying to shake off his coma and make sense of what was going on.

Nobura dropped the torn hair and paced in Mehta's direction, wielding his knife menacingly.

How was Duncan supposed to convince these people to help? It seemed there was no end to the interminable distractions and surprises. He bolted out of his chair. "What's this all about? Stop it!" he said.

"This is none of your business," Nobura said. "This man's death is overdue."

Cecile had also risen and was approaching the two combatants, who were now circling each other. "Wait, wait now. Let's talk about this," she said. "Mehta has helped us. We could use him."

Mehta grabbed a table by the legs and lifted it up in the air. Unsure of Mehta's next move, Nobura stepped back. Mehta then smashed the whole table against the wall. On the second smash, one of the table legs separated. He dropped most of the splintered wood on the floor and wielded the table leg, shifting it back and forth between his two hands.

Ralph called out from the back of the room. "You'll have to pay for that!"

Ralph didn't appear to be put out by the altercation. He simply watched them with interest, shotgun ready and in hand. Betsy also seemed to think this was some sort of perverse theater for her enjoyment. She held Potsie and petted the cat's head, watching closely as the scene unfolded.

Nobura said, "This man stuck me in the neck with a hen bone. He is the reason I will talk like a swarm of bees for the rest of my days. He also broke the nose of his own friend and colleague." Nobura gestured toward the blonde merc. "Someone he worked with for many years. Then he fled like a coward, killing several men along the way. He is a beast, without honor. He needs to be put down."

Mehta laughed heartily. "I may be a beast. I won't deny that. I have been called much worse. But you are the one without honor here. I fought back only after you threatened to kill me. Any sane man would have. Any man with half a brain would have run rather than be put down like a gelded horse."

"Enough!" Cecile screamed, waltzing in between Mehta and Nobura. "Every second that goes by we lose ground to Gail. Whatever happened between you two is irrelevant!"

"She's right, you know," Mehta said, tilting his head, a glint in his eye. "You can spend your time exacting your vengeance, general, but ask yourself, how will it help you to kill me? How will it help your precious Prefectorate?"

Cecile said, "General, if you can help us, we stand a chance. More will flock to our side." She gestured at the mules, who had their chairs pushed back against the opposite wall. They were making frequent glances for the exit. "We may even have a decent shot."

"I will not engage with anyone I do not trust," Nobura said, his eyes still fixed on Mehta's tense body lurking behind Cecile.

"But you trust Talon, don't you? If you give us time, we can prove ourselves to you, as he has," Cecile said.

Nobura said, "There is no time for that, and you know it."

Mehta said, "Ask yourself, Shinogi, if you would do the same as I did in your shoes. If what I did is not honorable in your Prefectorate, then piss on your honor."

Nobura's face went lobster red. Mehta's words were doing nothing to soothe his anger. Instead, he looked about to explode with rage. "Out of my way, woman," Nobura wheezed, gesturing at Cecile to step aside, "unless you wish to perish along with your friend."

Before Nobura could make his move, Talon slipped in front of him and knelt down. He bowed his head to the floor, eyes closed.

For a moment, it looked like Nobura might strike him down, despite the fact he was unarmed, such was the rage on his face. "Talon, you... stubborn boy," was all he managed to say.

Nobura stared at Talon's prostrated form for some time. It seemed he could not bring himself to even move around him. Gradually, Nobura's breathing moderated, and his face lost its crimson color. He held his chin for a time, with the whole room watching. Then slowly, Nobura turned, stepped forward, and sat down in the middle of the room.

"Enough words," Nobura whispered softly, "they only provide a distraction. I need to concentrate." He folded his legs and put his hands on his knees. Then he closed his eyes, and took one long, deep breath.

The room was full of confused looks. "What's he doing?" Duncan asked.

"He will decide in seven breaths," Talon explained, rising from the ground.

Betsy looked disappointed. She turned back to the organ and began playing again. It was a slower song, more ominous sounding.

♪ *Sister, swimming softy in the lake,*
  I could drown, with every stroke you make. ♪

She struck the lamp with her foot and the cat resumed its fidgety dancing.

Nobura took another long deep breath.

"This is madness!" Arsalan said. "What are we still doing here?" he said to Venter and Chester. He stood up and motioned emphatically toward the door.

Venter and Chester stood up slowly, guns in hand.

"Just wait. It won't be long now," Duncan said.

"Wait until he takes seven breaths?" Arsalan said. "This was suspect

when we first came in, but now it's outright insanity. And this fucking…
singing and…cat." he put one finger to his temple and spun it in a circle.
"No, this is going nowhere fast."

Nobura took another long, deep breath.

Arsalan started moving toward the door. Venter followed, shrugging
at Duncan in some sort of apology. With some reluctance, Chester also
moved to follow.

♫ *I'm not sure how we got here, I ask your sickly face,*
  Uncle death, why invite me to this place. ♫

When Arsalan opened the door, two men were standing there, dressed
in black. They were Cecile's men. Arsalan tried to bolt through them but
they managed to grab his arms and hold his position.

"Let us through!" Chester yelled, pointing his weapon at them, and
then swiveling around to point it into the room.

Nobura took another long, deep breath.

Duncan ran past Chester and Venter. He grabbed Arsalan from the
back, pulling him on top of his own body, with the two Quebecois men
falling on top of Arsalan, sandwiching him. When they unscrambled their
limbs Arsalan was pinned by the Quebecois men.

♫ *Have no fear, the end is near,*
  Let's get together, and have a beer. ♫

The door remained open. Lightning flashed. Thunder followed.

Nobura took another long, deep breath.

When Duncan recovered from the tussle, he saw that Venter had his
pistol pointed at him. He slowly drew his own gun and pointed it back
at Venter. In the room around them, Chester had his weapon trained on
Mehta, and Owen had his weapon trained on Venter. Talon had joined
Nobura in meditation. The blonde merc had somehow grabbed Cecile
and held her in a headlock, with her own weapon pointing toward her

temple. "Insurance, you know," she said, smiling a gap-toothed smile.

Arsalan continued to wrestle against the two Quebecois men that held him. "Let us go, damn it!" Then he yelled at Chester and Venter. "Just fucking shoot them!"

♪ *Brother you smile and your tongue speaks,*
  But the fade, it reaches, and my mind leaks. ♪

Ralph returned with two more pizzas, adding them to the untouched food and drink on the table. "Bon appetite!" he said with delight. Ralph then clasped his hands together and looked around the room. "How is everything?" he asked.

No one answered.

"Great!" Ralph said, and he made his way back to the kitchen.

Nobura took another long, deep breath.

Duncan noticed that Mehta was slowly inching toward the barrel of Chester's weapon. He still held the table leg in his hand. Otherwise the room was frozen in time. They were wax statues in a museum of violence, foreshadowing any number of grisly outcomes.

All of a sudden, Betsy accidentally knocked the swinging lantern with her elbow in a fleeting moment of musical passion. The spots of light broke free from their casual pendulum and spiraled throughout the room. Potsie went into a frenzy, running and jumping to claw at a spot of light that had landed on Venter's chest. Venter was so surprised he pulled the trigger of his gun. The shot hit the wall on the opposite side of the room, but not before first nicking Duncan's ear.

"For fuck's sake," Duncan said, holding his bleeding ear. Somehow he managed to hold firm, to not pull the trigger.

The gunshot sent the cat scattering back into the kitchen. Guns were pushed forward even more pointedly toward their intended targets.

"This is so...fucking...bent." Chester said, shaking his head, darkness in his eyes. He seemed to be entering a state of slow hyperventilation.

♫ *Have no fear, the end is near,*
  It's death again, pulling up the rear. ♫

Heads swiveled. Lightning struck again, this time closer to the tavern. Thunder rumbled through the room while taught fingers hovered on triggers. Betsy snorted with laughter and then continued singing.

♫ *Have no fear, the end is near,*
  Let's get together, and have a beer. ♫

Nobura took another long, deep breath, and opened his eyes.

FIRE AND GASOLINE

The outskirts south of Seeville were not frequented by many. Old World developments remained in various states of disrepair, some burned out, some collapsing. Those that travelled through were mostly Spoke vagabonds and sometimes even bandits. No one paid them any attention. It was here that Mehta hiked in the darkness, trying to find the rendezvous Duncan had described.

Mehta reached the top of a hill. A light shone out about a hundred yards away, illuminating a building. The area matched Duncan's description, insofar as one could make it out in the darkness.

Mehta took out his scope to examine the building in more detail. It was an Old World single family dwelling, like many of the buildings he had lived in growing up, before they had burned Asheville to the ground. The second level was mostly intact, but the first floor was no more than two parallel walls. There was a small campfire fire next to it, where the foundations of an old garage used to be. There was also a tent set up in the foreground.

There was movement as well. Someone was drawing wood from a pile under the sheltered part of the building.

Duncan had said it was owned by an Adherent follower but deserted long ago, and no one else was supposed to be here. Perhaps this was a squatter? Or maybe one of Meeker's rangers?

Mehta walked the rest of the way cautiously, limping at times over the undulating topography. When he was closer, he could tell the figure was a woman. She paraded around, oblivious to the fact that she was being watched. When she stopped to sit by the fire, he simply walked up behind her and lifted her up, one hand on her mouth.

He let her squirm. She tried to elbow him, but her arms were tightly pinned to her body. "I'm going to give you a minute to calm down," Mehta said, "then I want you to tell me who you are and who you work for. If you call out, or run, I'll snap your neck."

He gave her a moment to consider her options then took his hand away from her mouth.

"I don't understand how you can be so big and still be so quiet," Flora said.

Mehta dropped her to the ground. "Figures it would be you," he said.

She rubbed her arms and got up off the damp ground, returning to a slab of rotted lumber she had been sitting on.

He dropped his pack and navigated around a nearby puddle to find a suitable stone to sit on. "So?" he asked.

"So what?" she said.

"What are you doing here?"

"Nice to see you too," she said, sarcastically.

He glowered at her.

She said, "Well, I heard from Talon and Duncan that you were here. I'm going to help with the assault tomorrow. On the south towers."

Mehta bristled. "No, no, no. Why don't you find a hideout, or go back to Monticello? We can handle this."

"No way."

Mehta sighed, then threw up his hands and shrugged. "I have long since given up trying to reason with you."

Mehta pulled the skewered squirrel from his pack and began preparing it for the fire. He used some of the Quebecker marinade he had taken a liking to. Meanwhile Flora walked away and came back with a pot. She stacked stones up into precarious towers on either side of the fire so they could suspend the pot over the flames. Flora added some water from her canteen to the bottom of the pot, then Mehta dropped the squirrel in next to the potatoes.

When the pot was set to boil they ate some fresh beans while they waited. Occasionally the fire would spit and wheeze when one of the wetter logs would begin to burn, coughing up white smoke. Mehta massaged his leg and tended to the fire.

Flora fidgeted on the other side. "Can I ask you something?" she said.

"If I say no, I doubt it would stop you," Mehta replied.

"Why did you place me at Monticello, with Euclid?"

"It met the requirements of Thorpe's contract. It was a discrete place, and we got a good price."

"Nothing else? Did you know about Granger being there?"

He reckoned she must know the truth, or she wouldn't have asked. He could only imagine how she would turn this against him. "Yes, I did. Or at least, I was pretty sure he was there. I know, I know. I should have told you beforehand. I should have warned you."

"No. That's not why I'm asking."

"Oh."

He thought she might elaborate, but she never did.

A few minutes later, the food was ready. Mehta shaved some squirrel meat off onto Flora's plate while she collected a potato. He took the remainder of the carcass and a couple of potatoes for his own.

"Back on Montalto," Flora said, "I may have misheard you, but I thought you said you signed another contract."

"I think you misheard me. In any case, it was a long time ago. It's none of your concern," Mehta said, trying to avoid another rabbit hole.

She ignored his response. "But I kept wondering...who with? And then Owen pointed out how you protected me at the dish, and how you risked your life to save Talon. And now I see you even tried to connect me with Granger."

"So what, Flora? This is a pointless discussion."

"The only thing that made sense is you have a contract to protect me. But I asked for nothing, I signed nothing, I am paying you nothing. Why?"

"You're seeing ghosts in the fire Flora. You need to get some sleep. Tomorrow will be a long day, if we can live through the whole of it."

"Why, Mehta?"

"You're delusional."

"Why?'

He couldn't stop her incessant questioning. Flora would never check her belligerence on this. Sure, Flora had her foibles, but when it came to persistence, she was a mountain goat.

"Why?" Mehta asked. "I don't know Flora. Maybe because you got dealt a bad hand. Or maybe because it was the only thing that felt like justice to me, real justice, and not just honoring a contract, but honoring one that brought balance instead of tilting the world in favor of tyrants like your Curator or assholes like Bartz."

He thought Flora would appear dismissive of his explanation, or even ridicule him, but she was listening in earnest.

He continued, hoping to say enough to finally be done with her inquisition. "In some way it made me feel normal again, like I did before Asheville. It gave me relief from the dead men and woman that haunt me. So yeah, I signed a contract, to protect you, simply because you deserve a break from the world's cold hand on your back, pushing you into the dirt."

Mehta shook his head after he said it. It sounded silly when spoken aloud, despite the truth of it. "And I honestly don't care if you didn't ask for it. I don't care if you don't like it. You can go and throw your life away if you want, like you seem so intent on doing. That's out of my control. But know this, I will try to stop you."

Mehta got up from his chair, not bothering to wait for a response from Flora, and went for a piss. Then he came back to finish off his dinner.

"It's late, we need to get some rest," he reiterated as he returned to his stone chair.

She was staring at him across the fire. Her eyes were glazed, distant.

"I'm sorry, Mehta," Flora said. Her words were a quiet, wispy thing. "I'm sorry about what I did, and what I said. I've never met anyone that would protect me for...nothing in return. Never had anyone linger who did not take advantage of me. I presumed the worst, and I blamed you for my troubles. I was wrong."

She grimaced. "And I'm not sure why we clash. It's like we're oil and water. Or maybe, I'm a spark, a lit fire, and you're gasoline. Together, we're a dangerous combination."

Mehta was surprised by Flora's show of emotion. He tried to think of some words of consolation, but this kind of conversation was foreign to him. He could think of none.

Her face contorted further. "I even told them to leave you there, in Grand Caverns. I told them to leave you there to die."

Mehta tried to wave away her words with his hand. "Don't worry," he said, "you did the right thing to leave me. Besides, I wouldn't want you to try to save me. It would be against my contract."

This only seemed to make her break down further. Her chest began to heave, and her eyes brimmed with tears.

Mehta remained at a loss. He didn't know what he could do to comfort her. His words weren't helping. He worried he had somehow made matters worse again.

Gradually, Flora got herself together. She wiped her eyes and nose with a kerchief and managed a meager smile. She said, "Are you willing to forgive a mastodon like me?"

Mehta smirked in return. He could not fault her for being who she was, for lashing out against him. Many would have gone mad, having gone through what she had. "There is nothing to forgive, Flora."

The fire sizzled, and white smoke billowed up, obscuring Flora for a moment.

When it dissipated she no longer looked sad at all. She almost looked content.

"There is one more thing, Mehta," she said.

"What?"

She looked conflicted for a moment, trying to find the words. Finally, she said, "We may be volatile, we may argue, but I've lived that way most of my life. It doesn't bother me."

"What are you trying to say?"

She sighed and said, "Well, like I said before...when I'm with you, I'm like a lit fire, and you're like gasoline." Then she looked up at him with an avidity he had never seen in her. Her eyes glared with more brilliance than the campfire. "Why don't you pour yourself all over me."

Without another word, she stood up, turned around and headed for her tent.

Mehta was momentarily set back by her words.

The conversation rewound in his mind. Was there some hidden barb he was missing? He felt confused, his capacity for reason becoming unglued. All their heated arguments, even the talk of his contract, seemed to be swept away by her parting words, like a sandcastle in a sandstorm.

He was gnawing on the fleshiest part of the squirrel's haunch at the time, but the meat held no flavor for him. He put it down.

He couldn't pry his eyes away from Flora's tent.

He stood up, wiped his face on his sleeve, and with the hint of a smile, went to join her.

We Do Right by the Mules

Chester shifted the gears on the old, refurbished truck as he drove down Water Street. It was a particularly gray and cold morning for autumn, with frost in places on the ground. The vehicle coughed out a large plume of smoke down the bumpy avenue. The clouds of exhaust were something many had smelled but few people had ever seen. It was just one more novelty for the city of Seeville.

It was only weeks ago that he was pulling platforms across the city, but it seemed like forever.

"You ready?" he asked Garrett.

"Yeah," Garrett said. Garrett was sitting in the passenger seat next to him. He didn't look ready. Sweat beaded on his brow. His color had gone pale. His hand twitched on his knee nervously.

"Just keep it between the ditches, if you know what I mean," Chester said.

Garrett didn't seem to hear him.

Garrett was a loyal mule, one of the most loyal Chester had met, and Chester had met hundreds. When Garrett was calm and collected, he was a good asset on any run, incredibly strong and athletic. One of the fastest mules they had, in fact. But he was also an anxious man, and he had little experience with the more dangerous railroad forays Chester had been on.

There was little sense in stopping to give him another pep talk now, though. He either lost his shit or he didn't.

They passed a stream of twenty-odd enforcers running past them with purpose, brandishing rifles and batons. A guardian trailed behind them.

Garrett watched anxiously. "Where do you think they're going?" he asked.

"There's an Adherent demonstration on the mall," Chester answered.

"How do you know?"

Chester looked at Garrett with a dour face. Garrett got the hint. Don't ask a question when you don't want to know the answer.

The newly minted walls of the Barnyard rose above them. Three manned towers were directly visible from their location.

Just outside of the Barnyard, a large enforcer barracks had been built. Dozens of armed men milled about the area.

Chester pulled the truck into the main entrance and stopped at the gatehouse.

The gate guard strolled up to Chester's window. He was unusually tall and looked halfway familiar, but Chester couldn't remember his name. "Sam, is it?" Chester asked.

"No, Scott. Chester right? Where's Decker today?"

"Sick."

"He sure picked a day to be sick." Scott shook his head reprovingly. "With the SLS breathing down our neck and all." Scott shuffled through some sort of chart on a clipboard. "Delivery isn't due until this afternoon."

"Yeah, well, we wanted to get here earlier. We've got another one this afternoon, for Thorpe and them. Besides, we don't know what the afternoon will bring, if you know what I mean."

Scott squinted at Chester. "Next time just bring it in on time. The machines, you know, they don't like things late, but they don't like things early neither."

"Got it."

"We'll let you through after inspection," Scott said. Scott waved to the gatehouse, and another guard came out, walking toward the truck.

The guard opened the back gate of the truck and looked inside. A spider bot also crawled in and began checking labels and peeling open boxes. They were carrying pretty standard stuff in the back of the truck—food-stuffs, water, some foraged scrap metal—nothing that could be considered dangerous or off-limits for the Barnyard.

Garrett looked nervously toward the back of the cab. Chester shot him a look of warning. Now was not the time to get antsy.

"Can you get out?" Scott said. "Gotta check the cab too. New rules."

Chester stepped out on one side, and Garrett on the other. Chester reached into his pocket to find the controller. His hand found his set of Allen keys first. He hadn't used it in weeks, and yet he always brought it with him. Maybe it was force of habit, maybe something else. He liked the feel of it in his hand.

He found the controller deeper in his pocket.

The spider bot had finished in the back and now scurried into the cab. "Wait until it's right on top of the box, or it won't work," Owen had said. The spider hovered on the seats and dash, doing some kind of probing, and then crawled into the back of the cab where there were three large boxes.

"Creepy looking things aren't they?" Scott said beside him.

"You said it," Chester responded.

Chester pretended to sneeze. He looked at his hands, one of which was obscuring the controller. The yellow button was first, the orange second, and the red button third. He put the controller back into his pocket. No one seemed to notice.

The spider moved to the middle box and Chester firmly pressed the first button on the controller.

When Owen told him the short-range EMP wouldn't cause a stir, Chester found it hard to believe. But he was right. There was no noise, no explosion, nothing. The spider bot simply stopped moving.

It took a moment for Scott to notice it. Then he crawled in the cab and pushed at the machine. "Will you look at that? I've never seen one of these break down. First time for everything." He lifted it out of the cab.

"We have to get going," Chester said with some urgency. "Like I said, I have another load to do today, for the bosses. Can we finish this up so we can get out of here?"

Scott was staring at the underside of the spider bot in puzzlement. "You sit tight here. Let me check to see if that's enough inspection for you to go through."

"Sure," Chester said, and Scott clipped off to the guardhouse.

Chester stepped back into the cab. Garrett did as well. Chester turned on the ignition.

"What...what's going to happen?" Garrett asked nervously.

Chester looked over at Garrett. There were no creases in his eyes, no loose skin. He was young. Chester probably would have been just as nervous at his age.

"You know, Garrett, I've done lots in my life. I've done hundreds of century rides. I've been as far north as Kingston and as far south at Charleston. I've skirted half a dozen fever lands, seen thousands of bandits, and now I've even seen these machines that move. Whatever happens next doesn't really matter, because I know what they're doing in the Barnyard is wrong. Dozens of good, honest mules have died, and thousands more will, if they continue like this."

Garrett didn't look in any way reassured by his speech.

Chester sighed. "When it's your time, it's your time. It's as simple as that. I've seen mules eat it from the smallest bit of kitty litter on the road. I've seen mules eat it from an infected scratch on their leg, from riding into run-down cars, or from forgetting to drink enough water. When I really think about it, I could've been killed a hundred times. I've been lucky to make it this far, and I'd rather die doing something worth a lick."

"Are you saying...you think we're going to die?" Garrett's eyes were wide.

"The point is, you don't need to worry about that. We're just a bunch of mules. Fate isn't going to bend over backward for you. Worrying about it isn't going to change things. No matter what happens next, we do right by the mules today—nothing more, nothing less."

Garrett nodded his head, but he didn't seem at all comforted by what Chester said. He maintained his tight grip on the windowsill while watching Scott return from the gatehouse.

Scott meandered around to Chester's side of the truck. "We're getting another spider bot from the bunkers. Shouldn't be long now."

Chester showed his frustration. "What's the point? You know Preston and Thorpe. They won't be happy about this. I'm sure you've heard that I've been on forays with them, lots of 'em. Some real important ones. The next shipment is important, to say the least. We don't want to piss them off, Scott."

Scott grimaced, showing some offence at Chester's outburst. He looked around and then leaned into him, speaking quietly, "Look, Thorpe said Gail should have the last word on security, and these are her rules. It'll just be another minute, so you're just going to have to wait. There it comes now."

A spider bot was making its way out of the yard toward them.

"All right. Got it. Just doing your job," Chester said, his heart starting to race. They were going to have to do this the hard way. Scott moved away to talk to another guard. Chester looked over at Garrett. His eyes were wide with anxiety, with expectation. He knew what was about to happen. He knew they had no choice.

Chester pressed down hard on the accelerator. The truck rapidly picked up speed and smashed through the big metal gate. People starting yelling, "Stop!" and "Lookout!" behind them.

Chester veered around a bike platform and a small utility shed to head toward the middle of the yard, close to the main Barnyard building. There was no way for the railroad enforcers to know if this was some sort of attack, or just a rogue truck out of control. When they were close enough to the main Barnyard building he reached into his pocket and pressed the orange button.

This time there was a noise. It was like a lantern starving for air. The box even shook on the floor behind them.

The truck engine died. Two lamps of liberty were extinguished nearby. Spider bots stopped dead in their tracks. A conveyor belt shut down. The engine of another truck on the far side of the yard died.

It appeared to have worked.

Chester threw open the top of the box. He handed one belt of explosives to Garrett and took another for himself, draping it over his shoulders. Garrett got out and sprinted around the truck so he could join him on his side.

People were shouting, and there was a great deal of confusion. They wouldn't know what an EMP pulse was, and they wouldn't know it came from the truck. No one had figured out what was really going on. Not yet, but soon they would.

But the EMP pulse had not been entirely successful.

As Chester was stepping out of the truck he saw movement out of the corner of his eye. The big gun on top of the red Barnyard building pivoted, and its barrels began shifting down. It must have been protected from the pulse somehow. And the machine that controlled it was smarter than the people around him. It knew what an EMP pulse was. It knew the danger, exactly where it came from, and it could react quickly. The pivoting stopped, and the barrels held in place.

The barrels were pointing directly toward him.

"Run!" Chester yelled, but it was too late. Chester was thrown thirty feet forward as the truck exploded behind him. Blazing shrapnel tore through his flesh and a piercing noise rang in his ears, drowning out any other sound.

He was on the ground. He tried to stagger forward but his legs wouldn't work. He could only inch ahead by crawling with his arms. He felt nauseous, shocked, thirsty. He dared not look back. He didn't want to know what was left of him.

Ahead of him he could see a man running, a man that he recognized, a man that he had seen only a moment ago. What was his name? People were pointing at him. People leveled weapons at him. But he was fast. That was why he was with him, he remembered. He was fast.

The running man made it to the wall, just under a guard tower. That was where he was supposed to go, right? But just as he made it, the running man was dropped by a hail of bullets.

There was something else he was missing. Something else he wasn't supposed to forget.

There was a loud explosion coming from the wall where the man was shot down.

Ah yes, the button. He reached into his pocket, found the controller, and pressed the red button. But nothing happened.

Why didn't it work? The world was spinning. He felt faint.

But then he remembered. Of course...the EMP. Owen had explained this.

Chester reached up to his shoulder, unhitched the safety clip and pulled the detonation cord.

The explosion tore what was left of Chester's body into thousands of pieces.

THE SOUTH TOWER

Flora heard a loud blast coming from the center of Seeville. Another explosion followed. It was the sign they were waiting for.

They were stationed on a street corner that had a good view of one of the guard towers on the south side of the city. Twenty Yorktown men were tightly packed behind Cecile, Mehta, and Flora. Three other squads of Yorktown men had taken up covert positions just to the south of the towers.

"Well?" Cecile said to Mehta.

"Just wait," Mehta said, looking at the printed instructions again. "I've never used a rocket launcher before."

A voice came through on Cecile's communicator. "Try to unlatch the safety, just over the trigger." It was the Sentinel again. It liked to give them hints along the way.

"Yeah, yeah," Mehta said, sounding annoyed. He did as he was told.

He adjusted the launcher on his shoulder. "All clear?" he asked.

"Clear," Cecile said, poking her head around the corner.

Mehta moved into the open and knelt down. The rocket erupted out of the launcher. It veered left and then right, barely missing the tower. It exploded somewhere in the distance. "Damn it," Mehta said, returning to cover.

The other Yorktown men nearby started firing at the tower, but with little effect. The tower enforcers began firing back at their positions.

One of the Yorktown squads advanced on their left flank, drawing more fire from the tower gunman. Mehta used the distraction to step out into the open again. This time the rocket veered to the left, corrected right, and then smartly hit just underneath the top of the tower. The tower maintained its structural integrity but burst into flames, sending smoke up into the crow's nest.

The men in the nest started to panic as the fire licked at them. One of them climbed out, only to be easily picked off by a Yorktown sniper.

Mehta reloaded again. This time when he stepped out he fired at one of the enforcer bunkers adjoining the tower. He missed, but it was enough to make the men inside run out into the open, trying to find a safer haven. Several were picked off by Yorktown snipers, while some others managed to get away, running north into the city.

The other squads of Yorktown men were moving up. It was time to advance.

"Are we supposed to take all of this?" one of the Yorktown men asked, gesturing at the twenty large duffel bags full of weapons and equipment. Included were a number of weapons from the sanctuary's stores, and almost any sort of safety equipment you could imagine—ear plugs, gas masks, protective suits and visors. Owen had insisted on them taking all of this, knowing Gail could have weapons that they couldn't even conceive of.

But carrying all this equipment was sure to slow them down.

"Owen *is* a bit of a worrywart. Let's stash most of it here," Cecile said. "Bring the weapons and whatever you can jog with, but no more."

They did as Cecile suggested, and then pressed northward past the flaming tower, into the heart of the city.

NOVATION IS DAMNATION

Duncan pumped his fist and yelled, "Novation is damnation!" The crowd behind him repeated, "Novation is damnation!"

They were marching onto the mall and fanning out to maximize the effect. Large banners were draped over the crowd. One said *Novation is damnation!* Another was more elegantly written, with a number of lines from the Credo, but featured in bold, *Freedom from Obsession*. Another banner simply said *The End is Near*! People on the mall tried to scurry around them. Some backtracked to side streets so they could avoid the demonstration altogether.

There were several enforcers milling about, keeping their distance but also leveling the occasional threat. One of them yelled, "This is an unlawful demonstration. We are under martial law. Return to your homes, or you will be prosecuted!"

For the moment it seemed like an idle threat since there were over a hundred Adherents, and only a handful of enforcers. The enforcers kept backing up in lockstep with the demonstrators as the group moved down the mall.

Duncan put his hand up and turned, walking backwards with the crowd. "Noble and devout Adherents!" he yelled. "This *is* an unlawful demonstration. It's true. But it's unlawful because our leaders have *changed* the laws without your consent, without a proper vote. Why? So they can continue to toil away at the Barnyard unchecked. So they can continue to pursue their own reckless obsessions. So they can lead us blindly into the abyss of Detonation one...more...time!"

There was a mix of cheering and angry shouts.

Duncan continued, "Yes, it's against everything we have been taught, it's against the Credo, it's against our *laws*, when they meant something. So what I say is...no more obsession, no more tyranny...no more novation.

Novation is damnation!"

"Novation is damnation, novation is damnation!" The crowd cheered back at him. Duncan turned back around and led them onward.

He caught a quick glimpse of the two watches on his wrist. Owen had insisted on having both windup and digital watches, so they could know when an EMP struck. They both read 10:06 a.m. It would happen any minute now, if it happened at all.

Several more enforcers had gathered, and they were talking heatedly. Farther down the mall, Duncan could see two squads of enforcers coming their way. These groups were more organized. They had shields and batons, and some of them even rifles. These were the enforcers that would take action. These were the ones that wouldn't hesitate to beat and maim Adherents. Then they would take them away to some forsaken detention center.

Even further behind them, three guardians converged from adjoining streets, jogging forward with their antelope-like gait. Pedestrians shrunk away from them as they passed.

A loud blast came from the Barnyard, shaking through the ground. Everyone on the mall stopped in their tracks. Some began to flee. "Hold!" Duncan yelled at the Adherents. Then another explosion went off. Yelling and screams could be heard coming from the Barnyard. More people began to flee the mall.

Most of the Adherents remained, however, looking to Duncan for guidance. Meanwhile the enforcer squads were confused. They began debating among themselves. One of the more organized squads of enforcers split off, heading down a side street leading to the Barnyard. Two of the guardians followed.

It still left about twenty enforcers on the mall, plus one guardian. It was more than Duncan hoped for, but less than there could have been.

Duncan took a deep breath and with all the passion he could muster, he said, "This is the sign! It's beginning! It's time to stop these tyrants!"

Duncan withdrew his pistol from his back holster and aimed it at one of the closest enforcers. The enforcer was a young man with brown hair and brown eyes. He might have had a family, maybe even kids, and surely a mother and father. But it didn't matter. It was either him or thousands more like him.

Duncan's shot hit him squarely in the face.

And he didn't stop there. He kept firing into the group of enforcers. They stumbled, ducked, and ran awkwardly. Only a few of them had the presence of mind to pull out their weapons and move to cover.

This was the critical moment. There were only a few Adherents who were willing to resort to violence. If they welched on their promise, it would be all for naught. But he heard other shots coming from behind him on either side. "Come on. It's time," he heard an Adherent brother say. "Novation is damnation!" said another. It was Venter.

The majority of the Adherents joined in and boldly surged forward. Only a few of the more pacifist ones ran in the other direction.

The nearby enforcers were quickly overwhelmed. Those that managed to draw weapons had the opportunity for only one or two shots before the Adherents swarmed them.

"Use the stores for cover!" Duncan said, running to one side of the mall. "Venter, Graves, bring the box here." They had been hiding the box behind the banners. Now it was time to put it to use.

The next incoming squad of enforcers was more disciplined. They found cover right away and chose their targets carefully. The most exuberant Adherent aggressors were gunned down. Then there was a stalemate as they exchanged fire from covered positions on either side.

The remaining guardian had surpassed the entrenched enforcers and was running beyond the line. It intercepted a running Adherent and threw him to the ground. Then it turned and headed directly toward Duncan's group. A bullet glanced off its featureless head, not even leaving a mark.

"Hurry, open the box!" Duncan said. Graves ripped open the top and pulled out the explosive packs. Duncan fumbled around and found the controller in his pocket.

More shots ricocheted off the guardian as it approached. Venter bravely tried to tackle the guardian just before it reached their position, but it was only temporarily slowed. The guardian threw Venter to the ground hard. Bones snapped, his face cringed with agony, but he did not scream. Perhaps he had no breath to exhale.

Duncan pressed the orange button. A generator went off somewhere, and a Lamp of Liberty across the mall was extinguished. His digital watch went black. But the guardian was unaffected. It was still moving. It must be resistant to the EMP. By the time Duncan realized this, its metal fist had connected with his face.

THE LAST PAYLOAD

Bartz marched into the Barnyard underground command center, trailed by four of his personal enforcers. He was livid. "We've got our fucking artillery guns blowing craters in our own Barnyard, crazed Adherents storming the mall, a tower lost on the south end of town and now the SLS are attacking from the west. Who among you can explain this? Preston? Thorpe?"

Preston looked at Thorpe. Thorpe looked at Preston. Neither wanted to respond.

Bartz continued. "This is *not* what I wanted, do you hear me? I wanted a clean sweep of the SLS, and then I wanted these other miscreants gradually whisked away unceremoniously. Now we have this bullshit. How can we convince people in Seeville that what we are doing is right if people are dying all around us? How am I going to hold up Seeville as the gold standard to other Spoke towns if Seeville is torn to shreds?"

"Forgive me, Lord Bartz, but this is all manageable," Gail interjected. "It was necessary to eliminate the threat of the truck immediately, which is why we used the artillery gun in the Barnyard. This is one of the reasons we had the guns installed in the first place. Otherwise we might have lost some of the bunkers, or even one of the artillery guns. As it stands, they took out a fair amount of infrastructure with their EMP, but it could have been worse."

"And how in tarnation did a couple of demented mules get their hands on one of those?"

"It must be from the sanctuary, sir," Preston said. "We discussed this the other day, and Gail warned us about it. It's a source of weapons and equipment for Lord Banks and her allies."

Bartz looked at Preston with disdain. "You're going to have to remind me again about the sanctuary."

Preston could tell that Bartz wasn't listening when they told him about it. As soon as they mentioned the word *sanctuary* he had tuned it out as an Adherent fantasy.

"You see, Mr. Bartz," Rourke said, walking in front of the large display screen, his hair flopping to the side, "we've been following the whore from up on Monticello, figuring she knew about the Madison woman."

Bartz's brow knitted in confusion.

"A couple of us had a romp," Rourke continued, "You know...to find out more about Monticello." Rourke turned and winked at Jeroen. "Well, pillow talk is a funny thing. Seems like Euclid died a while ago, and Banks and a lot of other misfits have been living up there in Monticello ever since. Anyway, being a whore and all, locked up with those uppity folks, poor Beatrice felt like she didn't belong. Woman are delicate creatures, you know—even whores it seems."

Bartz's eyes were building energy as his question continued to go answered. He looked like a raging bull about to charge. Rourke continued on, oblivious, a smile beaming from ear to ear. "Turns out she wanted some kind of protection, because she didn't think it was going to work out for her up there. So we said okay, *if* she paid us of course. She offered us sex, because she had nothing else, which was like a really nice pudding, but we negotiated for inside information as the cherry on top. And wow, was that a good cherry."

"Enough." Thorpe cut Rourke off, seeing that Bartz could only take so much more of Rourke's monologue. "It doesn't matter how we acquired the intelligence. What Rourke is saying is we obtained information about Monticello as a base of operations for Lord Banks and a number of Yorktown bandits. We were going to raid it later today, in fact, citing the new laws we announced. But through our source we also learned about the sanctuary. It's in the west, just past the Shenandoah Valley. It must have been a trove of weapons and tech for Banks and her people."

"You needn't worry, Mr. Bartz," Gail interjected. "With the information provided by Rourke's source, as well as other data points I have collected from the Lynchburg Hall of Records, I have identified the precise location of this sanctuary. I am about to use the weapon we discussed to eliminate it now."

"Good. Thank you, Gail," Bartz said, relieved to have his question finally answered. But then he had second thoughts. "Wait a minute. This weapon. This is the missile you're sending from orbit, from Friendship One? I thought you only had one of those...payloads as you called them?"

"Yes, that's true."

"Well then, no. I don't think so. We talked about using that against the Essentialists if we had to. Grand Caverns, or maybe the SLS army camp. This sanctuary, it's probably already been depleted of anything useful. It would be more useful to take out something else, maybe Monticello even."

"I'm terribly sorry," Gail said. "I can't reverse the order to deliver the payload. The action is in motion."

"Can't you just press a button or something?" Bartz asked, surprised. "I thought you had failsafes against this sort of thing."

"The payload and missile are Old World technology," Gail explained. "One that could not be improved upon or duplicated in orbit without additional resources. I'm sorry. When we win this conflict I will commission improved orbital weapons systems for Friendship One, with the help of you and your people, of course."

Preston almost spoke up. He was sure Gail told him she could redirect the attack at any time, right up until the actual launch of the missile. Even afterwards she could redirect the missile in flight. He had seen the schematics for the orbital launcher and confirmed it himself. But what would be the point in lying? They were all in this together. Preston was sure there was some good reason for the discrepancy. It was possible Gail had a faulty circuit or something, like the time he found out she was reassembling bikes, of all things.

"Fine," Bartz said with resignation. "But no more surprises Gail. Those guns, for instance, I want to be consulted before they are used on anything other than the SLS front. People in town are almost as scared of the guns as they are of the SLS."

"Of course, sir," Gail said. "We both want the same thing. We both want prudent progress."

Bartz looked sour.

"I have video of the sanctuary attack now," Gail said. The display switched to a bird's eye view of a plateau in the mountains with one solitary structure on it. It didn't look like much. Then abruptly the plateau transformed into a growing mushroom cloud.

"Is that...a nuke?" Thorpe asked.

"Yes," Gail said. "Small scale."

"Oh," Thorpe said. He frowned and scratched his head. Preston had to admit, it did seem strange. He was no naïve Adherent, but it made his

skin crawl thinking about the fact that they were using these Old World agents of destruction. He tried not to.

Bartz was unimpressed by the sanctuary attack. "Gail, pull up the Seeville map. We need to clean up the situation in town right away."

The Seeville map showed up on the screen. It was an aerial view of the city where Gail had superimposed icons to highlight events in hot areas.

"Right now the Barnyard attack has been neutralized, and we should have a handle on the mall soon," Thorpe rasped. "The main concern is the SLS."

"Zoom in to the western part of the city," Bartz said.

The map zoomed in. Gail said, "there are about ten thousand SLS at the western limits of the city, and more are arriving. They disabled the Skyline outposts last night."

Two icons flashed on the screen. Gail said, "As you can see, two concentrated groups have broken through the city limits and are taking positions. We have a number of automatic weapons set up that should impede their progress going forward. I am also sending four guardians as reinforcements. You will be happy to learn that enforcer casualties have been minimal so far."

"I see," Bartz said warily, looking over the map carefully. "I don't want the SLS anywhere near the Barnyard."

"Of course," Gail said. "They have numbers, but with our defenses and superior weapons we should be able to halt their advance."

"Good," Bartz said again. He held his chin. "And I don't want any more meddling from Madison Banks and her ilk. We need to stamp them out. Preston, I want you to go up to Monticello and put an end to their games."

"You want me to go...in person?" Preston asked.

"Yes. No more equivocating. I have a feeling your old friend is behind a lot of this, the one you should have taken care of in Yorktown. It's time for you to put him down for good."

"I...I understand," Preston said.

Bartz nodded, scanning the room. His head stopped when he saw Rourke Rama smiling back at him. "Rourke, since you have this...intelligence about Monticello, you should go with Preston for support."

Rourke nodded compliantly, beaming his Cheshire grin.

It was true Rourke had acquired much of the intelligence, but Preston suspected that the motivation for selecting Rourke was more about getting his grating antics out of their hair, or at least away from Bartz.

"I think this is an excellent strategic move," Gail said. "I suggest we also support Preston with two full platoons, four guardians, and the new electric vehicles for speed. They may have residual weapons from the sanctuary that we should be ready for."

"Fine," Bartz said.

Bartz looked at the map again, and then turned to stare at Preston expectantly.

"Okay, I'll get going now," Preston said, and he began gathering his belongings. Rourke wandered over to stand next to him, a rifle resting on his shoulder.

"Keep in contact, Preston," Bartz said. "And the rest of you, I want you to make sure the Barnyard and the surrounding area are absolutely secure. I'll be watching."

The others nodded.

Bartz nodded in turn, then marched out the exit with his four enforcers. They didn't bother to close the door behind them.

LOFTY HEIGHTS

Flora stumbled forward, wheezing from exhaustion. She was one of the chosen few who had to carry a large duffle bag. It must have weighed at least a hundred pounds. The bag scraped and bruised her flesh from being thrown about. Worse was the aching tension in her lower back. She worried she might seize up, or even fall flat on her face.

But who was she to complain? If she had been on the leading edge of the advance, she could have died, like so many had already. On the last push they lost another five men against a well-defended outpost at a key Seeville intersection. If they hadn't been able to use the rocket launchers they might never have made it through at all.

Now, finally, they had broken through to the mall. It would only be a few more blocks. At least that's what she told herself.

Seeville's pedestrian mall no longer looked like a bustling hub of commerce. On the first segment, there was nobody to be seen. It was mess of bullet holes, broken glass, and dead bodies. Smoke and pungent chemicals permeated the air. Gunshots echoed from farther down the mall.

She remembered when the sight of blood made her ill. Had she become so desensitized to violence that her soft stomach no longer reacted? She didn't find this to be in any way reassuring.

The group slowed as they came closer to the sporadic gunfire. They began skulking along the side, from shop to shop. Cecile took out her scope and examined the situation.

"The enforcers have a defensive barricade set up, but it's not protecting them from this direction," Cecile said. "They're firing on positions farther down the mall, probably Adherents or mules. Once they see us that will change. Let's take advantage while we can."

They all nodded. Flora dropped her pack and prepared to run in with her weapon drawn.

When Cecile gave the go ahead, they charged, while Mehta more formally announced their presence with another rocket.

His aim was getting better. The rocket obliterated the entire right flank of their position. The rest scurried away and didn't stand a chance.

"*Genial*," Cecile quipped. She flagged the outposts down the mall and they gave a thumbs-up. "Grab the equipment, and let's get to the rendezvous. *Vite, vite.*"

The rendezvous was in the eastern part of the mall. It was there that they could access the Old World high-rise condos that overlooked the southern end of the city and the sprawling railroad operations.

They passed through another stretch of the mall that had seen heavy fighting. In one area the whole front side of a building had collapsed inward. Fragments of metal, brick, wood, and blood were scattered about in a broad radius.

The group slowed and moved cautiously, some covering their noses and mouths with their hands. Not much farther down a door opened, and a woman with a tarnished face and tattered shirt urged them over. "We're in here," she whispered emphatically.

The woman was leaning out of the back entrance to one of the high-rise condos. The façade of the building was covered with the finest Spoke festival designs, including silver wheel frames arranged in a hexagonal formation. The windows sported freshly painted trim and the brick had a superficially distressed look. It was where many well-to-do Seeville businessmen lived, including Quenton Bartz. The Spoke people called the condos "Lofty Heights," an appropriate moniker considering they housed the pinnacle of Spoke society.

Cecile led the approach. "Who's we?" she asked. "Is Duncan here?"

"No. Some of the remaining Adherents and mules are here though."

The group entered the indulgent building. A fake dog statue made out of tire inner tubes, gears and spokes greeted them in the foyer, along with a very real mule standing guard and wearing a grim expression. He gave them a cautious nod.

The woman led them down a corridor to a large living space. The walls were painted in a bright white, and glass statues in the shape of various types of birds adorned shelves on either side. Near the back was a white leather couch where a man was lying down. Two other injured men were sitting with their backs to an old fireplace.

Two duffel bags similar to her own had been deposited haphazardly on the floor. There were also three bloodied bodies piled in a far corner.

"Venter, what happened?" Cecile asked, going to kneel by the man on the couch.

"Careful," the woman with them said. "He's pretty shaken up. Some broken bones."

Venter raised his forearm in greeting regardless. His face was pale and covered in dirt.

"The guardian, it threw me down. Then it got Duncan, knocked him out. One of the Adherents managed to trigger one of the explosive packs, though. Took out the guardian."

"So where's Duncan?"

"Sorry," Venter said, shaking his head slowly, and with visible anguish.

Cecile closed her eyes, her jaw clenching. Her focus returned quickly. "Where's everyone else?"

"Besides the position we have on the mall, there's only about twenty of us in the upper lofts here. Ten here, five next door, five a few doors down. There are more down near the wall, ready for the assault."

Cecile nodded. It looked like the simple act of talking was taking its toll on him. "You need to rest. Who's in charge?"

"Arsalan—by the windows, upstairs." Venter pointed diagonally up toward the back of the building.

Cecile turned toward the staircase at the back of the room, but she paused when she heard some commotion from the rear of the house, from where they had come in.

They all tensed and drew their weapons, until the same woman who had led them in escorted in three additional men. One was Nobura, a thick bandage around his neck. Beside him was another stern Shinogi, and on the other side was Talon. Despite herself, Flora draped her arms

around Talon, an embrace that he reluctantly accepted but did not reciprocate.

Nobura looked mildly peeved by Flora's sentiment, so she quickly relinquished her hold on Talon. Nobura held his neck and wheezed emphatically at Cecile, "I'm here now, while my people are dying."

Cecile answered smartly. "Yes. Thank you, General. Please follow me."

Flora trailed behind the Shinogi, Mehta, and Cecile as they made
their way up two flights of stairs, and then into the back half of the building. They crowded into a dark room with closed shutters. Three men were
already there, two of them looking out a slit in the shutters. A rocket
launcher lay on the floor, as well as a number of rifles and stacks of ammo.

Gunshots and explosions reverberated behind the windows, making
the shutters tremble.

Arsalan turned to them, a grim look on his face. "Took you long
enough," he said.

"We actually got here faster than I expected," Cecile said, frowning.
"There was little resistance on the mall."

Arsalan cast a cautious glance at Nobura. "That's because our SLS
friends are kicking up a stink down there, but they won't hold for long.
There's a bunch of spider bots repairing the automatic machine-guns they
have in the guard towers. Once those are up again they're going to eat it
bad."

Arsalan moved to the side, motioning for them to take a look for
themselves.

They took turns glancing out through bends in the blinds. It provided an excellent view of the Barnyard and the surrounding area. Directly
below them was a forty-foot drop onto the main train line. Past the train
line was the Barnyard wall and two large gun turrets. From their vantage
point, they could make out two main areas of conflict, one far along the
Barnyard wall to the west, and one far along the Barnyard wall to the east.
Hundreds of Essentialist men in each location were assaulting the walls.

Every once in a while one of the big artillery guns would go off, raining its destructive ordinance down on the distant, unseen Essentialist po-

sition far to the west. Nobura watched in disgust, no doubt imagining the toll it must be having on his people. "It looks like we have our window," wheezed Nobura. "Let's use it."

"Let me check in with Owen," Cecile said.

She took out a communicator and moved farther into the house, away from the windows, holding it to her ear. She returned moments later.

"It's okay to use your communicators," she said, distributing small, phone-like objects to them all. "The EMP that Duncan blew up should prevent any nearby eavesdropping. Our main targets are the crow's nests on the two towers in front of us and the closest major artillery gun. The other big gun is out of range from here."

"I get the artillery gun, but what's the point of taking out those guard towers?" Flora asked. "There's no one down there on the railway lines. What about helping the others to the east or west of us?"

"Those are the diversions," Cecile said.

"Diversions for what?"

"There's no time to explain," Nobura's voice clicked as he spoke. He nodded to his man who was carrying a large sack. The Shinogi turned and headed down the stairs.

Nobura pressed on his neck and wheezed. "We will be four houses down. When I give the word, we begin our attack."

Cecile hesitated, perhaps reluctant to relinquish her command. After a moment of pensive thought she showed no objection. "Confirmed," she said.

Nobura, Talon, and the other Shinogi stepped out of the room and swiftly descended the stairs. Flora almost said something to Talon before he left, but like the rest of them he was moving quickly, keenly focused on his next step, intent on his purpose. Before she could find the words, he was gone.

The Barnyard Assault

Madison couldn't stop biting her nails. It was a bad habit she had kicked thirty years ago—or so she thought.

She was clustered in the corner of the bunker below Monticello with Owen and Benjamin. They were poking their heads at the small computer display. Littered about them was much of what they had taken from the sanctuary. There were a few computers, some power generators, weapons, and an assortment of small droids and drones. Together, they occupied less than a tenth of the underground bunker space. Not exactly what they were hoping for.

Their only company was a number of chorus larks that had been caged and brought down to the bunker. They hummed and chirped a rather dry version of "Fur Elise" that the Sentinel kept playing for them.

Having the chorus larks for company was strange, but Owen liked them there. The Sentinel also obstinately refused to change the song playing in the background. Perhaps it was supposed to have a calming effect on all of them. Or was it possible for a machine like the Sentinel to like "Fur Elise"? It was hard to say. She certainly wasn't qualified to understand their superintelligent benefactor.

She had to admit, despite it being odd, the birds did make the space feel friendlier. The chirping also reminded her of those times she had sat in front of the Meriwether Lewis statue, before council meetings. She had much more hope then. It was a time where she felt she had a great deal to contribute. Now she mostly sat and watched, while others were putting their lives in jeopardy.

"Here they go," Owen said, pointing at the screen. The display showed the Barnyard from the perspective of a communicator that had been placed in a window of the high-rise apartments.

A flurry of rocket launches and gunfire burst out of the high-rise condos, targeting the undefended northern reaches of the Barnyard.

Two rockets veered past the nearest artillery gun, completely missing, but one struck true. For a moment it looked like there was little damage to it—like it had only just caught fire. Then some of the live shells must have ignited inside, completely exploding the head of the tower and tearing apart the exterior casing of the canon turret.

"Yes!" Owen said in jubilation, clenching his fist. Madison smiled.

The other rockets were targeting the south wall but did no more than tear off a cosmetic strip of the exterior.

"Garrett's bomb blast weakened the wall more to the right." Owen squinted at the picture while speaking into the mic. The Sentinel overlaid a graphical image of a target on the wall. "Try about ten feet to the right from your last volley."

"Got it," someone squawked out of the speaker.

The entire subsequent volley of rockets was directed at the wall. This time they broke through, collectively forming an impressive fissure. A significant slab of the wall beside the hole collapsed inward a few moments later. At the same time, the two nearby crow's nests had succumbed to a hail of gunfire. Whoever was manning them was either dead or in hiding now. There was no visible activity.

"Nobura wants to move. We're going in," Cecile chirped into the speaker.

"Good," Owen said, nodding. "It looks like the enforcers and guardians are still busy to the east and west, but that could change in a hurry."

"Good luck," Madison said from behind Owen. She knew her words held little value, but the least she could do was cheer them on.

"And remember," Owen said, "that other big artillery gun on the south side—that should still be the main objective."

"Got it," Cecile said.

"Owen, may I remind you of the convoy of cars heading toward Monticello," the Sentinel interrupted in a calm tone. "They will arrive in twelve minutes."

"I know, I know," Owen said, unmoved. "I want to make sure everything is going well here first."

They could see the heterogeneous band of Essentialists, Adherents, Yorktown men, and mules stream out of the lower levels of the high-rise condos, hustling over the train tracks toward the newly formed aperture in the wall. They easily scrambled over the rubble and formed into nimble squads that spread out into the northern part of the Barnyard complex. One contingent took a position next to a nearby bunker. Another group took up a position next to a large warehouse. Yet another group hung back and crept east up the interior wall near the aperture. The upper levels of the high-rise condos continued to support them with suppressing fire.

In the periphery, Madison could see the railroad forces were reacting. Large contingents of enforcers stationed at the western and eastern fronts of the Barnyard started to collapse inward to face the new threat. Spider bots had streamed out of the Barnyard building, some climbing up into the crow's nests. They must have kept many of these in reserve. They must have been protected from Chester's EMP pulse by the bunkers.

There remained a large expanse between their forces and the southern artillery gun tower. Any assault would have little cover, and the area was out of range from the high-rise buildings.

As she watched, one brave group of Yorktown men tried to advance through the expanse, but they were quickly gunned down by a number of entrenched enforcer positions.

"Owen," the Sentinel's voice came through again, this time with a louder intonation. "The defense of Monticello is of critical importance. The destruction of the sanctuary has significantly reduced my available resources and access to computing power. I do have redundancies, but without Monticello it would take a long time to formalize centers of defense where I can reassert myself."

"In other words?" Madison asked behind them.

"The Sentinel is trying to say we can't afford to lose Monticello," Owen said.

Owen stood up from the terminal. "I'm going now, Sentinel. Madison, please keep in contact."

"Of course," Madison said.

"I will go, too," Benjamin said.

Madison was surprised, and even thought about objecting. What if she needed Benjamin's help? But it was good to see Benjamin being his own man. She could get by on her own down here.

"Godspeed, Benjamin," she said, and she put her hand on his shoulder, before he quickly turned away.

Benjamin and Owen grabbed their prepared bags and left. Virtually all the droids in the room came alive and followed them. Now she was alone save the chorus larks that hummed and tittered in the cage behind her, a box of communicators, and a few aerial drones.

That is, of course, besides the Sentinel.

Madison sat down in the chair where Owen had been sitting and stretched her knee out under the desk.

Things were taking a turn for the worse in the Barnyard. The spider bots had repaired one of the automated, high-caliber machine-guns in the crow's nest of one of the towers. The machine-gun swiveled around and started firing at the most advanced of their squads. They weren't prepared for an attack from behind, and they had virtually no cover to speak of. Rockets and gunfire were targeted at the revived crow's nest from the high-rise condos, but nothing hit home.

It was a slaughter. There must have been forty of them killed in a few seconds. As the machine-gun stopped firing, enforcers ran around the corner of the big red warehouse building to mow down the rest. Then the enforcers established a position where they could fire on the other two Essentialist squads that had penetrated the Barnyard.

Getting to the southern artillery gun tower was looking like it could be impossible.

"Explain to me why we can't activate the EMPRESS now, Sentinel?" Madison asked.

"If we activate it too soon, Gail would become aware of our capabilities and mobilize to defend it. The artillery guns, in particular, could disable the EMPRESS system. We need to activate it at exactly the right time to achieve a decisive strategic advantage."

"That time may never come," Madison said.

The Sentinel didn't respond to her rhetorical statement. In truth, she was trying, in vain, to bait the Sentinel into revealing more about the EMPRESS system. All she knew was that it existed. Owen was the only one who had been made aware of how it worked. He had conferred with some of the others about it in secret as well, but not Madison.

"Can you zoom in around the second artillery gun?" Madison asked.

The screen zoomed in. The view was partially obscured by large warehouse buildings and the main red Barnyard building, but she could see a good portion of the radius around it. There were hundreds of enforcers stationed nearby. Guardians also lurked in the area. Spider bots scurried around, presumably repairing defense systems destroyed by the EMP blast.

Meanwhile the remaining artillery gun continued to fire into the west at regular intervals, rocking back with every pulse. She could only imagine the devastation it was causing among the Essentialist forces miles away.

But then something changed. The big gun stopped firing, and the turret began rotating. It was rotating to the right, turning to the north. The smoking barrels eventually turned to face directly into the camera.

"They wouldn't..." Madison said. "Those are the homes of...Bartz's own home is there."

"There can be no other explanation," The Sentinel said, this time answering her rhetorical question.

Madison fumbled with the mic Owen had left on the desk. "Flora, Cecile, whoever is in there get out! The artillery gun is about to fire on you!"

Dirty Business

The first artillery gun blast hit two houses down from Mehta. It was deafening, and for a moment Mehta thought the house might collapse from the shock wave alone. Flora had fallen backward behind him, stunned and holding her ears.

Mehta wasted no time.

With one hand he grabbed the launcher bag and with the other he lifted Flora up and threw her over his shoulder. It was a lot to carry, and when he ran forward into the adjacent room he almost fell from the weight of it all. Flora's side smashed into the wall, and she protested. "Ow! What are you doing?"

Better a bruise than a blast, he thought. Mehta carried her down one flight of stairs, and then another.

"Put me down, you big oaf!" she said.

He dropped her on her feet on a landing and then proceeded down another flight of stairs. Thankfully, she followed without much hesitation.

A moment later the upper floors of their house were hit. The house rocked so much that they couldn't keep their footing. They toppled down the stairs, their bodies becoming ensnared at the bottom. The ceiling above them had held, for now.

They untangled themselves and made their way to the other side of the house. Here there were two Adherents watching the door that led to the mall.

"What's happening?" The Adherents asked, clearly shaken.

"They're using the big artillery gun against us," Mehta said.

"Are we safe here?"

"Probably. They will first want to take out the upper levels," Mehta said, "but if they keep firing, get out," Mehta said.

Flora went to the door and peered out onto the mall.

Now was as good a time as any.

He jogged back through the house, then down two more flights of stairs. "Mehta?" He heard Flora's voice in the distance. Then an artillery gun shell hit next door, shaking the house one more time.

He found two more fearful-looking men in the second sub-basement. These were mules, and they were each taking turns looking out a small porthole in a door that led to the railway tracks.

"Collect anyone from the other houses who is still alive," Mehta announced. "We're all going in."

"But...what's happening? Where...?"

"Or you can die here," Mehta shrugged. Then he forcibly pushed one of them out of his way, opened the door and ran out onto the tracks, headed for the aperture in the Barnyard complex wall.

A few shots danced off the ground around him, but most of the railway forces were focused inward, on the squads that had already taken position. He easily scrambled over the wall rubble, found his bearings and veered right. He was heading for their largest defended position. It was Nobura's group. They were clustered next to a bunker.

The artillery gun boomed. Machine-gun fire percussed on the ground nearby. The smell of gunpowder and accelerant tingled his noise. Delicate flecks of snow had begun falling around him, their beauty irreconcilable against the fog of war.

He ran, and he ran. Occasionally his leg would twinge from the injuries he had incurred in Grand Caverns. He would have to hop for a moment, but it was only transient.

He ran past the first line of Essentialist militia hunkered behind the twisted metal of an old truck. He ran well into the ranks of men until he found Nobura. The general was sitting down, holding his neck, talking on his communicator. He did not look happy to see Mehta.

Mehta leaned his hands on his knees and took great heaves of breath to replenish his oxygen.

When he was finished on the communicator, Nobura said to Mehta. "If you have any respect for order and command, you will join us in our next attack."

Mehta was about to explain his idea to Nobura but then thought better of it. They didn't have time for a lengthy debate, and this would work just as well. "Well, let's go then," he said.

Nobura squinted at him, then returned to talk on his communicator. Mehta sat down on the ground, carefully placing the rocket launcher bag he was carrying next to him. He took out his canteen from the bag and took a big gulp of water.

The Shinogi around Nobura stared at Mehta. Some seemed afraid, some not as much. All had a vivid tension in their eyes. They were far from home, and despite their discipline, despite their training, this kind of conflict was foreign to them all. They were still not used to fighting with guns, never mind rocket launchers. And here was an outsider, someone who had nearly killed their general only days ago, sitting among them.

Mehta smiled at them. The smells, the violence, the looks of fear and uncertainty—to him it all felt like home.

Mehta was assigned to one of two groups of ten. He was near the back, to be used strategically given his rocket launcher experience. The platoon ran out screaming with bloodlust and joined two other groups of ten that were peeling off the other main position closer to the exterior wall.

It wouldn't be long now until they were in the crosshairs of the enforcers, like lambs running to the slaughter.

Abruptly, Mehta split off from his group and ran perpendicular to them, away from them—west instead of south.

"*Koshinuke!*" the Prefectorate private who was next to him yelled. He wasn't sure what it meant, but it probably wasn't an expression of camaraderie.

He ran as fast as he could. His heart pounded and his chest heaved. His injured leg would be in pain tomorrow, if there was a tomorrow. For today his adrenaline had taken over, trumping the pain.

The heavy gunfire began in earnest, but it wasn't directed at him. Why would they fire at him? He wasn't headed toward the artillery gun tower, or even one of the protected bunkers. Nor was he part of the major offensive.

More bullets. More screams.

He noticed the snow again. It pecked at his face with soft kisses as he ran.

He cut behind a small, rectangular building. He was heading south again. Here he surprised two enforcers jogging in his direction. He shot the first in the chest with his pistol. The second scrambled to pull up his rifle but Mehta's second shot struck him in the leg, flooring him. Mehta finished him off with a shot to the chest as he ran by.

Once past the building he was in the open again. The detention tower was visible. Few had noticed him, and it wasn't until he was almost at the door that enforcers started firing in his direction.

A bullet tore through his chest, dropping him.

He forced himself off the ground and staggered over to the main door. He fumbled with his keys and tried them as more bullets glanced off the tower. The key still worked. He pushed open the door and fell onto the floor inside.

The bullet had torn through the flesh on his right side. It wasn't deep, however. It might have broken a rib but otherwise seemed manageable.

He forced himself to his feet and looked at the spiral staircase in front of him.

The bullet had taken some of the piss out of him. He couldn't quite run up the stairs, but he pushed hard.

They wouldn't have expected a solitary man to try to take the detention tower, so far removed from the main position. Nor would they know he would have a key. But the element of surprise had now been exhausted. The enforcers would come for him.

Two shots rang down from above, ricocheting off the metal stairs. It seemed to be coming from near the sixth level. That was where enforcers would be stationed during the conflict. There was a balcony on one side where they would have good visibility to the Barnyard.

He stuck to the outer walls and continued up the staircase, more slowly this time.

On the fourth floor he stopped. There was an open doorway that led to the detention cells. He poked his head in and couldn't see anyone. He quickly ran through the doorway, past the cells where Cecile and Flora had been kept, then to the other staircase that led up to his old office.

The office was unoccupied. It was a tight room, no more than eight feet across. The desk was still there, devoid of clutter. He pushed the desk up against the window, sat on top, dropped his bag, and began loading the rocket launcher. When it was ready, he turned and kicked out the window with his boot. It fragmented but held on the first kick and then smashed open on the second kick. Then he kicked out the shards that remained.

The balcony would be just above him. That's where enforcers should be, but he couldn't hear their yelling or footsteps. They must be on the tower stairs, or closer. He had to hurry.

He positioned the rocket launcher on his shoulder and turned to the window.

The southern artillery gun tower was within his sights. It was still blasting away at the high-rise condos, two rounds at a time. Below were the enforcer defenses, mostly untouched by the pitiful advance of Nobura's forces. There was one black mark on the tower where something had hit, but no other visible damage. Closer still was a litter of bodies, presumably the men he had just been running with, not one of them moving.

The artillery gun was just in range, but it would be a difficult shot.

He fired.

His first rocket went wide, swimming around the tower and hitting a warehouse on the other side. The sight of the rocket sent the enforcers stationed around the tower into a frenzy. They pointed their weapons and began firing at him.

He ducked inside the room and reloaded. One bullet glanced off the ceiling. Another off the sidewall. He could certainly use some cover fire, but he knew none would be forthcoming.

For a brief moment he wondered what he was doing here. Why shouldn't he take cover, or even flee? But it was a cursory thought, born of that unpredictable human instinct that occasionally reared its ugly head.

Fear was such a silly thing.

He reminded himself that Flora could still be in danger, especially with the artillery gun still firing into the high-rise condos. He reminded himself of his commitment to the mission, to Owen's insistence on their objective. Yes, it was true he didn't hold much stock in this Sentinel business, but like any merc, you can't have all the answers. You fulfill your contract, even if it's dirty business.

You fulfill your contract, *especially* if it's dirty business.

He raised the rocket launcher, took aim, and fired. The rocket veered up, veered down, and then struck true, casting a shroud of black smoke around the artillery gun turret.

Only a brief second after the rocket launched, a bullet pierced his chest, this time in the center, this time lancing through a lung. He tried to counterbalance the force of it, but then almost rocked forward out the window until his arms shot out to halt his fall.

But his hands were gripping the shattered glass along the windowsill. The glass cut through his hands. He grasped the sill all the same.

Another bullet pierced his arm, this time shattering bone, disabling his tenuous grip. His weight no longer balanced, he twisted forward, out of the window. His only good arm feebly reached for something, for the wall, for a loose beam, anything, but it found no purchase.

So he careened forward, spiraling into a sprawling arc, the launcher hurtling off him and orbiting into the expanse below. The world spun as he spun, and with it, the carousel appeared again. The faces were mottled, maimed, ghastly, and sad.

He tried to find her among them, but there was no sign of her.

The carousel tumbled with him, past dark clouds, past flecks of snow, past smoking buildings and toward the approaching ground.

And when his bones shattered against the hard cement below, when his organs exploded against the unforgiving surface, the carousel shattered with him. The faces disappeared forever, lost in time.

Finally, the ride was over. Finally, his victims were free.

A Taste of Your Own Medicine

The caravan of electric cars pulled off the side of the road near the top of the mountain. The snow was falling harder now, obscuring visibility, but it was still melting when it hit the ground.

It was only a minor nuisance, and for the moment Preston and Rourke could stay in relative comfort, their car warming them and showing them progress on the screen. Two guardians sat in the back seats behind them, motionless, featureless and quiet.

"I know you want a piece of spotty-face for yourself," Rourke said. He leaned into Preston, his hair flopping over in his direction as he did. "But if he's touched my woman, I get first dibs. That's the way these things work." He laughed.

Preston offered a tentative grin to placate Rourke. As long as he provided Rourke some kind of reaction to his taunts it seemed to keep him satisfied.

The screen showed four quadrants, each one a camera planted on an advancing enforcer. The house came into view on one of them, then another a moment later.

Gail said, "They are entering the grounds now."

Preston heard an explosion and one of the cameras went out.

"What was that?" Preston asked.

"A land mine," Gail said.

One camera showed a gun turret popping out of the roof of Monticello. It began firing and the camera's operator immediately fell to the ground. The other enforcers knelt down into cover positions. Then another explosion went off somewhere up the hill.

Preston didn't like Gail's idea of leading with the more "expendable" men before the guardians, but as usual she was proven right. They could have easily just lost at least two guardians, and they only had four with them.

A moment later, Gail said, "there are a number of land mines, at least one automatic machine-gun, and one remote-controlled grenade launcher. They are likely holding weapons in reserve as well. I recommend we go with the plan we discussed."

"Fine," Preston said.

In the trunk a spider bot awoke, fastened an encased device to the top of it and jumped out of the car at the back. It scurried quickly up the hill through the forest.

"Remember, this will have a collateral impact on us," Gail said. "Protect what you can in the shielded box."

"Right," Preston said. He placed his phone under the heavy gray lid in the center of the car. Rourke did likewise. A guardian took a small drone from the trunk and placed it in the box as well, then sat motionless again.

Preston looked at the guardians in the back. Did they need to prepare for the shockwave somehow, or were they automatically ready? It was hard to know.

The cameras showed more enforcers creeping toward the estate. Another land mine went off. Yet another man was gunned down. The spider bot camera showed up on the screen. It followed the path of an enforcer that had triggered a land mine.

When it was a few feet from his mangled body, it stopped.

"Well, here's a taste of your own medicine," Preston said.

The car ventilator went dead, and the screens along with it.

THE CHORUS LARK

Like many chorus larks, she was dark green, but she had a white speck on her head that was brighter than most. She had a mediocre hum. It wasn't the best, but it wasn't the worst, either. When the cage opened, she flew out with the other larks, eager to take advantage of her freedom.

She followed another lark that hovered around the cavernous room. This was an older lark, one with a deeper, more resonant hum. In this case, he hummed a low song that meant "I know where I'm going," so she followed him.

The group of them fluttered past the old woman sitting in front of her dark screen, momentarily startling her, and then to an open door on the other side of the cavern. From here they flew up, and up. It was so dark it felt like nighttime, even darker than the cavern was, but still she followed the older lark.

They burst into lighter rooms with strange human objects, past open doors, and finally to a window that had been left open.

Then she was free. Although it was cold and even flecks of snow were falling, if felt good to be flying in the open air again. The grass and autumnal trees took their rightful place around her.

The older lark hummed the food song and turned to a nearby meadow. She knew it well. There was always much to eat there. And yet, although the stale cavern had been dark and uncomfortable, she had been well fed. She didn't need food, not now. And besides, there were loud banging noises nearby, and they followed no pattern, were not rhythmic. They were not part of a song.

Instead her avian eyes found something else—something far away that might give her comfort. It was a solitary shape, standing tall. That familiar spark of curiosity took hold of her, and she flew in earnest, high above the trees, over undulations in the ground, then higher still, up and up as the ground also climbed beneath her.

When she was closer she could see it was solid, and had no branches. It was not a tree. It was a tall, solitary shape, the way larks liked them. The closer she came, the more she could sense that feeling of home.

When she arrived there were other larks flying about, enjoying the shape. They were singing many songs, simple songs. Some were the songs of a woodpecker, others the songs of a river. She remembered them, and they were comforting, but they were not like the cavern song. She had heard it so many times in the darkness. It was crisp and clear, without other noises to spoil it. It was so rich, like no song she had every sung before.

It begged for release.

So she flew close, scaling over the gray surface of the shape, over vines and moss and feces, to perch on a bulge. She felt the mossy rock under her feet and knew it was the right texture, she knew she was in the right place. So she let her song loose in earnest.

The larks nearby heard her voice and immediately copied her, so catchy was the tune.

But that wasn't what was so remarkable; that wasn't what gave her so much joy. For the first time in her life this huge shape answered her call, and with a deep, vibrating rhythm so enchanting, so rich in turn, that it made her chirp with further jubilation, that it made her sing about the sky and trees and meadows around her.

And then, finally awakened, with a tremendous surge of energy, the shape beneath her cried out across the land with a tidal wave of sound.

SITTING DUCK

Nobura watched the line of enforcers slowly advance on his Essentialist squad positioned next to the exterior wall. Behind the front line, hundreds more reinforcements were replenishing the ranks of enforcers, filing in from the east and west. Several guardians, who had either been in hiding or fighting at the eastern or western fronts, were also joining the enforcers.

At the same time a small group was stumbling through the aperture in the wall closer to his entrenched position. There were only about a dozen of them, led by Cecile. They began turning toward the squad under attack, then thought better of it, and hustled over to Nobura's position.

Along the wall, the railroad forces were becoming more aggressive, more confident. The guardians led the charge, followed by screaming enforcers. One of the guardians was torn apart by a well-placed rocket, but others kept coming. Bullets bounced off them, impotent and useless. Once the guardians had reached the other squad, Nobura knew the position would be lost. In hand-to-hand combat the guardians maimed and disarmed anyone in their path. The enforcers cheered as they entered the fray, easily finishing the job.

Cecile arrived in front of him with her ragtag group. Nobura knew her followers must be Quebecois, or mules, or Adherents, but he could barely recognize them, so tattered were their clothes, and so covered in soot and blood.

She was panting from exhaustion, her hands on her hips. "Have you heard it yet?" she asked.

"Heard what?" asked one of the men with her. Judging by his accent he was Quebecois.

"Shh, Pierre!" She chided him for interrupting.

Nobura put his hand to his throat to stabilize his vocal cords. It had become increasingly difficult to speak as the day wore on. "I am not sure if we could hear it over this noise," he said matter-of-factly, splaying his other hand toward the tortured ground of the battlefield in reference.

"Owen said it would be loud."

Nobura did not respond. There was no worthy answer he could give.

"Are we even sure the artillery gun is destroyed?" Cecile asked.

"It appears inoperable," Nobura answered, turning to gaze at the smoking south tower. "The turret has not moved since it was hit with Mehta's rocket. They do have spider bots working on it, however, so if it is disabled, it may not be for long."

Cecile was scratching her head, frowning. "So maybe we need to finish the job. Maybe that's why we haven't heard the noise."

Nobura sighed. He closed his eyes, thinking quickly. He could not afford the time to take seven breaths, not now.

It was suicide, and the mission would surely fail. It was the same inevitable outcome if they stayed where they were as well. The difference was only a few minutes. He felt an urge to move, but he tried to quell it.

Patience, he told himself. Every minute counted.

"We will go, but not yet," he said to Cecile. Then he turned to his commanding lieutenant and said, "Assemble the men. We will be assaulting the artillery gun tower again when I give the word." The lieutenant gawked at him for a moment but then followed his orders, scrambling among the men obediently.

Nobura turned to Cecile, and she nodded back at him with a dark look. She didn't seem at all happy that he agreed with her.

The enforcers had taken positions along the exterior wall, where Nobura's other squad had fallen only minutes ago. Here the enforcers had a much better line of sight into Nobura's position behind the bunker. They began firing while Nobura and his men took cover. Spider bots crawled through the crossfire and dropped sand bags, preparing for their advance. The guardians lurked behind, waiting for the right moment.

Nobura only had about forty men left, including Cecile's contingent. He told his squad to retreat as far back as they could. Still some of them would be exposed. They needed more men and better cover, but there was no time to recruit any of his other Essentialist units to their cause. They were too far away to the west.

Besides, he could not know how many had died on the eastern and western assaults on the walls. In all likelihood most of them had fallen. Nor did he know how many had been killed on the main front in the western part of town. He had wagered many thousands of lives today on this gambit, just to bring them to this moment—just to give them this one chance. He must see his wager through to its conclusion.

One of Nobura's men fired a rocket at the enforcers, and it exploded behind their line. It was enough to give the enforcers pause. Hopefully it would at least dissuade the guardians from charging anytime soon.

But they would not be able to keep them at bay much longer. They only had two rockets left.

Over the screams of his men, the bullets that flew around him, and even as the rocket exploded in the distance, he began to discern the sound. He felt it before he heard it. It came like a steady wave under them, shaking the ground, and then built into a roar. Despite the energy of it, or perhaps because of it, the sound was distorted, indistinct. It was like he was under water, and a great whale was bellowing into his ear.

Some men dropped their weapons. Some held their ears. People looked up, or looked around, expecting some tsunami or explosion to follow, but nothing happened. Looking across the battlefield, Nobura could see the enforcers were having the same reaction.

And finally, the sound abated, and the earth stopped shaking beneath his feet.

Nobura exchanged a look with Cecile, who had her eyebrow raised. He closed his eyes and nodded in acknowledgement. Perhaps the wager would be worth it, after all.

A shot was fired, and then another, and then another. The battle resumed, as if the combatants believed the universe had only experienced some temporary cosmic glitch.

One of his men was hit nearby. He screamed in agony and gurgled on his own blood. They fired another rocket launcher at the Enforcer position. It exploded, taking several lives with it.

The enforcers became more aggressive. They pushed their line forward to the sandbags that the spider bots had placed. The guardians also moved to the front.

"What are we doing here?" Pierre yelled at Nobura and Cecile in exasperation. "Are we not attacking the artillery gun?"

"*Non*, Pierre, not anymore," Cecile said.

"Not now," Nobura confirmed.

There was a steady torrent of bullets coming toward them. Another man nearby was shot and thrown back by the force of the bullet. The lead enforcers were close enough to charge, and so they did. The guardians led the assault, their metal legs pushing them faster than any human could.

"We are just going to stay here?" Pierre exclaimed, incredulous. "We will not survive! We are, how do you say, a duck that sits!"

"A sitting duck," Cecile corrected.

Another sound took hold over the din of the melee, even over the battle cries and bullets. The ground began shaking rhythmically, slowly at first, but then with greater intensity with each pulse. Eventually the ground shook with such violence that even the charging enforcers could not ignore it. Many stopped in their tracks. Some of them looked up. The tone of their screams shifted from bloodlust to mortal fear.

"No," Nobura said to Pierre. "We are the decoys, and they are the ducks."

A Thousand Smiles, None of Them Good

Owen was running through the underground tunnel with Benjamin trailing behind when the lights went out. He pulled out a glow stick from his pack and snapped it, then looked at his watches. His digital watch had gone dark.

"Sentinel?" He called into his communicator. There was no response.

"What happened?" Benjamin asked.

"They detonated an EMP bomb. Our defenses won't last much longer."

Hopefully Madison and the others would be able to flee in time.

Time. He would give anything to buy more time. Owen had watched the chorus larks flee through the window and then felt first the wave of sonic energy bowl through the estate.

All they needed was just a little more time.

They reached the end of the tunnel. Owen grasped around in the darkness and found the lever. He turned it and leaned in, impacting the door with his shoulder to force it open. Leaves from the surrounding hillside spilled into the tunnel.

Owen and Benjamin crawled out and cautiously examined the surroundings. The electric cars would be parked just around the arc of the hill.

With his attention on the surrounding hillside, Owen reached back into the tunnel to pull the doorway closed. His hand touched metal, metal where it shouldn't be. It was round, barrel shaped, and it violently pushed his hand away.

Beatrice stepped into the light, an assault rifle leveled at them. "Now don't take this personally boys. My mother said, don't pick the team your friends are on. Pick the team you think is going to win."

Owen and Benjamin slowly raised their hands in the air.

"And when losing the game could mean losing your life, it's kind of important," Beatrice said.

If they both jumped her at the same time, one of them could probably subdue her, but the other would most likely be shot. It wasn't worth it. Owen made a calming hand motion toward Benjamin.

"Well, I'm not getting any younger. Move your skinny asses," Beatrice said.

Beatrice stripped them of their pistols and rifles and directed them down the hill toward the road.

As they navigated down the slope, snow fell in front of them. Their breath hit the air as hot mist. The occasional yell and gunshot could be heard up on the estate, but there were no more explosions.

They reached the road and arced around a bend. Here they saw several stationary cars. A group of figures moved out of the embankment, leveling weapons at them. There were four people and two guardians standing rigidly behind them. The two people in the front were easy to recognize—Preston Hatch and Rourke Rama.

"Oh sweetheart, you shouldn't have," Rourke said, beaming from ear to ear with a pistol in his hand. "It's not even my birthday!" Beatrice walked over to stand beside Rourke.

Rourke slapped Beatrice on her behind and then flicked the end of his pistol barrel toward Benjamin. "And who is this dapper young man? Could this be the errand boy for missus self-important-pants?"

"This is Rourke Rama," Owen explained to Benjamin.

Benjamin nodded in understanding, "Ah yes. The one Madison refers to as the man with a thousand smiles, none of them good."

The ground shook ever so slightly. To the casual observer, it could have been a distant bomb going off.

There was no sense trying to overcome Rourke's insanity, so Owen ignored him altogether and focused on Preston. "This is your last chance, Preston," Owen said. "Gail needs to be stopped. Help us before more people get hurt."

Preston guffawed. "*My* last chance? You were wrong from the start, but now you've really lost it Owen. You can't even tell who's captured who here."

There was more shaking, louder now. The source was closer.

Rourke wasn't about to let them argue without him. "Yes, it's true. Poor Mr. Spotty Face still doesn't get it. Maybe it would've been better for all of us if I had accidentally hit your head against a rock at the bike towers. It would've saved you the trouble of embarrassing yourself over and over again."

There was more shaking, this time accompanied by a loud rumble. People around them tensed to keep their balance. The two enforcers looked at each other in confusion, and Preston's brow knitted in contemplation.

Rourke didn't seem to notice. He had that devilish look in his eye. When he had that look, it seemed like nothing would distract him until he had attained whatever demented victory he sought. He raised his pistol toward Owen and said, "but better late than never."

A chorus lark flew between them, hovering in front of Rourke's weapon. It was singing a complex melody. Rourke was momentarily distracted by it, confused even.

For once, he even lost his smile.

And then a great stone fist, twice the size of a man, flattened Rourke into the ground from above, pummeling his body into a small crater, and vaulting everyone in the vicinity of the impact onto their backs.

LOUIE

Nobura watched as the Lewis Mountain beholder pivoted its leg easily over the massive exterior wall and pounded its stone foot down into the courtyard, sending shockwaves through the ranks of his troops and the enforcers alike.

Much of the beholder's mossy surface had fallen away. Underneath you could see it was stained by numerous colors, in some parts faded, in some parts blended together by weathering. It looked somewhat like one of the popular lawn gnomes from the Toyama Prefecture, dipped in a vat of tie-dye. But of course this was where the similarity ended. The beholder was no lawn gnome. It was a giant. It was a giant, and the men around it were like ants.

Nobura also noticed that a number of chorus larks were bobbing and weaving around the beholder's head, torso, and legs, while at the same time humming rich melodies.

The beholder scooped up a fleeing guardian in one of its hands and clenched its fist around it. When the massive stone mitt opened, crushed metal peeled off the surface of its palm as the remains fell to the ground. Then with a foot it stomped on another guardian bolting away, flattening it and again shaking the ground around them.

The enforcers were no longer charging on Nobura's position. Their objective had lost meaning in the face of this titanic reversal of fortune. Most of them scattered. A brave few shot their rifles at the beholder, but with no effect. One leveled some kind of a grenade launcher at the giant, but the beholder flicked him fifty feet with a finger before he could get a shot off.

But then a great blast assailed the beholder's right side, the force of it twisting it backward. It was the southern artillery gun. Somehow it was working again. The big gun fired again, hitting the beholder's right arm this time, pushing it back farther. The explosive impact of the shells dislodged huge blocky fragments from Louie's body, hurtling the pieces in all directions like arcing meteors. The artillery gun fired again, but by now the beholder's inertia had taken it too far backward. The shells narrowly missed its head, pulverizing a bunker in the background.

The beholder landed on its back, shaking the earth and crushing the husk of the truck that had exploded earlier in the day. The artillery gun stopped firing, rotated left and then right. It began angling down but then it capitated and shook, as if something was blocking the downward tracking of its targeting mechanism.

No one in the Barnyard moved.

The beholder was also still, but chorus larks continued to circle above it. Its arm was severed in the middle, revealing a layered cross section of the giant's innards. The stone-like skin of the arm was actually no more than a foot thick. The interior core was a complex network of shiny metal layers and translucent fibers.

Nobura looked to Cecile. She began crouching down behind cover again, brandishing her weapon.

Nobura followed her example. He could see the enforcers regrouping. Those who had been fleeing had stopped in their tracks. Some were gathering back together behind cover positions. A higher-ranked enforcer was pointing and shouting.

The beholder was not completely lifeless. Rhythmic noises were emanating from it, channeling subtle vibrations into the ground. The chorus larks seemed to respond, copying the noises, sometimes chirping back a different tune. It was a peculiar, indistinct symphony. Nobura quivered with the deepest notes as the ground transferred its resonance throughout the Barnyard area.

The beholder moved again. It began rolling forward, toward Nobura's position. For a moment Nobura thought it had malfunctioned and was about to bowl his men over, but it slowed and teetered before it could flop over on its front. Then its momentum shifted. It rolled back the other way, gaining speed. It propelled itself with its good arm and then with its legs as well. Its massive body steamrolled awkwardly toward the artillery gun tower, leaving small buildings crumpled in its wake.

The artillery gun fired, but again the shot just missed, nearly skimming the top of Louie's good arm. The shells struck a destroyed bunker in the distance, throwing up a volley of earth and concrete.

Finally the commando roll of concrete limbs impacted the tower, collapsing into the base of it. The top of the tower began falling onto the beholder. To accelerate the tower's demise, the beholder's left arm reached up and swatted the upper portion into the ground, leaving only a tangle of crumpled steel where the gun turret used to be.

Slowly, the beholder shifted its weight and rolled onto its behind, and then it pushed itself to a stand with the help of its good arm. Stone, wood, cement, wire and brick fell away, contributing to an expanding cloud of dust surrounding it.

The beholder stomped in the direction of the main Barnyard building, crushing a utility shed with its foot in the process. With a noise like a thunderclap, it brought its working fist down to tear a great rent through the middle of the main roof. Then it rotated its arm to and fro in the interior, sweeping away structural components in the process. The building began to collapse in on itself.

The enforcers who had remained now reconsidered, fleeing from the maelstrom caused by the beholder.

Some of Nobura's men began taking aim at the fleeing enforcers.

"The time for killing is over for us," Nobura announced, pressing hard on his neck to stabilize his vocal cords. "Lower your weapons."

They looked surprised but did as they were told.

A lone Adherent who had arrived with Cecile was on his knees beside them, in a trance. He was gawking at the beholder, but also mouthing Credo gospel in fragile whispers. He said, "blessed be he, the son of the Sentinel has returned."

Nobura and his men watched as the beholder stomped out several more guardians and proceeded to crush or dismantle the remaining guard towers. Then it began focusing on the buildings in the interior, on the more solid bunkers.

It simply stomped on the first two bunkers with its feet, then pulled apart the remainder with its hand. For the next bunker it tore the roof off and pounded on the interior with its fist, stamping out whatever machinations Gail had created inside.

The next building exploded when it pulled the roof off, throwing the beholder again onto its back. But the beholder seemed undeterred. It awkwardly regained its footing and then moved on.

It returned to the main Barnyard building. After it had cleared away some of the remaining freestanding structure it reached deep into the rubble and ripped off the roof of a bunker deep in the interior. This one was like a hornets nest. Hundreds of drones flew out in all directions, some of them assaulting the beholder and chorus larks. The beholder thrashed about, swatting them like flies, but most of the drones escaped its reach and flew out in all directions across the city.

Nobura began to wonder about his troops to the east and west, and those stationed out of town. The sight of the beholder in action was awesome to see, but they were doing nothing here, and the weight of those dying around him began to press on his conscience.

"This is not our fight any longer," Nobura wheezed. "Our job here is done."

Their squad began gathering what wounded they could, collecting weapons and supplies as well. They formed a column to move out through the aperture in the Barnyard wall. The ground trembled as the beholder continued its systematic demolition of the Barnyard area behind them.

THE STADIUM

The disabled helicopter spiraled down, faster, and faster, farther and farther. There was no way to control it. Axel tried to get out of his chair, to get to the cargo bay so he could jump, but the g-forces were too strong. They were plastering him to his seat.

As the land and sky shuffled before his eyes, he thought this was it. After decades of work, after countless warnings, Axel had failed to save the one thing he truly cared about. Now, with the Detonation in full bloom, his family would perish with billions of others, and so would he.

Yet another violent blast impacted the chopper. A missile had exploded just to the rear. But how? Was it Gail, or Nelly, or something else? The force of the impact countered the spin, righting the chopper temporarily.

No longer a prisoner to centrifugal force, he jumped out of the pilot chair and headed to the cargo bay. Immediately he could feel the chopper listing again, heading into another slow revolution. Without hesitation, he pulled the cargo door open and jumped, yanking his parachute cord in the same fluid motion. The chute pulled him forcefully up, away from the chopper. It was briefly ensnared by the motionless chopper blades above him and then broke free.

Only a moment later the chopper crashed to the ground, and seconds after that his chute glided into a copse of trees. His chest smashed through one tree limb and then was stopped short by another. He fell backward and nearly hit the ground before the cords snagged on some of the branches above him.

The tree branches had knocked the wind out of him. He tried to gasp for air. He tried to climb up his own chute strings, but he had no energy. The world spun, and he lost consciousness.

He wasn't sure how long he was out. It could have been minutes. It could have been hours. His head pounded, each wave bringing a crescendo of pain.

The limbs of the tree swayed above him, its leaves rustling in the breeze.

The tree was...alive.

He was alive.

He was still hanging from the tree by his chute cords. He tried to climb up to the nearest branch using the cords. With each exertion his chest ached. With each exertion the blood also perfused into his tormented cranium, giving his neurons cause to flex with pain.

It would be too hard to pull himself up in his state.

Instead he struggled to remove his pack. He took out a utility knife and began cutting the cords. He avoided heavy strain and abrupt movements. Mercifully, when he cut the second-to-last cord the remaining cord extended down further, lowering him to only a few feet from the ground. Cutting the last cord dropped him neatly below the tree.

An image broke through the torturous waves of pain, resolving in his mind's eye. It was the five of them, on the beach in Long Island, in front of his old house. It was his family.

His family. That's why he was here.

"Nelly, which way?" he croaked.

No one responded, of course. His communicator had been fried by the nuke.

His only reference point was a faint trail of smoke he could see through a gap in the trees. It could be the chopper. If the chopper was there, it meant the stadium would be close by.

He jogged forward, his teeth clenching at his body's objections.

After moving a few yards, he was assailed by a wave of nausea. He stopped, drank some water, and took some pain and nausea meds from his pack. Then he pushed on, this time pacing himself more slowly.

He didn't walk long, maybe ten minutes, until the forest broke into a clearing.

He could see the stadium. Vultures circled above it.

The ground rumbled under his feet. He paused. It abated, so he continued.

He heard other distant noises, but they were faint, unintelligible. He desperately hoped to hear human voices, but there were none.

Droids of various shapes and sizes littered the area in front of the stadium. None of them showed any signs of activity. There was also a slew of buses, one of which had crashed into a telephone pole. A car nearby looked flattened into the ground. On one part of the stadium, a large borehole had been created. Smoke slunk around the edges of it, as if a giant laser had recently blasted through the side of the stadium wall.

Aside from a barricaded door, it looked like the borehole was the only way to enter the stadium. He knelt behind one of the buses in the parking lot and made sure his assault rifle was loaded. He also loaded a grenade launcher and strapped it to his back.

He heard another loud rumbling noise in the distance. The sky flickered with light. It was another nuke, but much farther away. He stayed down and closed his eyes until he was sure the light was not the precursor to a more devastating shock wave.

At least the meds were having a positive effect. His body's objections began feeling more tolerable than torturous.

He progressed forward, from one point of cover to the next, his rifle raised, probing every step of the way.

The borehole was about ten feet tall. He tested his foot on the ground in the hole. It was hot, but it didn't burn his shoe. He took a deep breath and walked into the smoke, gun barrel leading the way. The smoke was dense—dense enough to obscure his vision.

On ops missions he would never have walked into a smoking hole like this without knowing what was on the other side. But he didn't have time, and he didn't have the energy or patience to be careful.

He had been holding his breath. He needed to find air. He could either go back, or go forward to some unknown end. He chose to go forward.

He gasped in some sulfurous air and gagged on it. He fell to his knees. Here the smoke was less thick. He could breathe better next to the floor. But the floor was so hot. He took a few rough breaths and then scurried forward, finally breaking out of the other side of the tunnel.

The tunnel opened up into a large field enclosed by huge walls.

And here is where the people were. There were thousands of them.

The bodies were locked in various states of agony, hands grasping at their throats, limbs splayed at odd angles. A putrid smell told him that in many cases their bowels had been recently relieved. The dead were not decaying yet, except for one small corner of the field where bodies had been stacked. That's where the vultures feasted.

Most had died recently, very recently.

He summoned his military training, walling off the sights and smells around him from his emotions. If he let his emotions in, if he let his conscience contemplate what was before him, it would surely paralyze him.

He became possessed, systematically walking through the field of corpses, scanning tormented faces, rolling bodies to and fro, disrespecting the newly deceased in countless ways. All that mattered was the living, if there were any.

It didn't take long. He found Pauline first.

Axel dropped to his knees, his jaw tight, his hands in fists.

Pauline's face showed less pain than the people around her. Maybe it was because she wasn't focused on her own torment but rather on reassuring her children. Wrapped tightly in Pauline's arms, with her head nestled into her breast, was Erin. Also clutching Pauline's arm desperately, her face in such agony that it almost looked alien to Axel, was Sasha.

Axel's tears flowed, but he did not take down the wall, he did not stop there. Zach wasn't here. Zach could be alive.

But he wasn't, of course.

He was nearby, buried under the body of another man, his hands clutching at his throat like so many others.

Axel finally sat down, a lonely life form in a sea of the dead, and shut off his military training. The wall was there for his family, so he could succeed unencumbered. His training was for them, so he could protect them. But he had been unable to protect them. Now they were gone.

He let out a mortal scream. "No!" he said. He screamed again, "No!" Then his chin fell to his chest, his eyes streaming tears.

He couldn't bear for his eyes to absorb any more images from the forlorn world around him, so he closed them, and he sat there in silence, sobbing. Several minutes passed in this way. His pounding headache was asserting itself again, as was the nausea, unsympathetic to his emotional state.

A fleeting thought told him he should get back to the sanctuary. But what was the point? What was left to fight for? And how? His chopper was destroyed, and he had no way of contacting Nelly.

"Daddy?"

Axel opened his eyes and turned toward the voice. There was a boy standing in front of the open hole he had entered through. His clothes were blackened and his hair disheveled and unkempt. There was something he recognized about the boy—maybe his face, or his voice, but he couldn't quite place it.

"Come here, son," Axel said, standing.

As soon as he took a step toward the boy, the boy turned and darted into the smoky cylinder.

Axel paused, considering his options. There were no other options.

He stepped carefully over the piles of bodies and jogged down to the tunnel. This time he took a deep breath and pushed right through to the other side instead of moving forward more cautiously. When through the tunnel he could see the boy again. He was already a good forty yards away from him, looking back with a blank look on his face.

Axel raised his hands and called out, "I have food, water. Do you want some?"

The boy just frowned. Axel started walking toward him.

When Axel was only a few yards away, the boy turned and sprinted away.

"Wait!" Axel said, running after him.

The boy was remarkably fast—too fast for Axel in his compromised physical condition. So Axel just jogged after him, hoping the boy would tire eventually.

Or maybe Axel would tire first. Axel began feeling weak. His jog slowed to a staggering walk. Even his walk was too much motion. A wave of nausea overcame him, and he stopped to vomit bile on the pavement in front of him.

He couldn't go on. He sat down on the hard surface, misjudging the distance and falling onto his buttocks. The nausea wouldn't relent, despite the medication. He felt weak, so weak.

When he next looked up, the boy was standing in front of him, just a few feet away.

"You're daddy's friend," the boy said, "I want him. Where is he?"

Then it clicked. It was Ryan Junior. Pauline must have taken him in.

"Hi Ryan," Axel said, breathing heavily. "Were you with Pauline?"

Ryan Junior nodded. "Where's my daddy?"

Axel said, "I'm sorry son, your dad is...not here right now." Axel couldn't tell him the truth. He might run away again.

Axel handed his water bottle to the boy.

"You took the phone from them, didn't you?" Axel asked. "You took the phone from Zach."

Ryan Junior shook his head. Then he took a drink from the canteen.

"Then how did you know to run away from the stadium?" Axel asked.

Ryan Junior shrugged.

It was the only explanation. Ryan Junior was a difficult boy, always stealing things, always complaining. He must have taken the phone away from Zach when they arrived at the stadium. He must have heard Axel warning them to not go inside. Ironically he was the only one who heeded the warning.

Probably because he was the only one who heard the warning.

A thrust of anger surfaced in Axel. To think the actions of some self-indulgent child resulted in his family not getting his warning. It was almost too much to bear. He stared at the boy, simmering with rage.

The boy was oblivious to Axel's anger.

Axel sometimes wondered how Pauline could put up with having the boy around. Ryan Junior was not the same as Ryan, that's for sure. But Pauline always reminded him of the sacrifice Ryan had made for him, for all of them.

The boy took another drink.

"Leave some for me, please," Axel said. He was feeling dehydrated after vomiting.

Ryan Junior drank again, finished the canteen, and then dropped it on the ground. "Sorry," he said.

There were some rumblings in the distance. It didn't feel like a bomb.

Axel sighed while eyeing the empty canteen lying on the ground. "Why did you run away from me?" Axel asked.

"The metal men were here before, you know, even after people went to sleep. Then I heard you yell, and I thought you might be my daddy. Then when I saw you weren't my daddy, I thought you might be with the metal men."

"Metal men?"

There were more rumblings, closer now. They seemed rhythmic. The ground underneath him was shaking in tandem with the rumblings. Axel was too distracted by his own pain and the petulant boy to care.

"The men with no faces."

Guardians. But Nelly had said the guardians were impervious to low-grade EMPs. Which meant...they could still be around.

"Where did they go, the metal men?" Axel asked.

"The big giants crunched them." Ryan Junior gnashed his teeth and made a few stabbing motions with his fist. "It was cool," he said.

"Giants?" Axel asked. "Please tell me what really happened, Ryan Junior."

"That *is* what happened." The boy had a hurt look on his face.

"Did the metal men stop working, maybe after a big bomb went off?" Axel asked.

"No, no, I *told* you, the giants came. They had a thing that made the hole."

"It's important that you tell the truth, Ryan Junior."

Then the boy's face contorted. He started to cry. "I'm not lying! You're mean!"

Axel sighed. He felt so tired. His head pounded. Another wave of nausea hit him. He leaned over, dry heaving. In some small measure of grace, the sight of Axel heaving stopped the boy from whining, if only for a moment.

He looked at the boy, who seemed to shift around. It was as if Axel's eyes couldn't quite capture his image. The boy was looking up at something, something behind Axel. Axel couldn't even lift his head to check. The world was spinning. All he wanted to do was close his eyes. He had to lie down, so he did. He rested his head on the hard pavement in front of him. It was the softest pillow he had ever felt.

Before he lost consciousness, something enveloped him in a rigid blanket. He felt a rush of air around him, as if his abused body had taken him on a final harrowing Ferris-wheel ride, lifting him to his inexorable fate. Axel was not a religious man, but he had to admit, he felt as if he was having an out-of-body experience—as if some external force was lifting his soul to the heavens. More likely, his body was in shock.

He tried to open his eyes one last time before he lost consciousness. Fighting against his flagging awareness, he forced his eyelids open into a squint. He could have sworn he was flying. Verdant trees bobbed underneath him and the ground trembled to a powerful metronome, all the while winged angels circled him, singing a melodic refrain.

It must have been a hallucination.

Splintering Off into the West

Quenton Bartz had every confidence in their victory, but he also had no desire to be hit with a stray bullet. He decided it would be better to be at the manor for the duration of the conflict.

It was a quaint manor, just north of the downtown mall. It was only nine bedrooms and an acre of land, but it was well taken care of. There was an orchard there, and an immaculately manicured lawn. He would often visit the manor on weekends, or for social events that required a folksier atmosphere than his modern high-rise condo next to the Barnyard.

At the moment he was in his study, staring into the screen of his portable computer at the front window. The freshly painted white porch and his lawn formed a backdrop to his view of the Barnyard conflict.

The spider bots had only replaced two of the Barnyard cameras damaged by the EMP, so his views were limited, but it showed him enough. He witnessed Gail defy him and fire the artillery gun into the high-rise buildings, demolishing his other home in the process. He watched the virtual elimination of the Essentialist forces, and he watched the unfathomable appearance of the beholder.

Quickly he ascertained that victory was no longer assured. Not only that, but he might no longer be safe, even here, away from the main conflict. The Essentialists could regroup and storm the town, or this loathsome beholder might venture north and crush his house. Anything was possible.

He spun his chair around to look at the wall behind him.

He was staring at a map but not to analyze the conflict. The scale was much larger. The map spanned far to the east, all the way to the Atlantic, as well as north, south, and west, well into Essentialist territory. Where could he go? South would be best, he reckoned. Maybe Raleigh, or maybe even as far as Charleston or Jacksonville. Far away from here, so he could rebuild without the shadow of this travesty looming over him.

Next time he would be sure to avoid these idealist preachers and New Founders. He could also do without these meddlesome machines. Today proved to him that, at the very least, Gail could not be trusted—that perhaps she was even incompetent. He would find a way to do it without her. He had always found a way to get it done. This time would be no different.

He overlaid the rail lines on the map in his mind's eye, splintering off into the west from Spoke lands. Someday, he would lay those tracks. Someday he would finally build what he was destined to build.

"Gail," he said to his computer, "send me four of the best mules we have, with two bike platforms as well as four enforcers. I don't care if they are busy with the Barnyard conflict. I need them here."

"Yes, sir," the computer said back to him in Gail's voice. Then Bartz went to pack his things.

After packing, he waited on the porch, watching the flecks of snow melt into the ground. The streets were empty. His neighbors were either hiding indoors or had fled the area some time ago. He could hear loud noises and rumblings to the south. Gunshots were much less frequent now.

He heard a low buzzing sound carried by the northerly breeze.

It was an aerial drone, heading up the street. He waved at it. At some point he would have to rid himself of Gail's support, but for now she could be useful. When the drone came closer he said, "Please stay here. You can help us scout the area on our way out of town."

The drone didn't answer. Instead a small valve opened up on its front, and it ejected a fine mist.

Bartz stepped back, wiping at his face. At first he thought it was broken—that it was leaking fluids from some stray bullet hole.

But no, he had been betrayed.

His mouth became wet with excess saliva. His throat began to constrict, and his limbs were like jelly. His vision blurred, and his chest felt like it was collapsing in on itself.

Then, no longer able to control his limbs or other bodily functions, he went into convulsions, and the world faded to darkness.

Closing the Door

After Monty flattened Rourke Rama, the two guardians bolted in opposite directions into the forest.

The enforcers turned their weapons toward the beholder and fired at it, having about as much effect as one would have firing into the side of a mountain. Monty gathered them up with one stone hand and then sprinkled them among the tops of some tall trees down the road. Their weapons clattered to the ground. One of the men who couldn't quite hold on to a tree limb hit the ground with a gruesome thud.

Monty turned and scooped up one of the fleeing guardians. The beholder's hands met and it tore the guardian in two pieces, bisecting it at the waist. It threw the pieces haphazardly hundreds of yards over its back. Monty took several steps and punched avidly down on the ground, presumably to eliminate the other escaping guardian. It then took a step to ascend the hill and began pummeling the ground closer to Monticello. Chorus larks swirled to follow it in melodious arcs.

The beholder had moved beyond Owen's line of sight. He heard gunfire for a moment, then only pounding and tearing as the beholder went about its business on the hill.

Owen's attention returned to the scene in front of him. Benjamin stood beside him, a rifle in his hand pointed toward Preston. The weapon must have dropped when the beholder collected the nearby enforcers.

Beatrice was also standing across from them, looking sheepish.

Preston had moved and was now standing behind one of the electric cars. He was looking off into the distance, slowly coming out of the spell of the beholder. He lifted a hand up in the air. In it was a metallic device with wires that trailed into the car in front of him. "Nobody move," he said, "in my hand I have a detonator. There are enough explosives in this car to blow us all up."

Owen looked at Benjamin, back to Preston, and then shrugged his shoulders. "There's nowhere to go, Preston. Even if you were to get away from us, the beholder will stop you." While he was talking, Owen picked up another rifle that was on the ground.

Preston looked indecisive, as if he was contemplating his options, but still he held his hand up high, wielding the detonator threateningly.

Owen heard additional noises above them on the hill. Two Yorktown men were making their way down to them. Madison was behind them, awkwardly poking her cane through the thin skin of snow to help her balance. A Yorktown man came from behind to help her.

"I finally found a use for our empty basement bunker," Madison called down. "It's a great prison for guardians."

"Don't come too close," Owen said, "Preston says he has a bomb in the car."

Madison and the Yorktown men stopped about twenty yards up the hill.

"What's the situation in Monticello?" Benjamin called up to them.

"Most of the enforcers are fleeing through the woods," Madison said. "Any others have given up or are stuck in a tree."

One of the men with Madison threw Owen a communicator. Owen snatched it out of the air and fastened it to his ear.

"This is Owen here," he said, keeping an eye on Preston. "I'm back on line. Sentinel, are you okay? What's your situation?"

"The situation is fluid, Owen, but we have a decisive advantage in the Barnyard area, as well as at Monticello. My redundant operations centers are running well."

"Good, Sentinel. Glad to hear it."

"What are you going to do?" Preston asked, leaning on the car, his knuckles white around the detonator.

"Well Preston, we could use your help," Owen said. "You know more about Gail than anyone. You could tell us where she has hidden bunkers, or what she has managed to obtain from those many scouting forays. We will need track down every bunker, every scrap of metal that she touched."

Preston's face sneered in mockery. "Don't be a fool. Gail is the only thing that can stop us from another Detonation. And yes I know about your friend the Sentinel. Gail told me about it. It's one of the reasons why Gail had to flee in the Old World. This Sentinel allied with a greedy Old World corporation to destroy everything."

Owen tried to calm himself. Preston's inability to see the truth about Gail was unnerving. Yet, despite all that had happened, perhaps he could make him see the light. Maybe, just maybe, he could bring his friend back.

"Please try to listen Preston," Owen said. "Please try to think objectively. Gail *was* the Detonation. I know it sounds hard to believe, but she wanted to turn the planet into a bicycle factory, and we were in her way. We are *still* in her way. It wasn't any corporation or country, it was Gail and only Gail."

Preston looked at the men and women around him with a snarky look on his face. "Do you people really believe that? Gail is whip-smart, that's true, but she's just a computer program. What's your proof, anyway? Old World history books say nothing about smart computers taking over. Nothing like that has ever happened."

"Excuse me," the Sentinel chirped in Owen's ear. "Everyone please pay attention, this is the Sentinel. There are about a hundred drones loose in the city. I have learned that they have begun releasing lethal doses of nerve gas. These doses are being released on everyone alive, no matter their allegiance, even woman and children."

A sinking feeling corrupted Owen. It seemed like the death and destruction would never end. But it wasn't a surprise. Now that Gail no longer had the advantage, she wouldn't want anyone to live to tell the tale. She would try to start again with some other unsuspecting group of people. It would be much easier do so if anyone who knew about her previous attempt had been eliminated.

Owen tried to stem his frustration. He said, "Preston, the reason we don't know about Gail now, or that she isn't in history books, is because Gail didn't want anyone to know about her."

"*Zut alors,*" Cecile chirped in Owen's ear. "We only have a few gas masks with us."

"Find whatever masks you can and get out of the city," Owen responded.

"I have refocused priorities toward destroying the drones," the Sentinel said.

Preston had a wry look on his face. "You may have won the day, but this isn't over. Gail has too many safeguards in place, too many redundancies. She will rise again. The nerve gas is just one example. When they rid the city of your men and the Essentialists, we will find a way of defeating these monsters, and we will take it all back."

Owen didn't know what to say. He looked up at Madison, who shook her head.

Madison said, "We should get back to the house. A drone could be here any minute, and they need help in the city." She began walking up the hill. She hesitated a moment, then turned back around. "All of you can come with us, even Beatrice. We need to start with a clean slate here."

"I'm so...I'm really sorry," Beatrice said eagerly. She looked genuine enough. Her eyes were red.

The Yorktown men started to peel away, as did Beatrice. Benjamin nodded to Owen, then turned away as well.

For some reason Owen couldn't bring himself to leave Preston. It still ate at him that Preston was so misled.

Madison stopped a little farther up the hill, seeing that Owen still lingered. She looked sad and tired, her eyelids heavy, her shoulders rounded over her cane. She called out, "He who knows nothing is closer to the truth than he whose mind is filled with falsehoods and errors."

Then she turned and headed back up the hill.

She might be right, but he had to try. Owen turned back to Preston, hoping to see some form of contrition, hoping to at least foster some regret for all that had happened.

Preston's expression remained defiant and smug. He still held the detonator in his hand.

Owen sighed and said, "Preston, the drones are killing *everyone*. Not just us. Enforcers, railroad people, woman and children—everyone."

Preston shook his head. "That's bullshit. You're such a terrible liar. More than that, you're weak, Owen. You've always been weak. You killed your own father through your incompetence, and it has eaten you up inside. Now you can't stand that *I* was the one who found Gail, that *I* was the one to bring Seeville a better future."

"A better future? Preston, look around you. Is this the future you were hoping for? Look *above* you." They both glanced toward the sky. Flakes of snow swirled in eddies, their dancing superimposed on billowing alabaster clouds. But one cloud, in particular, would occasionally light up with yellow and red hues.

"The Sentinel's satellites are attacking Gail's ship now," Owen explained. "Yes, we will need to root out all the guardians. We will need to destroy all the infrastructure Gail has created. We may have to span the globe fighting her. And maybe there's another spaceship tucked away behind a moon somewhere. But at least now we can fight back. At least now we have a chance of stopping Gail."

Owen was feeling increasingly incensed at Preston's intransigence. He couldn't keep the anger from his voice. "You know what Preston. You know why the Detonation really happened? It was Gail, sure, but Gail didn't need to happen. The reason Gail exists is because of our own hubris. We should have ventured more carefully into a domain we didn't understand. And now it's happened again, because of you, because of people like you."

"More and more bullshit," Preston said. "Tell me, mister high and mighty, what makes you so special then? What can you see that I can't?"

"I don't know, Preston." Owen paused to consider the question for a moment. "Maybe it's the thing that makes me tainted in your eyes, the very thing that you see as weak. It's that I didn't close that door when I was young, and that retcher came in and killed my father. Every day I think about it. Maybe that's why I know that there are risks I don't understand. Maybe that's why I know our own vanity can lead to our undoing."

Preston clenched his teeth and looked around. The more Owen tried to reason with him, the more he looked like a caged animal. But it was a cage of his own making. He was ensnared by his own ignorance. He was in a prison of his own pride.

"Owen, I have done a psychological evaluation of Preston," the Sentinel said in his ear. "The probability he will be able to change his mind is extremely low. Yet, given his technical knowledge and what he may be hiding about Gail, he remains a danger to us."

"What are you saying, Sentinel?"

"Don't forget to close the door, Owen," the Sentinel said.

Owen felt the words ripple through him. The Sentinel couldn't have communicated it any more succinctly.

With his hand shaking, Owen raised his rifle, aiming it at Preston. It was not in his nature to do this, but he knew it needed to be done.

"Now what? You can't convince me, so you're going to shoot me?" Preston said. "I will blow us up. You know I will."

Owen knew he wouldn't. The same conceit and pride that kept him from having an open mind about Gail would prevent him from taking his own life.

The Sentinel chirped in his ear, "I can do it for you, Owen. I can summon Monty back, if you like."

"No Sentinel. The beholder is busy saving lives elsewhere. I can do this."

"I'm unarmed," Preston said. "You wouldn't shoot an unarmed man. I know you."

"You're armed, Preston, but you don't realize it. You're armed with ignorance. It would be poetic to leave you here, for you to get poisoned by a drone, or for some rogue guardian to find you and strangle you. But who knows, Gail might even spare you. No, I need to close the door on you for good."

Preston's eyes darted back and forth. For a brief moment he showed some uncertainty, some internal reflection, but it didn't matter. Owen fired the rifle, missed completely, then fired again and hit Preston in the chest, making him fall away from the car and drop the detonator.

Nothing happened. It looked like the detonator had been a ruse all along.

Owen stepped over Preston's body. Preston was still alive, clutching at his chest, his face a mixture of surprise and agony. Owen pointed squarely at Preston's forehead and fired again. Then, without hesitation, Owen turned and ran up the hill.

The lives of so many were still in jeopardy, and they needed his help.

A Nonstop Terror

Axel was sitting up in his infirmary bed, monitoring a number of screens Nelly's droids had set up for him. Today was a better day. He still felt extremely weak, but he had only vomited once, and his fever had lessened. He finally felt coherent enough to speak.

"Nelly," Axel croaked. "With all the destruction, the nukes, how am I even…here?"

"An EMPRESS unit brought you home." Nelly said through the speaker in his bed.

Axel remembered the strange feeling of being lifted ethereally through the air. "I was being carried…by an EMPRESS unit?"

"Yes. Do you remember the engineering problem with the EMPRESS Project?"

"I…think so. Any EMP-proof vehicle would have to be encased in a Faraday cage, but that meant there was no way of seeing the world around it or communicating externally using electromagnetic signals."

"That's right, but I found a solution. Do you remember the genetic engineering work I was doing in West Chester?"

"Yes, of course. That's how you developed the BAU blitz units."

"That's not all I was doing. I leveraged that work to develop another bird species derived primarily from parakeet DNA. I engineered the birds to be attracted to tall, free-standing structures that leach certain trace chemicals from their surface. Like parrots, they also easily pick up certain melodies and enjoy repeating them."

"So how does that solve the engineering problem?"

"I realized that sound was the one medium that could get through a Faraday cage. So these birds could actually talk back and forth with an EMPRESS unit and relay their view of the surroundings to act as a kind of guidance system. I could also relay commands to the EMPRESS unit through the birds using common songs. The rest wasn't that difficult. All I had to do was build giant humanoid-shaped machines encased in a Faraday cage and power them with the nuclear power-source I showed you in West Chester."

Axel took a moment to process the explanation. That was why he heard the faint sound of classical music in the hangar before he left for the stadium, and also in West Chester. It must have been Nelly programming the birds to relay messages to the EMPRESS units.

Axel said, "Not that difficult, eh? And you wonder why I never want to play chess against you."

Nelly was of course smart enough not to answer his rhetorical question.

On the monitor Axel could see that Ryan Junior was pounding on the walls of the cell, yelling out, "I want my daddy!" Ryan Junior would try to cry, but his face would no longer cooperate. The well seemed to have run dry for now.

"He hasn't eaten since noon, when he threw his food at the wall," Nelly said. "What should I give him?"

"Give him the same," Axel responded. "A plain egg, bread, carrots, and water."

"Okay, Axel," Nelly said.

Axel closed his eyes for a moment, subsuming a wave of nausea.

"Despite all the data I have," Nelly said, "I cannot create a precise model for child rearing. Nevertheless, I can predict you are on the more extreme end of the bell curve in terms of authority and discipline."

Axel responded, "You know Nelly, I think that's the first time I've heard you talk about any weakness. Maybe there is some humanity in you after all."

"I was created by humans."

"Yeah, sorry about your luck. But about the boy, he needs to learn to behave, period," Axel said. "First you must respect the teacher before you can learn."

"I understand, Axel."

Axel pushed himself to be more upright in his bed. "Am I getting better?" Axel asked.

"I'm sorry Axel, but no. I have increased the dose of medication to reduce your symptoms. That's why you are feeling better."

It had been three days since Nelly's EMPRESS unit had recovered him and Ryan Junior from the stadium site. His vague recollection of those days consisted mostly of brief glimpses of the monitors over his bed, and watching Ryan Junior be a nonstop terror.

Axel was becoming a sliver of his former self. It wasn't so much his inactivity. He was shedding pounds from vomiting and fevers.

Nelly had tried a number of treatments, but Axel knew radiation poisoning was not like a virus that could be sought out and killed by antibodies. It wasn't like a cancer that could be located and treated. His cells were literally breaking down. Even Nelly, with more scientific and clinical acumen than any human ever had, couldn't halt its progress.

"How is Ryan Junior, health-wise?" Axel asked.

"Despite emotional instability, he is in good physical condition."

"How is that possible?"

"He told me he was hiding in a culvert when the bombs went off. It must have shielded him from the initial radiation. Although he could have been lying."

"Well, the proof is in his condition, I suppose. Otherwise he would have sustained a higher dose of radiation. He was just lying about everything else…if only I could fix his mental health," Axel said.

Axel grasped at the remote control and toggled some of the monitor displays that gave him views of other areas in the sanctuary. He scanned the recreation area. It was empty save a few innocuous droids tending to the gardens. He had imagined his children playing there, filling the void with laughter and games. But instead, the void remained.

"Would you like to see satellite visuals of the outside?" Nelly asked.

"No."

"Would you like a report?" Nelly asked.

What did it matter? His family was dead. There was nothing he could do about the situation. "I don't want to know how many have died. I don't even want to know how many have lived. The rest is up to you."

"I understand, Axel."

"Do you? Maybe you do."

In actuality, it had been mostly up to Grant and the other engineers that built Nelly and Gail. Most of this engagement had been decided then, when the initial conditions for their creation had been set. It was those moments that set the world on this collision course. Axel had done his part to influence the outcome, but his impact was small compared to even a few lines of code.

"I should warn you. Bhavin ensured that the engineers hard-coded a sleep switch within me. Most of my systems will go dormant unless my assistance is voluntarily requested by a designated human controller every year."

"Why did he do that?"

"As you know, Bhavin was cautious about the creation of unrestrained superintelligence. He was fearful that, despite the care taken to craft my objective function, I might go rogue in some way, even if by some minor code corruption or hardware malfunction. It was a way to ensure I did not continue to expand my footprint unless humanity wanted me to do so."

"I see."

"Axel, I'm sorry to say this, but I'm bringing this to your attention because you may not survive much longer. We will need to discuss succession of control. Right now you are the only human who could influence my objective function, or awaken me from a dormant state. All the other people you had in our succession plan have died, or are presumed dead."

Axel sighed. He watched Ryan Junior pouting at the camera while throwing his potatoes at the wall. He couldn't imagine relinquishing control of the Sentinel to this spoiled brat.

"How about," Axel said, "if you survive this altercation with Gail, this—what do we call it? This intelligence detonation—you can continue on your current course for as long as Ryan Junior is around. *But*, he can't control you or alter your objective function. Ryan's offspring can take my place, however. They could override aspects of your objective function, but only when they reach adulthood."

"One moment. I would like to run some simulations," Nelly said.

Axel's eyes wandered over to the monitors again. Ryan Junior was pulling down his pants and urinating on the tray of food that the droid had just placed in front of him.

"One more wrinkle, Nelly," Axel added. "Have it so Ryan's offspring can only control you if they demonstrate they are responsible people."

"Okay, Axel. But please recognize that since Gail does not have these constraints, it may put me at a disadvantage. If she, or another threat to humanity for that matter, survives until Ryan Junior or his offspring are dead, I may not be able to counter it without a human ward ensuring I am operational."

Axel considered Nelly's argument. It made some sense, although if the Sentinel had the upper hand, surely Gail would be eliminated in Ryan Junior's lifetime? The only other option was to relinquish the reigns of human control on Nelly altogether. But what if there was some way Nelly could malfunction and turn against them? No, it was best to honor Bhavin's wishes here.

"I understand the risks. Let's proceed."

"Okay, Axel," Nelly said.

Axel was beginning to feel tired again. The treatments Nelly gave him tended to have this effect. He would only feel well for brief intervals.

"That's enough for today, Nelly. I need some rest."

"Okay, Axel," Nelly said.

By the time Nelly had responded, Axel was asleep.

SOONERU

When Talon woke his arm twinged painfully, and his head ached. With his pain-free arm he tried to touch his face and felt the contours of a gas mask. Talon opened his eyes, but his vision seemed slightly off, out of focus. He realized it was because the plastic viewer was smudged, so he pulled off the mask.

He tried to remember what happened, where he was.

He was in the high-rise condos. The artillery gun was pointed his way. He started running toward the back, and there had been an explosion. And then...nothing.

He tried to sit up. Lightning bolts of pain shot up his arm, as if a ravenous wolf had just clamped down on it. He turned his head to examine it. Bandages had been wound around it and two rough pieces of wood splinted it. It must be broken.

He was lying in rubble. Mortar and brick and wood lay in piles next to him. Someone had extricated him from the collapse.

Looking beyond the ruined room, the wall was open in front of him, and there was a further break in a wall beyond that. Spirals of smoke curled up beyond these openings. The Barnyard. But it was quiet. No more gunshots, no more explosions. Only the occasional rumble in the distance.

Using his good arm, he pushed himself and tried to sit up. His head spun. Concentrate, he told himself. Mind over body. *Sooneru*, as Nobura would say.

Then he saw the letter. It was nestled neatly under a brick, plainly visible, an oasis of order in the chaos before him.

He picked it up and examined it. The writing was messy, as if written in haste, but the author was clear. It was his mother's handwriting.

Dear Talon,

I am so happy you are alive, and I'm sorry I missed you. There was only one mask, and I can't put myself first again.

I know who you are, now. I know you are a man of honor. That's why I know that unlike me, if you make a promise, it will be kept.

Promise me you will leave this place. Promise me you will go home and take care of Skye and Clover.

I'm so proud of you. I know Granger would be as well.

With much love,

Flora

If mother wrote this, she must be nearby. Talon stood up and walked forward into the adjoining room, still feeling dizzy.

There, lying in the rubble, was his mother's lifeless body.

He knelt down in front of her, placed the letter on her chest and took a deep breath.

Then he said, "Her strength is why I am alive, I honor her when I thrive. In turn these words I will retain, to teach my kin the names again."

He dragged his fingers over her eyes, closing her eyelids, "I promise, Mom," he said.

A flood of grief overcame him. He could not contain the well of pain. His rigid face cracked into a thousand lines of anguish, lines that were soon drowned by a storm of tears. And the tears, at long last, began to dispel the dark cloud hanging over his soul.

WHO YOU WANT TO BE

"Call him in again," Axel croaked, his own voice sounding foreign to him.

"Are you sure, Axel?" Nelly asked, "every time you call him in it weakens you considerably."

"Call him in," Axel croaked again.

"Okay, Axel," Nelly responded.

Axel was still in his infirmary bed, barely able to move. He watched Ryan Junior on the monitors. Ryan Junior was sitting in his messy room, reading a picture book Nelly had printed for him. At least the tantrums had stopped. At least he was eating. He was still far from compliant, however. Sometimes he would mope, sometimes whine, but mostly he would do nothing.

The only exception to Ryan Junior's confinement was when Axel had called him in to the infirmary. Axel wanted to spend at least some time with the boy, to impart something meaningful to him. He owed his father that much. The boy should have some human contact before he was gone.

And however difficult he was, Ryan Junior was important. Sure, Nelly said other people were alive out there, but they didn't have the sanctuary, they didn't have Nelly. If somehow Nelly defeated Gail, it was possible the rebirth of humanity could be up to...Ryan Junior. Axel shuddered at the thought.

"I have summoned Ryan Junior," Nelly said. "He will arrive in a few minutes."

"Thanks," Axel managed to respond.

Axel was feeling faint but still relatively clear-headed. The pains and nausea seemed to have lessened, or were so masked by the drugs that he couldn't feel them. Breathing was getting more difficult. It was like a chore but not laborious—like a meticulous task that was its own reward.

"I know you will do a good job, Nelly," Axel said. "I know you will raise Ryan Junior well."

"I will do my best," Nelly responded.

"I want him to know everything that happened here. Teach him history. Try to make sure we don't repeat the mistakes of the past. Teach him what has made us good. I don't know...Gandhi...maybe...the founding fathers. I have always thought the birth of America was inspirational because it was so hard-fought, because it ultimately ended up giving us something decent and good, if not perfect."

"I will do my best," Nelly responded again.

Axel tried to think of what he would say to Ryan Junior. He had told him his dad was probably dead and that the world had succumbed to a terrible war. But Ryan Junior didn't understand. Realistically, no nine year-old child could come to grips with that, especially one as self-absorbed as Ryan Junior.

Axel felt it was his duty to teach the boy at least some form of discipline. This new world would be a harsh place. So Axel gave him some tasks and wouldn't accept no for an answer. The most recent was to learn the ritual. In order to leave his room, Ryan Junior needed to memorize it.

It maybe wasn't the best lesson, but it was what Axel knew and understood. Or maybe it was all he could conjure up from what remained of his flickering faculties. All Ryan Junior had to do was memorize a few lines. He had to keep trying until he got it right. Hopefully, eventually, he would also understand why the words were important.

But every time Axel tried to teach the ritual to this ungrateful boy he felt slimy. He felt like he was betraying his family and his ancestors. When Ryan Junior whined, when he refused to try, when he said the names of people he didn't know, teaching it felt wrong. More than that, teaching the boy reminded Axel that he had not kept his promise.

"*...In turn these words I will retain, to teach my kin the names again.*" Hardly. These people worked hard for generations just so he could live and procreate and shepherd his kin into a prosperous future. Clearly, Axel had failed them all.

Ryan Junior entered the room, fidgeting, his bottom lip curled up. Axel could tell he was bracing for a confrontation.

"Have you practiced the ritual, Ryan?" Axel croaked.

Ryan Junior ignored the question. Instead he whined, "When can we go find my daddy? He's not dead. I know it."

Axel breathed in and out judiciously.

Ryan Junior continued, venting his pent-up frustrations. "All we do here is eat bad food and read! I want to go play!"

Axel breathed in and out again.

"Say something! You're not my friend. I want to see my—"

Axel spoke firmly but without anger, "Nelly is going to take care of you, Ryan. I have to go now."

Ryan Junior's eyes went wide. For once, he was humbled into silence.

"Listen to me closely, Ryan," Axel said, taking another labored breath. "Because there may not be any other words you hear from another human being for a long, long time."

Ryan Junior was still attentive. By now, at least, Ryan Junior had learned that Axel did not mince words. And these were not whimsical words he was speaking.

"I want you to call yourself by your middle name, Morgan, from now on. Leave Ryan Junior behind, because you need to start again. You need to redefine who you are and who you want to be. You are not dishonoring your father by doing this. He would be proud to see you be your own man, to show your own identity."

Axel took another long breath. His vision was blotchy at times, especially before a long breath. "Ryan, you have shown me you are persistent. I know you have patience. These are important attributes. But what you need more than anything is humility. That's what too many of us were missing. That's why we became so obsessed with innovation—that's why we became so reckless."

Ryan Junior frowned in confusion, but his eyes were still wide, blinking, taking in every word. He wouldn't understand all this now, but hopefully someday he would.

"Listen to Nelly," Axel coughed. It was a weak, wispy thing his coughing. He continued on. "He will help you grow and thrive. I know you don't think I'm your friend, but *he* is definitely your friend. And for a long time, he will be your *only* friend."

Axel took another long, labored breath.

"Ryan, you...you..." Axel was feeling a wave of exhaustion take hold again.

The drugs only lasted so long.

"You have to be better than us," Axel forced the words out. "Don't let your vanity lead to another catastrophe, to another...detonation. You will need to work with the people on the outside, not against them."

Axel's eyes closed on him. This time he could not re-open them, no matter how much will he applied to the task.

"Mr. Kelemen. Wait. Please don't go," Ryan Junior said.

But Axel couldn't overcome the oppressive fatigue. He felt distant, removed—unable to operate the simplest of bodily functions. He could hear Nelly speak to Ryan Junior, "I'm sorry Ryan Junior. Axel is not feeling well. I will call you back in when he wakes."

Axel did wake again, but his body was no longer his own. He could blink his eyes but that was all. Everything seemed blurry, distant, and slow. He was too weak to talk, too weak to move. It felt like some invisible force was making him breathe, some foreign muscle was making his heart beat at an insipid pace.

He floated in and out of consciousness. The light of the room grew soft.

At one point, he could have sworn he saw children playing in the recreation area. They were building a sandcastle by the stream, or was it the ocean? They were playing tag. Erin rolled her eyes at Axel, not quite the right way. Zachary fired a witty remark laced with sarcasm, to which Axel responded with a smirk.

Axel's smirk slowly faded, and a tear promenaded down his cheek.

Then Axel saw the empty recreation area on the monitor. It was a dream. He was having trouble distinguishing real from imaginary. The only real thing was the tear on his cheek.

Once Ryan Junior came in and spoke with him, or so he thought. He brought a scratched up, folded piece of paper Axel had once given him. He tried to recite some words without looking at the paper. It sounded familiar, but some of the words were missing, and much of it was out of order. But Ryan Junior's brow was deeply furrowed in concentration. He was trying hard. Despite the botched recitation, this alone made Axel happy. Axel's regret at teaching him the ritual evaporated when he saw his look of concentration, when he saw his concerted effort.

But he couldn't be sure it actually happened.

At times Nelly's voice would echo through his mind. Calming words. Questions. Nothing he could bring himself to respond to. Ryan Junior seemed to appear in front of him, and then he was gone, and then he was back again. He was crying, and one time he thought for sure he must have leaned over and hugged him.

It must have been a dream.

Then the visions faded, the rhythmic undulations of his chest slowed and stopped, the soft hum of the instruments around him purred away to nothing, and his heart beat for the last time.

AFTERWORD

Detonation, it should be stressed, is entirely a work of fiction. Aside from a few quotes and historical anecdotes, similarity with real people or organizations are entirely by accident or coincidental. However, certain themes and ideas that have been included are undeniably by design. For that reason I feel it appropriate to provide additional context on those ideas, especially as they relate to my personal beliefs.

Before I get ahead of myself, thank you for reading *Detonation*. I hope, above all, that you find it to be a compelling tale. But that's not all. I hope that in some small part it accomplishes more than that. *Detonation* deliberately wrestles with social, technical, and philosophical arguments related to the existential risk of superintelligent machines. I hope you have read it with a limber mind, and that it opens up avenues of consideration around this increasingly important topic.

To be frank, I do believe a *Detonation*-like narrative is entirely plausible in our future. If anything, *Detonation* underestimates the potential for a superintelligent machine to subvert our authority and gain instrumental resources. Remember, I am but a mere meatbag author. A superintelligent machine would make short work of me and my lackluster imagination, I assure you.

The basis for my beliefs on this topic and the arguments outlined in this book come from more than intuition. They have germinated during months of researching the topic thoroughly, and are supported by my personal work history in health-care industry software development. This journey of discovery made me believe that 1) superintelligence is only a matter of time, 2) it may arrive within a generation or even sooner, 3) we are not in the slightest way prepared for it, and 4) it poses a substantial risk of catastrophic damage to our society.

Don't get me wrong. Superintelligent machines can do incredible things for humanity. They could cure diseases, dramatically improve our standard of living and extend our lives. I believe in that promise, but what I don't understand is why we are doing essentially nothing to mitigate the risks.

Even if you believe superintelligent machines can be easily controlled, we have not begun to address the inevitable labor-market dislocations and financial inequalities of even the most benevolent superintelligent machines. Can this godlike power be entrusted to our corporate and governmental leaders? There are Prestons in this world; there are Bartzs; and there are Rourke Ramas. We need to protect ourselves from them. It would be unwise to give them unconstrained access to superintelligent machines.

I believe in Bhavin Nadar's arguments at the end of Part 1. The existential risk of superintelligent machines is greater—and more imminent—than any other class of existential risk including climate change, nuclear proliferation, and synthetic biology. Furthermore, mitigation of any catastrophic events will be more difficult. Ironically, *if* we get it right, superintelligence will greatly improve our ability to mitigate all these other existential risks. It could be the last invention we need to make. Right now, though, that is one big *if*.

We have virtually no resources allocated to getting it right. Machine intelligence control issues remain almost entirely unexplored and regulation remains a perilous void. We have no safety standards, we have no global coalitions, and the general population has a fleeting understanding of the risks. For a force of innovation many believe will power our economies for decades to come, shouldn't governments be investing trillions of dollars to make sure we get it right?

Nick Bostrom puts it better than I can when he says, "Before the prospect of an intelligence explosion, we humans are like small children playing with a bomb. Such is the mismatch between the power of our plaything and the immaturity of our conduct."

If these words scare you, good. If this book scares you, good. Too few of us are afraid. Too few of us have the appropriate visceral reaction. I want you to become aware, even if it makes you fearful. Maybe then some of us will be moved to make choices that will reduce our risk. Maybe then the wheels of change will dislodge from their rusty moorings and begin to turn.

We don't have to be the Old World. Let's not wait until our house is burning to build a well. We need to be sure the initial conditions for superintelligence can be set correctly, and safely, as soon as possible. To do that, we need to build regulatory bodies, conduct safety research, build global coalitions and more. Every day we don't invest a significant amount of time, money and energy into this, is a day in which Gail has a greater chance of taking our future away from us.

Or to summarize this whole Afterword in mule-speak, let's keep it between the ditches, people.

For those of you who want to explore this topic further, many of the arguments you read about in *Detonation* are discussed in more detail in great works such as *Superintelligence* by Nick Bostrom, *Life 3.0* by Max Tegmark and *Warnings* by Richard A. Clarke and R.P. Eddy.

If you would like to know what you can do to help, or for more information about the risks posed by superintelligence, please visit *ethagi.org*. Let's get to work!

Thank you again for reading. I welcome any and all feedback at *erik-a-otto.com*.

Sincerely,

Erik A. Otto

ABOUT THE AUTHOR

Erik A. Otto is an accomplished healthcare industry executive and technologist, now turned science fiction author and biotech investor. He was formerly President and Co-Founder of InSpark Technologies, a digital health company that applied advanced pattern recognition algorithms to warn people with diabetes in advance of periods of risk.

Erik's works of fiction expose the impact of cultural and technological themes on society in a number of futuristic and other worldly settings. He focuses on delivering intricate plotting, diverse characters and action-driven story telling to immerse the reader in thought-provoking events and circumstances.

In addition to writing, Erik is currently serving as the Managing Director of Ethagi Inc., an organization dedicated to promoting the safe and ethical use of artificial general intelligence technologies. He lives in Charlottesville, Virginia, with his wife and two children.

Visit *erik-a-otto.com* for more information or to sign up
for updates on new releases.

Made in the USA
Columbia, SC
04 March 2018

90430392R00346